THROUGH THE EYES OF
SOCIAL SCIENCE

FIFTH EDITION

Frank Zulke

Harold Washington College
City Colleges of Chicago

WAVELAND
PRESS, INC.
Prospect Heights, Illinois

For information about this book, write or call:
Waveland Press, Inc.
P.O. Box 400
Prospect Heights, Illinois 60070
(847) 634-0081

Chapter 1 through 16, 19, 25 and 38 were written specifically for *Through the Eyes of Social Science*. I am very grateful the authors gave me permission to use their work. Sources for other chapters are listed at the bottom of the first page of each specific chapter.

Printed in the United States of America

7

Contents

─── Index to Boxed Material ───

Preface

This revised collection of readings, like previous editions, is designed to introduce undergraduates to the point of view of social science. It is designed for students who do not necessarily specialize in the social sciences. Nineteen articles were written directly for *Through the Eyes of Social Science*. Other articles are from both professional and popular publications. Authors range from anthropologists, sociologists, psychologists, economists, political scientists, historians, and geographers, to educators, journalists, and futurologists. I have aimed for diversity and balance. Most of the articles contain "boxes"—maps, quizzes, experiments, tables, alternative views, census information, updates, etc. They are included because they deal with topics or areas of concern that my students wanted to discuss. In addition, almost every article is followed by study questions. They can be used as homework assignments and as a focus for classroom discussions. A glossary at the end of the book defines and explains some of the most frequently used words and concepts in social science writings. While the emphasis is on American society, particularly on multicultural issues, many of the articles discuss cultures beyond the North American continent.

Because some of the selections are fairly complex, each "part" of the book has an introduction to help the student place the article within a framework. Some of the introductions are "substantial," defining basic terms and/or offering different theoretical perspectives; other more "succinct" introductions merely tie together the articles within a part. The parts are not arranged at random but form a progression. When possible, I have attempted to identify relevant biographical information about authors, usually in the introduction to each part.

Part I provides an introduction. I find the quotations in Chapter 1 very useful for that early time in the semester when an overview of course topics is needed. Chapter 2 tests geographical literacy or, in some cases, illiteracy. Chapter 3 introduces the student to science and social science in general and suggests possible research designs to gather information. Part II defines the various social sciences. This is difficult to do in short articles, but I think the authors have succeeded. Parts III and IV consider historical and theoretical issues. Part V deals with human and sociocultural evolution. All authors of Chapters 1 through 16 are from Harold Washington College with the exception of geographer John Alwin who hails from Central Washington University in Ellensburg, Washington.

Part VI gives an overview of America that is satirical and serious. I sometimes, usually with great success, assign Chapter 17, "One Hundred Percent American," and Chapter 18, "Body Ritual Among the Nacirema," at the beginning of the term. While many articles in the book emphasize multicultural issues, Part VII tackles them head on. Asian-Americans, Latinos, Native Americans, and gays are the multicultural groups viewed here. Chapter 25 in Part VIII considers the meaning of culture all over the globe, always warning not to be ethnocentric. The three concluding articles in this part all deal with one culture: the !Kung of the Kalahari desert. It was felt that such depth would help us better understand this culture and the vast cultural change through which it is going. Part IX continues the cross-cultural perspective as it examines the position of the elderly in Russia and the United States. Part X brings up ethical issues as it examines three experiments in which the researchers used deception with their subjects. Part XI tackles social issues such as poverty, the African-American and Puerto Rican underclasses, and homelessness. Part XII focuses on the individual and raises the question of whether we are basically biological or social animals. Part XIII opens the discussion to the future, focusing on the family, schools, cities, and overpopulation.

Any merit this reader has derives from the authors of the selections. I thank them for allowing me to include their work here. I also wish to thank my colleagues and students. Both have helped me, directly and indirectly, to hasten the gestation of this fifth edition. All errors of omission and commission rest, of course, upon my shoulders.

Frank Zulke
Harold Washington College
City Colleges of Chicago

Part I

Introduction

The first selection, "Science and Social Science, Pro and Con," is a sequence of quotations which reflect the hopes and despairs of attempting to see through the eyes of science in general and social science in particular. The quotations summarize many important themes that will be taken up in the book. As you read through them, see how many of the authors you can recognize by name. See if you can place any of them into specific historical and/or social contexts. The quotations are presented to start you thinking. "Lost on Planet Earth," the second reading, is presented to start you thinking about your geographical literacy. Some recent surveys have pointed out that some college students couldn't locate the United States on a world map, let alone Chicago or Los Angeles. The final selection, "Science, the Scientific Method, and Research Designs in the Social Sciences," supplies a few essential definitions. After pinpointing the steps necessary to do research, the article follows these steps through an actual research project. Four commonly used research designs in the social sciences—experiments, surveys, observational studies, the use of already existing data—are described. This background information should help you to begin seeing through the eyes of social science.

Chapter One

Science and Social Science, Pro and Con

Science

1. Where there is much desire to learn, there of necessity will be much arguing.

   Milton

2. We are not simply contending in order that my view or that of yours may prevail, but I presume that we ought both of us to be fighting for the truth.

   Socrates

3. The philosophers have only interpreted the world in various ways. The point, however, is to change it.

   (from the tombstone of Karl Marx)

4. In our time and for some centuries to come, the natural and social sciences will be to an increasing degree the accepted point of reference with respect to which truth is gauged.

   George Lundberg

5. Science is a body of knowledge about the universe obtained by objective, logical, and systematic methods of research.

   Olga Petryszyn

6. Scientific knowledge is based on empirical evidence.

   John Macionis

7. Equipped with our five senses, we explore the universe around us.

Edwin Hubble

8. An actually existing fly is more important than a possibly existing angel.

Emerson

9. Science recognizes no ultimate final truths.

Ian Robertson

10. In science, each of us knows that what he has accomplished will be antiquated in ten, twenty, fifty years.

Max Weber

11. The entire history of science is a progression of exploded fallacies, not of achievements.

Ayn Rand

12. The exact contrary of what is generally believed is often the truth.

Jean De La Bruyère

13. Science never solves a problem without creating ten more.

George Bernard Shaw

14. Too many seem to have either a global perception of science as some variant of magic, or else an understanding of the specifics of a *particular* science, but no fundamental grasp of it as a generic process of knowing.

Charles Hughes

15. Always simplify.

Henry David Thoreau

16. Theories should be as simple as possible, but not more so.

Albert Einstein

17. It is a capital mistake to theorize before one has data.

Sherlock Holmes

18. There is in science, as in all our lives, a continuous to and fro of factual discovery, then of thought about the implications of what we have discovered, and then back to the facts for testing and discovery.

Jacob Bronowski

19. The true scientist is able to look into the face of Hell and not be afraid.

Bertrand Russell

20. The best way to grasp what science "is" is to see what scientists do.

Leslie White

21. We simply collect the facts; others may use them as they will.

W. E. B. DuBois

22. Science should not be an egoistic pleasure.

Karl Marx

23. Nothing in science has any value if it is not communicated.

Anne Roe

24. All observations must be for or against some view.

Charles Darwin

25. Science commits suicide when it adopts a creed.

T. H. Huxley

26. Science is amoral; scientists, however, are not amoral.

E. R. Babbie

27. The intention of the Holy Spirit is to teach how to go to heaven and not how go the heavens.

Galileo (quoting a churchman of his day)

28. There are no irreconcilable differences between science and faith.

Pope John Paul II

29. Scientists leave their discoveries like foundlings on the doorstep of society. The step-parents do not know how to bring them up.

Ritchie Calder

30. Unless scientists are willing to give hard thought—indeed, their hearts—to their social responsibilities, they may find themselves someday in the position of the Sorcerer's Apprentice, unable to control the forces they have unleashed.

René Dubos

Social Science

31. Social science is the study of human behavior. Anthropology, sociology, psychology, economics, history, and political science have developed into separate "disciplines," but each shares an interest in human behavior.

Thomas Dye

32. Social scientists should differ from other scientists only in their concern with human behavior rather than the behavior of viruses or electrons. The situation, however, is more complicated. The scientist will not have a brother or sister married to a virus.

Reid Luhman

33. Social scientists have destroyed the delicacy and intricacy of their subject matter in coarse-grained attempts to imitate the methods of natural scientists.

Margaret Mead

34. Executed properly, social science is the quality of mind whose more adroit use offers the promise that human reason itself will come to play a greater role in human affairs.

C. Wright Mills

35. Social scientists . . . maintain a flow of information and an understanding of alternative modes of action that keeps policy-makers in line with reality.

Paul Bohannan

36. Social Science can provide us with rules of action for the future.

Émile Durkheim

37. Social Science is a tool of the establishment and, consciously or unconsciously, a way of supporting the status quo.

James Rankin

38. Social life is so complex that researchers cannot observe everything; they must select what is relevant.

Helen Hughes

39. To the social scientist, a humble cooking pot is as important as a Beethoven sonata.

Judith Nielson

40. All social research represents a potential invasion of privacy.

M. Bassis

41. Not everything that can be counted counts, and not everything that counts can be counted.

Robert Cameron

42. The regularities social scientists find do not have the firm general validity of laws of nature.

Gunnar Myrdal

43. There are three kinds of lies: lies, damned lies, and statistics.

Disraeli

44. We·must not view people's behavior as a finished product, as a relationship of an independent and a dependent variable.

Herbert Blumer

45. The systematic gathering and analysis of evidence allows social scientists to explain how they came to know what they know. Thus, we can evaluate if we should trust their knowledge.

Susan Jablonski

46. One common attribute of social scientists is a somnambulant dullness combined with a wordy concern for things everybody else already knows.

Ray Cuzzort

Chapter Two

Lost on the Planet Earth

Frank Zulke

Knowledge of geography is essential information. Without understanding geographical relationships, one cannot understand historical or current events. Put as simply as possible, you must understand where you are to understand where you are going or even where you want to be. Yet, consider these findings from recent surveys. A 1988 survey by the National Geographic Society compared American geographic literacy with neighbors Canada and Mexico and six other industrial nations. Respondents were given a world map and asked to identify sixteen geographic locations. The winners among 18- to 24-year-olds, from first place to last, were Sweden, West Germany, Japan, Canada, Italy, France, United Kingdom, Mexico, and the United States. About 14 percent of the Americans could not pick out the United States on a world map. Only 5 percent could locate Vietnam. A 1989 National Geographic survey pitted the United States against the Soviet Union. While Soviet adults in general scored slightly lower than American adults, younger Soviets between 18 and 24 did significantly better than their American counterparts.

The unlabelled world map on the next page is intended to start you thinking about your geographical literacy. Study it for a few moments. See how many continents you can locate. (That's Antarctica peeking up at the bottom.) Try to get some idea of size of countries. (The Soviet Union has a land area over twice the size of the United States.) Compare population size of various countries. (The United States population of 250 million is minuscule compared to China's 1.5 billion). Get a feel for distances between countries. (Cuba is only 90 miles from the United States.) Finally, see how many numbers you

7

can pin on the countries below. If you get stuck, you can figure out the answers by consulting the maps in the appendix. Consult those maps often while reading this book. Don't get "lost on the planet earth." (Keep in mind, however, that the world is not static: countries change names, boundaries, etc. Just recently, for example, Burma changed its name to Myanmar, East and West Germany were reunited, and many republics of the former Soviet Union have become independent.)

☐ United States	☐ Germany	☐ Vietnam	☐ Japan
☐ United Kingdom	☐ Canada	☐ Soviet Union	☐ Mexico
☐ France	☐ Italy	☐ Sweden	☐ Brazil
☐ South Africa	☐ Australia	☐ China	☐ Egypt

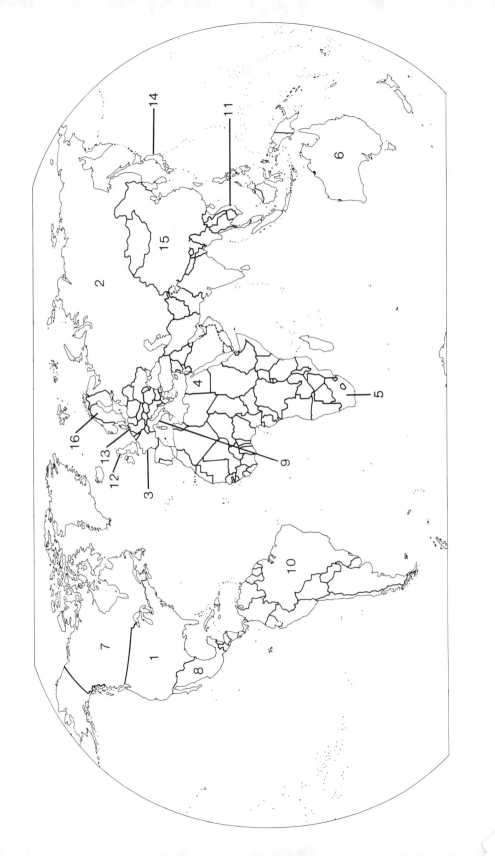

Chapter Three

Science, The Scientific Method, and Research Designs in the Social Sciences

Frank Zulke

The world we live in is changing. It is changing at a more rapid pace than at any other period in history. Compare life today with the not too distant past. Imagine an age where values were stable, when the divorce rate was low, when one could go downtown at night without fear of being mugged, when a cross country flight took eight hours, and when a typical American did not have their television on for seven hours or more each day. Indeed, try to imagine life without the airplane or television. Or, better yet, think of what life could be like for your children. The next twenty-five years may bring further megalopolitan growth, test-tube babies, the "electronic church," increased longevity, transsexualism, global warming, the threat of nuclear destruction, the colonization of space, and maybe even communication with extraterrestrials. To continue boggles the imagination. Virtually every human institution and cultural practice accepted in the past will come under scrutiny and be subject to change. Will we be ready for these changes? Will we have any control over the direction of these changes? Will the changes affect us and, if so, how? Will the new society be a better one than the one that exists now?

Since our relationship to the universe and to each other is constantly evolving, these questions are, of course, not new. Neolithic cave dwellers in 10,000 B.C., inhabitants of the *polis* in ancient Greece, theologians in the Middle Ages,

11

hunters and gatherers in the Kalahari desert in Africa, and Chicagoans and New Yorkers at the dawn of the 21st century have all attempted answers. Indeed, "ancients" and "moderns" alike have wrestled with the problem of change so life might be more meaningful and have a greater sense of direction and purpose. But, and this is a very important but, the pace of change has accelerated and no one would doubt that the world is undergoing a major transformation. We no longer even speak of trends today but, as Box 1 points out, "megatrends."

Some authors, like Alvin Toffler in *Future Shock* and *The Third Wave*, Joe Cappo in *Futurescope*, and Bill McKibbons in the elegiac *The End of Nature*, fear a dehumanization of society as people's lives become regulated by new technologies and impersonal bureaucracies. They see poverty, overpopulation, ecological devastation, secularization and loss of community. Even an increase in mental illness is predicted. Such dire pessimists warn against getting caught up in materialism and narcissism. Other authors, like Marvin Cetron and Owen

---

Box 1

Megatrends 2000

One way to think about the future is to consider new directions in which our society seems to be moving. Futurists John Naisbitt and Patricia Aburdene have pinpointed some megatrends that they believe are transforming our lives. Read through the list below and see if you agree. As you try to think of examples, consider the positive and negative consequences of each megatrend.

1. We are shifting from a manufacturing society to one in which service and information related jobs will predominate.

2. We will live more and more in a "high tech" world and have an ever increasing need for a "human touch."

3. Cities in the southern and western areas of the country will "win" over the old industrial cities of the north.

4. We are moving from a national economy to a global one.

5. The Pacific "rim" of the world will become increasingly more important in the world.

6. A free market socialism seems to be emerging worldwide.

7. There will be a religious revival in the third millennium.

8. Women will move into positions of leadership in record numbers.

SOURCE: John Naisbitt: *MEGATRENDS* (New York: Warner Books, 1984) and John Naisbitt and Patricia Aburdene: *MEGATRENDS 2000* (New York: William Morrow), 1990.

Davies in *American Renaissance*, Austin and Knight Kiplinger in *America in the Global '90s* or Richard Falk in *This Endangered Planet* offer a more upbeat mood. They see the shifts taking place in today's world as offering unprecedented opportunities for a humanism that will eventually prevail. These exuberant optimists point to stabilized populations, harmoniously used resources, new technological developments, and a sharing, cooperative world where satisfaction might be achieved by all. Since both the pessimistic and optimistic points of view are reasonable, only the future will tell which is more correct.

Science

What is new about the modern attempt to pose and answer fundamental questions regarding possible changes is that we rely more and more on the use of science to do so. It is not that we cannot learn much from mythology, folk-sayings, religious maxims, intuition, common sense, poetry, philosophy, or even movies and television, but rather that science offers a "new" way to obtain and organize our knowledge. While other approaches are feasible, of course, few would argue with the position that science increasingly affects our lives.

Science may be defined as an objective, logical, and systematic method of analysis of phenomena devised to permit the accumulation of reliable knowledge. So defined, two components of science stand out. Science is both a body of knowledge about some aspects of the universe in which we live as well as a method by which that knowledge is obtained. Conceived of this way, we usually speak of the natural sciences and the social sciences. The natural sciences include those which focus on the nature of the physical universe (for example, astronomy, chemistry, physics) as well as those that study living organisms (for example, biology, botany, zoology). Generally included among the social sciences are anthropology, psychology, sociology, economics, history, and political science. Some feel the subject matter of geography overlaps enough so that it should be included as well. All the social sciences are concerned with the study of people, both individually and in groups, in cultures and societies, and in the past and the present.

Regardless of whether we talk of the natural or the social sciences, scientists attempt to "discover" basic data and to generalize or "explain" their meaning, that is, they do research and theorize. Research refers to the actual tasks involved in the way scientists have chosen to study the world. Put another way, scientists must collect the facts. A theory is a general explanation of phenomena that, hopefully, will have predictive value for future research and theorizing. Whereas research tells us "what," theory tells us "why." Theory gives meaning to facts that might otherwise simply be units of information; research makes theory more than a set of abstractions. The two are thus complementary: research is meaningless without theory, and theory without research is simply speculation.

The Scientific Method

Although the way of studying or knowing a subject hardly seems as important as the subject itself, it is clear that what one learns depends on the way one approaches the material. The scientific method is a set of rules for ensuring that research will lead to valid theories. It proceeds from the inception and first formulation of a problem to publication of its results. Executed properly, it can serve as a safeguard against the possibilities of arriving at false conclusions or of accepting generalizations that have not been adequately supported by evidence.

Step one: Choosing a Topic and Defining Basic Terms

The first goal of the scientific method is to identify an area of concern that the research will investigate. Although this sounds relatively simple, it is often more difficult than one might think. Enthusiasm and curiosity are not enough. The researcher must have both the insight to see possible relationships between complex phenomena as well as the ability to define terms in such a way that the topic can be studied logically, objectively, and systematically. *Try to think of a topic on which you would like to do research.*

Step two: Getting Oriented on the Topic

The next step is to compare existing knowledge about the topic with the researcher's ideas. A survey of the literature will show what research and thinking has already been done on the topic and may expand or change research plans. More and more libraries now offer computerized literature searches that speed up this step. The idea here is that we do not want to "rediscover the wheel." *Where would you look to see how others have studied similar topics?*

Step three: Formulating a Hypothesis

Having chosen a topic and reviewed what work has been done on it, the researcher now formulates a hypothesis or hypotheses. A hypothesis is a statement specifying a particular relationship between two or more variables (or factors) thought to be important. Usually, an independent and dependent variable are involved. The independent variable is the factor thought to affect the dependent variable; the dependent variable is the factor expected to change in relation to the independent variable. The hypothesis is phrased in such a way that it can be "tested," i.e., proved or disproved empirically. This involves sense perception: the information must be visible, smellable, hearable, feelable, or tastable. This is crucial because observations made in this way can be checked for accuracy by other persons using the same senses. Remember that many propositions are not testable because they are outside the realm of empirical evidence. The existence of angels or God, for example, can be neither supported nor refuted empirically. In summary, then, a hypothesis is an expectation or educated guess that acts as a guideline in suggesting what might be encountered as research proceeds. It may be just a "hunch" or it may be part of a previous theory. *Have you come up with at least one testable hypothesis for your topic?*

Step four: Choosing a Research Design and Collecting the Data

Once the hypothesis is formulated, the researcher must decide how to collect information that will prove or disprove it. Box 2, below, "Collecting the Facts," gives some idea of unobtrusive ways to do this, i.e., designs that involve little contact between the researcher and the subjects of the research. Other designs may be more obtrusive. Many commonly used designs in the social science—experiments, sample surveys, and observational studies—involve situations where the researcher may influence the behavior of the persons being studied. Sometimes researchers make use of sources of data that already exist to avoid this potential pitfall. Each of these designs will be discussed in greater detail later in this article. *Will you use an obtrusive or unobtrusive design to gather your information?*

Step five: Analyzing the Data

After the information has been collected, it must be summarized and interpreted. (The use of computers increasingly plays a large role here and social science majors are encouraged to take statistics and data programming courses). The attempt is made to draw logical conclusions and, on the basis of those conclusions, either support or reject the original hypothesis. Equally important is to determine if the findings add to or suggest revision of established theory. *Did your analysis prove or disprove your hypothesis? Why or why not?*

Step six: Reporting the Results

Once the data is analyzed, it is important that the results be made public. Communication within the scientific community cannot be overestimated as the value of a study lies both in the information collected and analyzed as well as in new investigations the study stimulates. In this way, scientists can systematically build on one another's work. Many great scientific achievements were accomplished by building on the findings of others who lived and worked

---

Box 2

Collecting the Facts

Determine the independent and dependent variables for each of the studies listed in this box.

One investigator wanted to learn the level of whiskey consumption in towns which were officially "wet" or "dry." Empty bottles were counted in ashcans.

The degree of fear induced by a ghost-story-telling session can be measured by noting the shrinking diameter of a circle of seated children.

The floor tiles around the hatching-chick exhibit at Chicago's Museum of Science and Industry must be replaced every six weeks. Tiles in other parts of the museum need not be replaced for years. The selective erosion of tiles, indexed by the replacement rate, is a measure of the relative popularity of exhibits.

Chinese jade dealers have used the pupil dilation of their customers as a measure of the client's interest in particular stones. Others have noted this same variable as an index of fear.

Library withdrawals were used to demonstrate the effect of the introduction of television into a community. Fiction titles dropped, nonfiction titles were unaffected.

Children's interest in Christmas was demonstrated by distortions in the size of Santa Claus drawings.

Racial attitudes in two colleges were compared by noting the degree of clustering of blacks and whites in lecture halls.

SOURCE: E. Webb, D. Campbell, R. Schwartz, and L. Sechrest, *Unobtrusive Measures* (Chicago: Rand McNally, 1966).

---

in different places. *Where will public dissemination of your conclusions do the most good?*

Psychiatrist Thomas Szasz observed that when you put on a shirt, "if you button the first buttonhole to the second button, then it doesn't matter how careful you are the rest of the way." So it is with the scientific method. If these steps are not followed—if basic terms are not defined precisely, or if the hypothesis is not defined in a way that can be tested empirically, or if an inappropriate research design is chosen—then all the brilliant analysis in the world will not make things right. The scientific method is a way to make sure "to button the first buttonhole to the first button."

Application of the Scientific Method to a Problem

To understand the scientific method more concretely, let us attempt to follow these steps through on an actual research project. The project chosen is a classic example of sociological research: Frenchman Emile Durkheim's *Suicide*. Although originally published in 1897, the findings seem as important today as when the study was first published. Before you continue reading, jot down some of the reasons why you think people commit suicide. Then, after you read this section, you can see if you have a different view.

In Durkheim's time, suicide was thought to be caused by such factors as insanity or heredity, or even a full moon. Investigators usually explained suicide by referring to the motives of people who had taken their own lives. Some had committed suicide, for instance, after a doctor had diagnosed a fatal illness, others had failed in business, and still others may have had unhappy love affairs. Durkheim was not satisfied with such explanations. He believed the reasons for suicide lay outside the individual and sought to investigate this.

Having *chosen a topic*, Durkheim had to *define his terms* more precisely. Of primary importance, of course, was to define suicide. He said it referred to "death resulting from some act of the victim which he or she knows will produce the result." He wanted to measure it in terms of rates such as the number of suicides per 1,000,000 population. Lastly, he had to define the reasons for suicide that "lay outside the individual." This was harder to do. He finally decided he would concentrate on the "social context" within which suicide occurs, that is, the type of society and the kinds of groups to which people belong.

His next step was to review the literature in order to *get oriented on the topic*. He found that suicide rates varied from one time period to another and from one country to another. Those countries that had the highest suicide rates surprisingly had the lowest rates of mental illness. This suggested that insanity alone did not explain suicide. He found, furthermore, that while more women than men were confined to mental asylums, more men than women committed suicide. He was not able to accumulate accurate information that compared suicide rates of parents and children. While Durkheim's survey of the literature did not allow him to disprove that suicide rates were related to insanity and heredity, his findings were suggestive enough to make him suspect that previous researchers had been looking in the wrong direction. Thus, Durkheim decided to pursue his idea that suicide was related to a person's relationships within the groups to which they belong.

Durkheim could now *formulate some hypotheses* to be investigated. He used factors such as marital status (unmarried and married), religious affiliation (Protestant and Catholic), military involvement (being in the armed forces and being a civilian), and societal stability (a rapidly changing society and a stagnant society) as his independent variables and specific suicide rates as his dependent variables. Examples of hypotheses he sought to test were: fewer married people will commit suicide than single people; more Protestants than Catholics will commit suicide; fewer civilians will commit suicide than people in the armed forces; periods of rapid social change will have higher suicide rates than periods of slow change. Durkheim tested many other hypotheses as well.

To test these hypotheses, Durkheim *chose an unobtrusive research design* that utilized already existing data. He examined official government suicide records in various European countries over a period of years. The records listed numbers of suicides and gave information about the people involved — their age, sex, nationality, marital status, and so on. Statistical records available at the time were scattered and incomplete and Durkheim, without the aid of today's computers, *collected the data.*

Analysis of the data supported many of Durkheim's hypotheses. He compiled percentages and constructed elaborate tables, maps, and graphs to illustrate his findings. The table offered in Box 3 is a good example of his analytical approach. From this table we see a relationship between male family relationships and the suicide rate. Men who are married and have children have the lowest suicide rate; widowers without children have the highest suicide rate; husbands without children and widowers with children have intermediate rates. (He compiled female rates as well as rates for hundreds of other groups).

What many regard as Durkheim' s most lasting contribution to social science was his ability to consistently relate his factual information to theoretical and practical issues. Box 4 below gives a general idea of how he did this.

We might look now at some of the conclusions Durkheim made as he *reported the results of his findings.* He explained that unmarried people are more likely to commit suicide than those who are married because the unmarried are likely

---

Box 3

Family Relationships and Male Suicide Rate: France, 1861-1868

Family Relationships	Male Suicide Rates (per million)
Husbands with children	336
Husbands without children	644
Widowers with children	937
Widowers without children	1258

SOURCE: Emile Durkheim, *Suicide* (New York: The Free Press, 1966).

Box 4

Why Study Suicide Rates?

"The study of suicide rates shows that the individual is dominated by a moral reality greater than himself: namely, collective reality. When each society is seen to have its own suicide rate and when it appears that the variations through which it passes at different times of the day, month, year, merely reflect the rhythm of social life; and that marriage, divorce, the family, religious society, the army, the economy, etc. affect it in accordance with definite laws—then these states and institutions will no longer be regarded as characterless, ineffective ideological arrangements. Rather they will be felt to be real, living, active forces which, because of the way they determine the individual, prove their independence of him.

If, instead of seeing in suicide only separate occurrences, unrelated and to be separately studied, the suicides committed in a given society during a given period of time are taken as a whole, it appears that this total is not simply a sum of independent units, a collective total, but is itself a new fact *sui generis*."

SOURCE: Emile Durkheim, *Suicide* (New York: The Free Press. 1966), p. 46.

---

to have a lower level of social integration and group involvement. Since the emotional attachment of single persons to a family group is less intense than that of married persons, their barrier against suicide in times of personal stress is weaker. The logic here is that when the father in a tightly knit family comes home with the news that he has been fired, the wife and children rally around him, "hold his hand," and assure him of love and support. The answer to why suicide rates differed for various religious groups was not so obvious. Durkheim had to look beyond specific religious beliefs since both Protestantism and Catholicism condemned suicide. Instead, he concentrated on how the two religions interpreted the relationship between the individual and God. For Protestants, a central concept was that each individual stood alone before his Maker; for Catholics, a hierarchical order of the priesthood intervened. Thus, according to Durkheim, the Protestant was more susceptible to suicide than the Catholic because he was less intimately associated with a traditionally organized Church and placed largely on his own resources. Durkheim referred to suicide for the unmarried and for Protestants as *egoistic suicide*—such individuals will commit suicide because they perceive themselves as isolated.

Durkheim's explanation of why men in the armed forces commit suicide more than civilians is referred to as *altruistic suicide*. When you belong to a group in which its importance is stressed and the individual is viewed as insignificant, you will not value your own life as strongly. Thus, provocations that would not motivate others to commit suicide may affect you. The Indian widow who is expected to burn herself to death on her husband's funeral pyre, the Kamikaze pilots in World War II, or the self immolating Buddhist monks during the Vietnam War are examples of this.

One other major type of suicide that Durkheim discusses is *anomic suicide.* He posited that a rapid change in either the society as a whole or in an individual's social situation would create a state of anomie or normlessness. This would increase the probability of committing suicide. This is because individuals are most satisfied with their lives when their day-to-day behavior is oriented toward a set of meaningful goals and is regulated by a set of rules or norms. When goals lose their meaning or when norms are uncertain, life seems without purpose and suicide is more likely. The theory of anomic suicide could explain, for example, the increase in suicide rates during a period of economic instability as existed after the stock market crash of 1929.

You might wish to return now to the reasons you thought that people committed suicide. Most likely you had listed individual causes like unhappiness or depression. Did Durkheim make you change your mind? Do you agree now that a private act like suicide can be explained in terms of social causes? Which, if any, of Durkheim's types of suicide might account for the current increase of suicides in high school and college age populations in the United States?

Current Research Designs in the Social Sciences

Social scientists currently use one or more of four basic research designs: the experiment, the sample survey, the observational study, and the use of existing sources of data. The first three of these involve researchers personally collecting their own data; the fourth does not. Each design has its own advantages and disadvantages. While each are discussed separately, keep in mind that there is often an overlap between them when actual research is being done.

The Experiment

The experiment is the most precise and rigorous of the research designs. It seeks to specify cause and effect relationships between two variables under carefully controlled conditions. In a typical experiment, three basic steps are involved. First, two comparable groups are set up. Second, one group is exposed to some stimulus and the other group is not. Third, both groups are measured and compared to see what effect the stimulus had. Conducted properly, the experiment should be able to prove or disprove if one variable "caused" a change in another variable. The next few paragraphs attempt to pinpoint some of the more salient aspects of this technique in a hypothetical situation.

Let us suppose a major pharmaceutical company has developed Expando, a drug it believes will expand human memory so as to retain much more material. So far, the company has tried Expando on many animals with positive results and no negative consequences. Since a similarity between animal and human reactions is assumed, the company now wishes to see if Expando works on humans. Psychologists, who have pioneered in the use of experimentation to study human behavior, are consulted to help set up a laboratory experiment.

The experimenter obtains "subjects" and divides them into two groups, the "experimental group" which takes Expando, and the "control group" which is given a false medication. (Taking or not taking the drug is the independent variable.) The researcher may not want to know which group got Expando and which the "placebo" so that he or she will not subconsciously influence the results as testing commences. Another consideration for the researcher is to be certain that the groups were similar in terms of sex, age, race, social class, scholastic aptitude, previous success in studies, etc. After all, these variables might play a part in the subjects' memory retention. At this point, tests measuring retention of information can be given to the two groups and we should be able to see if the drug works. If it does, the experimental group should perform better on the tests than the control group. (Improved or unimproved memory as measured by the tests is the dependent variable).

While the situation above is hypothetical, properly constructed experiments can help to disentangle cause and effect relationships. To the extent they do this, whether in a "laboratory" type of setting (as described above), or in a more "naturalistic" setting (as described in Box 5), they are very important. Keep in mind, however, that there are always potential disadvantages in conducting experiments: usually only very few subjects — often pigeons or college sophomores — can be "tested"; designs must frequently be modified for reasons of time, costs, etc.; "labs" are often artificial; "naturalistic" situations can't always be controlled; the experimenter may unwittingly influence the results, etc. The point is that the experiment is not a fool proof way to collect information but one of several possibilities. Ask your instructor if your class can perform the "Landing on the Moon" experiment described in Box 6. You may have fun and there may be some surprises for you.

The Sample Survey

The sample survey, while lacking the precision of an experiment, is another frequently used research design in social science. It is a method in which people are asked questions in order to systematically gather standardized information about their behavior, opinions, attitudes, values, beliefs, or other characteristics. It is useful for gaining information about issues that can't be directly observed. In simplest terms, its asking people "what's going on out there." Since it can deal with a large number of subjects in a real community, its results can often be easily compared and/or generalized to the wider society. Whereas psychologists most often use the experiment as their way of gathering information, sociologists, political scientists, and economists usually use the sample survey.

One key word here is "sample." A "sample" or portion of people is chosen from a particular "population," for example, Americans, Chicagoans, doctors, college students, etc. The way the sample is chosen is of paramount importance if the sample is to accurately reflect the population. An example of how *not* to choose a sample was offered by a poll conducted by the magazine *Literary Digest* in 1936. The magazine sent ten million postcard ballots to respondents chosen from telephone directories and auto registration lists. On the basis of returns, the magazine predicted that Alfred Landon would beat Franklin D. Roosevelt in the presidential election. Think of how many people would have telephones and drive automobiles during the Depression and you can guess why the magazine's prediction was so inaccurate. For reasons like this,

---

Box 5

The Hawthorne Effect

Sometimes, researchers are able to conduct their experiments in the field in a naturalistic setting. This is often desirable because there may be a tendency for people to behave differently when they know that they are participating in experiments than they would ordinarily behave in real life situations. In one famous study, researchers went into a factory to see how lighting (the independent variable) affected worker's output (the dependent variable). To the investigator's amazement, findings indicated that the productivity of the subjects increased regardless of increases or decreases in lighting. Even when working in almost complete darkness, productivity increased. The experimenters concluded that the high degree of personal attention was a more important influence on behavior than the physical setting. Workers changed their behavior to fulfill what they believed were the researcher's expectations. This change in behavior is known as the Hawthorne effect (after the factory in which the experiments were conducted). Social scientists today strive to avoid it.

SOURCE: F.J. Roethlisberger and W.J. Dickson, *Management and the Worker* (Cambridge, MA: Harvard University Press, 1939).

Box 6

An Experiment to Compare Individual and Group Decision Making

You are to imagine yourself a member of a space crew originally scheduled for rendezvous with a mother ship on the lighted surface of the moon. Mechanical difficulties, however, have forced your ship to crash-land at a spot some 200 miles from the rendezvous point. The rough landing damaged much of the equipment aboard. Since survival depends on reaching the mother ship, you must choose the most critical items of those available to take with you on the 200 mile trip. Below are listed the fifteen items left intact after landing. Your task is to rank the items in terms of their importance to your crew in its attempt to reach the rendezvous point. Place a number 1 by the most important item, the number 2 by the second most important item and so on through number 15, the item you feel to be the least important.

___6___ A. Box of matches

___8___ B. Food concentrate

_____ C. 50 feet of nylon rope

_____ D. Parachute silk

___7___ E. Portable heating unit

_____ F. Two .45 calibre pistols

_____ G. One case dehydrated milk

___1___ H. Two 100 lb. tanks of oxygen

_____ I. Stellar map

_____ J. Life Raft

___9___ K. Magnetic compass

___2___ L. 5 gallons of water

___4___ M. Signal flares

___3___ N. First aid kit (with injection needles)

___5___ O. Solar powered FM receiver-transmitter

After you have done this individually, divide up into working groups of four to eight students. The group will then work together to provide a ranking from 1 to 15, as has previously been done individually.

When both individuals *and* groups have completed their work, look in the appendix to see how the National Aeronautics and Space Administration would have ranked the items. Compute scores for individuals and groups and try to answer these types of questions:

1. Did individuals or groups do better?

2. Does the make-up of the group affect its score? Age, sex, year in school, etc.

3. To what extent do emotional factors affect the group's score?

4. To what extent does basic knowledge play a part in either the individual's or the group's score?

researchers will usually have trained statisticians help them choose a representative sample, i.e., a subgroup drawn from a population so that it has essentially the same distribution of characteristics as the population at large. If a sample is to be representative, all members of the population must have the same chance to be selected for the sample. The sample in effect must be random. A young George Gallup, incidentally, correctly predicted the Roosevelt landslide using a much smaller random sample than that used by the *Literary Digest*.

The other key word here is "survey" and, as you have undoubtedly guessed, people in the sample will be asked to complete a questionnaire or take part in an interview. Questionnaires, which respondents fill out, are popular because they can be collected relatively fast and inexpensively. A problem arises, however, because although all respondents fill out the same questionnaire, there is no guarantee that they will understand and interpret each question in the same way. A question such as "do you approve of legalized abortion?" usually poses little difficulty. About 50 percent of Americans answer yes. Questions such as "do you believe there should be an amendment to the Constitution protecting the life of the unborn child?" or "do you think there should be an amendment to the Constitution prohibiting legalized abortion?" may involve difficulties in interpretation. While essentially the same question, over 60 percent of Americans said yes in the first version and under 25 percent answered yes in the second version. It is important that survey questions be phrased in a neutral way. Additional potential problems in using questionnaires are that unanticipated responses or information often cannot be included, people may give false information, or people may not return the questionnaires. To complicate matters even more, between 10 percent and 20 percent of American adults are not sufficiently literate to complete a questionnaire.

The interview differs from the questionnaire because the questionnaire is completed by the individual respondent whereas the interview is carried out by a trained interviewer who asks the subject certain questions. This is more time-consuming and expensive but there are several advantages. The problem of nonresponse is limited; more intimate questions can be asked; the interviewer can explain questions and thereby reduce misunderstandings on the part of the respondent.

Once the data is collected, the sample survey is an excellent source of information about social characteristics. In addition to basic distributions (for example, the number of people who approve or disapprove of abortions), sample surveys can provide clues to relations between variables (for example, attitudes toward abortion do or do not vary with sex, age, social class, religion, etc.). Furthermore, if the survey is repeated over a period of time, social scientists may be able to draw certain conclusions about changing attitudes (for example, attitudes toward abortion are more tolerant or less tolerant in the 1990s than in the past). Use of modern computers makes it possible to pinpoint relationships between many different variables for large populations. The relationships are usually correlations. As Sydney Harris points out in Box 7, there are major differences between correlations (when two factors vary together) and cause-and-effect relationships (when one factor causes the other to happen).

The Observational Study

Some social scientists argue that they would prefer to study fewer people than those involved in the typical sample survey and to probe more deeply into the context of the behavior being studied than is usually allowed in an experiment. The observational study provides an opportunity to do this. It is an intensive examination of one unit—person, event, gang, ghetto, religious cult, etc.—firsthand in a natural setting. It allows the researcher the opportunity to observe behavior while it is actually taking place. The goal of such investigations is to learn "all" one can about the particular subject. Sometimes the social scientist simply watches without getting involved in the activity itself. This is called "detached observation." Other times, and it is this approach

---

Box 7

"Correlation" and "Cause and Effect"

Few laymen really understand the difference between "correlation" and "cause and effect." Most people take the one for the other, and commit a huge blunder in doing so.

There is a clear and steady correlation between the amount of formal education you have and the level of income you achieve. This correlation has led many people into the fallacy that education is the "cause" and income is the "effect" in this common equation.

It is not so. Young people with more formal education win better jobs and higher income not so much because they know more and can do more as because they know more people who can do more for them. Most have little difficulty in finding a white-collar job—through family, friends, college connections or the general social milieu in which they have grown up and live. It is not education per se that raises the quality of the job or the level of income, but the whole social fabric and pattern of the community.

The old cynical slogan "It's not what you know but who you know" still operates to decide which youngster trudges off to the car wash and which walks briskly into the anteroom marked "Executive Trainee."

Sydney J. Harris: *Chicago Sun-Times*, 9/20/83.

that anthropologists and some sociologists have developed extensively, the researcher finds it useful to actually join and participate in the group or community being studied. Such "participant observation" often allows the researcher more insight into the way of life of the people he is observing since it provides a better opportunity to experience and understand the world from the point of view of the subject. Let us take an imaginary trip to the Kalahari desert in Africa to indicate how an observational study of the culture of the !Kung people might be carried out. (The exclamation point before Kung indicates a clicking sound in these people's language for which there is no English equivalent).

We leave Johannesburg, South Africa to spend a year among the !Kung. We have jeeps, food, water, medicine, camping equipment and even rifles. We have a guide who knows the land and speaks the !Kung language fluently. The guide is probably the only person we take with us, for "the fewer people along the better" is a good rule of field work. One or two people stand a better chance of making friends with the !Kung and observing their life without disrupting it than do half a dozen. Of course, our arrival will affect their activities no matter what because they are a shy people who live in small bands of about 20-50 people. Nevertheless, we want to minimize our effect.

We will have read everything that has ever been written on the !Kung and even have tried to learn their language. Because so much has been written, we may even anticipate proving or disproving some hypothesis. We certainly can't wait to practice speaking our new found "clicking" language.

When we find a band of !Kung, our first problem will be to make friends with them. Previous research reports indicated that tobacco serves this purpose well. Since the Surgeon General has warned us about possible ill effects of this, we may have qualms about giving them tobacco. (Box 8 discusses "ethical questions" that arise in the social sciences). Hopefully, we will find some alternative way to gain their confidence and become accepted. This may not be easy. Think of how we would react if a !Kung came into our neighborhood with trucks, cameras, notebooks, tape recorders, and rifles to study our way of life. Eventually, when they get used to our odd ways, they probably will let us write down, photograph, and record what we want. They may even laugh at our attempts to speak their language.

At first, everything we see will seem unique: a small boy shooting arrows at an ant hill, two men jogging across the veld, a circle of men dancing around a campfire at night with women singing in the background. Gradually, a pattern will emerge and we will learn that small boys spend hours amusing themselves with bows and arrows in anticipation of future roles as hunters, that men sometimes try to run down game, and that dancing and singing are an important part of !Kung religion, recreation, and even medicine. These learned, shared patterns of life are the !Kung culture and that is what we have come here to study.

As with the other research designs considered, there are pluses and in doing observational studies. They are very useful if we want to study thing that we don't know much about. They cannot be matched in their a to reveal the meaning of a social situation from the angle of the people involv Behavior studied in this way is relatively uncontaminated by the presence o

---

Box 8

Ethical Questions: Tea Rooms

Certain ethical questions arise for social scientists doing research: Should animals be used? What if it is necessary to terminate their lives? How does one respect the privacy and integrity of the people being studied? Is there the potential for emotional suffering? Who will make use of the findings? Might the findings be used for policy formulation that is detrimental to the group from which the findings came? Should secret agreements with sponsors be allowed? Must all reports be public? Not surprisingly, because of these and other questions, there has been a hot debate among social scientists over the past decade on the subject of ethics. Professional organizations such as the American Anthropological Association, American Psychological Association, American Sociological Association, etc., have now adopted codes of ethics which offer guidelines for "proper" research so that there will be no damage to either the people studied or to the scholarly community. The codes often have provisions for censure of unprofessional conduct.

Despite safeguards, the mere possession of confidential information about people introduces certain risks. One controversial study involved an investigation where sociologist Laud Humphreys observed homosexual encounters in "tearooms," that is, public restrooms in forest preserves. Subsequently, he followed the men to their cars and used their license plate numbers to find out their names and addresses. A year later, he changed his appearance and went to their homes and interviewed them—without revealing his knowledge of their sexual activity. Had the names of his subjects become public, there was always the possibility of personal embarrassment, not to mention the risk of family disruptions or threats to careers. Some social scientists opposed Humphreys' approach because they feel people have a right to know when they are being studied and a right not to be studied if they don't want to be. Others argue, however, that when people are in a public place, social scientists have the same right to observe them that anyone else has. What do you think?

SOURCE: Laud Humphreys, *Tearoom Trade: Impersonal Sex In Public Places* (Chicago: Aldine, 1970).

umber of strangers and interviewers. They are adaptable, furthermore, e extent they are relatively unstructured and can easily be altered when essary. Still another advantage is that the detail and depth of information ake them particularly rich in clues and insights. In this way, observational studies often suggest hypotheses worthy of future testing by more precise methods.

A major limitation of the observational study is that the results are often based on one case, which makes it difficult to generalize to another situation. The potential for bias on the part of the researcher is another possible problem area. Often, he or she must rely on personal judgment and interpretation and thus may not accurately see what is actually happening. Finally, the lack of standardized procedures could make it difficult to duplicate or replicate additional observational studies.

Use of Existing Sources of Data

The three research designs discussed so far emphasize collecting data from scratch, that is, with researchers personally collecting their own data. Sometimes this may be unnecessary. Relevant data may already exist which has been collected by other researchers. Various research centers throughout the world such as the National Opinion Research Center in Chicago or the late George Gallup's American Association for Public Opinion Research in Princeton, now maintain data archives whereby they collect, exchange and sell data sets stored on computer cards and tapes. The records of universities, corporations, hospitals, government agencies, etc. present other sources where data is available. One of the richest sources of data would be the United States Census which gathers detailed information about every citizen every ten years. If we think of Durkheim's research dilemma, it may make what is being said more clear. Durkheim found it impossible to conduct an experiment, survey, or observational study because the people whose behavior he wanted to study were dead. His solution was to analyze government death certificates. He did it so brilliantly that many consider his research to be the first great empirical breakthrough in sociology.

There are some already existing sources of data that are less "quantitative" than those mentioned above, but of equal potential importance for social science research. Useful information can be found in newspapers, books, magazines, movies, television programs, advertisements, speeches, letters, diaries, song lyrics, paintings, school textbooks, the yellow pages, or even garbage. Newspapers, for example, can be a time machine to another century. If we analyze the newspapers published 100 years ago, we can find out how people at that time lived. Another imaginative study dealing with this more "qualitative" type of data had sociologists study the images of men and women in rock music videos. They looked at lyrics, clothing styles, gestures, and the like and found that most rock music videos portrayed women in subordinate roles, as sexual objects, or as targets of violence.

As was true for the other three research designs, there are advantages and disadvantages to using precollected qualitative and quantitative data. Certainly, in some circumstances, a lot of time, money, and effort can be saved. There are also the distinct advantages of making historical research possible and giving the researcher the opportunity to be "creative." Also, since the data have been collected by others, the researcher cannot influence answers to questions he or she is using.

On the negative side, however, there are several potential problems. Quantitative data, often collected for a different purpose than the researchers, may not be sufficiently accurate or reliable. The official statistics on crime, for example, overreport lower class crimes and underreport crimes committed by members of the middle and upper classes. Qualitative data, on the other hand, may require undue subjective interpretation. Assume, for example, that we wanted to see if public attitudes toward sex had changed in the last 20 years. We might compare the erotic content (vocabulary, themes, descriptions of sexual acts, etc.) in best selling novels of today with those of the past. But how do we deal with the fact that what may be erotic to one researcher may not be erotic to another? These types of subjective issues could arise when using already existing sources of data.

Summary

Scientists in general and social scientists in particular are interested in finding out what is true and why it is true. Adherence to the scientific method keeps them on the "right track" in this search for truth. Specific research designs used by social scientists include experiments, sample surveys, observational studies, and the use of existing sources of data. Experiments can disentangle or explain cause-and-effect relationships both in laboratories and naturalistic settings. Sample surveys generally provide correlations that allow us to explore the current scene. Observational studies give descriptive depth. Already existing sources of data may be useful for explanatory, exploratory, and descriptive types of research. Overall, no single research design is superior to any other. Each has its own strengths, drawbacks, and limitations. Sometimes the best way to conduct research is to combine several of these designs.

Questions

1. What is the difference between the way that "ancients" and "moderns" conceive of change and upheaval in life?

2. What did you think science was before reading this article? What definition of science do you have now? Is astrology a science?

3. To what extent are *all* sciences alike? To what extent are they different?

4. What are "discovery" and "explanation" in science and how are they related to research and theory?

5. What is the scientific method? Why is it important?

6. What is the difference between an independent and a dependent variable? Give examples.

7. What are the differences between obtrusive and unobtrusive research designs? Which are better? Did Durkheim use an obtrusive research design?

8. Explain the difference between a scientific and an unscientific hypothesis.

9. What is the difference between egoistic, altruistic, and anomic suicide?

10. Why has the experiment always had a central place in the history of science?

11. What is the Hawthorne effect?

12. What kinds of questions can a sample survey answer that an experiment cannot?

13. What are the differences between correlations and cause-and-effect relationships?

14. What problems are involved in picking a representative random sample?

15. The telephone is increasingly used to interview people today. Some jokingly call these "telephone polls." List the pros and cons of using telephones in survey research.

16. Why is it difficult to be both a participant and an observer of a society or culture?

17. Assume someone gave you a stack of comic books that date back to 1930. Design a study that would make use of this existing source of data.

18. What are the advantages and disadvantages of using the experiment as a research design? The sample survey? The observational study? The use of existing sources of data?

19. Do you think that increased use of computers in social science will have positive or negative effects?

20. What types of ethical questions arise in doing social science research?

Part II

Seeing the
Social Sciences

Social science investigates human beings and their social world. Its subject matter is the entire range of human behavior and the social institutions which mold it. Since this is a very large subject, social science is divided into disciplines, or specialized areas of study. Different perspectives and emphases distinguish one from another, though the divisions between these disciplines are somewhat arbitrary and subject to change. Generally included among the social science disciplines are psychology, sociology, anthropology, political science, economics, and history. Geography is sometimes included as well.

This brings to mind an ancient Indian or Pakistani folk tale in which six blind men, touching various parts of an elephant's anatomy, attempt to identify the object. The first man, grasping the tail, declares it to be a rope. The second, third, fourth, and fifth men grasp, respectively, the elephant's tusk, ear, trunk, and knee, and believe it to be a stone, leaf, snake, or tree. The last man, running his fingers over the sides of the elephant, says he does not really know what he has touched, but he does know it has no beginning or end. Social science is something like that elephant. Beginning students, like the first five men in the tale, often find it difficult to conceive of social science as a totality. Even when they do, like the last man in the tale, social science may appear to be without beginning or end.

The articles in this section will, hopefully, clear up some of this elusiveness. Each deals with a specific discipline. As you read them, keep in mind that social science is a general term applicable to those disciplines which by their methodology attempt a systematic study of the institutions of human societies and the behavior and interrelationships of human beings. In this sense, social science is a totality.

31

Chapter Four

Psychology

Jacqueline P. Kirley

Cathy put down her sandwich. She was full. She kept turning certain events of the afternoon's meeting over and over in her mind. "Why didn't I speak out to make that point. Why didn't Greg wait another five minutes to make the point when he knew I planned on making it. Then he comes off as a leader and all I do is nod my head in agreement. If I keep this up, I'll never get ahead! Why do I always do this? Oh, I can't let myself keep thinking about it—it'll drive me crazy!" With that, she got up, put the rest of her sandwich away, and went to her desk to finish a report.

But, in fact, Cathy *had* gotten ahead. After college she'd taken a master's degree in business administration, graduated in the top 10 percent of her class, and been hired by a toy and game manufacturing company. In five years she had made two major moves up the corporate ladder. And yet she was, or she saw herself as, unassertive.

Concentrating on the report proved beyond her powers at this moment. She decided to call her boyfriend, which she'd avoided doing up to this point. Somehow, she didn't want him to see her in the midst of a silly personal trauma. When there was no answer, she was almost relieved. "I'll repot some plants; they need it," she thought. Soon she lost herself in deciding which plants should go into which pots, taking into consideration the size of the pot, the plant's need for water, and whether the pot was plastic or clay. She carefully knocked the plants out of the pots and checked for root damage as her uncle, the gardener, had done. Working with plants was a real pleasure for her and she'd even had a few of her more creative thoughts about her work while washing pots or mixing soil. But today something in the tangled roots of the plants reminded her of the tangled relations at work and her mind jerked back to the meeting. In no time she was upset again—with herself, with Mr. Genovese her boss, with Greg Thompson, with the way her mother criticized some of her suggestions—and before her thoughts really jelled, she'd dropped one of her favorite clay pots and cut her hand reaching down too fast and grabbing a pointed shard.

Just then the phone rang and Cathy answered, "Hello . . . . Oh, hi, Greg . . . . Just fine, and you?" all the while fighting the urge to scream or cry.

Some of the events in the above story may be used to illustrate important interests of the intriguing social science discipline called psychology. Psychology is defined as the science of behavior. Most psychologists would agree with this definition as long as the word behavior is defined so as to include not only observable behavior—actions, gestures, spoken words or sounds—but also internal behaviors of the nervous system or glands and unseen mental processes such as conscious or unconscious thoughts. There is, however, an important division among psychologists. Some believe that psychology can only study observable behavior and events in the environment, both of which are empirically knowable. Others believe it is possible, and certainly necessary, to study internal mental processes.

All psychologists would be interested in understanding why Cathy has been ambitious, why she likes to pot plants and how she learned to do so, why she is or perceives herself to be unassertive, and why she is so upset at her co-worker, Greg. But the psychologists who believe we can know what is inside would explain the events in the story in terms of types of thought processes Cathy exhibits, such as imagination, cause-effect thinking, and verbal and non-verbal thinking. They would also consider internal motivation such as drives and wishes. They might analyze her behavior in terms of an achievement drive or in terms of an unconscious wish to hurt herself or someone else. In contrast, the psychologists who prefer to deal with observables would want to carefully observe and log her behavior and analyze how her environment, especially her human environment, interacted with that behavior in the past. They might want to know how her parents acted towards her when she was assertive. They might want to know what events had occurred when she was learning to pot plants so that she had such pleasant associations to it.

Today psychology is a huge discipline which has carved out a territory that stretches from the biological to the social. It takes as its subjects human beings as well as animals, from the chimpanzee to the lowly cockroach. Basic research and theory in psychology can be divided into five major areas: the behaviorist, the dynamic, the social, the physiological, and the cognitive. The interests of each of these five areas will be briefly described below. After each description there will be some suggestions as to how the psychologists in that area might regard the incident with Cathy. Some final considerations will focus on how basic psychological knowledge can be applied to areas of daily life.

Behaviorists

Behaviorists believe that it is possible to understand human beings or animals by studying observable behavior as it relates to the environment. Therefore they take the position that psychologists should avoid vague and abstract concepts such as mind, drive, wish, intuition, and imagination because these concepts are not observable, and hence cannot be empirically validated. Behaviorists use the term "conditioning" to describe the kind of learning that goes on, either through simple association of two events or stimuli or through rewards and punishments which follow a behavior and thereby control it. For example, a person can associate a high-pitched whirring sound (one stimulus) with the dentist's drill in action (a second stimulus) and learn to feel a little queasy on hearing that sound—even if it is made by a drill which is working on bricks on a building. We call that a learned reaction because before the events in the dentist's office that person had no particular reaction to the drill on the building. Another type of learning occurs when little Billy learns that when he has stuck his tongue on some freezing metal, he should wait a couple of seconds before pulling the tongue away. If he waits that couple of seconds, his behavior is rewarded by having the tongue come away quite easily and painlessly. If he pulls on it immediately, he experiences intense pain and might even lose a small piece of skin from his tongue. We can say that the response of holding the tongue there longer has been "reinforced" by being able to remove it painlessly. Because behaviorists believe that virtually all behavior and feelings are learned, they are often called "learning theorists."

Behaviorists might be interested in how Cathy's environment is reinforcing (encouraging, rewarding) her unassertive behavior. Alternatively, they might wonder what kinds of reinforcements she gets from *perceiving* herself as unassertive. They might want to know what conditioned her ambitious behavior. They would want to know how she learned to pot plants and what made her enjoy the activity. In each case, behaviorists would turn to their models of conditioning to understand how Cathy learned to feel and behave as she does.

Dynamic Psychologists

Dynamic psychologists focus their interest on the motivations of human beings. Some, like Carl Rogers, who are called humanists, believe that people are motivated by a need to fulfill themselves. Rogers' theory, known as "self theory," holds that each person is born with a desire to realize his or her potential. He believed that in order to accomplish this, a person needs a strong, positive self concept. Rogers would consider Cathy's self concept to be too negative. When something goes wrong or if she herself does something which is wrong, she goes beyond criticizing the act or behavior and becomes critical of her whole "self." At that point she can no longer think constructively or comfortably about the issue. If she could maintain a strong self concept in the face of occasional failures or reverses, Cathy would be much more likely to achieve her potential.

A different kind of dynamic psychology is offered by psychoanalysis. Psychoanalysis is a theory of personality developed by an influential Austrian physician named Sigmund Freud. Like Rogers' self theory, psychoanalysis also considers motivation important, but instead of seeing people pulled towards self fulfillment, it sees people as being driven by instincts which are largely unconscious. Freud believed that a few, fundamental instincts support a broad range of activities. The instincts go through a series of modifications before they are put to use. For example, the sex drive might "fuel" creativity. In other words, some people, unable to express all their sexual energy directly, may redirect some of it into producing something new—perhaps an idea, a product, or even a book or painting. It is not uncommon to refer to this new creation as that person's "baby," even though the connection between sex and creativity remains unconscious.

A psychoanalytically oriented psychologist might ask whether Cathy's accident with the pot was really an accident. Could it have been that Cathy was trying unconsciously to punish herself or someone else? Does her controlling personality reflect childhood experiences? Since her mind so readily jumped from her boss to her co-worker Greg (who had "taken over" what she wanted to do) to her mother, did some of these problems begin in childhood, and does she perhaps unconsciously transfer feelings about her mother to people—male or female—who try to "take over"?

Social Psychologists

Social psychologists begin with the premise that people are social animals and that their thoughts and actions reflect that they are members of groups. Social psychologists can be thought of as cousins to sociologists. The difference between them is that the former focus on how the group affects the individual while the latter attend more to group processes. Issues in social psychology include decision making, interpersonal and group influence, compliance, attitude change, discrimination, and social status. While they measure observable behavior and consider environmental factors, they do not shun internal, mental concepts since attitudes and values are central to social behavior.

A social psychologist reading Cathy's story would ask about the role of women in the general society and in the corporate world. How is influence wielded among board members? Does Cathy's behavior violate the norms (rules) of that setting? What is the basis of leadership on that board? What kinds of exchanges of power exist in that setting? Is Cathy's position on the board adequately defined? Does the way the board is set up automatically put the position Cathy holds in competition with the one Greg holds?

Physiological Psychologists

As social psychologists are the cousins of sociologists, so physiological psychologists can be considered close relatives of the biologists. They concern themselves with how the nervous system, including the brain, works and how the nervous system interacts with the glands, which are part of the hormonal system. For example, they might study the electrical patterns the brain makes during different stages of sleep, including dreaming. When we have an electroencephalogram (EEG) taken of our brain, the marks which the pen makes are driven by the electricity in our brains. It is the same electricity which allows us to feel a soft kitten's fur or to regulate how far we move our foot when we're walking downstairs. It is also possible to study our physiology in chemical terms because when nerves send impulses electrically, they release chemicals at the nerve endings to make the connection from one nerve to the other. Appropriately, these chemicals are called "neurotransmitters" because they transmit messages within the nervous system. Neurotransmitters are associated with certain feeling states, such as aggression, fear, or depression. There is evidence that certain mental disorders, such as extreme depression, are due to an overabundance or a deficiency of certain of these chemicals. Whether physiological psychologists are studying human beings or lower animals, what they care about is how the system works. If we use computer terminology, physiological psychologists care about the "hardware" as opposed to the way the machine is programmed.

A physiological psychologist would wonder what kind of neurotransmitter was present when Cathy was upset. Was it the same kind which exists in more aggressive people when they are upset? What signalled her that she was "full" after eating—was it her stomach or her brain? Is the memory of her uncle stored as a unit in a single location in the brain? Or is the memory of her uncle re-created with the entire brain each time she thinks about him? When she hurt herself on the pointed shard, what registered her pain? When she reads or speaks or otherwise processes language, which side of her brain is active—the left side, like most people—or the right side?

Cognitive Psychologists

Cognitive psychologists have a different way of looking at all this. They accept the "hardware" of the nervous system with its biochemical operations and then hone in on the way the system is "programmed," what routines and procedures the system uses to acquire and manipulate information. They are interested in mental representations—images, words, and symbols—as well as mental processes—sensation, perception, recall, and thinking. Cognitive psychologists would ask questions like: How does Cathy use her senses to get the information she needs from the environment? For example, when she looks at and "sees" a clay pot or a word on a page, is everything she needs to "see" (apart from her eyes) out in the environment or must she bring certain expectations and knowledge to her perceptual encounter? How are mental representations recalled? Are memories, such as Cathy's memory of her uncle or even of the more recent board meeting, always the same or do they change? What are children's minds like—are they like adult minds or are they qualitatively different? When Cathy was four or five years old, did she have a different way than adults of understanding what "more" means? What rules do people follow when they generate sentences in speech? What is language? When Cathy speaks a sentence which she has never spoken before, how does she know in what order to put the words? How is her creativity different from her problem solving? Is Cathy's thinking about which plant to put in which pot different from the thinking she does when she invents a new toy?

As you can see, different areas of specialization can ask different questions about the same issues. Questions about memory, for example, were raised by more than one area of specialization. Furthermore, the same questions are capable of being answered in different ways depending on the theory the psychologist uses. For some people this lack of certainty and clear answers makes psychology a frustrating field. Others consider that each branch of psychology gives us certain kinds of information and explanation and no one branch can offer us the whole truth.

Applied Psychology

While many psychologists try to answer the type of basic questions described above, there are others involved in what is called "applied" psychology. This branch of psychology is not trying to learn about animals or human beings and how they function, but rather to take what psychology has already learned and apply it to areas of everyday life. Areas influenced here range from advertising to the best way to help a person cope with life in times of stress.

Advertising is one prominent area which uses the findings of psychology. Even if we know that driving a particular make of car will not lead to a wonderful sex life, we are still influenced by seeing sexually attractive people associated with a particular product. And why do businesses pay famous sports figures to recommend a breakfast cereal? Obviously, they play upon our identification with that figure.

Besides advertising, psychologists play important roles in the school and workplace. Educational psychology deals with trying to optimize educational settings so that children (and adults) can learn better. They compare learning individually from computers or teaching machines to learning in groups. They examine the effects of tracking students by ability level for teaching such classes as reading and math. Psychology in the workplace asks many of the same questions as social psychology, with an emphasis on people operating in an organization. They are concerned with employer-employee relations, with using the personnel department to match people to jobs, and with maintaining good morale in the workplace.

The best known and by far the most numerous type of applied psychologist is the clinician who offers psychotherapy or counseling. It is estimated that 50 percent of the 70,000 psychologists in the U.S. are clinicians, some with private practices and others working in settings such as hospitals and clinics. Clinical psychologists address a wide range of emotional and behavioral problems. They are engaged in diagnosis of mental illness as well as its treatment. Their clients can be criminals or drug addicts, as well as people who have less serious problems of adjustment. To an outsider, Cathy appears to have every reason to be happy. She seems successful at work, she has friends, and a boyfriend. Yet we see that she worries about herself and her performance on the job and she spends an inordinate amount of time brooding about certain issues. If this should get to the point where it is interfering too much in her life, she may choose to get some therapy. In this capacity psychologists help people deal with issues of stress. (See Box 9 to see what different kinds of therapies exist.)

Box 9

Types of Therapy

Therapy can be offered in a setting for an individual or for a group. The kind of approach the therapist takes depends primarily on the theoretical framework in which that person was trained.

A person in individual therapy quite often sees the therapist once a week but it may be more or less often than this. In long-term therapy, the therapist is likely to primarily listen to the patient and to interpret what the patient says.

If the therapy is going to be short term, the therapist may play a more active role, making suggestions and helping the patient problem-solve. Behaviorist therapists may ask their patients to keep logs of certain events which they find troublesome. Analysis of the events may suggest that it is possible to modify the environment which controls some unwanted behavior so as to change that behavior. Rogerian therapists may listen and affirm their client so that the person develops a better self concept and in that way is more likely to attain self-fulfillment. Psychoanalytically oriented therapists strive to have patient and therapist recognize meanings which the patient unconsciously attributes to the external world — meanings which are born out of unconscious needs. Treatment largely consists of analyzing those wishes and meanings as they almost inevitably attach themselves to the therapist. If a person undergoes an analysis, he or she can expect intensive, long-term treatment in which the therapist is seen about four times a week and the treatment lasts a minimum of one year, more often from two to four years. The goal of analysis is to examine and, to some extent, restructure the personality.

In group therapy people express their ideas and feelings and get the reactions of fellow group members as well as the interpretations of the therapist or therapists. (Many groups have two; usually one is male and the other is female.) Ideally, group members provide a warm and supportive atmosphere for each other but also serve a "reality" function of telling a person in the group how what they do or say affects others. Some groups encourage acting out one's feelings and ideas, almost like a drama; others have the members talk out their feelings toward a parent, for example, while addressing a pillow. Some groups are "sensitivity groups" which may be short lived and which try to get people in the groups to be more open to their own and others' feelings. They may also engage in "trust" exercises, such as letting themselves be led around blindfolded by someone else in the group or falling backward and trusting someone to catch them.

Family therapy is a version of group therapy. Families constitute special groups in that they have a past history and are expecting a future together. In family therapy, with all the members who live together present, it is sometimes possible that solutions can be worked out with the help of the therapist.

Whatever the type of therapy, the person seeking help must want to change and be willing to work at it, even though the old feeling and behaviors may be more comfortable. Psychotherapy isn't like getting an injection and then waiting for the medicine to work. In most cases drugs are not prescribed in psychotherapy, but even where they are, they aren't the whole story. Psychotherapy is a kind of re-education and, like education, cannot be done to anybody. For a person to benefit from therapy, he or she must be willing to change — not always an easy task since known miseries are often preferable to what is unknown.

Questions

1. What is psychology? Why does it stand midway between the biological and social sciences?

2. What could psychologists learn from chimpanzees and cockroaches?

3. What are the similarities and differences between each of the five areas in psychology? How would each analyze the incidents in Cathy's story?

4. Classify the following three examples as either "stimulus-stimulus" conditioning or "behavior followed by reward or punishment" conditioning:

   a. A dog that has heard a bell ring every time its food is delivered learns to salivate to the bell.

   b. A child learns to say please because adults give him what he wants.

   c. CTA riders learn not to push the back door of the bus until the light above it is green.

5. Describe someone you know who has a strong positive self concept and someone who has a strong negative self concept. How important do you think self concept is to our mental health? Do you agree with Rogers that human beings have an inborn desire to fulfill themselves?

6. In addition to a sex instinct, Freud posited an aggressive instinct. How might an aggressive instinct be expressed in a socially acceptable manner in society?

7. Do you believe that some accidents — household, car, or losing objects — are unconsciously motivated? What is your evidence?

8. Men and women have different styles of wielding influence. Is this difference learned or inborn?

9. The 1980's brought therapy groups that were just for women; it is predicted that the 1990's will do the same for men. What benefits might men derive from a "men only" group that they could not derive from a mixed group? Would the same reasoning apply to racial groups?

10. Research has found that urban dwellers are more individualistic than people who live in the country. What is there about those two social settings that promotes this difference?

11. Certain neurotransmitters predominate during aggression and different ones predominate during fear. List five animals which would have a preponderance of the former transmitter (start with lions), and list a different five which would have a preponderance of the latter (start with rabbits).

12. To test if children think differently from adults about the concept "more," try this experiment with 4- and 8-year-olds. Test each child individually and be sure to ask for reasons for answers.

    Show the child five pennies in one hand and one dime in the other. Ask the child which he or she would prefer. Follow up with "why?"

13. What implications arise if memories are created anew each time we think them? Think about witnesses testifying in court.

14. Besides the two examples given in the article, think of five other ways that advertising uses knowledge from psychology to get us to buy products. Study the ads for Virginia Slims cigarettes in magazines. What is its message? Look at the models they use and check to see if they are always tall, thin, and white. If that is so, why do you think it is?

15. Is psychotherapy closer to the process of education or to the process of curing an illness such as appendicitis? Why?

16. What does it mean to say that "known miseries are often preferable to what is unknown"? Can you think of examples?

Chapter Five

Sociology

Frank Zulke

Sociology, defined broadly, is the scientific study of society, social groups, and social behavior. A basic premise is that behavior is determined by the groups to which people belong and by the societies in which they live. In other words, we behave the way we do because we belong to particular groups in a particular society at a particular point in space and time.

Groups can be primary (a small number of people who interact on an intimate basis) or secondary (a small or large number of people who interact on a temporary, anonymous, and impersonal basis). Think of dyads such as two people in love, or larger collectivities such as baseball teams, churches, audiences at a rock concert, or corporations. The kinds of questions that would interest sociologists studying such groups are: How did they form? How are new members brought in? Do they influence members consciously or unconsciously? Is there pressure to conform? Will behavior of members change as the group gets larger? Are there leaders? Are secondary groups becoming more important than primary groups today?

These groups combine together to form societies. Societies can range from small bands of twenty to fifty people who survive by hunting animals and gathering nuts and fruits to highly developed industrial societies teeming with millions of people. While sociologists are interested in both types of societies, they will usually leave the "bands" for the anthropologists to study. The sociologists will concentrate on the modern, complex, technologically advanced societies and attempt to see how the societies meet basic social needs of their members. Thus they will look at such universal institutions as the family, religion, education, government, and the economy.

As an aside, it might be of interest to note that the development of sociological research and theory has occurred only in countries which have democratic political regimes. The word sociology itself, in fact, was coined in France by Auguste Comte in the time period immediately following the French Revolution. This may be changing at present. In 1989, the Presidium of the Communist Party in the U.S.S.R. passed a resolution making the development of sociology a national priority. For the first time in Soviet history, graduate students were sent to the United States to study sociology. Sociology in China has also made dramatic strides. Since the death of Mao Ze-dong, a Chinese Sociological Association was founded and government funds for research were made available. Events like Tiananmen Square in China and the break up of the Soviet Union, however, may mean that the future of sociology in those countries is still precarious.

There are two levels of analysis at which sociologists work. One level is microsociology, which focuses on everyday patterns of behavior, face-to-face interactions and the like. The sociologist here might examine workers on an assembly line, men and women in a singles bar, or college students who join a cult. No aspect of social life is too small for this level of analysis. The second level of analysis is macrosociology, which focuses on relationships between and among groups and the overall social arrangements in society. The sociologist here might explore how subsistence technology is related to the stratification system or the long-term effects of industrialization on a society. Microlevel and macrolevel analysis often complement each other and to ignore either would give a lopsided view of what sociological analysis is about.

Still another way to find out even more about what sociology is would be to check the table of contents of an introductory sociology text. Besides topics already mentioned above, typical topics found here include culture, socialization, race, ethnicity, gender, bureaucracy, crime, delinquency, ecology, stratification, demography, minorities, etc. By now, it should be clear that sociology is a broad field.

In its approach to the study of behavior, groups, and society, sociology strives to be scientific. This means that sociologists are sometimes distrustful of common-sense explanations. (See Box 10.) One wag has wryly suggested that common sense is no more than yesterday's opinions. While one could debate if this is true or not, sociologists prefer to use an explanatory approach which can be verified by empirical evidence. They want to use an objective, logical, and systematic method to collect, organize, and analyze their information. It is this use of the "scientific method" that separates sociological thought from casual reflection. In terms of specific research designs, it is estimated that 90 percent of the data collected by sociologists is done by means of interviews and questionnaires.

Box 10

Sociology Versus Common Sense

Since people live in society, they feel they know a lot about what's happening within it. Didn't many believe, not too long ago, that the average female — because of "innate inferiority" — could not do college work as well as the average male? "It's simply common sense," it was said. But just because many believed it did not "prove" the biological inferiority of women. Because we tend to believe what we want to believe, we sometimes accept as fact that which has not been investigated. Such a common-sense approach to social knowledge can be vague, oversimplified, contradictory, and even illogical. If "he who hesitates is lost," why should you "look before you leap"? How can "absence make the heart grow fonder" when "out of sight, out of mind"? Do "opposites attract" or do "birds of a feather flock together"?

Common sense may tell us that "early to bed, early to rise, makes a man healthy, wealthy, and wise," but the sociologist who did research to examine this would probably tell us that the man in question is most likely to be an unskilled worker who will not live as long as those in higher occupational groups, who barely earns enough money to feed his family nutritiously, and who is functionally illiterate. Because common sense may lead to distortions, misinterpretations, and falsehood, sociologists approach their subject matter scientifically. A true understanding of how social life operates must be based on facts. Note well: this is not saying that common sense is necessarily wrong. It is saying that it can't always be verified by empirical evidence.

SOURCE: Glenn Vernon: *Human Interaction* (New York: Ronald, 1965).

In his classic *The Sociological Imagination* (1959), the late C. Wright Mills suggests that sociologists have a special insight into the social world because they have the ability to understand the subtle linkage between personal experience and the structure of the society as a whole. Mills feels that people have problems seeing beyond their immediate situation. They see themselves and their world from the limited perspective of family, friends, classmates, and fellow workers. People have no idea how they are connected to larger groups and the general society. Mills feels that use of the sociological imagination opens up this cramped vision of the world because it makes people aware that personal lives are shaped by larger historical and social forces which are sometimes beyond personal control. In simplest terms, the sociological imagination shows how individuals fit into the "big picture."

Mills offers examples dealing with unemployment and divorce. When only one man is unemployed, he says, that is his personal trouble. His problem can be explained by lack of skills, opportunities, or willingness to work. When ten million American workers are jobless, however, that is a social problem which goes beyond the failings of individuals. Either the economy is not producing enough job opportunities or the educational system is not turning out enough qualified workers or some other impersonal social force is at work. Or consider the general rise in divorce rates in American society today. A couple may be unhappily married, but when one out of two American marriages end in divorce, it is time to look beyond a particular couple's personal troubles. The sociological imagination suggests the causes of divorce must be understood in terms of social developments that have made married life less satisfactory. It guides us to think about "subjective" reasons such as feminism, an increasing emphasis on "self-fulfillment," and a decline in common values as well as more "objective" reasons such as increased job openings and higher salaries for women. We will not be able to understand ourselves or the world, Mills says, without understanding the groups to which we belong and the society in which we live.

In another classic work, *Invitation to Sociology* (1963), Peter Berger pursues Mill's idea and suggests that the sociological imagination becomes like a "demon that possesses one." It will induce skepticism about "common sense" explanations of human society and allow us to see through facades and conventional wisdoms. It will make us see ourselves and others in a new light.

Box 11

A True-False Quiz on Sociological Research

T 1. The population explosion in newly developing countries of the world is caused by their high birth rates.

F 2. The rate of murder will be lower in states that have capital punishment.

F 3. Reading pornography increases the likelihood of committing sex offenses.

F 4. Young people are more likely to vote than people over 65.

F 5. A person is more likely to be murdered by a stranger than a family member.

T 6. People on welfare could work if they wanted to.

F 7. The income gap between male and female workers has narrowed significantly.

F 8. Men engaging in public homosexual acts tend to be single rather than married.

T 9. When a racial minority group moves into a previously all-white neighborhood, property values decline.

T 10. People who live in the southern part of the United States drink more alcohol than people who live in the North.

Even the social world into which we were born and in which we have lived all our lives may appear different.

To test if what Mills and Berger say is correct you might wish to discuss with your instructor whether the statements in Box 11 are true or false. All deal with areas of research that sociology has investigated. While answers are listed in the appendix, don't look them up until you have "tested" yourself.

Another question to be considered is "what can this stuff be used for?" While sociology is a *basic* science dedicated to the accumulation of fundamental knowledge about society, groups, and behavior, it is also an *applied* science. Sociology can be used to solve practical problems, guide policy decisions, or serve particular clients. In fact, many of the 15,000 professional sociologists in America are quite active in the applied area. This is true for the 70 percent who teach in colleges and universities and for the steadily increasing 30 percent who are employed in government, industry and nonprofit organizations. Sociologists involved in applied research collect, analyze, and interpret data that enables manufacturers to anticipate consumer preferences, candidates to predict voting behavior, companies to make personnel decisions, and courts to render informed and just decisions. One landmark court decision was made, for example, in *Brown versus Board of Education* in Topeka, Kansas, in 1954. Topeka had segregated schools at that time. Six-year-old Linda Brown was forced to travel 20 blocks to an all-black school rather than attend an all-white school in her neighborhood. Her father challenged this and brought the case before the Supreme Court. Using the research and testimony of sociologists and other social scientists as the basis for its decision, the Supreme Court stipulated that racially segregated schools were unconstitutional because of harmful effects on the potential educational achievements of African-American children. I hope this point is made: sociological theory and research has important implications for social policies and programs. In terms of the ten items in Box 11, research and theory could contribute to policies and programs in such areas as welfare, crime, and the workplace.

In closing, it might be useful to consider some similarities and differences between sociology and the other social sciences. Sociology is like history in that both are interested in the social contexts that influence people. It is similar to political science in that both study how people govern one another. It is like economics in that both are interested in how goods and services are produced and distributed. It is similar to anthropology for both study culture. It is like psychology since both are concerned with how people adjust to the contingencies of life.

Unlike historians, sociologists are primarily concerned with events in the present. Unlike political scientists and economists, sociologists do not concentrate on only a single institution. Unlike anthropologists, sociologists primarily focus on industrialized societies. Finally, unlike psychologists, sociologists stress variables external to the individual to determine what influences people.

Questions

1. Define sociology. How does it differ from socialism or social work?
2. What types of groups and societies is the sociologist interested in? Why?
3. Why is sociology most highly developed in countries that are democracies?
4. What is the difference between microsociology and macrosociology?
5. Why might a common-sense approach to social knowledge lead to distortions and misinterpretations?
6. In what sense is sociological thought different from casual reflection?
7. What is the "sociological imagination"? How might use of it add to our understanding of such controversial issues as affirmative action or bilingual education?
8. Were you surprised by the answers to the ten questions taken from current sociological research? Why or why not?
9. "What can this stuff be used for?"
10. Can you see any disadvantages to using social science research as evidence for legal decisions?
11. How is sociology different from, and similar to, the other social sciences? Apply the approach of each to juvenile delinquency.

Chapter Six

Anthropology

Frank Zulke

Anthropology is most frequently defined as the "study of man" (in the sense of human being). It includes everything that has to do with human beings, past and present. Since, needless to say, no single anthropologist would be able to investigate such a broad field, the discipline is divided into at least two subfields: physical anthropology and cultural anthropology.

Physical anthropology focuses on humans as biological organisms. Whether the emphasis is on extinct ancestors or the study of living primate groups (mammals including lemurs, apes, monkeys, etc.), the attempt is made to examine the evidence for human evolution. The human animal is seen as evolving through gradual processes of "natural selection" — developing upright posture, a large complex brain, finely tuned eye-hand coordination, etc. The time span of interest here, as Box 12 indicates, may even go back 4½ billion years ago to the birth of the world. The time span of interest for humans, as traced through fossils, will be less. Fossils are bones, impressions, or traces of animals or plants of a former geological age found in the earth's crust. They provide clues to the human past. Fossils of humans have been found that are 35,000 years old. Other fossils that show "links" to humans have been dated at 500,000 and even millions of years old. Anthropologists, thus, have been the caretakers of human history for a very long period of time. Remember, too, that there are "written" records for only about 5,000 years of human existence.

Although humans are biological organisms and, therefore, similar to other animals, humans are also quite unlike any other animals. One distinctive feature

---

Box 12

Origins

"If we were to document the history of the earth, day by day, year by year, since its birth as part of the solar system some 4 ½ billion years ago in a single volume exactly 1,000 pages, each of those pages would cover 4 ½ million years. Almost the first ¼ of the book, about 220 pages, would describe how conditions propitious for the emergence of life slowly came about after the gases had condensed to form our hot seething planet. At this point, blobs of jelly, unmistakably living, yet very primitive, would be seen in the swirling tide pools of the warm oceans. But life in the sea in a form with which we are familiar would have to wait until we plowed our way through ¾ of the text—the Age of Fishes was 500 million years ago. And the first land creatures, descendants of fishes that deserted their aquatic habitat turn up 30 pages later, at about 350 million years ago. One of the most exotic periods, and certainly the most awe-inspiring, of the earth's history, the Age of Dinosaurs, would consist of about 30 pages describing the period between 225 million and 70 million years before the present when with unusual abruptness, they disappeared to be replaced by the Age of Mammals. It was at this point, 70 million years ago, that the first primates evolved, small rat-like creatures that abandoned ground living and took to life in the trees; it was from such simple beginnings that monkeys, apes and humans evolved. . .

The most distant of man's identifiable ancestors (the first hominid) put in an appearance about 3 pages from the end of the book, at 12 million years. The *Homo* lineage comes at the bottom of the penultimate page, and the first stone tools would be described half way down the last page. And, testing our powers of literary compression to an extreme degree, the whole rise of modern humans would have to be crammed into the last line of the book, with the esthetics and symbolism of the stone-age cave paintings, the advent of agriculture, the intellectual excitement of the Renaissance, the turbulence of the Industrial Revolution, the polarization of the Superpowers, the birth of space travel and everything else that constitutes our recent history somehow telescoped into the final word."

SOURCE: Richard Leakey and Roger Lewin, *Origins* (New York: E.P. Dutton, 1982), pp. 12-14.

---

that makes humans different is that they possess culture—socially learned and shared patterns of behavior passed on from one generation to another. Without a culture transmitted from the past, each new generation would have to solve again elementary problems of existence. Each generation would have to rediscover fire, reinvent the wheel, relearn to domesticate animals, devise again a moral code, etc. Cultural anthropologists study humans in terms of their culture. Three areas of interest for cultural anthropologists are archeology, linguistics, and ethnography.

Archeologists study past cultures. They are interested in those which left written records as well as those that existed thousands of years ago that did not. To study these cultures, anthropologists look at material objects, or artifacts, that people have left behind. Often these remains are buried in the ground, so archeologists carefully dig them up, date them, and try to reconstruct what life was like in the past. Tools, weapons, pottery, and even "garbage" can tell much about how people lived. Think of what archeologists 500 years in the future might conclude if they were to find a copper disk we Americans call a "penny." Or what if they found a condom?

Linguists study human languages. They are not so much interested in learning to speak foreign languages fluently but in understanding how the language used affects a culture. Without language, culture could not exist. It allows knowledge to be passed from individual to individual and from generation to generation. Some go so far as to say we know the world only in terms that language provides. We can tell how important something is to a culture, for example, by the number of words the culture has for it. Consider that Eskimos have twenty different words for snow, Bedouin Arabs have hundreds of words related to the care of camels, and Americans have an ever increasing number of words related to the computer.

Ethnographers concentrate on cultures of the present. They often go into the "field" to complete an observational study firsthand. Sometimes they use detached-observation but more often they use participant-observation. Here they eat, sleep, work, and make friends with the people in the culture they are studying. Anthropologists use this research design much more than other social scientists. Box 13 gives some idea of the "culture-shock" that might beset such a researcher.

Although best noted for studying relatively small, isolated, nonliterate, faraway, "exotic" cultures—the last surviving stone age tribe, lost cities, etc., anthropologists are increasingly interested in large, complex, technologically developed cultures. At least two reasons may account for this. First, many traditional cultures are disappearing or else are finding it necessary to adjust to a rapidly changing world. Second, there is greater recognition that some questions that must be dealt with in modern cultures can only be answered by the kind of understanding that comes from the use of an anthropological perspective.

The anthropological perspective constantly reminds us that ours is not the only existing culture and that we should not be ethnocentric, i.e., we should not consider our way of life superior to all others. If we judge other life styles in terms of our own conceptions, we may see those who are different as inferior,

---

Box 13

Culture Shock

Culture shock refers to the feelings of disorientation and stress that people experience when they enter an unfamiliar cultural setting. Even anthropologists have this experience. Napoleon Chagnon describes his first meeting with members of the Yanomamö tribe of Venezuela and Brazil:

> My heart began to pound as we approached the village and heard the buzz of activity within the circular compound. . . . The excitement of meeting my first Indians was almost unbearable as I duck-waddled through the low passage of the village clearing.

> I looked up and gasped when I saw a dozen burly, filthy hideous men staring at us down the shafts of their drawn arrows! Immense wads of green tobacco were stuck between their lower teeth and lips making them look even more hideous, and strands of dark-green slime dripped or hung from their noses. We arrived at the village while the men were blowing a hallucinogenic drug up their noses. One of the side effects of the drug is a runny nose. The mucus is always saturated with the green powder and the Indians usually let it run freely from their nostrils. My next discovery was that there were a dozen or so vicious, underfed dogs snapping at my legs, circling me as if I were going to be their next meal. I just stood there holding my notebook, helpless and pathetic. Then the stench of the decaying vegetation and filth struck me and I almost got sick. I was horrified. What sort of a welcome was this for the person who came here to live with you and learn your way of life, to become friends with you? . . .

> I am not ashamed to admit. . . that had there been a diplomatic way out, I would have ended my fieldwork then and there.

SOURCE: Napoleon Chagnon, *Yanomamö* (New York: Holt, Rinehart and Winston, 1968), p. 5.

---

ignorant, crazy, or immoral. "Early anthropologists" in the guise of Christian missionaries, for example, were appalled at the sexual habits of Polynesian peoples.

An important step in reducing ethnocentrism is to understand that values, norms, beliefs, and attitudes are not in themselves correct or incorrect, desirable or undesirable. They simply exist within the total cultural framework of a people. This is why anthropologists tend to be "holistic" in their examination of various cultures. Everything should be considered in relation to how it fits into "that" culture rather than how it fails to fit into "our" culture. This is known as cultural relativism. By attempting to understand how lending one's wife to strangers fitted into traditional Eskimo culture, for example, you would discover its usefulness in that climate. Below, the quotation from Hans Ruesch's *Top of the World* has an Eskimo explaining to a non-Eskimo why wife lending makes sense: "Anybody would much rather lend out his wife than something else. Lend out your sled and you'll get it back cracked, lend out your saw and some teeth will be missing, lend out your dogs and they'll come home crawling, tired—but no matter how often you lend out your wife she'll always stay like new." Wife lending seems the reasonable thing to do—albeit a sexist solution to be sure—within the harsh climate of the Eskimo culture.

In advocating cultural relativism, anthropologists are not suggesting that we can or even should condone everything people in other societies do. We do not, for example, have to lend our wife to a stranger. Practicing cultural relativity does not mean the abandonment of our own moral standards, but rather the attempt to understand the standards of other cultures. We can learn a great deal from the study of other cultures, no matter how simple or complex. The more we learn, the more we eventually see that it is impossible to gain complete knowledge about ourselves without examining cultures other than our own.

There are about 7,000 professional anthropologists in America, many of whom are women. About 80 percent of them are college professors who do research in addition to teaching. The other 20 percent work and conduct research for government, private industry, or nonprofit organizations such as museums. Anthropologists are particularly useful in jobs which require a cross-cultural orientation and/or where there is work that requires humanistic social planning.

In closing, I leave you to ponder this anecdote. My social science professor in college asked students to choose which of the social sciences was the "best." It had to be anthropology, she said, because anthropologists were the only social scientists with a sense of humor!

Questions

1. What is anthropology? Why is it considered the broadest science?
2. Distinguish between physical and cultural anthropology.
3. How long have humans been on earth? How do we know?
4. Distinguish between archeology, linguistics, and ethnography.
5. What other items in addition to a penny or a condom might a archeologist find if she was digging in the U.S.A. 500 years from now?
6. Do you think Chagnon's culture shock eventually wore off?

7. Why do anthropologists usually focus on small, isolated societies?
8. What is ethnocentrism? Why should we avoid it?
9. Why is cultural relativism desirable?
10. Compare job prospects for the various social sciences.
11. Can you think of any reasons why anthropologists might have a better developed sense of humor than other social scientists?

Chapter Seven

Political Science

Brady Twiggs

Political science is the study of the process of governing. As such, it is highly varied. Unlike most of the other social sciences, there are widely divergent positions among its practitioners as to exact subject matter and proper methodology.

Certain historic developments can help us understand why such diversity exists. Humankind has, after all, evolved an almost unending variety of ways to enable some humans to exercise rule over others. Partially, this involves institutional variations such as: clans, tribes, city-states, empires, kingdoms, nation-states and leagues—each of these having many possible sub-types. There have also been differences in the instrumentalities of rule: physical force, divinity, consensus, wealth, wisdom, prestige, numbers and negotiations. Finally, variation has developed in terms of what aspects of human activities are a part of political life. At times, only a limited number of human actions have been viewed as proper subjects of rulership, and yet, at other times, no area of human activities are excluded (care of the aged or unemployed, etc.).

To accompany such variation in subject matter, there have evolved widely divergent conceptions as to the best way to seek understanding. Among the intellectual approaches to the study of political life, the concepts, methods, and tools of such fields as theology, philosophy, law, psychology, sociology, anthropology, economics, history and biology are employed.

In the light of such diversity it is perhaps understandable that any attempt to specify "the" subject matter and "the" method of studying the subject is bound to frustrate and lead to arguments among practitioners. Despite this, it is possible to state some common subject concerns that consistently appear in the works of political scientists. First, political activity is always directed toward something, whether it be the good, salvation, equality, freedom, security, power or material well-being. Much of political thinking is devoted to identifying, defining, questioning, measuring and judging these values or purposes as a part of political life.

Other subjects for political scientists are institutions or structures. Political activities are organized human activities even though humans can and do participate as individuals. Here, the concern is with such phenomena as assemblies, parliaments, presidencies, bureaucracies, courts and police, political parties and pressure groups. Indeed, almost any form of human organization has the potential to function politically and thus come under the scrutiny of political study.

Finally, political life involves humans behaving or doing things. Some human actions that have been the focus of political studies are: warfare, voting, bargaining, terrorizing and administering. Again, almost any human activity can involve political life and part of political study is devoted to discovering and explaining what actions are necessary to understanding.

It is possible to identify philosophical, behavioral, and policy approaches to the study of political life. (Box 14 illustrates how the approaches might view abortion.) At times, one of these approaches is more dominant than the others, but all of them are currently represented among today's political scientists. Philosophical questions raised involve the moral nature of political behavior: What should be the relations among differing human groups? What are the limits of demands for obedience? What are the rights of individuals and groups? In trying to explore such issues the tools of philosophy are employed and this area is referred to as Political Philosophy (or Political Theory).

Secondly, we find an approach classified as the Behavioral Method. This includes a wide range of specific approaches. Generally, however, the emphasis is in developing and using concepts, tools and theories of science. The search is for patterns and systems of behavior. The tools used in such studies tend to be adapted from sociology, economics and psychology.

Finally, we have what can be called the Policy approach. This approach arose from a concern with the effects of political activities and interest in trying to solve some of society's problems. These studies start with certain generally accepted values and attempt to see how the political process furthers their achievement and/or how it can be formulated to do so. Perhaps the most distinctive characteristic of this methodological approach is the concern with the process of decision-making: who makes decisions; why they make them; and what are the results.

In conclusion, political science is one of the broadest studies of those who are students of human existence. As such, its scope of subject is almost as wide as all of human life and it makes use of almost every variety of intellectual skill.

Box 14

Abortion

The controversy surrounding the issue of abortion may be viewed as an illustration of the differing approaches to the study of political phenomena. Below are the differing ways the controversy might be viewed.

Political Philosophy –
The problem is one of conflict of values (freedom of choice versus protecting the unborn) and the role of government in this conflict.

1. What are the moral foundations of the respective values?
2. Should government attempt to resolve such value conflicts?
3. If so, upon what basis?
4. Can government effectively impose a settlement and retain the support necessary to popular government?

Political Behaviorism –
The problem is one of political conflict in which the government has become involved.

1. What groups are identified with each position?
2. What is the legislative record of abortion related bills?
3. What is the state of public opinion?
4. What are the positions on the issue of the candidates for political office?

Policy Approach Solution
Government decisions are going to strengthen or injure either the achieving of the freedom of choice or safeguarding the rights of the unborn.

1. What do the statistics on abortion suggest is needed? (How many; trends; related deaths; age and socioeconomic groups involved; etc.).
2. How has the Supreme Court decision impacted on the abortion statistics?
3. What would result from a change in the current legal status of abortion?
4. What public policies should be pursued to (change or sustain) the current situation?

Questions

1. What is political science, What are some common "subject concerns" of political scientists?
2. What does it mean to say that "At times, only a limited number of human actions have been viewed as proper subjects of rulership, and yet, at other times, no area of human activities are excluded?"

3. What is the difference between philosophical, behavioral, and policy approaches to the study of abortion?

4. What might each of the above approaches have to say about "Prayer in School" in America?

Chapter Eight

Economics

Daniel C. Reber

I'm sure that you would like a new car. But, the odds are that you don't have one. The reason? You say, I can't afford it; new cars are so expensive. Now, truth to tell, if you committed all your resources and took out a big loan, you probably would be able to buy a new car. What stops you is the thought of all the other things you would have to give up in order make that downpayment and pay those backbreaking monthly installments.

This scenario displays the heart of the study of economics. Economics is sometimes called the "dismal science," perhaps because economics always reminds us that every good thing that we want has a *cost* in the form of the sacrifice we have to make to get it. Ordinarily we think of costs in terms of the price in dollars. But the real cost of anything for which you spend your money is the opportunity to spend that money on something else. Just like you, I'd like to have a new car; but when I think of all the other things that I can have, that I would like to have, for the same money as a new car, I decide that I'd rather have the other things instead. Of course, not all costs are in money. The biggest cost of the course for which you're reading this book is probably the *time* that you have to give up in order to get a decent grade. The time you spend reading the book, going to class, and doing the homework could have been used for something else. Giving up that something else is your cost. If you work to get money, you have to give up leisure; if you buy a car, you have to give up many other good things that you could have bought and now can't; if you plan to get an education, you will have to give up some of your working hours, some time with family, or something else. You are like everyone else: there's never enough time to do all you want to, never enough money to buy everything you'd like. So you have to choose, and when you choose one alternative you necessarily give up another. This is the economic problem: the things we want are always more than the things we can get. Economics at its most basic level studies how people behave when they *must* choose among their alternatives.

The academic field of economics is usually divided into two categories, *Microeconomics* and *Macroeconomics*. Microeconomics is also called price theory. It studies the costs of individual goods, usually in money terms, and investigates what happens to the quantities that are bought, or produced, in response to a change in price. So price theory is concerned, for example, with what happens to the quantity of gasoline sold when the price goes up? Does a higher price cause consumers to buy a lot less gasoline, or just a little less? Why? Would sales of pretzels behave in the same way? If the price of pretzels goes up a little, will consumers buy a lot less, or a little less? What about the quantities of goods that producers are willing to bring to market for sale? If the price of lumber rises a lot, will that lead to much more lumber for sale? If the price of typing services goes up will many more people look for typing jobs, or just a few? If we raise the minimum wage, will that increase unemployment? What will be the effects of a law that requires women's wages to be equal to men's? If I open a restaurant, what are the costs I will face? What are the risks I run? How will I know if I'm making a profit or not? [The answer to that question is not as easy as you might think.] Microeconomics as a field is one in which economists are largely in agreement. Economists don't spend time arguing, for example, about whether, as consumers' incomes rise, they will buy more cars. Economists agree that they will.

Macroeconomics concerns the "big picture" topics in economics such as national economic growth; the general level of prices and inflation; the effects of taxation on work, output and the distribution of income; the effect of government spending and various government programs on the economy; the importance of interest rates and the causes and the effects of interest rate changes.

Economists are sharply divided over macroeconomics theory. One school of thought, called the *Keynesian* school, is named after a famous British economist, John Maynard Keynes, on whose views it is based. Keynes' theories are intricate, but the basic notion that has influenced public policy is that, when the economy is producing at less than maximum capacity, the government can, by spending more money in various ways, stimulate the economy to increase output and reduce unemployment, thereby making people better off. A corollary idea is that, in some cases, government can spend money better than individuals can.

Another view, the *Neoclassical* school, has lately been gaining increased credibility. This view of economics is associated with University of Chicago,

Box 15

Does Politics Make a Difference for the Economy?

The election of Ronald Reagan to the Presidency in 1980 brought with it a government economic policy very different from that which had guided U.S. policy in the 1970s. Under Reagan, policy was guided by economic ideas associated with the University of Chicago, the neoclassical, or "supply side" and "monetarist" approaches to government economic policy. The new President's policies were based on at least the following goals: 1) as little government involvement in private economic decisions as possible; 2) much lower marginal income tax rates; 3) a tough policy against inflation through tight money at the Federal Reserve; 4) a reduction in the percentage of national economic activity controlled by federal government spending and mandates; 5) free markets and letting consumers spend their money as they choose and not the way government directs.

Whether or not because of the Reagan administration policies, the 1980s saw some remarkable economic results: the rate of inflation fell spectacularly, from a high of 11.4 percent annually in 1979 to a mere 0.6 percent in 1986, rising again somewhat toward the end of the Reagan years. The rate of interest on U.S. Treasury 30-year bonds fell from 14 percent in 1981 to 6.7 percent in 1988. Perhaps most astonishing, the marginal rate of taxation on income fell from a variable rate as high as 70 cents on each additional dollar earned to a maximum of only 28 cents on the dollar. Beginning in 1982, the economy experienced strong, uninterrupted economic growth, and created at least 18 million new jobs—some commentators count even more. The rate of unemployment fell from an average of 7.3 percent in 1978-1982 to 5.8 percent in 1988-91. A huge wave of income tax dollars poured into government coffers from the top 1 percent and the top 10 percent of wage earners as stimulated by the new low rates, they strove even harder to get rich and abandoned old tax shelters, now worthless at the new lower tax rates. Meanwhile, through Reagan's changes, most very low wage earners were dropped from the income tax rolls altogether. The minimum wage, never raised during Reagan's years from $3.35 an hour, became a virtual dead letter.

George Bush was elected in 1988, ostensibly to continue the policies of the Reagan administration. "Four more years." "Read my lips, no new taxes." But Bush signed into law many measures that would have been rejected by the Reaganites out of hand. He raised taxes and marginal rates. He signed an increase in the minimum wage to $4.25 an hour. He agreed to the Clean Air Act, the Americans with Disabilities Act, and a so-called Civil Rights Act that greatly increased the ease with which minority and women workers can sue their employers for job discrimination. Each of these measures increases government control of the private economy and imposes very substantial new costs on the private sector. Bush increased non-defense government spending at a rate much greater than inflation or the growth of the economy. He greatly increased the number of Federal employees whose jobs regulate and oversee private industry. Bush also signed an extension of unemployment compensation benefits. All of these measures would be poison to Ronald Reagan's advisors, because they expand the role of government in the economy and interfere with markets and private economic decision making.

Although Bill Clinton defeated George Bush in 1992, his economic policies closely resemble those of Bush. Clinton obtained the passage of the Family Leave Act and a big increase in marginal tax rates on higher income earners. He wanted, although he did not get, a big new program of government spending "to stimulate the economy." He proposed a huge new government-managed national health care plan, which, if it had been approved, would bring 14 percent more of Gross National Product under government control. The President has nominated two economists to the Federal Reserve who have both written approvingly of inflation as a means of stimulating the economy and reducing the level of unemployment. So, the one element of Reagan's policies that Bush did continue, the fight against inflation, may be about to change as well.

In the 1996 Presidential election the Republicans may nominate a candidate in the Reagan mold of economic policy. If we assume that Clinton will be running for another term, we will get to see how the voters decide between these two very different approaches to national economic policy.

where over the years no less than six neoclassical economists have won the Nobel Prize in Economics. It also attained political importance with the election of Ronald Reagan as President (see Box 15). The neoclassicists generally hold that the causes of less-than-full output can only be worsened by government action. They hold that government spending is inherently inefficient, because people can decide for themselves how to spend their money better than the government can. Neoclassicists point out that government doesn't spend its own money, isn't subject to the iron discipline of profit and loss, and lacks any incentive to get rid of losing operations, or even shape them up. The postal service, the farm program, and the public schools provide typical examples of government inefficiency and waste. Neoclassicists say that obedience to Keynes' theories has led governments to spend more, seeking to stimulate the economy, and then to print money to cover their expenditures, causing inflation. Some of Keynes' followers assert that inflation reduces unemployment; but the neoclassicists say that inflation has but a temporary effect at best, and leads to higher unemployment later on.

Microeconomics matters to you, because clearly understanding the tradeoffs in decision making will help you to allocate your money and your time better. Macroeconomics matters to you because theories about it will guide national economic policy, and partly control whether, in the years ahead, we experience increasing prosperity and job opportunities, or declining options and a lower standard of living.

Questions

1. What is economics? Why is it sometimes called the "dismal science"?
2. According to economists, is money alone the cost of something?
3. Distinguish between Macroeconomics and Microeconomics. How does each affect us?
4. Contrast the differences between the Keynesians and the Neoclassicists on how the macroeconomy works.
5. Contrast national economic policy under Reagan, Bush and Clinton.

Chapter Nine

History

Jean Hunt

Virginia Woolf said that "Everyone is partly their ancestors" and Cicero warned us that ("Not to know what happened before one was born is to remain a child.")

History can be said to be the memories of the human race and it is also the touchstone of our identity. In order to think and act and decide, we must know how others acted, what others valued, how others failed, succeeded, invented, destroyed, created and persevered. History is our best definition of what it is to be human. History tells us the best and the worst; the stupid and the crafty. History insists on our shame and remembers our glory. We can not really know or appreciate our potential, for good or for evil, until we can put today into the perspective of the past.

A good historian is a good detective. The job is to look at the remaining and probable evidence and to try to reconstruct what really went on. How did people live? What did they think? Where did people get the courage, the drive, the madness to be explorers, pilgrims, revolutionists, pioneers, or immigrants? How did people work? Why did people sing?

History tries to come up with some answers. The biggest question is how and why do we have changes? How different is our life today from the lives and problems of our grandparents or our great, great, great grandparents? Just what has changed? Beliefs? Conditions? Life styles? Politics? History helps us see what is unique to a particular group or event and it also helps us understand the consequences, expected and unexpected, of action, planning and even of inaction, accident and error.

Change is often obvious; continuity is often more difficult to explain. What do we mean when we talk about tradition? What values, ideas, customs persist and just how do they affect us in the 1990s? Do these links with the past bind us or are they too tenuous to matter?

Historians do try to provide various answers, but the discipline of history has another important task because it trains us to ask questions. We all start with curiosity but thinking about the past requires a rigorous process of inquiry. And perhaps that is the most important skill we can ever learn, the skill of asking apt questions or an appropriate sequence of questions. We cannot learn if we are not trained to probe and poke, to scrutinize and review.

All of the above can be considered the "uses" of history. But we are also obliged to know something about history because of the ways that history is "abused." Selected historical facts can become propaganda. Sometimes history is written as special pleading for one group or cause or ideology or country. Often national history is chauvinistic. Not infrequently historians push their view of patriotism. It is possible to read historical accounts based on insufficient evidence, distorted facts or with self serving interpretations. There are many ways that history can be abused; it often is.

The remedy is honest inquiry. Neither the uses nor the abuse of history can be avoided. So we are constrained to grow up; to stop being a child; to deal with the facts and hone the skills and train ourselves to make both the past and the present work for us.

Questions

1. What is history? Why must historians deal with the questions of chance and of continuity?

2. What do the quotations by Woolf and Cicero mean?

3. Are answers or questions more important in history?

4. How is history "abused?"

Chapter 10

Geography

John A. Alwin

Even though many Americans only now are beginning to appreciate the importance of geography, its roots in the Western world are deep, reaching back to ancient Greece. Such scholars as Homer, Hippocrates, Plato and Aristotle knew the importance of geographical knowledge and understanding and discussed geography in their writings. In fact, it was Eratosthenes (c. 273 to c. 192 B.C.), the Greek scholar who spent his career in Alexandria, Egypt, who coined the term "geography," Greek for "description of the earth." Two thousand years later a contemporary definition of geography as "the study of the earth as the home of people" is surprisingly like the original.

A Spatial Perspective

Unlike most other social sciences, geography is more defined by its approach than by what it studies. Geography is the social science with the persistent spatial perspective. Geographical inquiries commonly share three basic and organizing questions: 1) Where? 2) Why there? and 3) What is the significance? Inquiries routinely begin with gathering data and establishing the patterns and distributions of the phenomena studied. This might be the locational aspects of subjects as varied as AIDS, wheat production, crime statistics or movement of international trade. Maps, which so graphically show spatial distributions answer the first question: "Where?" They are understandably the discipline's most powerful tool.

Once patterns are identified, the geographer then poses the second question of "Why" that pattern or distribution "there?" In searching for answers, geographers aren't shy when it comes to considering a wide range of causal factors. With detective-like sleuthing, they consider contributing factors as diverse as soil types, history, climate, ethnic background, environmental perception and religion. Patterns rarely can be explained by a single factor. More commonly, it is an understanding of the interplay of multiple causes that adds explanation to observed patterns. For example, a study of the geography of America's Midwest Corn Belt, might consider climate, soils, topography, transportation and international economics.

Increasingly, more socially and environmentally conscious geographers continue on in their studies to ask the third and often most important question, "What is the significance" of this geography? A geographer may ask, for example, what implications a changing pattern of farming in a developing country has for local diet, or query the implications a rapid spread of suburbanization has for groundwater quality.

A Threefold Division

Geography is a wide-ranging and diverse social science, and it is useful to think of the discipline in terms of its three major subfields: 1) Human Geography; 2) Physical Geography and 3) Geographic Techniques.

We *Homo sapiens* are spatial creatures, and the way that we organize ourselves and our activities on the surface of the earth generates the patterns and distributions that so intrigue human geographers. Practitioners in the subfield of human geography have similar interests with other social scientists, studying many of the same topics. Always, however, they bring a distinctive spatial perspective to their inquiries into human behavior. For example, an economic geographer interested in spatial aspects of economic behavior may map a city's retail trade area, determine the distributional aspects of wheat production in the American Great Plains or map the global pattern of international air travel.

Physical geographers are interested in the natural world in which humankind makes its home, primarily the earth's surface and the lower section of the atmosphere. These geographers share many interests with their kin in the natural sciences. As always, they bring a spatial perspective to their studies. The physical geography subfields of climatology, geomorphology and biogeography offer examples. Climatologists have a special interest in classification of climates and their distributions and implications for human occupancy. Geomorphologists are intrigued by the earth's landforms and how they vary from place to place. Biogeographers study the distributional aspects of plant and animal life.

Geographers specializing in geographical techniques range from cartographers who construct maps to experts in interpretation of aerial photographs, to remote sensing specialists who can decipher and interpret images of the earth's surface generated by satellites. In fact, computers have revolutionized geographical techniques. Pen and ink drawings of maps are now passé, with computer cartography the standard. GIS (Geographic Information Systems) has been an especially fast growing and useful computer-related specialty in geography (see Box 16).

Box 16

GIS (Geographic Information Systems)

One of the geographer's most powerful tools is GIS (Geographic Information Systems), which is an integrated computer system for the input, storage, analysis and display of spatial information. Rather than laboriously overlaying a series of standard paper maps to consider numerous geographic patterns and their interrelationships, GIS allows geographers and others to produce composite and graphic color maps on a computer screen.

A geographer hired to help a corporation locate a new downhill ski area might call upon GIS to make the job easier and quicker. Provided the right spatial information has been stored, the geographer can direct the computer to locate and highlight all locations that meet all the prescribed site attributes within a given area. These may include a minimum elevation, snowfall, slope, northern exposure, location within a prescribed distance of power and of a of paved road, and any other relevant variables.

Although its innately spatial nature makes GIS a logical specialty for geography, this computer tool has seemingly unlimited uses both in and out of geography. It has, for example, been used to trace agricultural pollution, to track the endangered snow leopard, to site hospitals for the most cost-effective health care and to monitor Singapore's microclimate.

Themes Old and New

Since the time of their Greek predecessors, geographers have had a fascination with places and regions, large and small, near and far. Geographers hope to understand what gives places distinctiveness, how they function and how they interact with other places.

Individuals applying to become one of the several thousand members of the Association of American Geographers are asked to indicate up to three regional specializations on their application form. They can choose from dozens of "official" regional specialties—Europe, Canadian Prairie Provinces, East Asia, Caribbean and Pacific Rim to mention just a few. During their careers, geographers work to better understand their regions and travel to those places for research when possible.

At least since the time of Hippocrates, the fifth century B.C. Greek physician whose *On Airs, Waters, and Places* introduced the notion of a possible link between human character and the natural environment, geographers have sought to understand the connection between people and the natural world. In North America, George Perkins Marsh's 1864 book entitled, *Man and Nature, or Physical Geography as Modified by Human Action*, awoke Americans to the adverse environmental impact of human actions and launched our national conservation movement. Today geographers still routinely engage in studies that bridge human and physical geography (see Box 17) and continue to be leaders in the areas of environmental degradation, land use planning and natural resource studies. A growing global awareness of the serious implications of people's impact on natural systems should provide many challenging opportunities.

Like the other social sciences, geography has become more quantitative and theoretical since the 1960s. A growing contingent of geographers now are fully engaged in searching for regularity and predictability in human spatial behavior.

Box 17

The Cultural Landscape

As soon as people move in and occupy a previously unsettled area, they set about converting the natural landscape into a cultural landscape. This is especially true of more technologically advanced cultures which subdivide the land, build highways, bridges, houses, fences, golf courses, airports and factories, and plant agricultural fields. Each people-induced modification to the natural landscape is an element in the mosaic that is the region's cultural landscape.

From the air, cultural landscapes are all the more apparent. Checkerboard fields, road networks, strip cropping, irrigated green fields, forest clearcuts, towns and cities all provide silent testimony to humankind's power to remake natural landscapes into cultural landscapes.

The patterns and processes associated with cultural landscapes are of special interest to geographers, many of whom become experts in reading the cultural landscape. Noted Pennsylvania State University geographer, Peirce Lewis, has described the cultural landscape as a people's unwitting autobiography. Among other things, the cultural landscape conveys information about a society's history, means of livelihood, level of technology and relationship with nature.

Geographers find it difficult, however, to repeat experiments in controlled laboratory environments. To compensate for this, more theoretical geographers have developed numerous graphic models that simplify spatial aspects of reality, and allow them to test causal factors. Models help lead to theories relating to everything from the land use patterns of cities in Southeast Asia and Latin America to the development of transportation networks in less developed countries.

Unfortunately, most Americans view geography as a grade-school-like discipline dominated by place name geography, i.e., knowing the names and locations of countries, cities, rivers and mountains. Those who go on to study geography at the college level quickly learn that such place knowledge is the most mundane aspect of the field. It merely provides a spatial skeleton around which geographers build much more interesting and more relevant geographies that have direct bearing on humankind's well-being.

In our increasingly more interconnected global village, geographers are in a unique position to help us understand new neighborhoods and neighbors. Such knowledge is essential for residents of our shrinking world.

Questions

1. Some of the most interesting kinds of maps are those we carry in our heads, what geographers call mental maps. Without consulting an atlas draw a map of the world on a blank sheet of paper. Show major land areas; locate and label any 30 countries. Draw in the Equator and add a map scale. Is your mental map sufficiently developed for an educated resident of our increasingly more interconnected global community?

2. How might a geographer's spatial perspective assist with helping to deal with such current global issues as rapid population growth? Destruction of tropical forests? Loss of biodiversity?

3. What is a current social issue/conflict in your city/neighborhood? How could a geographer assist in resolving this problem?

4. What is a current environmental issue/conflict in your city/neighborhood? How could a geographer assist in resolving this problem?

5. Explain how GIS might assist you in deciding where to locate a new fast food restaurant in your community.

6. Write a brief essay describing the cultural landscape of your neighborhood or community. How do you think that landscape differs from a counterpart landscape in Sub-saharan Africa? Why the differences?

Part III

The Foundations of Social Science

The first selection, "European Foundations of Social Science," is a survey of the precursors and founding fathers of social science. The article has a dual purpose: first, to show the growth of social science as an attempt to understand the rapid social change engendered by the French and industrial revolutions and second, to illustrate the background of some current preoccupations of social scientists. It illustrates the change from social philosophy to social theory and, finally, to an empirical methodology for the systematic, even quantitative, study of humans and society. Social science, as we know it today, is the result of this process.

The second selection, "Objectivity in Social Science: Beyond European Assumptions," moves the discussion of the foundations of social science to another continent: Africa. James Heard feels that a truly objective attitude toward social phenomena was lacking in research assumptions in the past and that this has affected social science theories. Until this Eurocentric perspective is balanced with an Afrocentric perspective, he maintains, we will not understand that "American civilization as well as world civilization has been the creative effort of many different ethnic and/or racial groups." His essay is both polemical and thought provoking.

Chapter 11

European Foundations of Social Science

Frank Zulke

Social science, as we know it today, is a fairly recent phenomenon on the horizon of human thought. It was less than 200 years ago that the empirical method—one of the hallmarks of social science—became an acceptable tool for the study of humans and society. Historical events of the late 18th and 19th centuries, such as the French and industrial revolutions, and consequent changes in political, social, and economic conditions, were responsible as well for the rise of social science.

This is not to say, however, that humans prior to this time had not previously speculated about themselves and their world. Since they assuredly did, let us begin our examination of the foundations of social science in the distant past and from there trace its development. Box 18 summarizes some events and dates to keep in mind as we do so.

Social Thought Prior to the Revolutions

Our paleolithic ancestors—and most of human existence was in the stone age—spent their time coping with an often hostile environment. They practiced a way of life characterized by nomadic hunting and gathering. (There is some conjecture here as to whether they were the hunters or the hunted). As long as they ate only what they could kill or pick in the wilds, they depended on the precarious balance of nature. Their numbers were limited by the numbers of other living things: they flourished when nature was bountiful and declined

---

Box 18

Important Dates and Events to Remember

This box pinpoints important dates and events in the history of western civilization. All of the dates, particularly the earlier ones, are estimates and, in some cases, "guesstimates." Approximate "beginning" dates are offered for the civilizations.

Paleolithic era (old stone age)	1,000,000 B.C. or earlier
Mesolithic era (middle stone age)	35,000 B.C.
Neolithic era (new stone age)	10,000 B.C.
Invention of agriculture	10,000 B.C.
Development of metallurgy	8000 B.C.
Mesopotamian civilization	3500 B.C.
Egyptian civilization	3000 B.C.
First "cities"	3500 B.C.
Development of writing	3000 B.C.
Greek Civilization	800 B.C.
Roman Civilization	750 B.C.-500 A.D.
Middle Ages	500 A.D.-1500 A.D.
Renaissance	1400 A.D.-1600 A.D.
Beginning of Protestant Reformation	1517 A.D.
Rise of Natural Sciences	1600s on
Industrial Revolution	1750 A.D.
French Revolution	1789 A.D.
Empirical Revolution	1800 A.D.
Rise of Social Sciences	1800s on

---

in times of scarcity. All energies were focused on the life-or-death business of getting food. Probably the greatest accomplishment of the Paleolithic era was human beings' acquisition of the knowledge and skills to create weapons from stone and wood that made them effective killers. By the mesolithic era, the human species assumed its present physical form and was capable of creating cave paintings, sculpture, and even musical instruments. Nevertheless, the environment still dominated human existence.

During the neolithic period human life stabilized as the domestication of animals and the invention of agriculture allowed for the growth of more permanent settlements. Farming at even the most primitive level, "slash and burn techniques," for example, tends to bind people to a piece of land. With metallurgy and the development of the plow, there could be a sizeable surplus of food. With "surplus" food there could be "surplus" people, enough to run the farms, to build houses, to make sculpture, to paint, and — eventually — to write. Indeed, it is within these early settlements, particularly the first "true" cities around 3,500 B.C., that we begin to find "written" records that show attempts to answer questions of a social nature. While high civilizations developed, as may be witnessed by the Code of Hammurabi in Mesopotamia (modern day Iraq) or the great temples and pyramids in Egypt, it is in classical Greece especially that humans turned to "reason" to answer fundamental social questions.

Whether it is true or not that all modern ideas are footnotes to Plato (427-347 B.C.) and Aristotle (384-322 B.C.), social scientists would agree that Greek thought regarding human nature and the social order is based, not on chance, religion, tradition, and/or authority, but on reason. Plato's *Republic* and Aristotle's *Politics* were written for an Athenian city-state subject to problems similar to those of America today, i.e., the search for new foundations of social order to replace those that had been destroyed by war, revolution, and stasis. The *Republic* is a blueprint for a utopia ruled by humans of reason; the *Politics* is a manual for politicians to guide them in ruling wisely. Together, they offer comprehensive ideas about humans and their behavior: one can't be human without society; to be human is to be social; the good society is in principle possible if it is based on reason. These ideas, important and imaginative without a doubt, are concerned with what ought to be, rather than with the way things are. That is why, finally, Plato and Aristotle are unacceptable to the social scientist. Plato and Aristotle are, primarily, philosophers and, although they transcend mere descriptions, their approach to the study of social phenomena is not disinterested and objective.

Because its scope was so comprehensive, Platonic and Aristotelian thought started a tradition that took almost 2000 years to change. While Rome conquered Greece militarily, it adopted Greek ideas philosophically. Christian thought, as presented by Augustine or Aquinas in the Middle Ages, continued this tradition and was further unacceptable because the emphasis was on the creation and maintenance of society by Divine Will. Things were the way they were because that was God's will. With the Renaissance, philosophers again turned their attention to earthly events, but this "rebirth" was often a paean to the ideals of Greek and Roman thought and, hence, not a step toward a new understanding of the world. Think of Queen Elizabeth I, Martin Luther, Leonardi da Vinci, William Shakespeare, and Christopher Columbus and you will get some flavor of the Renaissance.

By the early 17th century, however, we find an imposing array of discoveries (gravity, etc.) and inventions (telescope, etc.) in the biological and the physical sciences. A question frequently being asked was this one: if the methods of the natural sciences make so much sense of the physical and biological world, could not these same methods be applied successfully to the social world? The answer to this question had an effect on the development of social science for at this time we find perhaps the earliest major break with traditional social philosophy. For Plato and Aristotle, the state was natural and prior to human life, because humans, social by nature, could not be considered human outside of and apart from their community. Thomas Hobbes, in the *Leviathan* (1651), and John Locke, in *Two Treatises of Government* (1689), on the other hand, assert that humans are by nature free, that government is established by contract, and that the function of the state is the protection of individual rights. Although Hobbes stresses the right of self-preservation (because humans, brutish by nature would without government live in a state of war against each other), Locke emphasizes the right to property; they agree on the purpose the state must serve. Hardly empirical themselves, Hobbes and Locke assert that government should be based on an empirical understanding of humanity. In this way, they laid the philosophical groundwork of the social sciences, but the empirical revolution waited another century.

Daniel Lerner, in *The Human Meaning of the Social Sciences*, describes succinctly the changes that had occurred up to the 18th century:

> With the secularization of thought in modern times, theology in the grand manner gave way to more specialized inquiry under the titles of natural philosophy and social philosophy. As our complex, national societies evolved, even philosophy changed its character. Natural philosophy gradually became natural science. Social philosophy, changing its ways later and slower, became Social Science.

Let us now turn from the discussion of the philosophical underpinnings of social science to more historical events, and focus on the industrial, French and, for want of a better term, empirical revolutions. The cataclysmic nature of each revolution is plain enough—it is hard to find any area of thought or writing in the late 18th and 19th centuries that was not affected by them. Here we find a gradual increase of interest in social science and a growing intensity of intellectual labor spent on it.

The Industrial Revolution

The industrial revolution began in England in the middle of the 1700s and its influence quickly spread throughout the world. Before the 18th century, England was a rural, agricultural nation. What little manufacturing there was depended on manpower, rather than on machines. Merchants bought raw materials, which they gave to craftsmen. The craftsmen, working in their own homes, produced a finished product which went back to the merchant who sold it. In the 1700s machines began to change this quiet rural life.

England's textile industry was the first to feel the impact of industrialism. New inventions (flying shuttle, spinning jenny, cotton gin, etc.) made it possible to produce goods at a greater rate than had ever been possible before. Use of new machinery (steam engine, power loom, etc.) increased production even more. As one invention beget or led to another, the iron and steel industries became mechanized. Other industries followed quickly. Such new technology required the development of factories. People had to move to where the factories were located. Improvements in transportation (roads, canals, railroads, etc.) and communication (the "penny post," telegraph, telephone, etc.) were required to keep pace with industrialization. Changes as abrupt as these made established institutions such as the family, guild, church, and even the estate system itself — aristocracy, clergy, peasantry — give way to the pressure of industrial capitalism. These very institutions were questioned in terms of their origins and functions and their structures became the objects of critical analysis.

The movement from an agrarian-feudal to an industrial-urban society drastically changed people's lives. Many millions moved from farms, villages, and manors into cities and towns and from fields and crafts into factories. For centuries before, a person had expected to be born and to die in the same place and to follow his or her parent's occupation. People now worked for wages instead of exchanging their services for land and protection. They became aware that they could change not only their habitat but their position in society. Such physical and social mobility changed their self-image as well. Rather than playing one comprehensive role in which the values of work, leisure, religion, and family were rooted in a secure and binding social context, people now saw that they must often play separate and often conflicting roles — parent, factory worker, tax payer — within inaccessible bureaucracies and complex organizations.

Our discussion of the industrial revolution will consider two viewpoints: one offered by Karl Marx and the other by Herbert Spencer, two of the founding fathers of social science, who gave it much of its present identity. Although both writers conceived of the future positively, in that ideas of progress are implicit in their work, they saw the transformations occurring differently. Although both focused on England, where industrialism originated, they developed widely divergent points of view.

Karl Marx (1818-1883)

Karl Marx was a radical by any standard. We are interested in him, however, not as ideologist or political activist, but as an objective social scientist. To the extent that he offers a comprehensive statement about the basic elements and structure of society, it may be the history of social thought since mid-nineteenth century cannot be understood without understanding the ideas of Marx. Those who criticize Marx for over emphasizing the industrial experience of England, or those who view him as an economic determinist who ignored other relevant factors, may not agree with this statement. They would have to admit, however that in *The Communist Manifesto* (1849) and *Capital* (1867), he offered theories of society and history which make him a social scientist *extraordinaire*.

Marx wrote in the middle of the 19th century when conditions of life for the urban factory workers were probably at their worst. Wages were fifty cents for a week of seven eighteen-hour days. Contracts were made with orphanages for the employment of children. Sometimes the children were chained to their machines. It is not surprising, then, that Marx saw the movement from the medieval manor into the cities as a movement into squalor, slums, and alienation

---

Box 19

Karl Marx's New Society

"When, in the course of development, class distinctions have disappeared and all production has been concentrated in the hands of a vast association of the whole nation, the public power will lose its political character. Political power, properly so called, is merely the organized power of one class for oppressing another. If the proletariat during its contest with the bourgeoisie is compelled, by the force of circumstances, to organize itself as a class, if, by means of a revolution, it makes itself the ruling class and as such sweeps away by force the old conditions of production, then it will have swept away, along with these conditions, the conditions for the existence of class antagonisms and classes generally and will thereby have abolished its own supremacy as a class.

In place of the old bourgeois society, with its classes and class antagonisms, we shall have an association in which the free development of each is the condition for the free development of all. . .

The communists. . . openly declare that their ends can be attained only by the forcible overthrow of all existing social conditions. Let the ruling classes tremble at a Communistic revolution. The proletarians have nothing to lose but their chains. They have a world to win.

Working men of all countries, unite!"

Karl Marx, *The Communist Manifesto*

---

from work. His architectonic theory posits that the class structure of a society plays a strategic role in shaping the rest of its social organization and culture. All social institutions and activities (family, religion, politics, science, literature, art, philosophy, etc.) are built upon the foundation of the society's economy by the social classes which develop from the economy. The economic institution, including the available technology and the division of labor, is seen as the basic institution in society. Social change occurs when changes in the economy lead to the development of a new division of labor, which gives birth to new social classes, which may eventually overthrow the ruling class.

To move the discussion from the theoretical to the actual, Marx linked the change from agrarian to industrial society with the rise of the bourgeoisie in the late Middle Ages. This class of factory owners became large enough in numbers and strong enough by virtue of money and power to challenge the political control of the nobility, clergy, and monarchy. Eventually, these capitalists established industrial capitalism. Marx saw in the class struggle between the bourgeoisie and the workers, or proletariat, the necessary condition for the revolution which would ultimately bring about a classless society — socialism, eventually to become communism — which would no longer breed exploitation.

If one thinks of the former Soviet Union, eastern Europe, Cuba, China, etc., it is easy to see that Marx's millenialist philosophy has had worldwide impact. We should state immediately, however, that Marx would probably be dismayed at some of the policies and practices that are being pursued in his name a century after his death. Recent events in many countries, furthermore, make us wonder what the final evaluation of Marxist political and economic philosophy will be. We are interested in Marx, however, as a social scientist. His emphasis upon the importance of economic factors in the study of human behavior and the use of historical models as a methodological approach has had a great influence on social science. First of all, Marx felt that a valid study of society must take into account objective "material" conditions, i.e., the economic division into social classes, rather than "spiritual" forces. Defining phenomena in this way makes their scientific investigation possible, and is still in use today in studies of social stratification. Secondly, Marx saw social structures as not only influenced by past historical periods, but finally determined by the historical periods in which they are found. This allows us to conceptualize historical conditions not as unique events but as recurrent phenomena.

Marx is important, finally, because he was not inhibited by the arbitrary boundaries of academic disciplines. In his work, cultural anthropology, sociology, and social psychology (to name only a few of the disciplines of special interest here) all find their place. He describes not only the "culture" and structure of society in terms of "class," but he examines the roles of individuals in all their psychological nuances when he asserts that revolution will only occur when people become "class conscious" or motivated to carry it out.

Herbert Spencer (1820-1903)

Herbert Spencer, too, is a seminal figure in the development of social science. His primary contribution is the application of evolutionary principles to *all* human and social diversity. By evolution, Spencer meant change from simple to complex forms. Whether evolution is seen as one of the two or three most important ideas of the 19th century or as a theory which should be quickly discarded, its influence on social science is important enough to be considered.

In Spencer's major work, *Synthetic Philosophy*, he traces not only the transformations which occurred with the end of feudalism and the beginning of industrialization, but also the entire history of humanity in a way analogous to Darwin's tracing of the evolution of animal species. Since Spencerian logic can become very intricate, keep in mind as you read the paragraph below that his theory is that both humans and societies socially and biologically adapt to their environment. Both have changed and continue to change.

Briefly, Spencer assumes that the Darwinian "laws of natural selection," which operate in the "struggle for existence" and dictate the "survival of the fittest," apply for individuals and societies. In the past, humans were selfish or "egotistical" and societies were competitive and, hence, "militaristic." This was the best way to "survive." As technology advanced, however, an offshoot of "egotism" and "militarism" was the combination of small isolated groups into increasingly larger ones to permit part of the population to be industrially employed. With this industrialization developed a division of labor so specialized that people became dependent on each other and it was then to their benefit to be group oriented. "Altruistic" behavior replaced "egotistical" behavior. Spencer did not mean that this was conscious or intentional; it is simply a form of behavior that has evolved because it is adaptive, i.e., it enables the individual to survive. Those who survive are able to reproduce more successfully. As "altruism" becomes incorporated in human nature and transmitted through heredity, a "pacific" rather than a "militaristic" society will ultimately evolve. Such is the end of evolution as envisaged by Spencer.

He might agree with Marx that poverty, regimentation, and degradation were evident in 19th century England, but he saw these conditions as merely a beginning step in the evolutionary process. Spencer categorically opposed any kind of government interference in the natural growth of society as, for example, public education or even sanitary measures. To aid the poor and dependent would encourage survival of the unfit and, therefore, weaken society. The right to survive should be reserved for those best adapted to their environment. Such ideas appealed, obviously, to many industrialists of the time. Box 20 discusses some of the implications of this so called "Social Darwinism." Even considering all this, Spencer saw himself as an advocate of freedom who was zealously devoted to individualism.

Since Spencer wrote in nontechnical language and his work was imbued with the spirit of progress, his ideas were particularly well-suited to the late 19th century scene. Some contemporary social scientists, however, believe that his theory is invalid because he saw the stages of development—from militarism to pacifism, from egotism to altruism—as inevitable. One must wonder, furthermore, if such development is genetic. Another problem is that his emphasis on individualism and freedom contradicts the deterministic aspects of his theory. But despite possible objections to this theory, it was not until it took hold that the development of the various social sciences began.

The French Revolution

France was one of the richest and most influential nations in the world in the late 1700s. Discontent arose among the peasants and the small middle class,

---

Box 20

Social Darwinism

Spencer's ideas became part of what is referred to as "Social Darwinism." This is a doctrine or a social movement that uses—or, more often, misuses—Darwin's theory of evolution to justify existing forms of social organization. Beginning with Darwin's idea that there is a "natural selection" in the "struggle for existence," Spencer coined the phrase "survival of the fittest" to describe his viewpoint that people who could not successfully adapt to industrial society were really inferior. The "disappearance of the unfit" had a great attraction for many, particularly industrial entrepreneurs. It enabled dominant groups to oppose reforms or social welfare programs which they viewed as interfering with nature's plan. In the United States, Social Darwinism became a justification for the repression and neglect of African-Americans following the Civil War. It also justified policies that resulted in the decimation of North American Indian populations.

SOURCE: Richard Hofstadter, *Social Darwinism in American Thought* (New York: George Braziller, Inc., 1965).

however, from the maldistribution of wealth and privilege. Justice was capricious and corrupt. There were no juries. Torture prevailed. Taxation was unfair and arbitrary. Affairs got so bad that on July 14, 1789, a riotous Parisian mob marched on and destroyed the Bastille, a fortress prison that symbolized the arbitrary tyranny of the old regime. The revolution that ensued destroyed the French monarchy and established the first republican government in Europe. Between 1789 and 1795, laws touching literally every aspect of the social structure in France were passed. Not only was the monarchy guillotined, but popular sovereignty became a reality; not only was property confiscated, but new laws regarding the inheritance of property were instigated; even marriage was designated a civil contract and grounds for divorce were made available. The political upheaval that deprived the aristocracy of power, combined with the new democratic ideology which demanded equality, fraternity, and freedom for all, was at least as far-reaching in its effects on French society as the industrial revolution. The revolution came like a storm, and like a storm it passed, but nothing the revolution had touched was ever again what it had been. Institutions, which had seemed timeless and had never been questioned before, crumbled. An inexperienced government, in an attempt to break down ancient beliefs, introduced public education, a new monetary system, and even a new calendar (with new names for days and months).

These changes produced general unrest and presented new problems which could not easily be solved. Uncertainty and confusion prevailed. The crucial issue was how to preserve order in society without sacrificing progress. Many thinkers addressed themselves to this dilemma and, in our context, one French aristocrat is particularly important: Isadore Auguste Francois Marie Xavier Comte.

Auguste Comte (1798-1857)

Whereas Marx' and Spencer's theories of societal change were revolutionary and radical, Comte's theory is basically conservative. This is not to say that Comte favored a restoration of either the defunct old regime or the social order of feudalism, but his *Positive Philosophy* and *Positive Polity* are profoundly traditionalist.

Comte believed that explanations for societal change had to be understood as progressing through three stages: theological, metaphysical, and scientific. In simplest terms, answers to questions regarding "why things change as they do" would be: "God wants it, reason dictates it, and science proves it." Comte felt that people were just beginning to accept this last stage of explanation and he wanted to hasten its acceptance. He hoped to put the study of society on the same scientific foundations as that of the physical and biological worlds. Comte believed that human behavior, kinship, law, and even literature could be dealt with precisely as if they were forms of physical matter, such as atoms and molecules. Only by discovering facts can invariable laws which explain social change be formulated. His conscious and explicit aim was to separate the science of social behavior from philosophy, just as chemists and biologists had separated their inquiries from philosophy.

Unfortunately, Comte did not stop here. He infused his work with the conviction of his own messianic role in the new science so that some even refer to him as a latter day St. Paul. But, although his work is often more polemical than scientific, it went far in delineating major areas of investigation for social scientists.

Comte felt that the social sciences, which had developed late in history, had not made the transition from a metaphysical to a scientific level. Since he believed that the stage of knowledge in a given society determines the state of its social organization, Comte maintained that progress depends on the formulation of universal social laws which can be applied to society. His solution to the problems besetting France in the post-revolution era was offered in his maxim: "Progress is the development of order." The method for arriving at the laws of society was to be the same as that used in all science: observation, experimentation, and comparison. The focus, furthermore, should be on society and not on individuals. Comte was less interested in the individual because he believed that the study of only a part of society distorts its essentially unified and coherent character: the whole is different from, and greater than, the sum of its parts; the parts at any one moment in time are naturally and harmoniously ordered and mutually interdependent.

How do we finally evaluate the work of Comte? Comte's contribution consists of his brilliant insights into methodology (though he himself never did any research) and his idea that "social engineering" can achieve a "reconstruction" of society. But to accord the rule of the positive state to a "priesthood" of social scientists may seem overly ambitious and even pretentious. As to specific disciplines, the psychologist would certainly criticize him for his virtual dismissal of individualistic factors in society. The anthropologist would object to his emphasis on structure over culture, although he might commend him for his macroscopic views. The contemporary sociologist might think him too speculative, but he would be pleased that Comte coined the word "sociology," even if, originally, he wanted to call the discipline "social physics." All, however, would see him and his belief that there could be an all-embracing science of society as a persistent influence on the development of social science.

The Empirical Revolution

Although Marx, Spencer, and Comte provided the impetus for a fresh look at humans and society, they were mainly concerned with social theory. Their theories, however, necessitated a change in methods of investigation: knowledge of social phenomena could only be gained by collecting all relevant facts, by considering the grounds on which these facts were accepted, and by testing and investigating information that had previously been only casually observed. Such a change in how information is collected and investigated is often referred to as empirical to the extent the traditional five senses are involved. The information, in other words, must be visible, hearable, feelable, tastable, or smellable. This new point of view toward society may be referred to as the "empirical revolution" and, although we are now beginning to feel its impact, eventually it may be no less than that of the industrial and French revolutions. The development of the social sciences is unthinkable without this revolution in methodology.

To what causes can we attribute the rise of this empirical approach? In the 18th and 19th centuries, society had changed so rapidly and so drastically that the traditional standards and norms no longer seemed valid. The new theories which tried to make sense of the world often appeared abstract and academic and the only recourse left was to study the actual phenomena. Since the initial attempts to study society empirically proved useful, social scientists increasingly resorted to this method; the trend has extended into the present.

If Marx and Spencer provided us with an interpretation of the industrial revolution, and Comte with insights into the French revolution, there is no one of their stature to help us understand the beginnings of this revolution. Engaged in the painstaking task of assembling a detailed picture of social reality was a group of earnest and well-intentioned people, primarily in England but both here and in continental Europe as well, whose aim was merely to "measure" rather than to destroy or rebuild the fabric of society. They attempted not only to gather *all* the facts bearing on a particular phenomenon, but also to develop techniques that would make their interpretation meaningful.

This concern with simple facts began with the new discipline of "statistics" in the late 1700s. In 1801, the first English census attempted to determine the number of inhabitants of Great Britain and to conclude whether the population was increasing or decreasing. At that time, the first objections to child labor were raised in Parliament in response to the fact-finding endeavors of reformers. By 1834, the London Statistical Society was established. The first issue of its journal stated that ". . . In the business of social science, principles are valid for application only inasmuch as they are legitimate induction from facts, accurately observed and methodically classified." In the last half of the century, as the Factory Acts became more effective, government sponsored surveys investigated the conditions of the working classes, and private research, not directly concerned with governmental policy, was conducted on a wide scale. Charles Booth's *Life and Labour of the People in London* (1880-1900) is the first great empirical study which investigates living conditions in London.

A closer look at Booth's seventeen volume work might give us some indication of the nature of the empirical revolution. Since many debates in Parliament were vitally concerned with welfare legislation and with finding a way to relieve the misery of the poor, Booth found it advisable to find out, first of all, just how many poor people lived in London and, secondly, what their life was actually like. He felt that an abstract theory could neither answer these questions nor account for the causes of poverty. Thus, Booth set out to acquire the necessary information empirically. But the task was not an easy one. The census provided no answers to questions of income and rent and it was unthinkable to personally contact millions of families. He finally interviewed a number of families, as well as school inspectors who knew the families in their district, and for some time he even took up residence among the poor. The result of his investigation was a graphic picture that described the lot of the poverty stricken in London with authority and conviction. He established, first of all, the number of poor; secondly, statistical tables gave details of the living conditions, such as amount of rent paid, number of children, amount of employment, etc.; thirdly, he concluded, on the basis of the data he had collected, that poverty was due to socioeconomic conditions. Box 21 gives some idea of Booth's approach.

Had not Marx said the same thing? Perhaps so, but Marx relied on historical sources to support his thesis while Booth had empirical data. Marx's conclusion

---

Box 21

Charles Booth Describes London

"In little rooms no more than 8 ft. square, would be found living father, mother and several children. . . . Fifteen rooms out of twenty were filthy to the last degree, and the furniture in none of these rooms would be worth 5s. Not a room would be free from vermin, and in many life at night was unbearable. Several occupants have said that in hot weather they don't go to bed, but sit in their clothes in the least infected part of the room. What good is it, they said, to go to bed when you can't get a wink of sleep for bugs and fleas? . . . The passage from the street to the back-door would be scarcely ever swept, to say nothing of being scrubbed. Most of the doors stood open all night as well as all day, and the passage and stairs gave shelter to many who were altogether homeless. . . The houses looked ready to fall, many of them being out of the perpendicular. . . . Most people appear poverty stricken and all have a grimy look. . . . More was spent on drink than on rent, clothes, and heating."

SOURCE: Charles Booth, *Life and Labour of the People in London* (London: Hutchinson, 1969) pp. 35-60.

was, furthermore, that the only solution to alleviating the misery of the poor was worldwide revolution. Neither Booth nor most social scientists today would accept this point of view. Booth's laborious documentation of living conditions made the government more inclined to pass legislation affecting the aged, the sick, the handicapped, and the young. What may have seemed quantitative busy-work to prove "what everyone knew" eventually played a significant role in increasing the comfort of the underprivileged.

Stripping Booth's work to bare essentials, we must admire the simplicity of his approach. He collected a mass of detailed data and synthesized them into a significant whole. While some current social science studies turn up collections of trivia that are hardly profound, Booth's study indicates that an emphasis on fact-finding, along with insightful interpretation, is a worthy goal.

The empirical revolution surely affected the social sciences: they accumulate and report facts about human nature, culture, and society. Whether these facts are gleaned through small group experiments, participant observation, or survey research, they quickly turn into a search for explanations. Social scientists, thus, are rarely content with simple counting or straight reporting. The empirical resolution has awakened in them a desire to understand and explain, to move from descriptive fact-gathering to comparison, to interpretation, and to an assessment of the relationship between different aspects of our social world. Interpretation of facts, in other words, leads to theories.

Summary

Unlike social thought prior to the 19th century, which was primarily philosophical, modern social science looks at the world empirically. The emphasis is on facts. Comte, Spencer, Marx, and others laid the theoretical groundwork for this. When their ideas were combined with empirical research, we see the real start of social science.

Questions

1. Why would it have been difficult to carry out scientific investigations of human behavior in primitive societies or even in the Middle Ages? What basic assumptions underlay the use of the scientific method?

2. What is the difference between social science and social philosophy? Which do you think is more important?

3. Mobility at the beginning of the industrial revolution has been described as physical, social, and psychic. What do these terms mean?

4. What is "Social Darwinism?"

5. Why did the formation and early development of social science take place in Europe? What about the rest of the world?

6. Why didn't the American revolution, which takes place at approximately the same time as the French revolution, have a similar impact on the world?

7. Marx asserts that conflict between the owners of the means of production and the workers was inevitable and the resulting class warfare would bring about a classless society. What conditions have prevented this from occurring in the United States? Might it still happen?

8. In what ways is Spencer a Social Darwinist?

9. In what sense are both the theories of Marx and Spencer similar? In what ways do their theories differ?

10. Give specific examples of how Comte's three stages might explain social change.

11. Explain how Emile Durkheim's study of suicide, discussed in Chapter 2, was influenced by Comte?

12. Since the theories of Marx, Comte, and Spencer could most probably be proven wrong, why do we try to understand them?

13. Why are there no men of comparable stature to Marx, Comte, and Spencer in the discussion of the empirical revolution? Who was Booth?

14. Does the history of social science indicate that history is moving in a certain direction, that there is a pattern in the changes that occurred, or that social change is largely a matter of chance?

15. Why are most of the people mentioned in this chapter male rather than female? How many are DWEMs?

16. The foundations of social science in the 20th century have been American. Why do you think this is so?

Chapter Twelve

Objectivity in Social Science
Beyond European Assumptions

James H. Heard

Within science, all conclusions must be supported by facts. At odds with this position is the use of unwarranted assumptions, particularly those based on one's subjective feelings. This essay will consider how one's assumptions—in this case, European ones—might bias scientific investigation. After all, since it is difficult to prove or disprove assumptions, they may lead away from objective research and, consequently, theory, i.e., explanations or conclusions supported by objective research.

Assumptions affect our perception of our environment and our behavior. For example, if I believe that most murders are committed by strangers, I will lock my doors to keep out strangers who might be murderers. When outside my house, I will avoid all contact with strangers who might be murderers. I will ignore the criminological evidence that I am most likely to be murdered by someone I know. Such behavior is an attempt to validate an assumption that is not supported by the data. Any challenge to an assumption makes a person uncomfortable. People will, therefore, engage in all sorts of mental and/or physical behavior in order to keep their assumptions.

Should we shake loose an individual from unwarranted assumptions? This essay says yes. Psychologists who work on individual perceptions say any perception that is not based on reality is damaging both to oneself and to others. The cure for this is the often painful "Cathartic Experience," i.e., examining one's perceptions in the light of factual evidence. The "truth" could hurt because it is unsettling. Nevertheless, most psychologists believe that this experience will have ultimate beneficial effects.

This article is more concerned with group rather than individual perception. Both can be pathological and in need of a "cure." In fact, as this essay hopes to show, the modern anthropologist and historian could make life very uncomfortable for those whose group perceptions are based on untested assumptions in order to rationalize or justify their exclusion and/or oppression of other groups.

Our focus will be on Europe because, paradoxically, it has often been true that those Europeans who claimed to develop the scientific method to a fine art did not always follow their own lead. They assumed European primacy rather than choosing the more adventurous route of pursuing the truth objectively — no matter where it led, unsettling though it might be. It was easy and comfortable for them to believe that Europeans were first everywhere and in everything. Too often, this assumption of European primacy was the beginning point as well as the ending point of scientific inquiry.

The assumption of European primacy became a "foundation post" of European supremacy. Consider byproducts of European supremacy like apartheid in South Africa and more "subtle" discrimination in the United States of America. Such racist policies refer to the attempt by Europeans and their descendants and followers to discriminate against and/or exploit others who were deemed inferior because they did not originate from the official motherland, Europe. The logic seemed to be if one was not first, one deserves to be last. Following this logic, it was inevitable that Africa and Africans would have to be last. To determine that Africans were "first" in anything seemed to deny European primacy or supremacy in everything. The assumption could tolerate no dissenting opinion or evidence. Thus it took (and still takes) great objectivity and great courage for those scientists, both European and non-European, to turn away from the comfort of untested but assumptions and to chart a course into the uncharted and unpopular areas of African equality. After all, to grant universal equality to Africans might disturb the assumptions of black inequality in such European dominated societies as the Republic of South Africa or the United States of America. As anyone who reads the newspaper or watches television knows, the cultural, social, and political implications of African equality are far-reaching and perhaps truly revolutionary.

A first step towards restoring African equality in the world scheme has been made by a family of anthropologists named Leakey. Beginning with Louis and Mary Leakey and continuing with son Richard Leakey, this family has established that the earliest humans were probably African. Louis Leakey (who is one of the few if not the only white man to have undergone initiation into manhood in a Kikuyu ceremony) believed that Charles Darwin was correct in his theory that humans originated on the African continent. (See Box 22.) European scholars at the time of Leakey's research considered their own part of the world to be a much more likely location. Remains of Neanderthal man

(350,000 years ago) and Cro-Magnon man (35,000 years ago) had been found in Europe and it was even thought that a perfectly respectable ancestor, "Piltdown Man," had been discovered in England itself. (Later the Piltdown skull was shown to be a forgery). At any rate, Leakey persevered in Africa, excavating at many sites. He eventually discovered early fossils of human heads at Kunem and Kanjera in Kenya which dated millions of years ago. These discoveries seemed to validate Darwin's theory. Because they "disproved" previous assumptions, the findings at first were unaccepted by many of Leakey's colleagues. Today, they are accepted. Current important questions are just how old this early person is and when he or she began to walk upright. Both social scientists and natural scientists are researching these issues. Regardless of when and how this early person walked, it is agreed that he or she walked in Africa. Europeans were probably not the first humans to walk the earth! It is now necessary to revise our assumptions about Africa, African peoples, and early humankind. This could be difficult for those whose ideas were formed by a basically European shaped culture. But science requires us to go beyond subjectivity to objectivity. The Leakeys and their scientific allies are leading us from a Eurocentric to an Afrocentric view of civilization. This Afrocentric view will have far-reaching effects.

Take, for example, the practical effect the Leakeys' discovery will have on our pictorial and verbal representations of reality. Will those who place pictures of earliest humans in books go back and put some color into these representations? Are not Africans people of color and have they not been so

---

Box 22

African Genesis

Long before the first fragmentary fossil evidence came to light in Africa, Charles Darwin argued in *The Descent of Man* (1871) that: "In each great region of the world the living mammals are closely related to the extinct species of the same region. It is, therefore, probable that Africa was formerly inhabited by extinct apes closely allied to the gorilla and chimpanzee; and as these two species are now man's nearest allies, it is somewhat more probable that our early progenitors lived on the African continent than anywhere else." Only time and more years of searching outside Africa will prove Darwin right or wrong in his evaluation. But, at the moment, the signs are in his favor. So far, the fossils of hominids, i.e., members of the human family, have turned up only in Africa, nowhere else.

for centuries? Will museums change their displays to fit the new reality? Many representations of "early *man*" (another challengeable assumption) are white like Europeans who "discovered" them. Since only bones were discovered, we can certainly speculate about the skin color of our early human ancestors.

What about the teacher whose traditional explanation of the dark hued skin of "colored" people was their closeness to the sun? This teacher assumed that if these people did not live close to the sun they would not be colored but would be white like everyone else in Europe. Even the use of the subjective appellation "colored" has to be reexamined and reevaluated in the light of objective data.

Indeed, a more balanced approach in scientific inquiry, one that would include an Afrocentric perspective, might at first be disturbing. In the long run, however, such a perspective might make it easier for many to give up the destructive myth of black inferiority. History books for example, have long looked to the "fertile crescent" as the "cradle of civilization." Of course, what they failed to mention was that the kingdom of Egypt was a part of Ethiopian Africa which included what is called "Kenya" today. This made it easy for people to accept a Europeanized Cleopatra (in the guise of Elizabeth Taylor) and reject an Africanized Anwar Sadat (in the guise of Lou Gossett) in films. Box 23 suggests that ancient Greece, usually conceived of as the fount of European civilization, should be seen from a more worldly perspective.

Box 23

How European Was Ancient Greece?

There is no doubt that Greece has been the largest single source of the elements that compose modern European civilization. A question that must be answered, however, is: how European was ancient Greece? In physiological terms, the Greeks then looked very much like Greeks today. They were a mixed population containing Europeans and North Africans of a basically Mediterranean type found elsewhere in southern Europe and the Middle East. If one focuses on language, many words (demos, psyche, etc.), place names (Athens Sparta, etc.), and divine names (Aphrodite, Apollo, etc.) can be explained by Egyptian and Semitic etymologies. Certainly there is evidence of trade with coastal cities in Lebanon, Syria, and Egypt. One of the greatnesses of Greece may be that it was a wonderful melting pot!

SOURCE: Martin Bernal, *Black Athena* (New Brunswick: Rutgers University Press, 1987).

Once the proper scientific connections are forged, one's perspectives broaden. It is not too difficult, for example, to accept new scientific findings. Scientific evidence has already established that Columbus and his crew were not the first Europeans to discover America—the Norsemen were. Anthropologist Ivan Van Sertima, author of *They Came Before Columbus*, now presents scientific evidence (skeletal remains, language comparisons, types of plant life, etc.) of an African presence in America centuries before Columbus and the Norsemen. This information is not offered to downplay the European discoveries but to grant equal prominence to the African discovery of America. Perhaps what is needed is a "Discoverers Day" in order to recognize all of the discoverers of America (including the Native Americans who were truly "first"). In a sense, all of these explorers were scientists in their own time and fashion. Like all good scientists they braved the unknown to get to the known.

Objective observation establishes over and over again that American civilization as well as world civilization has been the creative effort of many different ethnic and/or racial groups. Although it is comfortable and comforting to assume that one's particular reference group was the first to do everything,

---

Box 24

What History Books Don't Say: There was a Black Pilgrim

Every Thanksgiving we are reminded of the history of the Pilgrims, who braved the wind and weather to cross the Atlantic, landing at Plymouth, in 1620, in search of religious freedom and economic opportunities. What is seldom mentioned in most chronicles is the fact that one of our "founding fathers" was black. The evidence comes from a printed transcription found in the "Miscellaneous Records" volume of the "Plymouth Colony Records." The transcription, "Abraham Pierce, the blackamore," appears on the military muster roll of 1643. Pierce's name there means he was capable of carrying arms in Myles Standish's small militia. Such military eligibility listings were reserved for free men, generally of high repute, and not for servants. Why has this seldom been reported in history books?

SOURCE: Mary Lee Benton, *The New Leader*, December 1, 1983.

this assumption may break down in the light of objective scientific inquiry. In this country, such facts as a black "founding father" of Plymouth Colony (Abraham Pierce), a black "founding father" of Chicago (Jean DuSable), a black pioneer in open heart surgery (Daniel Hale Williams), as well as black cowboys in the west or black soldiers and sailors in *all* of America's wars are much easier to accept if a proper attitude is the rule rather than the exception.

What should be the proper attitude? This essay demonstrates the need for a scientific, that is, an objective attitude that resolves that one will not assume anything until factual evidence has been gathered and evaluated. It is an attitude that further resolves that there will be a conscious attempt to free one's evaluation from the trap of one's own sociocultural bias, which in this culture tends toward Eurocentric bias. Thus, scientific attitude and scientific method are inseparable if one wishes to move from a hypothesis, a tentative statement of expectations which invites research, to valid scientific theory. It is only when we adopt this proper stance that we move beyond assumption to objectivity, the guiding light of the scientific method.

Questions

1. What is meant by scientific inquiry? Research? Theory? Objectivity?
2. How might assumptions mislead us? How can we get back on the right track?
3. Why is group perception of more interest than individual perception?
4. What is the assumption of European primacy? Is it objective or subjective?
5. Why and how might the research of the Leakey family shatter a Eurocentric world view? Has a Eurocentric world view had no positive effects?
6. In what ways are the Republic of South Africa and the United States racist?
7. Has this article proved that the first man or woman was black?
8. How African was Egypt?
9. How European was Greece?
10. Who did discover America?
11. What impact will knowledge of black pilgrims, heart surgeons, cowboys, or soldiers and sailors have on us?
12. What is the proper scientific attitude?

——————— Part IV ———————

The Consequences of Science

The two articles in this section offer a critique of modern science and its effect on human life. Gloria Carrig's "Science: Gift or Curse?" considers the relationship between science and belief and attempts to answer the question of whether science can be "value-neutral" or "value-free." Dan Reber's "Scientific Principles and Their Social Consequences" examines the moral, political and psychological consequences that arise from acceptance of certain basic scientific assumptions. The question both raise is: while it seems obvious that science has given us comfort and ease, was it worth paying the price for what we have achieved?

Chapter Thirteen

Science: Gift or Curse?

Gloria Carrig

Let us imagine the following two scenes taking place at the identical time at two places greatly distant from one another: early one afternoon the sun, having reached its high point in the sky, was beginning its descent. Though the sky was cloudless, it suddenly began to grow dark. Soon it was like night. In a small village, people emerged from their grass-thatched huts, huddling together, cowering, some weeping and moaning. They feared the gods in their anger were punishing them. Had they forgotten to reward the sun god with sacrifices? Had one of them thrown a spear before noon or eaten from a blackened pot? Was it too late to satisfy the gods and put off their punishment, the taking away of the sun?

Far away on top of a high mountain a great telescope was pointed at the sun. It would magnify the aurora, visible only during a total eclipse, when the moon passes between the earth and the sun, blocking for a few minutes the light of day. Newspaper and television journalists had reported for days the coming eclipse, accurately predicting the specific time when it would occur, its path across the nation, and warning citizens not to look directly at it lest they damage their eyes.

Such is the difference in response to one unusual event between a tradition-bound people, hardly touched by modern technology, and a modern society, urbanized and shaped by scientific technology. In the first, religion, mythology, folklore, and ancient traditional beliefs determine the reaction to events. All our ancestors thought like this. In the second, factual observations using up-to-date technology and scientific theory explain what occurs and predict what will take place.

Witchcraft, voodoo, myths and beliefs about gods and spirits help people explain and understand things they experience. Science does that for modern man. But science is based on empiricism, which means knowledge through the observation or experience of facts. The scientist knows what he sees, what he can observe and measure through experiments. And such observations of fact can be put together into a body of theory which provides material results in chemistry, biology, physics, mathematics and astronomy. We live amidst hundred-story buildings, miles-long bridges, jet planes, spacecraft that land on the moon and Mars, cures for diseases that once devastated mankind, vast increases in food production, television, and computers. Technology, the consequence of science, has increased our capacity to do and make things. We see farther than our eyes can with television. We can record what is seen on film. We can see things not visible to the naked eye with microscopes and stars millions of light years away through telescopes. We hear across great distances with radio and telephone, and we travel faster and farther with all sorts of earth-bound and air-borne vehicles. We can now hurl at our enemies, not the sharp stones of our ancestors, but giant ballistic missiles capable of enormous destruction.

Science and Religion

But from the beginning science has raised problems for man. The early scientists were men who had been taught the body of "truth" then in existence, the explanations of phenomena or events taking place in the universe, many of which explanations were religious. Fear and opposition first greeted their early discoveries. Nicolaus Copernicus, born in Poland in 1473, deduced that the planets of our solar system, including Earth, revolve about the sun. The Earth is not the center, he said, as men had long believed and the Christian Church had insisted upon. Why was the Church threatened by Copernicus's idea, so much so that for centuries afterward it fought as if its life depended on defeating that revolutionary discovery? Precisely because its life, the dominance of religion, *did* depend on defeating the new science. If the sun is the center, what does that do to the biblical teachings about the creation of the earth and man by God and in His image? And if the Bible is wrong in this matter, could there not be other false teachings contained in it? The authority of religion was in jeopardy.

Over a century later, the Italian Galileo Galilei built a powerful telescope and turned it towards the stars. His direct observations of the planets, never seen before, proved Copernicus right. All he had to do was show his discoveries and everyone would listen, right? No! They would not listen and instead warned him to stop speaking these heretical words or be punished as others had been, like Giordano Bruno, who in 1600 had been burned at the stake by the dreaded Inquisition of the Church for his ideas. The powerful Church believed that faith must dominate and scientific findings give way. Galileo somewhat naively sought to publish his proofs and for this he was tried in 1633 by the Inquisition, found guilty, and threatened with torture on the rack unless he recanted. He swore that his findings were false and was imprisoned in his home till the end of his life. The Church had won another victory, but hindsight tells us that it was short-lived. Scientific discoveries were mushrooming and would not be stopped. As Box 25 indicates—the Galileo judgment still haunted us in 1984.

But can we say that the Church was mistaken to oppose the new science? It could see the threat to its authority, to the central place of religion in men's minds, to the natural order of the world as they saw it. Centuries later religion confronted the scientific findings of Charles Darwin, the naturalist whose *Origin of the Species* published in 1859 set forth the theory of evolution by natural selection, "survival of the fittest." There is a common origin of life, Darwin said, and species have developed throughout time by biological changes, culminating in *homo sapiens*, man. Christian religion never accepted this view of man's origin which obviously conflicts with the story of creation and reduces the image of man to a relative of the apes. As late as the 1920s a Tennessee school teacher was accused of criminally teaching the pernicious doctrine of

---

Box 25

Galileo and the Church

In 1633, Galileo was judged by the Roman Catholic Church's Inquisition to have violated a church edict against espousing the controversial Copernican view that the sun, not the earth, was at the center of the universe. He became widely regarded as a martyr of science who had been humbled by backward churchmen. In 1980, Pope John Paul appointed a commission of scientists, historians and theologians to re-examine the evidence and verdict. The panel's findings acknowledge that the church was wrong in silencing Galileo. As John Paul noted, "the church has now paid a suitable tribute to Galileo by accepting a major contention of the pioneering astronomer: that the Bible does not contain specific truths, but speaks metaphorically about such events as the creation or the movement of the sun."

SOURCE: Frederic Golden, *Time Magazine*, March 12, 1984, p. 72.

evolution—the celebrated "monkey trial." That this is still an issue today is exemplified by the enactment of a law in Arkansas in 1981 requiring the teaching of creationism in schools where evolution is taught. Though the courts have declared the law unconstitutional, we will probably hear more about this in the future.

Man vs. Machine

Copernicus, Galileo, and Darwin challenged existing authority. They insisted that their observations of fact could only be explained by their scientific theories, before which all other theories, including those of religious faith, must give way. And their theories were "progressive," in that they produced tangible results for mankind, enabling people to produce more, do more, live longer, and change the earth on which they live.

The invention of machines that could vastly increase production led to the spread of industry, the "industrial revolution." From the 18th century on, inventions multiplied, technology developed and men, women, and children by the thousands went to work in the new factories in England. Industrialization spread, and as it did, the lives of men and women were unalterably changed. Cities grew and work became long and tedious factory labor for low wages, and under harsh and severe conditions. People hated and feared the machines, and some even tried to fight them, such as the Luddites, who thought that by destroying the machines they could end this thing that had ruined their way of life. But industrial production grew under the leadership of men who had new ideas, ambition, and a drive for profit and power. Working conditions have considerably improved since those times, but people still resent the mechanization of life. Much of the contemporary hostility to environmental pollution and the desire to undo the damage done to the earth and to people by scientific technology is based on the same hostility to science that the Luddites felt. Scientific progress, presented to the world as necessary, irrefutable and progressive, has been received as, at best, a mixed blessing. More details on the Luddites are presented in Box 26.

Social Science

The growth and success of scientific technology was destined to lead to its application to the study of human beings. Why not use the same approach to knowledge through theories based on factual observation to understand human emotions, social practices, culture, and all sorts of behavior? At one time, people whose actions were considered irrational were labeled "lunatics" (after

---

Box 26

The Case of the Luddites

An example of resistance to technological change is offered by the "Luddites." They were 19th century British artisans in the woolen and clothing trades who wrecked industrial machinery, following the example of a semimythical figure, Ned Ludd. Trouble began in 1811 when workers in the stocking trade protested unemployment and low wages and destroyed sixty stocking frames in Nottingham. From Nottingham, machine breaking spread throughout England. Even entire factories were destroyed over the next few years.

Were these incidents the work of ignorant and illiterate men reacting blindly and irrationally to technological progress? Investigations suggest that the destruction was carefully calculated only against machinery and factories that threatened the livelihood of local artisans, i.e., those factories where technological changes affected wages and employment. Some factories met little or no resistance. What appears to be a defiance to technological change may actually be the resistance of people who expect to be harmed. Can strikes in the American automobile industry, for example, be explained because of technological change?

SOURCES: E. Hobsbawm, *Laboring Men: Studies in the History of Labour* (Garden City: Anchor, 1967); E. Thompson, *The Making of the English Working Class* (New York: Vintage, 1963).

---

the Latin *luna* for moon; they were thought to become crazed by the full moon) and put away in asylums where they were subjected to harsh attempts to rid them of demons. Now, modern psychology, greatly influenced by the work of Sigmund Freud, substitutes therapeutic treatment based on scientific concepts concerning the functions of the mind.

All aspects of human behavior are the concern of psychology, sociology, anthropology, political science, and the other fields of study which together make up what is called social science. The social scientists wish to apply the principles and methods of science to the study of people. In doing so, they run into a problem of science that is made even more complicated when applied to people; that of scientific objectivity.

Objectivity

A chemist mixing chemicals in his laboratory observes a reaction, identifies and reports the result. There is little likelihood that he would alter his report because he didn't like the new mixture that was produced. Nor is it likely that he would describe what he saw in a critical manner, permitting personal feelings to affect his report. However, when the scientist is an anthropologist observing a remote tribe of people, their customs may be very foreign to him, and he might possibly consider them immoral by his standards. Should he include these moral judgments in his report? Should the psychologist call his patient a terrible person or the sociologist characterize the people under consideration as bad men or women? Scientific objectivity would have us answer, "No. Be free of value judgments. Leave your own ideas about good and bad out of your work."

Some Current Questions

But there are problems about the objectivity of the scientist or his being "value neutral." One of these problems arose during World War II after nuclear physicists led by Albert Einstein developed the theories that culminated in the splitting of the atom. (The first sustained nuclear reaction took place in a secret laboratory under the stands of Stagg Field at the University of Chicago.) The scientists did not want to have the atom bomb dropped on the Japanese people, but this was considered a political question which President Truman had to decide. The moral question was taken away from the scientists. In a way, science's own belief in avoiding subjective questions has led to the problem of how scientific work should be used by government and society.

Can someone be truly free of subjective values? And even if he could, would his observations and conclusions about other people be worthwhile without some element of personal judgment? A person might study the Nazi movement in Germany "objectively" and fail to conclude that it was monstrously evil. In fact, such questions as what is good, right, and just, does God exist, and how should human beings live, are just the sort of questions that science tells us are subjective and cannot be answered scientifically. So men and women of learning avoid these questions, even though almost everyone knows that they were and are still the most important ones that human beings face. Modern man thus finds himself in what some refer to as a "moral vacuum."

Conclusion

Today, we question whether science has truly benefited us. We have found cures for disease, extended the life span, found ways to produce more food. Technology in communication, transportation, and production of goods has eased our physical hardships. On the other hand, the harm done to the environment, overpopulation, the threat of nuclear destruction—these make us wish we could turn the clock back to a simpler time, a slower pace. We would like to reestablish some of the old values that made life richer and more human. But of course there is no returning. Scientific progress has brought us to this point and we cannot go back. The early scientists believed that human beings could control nature. Now it is feared that science controls us and there may be no escape.

Questions

1. How do "pre-scientific" and "scientifically based" people view an eclipse?
2. In what ways did Copernicus, Galileo, and Darwin challenge the Church?
3. Did science ultimately weaken the authority of religion? How?
4. Why are people unhappy with technology and the mechanization of work?
5. Can scientific objectivity be applied to the study of human behavior?
6. Should the scientists or social scientists be free of values in their work? Can they be?
7. What types of questions are considered to be unscientific and thus not subject to scientific study. Give examples.
8. Would you like to turn the clock back? To which time? What would you gain? What would you give up?

Chapter Fourteen

Scientific Principles and Their Social Consequences

Daniel C. Reber

Today scientific technology makes it possible for ordinary people to live far better than a prince or princess of long ago. Stretch your imagination and strip away the improvements in the material conditions of your life that science has made possible in just the last one hundred years. You will find yourself without a telephone, electric lights, air travel, computers, flush toilets, automobiles, and deodorants that don't wear off. You just might find yourself dead: scientific advances in medicine in just the last 50 years have eliminated or reduced diseases which used to maim or wipe out millions: smallpox, polio, tuberculosis, pneumonia, influenza. The list of the material benefits of science could go on and on.

Yet the effects of science on our physical environment, for all their obviousness, are not more sweeping and more influential in our lives than their moral, political and intellectual effects. Over several centuries, science has worked a great change in the attitudes towards God, religion, society, philosophy, and life style. Because we have grown up with science and accept its ideas as the received opinion, we take these social effects for granted and very often do not even see their connection with science. The purpose of this essay will be to present, at the most basic level, a sketch of what science really is, and indicate the changes it has produced in social and moral attitudes and values.

What is modern science? Modern science is a philosophy about knowledge, about the way that we know what we know. Every philosophy of knowledge, scientific or otherwise, has to begin with certain basic assumptions that cannot be proved but which form the foundation of all that is thought to be known. Philosophy, scientific or otherwise, is like plane geometry; which, as perhaps you remember from high school, has certain basic assumptions called *axioms* or *postulates* which cannot be proved but which form the basis of all proofs. For example, geometry assumes that the shortest distance between two points is a straight line; two parallel lines never meet; given a line and a point outside a line, only one line can be drawn through the point parallel to the line. These assumptions seem reasonable enough—they fit well with everyday experience—but the key point is that they cannot be *proved* and have to be taken, so to speak, on faith. Yet they are utterly important, because they are the starting point of all subsequent truth and knowledge. If they turn out to be false, so will all the proofs based on them; false, or else true just by lucky accident, as the child who makes several mistakes adding a column of figures sometimes ends up accidentally with the right answer. Geometry is in the uncomfortable position of being able to prove a vast number of subordinate truths, based on its first assumptions or axioms, but of having to assume without proof that its most basic tenets are true.

Since every system of knowledge whatsoever, like geometry, must rest on certain assumptions, showing what science most basically is requires a presentation of its postulates. From its postulates or premises we will be able to trace the more familiar features of today's social and intellectual climate, as we could also trace the scientific method and today's technology, if that were our interest.

The first premise of modern science, and the one with the most earthshaking consequences, is this: "We know what we know through the senses *alone.*" The key word here, of course, is **alone**. Previous influential philosophic approaches, Aristotelianism and Christianity, never denied that the senses were useful for many practical purposes of life. A Christian avoids eating dirt or falling into manholes with his senses, and uses them to find his way to church and recognize the pastor. But a Christian holds that knowing the *most important* things about life and the world depends on *faith*, and faith is not something the senses can detect. Aristotle, while not willing to take the word of God or anything except philosophic premises on faith, regarded the senses as just the first frontier of knowledge, beyond which the mind, unaided by the senses, could come to certainty about things which the senses could never detect.

Science insists that, if the senses can't confirm it, it cannot be known or regarded as true or real. For science to regard something as proved it must have a direct or indirect confirmation in one of the five senses: sight, hearing, taste, smell or touch. If a phenomenon, or an assertion, cannot in some way be ultimately grounded in the senses, then science will not accept it. Take God, for example. According to both those who believe in him and those who do not, God is not something the senses can detect: he cannot be seen, smelled, heard, tasted or touched. Nor is it possible to detect his presence indirectly through sensitive instruments which would in turn produce results the senses could detect. Science *will* accept indirect sensory evidence: gamma rays, for example, cannot be seen or felt by ordinary senses, but they can be made to make traces on photographic plates that the eye *can* see. But neither science nor its philosophic opposition think that there could be a "God-o-meter" or some sensitive device that could detect God or his influence and produce a sensory proof. According to science, there is no proof whatever that God exists, any more than there is proof of the existence of ghosts or spirits.

There are other sweeping consequences of our first postulate, but before passing on to them, let us focus our attention on the rest of the postulates of science, so that, when we turn to conclusions and consequences, we will have the whole picture of the scientific premises in our mind's eye. Science's second postulate is, "The mind has the power to receive, record and rearrange sensations." This second postulate deals with the nature of that which is trying to find knowledge, the mind. Some assumption about how the mind works is essential to knowledge, because it is only with the mind that we can be said to know anything. The senses detect, but cannot know. The eye sees red now, and can see it again tomorrow. It cannot imagine red when it is not present—only the mind can do that—and it cannot conclude, as only the mind can, that the red I see now on the postage stamp is the same color I saw yesterday when I cut my finger, and that the name of this color is red, and it is different than blue.

In fact, it is necessary to the good function of the senses that they "remember" nothing. As soon as the sound, or the sight, or the smell disappears, so does the sensation of it. When that does *not* happen, the function of the senses is temporarily impaired. When on a cold day you come in and put your freezing hands under the tap, you can't tell for a moment what the temperature of the water is, because your hands are feeling cold no matter what; "remembering" the cold, as it were. After you have had your picture taken with a flash camera, for a while, everywhere you look there is the flash bulb right in the middle, so it's hard to see what you're actually looking at. The senses *must* remember nothing, so they can detect each change as soon as it happens. Thus a well-working eye can follow the changing patterns on television as quickly as they happen, and the ear can hear all the notes even when the music is fast. It is up to the mind to remember and to comprehend the shape and order of the colors, that is, the pattern or picture; and up to the mind to remember and comprehend the pitch and order of the notes; that is, the music.

The third postulate of science is, "nature is orderly and regular." That means that anything that happens now under specific circumstances always will and always did happen under those same circumstances. The rules of nature, in other words, do not change. If water boils today at sea level at 212° Fahrenheit, it boiled at that same temperature at the time of the dinosaurs, and will boil again in the year 2032. If lead poisons people today, it poisoned the Romans in their heyday when they cooked in lead pots.

Although it cannot be proved, this assumption is essential to knowing anything. If the same circumstances produce different results, we will never know what to expect. If a temperature of 20° Fahrenheit froze water today, boiled it tomorrow, and turned it orange last week, we would never know what to expect, and could not really know anything. Although we might know that the circumstances now are the same as before, we couldn't be sure of the same result. Suppose you were up in an airplane and the laws of aerodynamics suddenly ceased to operate—it would be a headline and a plastic undertaker's bag for you. Knowing how to predict anything or getting anything to work right would be impossible.

From the premises of science flow consequences for the method of both social and natural science. From the same premises flow consequences in which we are interested here, influences on what people hold to be proper, right, just and good. Although science claims to have no views on what is right and wrong and to take no stand on social issues since right and wrong have no qualities the senses can detect, we will see that the premises of science produce an influence nevertheless.

Earlier, for example, we noted that scientifically speaking, God does not exist, any more than do ghosts or spirits. Officially then, science has nothing to say about religion, as being a subject about which nothing can be known. In practice, however, science's doctrine that God cannot be known leads to one of two important political attitudes.

Americans take it for granted that everyone is entitled to his or her own point of view on God and religion; but from a historical standpoint, this is revolutionary. When it was anciently held, as in Roman Israel or Medieval Spain, that the will of God could be really known, then to follow that will was supremely important. Consider: if God says you should not preach blasphemy, and the penalty for preaching blasphemy is eternal damnation, then you'd better not do it. Who is willing to argue with the Absolute Big Man of all time? And if God tells me that I should compel you to stop preaching blasphemy, even if it means maiming you, or burning you at the stake, I'm surely doing the right thing, if God *really* exists and He *really* says it. By burning you I purge you of your heresy and get you to heaven instead of to Hell, and I also show everyone else what happens to heretics, so others will say and believe the right things. How could I be a greater benefactor than to send you to Heaven and strongly encourage good behavior on the part of the rest of mankind?

The critical issue is, of course, does God really exist and is that what he really wants? Scientifically speaking, God cannot exist or, if he does, it cannot be known, since he does not appear to the senses. Since no one really knows, the solution to religious differences has been, at least in Western Europe and the United States, to let everyone believe what he wants about God and about religion, even if he chooses to believe nothing. Since no one actually knows, any man's opinion is as good as anyone else's. Thus tolerance as a social value has its roots in science, and although very few people perceive the connection between tolerance and science, almost all people, at least almost all Americans, support tolerance of different religious points of view as proper behavior.

From tolerance of religious views naturally develops tolerance of different points of view on what is moral and proper. Moral things, like God, are not sensory—good and bad have no qualities the senses can detect. If I differ from you, who is to say I am wrong? You must tolerate my ways, even if you disapprove. Really, you don't have any business disapproving: you go your way, I'll go mine; who is to say which is best? The limit to tolerance, scientifically is, of course, material things: you can do your thing as long as you don't hurt me, or damage my property, or imperil my health—or my lifestyle, since I am and should be free to live as I choose. You may say that if I continue to smoke I'll die of lung cancer, if I don't die first of cirrhosis of the liver from all my drinking. And I'll tell you that it's my business if I prefer a life that's short but sweet, compared to your prolonged but dreary existence.

While in America scientific ideas have led us to tolerance, there is another way of approaching the same question, which is the one chosen by the Communists. Their reasoning goes roughly like this: although there is no truth on morality or religion (speaking now always scientifically), it would be nice if everyone agreed. *If* everyone agreed, then no one would ever quarrel; if no one ever quarrels, no one ever fights; if no one ever fights, no one ever gets hurt and nothing material is destroyed. Therefore for the sake of material well-being, which requires civil peace and order, *let's require that everyone think the same thing.* To that end each schoolchild will be taught to believe what he should, which is to say, what the government says he should—after all, *someone* has to say what it is that we'll all believe, and since government has the power, it can enforce uniformity. So in the Soviet Union there is one newspaper, and the name is Truth (Pravda); not because it's really true—no one knows that—but because it's the line if we all take we'll all agree; that's what makes it true. How ironic that two nations so opposed should find, at the root of one of their fiercest differences, the same idea: that things invisible cannot be known!

Another result of scientific premises is a high social value put on material things. Nice clothes, a nice car, a large, comfortable and beautiful house or apartment, sex, beauty and expensive vacations: these are the things that Americans and people in other scientifically oriented societies are often criticized for placing a high value on. Of course, not every American fits the mold, but those who are more concerned about doing the work of God, or being virtuous, no matter how poor or how horny, are a distinct minority: observe the bemused, tolerant detachment with which most Americans view the Salvation Army.

This tendency of Americans and other scientifically oriented societies to prize material things has been criticized; but we, being knowledgeable of the premises of science, will not be surprised. "We know what we know through the senses alone." The senses detect only material things: God, truth, right, virtue or any other such thing may or may not exist, but have evidently no material characteristics. Hence, it is understandable that, to people raised in a society whose intellectual climate is dominated by science, the objects of the senses tend to become first in importance.

Another fruit of science is an emphasis on and an approval of variety, novelty, and change. This trend has more than one root. First, a scientific society expects progress: as time passes, continuing scientific experiments will yield new truth about nature and new ways to control her for the benefit of man. Although each of us can think of changes that he or she would not regard as for the better, in general science really has produced progress in the material world. Science has been so successful that we easily slide into the presumption that any change is progress.

Another root of this same notion lies in the way the senses work. As we earlier observed, the senses, when working properly, can keep up with rapid change and indeed delight in changing colors, sounds, scenes and flavors. Although the mind may have trouble keeping up with the rapid pace of change, in science the senses are emphasized.

That we do view change as good is hardly open to question. When we want to praise something, we say it is "new." Praising somebody, we say he or she is "innovative," "dynamic," "original," "creative." We don't often say people are "good," because that implies moral judgment; and being a "goody-goody" implies being deplorably moral, strict, closed to new things. Would a friend be complimented if you said he was "predictable" or "traditional"? He might hit you if you said he was "righteous," "Godly," or "virtuous."

Constitutionalism is another scientific development. The United States is the first modern country to have a written constitution. What made Americans think they should have one? The source is science once again. If we know what we know through the senses alone, then who's to say what is the right kind of government for me? Only I can say. Before I can give my consent, I need to know what I'm getting into, so I can decide if the system of government is acceptable to me. I need to see the plan of government, the basic rules by which it will operate; a *written* plan, so that there will be no doubt later on over what was agreed to. With the coming of science came the end of governments based on the notion that the ruler was God's appointed agent, or that some persons were entitled to rule because they were better or wiser than others.

One of the most sweeping social ideas coming from science is the notion that we are all equal. Now, as anyone with 20 years' experience in living can see, men are not actually all equal: some are richer, some have more pleasing jobs, some sail serenely through crises while others fret over trivia, some strive vigorously to accomplish while others sit and wish. But these are all environmentally caused differences, you say. But evidently some people are also better looking than others; or more talented, or stronger, or have greater aptitude for certain things; and some people seem to combine all these things while others seem to lack them all.

Whether people are equal in fact depends on what you want to look at. Science tends to look at those things in which people really are pretty equal. With regard to the five senses, mankind is remarkably equal. I know that I wear glasses and you don't; but when I put my glasses on I can see as well as you. With regard to our sense of hearing, most of us are extremely equal. With regard to touch, taste and smell, it's harder to compare, but the presumption is that we're quite equal on those counts as well.

Science appeals to other grounds for equality. Since all that we know comes through the senses, knowledge must begin at birth. Before birth, then, we were all perfectly ignorant, and zero equals zero, blank equals blank. Scientific social science tends to account for the observed differences among people as environmentally caused, and hence artificial. Also, we observed earlier that scientific principles leave everyone entirely ignorant on matters of religion and morality—equally ignorant. Since no one knows right or wrong, good or bad, just or unjust, everyone's point of view is of equal merit.

The scientific support of equality has worked sweeping changes to create the modern political and social scene. It has produced the emancipation of women from an inferior status, and the right to vote for everyone; rather than the richer, the better, the more educated, the older, the wiser or whatever. The same goes for the right to run for office. The idea that the observed inequality of mankind is a product of environment is the driving force behind huge government social programs like social security, federal housing programs, and free or cheap publicly supported education. Scientific thinking is behind the opening words of the Declaration of Independence, "We hold these truths to be self evident, that all men are created equal," which are remarkably accurate in saying that the truths are held to be self evident, as scientific premises require, rather than proved beyond a reasonable doubt, which would be impossible.

An intellectual outgrowth of science that leads to an important social result is a corollary of scientific principles which says that "nothing occurs without a *material* cause." If we know what we know through the senses alone, our experience and knowledge will be limited, as we have noted before, to material things—the senses can only detect material things. This means that the causes of events have to be material—not supernatural or beyond the range of the senses. Otherwise, there would be a field of knowledge that science would be incompetent to inquire into, because it would be unequipped to accept proofs of an extrasensory nature. Science also asserts that nature is orderly and regular. Miraculous or random events do not occur, because, if they did, they would violate science's third premise. The two premises together mean that nothing can occur without a material cause: material, in order to be detected by the senses; a cause, to prevent events from being spontaneous and erratic.

When this high-flying epistemology gets down to social applications, it results in this: that everything I do is or has been determined by the environment which has shaped me. I was born with a blank mind—nothing in it. I acquired what is in it by the forces operating on me through the senses. I did not control those forces—they control me. Hence I am not responsible for what I do.

This makes for sweeping social consequences when accepted. If I am unsuccessful in my life in whatever way, it is society's job to make me successful. If I sit on my duff and do nothing, and pity myself for the lack of those things I could get if I would try, I am not to blame, because I was shaped that way by my environment—that is society. Society has made me what I am; society should unmake me: with some special program of education; with financial aid to support me meanwhile; with housing to keep me warm, dry and comfortable while I'm trained; with janitors to clean up the mess I make because I've been emotionally misshapen by society. This will be expensive, and society will have to pay, but after all it's society's fault. Who else is there to blame? I am no more to blame than I would be if someone should seize my fist and hit you in the eye with it, totally surprising me. It's true that it was my fist: but it wasn't my agency, or my intention. Though I was the actual doer of the deed, actually as far as my personal involvement is concerned, I am an innocent bystander.

The same is true respecting criminal behavior. When I'm hauled into court on some charge, what is my plea? Something made me do it—I was "temporarily insane." Maybe I ate something this morning that demented my mind. Or my toilet training was poor when I was little. I was abused as a child. I've never known anything but poverty. Or a life of riches spoiled me. Or whatever. The excuse doesn't matter, because the principles dictate that there has to be some excuse. If I were free to control my own behavior, if I had free will, I would be an uncaused cause, violating the principles of science. Thus we see that scientific premises can lead in practice to excusing criminals and blaming the rest of society for their crimes. Whether that is right or good or not, one must concede a profound change from older attitudes, which held that the law-breaker was to blame and society was to be recompensed and protected.

It is up to you to decide whether you think these social and moral features of modern existence are fruits or scourges of science. But our survey would not be complete without looking into some of the difficulties with science, not practical problems but theoretical flaws in the underpinnings of science, the difficulties of which may some day cause science to lose some, or much, of its present-day overwhelming dominance in social thinking. Intellectuals of the future will probably not look back towards Christianity or another religion for an alternative to science, because Christianity holds at the bottom that there are things that are true that cannot be understood or comprehended. They are held to be true by the Christians (or other sects of believers) on a dogmatic basis. Thus the existence of evil in the world run by an all-powerful and all good God is a mystery. So are miracles, which are prima facie suspensions of the intelligible rules of nature and hence uncomprehendable. Christianity or any other doctrine relying on faith may always have many adherents, but it cannot easily make headway among intellectuals and scholars when it admittedly blocks the progress of intellect with mysteries it says that intellect cannot know. And what scholars think tends in time to become the received opinion of the common man.

The long-term threat to social science must come, and indeed is already evident in the field of political science, from the doctrines of Aristotle. This ancient philosopher's ideas dominated philosophy, even Christian philosophy, before the triumph of science. Aristotle subscribed to the last of science's postulates, that nature is orderly and regular, but he rejected the first two because they conflicted with his own first principle: that we can accept no contradictions; or, that we cannot assert and deny the same thing at the same time. Aristotle accepted this premise—he could not prove his premises either—on the ground that knowledge is impossible if this rule is not followed. Suppose I say it is raining and not raining. How can you know what is true? The mind is tied in a knot of ignorance when a contradiction is tolerated. "I'm a liar." If I'm a liar, I don't tell the truth. If I don't tell the truth, then what I said was a lie—and I said I was a liar, so I must have told the truth. But I said I was a liar. You see how a self-contradictory statement makes it impossible to figure out what the truth is.

With this example in mind consider the first of two postulates of science. Behold: the second violates the first. The first says we know what we know through the senses *alone*. The second says that the mind has the power to receive, record and rearrange sensations, i.e., more is required for knowledge than merely the senses. These powers to receive, record and rearrange are not themselves sensations and evidently did not come through the senses. They were there before the senses began to operate, and science admits it. Thus science is in the position of saying that the senses are everything, and they are not.

With observations like these Aristotle laughed the early forerunners of scientific philosophy literally out of school. Aristotle proceeded to consider the nature of the mind and what must be true of it if knowledge is to be gained. Since it is with the mind that we know, all knowledge that we can have must be consistent in some way with the built-in mode of the mind's operation. Since to know things the mind must have consistency, *the world, to be known, must be consistent also.* No other premise makes knowledge possible.

The senses are not needed for, nor can they contribute to, this understanding. Thus there is knowledge, of a most fundamental kind, about the world, which the senses do not bring us.

Another example will show us how the mind can transcend what the senses bring us. The senses bring us proof that chickens exist. The mind can go beyond this, and with its premise that the world is orderly and regular (on this Aristotle and modern science agree), to observe, that if chickens exist today, their existence proves that it is possible for chickens to exist, even if actual chickens did not always exist and might become extinct in the future. Hence the *possibility* of chickens being is eternal and unchanging. And real.

Having breached the fortress of science on theoretical grounds, let us consider some practical contradictions and problems which are likely to undermine its social influence. We have already seen that science claims to be value-free and to not prescribe or be able to prescribe about moral things, even though its principles lead to certain social views in practice. But science has a much worse problem with values, from its own point of view: values determine what science shall study. The world is filled with countless things that science could study. How many grains of sand are on the shores of Lake Michigan? How often do dogs wet car tires in the city of Chicago, How many bugs live in an average oak tree during July? You will probably agree with me that these are trivial questions. But science itself cannot say that these questions are any more trivial than, shall we spend money and effort to find a cure for cancer? Shall we fund a trip for spacemen to Mars? Would abolishing the minimum wage reduce unemployment? You will probably agree that these are important questions. But science cannot say so, and must depend for the choice of what it will study on the *values* of investigators. Hence all scientific research is subordinate to what values determine as important, and hence all scientific inquiry is a slave to what science says cannot be known, vis., is what we will study worth the trouble, and more worthwhile than something else we could spend our time and money investigating?

Earlier I said that the debate between the modern scientists and the Aristotelian thinkers has been kept alive in the field of political science while it seems that, for now at least, in all other fields, even philosophy, and not to mention physical science, Aristotle has been abandoned. In political science the problem of good and bad will not go away. Politics constantly presents situations in which human beings are being impoverished or butchered or having their relative status changed, and the political scientist cannot bring himself to say, "Whether this is good or bad depends on your personal opinion." He also faces situations in which economic growth is gratifying but the members of society do not share equally in it, and that violates his value of equality. He is also forced to judge between the long run and the short run: shall we spend more on defense now, and suffer a lower standard of living, to make sure we are safe later on? Considering and deciding these trade-offs is absolutely unavoidable in politics, and science can't tell the political scientist how to judge. He has to push on to the inevitable question, what is good for man overall? That question raises another, what kind of creature is man? And that brings the political scientist face to face with epistemology, that is, with the study of what premises about knowledge we will make; because depending on what basic premises we choose, we will come up with a different concept of what man is and hence what is good for him. Modern science, you can see, leads us to a conception of man that is purely materialistic. Aristotle, on the other hand, says that friends and good actions are more important for happiness than wealth.

Although in political science the debate has stayed alive, the showdown will probably come in psychology. Modern psychology purports to be fully scientific; it will not respect any psychological analysis based admittedly on non-scientific ideas. The clients of modern psychology, however, want to know, why are we not happy? Why are we suffering emotionally? Tell us what happiness is so that we can aim our actions at it. *What are we doing wrong?* To answer these questions, modern psychology is totally bankrupt as long as it stays true to its scientific principles: "we cannot tell you what to do—we are scientists and value-free—whatever you want to do is right for you; all we can do is point out alternatives." But the patients say, we know the alternatives: we want to know which ones to pick, and why. We do not know which way to turn. And we need to know because we are unhappy. The modern psychiatrist can offer drugs, which are not his but the fruits of physical science and medicine, but he can't offer advice. His very principles prohibit him. If the psychiatrist does try to tell his patient what to do or think, he is violating his principles as a scientist and imposing his own personal values, which have no higher rank or goodness than anyone else's. If he tells his patients what to do, he's not a scientist anymore; and if he is not a scientist, where will he get his answers?

Aristotle had answers; space does not permit us to go into them here. We can say that he described what happiness was and how it was obtained, not through faith or luck but understanding and practice. He purported to show what man's place in the scheme of the world is, and claimed to show that God must be, and must have invested men with a purpose for their existence. He may not have been right, but modern psychology has no alternative. Its own rules mean it has nothing to say. Aristotle could prescribe and be consistent with his own rules, without demanding belief in things that could not be understood. The absurdity of modern psychology, that its experts are prohibited by their very expertise from giving answers to questions inherent in their profession, coupled with the practical importance of those same questions, must sooner or later lead to the abandonment of trying to apply science to psychology.

Thus we come to the end of our discussion on the principles and social consequences of modern science. Those thoroughly acquainted with the subject may complain that we have painted with a broad brush that has obscured many details, and that for clarity's sake we have made the subject simpler than it really is. To that we plead guilty. But now the student can move from this broad outline into a more thorough investigation of the questions, a work to last a lifetime.

Questions

1. Why must every system of knowledge rest on certain assumptions or premises?

2. What are the basic premises of science?

3. Can one prove the existence of God scientifically? Is this important? How would the answer one way or another affect your life?

4. What kinds of consequences "flow" from the premises of science?

5. What connection is there between tolerance and science? Between materialism and science? Between change and science?

6. What are the political consequences of scientific ideas in America?

7. Are all men equal? How is the question settled by our decision about what factors to consider?

8. To what extent are we responsible for our actions scientifically speaking? Why?

9. In what sense do the doctrines of Aristotle pose a threat to science? How would they affect psychology and psychiatry? Why is modern psychiatry in a weak position to resist the challenge of Aristotelian ideas?

Part V

Human and Sociocultural Evolution

In the year 4004 B.C., at precisely nine o'clock on the morning of October 23, "God created man in his own image, in the image of God created he him; male and female created he them." So said two seventeenth-century scholars. To put a date to creation, specific even to the hour, gave it a comforting actuality. Historian/anthropologist Robert Clarke, in "Evolution and Natural Selection: The Human Animal's Tale," disputes these calculations and the creation story itself. He points out that there are as many different creation stories as there are cultures. Rather than an act of creation "at one time in fixed forms," he says, we must see where we came from through Charles Darwin's theory of natural selection. Humans, like other of the world's species, evolved from some lower forms of life. Dates, furthermore, must be recalculated. The beginning is not 4004 B.C. Instead we must think in terms of millions if not billions of years ago.

Sociologist Frank Zulke's "Types of Societies: Sociocultural Evolution," the second selection, attempts to pinpoint whether there are any "general patterns in societal development." Taking a macrosociological approach, six types of societies are noted: hunting and gathering societies, pastoral societies, horticultural societies, agricultural societies, industrial societies, and post-industrial societies. It is "concluded that there is a general historical trend of sociocultural evolution, that is, a tendency for societies to grow more complex over time as their means of subsistence changes."

Chapter Fifteen

Evolution and Natural Selection
The Human Animal's Tale

Robert H. Clarke

Thousands of cultures have taught creation stories which explain in mythological or religious terms how the universe and its creatures, including humankind, came to be. Cultural anthropologists study these tales for what they reveal about values and belief systems, but their content cannot be subjected to any serious scientific test. That is, we cannot formulate refutable hypotheses about myths and measure them against observed evidence. How can one measure a miracle or test an assertion of divine intervention? Here is a sampling of such traditional accounts of how the natural world was created and shaped:

West Africa (Yoruba)

The Yoruba of Nigeria say that in the beginning the world was all marshy and watery, a waste place. . . . But there were no men yet, For there was no solid ground. One day Ol-orun—Supreme Being—called the chief of the divinities, Great God (Orisha Nla) into his presence. He told him that he wanted to create firm ground. . . . When Great God went back to report to the Supreme Being the latter sent a Chameleon to inspect the work. . . . The making of the earth took four days, and the fifth was reserved for the worship of Great God. . . . Then the Supreme Being-Creator sent Great God back to earth to plant trees, to give food and wealth to man . . . . Meanwhile the first men had been created in heaven and were then sent to earth. Part of the work of making men was entrusted to Great God, and he made human beings from the earth and moulded their physical features. But the task of bringing these dummies to life was reserved for the Creator alone.

SOURCE: Geoffrey Parrinder, *African Mythology* (London: Paul Hamlyn, 1967), p. 20.

Ancient Greek Tradition

In the beginning, Eurynome, the Goddess of All Things, rose naked from Chaos, but found nothing substantial for her feet to rest upon, and therefore divided the sea from the sky, dancing lonely upon its waves. She danced towards the south, and the wind set in motion behind her seemed something new and apart with which to begin a work of creation. Wheeling about, she caught hold of this north wind, rubbed it between her hands, and behold! the great serpent Ophion. . . . [After making love with Ophion] she assumed the form of a dove, brooding on the waves and, in due process of time, laid the Universal Egg. At her bidding, Ophion coiled seven times about this egg, until it hatched and split in two. Out tumbled all things that exist, her children: sun moon, planets, stars, the earth with its mountains and rivers, its trees, herbs, and living creatures.

SOURCE: Robert Graves, *The Greek Myths*, Volume I (New York: Penguin, 1960), p. 27.

Hindu Tradition

"In order to protect the universe, He, the most resplendent one, assigned separate duties and occupations to those who sprang from His mouth, arms, thighs, and feet," stated the Manusmiriti. . . . In consequence of many sinful acts committed with his body a man becomes in the next birth something inanimate; in consequence of sins committed by speech, a bird or beast; and in consequence of mental sins he is reborn in a low caste.

SOURCE: Dilip Hiro, *The Untouchables of India* (London: Minority Rights Group, 1962), p. 5.

Pima Tribe of Southern Arizona

From the Pima tribe . . . comes "a song sung by the Creator at the beginning of the world": "In the beginning there was only darkness everywhere—darkness gathered thick in places, crowding together and then separating, crowding and separating until at last out of one of the places where the darkness had crowded there came forth a man. This man wandered through the darkness until he began to think; then he knew himself and that he was a man; he knew that he was there for some purpose."

SOURCE: Stanley P. Stocker-Edwards, Letter to *New York Times*, 10 March 1990.

Judaeo-Christian-Islamic Tradition:

In the beginning God created the heaven and the earth. . . . And God said, Let the earth bring forth grass, the herb yielding seed and the fruit tree yielding fruit after his kind . . . [He] formed man of the dust, and breathed into his nostrils the breath of life. . . And out of the ground the Lord God formed every beast of the field and every fowl of the air and the rib, which the Lord God had taken from man, made he a woman.

SOURCE: *Holy Bible*, Genesis I, II. (King James Version).

Most of these creation tales recount that all varieties of plants and animals were created at one time in fixed forms. But scientific observation reveals an evolving history of life, including the emergence, modification, proliferation, adaptation or disappearance of millions of species over nearly four billion years on earth. Meteorite showers, climatic changes and other events have punctuated this history with massive annihilations of as many as 95 per cent of all existing species; but so far the history of life itself has never stopped.

To this complex puzzle is added the problem of observing, classifying, and explaining the fantastic variety of surviving species and their interrelationships both with each other and the inorganic physical environment. And, since we are a uniquely self-interested species, we are especially curious to know the origin and development of one particular variety; namely, *Homo sapiens*— ourselves. Where do we fit in this tremendous mosaic of nature? How did we, so recently, emerge from the process of creation and destruction?

For over a century, the world scientific community has accepted that life evolves essentially as Darwin recognized in 1859, and that our species has no special history outside this broad process. Having observed the way animal breeders such as pigeon fanciers could "select" for certain characteristics in their pets or livestock, Darwin theorized that the much vaster selective forces of nature could, on the grand scale, account for the changes within and emergence of new species. This power of transformation he called "natural selection," probably the single most important organizing concept of the life sciences (see Box 27).

As now understood in the light of modern genetics, natural selection operates after some force, such as cosmic radiation, randomly alters or "mutates" the genetic material (DNA) within our cells. This genetic material is crucial because it lays out all the major expressed physical characteristics or "phenotype" of every organism. Most of these mutations or variations either are insignificant or actually reduce an organism's ability to reproduce within some space or "environmental niche" where it is not subject to lethal competition from other species. On the other hand, the organism's environment—weather, food

---

Box 27

An Idea that Shook the World: Natural Selection

Contrary to what a lot of people seem to think, Darwin did not "discover" or "invent" evolution. The general idea of evolution had been put forward by a number of writers, including his grandfather, long before Darwin's time. Nor is evolution a theory, as some people seem to think, any more than gravity is a theory. (T)he evidence in favor of evolution is overwhelming, even though there have been competing theories that seek to explain how it works.

Darwin's contribution was one such theory, that of evolution through natural selection. His was the theory that was best able to account both for change within species and for the emergence of new species. . . . Today, we can say that Darwin's basic idea has stood the test of scientific scrutiny remarkably well.

SOURCE: William Haviland, *Anthropology*, 5th ed. (New York: Holt, Rinehart, and Winston, 1989), p. 60.

The theory of natural selection is really three facts and an inference. First, that all organisms produce more offspring than can possibly survive. Secondly, organisms vary among themselves. Thirdly, at least some of that variation is inherited. From those three facts, Darwin deduced the principle of natural selection: on average, survivors will be those that, through their variations, are better fit, better adapted to changing local environments.

SOURCE: Stephen Gould, *DePauw Alumnus*, Spring 1990, p. 8.

This preservation of favourable variations and the rejection of injurious variations, I call Natural Selection. . . . It may be said that natural selection is daily and hourly scrutinising, throughout the world, every variation, even the slightest; rejecting that which is bad, preserving and adding up all that is good; silently and insensibly working, wherever and whenever opportunity offers, at the improvement of each organic being in relation to its organic and inorganic conditions of life.

SOURCE: Charles Darwin, *The Origin of Species by Means of Natural Selection* (London: Penguin Books, 1982), pp. 130-33.

---

supplies, predators, etc. — is constantly changing; and nature thereby "selects" some mutations which help the organism to survive and reproduce under the changed conditions.

In other words, natural selection preserves those mutations which carry reproductive advantages and winnows out the non-adaptive ones. A simple example would be the lengthening of the necks of the ancestors of modern giraffes. Since long-necked giraffes have better food sources in high trees than short-necked ones, they succeed better and have more offspring over time. Consequently, the average neck length slowly increases, and eventually all the individuals are relatively long-necked. But adaptations may not be permanently useful. For instance, the characteristics which made dinosaurs the dominant land species for so long rather suddenly stopped serving them well under a changed environment about 65 million years ago, and they disappeared from the planet. Their place was later taken by mammals, which grew increasingly large and successful.

Among large creatures, major evolutionary change is usually very slow and can be observed only through such evidence as a long accumulation of fossils. But among the simplest forms of life we can actually observe evolution in action. If we attack a population of living bacteria in a laboratory dish with penicillin, we drastically modify their environment; and most of them will die. Because they reproduce so rapidly, we can see, sometimes within days, that a mutation has permitted the appearance of a strain that goes on reproducing despite the antibiotic that terminates the great mass of the others. What matters here is the experience of modified *populations*. Individual organisms may be perfectly "fit" to survive the challenges but unable to reproduce (mules would be an example).

In the scientific model, these mutations interact with an environment which itself may "co-evolve" to fit in with the mutated organism. The scientific view also stresses that organisms do not "direct" their evolution, nor does evolution proceed in some fixed progression toward any higher purpose or complexity. Biologists and paleontologists increasingly reject the metaphor of a ladder leading to our own species. Indeed, there is little foundation for the belief that *Homo sapiens* had to happen at all. Theorists like Stephen Gould underline the extreme importance of chance and accidents which drastically change the environment. Sudden events such as meteor bombardments or massive volcanic eruptions can shift the patterns of survival-reproduction and at various moments have sharply reduced the number of basic anatomical designs or phyla. Thus, as Gould puts it, the origin of humankind is "a tiny twig on an improbable limb on a fortunate tree. . . we are a detail, not a purpose or embodiment of the whole. . . a wildly improbable evolutionary event well within the realm of contingency." [Source: *Wonderful Life: The Burgess Shale and the Nature of History* (New York: W.W. Norton. 1989), p. 29.]

Some sixty years ago, in his novel *Of Human Bondage*, Somerset Maugham captured this idea:

> On the earth, satellite of a star speeding through space, living things had
> arisen under the influence of conditions which were part of the planet's

history; and as there had been a beginning of life upon it so, under the influence of other conditions, there would be an end: man, no more significant than other forms of life, had come not as the climax of creation, but as a physical reaction to the environment.

Nor does evolution lead to any perfection of form or "exquisite design" of species. The human animal, for instance, has numerous redundant features and is far from perfectly designed. We have weak backs and are hernia-prone, poorly protected from the elements, practically without natural armor or weapons; our newborn require an extraordinarily long time to become viable; and until quite recently we had no way of knowing when a female is fertile, something any dog knows. On the other hand, our bipedal upright posture (walking on two feet) leaves our hands free; and we can invent, discover, and learn from each other, thereby compensating culturally for what we lack physically. As anthropologist Richard Potts put it, "when it comes to important traits like brain size and bipedalism, you don't get a package of perfection; you get a package of compromises." [Source: *U.S. News and World Report*, 27 February 1989, p. 59.] Others use the concept of "evolutionary trade-offs"to remind us that nature extracts a price for most of the adaptive advantages conferred (see Boxes 28, 31, and 32).

From these observations emerges the chastening view that the "tape of life" could as easily have been played out on an earth not only without us, but without any mammals, reptiles, birds or fish. Yet there would probably be an abundance of insects and "weird" marine life. Even today, a fairly small environmental change such as global warming induced by human industrial excesses could wipe us out and leave the earth to the hardier cockroaches.

As we zero in on the particular history of natural selection which produced *Homo sapiens* we are struck by how remarkably recent a growth we are upon the thin skin of life that envelops our planet (see Box 29). Increasingly reliable methods of dating indicate that life began on earth just under four billion years ago, that it evolved into multicellular form only about 570 million years ago, and that the rat-like early primate (a tree-dwelling visual insect predator) from which we and our ape cousins descend came onto the scene less than 70 million years ago.

Evidence from molecular biology—especially that showing the close match of human and chimpanzee DNA—indicates that the split from a common ancestor between hominids (the line leading to modern human beings) and apes occurred as recently as five million years ago—a mere speck in the span of geologic time. The spectacular bipedal footprints of Laetoli, Kenya and the early hominid "Lucy" skeletal material from Ethiopia are dated by the potassium-argon method to just under four million years ago (see Box 30). Both Lucy and the footsteppers were "Australopithecine" African hominids.

Box 28

Nature's Cruel Bargain: Sickle-cell Anemia

She was only eight years old, but suffered with a stoic resignation that was as poignant as her desperate condition. She had experienced similar crises of nausea, vomiting and piercing joint pains many times before. The medical team of the central city's hospital worked with rapid efficiency. Within a few minutes of her admission, the metal tree stood near to her bed, holding bottles of the blood and the glucose and salt solutions that were being slowly transfused into her fragile veins. . . . [She] was undergoing a crisis of sickle-cell anemia. The child was black, and her blood abnormality was the product a bargain evolution has struck with the most malignant of the malaria parasites affecting humans, *Plasmodium falciparum*.

SOURCE: Robert S. Dersowitz, *New Guinea Tapeworms and Jewish Grandmothers: Tales of Parasites and People* (New York: Avon Books, 1981), pp. 59-61.

An estimated three million African-Americans carry a defective gene which evolved to protect their ancestors from malaria. Since malaria does not now exist in the U.S., this gene is no longer "useful," but it persists along with its cruel evolutionary accompaniment: a certain percentage of carriers produce children with sickle-cell anemia. Over thousands of years in Africa, malaria was a potent environmental selector, favoring successful reproduction by individuals born at random with a slight alteration or "mutation" of the chemically coded DNA genetic tape which made their red blood cells more resistant to malaria. But this protection was in the form of the defect which afflicted some with anemia. Where malaria was a threat, nature's willingness to sacrifice some of the population was more than balanced by the larger number rescued by the defective gene. Now transplanted to a non-malarial area, these populations are continuing to pay the price without receiving the benefit.

They walked upright on two legs (in contrast to the four-limbed locomotion of all our ape-cousins) but had small brains. The first "true" members of our genus, *Homo habilis*, appeared about two and a half million years ago. Having evolved larger, more capable brains, they made use of primitive stone tools.

Within another million years, *Homo erectus* hominids were making sophisticated stone tools and beginning their initial emigration from Africa. *Homo erectus* was big-brained, bipedal, and successful for hundreds of thousands of years on several continents. Much fossil evidence of this species exists in Asia and Europe as well as in Africa, but there are no complete specimens.

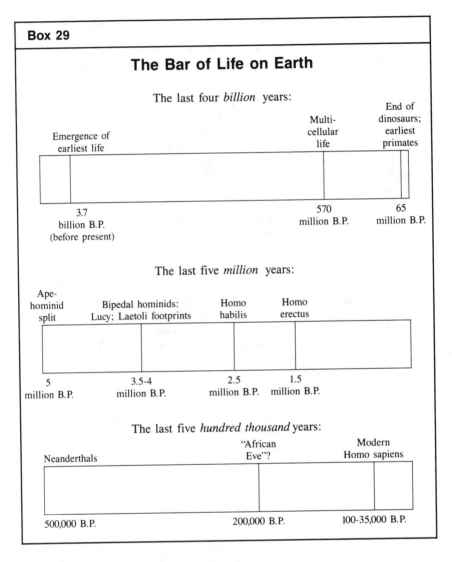

Box 29

The Bar of Life on Earth

(As one anthropologist lamented, "A good *Homo erectus* is hard to find.")
    What happened next in the evolutionary give and take is not altogether clear.
Of course we know that by 15-35 thousand years ago creatures exactly like
us, with equal intellectual and communicative abilities, were living in
communities and producing glorious works of art like the cave paintings found
at Lascaux in France. But what about the interval between *Homo erectus* and
Lascaux?

Box 30

Dating Fossils

When fossils are found in volcanic ash or lava, we can discover their age by observing the breakdown of radioactive potassium 40 into argon gas. The "clock" starts when the lava or ash cools. "It takes 1.265 million years for half the potassium in a sample to decay into argon. . . . The age of the rock can therefore be calculated with remarkable precision by determining the ratio of argon gas to potassium 40." This method "can be used to date fossils only from areas where volcanic eruptions occurred at about the same time as the fossils were deposited." Fortunately, in the areas of East Africa where the Lucy fossils and Laetoli footprints were found, volcanic activity was widespread.

SOURCE: Bernard Campbell, *Humankind Emerging*, 5th Ed. (Glenview, IL: Scott, Foresman/Little, Brown College Division, 1988), p. 30.

Many physical anthropologists conclude from primarily fossil evidence that *Homo erectus* evolved separately in Africa, Asia and Europe, producing early *Homo sapiens* species, including Neanderthals, from three to five hundred thousand years ago. Natural selection then modified these Neanderthals in a few significant ways and resulted in us—modern *Homo sapiens*—somewhere between 35 and 100 thousand years ago.

An alternative view, recently publicized under the "African Eve" headline, holds that all the mitochondrial DNA (found outside the cell nucleus and inherited only from females) in present human populations can be traced to a single African female who lived as recently as 200,000 years ago. According to this view, all but one of the descendants of *Homo erectus*, including the Neanderthals, far from being our ancestors, were in fact evolutionary dead ends. Only one line, arising in Africa, led to all existing human populations.

Adding to the uncertainty concerning the period since *Homo erectus* is the absence of agreement on exactly where to draw the line between modern *Homo sapiens* and our nearest predecessors. Human attributes such as high intelligence and culture are no longer used to explain early hominid adaptations like upright walking or the loss of daggerlike teeth. As Roger Lewin has suggested, where "they" end and "we" begin "is not a question for. . . biology. It is a question. . . of self-image." [Source: *Bones of Contention* (New York: Touchstone, 1987), p. 317.]

Wherever we draw this line, two major conclusions are gaining increasing scientific acceptance. One of them is that within our common species, variations

---

Box 31

An Evolutionary Combat

Despite our impressive brain development and our capacity for language, which gave us our "cultural edge" in the "struggle for survival," we can fall victim to organisms that possess no intellectual-cultural capacity whatsoever. For example, certain viruses mutate very rapidly, enabling them to survive our most determined medical assaults. Here we see our weapon of culture pitted against an enemy species' capacity for rapid physical mutation. For example, flu vaccines must be modified to counteract newly mutated virus strains undaunted by the combination of our immune response (physically evolved) or by previous vaccines (our "cultural" response) to the flu threat.

HIV (human immune deficiency virus), which is thought to cause AIDS, probably mutates faster even than the ordinary flu virus. Moreover, HIV has evolved a marker just like the one our own immune system uses to "notify" our bodies that "foreign enemies" are at the gates. Thus, the tiny brainless virus challenges our potent medical knowledge and our elaborately evolved immune defenses. It will, in fact, probably kill millions of us. Which species will survive this combat is still not certain.

---

like skin color or hair or size are remarkably small — in other words, human populations are remarkably alike physically, possibly because our recent emergence has not allowed time for more drastic differentiation. The differences *within* groups like Europeans, Asians, or Africans are greater than the differences *between* such groups. A second conclusion is that we are less different from our closest ape relatives than we used to believe. *Homo sapiens* is not as distinctive or unique as textbooks used to teach. Here are some reasons:

1. Ability to use language or symbolic communication, even including vocalization, has been demonstrated among apes. Chimpanzees have mastered a large range of American Sign Language (a true language like Russian or English).

2. Chimpanzees and even some species of ants and birds, both through genetic programming and learning, regularly fashion and use simple tools, including weapons.

3. Observations of chimpanzees have shown that they develop complex social hierarchies and learn their place within them. They even plot ways of using these social structures to their advantage, prompting one ethologist to suggest that they practice a form of politics that would be well understood by Machiavelli!

4. Pygmy chimpanzee females are sexually receptive much of the time, about half the days of the year, a trait once thought exclusive to human females. Moreover, females of some monkey species have been observed engaging in mutual masturbation, suggesting that they engage in sex purely for pleasure. Among females, sex unrelated to procreation was previously thought a behavior exclusive to *Homo sapiens*.

5. In general, the role of learned behavior, especially among higher mammals, is getting increased recognition. For instance, observers have seen Japanese monkeys quickly teach each other how to wash off food once one of them has learned this technique from a human teacher.

6. Human and chimpanzee DNA are 98 percent identical.

Box 32

The Sun Also Jeopardizes
Skin Pigmentation and Survival

Variations of skin pigmentation (color) among populations illustrate the relationship between evolutionary adaptations and environmental conditions. Darker skin has a higher content of melanin, a chemical that protects against the sun's damaging ultraviolet rays. In tropical zones, these ultraviolet rays strike directly and can cause skin cancer. In areas more distant from the equator, such as Scandinavia or England, lighter skin is more adaptive because it permits the body to absorb needed vitamin D from the sun's rays, making possible the assimilation of calcium. Inadequate calcium can lead to bone disease such as crippling rickets. It is instructive to note that dark-skinned south Asian immigrant children in England suffered a high rate of rickets while light-complected north Europeans who moved to sunny Australia (where the aboriginal people were very dark) have the world's highest rate of melanoma, a deadly form of skin cancer. Thus, the adaptations — *within* our species — evolved for one environmental zone were not successful for the other (see also Box 28).

But the story does not end here. *Homo sapiens* is the species *par excellence* whose survival depends upon adaptation through *culture* — learned behavior made possible by physical brain evolution. Using these possibilities, we can make the dark-skinned children in England healthy by giving them vitamin D supplements and spare the pink Australians cancer by persuading them to use sunscreens and spend more time in the shade! Such cultural adaptations can take place very rapidly. Of course, other things being equal, if we misuse our technological culture to destroy the earth's protective ozone layer, the resulting increase in ultraviolet radiation will change the environment so as to favor the reproductive success of darker-skinned members of our species and perhaps eventually lead to the disappearance of those of lighter hue. Under such conditions, black might be not only beautiful but also necessary for survival.

Of course, no evidence indicates that we are descended from existing species of apes. Rather, with common ancestors, we are their evolutionary cousins, perhaps having more in common than was previously appreciated. No evolutionist believes that when we look at a gorilla in the zoo we are "seeing our ancestors." Nevertheless, as Darwin wrote in the final words of *The Descent of Man*, "Man still bears in his bodily frame the indelible stamp of his lowly origin."

One egregious scientific fallacy, "Social Darwinism," was unfortunately long accepted by many anthropologists. This false interpretation of evolutionary data, now discredited, held that certain human populations (nations, females, so-called races) were more recently evolved or somehow less complex or developed than others. Such views, which were really prejudice disguised as science, were taken up by German leaders to justify their attacks on "inferior" European peoples even in World War I. In America, the claim of the evolutionary inferiority of Jews, southern Europeans or even African-Americans (especially ironic in light of the "African Eve" hypothesis) was used by employers and others to justify low wages or other forms of discrimination.

Indeed, it was this perversion of science, as much as his Biblical faith, that led the anti-militarist and pro-labor political leader, William Jennings Bryan, in the famous Scopes trial of 1925, to support a Tennessee law forbidding the teaching of evolution. Today, we can sort out the insidious lies about the inferiority of populations and make use of the scientifically validated view of evolution as a dynamic model to illuminate our understanding of where we come from, where we fit, and perhaps where we are going in the natural order.

Questions

1. Why are creation stories like those of the Yoruba or Jews not considered "science?"

2. Darwin was interested in the work that livestock breeders and gardeners did to select characteristics like fatness in pigs or yellow petals in tulips. How would you compare what they do with "natural" selection?

3. Do you agree or disagree with this recent critique of Darwin? "(H)ow does one test the claim that the fittest survive? . . . Whichever species survives is automatically declared the 'fittest' and this is invoked to 'explain' the survival . . . Darwin can't lose. And in science if you can't lose, you can't win." [Source: Steven Goldberg, Letter to *New York Times*, 15 December 1989.]

4. What do human beings have in common with apes? What traits are specific or unique to *Homo sapiens*? What do you understand Lewin to mean when

he says that the answers to these questions depend partly upon our "self-image?"

5. Can you think of any current examples of "Social Darwinism?" How can you relate the "African Eve" hypothesis to the problem of racist beliefs?

6. Review the definitions of the following terms, using a dictionary if necessary: genus; mutation; phenotype; hominid; melanin.

7. The reading gives several examples of human evolutionary adaptations based on culture rather than physical changes. What are three of these examples? Can you think of any others?

8. Review the concept of evolutionary "trade-offs" in the text. Try to identify some possible negative trade-offs or "prices" paid by our species for the following adaptations:

    a. bipedal upright posture

    b. large, complex brain development

    c. high language communication abilities

    d. prolonged dependency of offspring

    e. chronic sexual receptivity of females

9. What other methods of dating fossils and artifacts might the anthropologist use when the potassium-argon method is inappropriate?

10. How does the article help to understand the difficulty of finding a cure for AIDS?

11. Why might black be both beautiful and necessary for survival?

12. Today there is hot controversy over the teaching of evolution in the schools. What are your ideas about this controversy?

Chapter Sixteen

Types of Societies
Sociocultural Evolution

Frank Zulke

The term society is probably familiar to most of us. Yet it is one of those words that we use freely in our daily conversations but that may have different meanings for different people. Some may associate the word with "high society" and the lifestyles of the rich and famous. Some may think of an organization devoted to a specific purpose such as the "Society for the Prevention of Cruelty to Animals." Others may be even more vague when they say such things as "society disapproves of mercy-killing" or "society encourages patriotism."

In social science, the use of the word society is more precise than that of ordinary speech. For social scientists, society refers to a group of people who live in a given territory and who share a common culture (language, norms, customs, values, ideas, beliefs, artifacts, etc.). This definition is necessarily broad so as to include the many types of societies that have existed throughout world history. The 300 thousand people who lived in ancient Athens formed a society, as do the 250 million people who live in the United States of America today or the 1.2 billion people in the People's Republic of China. In the modern world, most societies are nation-states, like America or China. Societies and nation-states are not necessarily the same, however, as societies existed for thousands of years before nation-states were created, and some separate societies still exist *within* the boundaries of nation-states. The French and English speaking populations of Canada exemplify different societies within nation-states.

Societies can be classified by their means of subsistence, that is, by their means of obtaining food and other necessities such as shelter, clothing, and so forth. This classification yields five different types of societies: hunting and gathering societies, pastoral societies, horticultural societies, agricultural societies, and industrial societies. In addition, there also seems to be a sixth type, postindustrial societies, that is beginning to emerge in some parts of the world.

The following discussion of these various types of societies benefits greatly from the excellent analysis of this topic by Gerhard and Jean Lenski in their book *Human Societies: An Introduction to Macrosociology* (5th edition, 1987). Using historical and archaeological data, they examine how most hunting and gathering societies changed into other types of societies. They concluded that there is a general historical trend of "sociocultural evolution," that is, a tendency for societies to grow more complex over time as their means of subsistence changes.

A consideration of institutional change may illustrate what is meant here. Institutions are stable clusters of values, norms, statuses (positions), roles (ways in which statuses are "acted out"), and groups that develop around basic needs. They are routine ways of dealing with common dilemmas that people face. The family institution, for example, answers the basic need of how to care for children. An important value connected to the family in American society is marital fidelity. A norm is that a person can have only one spouse. Some statuses and/or roles might be "loving husbands" or "doting grandmothers." Some groups might be nuclear families or single parent families. In simple societies, one basic institution, the family or kinship group, answers all basic economic, educational, religious and political needs. Social relationships based on kinship obligations organize everything from producing and distributing food and goods, training the young, supplying answers about the unknown or unknowable, to maintaining peace and order. As societies grow more complex, the kinship structure is less able to offer solutions to all problems. The economy (capitalism, socialism, etc.), education (public, private, etc.), religion (Islam, Catholicism, etc.), and government (democracy, dictatorship, etc.) become fully developed institutions that exist separately from the family. Try to think of values, norms, statuses, roles, and groups that exemplify each of these institutions.

The Lenskis are not saying that it is inevitable that *all* societies *must* evolve in a certain way. Neither are they saying that the evolutionary process is necessarily uniform. They point out that some societies have changed faster than others, some do not seem to have changed at all, and some have even disappeared. What they offer is a useful way to classify societies based on their means of subsistence. This scheme can account for general patterns in societal development as well as individual variations.

Hunting and Gathering Societies
Living Off the Land

Perhaps the simplest solution to the subsistence problem is that offered by hunting and gathering societies. Using primitive weapons or tools, hunters and gatherers hunt wild game and forage for vegetation (fruits, nuts, roots, bird's eggs, etc.). Because they waste little of what they obtain directly from the natural environment, some say they live in harmony with nature. Hunting and gathering is certainly the oldest solution to answer subsistence needs and has been around since the beginning of human history. The exact dates when humans first inhabited the earth can be debated, but most social scientists would agree that a fully modern species of humans (*homo sapiens sapiens* — the doubly wise man) appeared about 35,000 years ago (Box 33 describes these people and their lives). From at least that time until about 10,000 years ago, *all* human beings lived as hunters and gatherers. Today less than 0.1 percent of people in the world do. Some of the remaining hunting and gathering societies are the !Kung of the Kalahari desert in southern Africa, some aborigines in Australia, some Eskimos in North America and isolated groups in New Guinea and South America. Those still around have often modified their way of life and are fast disappearing as more technologically advanced societies encroach on their lands. The Lenskis doubt that any will survive into the twenty-first century.

Box 33

The Way We Were—35,000 Years Ago

Do not think of *homo sapiens sapiens* 300 centuries ago as brutal grunting savages. Fossils indicate their frontal lobes—the seat of reasoning—were large and developed giving them the capacity for symbolic thought, adaptation, and invention. Artifacts from this period give further insight into the lives of these people. Artifacts range from the practical (sewing needle, spear thrower, etc.) to the ethereal (Venus figurines, musical instruments, etc.). While the total picture is incomplete, we see people who have a sense of community, language, art, music, trade, fashion, and even liquor and pornography. The physically evolving *homo sapiens sapiens*, furthermore, given a haircut, shave, and dressed in sweats and sneakers might be indistinguishable from the person sitting next to you in your classroom today.

SOURCE: Sharon Begley and Louise Lief, "The Way We Were," *Newsweek*, November 10, 1986, pp. 62-72.

Even though hunting and gathering societies have significant cultural and environmental differences, there are certain recurring features of social organization. In most such societies, members are nomadic, moving about a great deal as the food supply and seasons change. Their way of life cannot support large concentrations of people. Thus a typical "band" is small, having twenty to fifty people, with most members related by ancestry or marriage. The family is *the* most important institution in these societies. It provides for the emotional needs of members and most of the economic, political, educational, and religious needs that larger formal organizations assume in modern societies.

The entire band works as a unit. The division of labor is simple and is based on age and sex. The very young or old need not work; men usually make their own weapons and hunt; women gather and perform "home" chores. Food, particularly meat from the kill, is shared. While hunting brings in the most desirable food, most of the food that is eaten is gathered. This has led some to say that we should call these gathering and hunting societies to give proper emphasis where it is due.

Another consequence of relatively constant nomadism is that possessions are limited by the amount that can be carried. People own nothing but what they can wear on their backs or balance on their heads. No one acquires great wealth. Since people have few possessions to fight about, there is little chance of warfare. As a result, some hunting and gathering societies are often marked by equality and peaceful cooperation. One sign of sexual equality among the !Kung, for example, is that adults express no preference before birth for a child of either sex. Some hunting and gathering societies, however, go in the opposite direction. Central Eskimo groups, for example, control population by killing or deliberately starving female infants.

Hunters and gatherers must rely on whatever food they can find or catch from one day to the next. We should not assume, however, that life within these groups is necessarily one of constant hardship. In fact, because their needs are simple, members of some hunting and gathering societies might work merely two or three hours a day! One researcher has called these societies the "original affluent societies" and points out that they contain the most leisured people on earth. Nor need we assume that hunters and gatherers live on the brink of starvation. Research has shown that, when gathered foods are easily available, people get more than adequate nutrition. This would not be true, of course, for those societies where environmental restrictions might limit hunting and gathering. Eskimo societies come immediately to mind.

In summary, hunting and gathering as a subsistence strategy greatly influences those societies that utilize it. They are small and nomadic with a very simple social organization. The family assumes all major responsibilities. In some of these societies, there is little social inequality.

Pastoral Societies
Herding

Between 10,000 and 12,000 years ago, some hunting and gathering groups began to capture, breed, and raise animals they had previously hunted. These people established pastoral or herding societies which depend for their subsistence on meat, dairy products, and skin derived from domesticated herd animals (cattle, camels, horses, goats, sheep, etc.). This subsistence strategy is useful in deserts, mountains, and grasslands where plants are difficult to cultivate. Today, pastoral societies exist in areas of the world as diverse as the Middle East, central Asia, and central and north Africa. Like other preindustrial societies, however, they are vanishing as they are brought under the control of agricultural and industrial societies.

The advantage of pastoralism over hunting and gathering is that a surplus of food can be accumulated. A result of this is that these societies can be very large and may include hundreds or even thousands of people. Since livestock and animal products can often be converted into other forms of wealth (jewelry, carpets, etc.), some individuals within these societies can become richer and more powerful than others and can pass these benefits on within their extended families. Elaborate kinship patterns develop and determine not only marriage (for example, how many spouses one can have) and descent (for example, inheritance patterns) but political and economic alliances. Because males tend the animals, the source of the society's wealth, they often assume positions of authority and leadership. A man's prestige is based not only on the size of his herd but on the number of his wives.

Most pastoralists are constantly on the move, needing new grazing grounds for their herds. This brings them into contact with others. One consequence of this is the growth of trade and commerce. Another consequence of the need for more grazing land is that intergroup fighting often arises over grazing rights. Even slavery, unknown in hunting and gathering societies, appears in pastoral societies. The slaves are captives taken in battle who are used as cheap labor.

"Otherworldly" aspects of culture such as one's perception of god are also influenced by the subsistence strategy of a society. The god, or gods, that pastoralists worship are different from those revered by hunters and gatherers. Hunters and gatherers believe in many spirits equal to one another (gods of rain, giraffes, sickness, the desert, etc.). These spirits must be taken account of, but not necessarily worshipped. Religion in the pastoral society reflects the pastoral way of life. The word "pastor" originally meant shepherd. God is portrayed as a male who looks after his people much as a shepherd looks after his flock. The emphasis here on the masculine is intentional for pastoral societies are societies in which males dominate. Do not forget that the Hebrews who founded Judaism and Christianity, and the Arabs who founded Islam, used to be pastoral people.

In summary, nomadic pastoralism as a way of life greatly affects a society. A surplus of livestock and food allows population to grow larger and more diverse. A simple stratification system develops. The production of more goods is often accompanied by less willingness to share within the society. While still family-centered, political, economic, and religious institutions begin to develop and become more complex.

Horticultural Societies
Gardening by Hand

Horticulture is an alternative to pastoralism, although it is sometimes combined with it. Horticultural societies rely for their subsistence on cultivating plants by hand in small garden plots. A hoe or a digging stick is used to punch holes in the ground for seeds and careful tending of the plants hopefully leads to a successful harvesting of edible vegetation (grains such as wheat, rice, etc.). Sometimes trees and bushes producing edible fruits and nuts are also cultivated. Societies using this subsistence technique first emerged between 10,000 and 12,000 years ago when some hunters and gatherers became horticulturists. While few in number today, there are still horticulturalists in Africa, Asia, and Australia, as well as in the tropical rain forests in the Amazon area of South America.

Unlike hunters and gatherers or pastoralists, horticulturalists lead a relatively settled life. They live in permanent or semipermanent homes instead of in skin tents or grass huts. Nevertheless, they must move periodically because they typically use "slash and burn" cultivation. This means they clear an area, burn the vegetation they have cut down to help fertilize the soil, and raise crops for two or three years until the nutrients in the soil are depleted. They then move and repeat the process elsewhere. Environmentalists must note that once a tropical rain forest's cover is gone, rainfall leaches the remaining nutrients from the soil, leaving a "moonscape" where once was abundant life.

Ecological concerns aside, horticulture is more efficient than hunting and gathering because it can assure a food supply and a probable surplus. The surplus allows for larger populations, some occupational specialization, more highly developed political and economic institutions, and more permanent cultural artifacts (houses, thrones, monuments, etc.). There develops a class or caste hierarchy between the majority of the people, who must devote their full time to food production, and those few at the top. As these societies become more productive and better organized, we find an increase in social inequality, sexism, intertribal fighting, and even cannibalism and headhunting. The gods who must be worshipped, furthermore, are sometimes capricious and may need to be appeased with human sacrifice. Box 34 provides a chilling account of this dark side of the Mayan religious heritage. Technological progress, the Lenskis say, may be accompanied by ethical regression.

In summary, the use of a horticultural subsistence strategy has implications very similar to the use of a pastoral subsistence strategy. Both strategies yield a food surplus which allows for larger populations and more complexity in the institutional structure of the societies. Both strategies see an enormous increase in social inequality. The society utilizing horticulture differs, of course, in that this strategy permits a more settled way of life.

Agricultural Societies
Gardening with the Plow

Agricultural societies rely for their subsistence on large scale cultivation of crops through the use of plows and draft animals. Some say the plow, invented

---

Box 34

Human Sacrifice

Paul Rivet describes how a human sacrifice ceremony might have taken place in the Mayan Temple of the Jaguars in Chichen Itza, Mexico:

> The victim was presented in the nude, his body painted blue, his head decorated with a pointed headdress. The place of execution was either the precinct of the temple, or the summit of the pyramid where the altar was erected; the altar of sacrifice was a heavy stone with a convex surface. Four assistants or *chaces,* also painted blue, took hold of the four limbs of the victim and laid his back on the stone so that his thorax projected. The sacrificer or *nacom,* equipped with a flint dagger, opened the lower left part of the breast, put his hand into the incision, tore out the beating heart, placed it on a plate and gave it to the priest or *chilán.* The *chilán* quickly smeared with blood the image of the god in whose honor the ceremony had been celebrated. The *chaces* threw the still warm body to the bottom of the pyramid where the priests of lower rank stripped it of all its skin, except for the hands and feet. The *chilán* dressed himself in this bloody skin and danced in company with the spectators. When the victim had been a particularly valiant soldier, the scene was accompanied by ritual cannibalism. The hands and feet were reserved for the *chilán.*

There is evidence that such ceremonies occurred in horticultural and early agrarian societies in both the "old" and "new" world.

SOURCE: Paul Rivet, *Mayan Cities* (New York: Putnam, 1960), p. 78.

5,000 or 6,000 years ago, is a "prerequisite" of civilization. Box 35 suggests the time period when it came into use might be called the "dawn of civilization." When a plow is used, nutrients that have sunk into the soil are brought to the surface and weeds are killed and buried in the soil to act as fertilizer. This increases productivity. If farmers use animals to pull their plows, this additional muscle power increases productivity even more. By putting the nutrients back into the soil, people do not need to abandon their fields and a greater variety of crops can be grown. People must no longer be nomads, and a substantial food surplus can be produced.

Box 35

The Dawn of Civilization

The period in which the plow came into use, from 5,000 B.C. to 3,000 B.C., was an extremely creative one. During this time period we see the invention of the wheel for use in wagons and making pottery, the harnessing of wind power to propel sailboats, the expanding use of metals for weapons and artifacts, the use of money for trade, the construction of monumental pyramids, palaces, and temples, and the development of writing, numbers, and the calendar. Changes in human societies were so profound that some call this the "dawn of civilization."

This surplus means that societies can now contain more people. Roman Emperor Augustus conducted the first census of the world in 28 B.C. and estimated the population of the Roman Empire at 70 to 100 million people. Most agricultural societies, of course, will be much smaller and will not be empires. Because each farmer can produce more than enough food for one person, the division of labor expands. An increasing percentage of people are now able to give up food production and pursue other occupations such as priest, soldier, merchant, tax collector, artist, temple builder or prostitute. Larger populations means larger governments are needed to control the inhabitants of these societies. As power becomes concentrated, hereditary monarchies develop, as do military elites, state religions, elaborate bureaucracies, and complex stratification systems. Towns and cities as centers of power, religion, and trade emerge for the first time in history. Within these societies we sometimes find such monumental architectural achievements as the castles of Europe, the temples and pyramids of Egypt, the Taj Mahal in India, and the Great Wall in China.

The increase in wealth in these societies is not shared equally, however. In fact, the amount of inequality found in them is much greater than in any of the previously described societies. Though an extreme position, physiologist/ ecologist Jared Diamond has even gone so far as to call the advent of agriculture the "worst mistake in the history of the human race" (see Box 36). In some of these agrarian societies, castes and classes become rigid. Political leaders arise who extract unfair taxes and, in extreme situations, enslave and exterminate groups of people. Warfare becomes an almost constant state of existence. One historical survey of European nations during their centuries as agrarian societies computed that they had been at war well over 50 percent of the time. Even the status of women, "relatively equal" in hunting and gathering societies, declines in these societies. Men, generally bigger and stronger and therefore able to perform tougher chores, engage in important tasks like plowing, and women are relegated to subsidiary tasks like weeding and carrying water to the field. The end result is that authority and decision-making in the household become the province of the male.

In summary, just as pastoral and horticultural societies were more complex than hunting and gathering societies, agricultural societies are more complex than any of the earlier three types. While hard to measure in absolute terms, the magnitude of the differences is enormous. For the first time in history, the abundant agricultural surplus now allows for populations in the millions, the emergence of cities, and the creation of empires. While the family and kinship still serve as basic anchors, elaborate political, economic, religious, and military institutions develop to maintain the social order. Since these societies can take many forms, it is not surprising that they still predominate today in parts of Africa, Asia, and South America and have existed in diverse time periods from ancient Egypt to the Roman Empire to the Middle Ages to the present.

Box 36

The Worst Mistake in the History of the Human Race

There are at least three sets of reasons to explain the findings that agriculture was bad for health. First, hunter-gatherers enjoyed a varied diet, while early farmers obtained most of their food from one or a few starchy crops. The farmers gained cheap calories at the cost of poor nutrition. (Today just three high-carbohydrates—wheat, rice, and corn—provide the bulk of the calories consumed by the human species, yet each one is deficient in certain vitamins or amino acids essential to life.) Second, because of dependence on a limited number of crops, farmers ran the risk of starvation if one crop failed. Finally, the mere fact that agriculture encouraged people to clump together in crowded societies, many of which then carried on trade with other crowded societies, led to the spread of parasites and infectious disease. Epidemics couldn't take hold when populations were scattered in small bands that constantly shifted camp.

What evidence is there that malnutrition, starvation, and epidemic diseases are the offspring of farming? Jared Diamond feels that paleopathology, the study of signs of disease in skeletal remains of ancient peoples, can provide clues. A skeleton tells its owner's sex, weight, height, age, and health condition. In fact, "where there are many skeletons, one can construct mortality tables like the ones life insurance companies use to calculate expected life span and risk of death at any given age."

SOURCE: Jared Diamond, "The Worst Mistake in the History of the Human Race," *Discover,* Vol. 8, 1987, pp. 64-66.

Industrial Societies
Using Power-Driven Machines to Produce

Industrial societies rely for their subsistence on mechanized production. This mode of production originated in England about 250 years ago at the time of the Industrial Revolution. Industrialism is such a successful strategy that it now dominates throughout the world: most societies are either industrial or trying to become so.

The idea behind industrialism is to replace human and animal muscle power with machines using advanced energy sources such as steam, electricity, oil, and nuclear energy. Preindustrial societies used natural energy sources such as wind and water. With machine power harnessed, as one wag put it, people do not have to work harder, but can "work smarter." In building a road, for example, one bulldozer driver can do the work of hundreds of laborers using picks and shovels. With mechanical equipment, one farmer can produce enough food to feed fifty to seventy-five people. In the industrial society, thus, it becomes possible for a small minority to feed the rest of the people. The majority of the population, in turn, can expect nonagricultural employment with many members of the society producing manufactured goods in factories.

Industrialization has gone hand in hand with the rise of cities as economic centers. At its early stage, people migrate from rural areas to live in or near cities where the factories are located. This is happening currently in Mexico. Mexican peasants are moving into Mexico City so rapidly that it is fast becoming the largest city in the world, and one of the most problem-ridden as well. Over time, as industrialism advances, societies become so urbanized that large cities and their suburbs—metropolises and megalopolises—contain most of a society's members. Over 90 percent of the population of highly industrialized

Great Britain, for example, live in urban areas. While dwellers in a modern city tend to be highly aware of physical blight and urban problems, slum sections of cities in more advanced industrial societies are smaller and problems are less extensive than in other types of cities. Even the worst parts of modern cities such as London, Edinburgh or Belfast are an improvement on large sections of cities during the early stages of industrialism, to say nothing of the squalor of preindustrial cities. In large cities in India, which is just beginning to industrialize, there are special police forces to clear the streets of homeless people who died of starvation and malnutrition during the night. On a walk through the worst urban neighborhood today, no one will see dead infants lying on dung heaps, or even any dung heaps.

Increased manufacturing activities and urbanization are not the only consequences of industrialization. Another important consequence is rapid population growth (number of births minus number of deaths). Throughout most of history, population growth in preindustrial societies was slow. There was a high birth rate since people had large families, but there was a high death rate, especially among infants. Fertility and mortality in these societies balanced out and their populations remained stable in size. With the onset of industrialization, however, better food production and distribution along with improved health and sanitation measures begin to produce a sharp drop in death rates, but birth rates remain high. As a result, population grows rapidly. In some areas of the world, this stage can be called a "population explosion." In advanced industrial nations, the birth rate drops. Large families in urban areas are a liability and methods of birth control are easily available. The death rate remains low. The result here is that births equal deaths and population size remains stable. It is said that "zero population growth" is achieved when parents have only two children—just enough to replace themselves. This demographic transition, graphically depicted in Box 37, occurred or is occurring in most industrial countries. The big question, of course, is whether birth rates will drop in the rest of the world the way they have in Western Europe and the United States, Canada, and Japan. We need to know the answer soon, as twelve new babies were added to the current world population of 5.7 billion people in the five seconds that it took you to read this sentence. It is almost certain that world population will easily exceed six billion by the year 2000.

In addition to world overpopulation, the relationship between a society's stage of industrialization and ecological effects on the natural environment is another important topic to consider. In many preindustrial societies, people traditionally treated nature with respect. Hunters and gatherers, for example, sustained themselves directly from the environment. Industrial societies, on the other hand, often seem to view the environment as something that technology can "master" in the name of "progress." We are so used to dumping our waste products into the environment, for example, that we forget this can lead to

---

Box 37

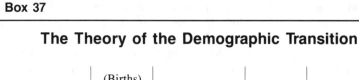

The Theory of the Demographic Transition

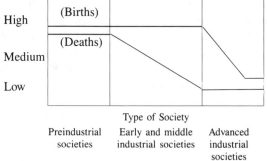

| | Type of Society | |
| Preindustrial societies | Early and middle industrial societies | Advanced industrial societies |

According to the theory of the demographic transition, preindustrial societies will have high birth and death rates and slow population growth. Early and middle industrial societies will have high birth rates, declining death rates, and rapid population growth. Advanced industrial societies will see birth rates decline to match death rates and slow population growth. If you think of the "baby boom" that occurred in the United States after the second world war, you will understand that this theory is not fool-proof. The theory also ignores migration rates. These, too, have an effect on population growth.

---

extensive pollution of air, water, and land with harmful effects on human health and the climate of the planet. One can hardly pick up a newspaper without reading about smog, the "greenhouse effect," global warming trends, acid rain, etc. Another problem is that we are so used to exploiting natural resources such as wood, oil, natural gas, and minerals that we forget they are limited and exhaustible. While the list could go on—species extinction, ecosystem destruction, negative health effects of synthetic chemicals, etc.—it is hoped this point is made: if we are not careful, industrialization may have devastating ecological effects.

A more positive side of industrialism is its long term ability to eventually reduce social inequality. When a society first becomes industrialized, there is a wide gap between rich and poor. A few can live in luxury with much leisure but, for most, working hours are long and wages are low. The majority, in fact, live under wretched conditions as has been brilliantly described by such novelists as Charles Dickens in the nineteenth century or Upton Sinclair in the twentieth century. Over time, however, inequalities are reduced. There is a dramatic long-term rise in the standard of living. As possibilities for upward mobility increase, the classes in the middle of the stratification system become the largest in the system. (Box 38 offers a general description of social stratification.) Material conveniences become available for many. Labor unions increase the power of workers. Public education becomes widespread. Voting rights are extended to those previously disenfranchised. More public accessibility is made available for the handicapped. While hard to measure empirically, the Lenskis maintain that *freedom* itself increases for average members of advanced industrial societies.

Box 38

Social Stratification

Some form of structural inequality exists in most societies. Sociologists refer to this as social stratification, a hierarchical system in which people are ranked into layers or strata. Stratification systems may be closed (caste) or open (class). In caste systems, such as in India, the boundaries between strata are rigid. Caste membership is an ascribed status on grounds such as skin color or parent's religion over which the individual has no control. The status is assigned at birth and will determine the person's "life chances" until death. In class systems, such as in the United States, boundaries between strata are more flexible. Class membership, dependent on such factors as wealth, prestige, and power, is an achieved status over which the individual has some control. In theory, one can move up or down within the system. While the exact number of classes can be debated, most social scientists would probably agree that designations described below are accurate.

The upper class is tiny (1 percent), containing the richest, most prestigious, and most powerful people in the country. Included here are investors, heirs, and corporate executives, many of whom have been educated at prestigious universities. Some feel there are actually two classes here: an elite with old money and those who have struck it rich.

The upper-middle class (14 percent) are college educated, high income business and professional families. They live in "comfortable" homes in "better" neighborhoods and are active in civic affairs. They are highly "respectable."

The lower-middle class (30 percent) consists of semi-professionals, lower level white collar workers, and skilled blue collar workers. They have completed high school and, in some cases, apprenticeships. A few have some college. They live in small homes, and are politically conservative. They are the "good common people."

The working class — so designated because they don't consider themselves middle class and don't want to be called lower class — consists of semi-skilled factory workers (15 percent) as well as low-level clerks and salespeople (15 percent). Their jobs are routine and they are susceptible to layoffs in times of recession. Few of them have gone beyond high school. They consider themselves simple but decent people.

The lower class is the stratum at the bottom of the stratification system. Included here would be the "working poor" (15 percent) as well as those who are unemployed and/or on welfare who are referred to by the almost caste-like designation "underclass" (10 percent). The working poor are unskilled laborers and low-paid operatives whose incomes oscillate from just above to just below the poverty line. The underclass suffers long-term deprivation from low income, low education, low employability, and eventually, low self-esteem. Many members of the lower class are members of minority groups.

Industrialization has a dramatic effect on the institutions of society as well as on lives of individual people. Almost overnight, it changes long established patterns of existence. The family, no longer the center for economic production or education of the young, loses some of its traditional importance. High divorce rates and an enormous increase in single-parent families perhaps exemplify how fragile the family has become. Secularization, that is, the erosion of belief in the supernatural, tends to make religion simply one institution among many. In the past, religion provided an all-enveloping set of beliefs and practices that affected everything one did. Education, on the other hand, takes on increasing importance in advanced industrial societies as occupational positions requires more know-how and training. The government and the economy, of course, become vast and pervasive. Other "new" institutions such as science, law, medicine, the military, and sports emerge. Rapid social change is the order of the day. Some observers call this "future shock" because they fear it will be difficult to adjust to.

In summary, industrial societies rely on machines for their subsistence. This subsistence strategy is so efficient and produces so much wealth that it makes for a way of life radically different from that of the preindustrial world. In preindustrial societies, the children of one generation grew up and lived a life very similar to that of their parents. In industrial societies, however, one cannot assume lives will be lived in an unchanging world. Children can expect a different job from that of their parents, an urban instead of a rural existence, a densely populated world, seemingly unsolvable ecological problems, an increase in equality, and vast changes in our basic institutions.

Postindustrial Societies
Making a Living by Providing Services and/or Information

Some social scientists feel that the most advanced, highly affluent, industrial societies, such as the United States, Japan, and some nations in western Europe, are so different from newly industrializing nations or even some at an intermediate or advanced stage of development that we must speak of a new, sixth societal type emerging at present. Daniel Bell has coined the term "postindustrial societies" to refer to them. They rely for their subsistence on the production of services and information. The majority of the population in such societies are not engaged in food production or in industrial manufacturing. Instead, most people spend their time providing services and/or creating, processing or distributing information. Important industries include such areas as trade, finance, insurance, transport, health, and scientific research, etc. Over 90 percent of Americans will have these kinds of jobs in the early twenty-first century. Box 39 gives some idea of occupational specialization that has occurred over time.

Agriculture and manufacturing do not disappear in a postindustrial society but they are made more efficient through automation. Industries that depend more heavily on manual labor will either decline in postindustrial societies or, alternatively, they will move their factories to less technologically developed societies where wages are low. In the early 1990's, an auto worker in America, for example, earned over $20.00 an hour compared to an auto worker in South

---

Box 39

Occupational Specialization

In the simplest preindustrial society, the number of specialized occupational roles — if any exist at all — can probably be counted on the fingers of one hand. Even in the early stages of industrialism in the United States, the 1850 census recorded a grand total of 323 occupations. In the postindustrial United States today, in contrast, the Department of Labor records over 20,000 jobs, including such highly specialized occupations as blintz roller, alligator farmer, oxtail washer, corset stringer, ear-muff assembler, gherkin pickler, chicken sexer, singing messenger, tamale-machine feeder, braille proofreader, environmental epidemiologist, and nuclear-criticality safety engineer. This list, of course, includes only legitimate occupations. It leaves out such jobs as dope pusher, pimp, pickpocket, counterfeiter, and con artist, all of which include many further subspecialties.

SOURCE: Ian Robertson, *Society: A Brief Introduction* (New York: Worth Publishers, 1989, p. 317).

Korea, who earned less than $2.00 an hour. This points to two key factors that account for postindustrial societies' success. First, they thrive in a global economy where labor, capital, and raw materials can be combined independently of national boundaries. Second, they thrive by supplying themselves and other societies with advanced theoretical knowledge and with products based on this knowledge. Consider that a computer designed in Silicon Valley and marketed in Poland may have its casing built in Mexico, its microchips in Japan, its circuit boards in Singapore, its keyboard in Taiwan, and its disks in Germany! Box 40 gives some idea of how the world is shrinking.

Let us put off further discussion of global issues for a moment and return to the discussion on the kinds of jobs that will be available in industrial and postindustrial societies. In industrial societies, most workers are unskilled, semiskilled, or skilled "blue-collar" workers. The future-oriented postindustrial society with its emphasis on research and development, will need new kinds of workers, *some* of whom can expect technical and professional "white collar"

Box 40

Our Shrinking World:
Transportation and Communication

While change is a constant fact of life, the rate at which things change has accelerated during this century. One change that profoundly affects everyone on earth is the increase in the speed at which people can get from one place to another. As the speed of transportation increases and travel time decreases, the relative size of the world continues to shrink. In 1750, the best average speed of horse-drawn coaches on land and sailing ships at sea was approximately 10 miles per hour. By 1850, steam locomotives averaged 65 miles per hour and steamships averaged 36 miles per hour. One hundred years later, in 1950, propeller-drive aircraft averaged 300 miles per hour. Just 30 years later, in 1980, jet aircraft averaged 500-600 miles per hour. By 1990, the Concorde averaged 1,500 miles per hour.

This information raises many questions. Is this increase in the speed of travel beneficial? How fast will we be able to travel in the twenty-first century? What will the transportation system be like then? Will there be ecological repercussions?

You might also want to think about changes in methods of communication over time for they, too, seem to shrink the world. Consider how the printing press, the telegraph, the telephone, radio, television, the computer, the "fax" machine, and satellite transmission affect people's lives. What will the next breakthrough in communication be?

jobs with high wages. Daniel Bell calls these jobs the "heart" of the post-industrial society and says the people who perform them will be preeminent in the class hierarchy. Those who want these jobs will need both applied and theoretical knowledge of the natural and social sciences. Technological innovation depends, above all, on scientific knowledge. These workers will also have to be computer-literate. They will have to document their educational achievements on paper. Speaking another language will increasingly be an asset as well. Geographic and occupational mobility will be a must. Workers must be willing to change their residence, from Los Angeles to Tokyo, for example, as well as to change their occupations several times during their work life.

Most service and informational jobs in the postindustrial society will be neither glamorous nor interesting. While "white collar," they will be routine jobs that do not require advanced degrees or offer high pay. In fact, they will be low-paying jobs such as secretaries or retail sales clerks. The outlook for many "blue collar" workers in the future is even less encouraging, as unemployment will continue due to foreign competition and automation. The only increase in blue collar work may be in the "McJobs" sector of the economy.

Positive aspects of these emerging postindustrial societies are governmental and corporate efforts to combat racism, sexism, and ageism. The more profitable knowledge becomes, after all, the more costly it is to exclude people with marketable talents and skills. Achievement, therefore, will assume increasing importance in postindustrial societies. In what some call a meritocracy, rewards will tend to be distributed according to ability and performance and not on the basis of such biological characteristics as race, sex, and age. It is probably no accident that all the postindustrial societies are highly democratic societies. It must be emphasized immediately that the changes spoken of above are trends rather than events which have already happened or will definitely happen. While income for African-American workers has improved, for example, it still lags behind that of white workers; women still work disproportionately at "pink-collar" jobs; there is still stereotypical thinking that the old are not such productive workers as the young. Some see the situation as unchangeable and point to a "permanent black underclass," the "feminization of poverty," and a general "lack of respect for the elderly."

Let us return to global issues. Just as was true for industrial societies, little more than lip service seems to be given to solving ecological problems in postindustrial societies. Environmental pollution, depletion of natural resources, and so forth are still issues of importance. Also of consequence has to be international political *and* economic cooperation between postindustrial societies themselves and between postindustrial societies and the newly industrializing nations of the third world. If a natural disaster, war, or economic collapse were to occur globally, the few remaining hunters and gatherers of the planet might be able to feed themselves but one has to wonder what would happen

Box 41 Sociocultural Evolution: A Summary

TYPES OF

	Hunting and Gathering Societies	Pastoral Societies	Horticultural Societies
Historical period	Through most of history; few remain today	From 10,000-12,000 years ago; some remain	From 10,000—12,000 years ago; some remain today
Technology	Primitive weapons and tools	Domestication of animals	Hand tools
Population Size	Small; 20-50 people	Small; hundreds to thousands	Small; hundreds to thousands
Settlement	Nomadic	Nomadic	Relatively permanent settlements
Occupational Specialization	Little-based on age and sex	Moderate	Moderate
Social Organization	Family-centered	Family-centered	Family-centered
Inequality	Little to high	High	High
Social change	Slow	Slow	Slow

SOCIETIES

Agricultural Societies	Industrial Societies	Postindustrial Societies
From 5,000 years ago; many remain in present	From 1750 to present	Present
Animal drawn plow	Mechanized production	Mechanized production; advanced energy sources
Wide variation; hundreds to millions	Millions	Millions
Rural primarily; some towns and cities	Urban; many cities and metropolises	Urban; many cities metropolises and megalopolises
Extensive	High	Very high
Family important; distinct political, religious, & economic institutions emerge	Family may lose some importance; other institutions take on importance	Same as industrial; education and science are increasingly important
Very high	High but starts diminishing	Diminishing
Slow to medium	Rapid	Very Rapid

in those societies in which people are not trained to produce food or goods. In summary, postindustrial societies rely for their subsistence on the production of services and information. They are a newly emerging type of society that the world has never before seen. While they are like industrial societies in many ways and carry positive and negative legacies from them, it is hard to predict what actual form these postindustrial societies will take in the twenty-first century. Important characteristics that will shape their form include a preponderance of service and information related jobs, extreme occupational specialization, participation in a global economy, and further reductions of social inequality.

Conclusion

Sociocultural evolution is a theory that links technological subsistence strategies to societal and cultural development. Box 41 attempts to summarize the changes involved. Use of this theory helps us to understand at least six types of societies that have existed from the earliest groups of people who banded together to hunt and gather food to highly industrialized societies such as the United States today. A massive transformation seems to accompany the advanced stages of industrialism and it will probably be decades before we grasp the significance of these changes.

Any merit the above discussion has owes so much to Gerhard and Jean Lenski that it seems fitting to close with their words:

> The study of societal evolution is much like the study of a giant mural. In both cases, we are almost overwhelmed by the many small details. If we are to grasp the picture as a whole and develop any feeling for it, we must stand back from time to time and view the picture in its entirety.
>
> A million years ago, the ancestors of modern man gave little indication that they were anything more than another variety of primate. There was nothing to suggest that this species would one day evolve into the dominant form of life, a creature capable of overcoming most of the limitations imposed on him by his environment and able to alter even the environment itself in major respects.
>
> Today, we take all this for granted. With the wisdom of hindsight, we see that man was destined for a unique role. We see, moreover, that the key to his accomplishments lay in his ability to use symbols . . . to mobilize energy and information. We also understand how he gradually escaped from the restraints of the genetic mode of adaptation and how sociocultural evolution finally replaced organic evolution as the dominant mode of human adaptation about 35,000 years ago.

The significance of this is hard to exaggerate. Sociocultural evolution, unlike organic evolution, has a natural tendency to "snowball." Despite occasional reversals of relatively short duration, this tendency has been manifest throughout man's entire history. As a result, we find ourselves today in the most revolutionary era of all. The rate of change is now so high that change has become the central fact of life.

Questions

1. Define society. How does the social science definition of it differ from that used in everyday life?
2. What is the difference between human and sociocultural evolution?
3. What were humans like 35,000 years ago?
4. List the main characteristics of each of the six types of societies.
5. Locate examples of the six kinds of societies on the maps in the appendix. Do some continents have more of one type than others?
6. What is a typical day like for males and females in these societies? For the young, middle-aged, and the elderly?
7. In which of these societies do we find the least amount of social inequality? Why?
8. How does the means of subsistence affect social institutions in the six societies?
9. Can agriculture *really* be the worst mistake in the history of the human race?
10. Why does manufacturing increase in industrial societies?
11. How has the means of subsistence affected urban development?
12. What is the theory of the demographic transition? How accurate is it?
13. The article says that classes in the middle of the stratification system increase in industrial societies. "Ph.D.'s that are driving taxis" would disagree. How can we reconcile this disagreement?
14. In what sense does "freedom itself" increase for average members of advanced industrial societies?

15. List characteristics and give examples of the newly developing countries of the "third" world. Do the same for "first" and "second" world countries.

16. What are ecological benefits and losses of the six societal types?

17. How does occupational specialization differ within the six types?

18. Is the world shrinking? Relate this to transportation and communication. How will it affect the global economy?

19. What are the advantages and disadvantages of living in each type of society?

20. What will most jobs be like in postindustrial societies?

21. The closing quote says that sociocultural evolution "replaced" organic evolution as the dominant mode of adaptation. What does that mean?

Part VI

America
An Overview

The first two articles in this part are "classics" in the sense that they have been reprinted more than any other articles in the social sciences. "One Hundred Percent American," satirically points out that most cultures contain within themselves elements of other cultures and other periods of history. That, as a matter of fact, is how most cultures have come by most of their ideas—by borrowing. Consider why 1937, a year still within the "depression" when the cities were teeming with immigrants, was a propitious time to publish this article. "Body Ritual Among the Nacirema," also describes America in a satirical fashion. Can it be that Americans are a group of people so immersed within their culture that many masochistic practices such as women baking their heads in small ovens and men scraping and lacerating their faces are considered to be desirable practices? Is this the America we know?

The third article, historian George Christakes' "All Mixed Up: Ethnicity in American Life," calls attention to the United States as a multi-ethnic nation with people from all over the world. As this thorough historical survey documents, xenophobia (hatred or distrust of strangers) was true in the American past and seems to be true in the present. Predictions for the future, however, are not necessarily pessimistic. Americans "will lead dual lives, with the ethnic part being reserved for family and private life and the common American culture dominating in work and school."

A common thread through all three articles is that we can learn much from other cultures and our own if only we are not ethnocentric. Rather than to pass sentence on other cultures, or our own, by measuring them according to "absolute" personal standards, it may be better to see culture as "relative," that is, to analyze each culture on its own terms and in the context of its own societal setting.

157

Chapter Seventeen

One Hundred Percent American

Ralph Linton

There can be no question about the average American's Americanism or his desire to preserve this precious heritage at all costs. Nevertheless, some insidious foreign ideas have already wormed their way into his civilization without his realizing what was going on. Thus dawn finds the unsuspecting patriot garbed in pajamas, a garment of East Indian origin; lying in a bed built on a pattern which originated in either Persia or Asia Minor. He is muffled to the ears in un-American materials: cotton, first domesticated in India; linen, domesticated in the Near East; wool, from an animal native to Asia Minor; or silk, whose uses were first discovered by the Chinese. All these substances have been transformed into cloth by methods invented in Southwestern Asia. If the weather is cold enough he may even be sleeping under an eiderdown quilt invented in Scandinavia.

On awakening he glances at the clock, a medieval European invention, uses one potent Latin word in abbreviated form, rises in haste, and goes to the bathroom. Here, if he stops to think about it, he must feel himself in the presence of a great American institution; he will have heard stories of both the quality and frequency of foreign plumbing and will know that in no other country does the average man perform his ablutions in the midst of such splendor. But the insidious foreign influence pursues him even here. Glass was invented

The American Mercury, 40, 1937, pp. 427-429. P.O. Box 73523, Houston, Texas 77090.

by the ancient Egyptians, the use of glazed tiles for floors and walls in the Near East, porcelain in China, and the art of enameling on metal by Mediterranean artisans of the Bronze Age. Even his bathtub and toilet are but slightly modified copies of Roman originals. The only purely American contribution to the ensemble is the steam radiator, against which our patriot very briefly and unintentionally places his posterior.

In this bathroom the American washes with soap invented by the ancient Gauls. Next he cleans his teeth, a subversive European practice which did not invade America until the latter part of the eighteenth century. He then shaves, a masochistic rite first developed by the heathen priests of ancient Egypt and Sumer. The process is made less of a penance by the fact that his razor is of steel, an iron-carbon alloy discovered in either India or Turkestan. Lastly, he dries himself on a Turkish towel.

Returning to the bedroom, the unconscious victim of un-American practices removes his clothes from a chair, invented in the Near East, and proceeds to dress. He puts on close-fitting tailored garments whose form derives from the skin clothing of the ancient nomads of the Asiatic steppes and fastens them with buttons whose prototypes appeared in Europe at the close of the Stone Age. This costume is appropriate enough for outdoor exercise in a cold climate, but is quite unsuited to American summers, steam-heated houses, and Pullmans. Nevertheless, foreign ideas and habits hold the unfortunate man in thrall even when common sense tells him that the authentically American costume of gee string and moccasins would be far more comfortable. He puts on his feet stiff coverings made from hide prepared by a process invented in ancient Egypt and cut to a pattern which can be traced back to ancient Greece, and makes sure that they are properly polished, also a Greek idea. Lastly, he ties about his neck a strip of bright-colored cloth which is a vestigial survival of the shoulder shawls worn by seventeenth-century Croats. He gives himself a final appraisal in the mirror, an old Mediterranean invention, and goes downstairs to breakfast.

Here a whole new series of foreign things confronts him. His food and drink are placed before him in pottery vessels, the popular name of which — china — is sufficient evidence of their origin. His fork is a medieval Italian invention and his spoon a copy of a Roman original. He will usually begin the meal with coffee, an Abyssinian plant first discovered by the Arabs. The American is quite likely to need it to dispel the morning-after effects of overindulgence in fermented drinks, invented in the Near East; or distilled ones, invented by the alchemists of medieval Europe. Whereas the Arabs took their coffee straight, he will probably sweeten it with sugar, discovered in India; and dilute it with cream, both the domestication of cattle and the technique of milking having originated in Asia Minor.

If our patriot is old-fashioned enough to adhere to the so-called American breakfast, his coffee will be accompanied by an orange domesticated in the Mediterranean region, a cantaloupe domesticated in Persia, or grapes domesticated in Asia Minor. He will follow this with a bowl of cereal made from grain domesticated in the Near East and prepared by methods also invented here. From this he will go on to waffles, a Scandinavian invention, with plenty of butter, originally a Near-Eastern cosmetic. As a side dish he may have the egg of a bird domesticated in Southeastern Asia or strips of the flesh of an animal domesticated in the same region, which have been salted and smoked by a process invented in Northern Europe.

Breakfast over, he places upon his head a molded piece of felt, invented by the nomads of Eastern Asia, and, if it looks like rain, puts on outer shoes of rubber, discovered by the ancient Mexicans, and takes an umbrella, invented in India. He then sprints for his train—the train, not the sprinting, being an English invention. At the station he pauses for a moment to buy a newspaper, paying for it with coins invented in ancient Lydia. Once on board he settles back to inhale the fumes of a cigarette invented in Mexico, or a cigar invented in Brazil. Meanwhile, he reads the news of the day, imprinted characters invented by the ancient Semites by a process invented in Germany upon a material invented in China. As he scans the latest editorial pointing out the dire results to our institutions of accepting foreign ideas, he will not fail to thank a Hebrew God in an Indo-European language that he is one hundred percent (decimal system invented by the Greeks) American (from Americus Vespucci, Italian geographer).

Questions

1. It is obvious that artifacts have been adopted from other cultures. Have cultural norms and values been adopted as well? Give examples.

2. List cultural traits and artifacts that have been added to American culture since the article was first published. Do you think the time period when the article was published affected what was written?

3. Have some countries or areas of the world influenced American culture more than others? Which ones?

4. What countries of the world are influenced by American culture? Is this influence increasing or decreasing?

5. What, in addition to the radiator, might be a purely American invention?

Chapter Eighteen

Body Ritual Among the Nacirema

Horace Miner

The anthropologist has become so familiar with the diversity of ways in which different peoples behave in similar situations that he is not apt to be surprised by even the most exotic customs. In fact, if all of the logically possible combinations of behavior have not been found somewhere in the world, he is apt to suspect that they must be present in some yet undescribed tribe. This point has, in fact, been expressed with respect to clan organization by Murdock (1949). In this light, the magical beliefs and practices of the Nacirema present such unusual aspects that it seems desirable to describe them as an example of the extremes to which human behavior can go.

Professor Linton first brought the ritual of the Nacirema to the attention of anthropologists twenty years ago (1936), but the culture of this people is still very poorly understood. They are a North American group living in the territory between the Canadian Cree, the Yaqui and Tarahumare of Mexico, and the Carib and Arawak of the Antilles. Little is known of their origin, although tradition states that they come from the east. According to Nacirema mythology, their nation was originated by a culture hero, Notgnihsaw, who is otherwise known for two great feats of strength—the throwing of a piece of wampum across the river Pa-To-Mac and the chopping down of a cherry tree in which the Spirit of Truth resided.

Reproduced by permission of the American Anthropological Association for the *American Anthropologist*, Vol. 58, No. 3, 1956.

Nacirema culture is characterized by a highly developed market economy which has evolved in a rich natural habitat. While much of the people's time is devoted to economic pursuits, a large part of the fruits of these labors and a considerable portion of the day are spent in ritual activity. The focus of this activity is the human body, the appearance and health of which loom as a dominant concern in the ethos of the people. While such a concern is certainly not unusual, its ceremonial aspects and associated philosophy are unique.

The fundamental belief underlying the whole system appears to be that the human body is ugly and that its natural tendency is to debility and disease. Incarcerated in such a body, man's only hope is to avert these characteristics through the use of the powerful influences of ritual and ceremony. Every household has one or more shrines devoted to this purpose. The more powerful individuals in the society have several shrines in their houses and, in fact, the opulence of a house is often referred to in terms of the number of such ritual centers it possesses. Most houses are of wattle and daub construction, but the shrine rooms of the more wealthy are walled with stone. Poorer families imitate the rich by applying pottery plaques to their shrine walls.

While each family has at least one such shrine, the rituals associated with it are not family ceremonies but are private and secret. The rites are normally only discussed with children, and then only during the period when they are being initiated into these mysteries. I was able, however, to establish sufficient rapport with the natives to examine these shrines and to have the rituals described to me.

The focal point of the shrine is a box or chest which is built into the wall. In this chest are kept the many charms and magical potions without which no native believes he could live. These preparations are secured from a variety of specialized practitioners. The most powerful of these are the medicine men, whose assistance must be rewarded with substantial gifts. However, the medicine men do not provide the curative potions for their clients, but decide what the ingredients should be and then write them down in an ancient and secret language. This writing is understood only by the medicine men and by the herbalists who, for another gift, provide the required charm.

The charm is not disposed of after it has served its purpose, but is placed in the charm-box of the household shrine. As these magical materials are specific for certain ills, and the real or imagined maladies of the people are many, the charm-box is usually full to overflowing. The magical packets are so numerous that people forget what their purposes were and fear to use them again. While the natives are very vague on this point, we can only assume that the idea in retaining all the old magical materials is that their presence in the charm-box, before which the body rituals are conducted, will in some way protect the worshipper.

Beneath the charm-box is a small font. Each day every member of the family, in succession, enters the shrine room, bows his head before the charm-box, mingles different sorts of holy water in the font, and proceeds with a brief rite of ablution. The holy waters are secured from the Water Temple of the community, where the priests conduct elaborate ceremonies to make the liquid ritually pure.

In the hierarchy of magical practitioners, and below the medicine men in prestige, are specialists whose designation is best translated "holy-mouth-men." The Nacirema have an almost pathological horror of and fascination with the mouth, the condition of which is believed to have a supernatural influence on all social relationships. Were it not for the rituals of the mouth, they believe that their teeth would fall out, their gums bleed, their jaws shrink, their friends desert them, and their lovers reject them. They also believe that a strong relationship exists between oral and moral characteristics. For example, there is a ritual ablution of the mouth for children which is supposed to improve their moral fiber.

The daily body ritual performed by everyone includes a mouth-rite. Despite the fact that these people are so punctilious about care of the mouth, this rite involves a practice which strikes the uninitiated stranger as revolting. It was reported to me that the ritual consists of inserting a small bundle of hog hairs into the mouth, along with certain magical powders, and then moving the bundle in a highly formalized series of gestures.

In addition to the private mouth-rite, the people seek out a holy-mouth-man once or twice a year. These practitioners have an impressive set of paraphernalia consisting of a variety of augers, awls, probes, and prods. The use of these objects in the exorcism of the evils of the mouth involves almost unbelievable ritual torture of the client. The holy-mouth-man opens the client's mouth and, using the above mentioned tools, enlarges any holes which decay may have created in the teeth. Magical materials are put into these holes. If there are no naturally occurring holes in the teeth, large sections of one or more teeth are gouged out so that the supernatural substance can be applied. In the client's view, the purpose of these ministrations is to arrest decay and to draw friends. The extremely sacred and traditional character of the rite is evident in the fact that the natives return to the holy-mouth-men year after year, despite the fact that their teeth continue to decay.

It is to be hoped that, when a thorough study of the Nacirema is made, there will be careful inquiry into the personality structure of these people. One has but to watch the gleam in the eye of a holy-mouth-man, as he jabs an awl into an exposed nerve, to suspect that a certain amount of sadism is involved. If this can be established, a very interesting pattern emerges, for most of the population shows definite masochistic tendencies. It was to these that Professor Linton referred to discussing a distinctive part of the daily body ritual which is performed only by men. This part of the rite involves scraping and lacerating the surface of the face with a sharp instrument. Special women's rites are performed only four times during each lunar month, but what they lack in frequency is made up in barbarity. As part of this ceremony, women bake their heads in small ovens for about an hour. The theoretically interesting point is that what seems to be a preponderantly masochistic people have developed sadistic specialists.

The medicine men have an imposing temple, or *latipso*, in every community of any size. The more elaborate ceremonies required to treat very sick patients can only be performed at this temple. These ceremonies involve not only the thaumaturge but a permanent group of vestal maidens who move sedately about the temple chambers in distinctive costume and headdress.

The *latipso* ceremonies are so harsh that it is phenomenal that a fair proportion of the really sick natives who enter the temple ever recover. Small children whose indoctrination is still incomplete have been known to resist attempts to take them to the temple because "that is where you go to die." Despite this fact, sick adults are not only willing but eager to undergo the protracted ritual purification, if they can afford to do so. No matter how ill the supplicant or how grave the emergency, the guardians of many temples will not admit a client if he cannot give a rich gift to the custodian. Even after one has gained admission and survived the ceremonies, the guardians will not permit the neophyte to leave until he makes still another gift.

The supplicant entering the temple is first stripped of all his or her clothes. In everyday life the Nacirema avoids exposure of his body and its natural functions. Bathing and excretory acts are performed only in the secrecy of the household shrine, where they are ritualized as part of the body-rites. Psychological shock results from the fact that body secrecy is suddenly lost upon entry into the *latipso*. A man, whose own wife has never seen him in an excretory act, suddenly finds himself naked and assisted by a vestal maiden while he performs his natural functions into a sacred vessel. This sort of ceremonial treatment is necessitated by the fact that the excreta are used by a diviner to ascertain the course and nature of the client's sickness. Female clients, on the other hand find their naked bodies are subjected to the scrutiny, manipulation and prodding of the medicine men.

Few supplicants in the temple are well enough to do anything but lie on their hard beds. The daily ceremonies, like the rites of the holy-mouth-men, involve discomfort and torture. With ritual precision, the vestals awaken their miserable charges each dawn and roll them about on their beds of pain while performing ablutions, in the formal movements of which the maidens are highly trained. At other times they insert magic wands in the supplicant's mouth or force him to eat substances which are supposed to be healing. From time to time the medicine men come to their clients and jab magically treated needles into their flesh. The fact that these temple ceremonies may not cure, and may even kill the neophyte, in no way decreases the people's faith in the medicine men.

There remains one other kind of practitioner, known as a "listener." This witch-doctor has the power to exorcise the devils that lodge in the heads of people who have been bewitched. The Nacirema believe that parents bewitch their own children. Mothers are particularly suspected of putting a curse on children while teaching them the secret body rituals. The counter-magic of the witch-doctor is unusual in its lack of ritual. The patient simply tells the "listener" all his troubles and fears, beginning with the earliest difficulties he can remember. The memory displayed by the Nacirema in these exorcism sessions is truly remarkable. It is not uncommon for the patient to bemoan the rejection he felt upon being weaned as a babe, and a few individuals even see their troubles going back to the traumatic effects of their own birth.

In conclusion, mention must be made of certain practices which have their base in native esthetics but which depend upon the pervasive aversion of the natural body and its functions. There are ritual fasts to make fat people thin and ceremonial feasts to make thin people fat. Still other rites are used to make women's breasts larger if they are small and smaller if they are large. General dissatisfaction with breast shape is symbolized in the fact that the ideal form is virtually outside the range of human variation. A few women afflicted with almost inhuman hypermammary development are so idolized that they make a handsome living by simply going from village to village and permitting the natives to stare at them for a fee.

Reference has already been made to the fact that excretory functions are ritualized, routinized, and relegated to secrecy. Natural reproductive functions are similarly distorted. Intercourse is taboo as a topic and scheduled as an act. Efforts are made to avoid pregnancy by the use of magical materials or by limiting intercourse to certain phases of the moon. Conception is actually very infrequent. When pregnant, women dress so as to hide their condition. Parturition takes place in secret, without friends or relatives to assist, and the majority of women do not nurse their infants.

Our review of the ritual life of the Nacirema has certainly shown them to be a magic-ridden people. It is hard to understand how they have managed to exist so long under the burdens which they have imposed upon themselves. But even such exotic customs as these take on real meaning when they are viewed with the insight provided by Malinowski when he wrote (1948):

> Looking from far and above, from our high places of safety in the developed civilization, it is easy to see all the crudity and irrelevance of magic. But without its power and guidance early man could not have

mastered his practical difficulties as he has done, nor could man have advanced to the higher stages of civilization.

Questions

1. What are the major institutions of Nacirema culture?
2. To what extent is Nacirema culture characterized by magical beliefs and practices?
3. How can one explain the emphasis on health and appearance in this culture?
4. Do Miner's values affect his interpretation of Nacirema culture?
5. Does Miner only observe overt actions of Nacirema and miss the symbolic nature of their actions?
6. Is Miner ethnocentric?
7. Does this article point to any potential disadvantages in the use of participant observation as a research design?
8. What elements of Nacirema culture can you trace to an origin in another culture?
9. What other Nacireman traits might surprise an outsider that was not familiar with the culture?

Chapter Nineteen

All Mixed Up
Ethnicity in American Life

George Christakes

I like Polish sausage, I like Spanish rice
Pizza Pie is also nice
Corn and beans from the Indians here
Washed down by some German beer

Marco Polo traveled by camel and pony
Brought to Italy the first macaroni
And you and I, as well as we're able
Put it all on the table.

(Song "All Mixed Up" is by Pete Seeger.)

As folk singer Pete Seeger's song indicates, Americans and their culture are "All Mixed Up." Today the United States is a multi-ethnic nation whose population includes peoples and religions from all over the world. While most Americans speak English as their first language, since many immigrants still communicate in their native tongue, we hear daily on the streets of our major cities Americans speaking a multiplicity of languages. This cultural diversity expresses itself in everything from food to religion. The way Americans eat and pray demonstrates the impact of the various ethnic cultures: people in the same city who work side by side go to pray (using religious forms which originated on other continents and were imported by immigrants) in Jewish synagogues, Moslem mosques, Catholic churches and a variety of Protestant

169

churches, etc. After their religious services they have the choice of eating their own ethnic foods—or those of other groups, such as Italian pizza, Polish sausage, or tandoori chicken from India.

While such cultural and ethnic diversity has certainly made life more interesting for Americans, it has also created social problems. Prejudice against ethnic and religious minorities has been a fact of American life throughout our history. Riots, lynchings, and murders have frequently been inspired by the hatred of one ethnic or religious group for another. On a less violent level, Americans have often divided on such questions as ethnic or religious intermarriage, job discrimination, and housing patterns. While Americans may like to eat each other's food, they often hate to live among each other or have their daughters and sons marry outside their own group.

A Nation of Immigrants

Understanding this ethnic diversity necessitates examining how it developed and the values and experiences of the various groups which are part of our multi-ethnic society. John F. Kennedy called America "A Nation of Immigrants." All people in the United States are either descendants of immigrants or immigrants themselves. Some come from families that migrated early and some are more recent. The oldest, of course, are the "native Americans" (American Indians), whose ancestors came from Asia more than 25,000 years ago. The next migration did not occur until the English established the Jamestown colony in Virginia during 1607.

During the colonial period most of the colonists had fairly similar origins. While there were a few Roman Catholics and Jews, as well as the Black slaves (introduced in Virginia in 1619) and a sprinkling of other ethnic groups, most colonists came from the British Isles, spoke English, and practiced some form of Protestant religion. In spite of this general uniformity in backgrounds, considerable strife occurred among both religious and ethnic groups. In New England, for example, the Quakers and the Puritans clashed over religion, while the Scotch-Irish, who populated the western frontier, divided their time between fighting Indians and resenting the British colonists along the seaboard. While ethnicity and religion were facts of American life during the colonial period, these factors were less important than in later periods because there was comparatively little ethnic diversity throughout the colonial and revolutionary period.

The Irish and Germans

It would not be until the 1830's and 1840's, over 200 years after Jamestown was settled, that America saw a major influx of new ethnic groups. Even then the influx still consisted of a people from the British Isles—the Irish. During that period many of the Irish migrated to America because of a famine in their home country, with Boston and New York being the most popular destinations. The major distinguishing feature of the English-speaking Irish was their Roman Catholicism. American nativists (Americans who were prejudiced against people who differed from the white Protestant majority) reacted to the Irish influx in a variety of ways, ranging from simple job discrimination to mob burnings of Irish Catholic churches and convents in Boston. Tolerance of differences has seldom characterized Americans. The fact that their native language was English, however, later proved to be a major advantage for the Irish over later immigrant groups.

Starting in the late 1840's and continuing through the Civil War, many Germans followed the Irish to America. Not being English speakers, they were conspicuously different from the other inhabitants of their new country. Their reasons for migrating ranged from political problems to draft dodging or the search for new economic opportunity. At first most of them were Protestant, but a minority of German Catholics and Jews came as well. The German Jews were the first large group of new Americans who were not Christians, and as such they faced prejudice from both the American nativists and the Roman Catholics, who were themselves despised by the nativists. The various types of Germans usually settled in northern cities, with Cincinnati and, later, Chicago being especially popular.

Blacks and Crisis

America's attention was diverted from the Irish and Germans, however, because of a crisis involving one of the older ethnic groups—the Blacks. While Black slavery had been a fact of southern American life since 1619, it had not become controversial until the nineteenth century. It was believed during the later part of the previous century that slavery would simply die out because of its economic inefficiency. Then, ironically, the invention of the cotton gin in 1793 by an anti-slavery Northerner, Eli Whitney, revived the "peculiar institution" of slavery by making cotton production economically feasible. The abolitionist movement grew in response and heightened already existing sectional animosities between the North and South. This ethnically inspired crisis eventually resulted in the Emancipation Proclamation (1863) which freed the Blacks from slavery, and the Civil War (1861-65) which destroyed the economy of the South. During the war the German and Irish fought in the Union Army against the South—frequently in all-German or all-Irish units.

After the war, the nation struggled with the problems of reconstructing the southern economy, reconciling the political differences between the federalists of the North and the states' rights advocates of the South, and the proper role of the freed Blacks. Eventually all of the southern states regained their status, and a compromise was arrived at in 1877 which allowed the southerners to maintain local control — which doomed Blacks to a subservient position in the South for another century. Such southern institutions as the Ku Klux Klan were at first used to insure white supremacy in the post-Civil War South, but these were later replaced by "Jim Crow" laws. (The name referred to a popular "blackface" minstrel show.) Like other historical problems, this one did not disappear but simply receded from the main stage of the American scene.

The New Immigration: 1880-1924

Starting about 1880 a new wave of immigration descended upon American shores. Emma Lazarus's poem at the base of the Statue of Liberty recommends, "Give me your tired, your poor, your huddled masses yearning to breathe free." The nations of Europe did. During the next few decades this "new immigration," as it was called, introduced the great variety of ethnic and religious groups that were to characterize the twentieth century in this nation. No longer would America be a nation of immigrants from the British Isles with a mere sprinkling of other peoples. Instead, the population of the nation's northern cities swelled with the new arrivals who became the workers in the industrializing, urbanizing new century.

This "new immigration" differed sharply from the old. Unlike the earlier Anglo-Saxon and Celtic immigrants, these newcomers came from southern and eastern Europe. They were often shorter and darker-complexioned, with brown or black hair and brown eyes. Even worse, in the opinion of the American nativists, they tended to be Roman Catholic, Jewish, or Eastern Orthodox in religion. They spoke many tongues — but not English. In spite of the misgivings about them held by the older Americans, they came, and then their relatives and countrymen joined them.

The young men usually came first, from Italy, Greece, Germany, Poland, Czechoslovakia and other southern or eastern European countries (see Box 42). Here, in the northern cities, they found jobs and tried to save their money. The young women followed them to the United States a few years later. Usually, their motivation was economic, but it was sometimes political or religious. An exception to both the pattern of young men migrating first and the economic reason for emigrating to the United States occurred among the Russian Jews. They fled at all ages, often as family groups, from the pogroms (violence against them, sometimes mob action, sometimes government-inspired) which were widespread in the Russia of that period.

The "new immigrants" most often lived and worked together in the United States, in part because of their inadequate knowledge of English. While they eventually learned English, it was more comfortable to communicate in their

---

Box 42

Immigration to the United States, 1820-1930, from Southern and Eastern Europe

Country of Origin	Number of Immigrants
Albania	1,663
Austria-Hungary	4,132,351
Bulgaria	64,918
Czechoslovakia	105,620
Estonia	1,576
Finland	17,447
Greece	421,489
Italy	4,651,195
Latvia	3,399
Lithuania	6,015
Poland	397,729
Portugal	252,715
Rumania	153,074
Spain	166,865
Yugoslavia	50,952

---

native language. Their children and grandchildren often were bilingual — but their language of choice was English. Generations further removed from the original "new immigrants" seldom were fluent in the ethnic group's tongue.

Since many of the "new immigrants" were Roman Catholic, churches and parochial schools were built to serve the ethnic groups of that faith. The Irish, since they had been early arrivals and were English speakers, occupied the higher clerical positions in the United States and, for similar reasons, dominated local politics. The local parish priests and the nuns who taught in the schools, however, tended to be of the same ethnic group and to speak the same language as the people in the parish. This helped preserve fluency in the native language among the second and third generations whose first language was English. The new immigrants who were not Roman Catholic, such as the Greeks and the Russian Jews, also established their own places of worship, but sent their children to public schools; these children learned the native language either at home or at special private schools.

Regardless of where their children attended school, the "new immigrants" lived apart from the older Protestant Americans and from each other. They established ethnic neighborhoods that frequently became known by such names as "little Italy," "Greektown," or "little Poland." In these neighborhoods, the churches, stores and schools catered almost exclusively to members of the ethnic group. Here they could feel comfortable in their own cultural setting and speak the language of their home country. At the same time, however, this segregation tended to encourage ethnocentric values (feelings of superiority about one's own group) which contributed to America's post-World War II ethnic problems.

At work, the members of a particular ethnic group tended to be almost as separate from the larger community as in their neighborhoods. This was at least in part due to language problems. Employers hired a group of people from the same ethnic group and appointed a foreman over them who spoke their language as well as English. Often employers manipulated the workers from different backgrounds against each other in order to prevent the formation of unions. Another reason for the separation of jobs by ethnicity was simply ethnic and religious prejudice on the part of American Protestants. Advertisements in newspapers as late as the 1950's carried such messages as "Nordics Only Need Apply" or specified American born Protestants. In later generations, as the children of the "new immigrants" achieved some economic success or established their own businesses, they in turn gave preference to their own, perpetuating a pattern which has had ramifications down to the present.

Reaction and Restriction of Immigration

Resentment towards the "new immigrants" on the part of American nativists was not confined to simple job discrimination. At times it even emerged as mob violence, with lynchings and riots. At a less extreme level was the organization of nativist societies with the goal of banning southern and eastern European immigration. Some, like the anti-Catholic, anti-Jewish, and anti-Black Ku Klux Klan, did advocate violence. Most did not. All of these groups basically agreed that America should be a white, Protestant nation. They achieved success when the National Origins Act of 1924 virtually eliminated all further immigration from anywhere except northern Europe. (Box 43 tells us where these white Protestants live.)

The "new immigrants" who were already here, however, stayed—as did their children, the Italian-Americans, Polish-Americans, etc. Ethnic neighborhoods, schools and churches likewise remained part of the reality of American life. The second and third generations, being English speakers, achieved greater economic and social acceptance in the larger community. Interestingly, they often adopted the ethnic prejudices that had been directed against them and simply focused such attitudes on groups that were still struggling up the American social ladder. Their children, nevertheless, as the generations went on, even married across ethnic lines, usually other descendants of the "new immigrants" — less frequently across religious divisions. Eventually, in the post-World War II period, many of the later generations moved to the suburbs, although the little Italys and Polands survived in the cities, often augmented by immigration from the old country after World War II. Identification of the later generations with the ethnic group varied with both individuals and American attitudes concerning ethnicity after World War II.

Ethnicity in Postwar America Until 1970

While the "new immigrants" and their descendants supplied the majority of the population in America's northern cities during the first half of the twentieth century, this situation began to change after World War II. First the

---

Box 43

The White Protestant in America

With our northern cities in the United States being full of ethnic Americans of one sort or another, the question arises as to where the white Protestants are, who after all are still the majority group in this country. The answer is simple: all over America except in large northern cities. The white Protestant is alive and well and living in the countryside. In farming areas and small towns throughout the country they comprise the overwhelming majority of the population. In the South, aside from the Black Southerners, most of the people in both urban and rural settings are white Protestants.

Power and wealth in the United States are still dominated by white Protestant Americans. Only one President of the United States, John F. Kennedy, did not come from this majority group. Corporate boardrooms also reflect the continuing central role of these Americans in the life of this country.

The only part of American life in which they are conspicuously absent, or only a minority, is in northern urban cities. They fled the central cities early in the century because of the influx of the "new immigrants," who in recent years have in turn been leaving the central cities to the Blacks, Spanish-speaking, and the new Asian immigrants. Part of both the white Protestant population and the "new immigrants" stayed behind and became, in the case of the white Protestants, a minority. Recent decades have seen a considerable immigration of poor rural southern whites to urban areas, which is counter to the general twentieth century pattern of the white Protestant abandoning the large urban areas for suburban or country life.

Black Americans from the South, then Spanish-speaking immigrants from several areas moved to the northern urban areas in search of jobs. As the country's largest minority group, the Blacks have had the greatest national impact to date.

The Blacks

Even though there have been small numbers of Black people in the North since colonial times, widespread migration from the South to the northern cities did not commence until World War I. Wartime demands for factory labor sent recruiters to the southern agricultural states to find young Black people to work in Chicago, Detroit, St. Louis, and other cities. But in 1918, at the war's end, returning troops returned to claim their old jobs. To make matters worse, the postwar economic depression meant fewer jobs for all Americans.

Some Blacks returned to the South; those who remained faced troubled times. Like the other ethnic groups, they lived in separate neighborhoods — usually the poorest. In the depressed economy they often found themselves out of work. They were used as strike breakers by anti-union employers, thus becoming even more unpopular among their fellow city dwellers, who were also competing for housing, as well as jobs, with the newly arrived Blacks. A series of race riots and mob actions resulted, including the Chicago race riot of 1919 and the East St. Louis race riot of 1917. Returning prosperity in the twenties, however, quieted passions, and American attention turned to other areas. Blacks continued to live and work in the northern cities, although migration from the South slowed to a trickle. In New York City, the Harlem Renaissance witnessed a flurry of Black music, literature and art during the 1920's.

The 1930's was a horrible decade for all Americans — including northern Blacks. The Great Depression, which began in 1929 and lasted for almost a decade, was a time of suffering for the entire nation. The second World War followed, and with it a situation similar to that of World War I developed. Again a demand for workers in northern factories caused thousands of southern Blacks to migrate North. Even they could not fill the insatiable need for workers, so women (both white and black) for the first time became a regular part of the nation's factory labor pool. The Black sections of the northern cities expanded in order to house the newcomers from the South, although in often pathetically crowded slum housing.

Again, as after the first World War, most Blacks did not return to the South but remained in the northern cities. Fortunately, economic conditions following World War II were not as bleak as after the previous global conflict, so Blacks and the ethnic Americans — descendants of the "new immigrants" — with whom they shared the cities did not come into direct conflict. Nevertheless, considerable antagonism existed over the old issues of jobs and housing. With the better economic climate following the 1940's, Black migration from the South to the North continued, although in smaller numbers than during the war. A steady influx from the South continued into the 1980's, when the economic hardships which spread through the northern cities discouraged migration and, indeed, caused an outflow of people to other parts of the country.

The Civil Rights Movement

The lives of Blacks and the entire nation were changed in postwar America by the emergence of the civil rights movement. Some steps toward integration had been taken during the war, such as President Truman's decision to end segregation in the military. But the modern civil rights movement is usually dated from the *Brown vs. Topeka Board of Education* Supreme Court decision in 1954, which mandated that the nation's public schools should be integrated. Following this ruling, all public schools in the nation, including the South, were integrated, but only after great struggles, with cities like Little Rock, Montgomery, and other southern cities becoming the center of the nation's attention.

The drive for integration and equality for Blacks did not stop with school desegregation. During the late 1950's and early 1960's new leaders of the movement emerged, such as James Meredith and Stokely Carmichael and, most prominently, the Rev. Martin Luther King, Jr. These leaders focused attention on integration in schools, churches, public accommodations and equal voting rights, as well as many other areas of American life. Dr. King went beyond civil rights for Blacks to broaden his fight for justice in many areas, including the struggle of American liberals against the Vietnam war, and was assassinated while in Memphis to support a strike by predominantly white sanitation workers. Marches and demonstrations for civil rights by both Black and White Americans — usually young, led by Dr. King and others (often accompanied by the music of Pete Seeger, Woody Guthrie, Joan Baez and Bob Dylan), became a frequent occurrence during the 1960's.

Three assassinations in the sixties had major implications for the civil rights movement. John F. Kennedy's death in 1963 resulted in the passage of several laws that he had advocated but had not been able to push through Congress, most notably the 1964 Civil Rights Act. A few years later, in April 1968 Martin Luther King was killed in Memphis; his murder sparked riots in many urban areas. In June, Robert Kennedy, then the leading Democratic presidential candidate, was shot after giving a campaign speech in California. At the Democratic national convention in Chicago later that year, a group of largely white anti-war youth had confrontations with the local police. Both the riots after King's death and the convention havoc were brought into the nation's living rooms by television, as was the emergence of an anti-King Black power movement that rejected the nonviolent tactics of the mid-sixties—and indeed the goal of integration. Instead, this movement, championed by Stokely Carmichael with the slogan of "Black Power," favored Black separatism and the maintenance of a distinct Black culture. It was short-lived. The seventies saw the beginning of a retreat—it would become a rout—of liberalism and the allied civil rights movement. Richard Nixon was elected president. Noted historian Christopher Lasch has argued that Americans believed political and social problems to be unsolvable, after the experiences of the sixties, and instead turned to a "culture of narcissism." While the problems and concerns of Blacks remained a central issue into the seventies, eighties, and nineties, the idealistic crusades of Blacks and Whites together in the civil rights movement faded from national view, as did many other liberal concerns of the sixties. (Box 44 describes a white ethnic "backlash.")

Spanish-Speaking Americans

Another group was becoming more visible in America during the period of the 1960's and 1970's when the civil rights movement rose and fell. This group was comprised of immigrants from several different Spanish-speaking countries. Spanish-speaking people from Mexico, of course, had long been a part of American life in the southwest—indeed, most of the area had been settled by the Spanish and ruled by Mexico until the 1840's. In our northern cities, in the East and Midwest, however, the presence of large numbers of Spanish-speaking people is a post-World War II phenomenon. New York City witnessed the growth of Spanish Harlem during the 1950's with immigrants from Puerto Rico (facilitated by the fact that Puerto Ricans are American citizens). Then, during the sixties, many Puerto Ricans went to northern cities further west and found themselves joined by other Spanish-speaking people fleeing from Cuba, as well as others from Mexico, the Caribbean, and South America.

In the cities, these immigrants followed the familiar pattern of the Europeans and Blacks who had come before them. They settled into ethnic neighborhoods with their own churches, stores, and schools. Cubans would live with Cubans and Mexicans with Mexicans, often in adjoining neighborhoods, but maintaining their separate identities. Although the Catholic Church and the common language served as unifying factors, the various groups retained their distinct identifications in their own communities. (Box 45 describes the attempts of the Spanish-speaking migrants to maintain their language.)

It is an oversimplification of which the media is frequently guilty to view all Spanish-speaking people as one and the same. There have frequently been bitter animosities between the separate groups, which have come from different countries. Education, class, status, skin color, and generation all serve to create

---

Box 44

Backlash and The White Ethnic Movement

During the last decade a new movement called the "white ethnic movement" has emerged. The Rev. Andrew M. Greeley and the columnist Robert Novak have assumed leadership roles. Arguing that the white ethnics (the "new immigrants" and their descendants) had been ignored, ridiculed, and discriminated against by advocates of the more visible minorities and "affirmative action" programs, Greeley and Novak have attempted to organize the movement to protect the interests of the white ethnics. Such organizing follows the lead of Black Americans who had organized during the 1960's.

Greeley, who is the director of the "Center for the Study of American Pluralism," has frequently argued the unfairness of programs like "affirmative action," which give advantages in hiring to minorities (often at the expense of urban "white ethnics"), rather than simply providing equal opportunity for all applicants.

While the movement had not gained wide membership or publicity, it does reflect a current in contemporary American life. The election of President Reagan in 1980, who has argued against "affirmative action," reflects the rejection of the liberal values of the sixties in such areas. Many of the "white ethnics," who have traditionally voted for the Democratic Party since the 1930's, voted for Reagan. A possibility seems to be emerging of their abandoning the Democrats for the Republicans. Indeed, this seemed to be the case in the election of George Bush in 1988 as Reagan's successor. This trend constitutes a major modification of voting patterns in America and may have important implications for political and social trends in the future. Whether this will actually occur depends on many factors such as economic trends, the ability of the Republicans to field other popular candidates, and "white ethnic" perceptions of their long-term best interests.

---

separate identities that are often stronger than the link of common language. The Spanish speakers, like the "new immigrants" before them, are far from unified.

The 1970's to the 1990's

Ethnicity since the 1970's has been characterized by a growing diversity and proliferation. The late 1970's (1977-1979) saw more immigrants enter these shores than has been the case since 1924. From diverse sources more areas of the world are represented in this recent immigration than ever in the past. While many immigrants seek economic opportunities, some have had to flee their

---

Box 45

The Spanish Language

An interesting sidelight of the Spanish-speaking immigrants is their attempts to maintain their language in America. The "new immigrants" had faced a similar problem over a half-century before, which they had tried to solve by having their own schools where their children could learn to speak Polish, German, or whatever their parents' language happened to be. Yet, these were definitely second languages rather than the first language for the children. In later generations, language facility tended to fade. Hispanics, however, tried a different approach to the problem by lobbying for bilingual education and having various forms and signs printed in Spanish as well as English. During the 1970's their efforts met with considerable success, and we frequently see results of this such as the printing of instructions on public telephones in both Spanish and English. During the 1980's, however, a backlash movement developed against this, as part of the generally conservative national mood, and we saw voters in Florida and elsewhere calling for an end to such practices.

---

homelands for their lives. Political factors account for much of the recent immigration and will be important in the future as well. (Box 46 gives immigration figures by continent from 1961 to 1987.)

Southeast Asians

Immigrants from China and Japan have long been part of American life, particularly on the west coast. They have been here for many generations, since the original immigration from those countries after the Civil War. The recent immigrants from Asia, however, have not come from China and Japan but from southeast Asia: from India, Vietnam, Thailand, Cambodia and other countries in that region. Their reasons for migration varied from the familiar desire to seek a better life that has motivated migration to the United States during the nation's entire history, to a desire to escape the political regimes and turmoil in their home countries. In the case of the Vietnamese, they are survivors of the disastrous war that ravaged their homeland.

Usually the southeast Asians follow the familiar pattern of immigrants to this country by living in their own neighborhoods with their own stores and places of worship. Learning the language of their adopted country is another familiar problem, as is the prejudice of the people with whom they are

Box 46

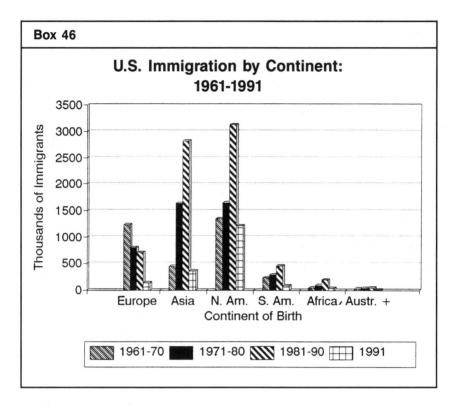

U.S. Immigration by Continent: 1961-1991

competing for jobs and housing. Again, as in the case of the Spanish speaking, Americans tend to lump these new arrivals together in one category—and again the reality shows they are distinct groups who have strong ethnic identifications of their own.

Among the southeast Asians, the immigrants from India and the Philippines depart from the pattern of poor, often uneducated, people seeking opportunity for themselves and their children. The Indians in the United States are primarily professional people—medical doctors, engineers, and scientists. Often they received their graduate education in this country and then decided to stay. Being English speakers has been an advantage in their adaptation to life in this country. Likewise, people who move here from the Philippine Islands, a former U.S. possession, are often educated and frequently in the medical profession. Both the Indians and the Filipinos, being English-speaking professionals, tend to live in a variety of places rather than in ethnic neighborhoods.

Box 47 gives a current detailed breakdown of the number of immigrants by country of birth from 1961 to 1987. National groups mentioned thus far are included as well as other groups still to be discussed.

Box 47

Immigrants, by Country of Birth: 1961-1991
(In Thousands)

	1961-70	1971-80	1981-90	1991
Austria	13.7	4.7	NA	NA
Cambodia	1.2	8.4	116.6	3.3
Cuba	256.8	276.8	159.2	10.3
Czechoslovakia	21.4	10.2	NA	NA
Finland	5.8	3.4	NA	NA
France	34.3	17.8	23.1	2.5
Germany	200.0	66.0	70.1	6.5
Greece	90.2	93.7	29.1	2.1
Hong Kong	25.6	47.5	63.0	10.4
Hungary	17.3	11.6	NA	NA
Iran	10.4	46.2	154.8	19.6
Ireland	42.4	14.1	32.8	4.8
Italy	206.7	130.1	32.9	2.6
Jamaica	71.0	142.0	213.8	23.8
Korea	35.8	272.0	338.8	26.5
Laos	0.1	22.6	145.6	10.0
Mexico	443.3	637.2	1,653.3	946.2
Philippines	101.5	360.2	485.3	63.6
Poland	73.3	43.6	97.4	19.2
Soviet Union	15.7	43.2	84.0	57.0
Sweden	16.7	6.3	NA	NA
Thailand	5.0	44.1	64.4	7.4
United Kingdom	230.5	123.5	142.1	13.9
Vietnam	4.6	179.7	401.4	55.3
Yugoslavia	46.2	42.1	19.2	2.7

SOURCE: Data drawn from *Statistical Abstracts*, 1990 and 1994 editions.

European Immigration During the Eighties

Eastern European unrest has resulted in Poles, Soviet Jews, and other eastern Europeans seeking new homes on our shores although, as Box 47 demonstrates, overall European immigration has declined in the seventies and eighties with increased economic opportunity in western Europe. The advent of *glasnost* and the political rearrangement of eastern Europe in the late eighties and the early nineties, with the end of the "Cold War," promises instability in eastern

Europe and Asia through the rebirth of nationalistic, ethnic and religious rivalries. The nineties could see the United States being the recipient of many people fleeing the breakdown of the old certainties of Communist countries. The recent softening of emigration restrictions in the Soviet Union has allowed many Jews to move to the United States. Frequently they are educated people who possess skills which are in demand in their new country. Of course, they do have a language problem—although many learned English in Russian schools. The Jewish-American community has aided them in adjusting and provided ethnic neighborhoods in which they can feel at home—except for the Russian language. Migration of Russian Jews to the United States has varied according to the current state of U.S. relations with the Soviet Union and Soviet emigration policy.

More traditional areas for immigrants such as western Europe continue to send people, but in smaller numbers and primarily to reunite families rather than for economic reasons. The success of the European economic community has provided greater opportunity than migration to the U.S. The decline in western European migration because of economic factors explains the decrease in the numbers of such immigrants to the U.S., as shown in Boxes 46 and 47. Nevertheless, the number of eastern European immigrants remains significant.

An Increasing Surge Across the Rio Grande

Central and South America have emerged as a growing source of immigrants, with an influx of boat people from Cuba and Haiti in 1980. The Dominican Republic, Jamaica, Panama, and of course Mexico, among others, have also contributed to the inflow of people. Many Americans, including the press, continue to gather all persons from Spanish-speaking countries under the heading of Hispanics without regard to country of origin, ethnicity, legality of immigration, educational levels, etc. Often such Americans express surprise when divisions among the Spanish-speaking surface, sometimes even with overt hostility. (Box 48 offers an example of one of these divisions emerging currently in the Spanish-speaking community.)

Black Americans in the 1980s

During the last decade Black Americans, or, as some now prefer to be described, African-Americans, have simultaneously faced both troubled times and political advances. The Reagan administration and the Bush administrations have been less concerned and are certainly less supportive of Black Americans in northern cities than previous Democratic administrations had been. Cuts in funding from the federal government for urban programs and education (which result in local governments having more to do with less money) have

---

Box 48

Religion and the Spanish Speaking

An interesting phenomenon which has emerged among the Spanish-speaking immigrants is the conversion of many of these people to Protestantism. While almost all of the migrants were raised as Catholics, many of the less educated members of these communities have been converted to evangelical and fundamentalist versions of the Protestant faith, frequently by preachers operating in storefront churches in the major urban areas. Such conversion seems to appeal to poor and uneducated people leading difficult lives surrounded by gangs, drugs, poverty and urban blight. Families have been divided because of such religious changes by some members. Not surprisingly, the Roman Catholic Church in recent years has been attempting a counter-campaign to halt or slow this trend.

---

resulted in the deterioration of such programs as Head Start, medical care for pregnant women, and other assistance for the more poverty-stricken in the community. Resulting declines in educational scores and soaring infant mortality rates (comparable to third world countries) have blighted the Black communities in the eighties. When such problems are combined with urban crime and drug usage, it is easy to see that Black inner-city life has been most difficult in recent years.

Nevertheless, in the eighties Blacks have been enjoying political successes in the United States greater than at any time since Reconstruction. These political advances have been both in urban politics and on the national scene. On the state level a Black American was recently elected Governor of Virginia. The large northern cities in the last few decades have seen white residents moving out of the central city to surrounding suburbs in large numbers. Hispanics, Asians, and other recent immigrants who have replaced the whites have often not been English speakers and frequently not citizens. The Blacks, being English speakers and long-time citizens, and being better organized, have seized the opportunity, in a manner very reminiscent of the Irish Americans in earlier periods, to capture many of the positions of urban mayors as well as lesser offices. During the last few years setbacks to the urban political achievements have occurred with the death of Mayor Harold Washington in Chicago and the drug related problems of Mayor Marion Barry in Washington, D.C. Yet, overall, Black Americans are doing well in the political arena.

On the national scene, the civil rights activist Rev. Jesse Jackson has emerged as a potential presidential candidate who in many ways (including oratorical talents and persistence) is reminiscent of William Jennings Bryan. While Jackson to date has won neither his party's nomination nor the presidency, he has managed to draw support from different economic, social, and ethnic groups to a degree that no Black American politician has previously done. Jackson's achievements are particularly noteworthy since he has drawn support not only from the Black community (which in 1987 comprised only 12.2 percent of the U.S. population) but from other minorities and the majority group as well.

Today's America
Melting Pot, Ethnic Battleground, or Multi-Cultured Society?

With all of these various people spoken of above living in the cities of the United States, the question naturally arises as to the future of our society and the ethnic groups within it. A popular view earlier in the century held that America was one vast "melting pot" in which the various ethnic groups would blend into a mixture, creating a new American — different from the old, perhaps, but sharing a common culture. Nativists rejected this and insisted that the "new immigrants" could never blend in and consequently should be excluded from the United States. A similar argument was used against Black Americans. Still another position (cultural pluralism) held that these various groups could live side by side, maintaining their own cultures and peaceably interacting. Refusing to accept the more moderate positions, extremists have at different times even predicted racial or religious warfare between the various groups in the United States. Today, with population mobility and immigration once again changing the population of our cities, competing views on this matter are being heard again.

While it is impossible to predict the future with certainty, the past often suggests patterns that are likely to be followed in the future, albeit in a modified form. From examining the impact of earlier immigration and the assimilation of those people into our society, certain patterns become evident. The original immigrants and, to a lesser extent, their children tended to live in separate neighborhoods, speak their own language, and patronize the businesses of their own community. Later generations spoke English as their first language (sometimes losing altogether the ability to converse in the original tongue) and tended to move out of the ethnic neighborhoods. Often they married out of their ethnic group, although less frequently out of their religion. They tended to think of themselves as Americans rather than Poles, Greeks, or Italians. Yet they did not lose their identification with the original group entirely. Many of their cultural values regarding such subjects as family, educational aspirations, and religion survived through multiple generations, as did the tendency to maintain contact, friendship, and identification with people who, like themselves, are descended from a particular ethnic group. In recent years we have witnessed a reawakening of this surviving ethnic awareness, which some have argued is a reaction caused by the prominence in American life of Black Americans. This resurgence of ethnic awareness also could reflect a feeling of powerlessness in contemporary American society that finds many old values and expectations being diminished, so that ethnicity is simply filling a vacuum. Clearly ethnicity remains a powerful force.

For many Americans this has meant a dual life. On one level — at work, in school, and even increasingly in their community — they speak English and share a common American culture. No group has been able to keep its language, except as a second language in which succeeding generations find themselves less fluent. Yet, at the same time, the later generations retain their ethnic identity, as can be seen in their weddings, friendships, memberships in organizations, and even their voting patterns. Products of cross ethnic marriages vary in their identification patterns. In some cases over a century after their ancestors migrated to America, people maintained their ethnic identity as well as their sense of being Americans. This, however, is only part of American's concept of self. We also identify with others as a part of a social class, a region, a profession, a skin color, an age group, and so on.

Most likely, considering the record of the past, ethnicity in America will continue to survive in the foreseeable future, as a significant feature in our society without all Americans either blending into a common culture, losing their sense of ethnicity and customs, or — as the extremists argue — descending into overt hostility. On the other hand, prejudice and discrimination between the various groups are also likely to continue on various levels, unless there is some major change in American life and education. Again, the past suggests that the people in the United States who will most successfully advance, materially and socially, will continue to be those who are articulate in the common language, English, and are acceptable in cultural terms in American society. This is not to say that they will have to relinquish their ethnic identities and values — but simply that they will lead dual lives, with the ethnic part being reserved for family and private life and the common American culture dominating in work and school. As Pete Seeger said, we'll continue to be "All Mixed Up." (Box 49 discusses in more detail whether there is a price to pay for success.)

Box 49

The Price of Success

Some of the ethnic groups in America have been successful in terms of both upward economic mobility and comparative acceptance in the larger United States society while others, to varying degrees, have not. A brief look at several of the successful groups may suggest some keys and strategies for those who desire mobility and acceptance. Some may feel the price required for social mobility may be too high and therefore unacceptable.

Among the ethnic and/or religious groups who have done relatively well in these two categories are the Jews, Japanese, Chinese, Indians (from India, not Native Americans) and the Greeks. Coming from different parts of the world with differing religions, skin complexions, cultures and historical experiences, these groups have all been successful in gaining an education and performing well in school, as well as succeeding economically. They have achieved a high degree of acceptance within American society. In contrast African-Americans and, to a somewhat lesser degree, Hispanics have largely been excluded from the American dream of success. The argument that ascribes this to genetic differences in intelligence has been shown to be without merit. This suggests that the explanation is likely to be found both in cultural patterns of that culture and those of the larger American society which has discriminated against minorities throughout the twentieth century.

What factors do the successful ethnic groups have in common which may explain their success in achieving their upward social mobility? A cursory look may provide a framework for further investigations. All successful ethnic groups appear to have developed dualistic cultures where the ethnic group identity, language, religion and cultural values have been reserved for interaction within the group. The English language, and other mainstream attributes are used in interacting with American society in the school, the workplace and in other areas when not exclusively among group members. A willingness to adapt to the larger American culture has been characteristic of all of these groups—most particularly a complete mastery of the English language. Their acceptance of American ways of life probably helps the general American society feel more comfortable with these groups. Yet, surely just the willingness to blend in on a daily basis cannot be the only factor.

Other factors shared by these groups are an emphasis on education and an affirmation of a "work ethic." Children are encouraged, sometimes almost driven, to work hard to obtain as much education as possible in order to achieve an upward economic and social mobility. The older generations worked hard and for long hours to achieve the economic means of furthering opportunities for the children. These values, as studies of the successful groups often emphasize, have meant hardship for both the original generations and a great deal of stress for the later generations who are trying to meet the expectations of the parents. Yet upward mobility and acceptance for later generations has been the reward.

Further comparative study of successful groups can lead to a better understanding of upward mobility and acceptance in American society. Just as valuable would be a comparison between these groups and those groups who have encountered frustration in this society and how their approaches have differed.

Questions

1. While the United States has many people within its borders, it is not a very tolerant society. Discuss this intolerance towards the successive waves of immigrants to these shores.

2. Discuss the similarities in the lifestyles of the various migrants to our nation's northern cities.

3. Discuss the role of Dr. Martin Luther King in both the rise and fall of the civil rights movement. What is the status of the movement today?

4. Opinion as to what should be done about minorities in America has ranged from schemes for assimilation to violence. Discuss the ideas presented for ways that Americans should cope with the problem of immigration.

5. Discuss the advantages and roles played by the Irish, as compared to the later "new immigrants."

6. Compare the Spanish-speaking immigrants to the "new immigrants."

7. Have some Latino groups done better than others? Which ones? Why?

8. What accounts for the fact that many Asian-American immigrants do so well in school and the workplace?

9. Many ethnic Americans lead a dual life today. Discuss this phenomenon from both the reading and from your own observations or experiences.

10. Using the reading, and your imagination, describe what American ethnicity will be like twenty years from now.

11. What do you think American immigration policy should be? Why?

12. What price must be paid for success in America? Is it a fair price?

13. Can all Americans obtain success?

Part VII

America
the Multicultural

The Pledge of Allegiance asserts the United States of America is "one nation, indivisible." Yet our country is remarkably diverse. People who call themselves "American" range from Native Americans who first populated the continent to slaves who were brought here involuntarily to over 60 million immigrants who have come here in the last 150 years. These diverse people are of different racial, ethnic, and religious backgrounds and even of different sexual orientations. To prevent the ideal of cultural unity—*e pluribus unum*, out of many, one—from clashing with cultural diversity, many now advocate multiculturalism. Multiculturalism is the recognition of American diversity along with efforts to promote the equality of all cultural traditions. "But," as sociologist John Macionis says, "precisely where the balance is to be struck—between the pluribus and the unum—is likely to remain a divisive issue for some time to come."

The five articles in Part VII start us thinking multiculturally. In chapter 20, sociologist David Bell focuses on Asian-Americans. They are this country's fastest-growing minority, numbering in 1990 at 7 million people and approaching 3 percent of the population. They account for almost half of all current immigration to the United States. The title of the article, "The Triumph of Asian-Americans," calls attention to the significant economic and social strides made by these people. Keep in mind as you read, however, that a "model minority label" may obscure the poverty of some Asian-Americans. A recent survey shows that for every Asian-American household with an annual income of $75,000 or more, there is roughly another earning under $10,000. Southeast Asian refugees, in particular, are a rapidly expanding segment of the Asian-American population, but assistance programs fail to address their special needs in the areas of language training and therapy for post-traumatic stress.

Chapter 21 looks at Latinos and politics. In 1990, Latinos, both legal and illegal, numbered around 25 million, representing one in ten people in the United States. If the trend of high birth rates and continuing immigration continues, Latinos will probably outnumber African-Americans early in the next century. "The Push for Power" indicates that, despite these huge numbers, Latinos in the past have "proved largely incapable of translating their numeric strength into political and economic clout." Whether this can be turned around is the question raised in this article.

Chapter 22, " 'Return' of Native Americans Challenges Racial Definition" provides census data which shows an increasing number of people—1.8 million—who have identified themselves as American Indians. One of the interesting things about this is that it is happening in "states that have no large tribal groups, tribal lands or reservations." Observers attribute the surge to better social acceptance, growing ethnic pride and possible eligibility for affirmative action benefits.

Chapter 23, "The Future of Gay America," deals with a group of people for whom we cannot get a census count. Whether 1 percent of the population, as claimed by some, or 10 percent of the population, as claimed by others, we are talking about anywhere from 2.5 million to 25 million Americans. Given such numbers, it is surprising that more than half of American adults polled believed that they do not know any homosexuals. Be that as it may, organizations like ACT UP, gay pride parades, and marches on Washington and the United Nations, will continue "testing the limits of this country's tolerance." "Gays," the article says, "won't let up in their quest for a more visible—and influential—place in American society."

The last chapter, "Whites' Myths About Blacks," uses survey data to point out that while some whites' views about America's 30 million blacks have softened, mistaken beliefs still persist. There has been poor communication and "too little discussion of racial misunderstanding and ethnic stereotyping." It is probable that "interracial contacts could eventually help diminish stereotyping by both races." Let us hope so, for as Martin Luther King, Jr. warned us: "we must learn to live together as brothers or perish together as fools."

Chapter Twenty

The Triumph of Asian-Americans

David A. Bell

It is the year 2019. In the heart of downtown Los Angeles, massive electronic billboards feature a model in a kimono hawking products labeled in Japanese. In the streets below, figures clad in traditional East Asian peasant garb hurry by, speaking to each other in an English made unrecognizable by the addition of hundreds of Spanish and Asian words. A rough-mannered policeman leaves an incongruously graceful calling card on a doorstep: a delicate origami paper sculpture.

This is, of course, a scene from a science-fiction movie, Ridley Scott's 1982 *Blade Runner*. It is also a vision that Asian-Americans dislike intensely. Hysterical warnings of an imminent Asian "takeover" of the United States stained a whole century of their 140-year history in this country, providing the backdrop for racial violence, legal segregation, and the internment of 110,000 Japanese-Americans in concentration camps during World War II. Today, integration into American society, not transformation of American society, is the goal of an overwhelming majority. So why did the critics praise *Blade Runner* for its "realism"? The answer is easy to see.

The Asian-American population is exploding. According to the Census Bureau, it grew an astounding 125 percent between 1970 and 1980, and now stands at 4.1 million, or 1.8 percent of all Americans. Most of the increase is the result of immigration, which accounted for 1.8 million people between 1973 and 1983, the last year for which the Immigration and Naturalization Service has accurate figures (710,000 of these arrived as refugees from Southeast Asia). And the wave shows little sign of subsiding. Ever since the immigration Act of 1965 permitted large-scale immigration by Asians, they have made up over 40 percent of all newcomers to the United States. Indeed, the arbitrary quota of 20,000 immigrants per country per year established by the act has produced huge backlogs of future Asian-Americans in several countries, including 120,000 in South Korea and 336,000 in the Philippines, some of whom, according to the State Department, have been waiting for their visas since 1970.

The numbers are astonishing. But even more astonishing is the extent to which Asian-Americans have become prominent out of all proportion to their share of the population. It now seems likely that their influx will have as important an effect on American society as the migrations from Europe of 100 years ago. Most remarkable of all, it is taking place with relatively little trouble.

The new immigration from Asia is a radical development in several ways. First, it has not simply enlarged an existing Asian-American community, but created an entirely new one. Before 1965, and the passage of the Immigration Act, the term "Oriental-American" (which was then the vogue) generally denoted people living on the West Coast, in Hawaii, or in the Chinatowns of a few large cities. Generally, they traced their ancestry either to one small part of China, the Toishan district of Kwantung province, or to a small number of communities in Japan (one of the largest of which, ironically, was Hiroshima). Today more than a third of all Asian-Americans live outside Chinatowns in the East, South, and Midwest, and their origins are as diverse as those of "European-Americans." The term "Asian-American" now refers to over 900,000 Chinese from all parts of China and also Vietnam, 800,000 Filipinos, 700,000 Japanese, 500,000 Koreans, 400,000 East Indians, and a huge assortment of everything else from Moslem Cambodians to Catholic Hawaiians. It can mean an illiterate Hmong tribesman or a fully assimilated graduate of the Harvard Business School.

Asian-Americans have also attracted attention by their new prominence in several professions and trades. In New York City, for example, where the Asian-American population jumped from 94,500 in 1970 to 231,500 in 1980, Korean-Americans run an estimated 900 of the city's 1,600 corner grocery stores. Filipino doctors—who outnumber black doctors—have become general practitioners in thousands of rural communities that previously lacked physicians. East Indian-Americans own 800 of California's 6,000 motels. And in parts of Texas, Vietnamese-Americans now control 85 percent of the shrimp-fishing industry, though they only reached this position after considerable strife (now the subject of a film, *Alamo Bay*).

Individual Asian-Americans have become quite prominent as well. I. M. Pei and Minoru Yamasaki have helped transform American architecture. Seiji Ozawa and Yo Yo Ma are giant figures in American music. An Wang created one of the nation's largest computer firms, and Rocky Aoki founded one of its largest restaurant chains (Benihana). Samuel C. C. Ting won a Nobel prize in physics.

Most spectacular of all, and most significant for the future, is the entry of Asian-Americans into the universities. At Harvard, for example, Asian-Americans ten years ago made up barely three percent of the freshman class. The figure is now ten percent—five times their share of the population. At Brown, Asian-American applications more than tripled over the same period, and at Berkeley they increased from 3,408 in 1982 to 4,235 only three years later. The Berkeley student body is now 22 percent Asian-American, UCLA's is 21 percent, and MIT's 19 percent. The Juilliard School of Music in New York is currently 30 percent Asian and Asian-American. American medical schools had only 571 Asian-American students in 1970, but in 1980 they had 1,924, and last year 3,763 or 5.6 percent of total enrollment. What is more, nearly all of these figures are certain to increase. In the current, largely foreign-born Asian-American community, 32.9 percent of people over 25 graduated from college (as opposed to 16.2 percent in the general population). For third-generation Japanese-Americans, the figure is 88 percent.

By any measure these Asian-American students are outstanding. In California only the top 12.5 percent of high school students qualify for admission to the uppermost tier of the state university system, but 39 percent of Asian-American high school students do. On the SATs, Asian-Americans score an average of 519 in math, surpassing whites, the next highest group, by 32 points. Among Japanese-Americans, the most heavily native-born Asian-American group, 68 percent of those taking the math SAT scored above 600—high enough to qualify for admission to almost any university in the country. The Westinghouse Science Talent search, which each year identifies 40 top high school science students, picked 12 Asian-Americans in 1983, nine last year, and seven this year. And at Harvard the Phi Beta Kappa chapter last April named as its elite "Junior Twelve" students five Asian-Americans and seven Jews.

Faced with these statistics, the understandable reflex of many non-Asian-Americans is adulation. President Reagan has called Asian-Americans "our exemplars of hope and inspiration." *Parade* magazine recently featured an article on Asian-Americans titled "The Promise of America," and *Time* and *Newsweek* stories have boasted headlines like "A Formula for Success," "The Drive to Excel," and "A Model Minority." However, not all of these stories come to grips with the fact that Asian-Americans, like all immigrants, have to deal with a great many problems of adjustment, ranging from the absurd to the deadly serious.

Few white Americans today realize just how pervasive legal anti-Asian discrimination was before 1945. The tens of thousands of Chinese laborers who arrived in California in the 1850s and 1860s to work in the goldfields and build the Central Pacific Railroad often lived in virtual slavery (the words ku-li, now a part of the English language, mean "bitter labor"). Far from having the chance to organize, they were seized on as scapegoats by labor unions, particularly Samuel Gomper's AFL, and often ended up working as strikebreakers instead, thus inviting violent attacks. In 1870 Congress barred Asian immigrants from citizenship, and in 1882 it passed the Chinese Exclusion Act, which summarily prohibited more Chinese from entering the country. Since it did this at a time when 100,600 male Chinese-Americans had the company of only 4,800 females, it effectively sentenced the Chinese community to rapid decline. From 1854 to 1874, California had in effect a law preventing Asian-Americans from testifying in court, leaving them without the protection of the law.

Little changed in the late 19th and early 20th centuries, as large numbers of Japanese and smaller contingents from Korea and the Philippines began to arrive on the West Coast. In 1906 San Francisco made a brief attempt to segregate its school system. In 1910 a California law went so far as to prohibit marriage between Caucasians and "Mongolians," in flagrant defiance of the Fourteenth Amendment. Two Alien Land Acts in 1913 and 1920 prevented noncitizens in California (in other words, all alien immigrants) from owning or leasing land. These laws, and the Chinese Exclusion Act, remained in effect until the 1940s. And of course during the Second World War, President Franklin Roosevelt signed an Executive Order sending 110,000 ethnic Japanese on the West Coast, 64 percent of whom were American citizens, to internment camps. Estimates of the monetary damage to the Japanese-American community from this action range as high as $400,000,000, and Japanese-American political activists have made reparations one of their most important goals. Only in Hawaii, where Japanese-Americans already outnumbered whites 61,000 to 29,000 at the turn of the century, was discrimination relatively less important. (Indeed, 157,000 Japanese-Americans in Hawaii at the start of the war were *not* interned, although they posed a greater possible threat to the war effort than their cousins in California.)

In light of this history, the current problems of the Asian-American community seem relatively minor, and its success appears even more remarkable. Social scientists wonder just how this success was possible, and how Asian-Americans have managed to avoid the "second-class citizenship" that has trapped so many blacks and Hispanics. There is no single answer,

but all the various explanations of the Asian-Americans' success do tend to
fall into one category: self-sufficiency.

The first element of this self-sufficiency is family. Conservative sociologist
Thomas Sowell writes that "strong, stable families have been characteristic
of . . . successful minorities," and calls Chinese-Americans and Japanese-
Americans the most stable he has encountered. This quality contributes to
success in at least three ways. First and most obviously, it provides a secure
environment for children. Second, it pushes those children to do better than
their parents. As former Ohio state demographer William Petersen, author
of *Japanese-Americans* (1971), says, "They're like the Jews in that they have
the whole family and the whole community pushing them to make the best
of themselves" (see Box 50). And finally, it is a significant financial advantage.
Traditionally, Asian-Americans have headed into family businesses, with all
the family members pitching in long hours to make them a success. For the
Chinese, it was restaurants and laundries (as late as 1940, half of the Chinese-
American labor force worked in one or the other), for the Japanese, groceries
and truck farming, and for the Koreans, groceries. Today the proportion of
Koreans working without pay in family businesses is nearly three times as
high as any other group. A recent New York magazine profile of one typical
Korean grocery in New York showed that several of the family members running
it consistently worked 15 to 18 hours a day. Thomas Sowell points out that
in 1970, although Chinese median family income already exceeded white median
family income by a third, their median personal income was only ten percent
higher, indicating much greater participation per family.

Also contributing to Asian-American self-sufficiency are powerful community
organizations. From the beginning of Chinese-American settlement in
California, clan organizations, mutual aid societies, and rotating credit associations gave many Japanese-Americans a start in business, at a time when most
banks would only lend to whites. Throughout the first half of the century,
the strength of community organizations was an important reason why Asian-
Americans tended to live in small, closed communities rather than spreading
out among the general population. And during the Depression years, they proved
vital. In the early 1930s, when nine percent of the population of New York
City subsisted on public relief, only one percent of Chinese-Americans did
so. The community structure has also helped keep Asian-American crime rates
the lowest in the nation, despite recently increasing gang violence among new
Chinese and Vietnamese immigrants. According to the 1980 census, the
proportion of Asian-Americans in prison is one-fourth that of the general
population.

The more recent immigrants have also developed close communities. In the
Washington, D.C. suburb of Arlington, Virginia, there is now a "Little Saigon."

Box 50

Asians and Jews

Comparing the social success of Asian-Americans with that of the Jews is irresistible. Jews and Asians rank number one and number two, respectively, in median family income. In the Ivy League they are the two groups most heavily "over-represented" in comparison to their shares of the population. And observers are quick to point out all sorts of cultural parallels. As Arthur Rosen, the chairman of (appropriately) the National Committee on United States-China Relations, recently told *The New York Times*, "There are the same kind of strong family ties and the same sacrificial drive on the part of immigrant parents who couldn't get a college education to see that their children do."

In historical terms, the parallels can often be striking. For example, when Russian and Polish Jews came to this country in the late 19th and early 20th centuries, 60 percent of those who went into industry worked in the garment trade. Today thousands of Chinese-American women fill sweatshops in New York City doing the same work of stitching and sewing. In Los Angeles, when the Jews began to arrive in large numbers in the 1880s, 43 percent of them became retail or wholesale proprietors, according to Ivan Light's essay in *Clamor at the Gates*. One hundred years later, 40 percent of Koreans in Los Angeles are also wholesale and retail proprietors. The current controversy over Asian-American admissions in Ivy League colleges eerily recalls the Jews' struggle to end quotas in the 1940s and 1950s.

In cultural terms, however, it is easy to take the comparison too far. American Jews remain a relatively homogeneous group, with a common religion and history. Asian-Americans, especially after the post-1965 flood of immigrants, are exactly the opposite. They seem homogeneous largely because they share some racial characteristics. And even those vary widely. The label "Chinese-American" itself covers a range of cultural and linguistic differences that makes those between German and East European Jews, or between Reform and Orthodox Jews, seem trivial in comparison.

The most important parallels between Jews and the various Asian groups are not cultural. They lie rather in the sociological profile of Jewish and Asian immigration. The Jewish newcomers of a hundred years ago never completely fit into the category of "huddled masses." They had an astonishing high literacy rate (nearly 100 percent for German Jews, and over 50 percent for East European Jews), a long tradition of scholarship even in the smallest shtels, and useful skills. More than two-thirds of male Jewish immigrants were considered skilled workers in America. Less than three percent of Jewish immigrants had worked on the land. Similarly, the Japanese, Korean, Filipino, and Vietnamese immigrants of the 20th century have come almost exclusively from the middle class. Seventy percent of Korean male immigrants, for example, are college graduates. Like middle-class native-born Americans, Asian and Jewish immigrants alike have fully understood the importance of the universities, and have pushed their children to enter them from the very start.

Thomas Sowell offers another parallel between the successes of Asians and Jews. Both communities have benefited paradoxically, he argues, from their small size and from past discrimination against them. These disadvantages long kept both groups out of politics. And, as Sowell writes in *Race and Economics*: "Those American ethnic groups that have succeeded best politically have not usually been the same as those who succeeded best economically . . . those minorities that have pinned their greatest hopes on political action—the Irish and the Negroes, for example, have made some of the slower economic advances." Rather than searching for a solution to their problems through the political process, Jewish, Chinese, and Japanese immigrants developed self-sufficiency by relying on community organizations. The combination of their skills, their desire for education, and the gradual disappearance of discrimination led inexorably to economic success.

SOURCE: Appearing with the above-cited article in *New Republic*, July, 1985.

Koreans also take advantage of the "ethnic resources" provided by a small community. As Ivan Light writes in an essay in Nathan Glazer's new book *Clamor at the Gates*, "They help one another with business skills, information, and purchase of ethnic commodities; cluster in particular industries; combine easily in restraint of trade; or utilize rotating credit associations." Light cites a study showing that 34 percent of Korean grocery store owners in Chicago had received financial help from within the Korean community. The immigrants in these communities are self-sufficient in another way as well. Unlike the immigrants of the 19th century, most new Asian-Americans come to the United States with professional skills. Or they come to obtain those skills, and then stay on. Of 16,000 Taiwanese who came to the U.S. as students in the 1960s, only three percent returned to Taiwan.

So what does the future hold for Asian-Americans? With the removal of most discrimination, and with the massive Asian-American influx in the universities, the importance of tightly knit communities is sure to wane. Indeed, among the older Asian-American groups it already has: since the war, fewer and fewer native-born Chinese-Americans have come to live in Chinatowns. But will complete assimilation follow? One study, at least, seems to indicate that it will, if one can look to the well-established Japanese-Americans for hints as to the future of other Asian groups. According to Professor Harry Kitano of UCLA, 63 percent of Japanese now intermarry.

But can all Asian-Americans follow the prosperous, assimilationist Japanese example? For some, it may not be easy. Hmong tribesmen, for instance, arrived in the United States with little money, few valuable skills, and extreme cultural disorientation. After five years here, they are still heavily dependent on welfare. (When the state of Oregon cut its assistance to refugees, 90 percent of the Hmong there moved to California.) Filipinos, although now the second-largest Asian-American group, make up less than ten percent of the Asian-American population at Harvard, and are the only Asian-Americans to benefit from affirmative action programs at the University of California. Do figures like these point to the emergence of a disadvantaged Asian-American underclass? It is still early to tell, but the question is not receiving much attention either. As Nathan Glazer says of Asian-Americans, "When they're already above average, it's very hard to pay much attention to those who fall below." Ross Harano, a Chicago businessman active in the Democratic Party's Asian Caucus, argues that the label of "model minority" earned by the most conspicuous Asian-Americans hurts less successful groups. "We need money to help people who can't assimilate as fast as the superstars," he says.

Harano also points out that the stragglers find little help in traditional minority politics. "When blacks talk about a minority agenda, they don't include us," he says. "Most Asians are viewed by blacks as whites." Indeed, in cities with large numbers of Asians and blacks, relations between the communities are tense. In September 1984, for example, The *Los Angeles Sentinel*, a prominent black newspaper, ran a four-part series condemning Koreans for their "takeover" of black businesses, provoking a strong reaction from Asian-American groups. In Harlem some blacks have organized a boycott of Asian-American stores.

Another barrier to complete integration lies in the tendency of many Asian-American students to crowd into a small number of careers, mainly in the sciences. Professor Ronn Takaki of Berkeley is a strong critic of this "maldistribution," and says that universities should make efforts to correct it. The extent of these efforts, he told *The Boston Globe* last December, "will determine whether we have our poets, sociologists, historians, and journalists. If we are all tracked into becoming computer technicians and scientists, this need will not be fulfilled."

Yet it is not clear that the "maldistribution" problem will extend to the next generation. The children of the current immigrants will not share their parents' language difficulties. Nor will they worry as much about joining large institutions where subtle racism might once have barred them from advancement. William Petersen argues, "As the discrimination disappears, as it mostly has already, the self-selection will disappear as well. . . . There's nothing in Chinese or Japanese culture pushing them toward these fields." Professor Kitano of UCLA is not so sure. "The submerging of the individual to the group is another basic Japanese tradition," he wrote in an article for *The Harvard Encyclopedia of American Ethnic Groups*. It is a tradition that causes problems for Japanese-Americans who wish to avoid current career patterns: "It may only be a matter of time before some break out of these middleman jobs, but the structural and cultural restraints may prove difficult to overcome."

In short, Asian-Americans face undeniable problems of integration. Still, it takes a very narrow mind not to realize that these problems are the envy of every other American racial minority, and of a good number of white ethnic groups as well. Like the Jews, who experienced a similar pattern of discrimination and quotas, and who first crowded into a small range of professions, Asian-Americans have shown an ability to overcome large obstacles in spectacular fashion. In particular, they have done so by taking full advantage of America's greatest civic resource, its schools and universities, just as the Jews did 50 years ago. Now they seem poised to burst out upon American society.

The clearest indication of this course is in politics, a sphere that Asian-Americans traditionally avoided. Now this is changing. And importantly, it is *not* changing just because Asian-Americans want government to solve their particular problems. Yes, there are "Asian" issues: the loosening of immigration restrictions, reparations for the wartime internment, equal opportunity for the Asian disadvantaged. Asian-American Democrats are at present incensed over the way the Democratic National Committee has stripped their caucus of "official" status. But even the most vehement activists on these points still insist that the most important thing for Asian-Americans is not any particular combination of issues, but simply "being part of the process." Unlike blacks or Hispanics, Asian-American politicians have the luxury of not having to devote the bulk of their time to an "Asian-American agenda," and thus escape becoming prisoners of such an agenda. Who thinks of Senator Daniel Inouye or former senator S. I. Hayakawa primarily in terms of his race? In June a young Chinese-American named Michael Woo won a seat on the Los Angeles City Council, running a district that is only five percent Asian. According to *The Washington Post* he attributed his victory to his "links to his fellow American professionals." This is not typical minority-group politics.

Since Asian-Americans have the luxury of not having to behave like other minority groups, it seems only a matter of time before they, like the Jews, lose their "minority" status altogether, both legally and in the public's perception. And when this occurs, Asian-Americans will have to face the danger not of discrimination but of losing their cultural identity. It is a problem that every immigrant group must eventually come to terms with.

Questions

1. What groups make up the Asian-American population? Are they increasing or decreasing?

2. In what ways do past and current immigration from Asia differ? Contrast it with immigration from other continents?

3. In what sense is Asian-American immigration triumphant?

4. Can the success rate of Asian-Americans maintain itself in the future?

5. Asian-Americans have avoided "second-class citizenship because of self-sufficiency." What does that mean?

6. Do stable families contribute to self-sufficiency? What about community organizations?

7. Will some Asian-American groups assimilate more easily than others? Which will find it difficult? Why?

8. Will there be an Asian-American underclass?

9. Compare the success of Asian-Americans with that of American Jews.

10. The 1982 movie *Blade Runner* presented a stereotypical view of Asian-Americans. Do current movies depict a more accurate picture?

11. Is the future of Asian-Americans positive or negative?

Chapter Twenty-One

The Push for Power

Eloise Salholz with Tim Padgett, David L. Gonzalez and Nonny De La Peña

It will be months before demographers at the Census Bureau produce their portrait of who we are in the waning years of the American Century. But when the results from the 1990 count are finally in, one statistic should come as no surprise: the number of Hispanics—the nation's fastest-growing group—could be approaching 25 million, or 10 percent of the total U.S. population. Latino leaders say the census will be their community's ticket to fuller participation in American life than ever before. It seems all the more ironic, then, that the forms arriving in mailboxes across the country recently were printed only in English—another reminder that, despite their vast legions, Hispanics remain an invisible minority.

Latinos were poised to make their mark once before. "The 1980s will be the decade of the Hispanics," declared Raúl Yzaguirre, president of the National Council of La Raza, in 1978. Pollsters predicted that Hispanics would soon become a "voting time bomb." But a dozen years later, Latinos have proved largely incapable of translating their numeric strength into political and economic clout. Today Yzaguirre says, "If anything, we retrogressed in the '80s." Reagan-era cutbacks and recession pushed many Hispanics deep into poverty, while conservative social climate permitted passage of "English Only" laws aimed at Spanish speakers. Last week, a report from Congress's

General Accounting Office confirmed what Hispanics have been saying for years: the landmark 1986 immigration law, which penalized employers of illegal aliens, has produced a widespread "pattern of discrimination" against job applicants with a "foreign appearance or accent"—even citizens and green-card holders.

Disappointed by their lack of progress in the last decade, Hispanics are now determined to salvage the 1990s. Activists have adopted a grass-roots strategy that has already led to successes in school reform and political redistricting. The Latino leadership is looking ahead to 1992, the 500th anniversary of Columbus's discovery of the Americas. The date holds great emotional significance for Spanish-speaking Americans, and activists hope it will lure diverse Hispanics—from cosmopolitan Miami and inner-city barrios to the planting fields of California—under a single political and cultural umbrella.

But the forces that made the "decade of the Hispanics" a nonevent continue to vex the Latino community. The first problem is one of definition. The term Hispanic is an imposed label, and remains more convenient than precise: it includes Mexicans, Cubans, Puerto Ricans and others (see Box 51) who, apart from speaking Spanish, often have little in common. And the black-white dichotomy that characterizes American thinking on minorities leaves little room for Latino concerns.

Though Latinos have had a continuous presence in this country for centuries, they have been slow to gain recognition. "Hispanic" appeared as a census term only in 1980. Relative to their numbers, they remain seriously underrepresented—there are no Hispanic senators and only 10 congressmen.

Box 51

Diverse and Growing

While some Hispanics trace their roots to Spain, most have some combination of Spanish, African, and Native American ancestry. Their cultures vary accordingly. According to 1990 census figures, about 60 percent (13 million) are Mexican-Americans, commonly called *Chicanos*. Puerto Ricans are next in population size (3 million), followed by Cuban Americans (1 million). Many other societies of Latin America are also represented (5 million). Because of a high birth rate and continuing immigration, the Hispanic population is currently increasing by almost a million a year. If this trend continues, Hispanics may outnumber African Americans in the United States early in the next century.

SOURCE: John Macionis, *Society*, 2nd Ed. (Englewood Cliffs, NJ, 1994), p. 224.

A 1989 study by the Southwest Voter Registration Education Project found that Latinos vote less, attend fewer political rallies and make fewer campaign contributions than other Americans. One reason is the extreme youth of the population. Young people generally are relatively uninvolved politically; with a median age of 25, many Hispanics are also simply too young to vote. And unlike blacks, whose churches and organizations provided an institutional base for the fight against segregation, Hispanics have lacked a political superstructure and a common enemy.

The few attempts at putting together a national platform have proved ineffective. In 1987, political and corporate leaders headed by Henry Cisneros, then the mayor of San Antonio, Texas, presented the presidential candidates with a National Hispanic Agenda. Although the document drew attention to concerns about employment, education and housing, the group proved somewhat ineffectual on account of bickering between Mexican-Americans and Puerto Ricans. Because Mexicans represent more than 60 percent of the Hispanic population, committee members felt they should have greater control over the document. In general, the nation's various Hispanic groups have complained about having to compete for attention and scarce government and philanthropic funds.

To be sure, Latinos have made some impressive strides on the local level: they have won elections in many predominantly Spanish-speaking areas and were crucial to the victory of Harold Washington in Chicago and, more recently, David Dinkins in New York. But there hasn't yet been a breakthrough, national leader. Latino political aspirations suffered a serious setback in the fall of 1988, when Cisneros announced he wouldn't seek re-election, then confessed to an extramarital affair with a political fund raiser (he is still married and living with his wife). Cisneros, 42, once touted as a Democratic vice presidential candidate in 1984, had been the ethnic group's great hope. As it happened, polls a month after the scandal showed only a slight drop in his popularity and he remains, says Hispanic Rep. Bill Richardson, "our most logical leader." But his temporary fall from grace was unsettling. "There is no savior that will lead the Latino community to some political, economic and social promised land," says Segundo Mercad-Llorens, a labor official in Washington. "It depends upon a community of leaders who work together."

Latino Talent

From New York to California, a new generation of Latino talent has emerged (Box 52). Meanwhile, local leaders have set their sights close to home. "Hispanics are going to galvanize around a set of issues more than race," says Daniel Solis, head of Chicago's United Neighborhood Organization (UNO). "And because we're made up of different nationalities and different opinions, we're being forced to do it the hard way—at the grass-roots level, with local institutions." Hispanics are being elected in growing numbers to city councils and school boards—or, as one activist put it, the "front line of democracy."

Last year's school fight in Chicago, which is more than 20 percent Hispanic, illustrates the new grass-roots strategy. Angry over the city's appalling public education, busloads of Hispanics descended on the state capitol with a reform plan centered on greater parental control. They proceeded to win nearly 25 percent of the seats on newly created parent councils. Partly as a result of their efforts, some 50 principals lost their jobs. In a key legal victory, the Texas Supreme Court last year ordered a more equitable distribution of school funding—a decision that will be an automatic boost to Hispanics.

Latino leaders are now vesting their hopes for the future in the 1990 census. A vast increase in the population should bring Hispanics new funds and additional political representation. Because the 1980 census resulted in a large undercount of Hispanics—perhaps 10 percent—a number of activists have formed a program called Hágase Contar (Make Yourself Count) to ensure a more accurate picture. They have their work cut out for them. Spanish speakers have to call to request a form in their native tongue. That alone could discourage Hispanics from participating in the count.

Box 52

Looking Ahead: Hispanics on the Move

The Hispanic community has yet to rally around a single national figure as blacks have done with Jesse Jackson. But a growing number of politicians—many in their 30s and 40s—have won power and prestige at the local level, and some could be candidates for a larger leadership role. A look at who's poised to climb the political ladder in the 1990s:

Lena Guerrero: Named as one of the state's 10 best legislators by Texas Monthly, Guerrero, 32, is political director for Democratic gubernatorial candidate Ann Richards. She will run unopposed in November for her fourth term in the Texas House of Representatives.

Xavier Suarez: A political independent, Suarez, 40, became the first Cuban-American mayor of Miami in 1985. He has steered the city through the tumult of riots, drug wars and waves of refugees.

Fernando Ferrer: Since taking office in 1987, the Bronx borough president's modest successes have lent optimism to a community riven by poverty and political scandal. Some predict Ferrer, 39, a Democrat, could become New York City's first Hispanic mayor.

Ileana Ros-Lehtinen: In a special election marked by an overwhelming Hispanic turnout, Miami's Ros-Lehtinen, 37, a Republican, last year became the first Cuban-American—and the first Hispanic woman—to be elected to Congress.

Nelson Merced: The first Hispanic elected to the Massachusetts state Legislature, Merced, 41, is a Democratic coalition builder who appeals to blacks and progressive whites in a district where Hispanics comprise only 20 percent of all voters.

José Serrano: The newly elected Bronx Democratic congressman is a champion of inner-city educational reform. A telegenic orator, Serrano, 46, faces hard work in his district, the nation's poorest.

Federico Peña: Peña, 43, a Democrat, broke the Anglo stranglehold on Denver politics by becoming mayor in 1983—even though Denver is only 20 percent Hispanic.

Gloria Molina: The first Latina on L.A.'s City Council, Molina, 41, is an uncompromising crusader and a polished speaker. A Democrat, Molina is touted by some as the next mayor of Los Angeles.

SOURCE: Appearing with the above-cited article in *Newsweek*, April 9, 1990.

Up for Grabs

Time and numbers may be on the side of Latinos as they sail toward the 1992 anniversary. Voter registration climbed 21 percent from 1984 to 1988. At the same time, voter turnout has dropped slightly. Hispanic organizers attribute the decline to the difficulty of keeping up with a 25 percent increase in the voting-age population, though political consultants wonder whether they simply can't get out the vote. In the coming decade, some 5 million Hispanics will become eligible for citizenship, thanks in part to the amnesty program that granted legal residency to undocumented immigrants who had lived in the United States for five years. Both the Democrats and the GOP have strengthened their outreach programs to win Hispanic votes, which are viewed as being up for grabs.

But Hispanic leaders have failed to galvanize their armies before. The '90s will be a make-or-break test of their political maturity. "We either get this nation's attention," says Elaine Coronado, Quincentennial Commission director, "or we continue being perceived as a second-rate minority group." Says Cisneros: "We don't want to ever look at a decade again and say, 'Where did it go?'"

Questions

1. How many Latinos are there in the United States? Are they increasing or decreasing?
2. What specific groups make up the Latino population?
3. Why didn't Latinos translate their large numbers into political clout in the 1980s?
4. Will they be able to do so in the 1990s?
5. Does the extreme "youth" of the Latino population have a political effect?
6. What is a political "grass roots strategy?" Will it be useful for Latinos?
7. Why do Latinos do better at the local political level than at the state or federal political level?
8. What is Henry Cisneros' current political position?
9. Have any other Latino politicians come to public attention besides those mentioned in Box 52?

Chapter Twenty-Two

'Return' of Native Americans Challenges Racial Definition

Carolyn Lochhead

Returns from the 1990 census reveal that several hundred thousand Americans reidentified themselves as American Indian after the 1980 count, apparently having changed their racial identification from white or other races to Indian when they filled out their census forms.

A continuing surge of pride in American Indian ancestry among those who previously disavowed it surely accounts for a large portion of the identity switch. As many as 10 million Americans, or one in 25, can claim at least some Indian ancestry. With social attitudes changing, many have begun to assert their lineage. Following a long history of anti-Indian discrimination, Indian culture has gained acceptance and even admiration among the public.

"It's OK to be Indian today," says A. Gay Kingman, executive director of the National Congress of American Indians.

Another factor may be at work too, however, As members of a minority group, American Indians are eligible for special benefits under affirmative action programs.

Given this fact, the census results highlight a troublesome social combination: The spread of racial preferences and the growing incidence of marriage across racial lines together make a person's racial classification economically more difficult to determine.

From *Insight Magazine*, April 22, 1991, pp. 20–22. Copyright © 1991 by Insight and Carolyn Lochhead.

"Race is a socially constructed category," says Matthew Snipp, a rural sociologist at the University of Wisconsin. As intermarriage erodes the once-strict boundaries between races, and as people cross those boundaries more freely, racial definitions become fuzzier. "One of the things that we're beginning to see," Snipp observes, "is that when you go over racial lines, then the whole idea of what race means becomes more and more problematic, in the sense that we don't know what our race is, or what racial groups are, or how you define membership in one or another."

Is someone who is one-sixteenth Asian, for example, Asian enough for affirmative action purposes? Is an Argentine less Hispanic than a Mexican? Such classification disputes have begun cropping up across the nation with increasing frequency. The question is particularly open-ended among those of American Indian descent, because historically, intermarriage between those of European and Indian descent has been commonplace.

This switch in self-identification to American Indian continues a three-decade census trend that began in the 1960s and apparently crested in the 1970s, but proceeded with considerable impetus in the past decade. Since 1960, it has led to a tripling of the American Indian population, to some 1.8 million.

Even accounting for high American Indian birthrates, natural population growth alone cannot explain the increase. The phenomenon is "demographically impossible," according to Jeffrey Passel, a demographer at the Urban Institute, a Washington think tank.

"The only thing we know pretty much for sure is that you can't start with previous censuses, add births and subtract deaths, and get to the next census," says David Word, a statistician and demographer with the Census Bureau. The 1990 census for American Indians is about 10 percent higher than would be expected from natural population increases, Passel estimates; the 1980 count was 35 percent higher.

Moreover, the biggest increases in the American Indian population are showing up in such odd places as New Jersey and Alabama, states that have no large tribal groups, tribal lands or reservations. By contrast, in the so-called Indian states of the West such as Arizona, Wyoming, Oklahoma or South Dakota, where some two-thirds of American Indians live, the population increases come in closer to expectations (see Box 53).

"One of the interesting things about this," Passel says, "is that it's not happening by and large in the states that we think of as having a lot of Indians."

The population figures are far too high to be attributed to improved census counts. Nor can immigration, which is swelling the tally of Asians and Hispanics, be an important factor among the indigenous Indian peoples. The only explanation demographers can point to is a voluntary change in self-identification.

Box 53

Another Decade of Pride

Increase in residents identifying themselves as American Indian, Aleut or Eskimo
from the 1980 census to the 1990 census

Alabama	117.7 %	Kentucky	59.8%	North Carolina	24.0 %
Arizona	33.2	Louisiana	53.7	North Dakota	28.6
Arkansas	35.5	Maryland	61.7	Ohio	66.3
California	20.3	Michigan	38.9	Oklahoma	49.0
Connecticut	46.8	Minnesota	42.5	Oregon	40.9
Delaware	52.0	Mississippi	37,9	Pennsylvania	55.7
District of Columbia	42.2	Missouri	61.0	Rhode Island	40.5
Georgia	75.3	Montana	27.9	South Dakota	12.5
Hawaii	84.2	Nebraska	35.0	Texas	64.4
Illinois	34.1	Nevada	47.6	Vermont	72.4
Indiana	62.3	New Hampshire	57.8	Virginia	61.6
Iowa	34.7	New Jersey	78.3	Wisconsin	33.5
Kansas	42.9	New York	58.3	Wyoming	33.6

SOURCE: U.S. Census Bureau; data on 12 remaining states not available.

The Census Bureau has no regulations governing how one should answer the race or ancestry questions. "The census doesn't make you prove that you're a member of a tribe or anything," says Wayne L. Ducheneaux, a Cheyenne River Sioux and president of the National Congress of American Indians. "It just asks you if you're Indian, and if you say yes, you're counted as one."

People may answer the census questions however they choose, and apparently, says Passel, "people are now considerably more willing to identify their race as American Indian than they used to be."

Demographers can only speculate as to why this should be, lacking any concrete evidence of people's motives.

It would be fair to assume, says Passel, that census counts reflect some spillover from affirmative action programs. "You can attribute this in part to the fact that people perceive there may be some benefits to them of their Indian ancestry," he says. "Whether there are or not is a different question, but the fact that they perceive that there might be some is what's important."

To be sure, individual responses to census questions are confidential; the answers cannot make anyone eligible for any affirmative action benefits. "Checking yourself off as American Indian on the census form buys you absolutely nothing," Snipp says. However, given that the census form is an official government document, there may be a perception, however erroneous, that how one answers the census has a bearing on one's racial classification for employment or other purposes.

Pride in Indian ancestry is also a major factor, Passel and other demographers believe. The 1960s civil rights movement kindled greater respect for nonwhite races. Before that time, American Indian culture was widely disdained. Such brutal episodes as the forced removal of the Cherokee from the Southeast to Oklahoma in 1838 and 1839 color much of early American history.

From the late 19th century until the 1960s, Snipp notes, the U.S. government believed Indians should be assimilated into the wider culture. "The federal government in particular implemented a number of fairly repressive policies designed basically to stamp out Indian culture," he says. These included a Court of Indian Offenses, administered by the Bureau of Indian Affairs, that existed until 1935. Its purpose, Snipp says, was to prosecute Indians who practiced traditional tribal culture, who wore traditional dress, lived in traditional homes or practiced traditional religion. Schools were also used as tools of forced assimilation and indoctrination.

As late as the 1950s, Congress legally "terminated" several tribes by taking them off the government's list of recognized tribes. As a result, the terminated tribes lost their sovereignty rights and other legal protections. Among those tribes were several California Indian rancherias, or communities, the Catawba of South Carolina and the mixed-blood Ute of Utah. Although most of them have since been restored to the government list, some remain unrecognized. The Ponca tribe of Nebraska was restored to the government list only last October. The federal government now recognizes 507 tribes.

In fact, says Ducheneaux, "We're in one of the cycles again where it's kind of fashionable to be an Indian. Characterizations of Indian culture in television and film have swung from disparaging to admiring, as a comparison between 1950s westerns and the recent film "Dances with Wolves" clearly illustrates.

In light of the general—not to say complete—shift in public attitudes, it is hardly surprising that more Americans would declare Indian lineage.

Reidentification can also work in reverse, say census analysts. For example, if the 1940 census had been taken in 1942, fewer people probably would have listed their ancestry as German.

The census patterns themselves indicate a rise in a kind of romantic fascination with American Indian ancestry among those who never claimed it before, notes Passel. The largest shifts in self-identification are showing up mainly in Eastern states, which account for just one-third of the Indian population. The 1990 counts there came in 30 percent above estimates based on birth and death rates, Passel says.

By contrast, in the states that account for two-thirds of the Indian population, the census count came in only 3 percent above expectations. Analysts believe that in the West even people who claim some Indian ancestry generally consider American Indians to be those who are enrolled members of a tribe.

Tribal requirements for membership are far more strict than the simple self-designation asked on the census form. Each tribe determines its membership criteria, much as nations set their own requirements for citizenship. Many tribes require some fixed percentage—one-half or one-sixteenth, for example—of Indian ancestry.

The certification process is often quite formal. The Cherokee Nation of Oklahoma, for example, requires that individuals trace and legally document their lineage back to the "final enrollment" of 43,000 Cherokee that took place from 1899 to 1906, says tribal registrar R. Lee Fleming.

Some federal benefits, including social services, welfare and health care, are directed specifically to American Indians, but people who receive tribal benefits must be enrolled members of a federally recognized tribe.

Moreover, beneficiaries must also live on or near a reservation, says Steve Gleason, assistant to the assistant secretary for Indian affairs. While the Bureau of Indian Affairs receives a few calls each week from people claiming to be Indian and asking where they can sign up for benefits, Gleason says there has been no unusual increase in such requests.

Eligibility for affirmative action, however, is determined by individuals' self-identification, and such benefits are much more widespread and valuable. A shift in self-identification, at least as reflected in the census, would be far more likely to appear among those of American Indian descent than those of African or Hispanic ancestry, most of whom are already identifying themselves as such. A large pool of people can claim American Indian ancestry but do not identify themselves racially as such; many of these can switch their racial identification if they decide to do so for whatever reason.

The census questionnaire itself reflects a greater social sensitivity to racial identification. The 1960 census, for example, had one race question with seven categories. In 1970, the race question expanded to a dozen categories, and a trial question on Hispanic origin was added.

By 1980, the race question had expanded to 14 categories. The question on Hispanic origin was extended to the entire census, and a new question on ancestry was added, with space allowed for open-ended responses.

"There's clearly a recognition in the census that this data is important," Passel says, "and the census usually doesn't lead in this regard. The census content follows."

As the use of racial preferences spreads, the definition of race becomes increasingly important to an individual's economic status; at the same time, intermarriage makes such definitions hazier. Reports of racial impostors are becoming more common, as are disputes over who exactly is entitled to preferences on the basis of ancestry. In San Francisco, a Hispanic fire fighter is even calling for a review board to determine racial eligibility.

These trends follow a typical pattern that has emerged in countries using racial preferences—from India, which grants special benefits to the untouchables and other "backward castes," to Malaysia, which favors Malays over Chinese, and South Africa, which discriminates in favor of whites. Walter E. Williams, an economist at George Mason University and author of a book on South African racial policies, argues that racial preferences create incentives to fraud and so beget legal rules delineating racial identity.

"Obviously, if you're going to create goodies by race," Williams says, "then people are going to try to sneak under the wire."

The proposal in San Francisco to set up a racial review board, Williams says, bears an unsettling resemblance to schemes used to defend South African apartheid. Early on in the apartheid regime, he notes, population registry laws were instituted to provide definitions of race. The government had a particular classification problem with so-called coloreds, people of mixed descent. Racial classification boards were also put in place, where individuals could legally challenge the racial classification of another person.

So far, U.S. preferences still rely on self-identification. Eventually, however, "you're going to have to give that up" to maintain the integrity of the system, Williams warns. Because affirmative action policies award jobs, contracts, admission to college and other economic benefits on the basis of race as well as individual competence, they inevitably create strong incentives to claim those benefits among those whose connection to the protected group may be tenuous at best.

The 1990 census results, showing a huge increase in those reidentifying themselves as American Indian, may reflect people responding to these incentives.

Questions

1. How many Native Americans are there in the United States?
2. How long have they been here?
3. Do censuses indicate their number as increasing or decreasing?
4. Can natural population growth account for the current increase?
5. In what sense does the "return" of Native Americans make us see race as both a biological and social category?
6. How does the census determine a person's race? How should it do so?
7. What has past governmental policy been regarding Native Americans?

8. What is present governmental policy?
9. How have Hollywood films depicted Native Americans?
10. Why might racial review boards rather than self-identification be necessary to determine eligibility for government programs such as affirmative action?
11. Is the future of Native Americans positive or negative?

Chapter Twenty-Three

The Future of Gay America

Eloise Salholz with Tony Clifton, Nadine Joseph, Lucille Beachy, Patrick Rogers, Larry Wilson, Daniel Glick and Patricia King

It is a chilly morning in Atlanta and, outside the Centers for Disease Control, the confrontation is just heating up. Mark Weaver, a minister who traveled from Texas, waves his "GAY IS NOT OKAY" placard at the demonstrators massing to protest some of the CDC's AIDS policies. The gauntlet is thrown—and so are some punches. "This man has just assaulted me, Officer, Officer," says Weaver. "Officer, Officer," some of the gay activists croon back in falsetto. "Hey, I talk in tongues too—look," says one, grabbing the nearest man for some explicit kissing. As Weaver and a policeman wearing AIDS-proof gloves approach, the crowd lets up a new chant: "Your gloves don't match your shoes. You'll see it on the news." Derision, outrage, civil disobedience—these are the hallmarks of ACT UP (the AIDS Coalition to Unleash Power), the gay community's shock troops in the war against AIDS.

Every May the Fritsch Rudser family of San Francisco celebrates its own whimsical tradition: the presentation, on Mother's Day, of the Michael Douglas Fritsch Rudser Surrogate Mother's Award. Michael, 6½, picks a woman he wishes to honor—his teacher, say—gives her a rose and a present, and serves brunch with Dad's help. But the holiday Michael, sister Crystal, 3, brother

Raphael, 2, and father Steven Fritsch Rudser observe with greatest fanfare is Gay Freedom Day. Fritsch Rudser, who adopted his children, is gay—one of a growing group of homosexual parents. "After having worked in the trenches in the AIDS crisis, I've become familiar with the end of life," he says. "I wanted contact with the beginning of it."

Since the first diagnosis nearly a decade ago, AIDS has threatened the very life and spirit of gay America. To date, at least 50,500 homosexuals have died; with a minimum of 82,500 already infected with the HIV virus, the death toll will continue to mount for at least another five years. But while black plagues don't have silver linings, AIDS has also galvanized the gay community in ways unimaginable just a few years ago. With the flip of the calendar from the '80s to the '90s, gays have leaped from political exclusion to a place in the corridors of power. And they have channeled their anger over what they regard as the government's inadequate response to the AIDS epidemic into a rebirth of activism. Today, says San Francisco author Randy Shilts, gays "are more interested in protest than in candlelight processions and quilt patches."

The No. 1 item on the political agenda remains AIDS. But gay leaders have also begun fighting for a slate of family rights including social security, medical benefits, inheritance, child custody and even gay marriage. For a growing number of homosexual men and women, such family concerns are a day-to-day reality: a new generation of gay parents has produced the first-ever "gayby boom." The gay community's goal is "integration—just as it was with Martin Luther King," says Harry Britt, president of the Board of Supervisors in San Francisco. "We want the same rights to happiness and success as the nongay."

By some yardsticks, gays are well on their way—not just in the gay meccas of New York and San Francisco but in the very heart of Middle America. Public attitudes toward the nation's estimated 25 million gays and lesbians are more tolerant than at any time since the AIDS epidemic triggered a negative backlash in the early 1980s. Certainly, ACT UP's provocations have offended many mainstream gays—and threatened to jeopardize their acceptance by straight society. But by and large, the devastation AIDS has created has led to greater sympathy in the straight world, and gays' responsible handling of the crisis has led to new respect for the community. According to a Gallup poll taken last fall, 47 percent of all adults believe that homosexual relations between consenting adults should be legal, up from only 33 percent in 1987; 71 percent of the respondents said gays should have equal job opportunities, compared with 59 percent opposed two years before. "The world has been genuinely transformed in two decades. It is not possible to live in the United States today and not be aware of gay people," says Tom Stoddard, executive director of the Lambda Legal Defense and Education Fund, which works for gay rights. "That by itself is a revolution."

Arguable, the most extraordinary development is the gay community's new political clout. There are 50 openly gay elected officials around the country, compared with fewer than half a dozen in 1980. The Human Rights Campaign Fund, a gay lobbying group, was the ninth largest independent PAC during the last presidential election, and 25th on the Federal Election Commission's list of fund raisers. Politicians have come to recognize the implications of the rise of an openly gay middle class—vast numbers of educated, articulate gays who can and do vote. "At the end of the '60s, most gays thought of themselves as outsiders," says John D'Emilio, a history professor at the University of North Carolina, Greensboro. "I don't think that gays then thought they could ever influence that system, or be a power within it."

Box 54

Milestones of a Movement

"Stonewall was our 1789," says gay advocate Tom Stoddard of the scruffy riot outside a Greenwich Village bar that set the quest for gay rights in motion. In the 21 years since then the struggle has moved forward—but over decidedly rocky terrain. A look at the milestones:

1950s: Mattachine Society and Daughters of Bilitis, organizations for homosexual men and women, formed.

1969: Police raid Stonewall Inn, a New York gay bar. Three days of rioting kick off gay-liberation movement.

1970: First gay parades in New York and San Francisco mark the anniversary of the Stonewall riots.

1975: Air Force Sgt. Leonard Matlovich discharged from military for being homosexual; wins case against the Air Force in 1981.

1977: Harvey Milk elected first gay supervisor of San Francisco. He was murdered the next year.

1981: AIDS, still unnamed, first reported in "Morbidity and Mortality Weekly Report." By 1990 at least 50,500 gay men had died of the disease.

1983: Massachusetts Rep. Gerry Studds announces his homosexuality amid a sex scandal, becoming the first openly gay congressman.

1984: San Francisco bathhouses closed during Democratic National Convention; 100,000 march in protest.

1986: U.S. Supreme Court upholds states' rights to outlaw sodomy.

1987: More than 250,000 gays and lesbians march on Washington for civil rights; AIDS quilt unfurled.

1989: ACT UP leads controversial protest against the Catholic Church at New York's St. Patrick's Cathedral.

SOURCE: Appearing with the above-cited article in *Newsweek*, March 12, 1990.

'Second Epidemic'

Yet most gay leaders would agree that there are many battles left—starting with the armed forces. Last week [just prior to the writing of this article] the U.S. Supreme Court refused to consider two constitutional challenges to the military's longstanding prohibition against gays in the service. Sodomy laws remain on the books in 24 states, and only two states—Wisconsin and Massachusetts—have passed measures banning discrimination against gays. And gay-bashing remains a fact of life in this country. "Homophobia is the second epidemic, says Robert Bray, a spokesman at the National Gay and Lesbian Task Force, an advocacy group. The Task Force says that gays are seven times more likely to be crime victims than the average American. Last month [again, prior to the writing of this article] the Senate passed a bill requiring the Justice Department to publish hate-crime statistics according to classifications that will include sexual orientation.

More than any other organization, ACT UP has become the voice of gay rage. The group got its start three years ago when, according to gay lore, activist playwright Larry Kramer happened to be addressing a community group in Greenwich Village. He told half of the gathered crowd to stand up, then screamed: "You could be dead in less than five years! What are you going to do about it?" The answer was ACT UP New York, a group dedicated to broadening the role of government and private industry in the fight against AIDS. Since Kramer's call to arms, offshoots have sprung up in about 40 cities here and abroad, with an estimated 6,000 members. Its accomplishments have been impressive. Members have sat on advisory panels at the Food and Drug Administration and played an important role in speeding the approval of experimental antiviral drugs, including DDI. When Burroughs Wellcome lowered the price of AZT from $8,000 to $6,400 last year, ACT UP received a measure of the credit. After months of internal debate, some chapters have lent troops to other causes, such as the repeal of sodomy laws, and even to the pro-choice movement in the abortion battle.

Drawing on a mix of guerrilla theater, passive resistance and state-of-the-art media manipulation, ACT UP uses tactics that shock—and often offend—many Americans. The group has halted trading on the floor of the New York Stock Exchange to protest drug pricing by pharmaceutical companies, staged traffic jams from Boston to San Francisco, even necked in Jesse Helms's Capital Hill office. At St. Patrick's Cathedral in New York shortly before Christmas, one member crumbled a communion wafer—a desecration of what Roman Catholics believe to be the body of Christ. "It is ACT UP's job to be disruptive and it is the job of other AIDS groups to pick up the pieces," says Greg Taylor, 23, a San Francisco member.

Officially, most mainstream gay leaders say that ACT UP's firebrand politics serve the cause well. "My view is that you need to use all the tactics available, even when you know that some of the things you do will antagonize and even repel potential supporters," says Urvashi Vaid, executive director of the Washington-based Task Force. But despite a certain reluctance to criticize another gay group, some prominent gays worry that ACT UP has created new tensions within the movement. They have questioned whether the more obnoxious actions—particularly the one at St. Patrick's—are counterproductive. Shilts, who wrote "And the Band Played On," a book critical of the establishment's response to the AIDS crisis, suggests ACT UP is at its best as an outlet for rage. But "the goals of political action are different from the goals of psychotherapy," he says. "We don't have time for ineffective tactics."

Perhaps the most controversial statement a member of the gay community can make is that it's time to move beyond AIDS. Longtime activist and author Darrell Yates Rist has argued that gays have become so obsessed with the disease that they have neglected other matters of vital importance for the community. The increase in anti-gay violence, the perpetuation of sodomy laws and civil-rights abuses, says Rist, "are going to destroy more lives than AIDS will ever destroy." Because epidemic-related cases could consume all its resources, Lambda long ago made the decision to split its docket 50-50 between AIDS and sexual-orientation cases.

How to Live

The tensions over tactics reflect a larger schism within the gay community today between the separatists and the assimilationists. Gay leaders all agree that "coming out" is the most important political and personal act anyone can make. Beyond that, however, there is widespread disagreement over how best to live outside the closet. Should gays pursue their own countercultural lifestyle in such urban ghettos as San Francisco's Castro district, or assimilate into the dominant straight culture? Should they continue—within the bounds of safe sex—to have multiple partners or emulate heterosexual monogamy? A certain amount of conflict is inevitable, suggests Martin Bauml Duberman, Paul Robeson's biographer and a history professor at Lehman College in New York. "You have to minimize your differentness from the mainstream in order to win acceptance," says Duberman. "But in fact the whole value of the subculture is in its differentness."

The debate reached a high pitch last summer, when two gay authors from Boston declared "the gay revolution has failed." In "After the Ball; How America Will Conquer Its Fear & Hatred of Gays in the 90s," Marshall Kirk and Hunter Madsen argued that certain extreme forms of homosexual behavior—for example, promiscuity or public sex—alienate straights and ultimately harm gays. Madsen, an advertising executive, and Kirk have suggested

Box 55

The Younger Generation Says Yes to Sex

For some gays, the slogan for the '90's is Just Say Yes. In New York City, 5,000 condoms rained down on guests at a "lust party" in a nightclub. Other clubs show gay-porn videos and hire go-go boys, dressed in skivvies and combat boots, to dance on bar tops. One gay group plastered posters of nude men on the San Francisco Federal Building last summer and an activist peppered the Yale University campus with similar artwork last fall. For nearly a decade AIDS has suppressed the collective libido of gay men. Now an avant-garde movement— partly political, party just trendy—has sprung up in New York and San Francisco, encouraging gays to practice safe sex but also to cultivate and celebrate their sexuality.

AIDS has struck hardest at a generation of gay baby boomers, now in their 30s and 40s. Watching friends and lovers die, survivors lost interest in the night life and sexual freedom that defined the disco and bathhouse hedonism of the '70s. For many, monogamy and celibacy became a way of life. "The only social activity was going to funerals," says Dave Ford, a gay journalist in San Francisco. Now a generation gap has emerged: many younger gays do not identify sex with death and believe sexual expression is a right worth fighting for, even though they may risk losing some of the public sympathy engendered by the AIDS crisis.

The pro-sex campaign doubles as a protest movement. During the controversy over the federally funded exhibit of Robert Maplethorpe's "homoerotic" photographs in Washington last summer, Sen. Jesse Helms proposed legislation prohibiting further funding for what he called "obscene" art. As a protest against Helms, a group of San Francisco artists called Boy with Arms Akimbo decorated the Federal building. William Dobbs, a New York lawyer and a founder of the protest group Art Positive, was arrested on misdemeanor charges for the Yale protest. Art Positive, says Dobbs, "stands for militant eroticism. We'll put our images and our culture out there for everyone to see."

Young lesbians also are part of the new sexual revolution. In the '70s, gay women, who in large numbers were feminists, tended to pair off, settle down and stay at home. To most of that generation of women, pornography was an absolute taboo, but now lesbians even have explicit erotica magazines. "Historically, radical feminism portrayed pornography as exploitative," says Laura Thomas, 23, of San Francisco. "Now we're saying it can be beautiful." Young lesbians are shattering other gay shibboleths. Many mix with gay men in the same clubs, and wear makeup and more feminine clothes. In New York, gay women on the fashionable cutting edge call themselves "lipstick lesbians" or "girlie girls," and wear clothes that both mock and salute the stereotypical past—motorcycle jackets and Hermès scarfs, garter belts and baseball caps.

As the pro-sex movement heats up, some alarming trends are emerging.

Recreational drugs play a large part in the movement. In New York, Ecstasy is in vogue; in San Francisco, the drug of choice is speed. "The fatal flaw of the sex-positive message is that some gay men are not engaging in safe sex," says Michael Shriver, 26, who works at a gay substance-abuse clinic in San Francisco. "Many of them are so stoned or drunk that their judgment is shot." With any luck that number will remain in the minority. In a decade of grim news, one of the few hopeful notes is that the rate of AIDS infection among gay men has been dropping since 1987—an encouraging sign that safe sex works.

SOURCE: James N. Baker with Nadine Joseph and Patrick Rogers. Appearing with the above-cited article in *Newsweek*, March 12, 1990.

that gays should mount publicity campaigns designed to allay straight fears—say, buying up ad space for pictures of great figures like Alexander the Great that ask: "Did you know he was gay?" Their critics have called them self-hating gays who have sold out their people to get along with society at large.

The ultimate act of assimilation would be marriage, a right some gays have placed on their future agenda. The impetus comes partly from AIDS, which revealed the degree to which gays did not have the rights straights take for granted. The partners of gay men who died intestate found they had no claims on property that would have gone to a spouse; others found themselves evicted from apartments because they weren't on the lease. "Gay men suddenly realized they needed the support systems which the state and society give as a right to heterosexual families," says Roberta Achtenberg, a lesbian activist and attorney in San Francisco. Seven U.S. cities, Los Angeles and Seattle among them, now have "domestic partnership" laws that grant gays a variety of spousal rights including insurance benefits, bereavement leaves and credit agreements.

Given the objections of church and state, legal marriage remains unlikely for the foreseeable future. In the meantime, gays themselves are divided over whether marriage hetero style is even desirable. Many in the community oppose quasi-straight unions, on the ground that they are too imitative and not uniquely gay. But Frank Kameny, a veteran gay activist, sees no reason why homosexuals can't have the whole package: "I've never heard a rational explanation for the prejudice against them—after all, marriage licenses aren't rationed, so we wouldn't be taking them from someone else." In *The New Republic* last year, Andrew Sullivan argued that marriage was not only good for gays but for society at large, because it would promote sexual and economic stability.

Parents' Concerns

While theorists debate the merits of marriage between gays, many are already living the settled-down life of their "breeder" peers. That includes children—either through adoption, artificial insemination or arrangements between lesbians and gay "uncles." There are an estimated 3 million to 5 million lesbian and gay parents who have had children in the context of a heterosexual relationship. But in the San Francisco area alone, at least, 1,000 children have been born to gay or lesbian couples in the last five years. A number of organizations have sprung up to meet their social needs. San Francisco boasts the Lesbian and Gay Parenting Group, storytelling hours for tots at gay bookstores and Congregation Sha'ar Zahav, a largely gay synagogue with a Hebrew School for member's children.

According to the parents, the concerns of gay families are both unique and quite routine. Tom White and his lover Dmitri (who didn't want his last name used) have a house in the suburbs, three dogs and a 4-year-old adopted son, Elliott. The men had arranged for the adoption when Elliott's mother was still pregnant. Present in the delivery room, Dmitri cut the umbilical cord, while White became the first person to hold the baby after his birth mother. Elliott calls White "Daddy" and Dmitri "Poppa." Dmitri, a coordinator for deaf-student services at San Francisco State University, has since cut his work schedule in half; "I'm on the mommy track," he says. Instead of going to parties, the two men organize picnics. While many American parents try to limit the time their kids spend in front of the tube, White says "we make sure Elliott watches enough TV so he can relate to the world."

While acceptance of such families has grown, the arrangement can lead to some difficult moments. When the teacher of 6-year-old Jacob Rios asked him who the man in the front of the classroom was, he answered, "That's my dad's husband." John Rios, 30, and Don Harrelson, 42, were united by a minister before moving in together two years ago. Harrelson, a trade-show organizer who became one of the nation's first openly gay adoptive fathers 13 years ago, had already raised two boys. Now he is helping bring up Rios's two kids from a heterosexual marriage, Jacob and Jennifer, 9.

Role Models

Psychologists have investigated the impact of gay parents on children with somewhat surprising results. In a 1980 Massachusetts custody case, a judge allowed testimony showing that all 35 studies on homosexual parents from the previous 15 years found no adverse effect on the kids. A study by Dr. Richard Green of the Long Island Research Institute found that the daughters of lesbians

---

Box 56

Lesbians: Portrait of a Community

In the past decade gay America has been preoccupied with the devastating effect of AIDS on male homosexuals. But now that the gay-rights movement is beginning to focus on couples' rights and family issues, more lesbians are moving to center stage: gay women have traditionally been more likely than men to settle down with one partner, and an estimated one third of lesbians are mothers, either from heterosexual relationships or by artificial insemination. These developments are just as critical to homosexuals in Middle America as they are to those in the gay meccas on both coasts. Columbus, Ohio, a large university town and the capital of one of the nation's most populous states, has a thriving gay community. In Columbus, lesbians have taken on key gay-rights roles as community leaders, career women and mothers.

Many Columbus lesbians work relentlessly to advance the gay-rights cause. The city's homosexuals are the largest per capita contributors to the Human Rights Campaign Fund in Washington, a gay and lesbian lobbying group. Just this past year a lesbian activist spearheaded Waging Peace, a multimedia public-relations campaign that stresses the positive contributions of the gay community. "We just want to be looked upon as ordinary citizens," a campaign spokesperson says.

One woman has been a key figure in the movement for many years: Rhonda Rivera, 52, a law professor at Ohio State University. Head of the Ohio Human Rights Bar Association, Rivera does pro bono work for people with AIDS and tries to draw attention to other problems that affect gays such as alcoholism, rape and physical abuse. For her human-rights advocacy, Rivera has received a number of awards from the general community, including a YWCA Women of Achievement Award.

Though lesbians are at a low risk for AIDS, the disease mobilized many of them into activism. Lynn Greer was a pro golfer living in Ft. Myers, Fla., when her brother, Mike, 29, was diagnosed with AIDS. On New Year's Day 1986, doctors in Florida gave Mike two weeks to live at most. He phoned his father, who was in Aspen, to take him home. "He wanted to die in Columbus," says Lynn. "Dad said, 'You can handle it. I'll see you in a week when I'm finished skiing.'" Greer, who moved to Columbus, has not spoken to her father since Mike died. She lobbies for AIDS legislation at the statehouse and is working with her national sorority on an AIDS education program for colleges.

Some women in Columbus avoid the front lines, choosing to live open but quiet family lives. After several failed attempts at artificial insemination, Linda Cahoon, 32, conceived a baby with a male co-worker, who legally forfeited paternal rights. Now Joel, 3, is being raised by Cahoon and her lover of 10 years, Cathy Carlisle, 31, in a middle-class suburb of Columbus, where they have found some acceptance among their neighbors. Carlisle works at a computer-software company. Cahoon, who has custody of a 14-year-old daughter from an earlier marriage, stays home. Despite their own experience, they hope Joel will be straight. "Because it's easier, but if he's not, that's fine," says Carlisle. "But we would like to have grandkids."

Losing customers: Homophobia also exists in Columbus, The city has had its share of violence against gays, but sometimes hostility takes other forms. Brenda Duncan and Alice Wing opened the Grapevine Cafe two years ago, attracting both straight and gay customers at first. Now the gay crowd mostly takes over at night. When straight customers find out the clientele is largely gay, some of them leave, explaining that they don't want to be mistaken for homosexuals. That the cafe exists unharassed shows how far gay America has come. But the reason that some straight customers give for staying away proves just how much further it has to go.

SOURCE: James N. Baker with Shawn D. Lewis. Appearing with the above-cited article in *Newsweek,* March 12, 1990.

tended to have strong female identities, while the boys like to hang out with the guys and play sports. But one prominent child psychiatrist questions whether the existing literature is indeed conclusive. "When one studies the children of such couples, you have to look at the totality of their development, especially as they enter adolescence," says Dr. Eleanor Galenson, a clinical professor of psychiatry at Mt. Sinai School of Medicine. Until more work is done, "we will not really know whether these children are faring well in their development, sexual and otherwise."

For gays coming of age in 1990, America is both infinitely scarier and immeasurably safer than it was for the Stonewall generation. Frightening because AIDS will continue to cut a deadly swath through the community. More hospitable because of the legal and social milestones that have made homosexuality acceptable in may corners of straight America. "In the past, before Stonewall, it was a matter of surviving in almost underground conditions, like the French Resistance in the second world war," says Adrienne Smith, president of the gay and lesbian division of the American Psychological Association. "Now the cry is, 'We demand equal rights in all areas'." As the decade progresses, gays will continue testing the limits of this country's tolerance. They have a long way to go: homophobia remains a serious problem, and even some Americans who oppose discrimination may have trouble accepting gay lifestyles. But as the rebirth of activism proves, gays won't let up in their quest for a more visible—and influential—place in American society.

Questions

1. How many gays are there in the United States? How do we know?
2. How many gays are there in the world? Are the numbers increasing or decreasing?
3. How do people acquire their sexual orientation? Is it biological or socially learned?
4. What is ACT UP? Will it win friends or make enemies for gays?
5. What is public sentiment toward gays? Is it more tolerant or less tolerant than in the past? Will a separatist or assimilationist approach hasten public acceptance?
6. Does the conception of AIDS as a gay disease affect the limits of tolerance?
7. Is gay political clout increasing or decreasing? What is the gay political agenda?
8. What are the pros and cons of gays in the military? What are current laws regarding this?
9. Is there a generation gap between younger and older gays? Give examples.
10. What are domestic partnership laws? Are they good or bad? Are legal gay marriages likely in the future?
11. What is safe sex? Does it work?
12. How common is lesbianism compared with male homosexuality? Describe similarities and differences between the two groups.
13. Should gays be allowed to adopt children? How might child rearing differ in heterosexual and homosexual households?
14. What are sodomy laws? Should they be taken off the books?
15. The last milestone in Box 54 occurred in 1989. Have there been any milestones since then?
16. Is the future of gay America positive or negative?

Chapter Twenty-Four

Whites' Myths About Blacks

Jeannye Thornton and David Whitman with Dorian Freidman

After the riots last spring [1992], the *Los Angeles Times* asked city residents a simple, open-ended question. What did Angelenos think was "the most important action that must be taken" to begin a citywide healing process? Poll results from nearly 900 residents showed that the two most *unpopular* antidotes were the standard solutions favored by liberals or conservatives: "more government financial aid" and a "crackdown on gangs, drugs and lawlessness." Slightly more in favor were the human-capital remedies of the economists to "improve education" and "improve the economy." But the No. 1 solution was the psychologists' remedy. What the city most needed, residents concluded, was to "renew efforts among groups to communicate [with] and understand each other."

That prescription sounds squishy, yet in all the post-riot analysis there may have been too much talk about the ostensibly "tangible" roots of the riots (such as cutbacks in urban aid or weak job markets) and too little discussion of racial misunderstanding and ethnic stereotyping. In 1964, Martin Luther King, Jr. warned that "we must learn to live together as brothers or perish together as fools," and the famed 1968 Kerner Commission report emphasized that narrowing racial inequalities would require "new attitudes, new understanding and, above all, new will." In the intervening years, however, those new attitudes

From *U.S. News & World Report*, November 9, 1992, pp. 41, 43–44. © 1992 by U.S. News & World Report. Reprinted by permission.

and understanding have been all too lacking. And continuing strife in cities may only further stoke racial prejudice and hostilities.

Changing Times

At first glance, recent trends in white attitudes toward blacks are deceptively upbeat. Fifty years ago, a *majority* of white Americans supported segregation and discrimination against blacks; just 25 years ago, 71 percent of whites felt blacks were moving too fast in their drive for equality. Today, by contrast, overwhelming majorities of whites support the principle of equal treatment for the races in schools, jobs, housing and other public spheres. Moreover, several national surveys taken after the riots contain encouraging signs of interracial accord. Most whites and blacks agree the Rodney King verdict and the violence that followed it were both unjust. The same polls show little evidence the riots initially made whites less sympathetic to the plight of poor blacks. For instance, both whites and blacks agree by large margins that jobs and training are more effective ways to prevent future unrest than strengthening police forces.

Yet much of the black-white convergence may be misleading for two reasons. For starters, blacks are still far more likely than whites to identify race discrimination as a pervasive problem in American society, especially when it comes to police and the criminal-justice system. At the same time, it seems probable that the riots at best only temporarily shifted whites' views of blacks. Annual polls taken by the National Opinion Research Center have found consistently since 1973 that most whites believe the government spends enough or too much to improve the condition of blacks (65 percent of whites thought so in 1991). Yet a *New York Times*/CBS survey taken *after* the riots found that a hefty majority of the American public (61 percent) now believes that the government spends too little to improve the condition of blacks.

In all likelihood, white prejudices are now evolving a bit like a virus. While the most virulent forms have been largely stamped out, new and more resistant strains continue to emerge. In the old racist formula, the innate "inferiority" of blacks accounted for their plight; in the modern-day cultural version, a lack of ambition and laziness do. Some modern-day stereotypes are simply false: others contain a kernel of truth but are vastly overblown. Regrettably, a large group of whites continues to harbor core myths about blacks based almost solely on their impressions of the most disadvantaged. Some examples:

The Work Ethic

The white myth: Blacks lack motivation. A 1990 NORC poll found that 62 percent of whites rated blacks as lazier than whites, and 78 percent thought them more likely to prefer welfare to being self-supporting.

Fact: For most of this century, blacks were actually *more* likely to work than whites, A greater percentage of black men than white men were in the work force from 1890 until after World War II, and black women outpaced white women until mid-1990. As late as 1970, black males ages 20 to 24 had higher labor-force participation rates than their white counterparts.

Today, the labor-force participation of the races is closer. After a 25-year influx of white women into the job market, white and black women participate in the labor force at nearly identical rates. Black men are slightly less likely than white men to be in the work force—69.5 percent vs. 76.4 percent. The only large gap between the two races occurs among teenagers: Last year, 55.8 percent of white teens were in the labor force, compared with 35.4 percent of black teens.

Blacks, who make up 12 percent of the population, are disproportionately represented on the welfare rolls; 40 percent of recipients of Aid to Families with Dependent Children are black, while 55 percent are white or Hispanic. However, numerous surveys have failed to find any evidence that most blacks prefer welfare to work.

In 1987, under the supervision of University of Chicago sociologist William Julius Wilson, the NORC surveyed 2,490 residents of Chicago's inner-city poverty tracts, including 1,200 blacks, 500 Puerto Ricans and 400 Mexicans. Roughly 80 percent of black parents surveyed said they preferred working to welfare, even when public aid provided the same money and medical coverage.

The most that can be said for white suspicions about black motivation is that a small segment of blacks has a more casual attitude toward welfare than do their low-income ethnic peers. In Wilson's survey, black parents were about twice as likely as Mexican parents to believe people have a right to welfare without working. And inner-city black fathers who did not finish high school and lacked a car were, in practice, twice as likely to be unemployed as were similarly situated Mexicans.

Crime and the Police

The white myth: Blacks are given to violence and resent tough law enforcement. The 1990 NORC survey found that half of whites rated blacks as more violence-prone than whites. An 11-city survey of police in ghetto precincts taken after the 1960s riots showed 30 percent of white officers believed "most" blacks "regard the police as enemies."

Fact: The vast majority of blacks have long held favorable attitudes toward the police. As Samuel Walker reports in the 1992 edition of "The Police in America," 85 percent of blacks rate the crime-fighting performance of police as either good or fair, just below the 90 percent approval rating given by whites. Some blacks, especially young males, tend to hold hostile views toward the police, and ugly encounters with young blacks often stand out in the minds of cops. Yet studies consistently show that white officers have "seriously overestimated the degree of public hostility among blacks," says Walker. Even *after* the recent riots, a *Los Angeles Times* poll found that 60 percent of local blacks felt the police did a good job of holding down crime, not much below the white figure of 72 percent.

Blacks, or at least young black males, do commit a disproportionate share of crime; blacks account for roughly 45 percent of all arrests for violent crime. Still, the disparity between black and white arrest rates results partly from the fact that blacks *ask* police to arrest juveniles and other suspects more often than whites do. The vast majority of victims of black crime are themselves black, and it is blacks, more than whites, who are likely to be afraid to walk alone at night or to feel unsafe at home. In fact, one of the gripes blacks have with cops is underpolicing. Walker writes: "Black Americans are nearly as likely as whites to ask for more, not less, police protection."

Job and Housing Bias

The white myth: Blacks no longer face widespread job and housing discrimination. Three of four respondents in a 1990 Gallup Poll said that "blacks have as good a chance as white people in my community" to get any job for which they are qualified, and a survey last year found that 53 percent of Americans believed that blacks actually got "too much consideration" in job hiring. In June, a national survey by the Federal National Mortgage Association reported that most whites also believe blacks have as good a chance as whites in their community to get housing they can afford.

Fact: Researchers have documented the persistence of discrimination by testing what happens when pairs of whites and blacks with identical housing needs and credentials—apart from their race—apply for housing. The most recent national study, funded by the Department of Housing and Urban Development, found that in 1989, real-estate agents discriminated against black applicants slightly over half the time, showing them fewer rental apartments than they showed whites, steering them to minority neighborhoods, providing them with less assistance in finding a mortgage and so on. According to University of Chicago sociologist Douglas Massey, 60 to 90 percent of the housing units presented to whites were not made available to blacks. Even more disappointing, the evaluators found no evidence that discrimination had declined since HUD's last national study in 1977. And last week [just prior to the writing of this article], the Federal Reserve Board reported that black applicants are currently twice as likely to be rejected for mortgages as economically comparable whites.

In the workplace, discrimination seems slightly less pervasive. Still, a 1991 Urban Institute analysis of matched white and black male college students who applied for 476 entry-level jobs in Chicago and Washington found "entrenched and widespread" discrimination in the hiring process; 1 white applicant in 5 advanced further than his equally qualified black counterpart.

Taking Responsibility

The white myth: Blacks blame everyone but themselves for their problems. Since 1977, a majority of whites have agreed that the main reason blacks tend to "have worse jobs, income and housing than whites" is that they "just don't have the motivation or willpower to pull themselves up out of poverty." Fifty-seven percent of whites ascribed to that belief when NORC last asked the question, in 1991.

Fact: When it comes to apportioning blame, blacks neither presume that big government is the answer to their problems nor shy away from self-criticism. A 1992 Gallup Poll of 511 blacks found that just 1 in 4 blacks believed the most important way they could improve conditions in their communities was to "put more pressure on government to address their problems"; 2 of 3 opted for trying harder either to "solve their communities' problems themselves" or to "better themselves personally and their families."

In fact, blacks are almost as likely as whites to "blame the victim" and invoke the virtues of individual responsibility. In a 1988 Gallup Poll asking, "Why do you think poor blacks have not been able to rise out of poverty—is it mainly the fault of blacks themselves or is it the fault of society?" 30 percent of blacks responded that black poverty was the fault of blacks themselves; 29 percent of whites said the same. A 1992 poll for the *Washington Post* found that 52 percent of blacks—and 38 percent of whites—agreed that "if blacks would try harder, they could be just as well off as whites." Often, the status of race relations is a secondary concern for black voters. A poll released just last week [again, prior to the writing of this article] by the Joint Center for Political and Economic Studies found that black and white voters both ranked the economy, public education and health care as their "most important" issues. Only 14 percent of blacks and 5 percent of whites cited the state of race relations.

A development with uncertain consequences is that both whites and blacks exaggerate the extent of white stereotyping. Both groups display a classic polling phenomenon—the "I'm OK, but you're not" syndrome. Whites are likely to overestimate other whites' support for racial segregation; blacks are likely to exaggerate whites' beliefs that blacks have no self-discipline or are prone to violent crime. Moreover, blacks and whites are far more sanguine about race relations and police fairness in their own communities than they are about other areas or the nation at large. A *New York Times*/CBS News poll after the L.A. riots found that just 1 in 4 Americans thought race relations were good nationwide, but 3 out of 4 believed race relations were generally good in their communities.

The downside to this syndrome is that it could make it easier for whites and blacks in suburban and upscale neighborhoods to write off blacks in poorer areas. A *Los Angeles Times* poll taken days after the riots found that nearly 80 percent of city residents felt they would suffer few if any hardships because of the riots' after-effects, and 2 out of 3 respondents said their lives were already back to normal.

On the other hand, the fact that whites and blacks mix more at work, at home and socially than in previous decades suggests that increases in interracial contact could eventually help diminish stereotyping by both races. More tolerance will not solve the nation's race problem by itself. But it sure wouldn't hurt if, one day, "them" became "us."

Questions

1. What do Angelenos think should be done to heal the city after the riots of 1992?
2. Are white attitudes about blacks upbeat or downbeat? What about black attitudes toward whites?
3. What about black and/or white attitudes toward other racial and ethnic groups and vice versa?
4. Are black-white attitudes about equality converging or diverging today?
5. Are these statements true or false?
   a. Blacks lack motivation.
   b. Blacks are given to violence and resent tough law enforcement.
   c. Blacks do not face job and housing discrimination.
   d. Blacks blame everyone but themselves.
6. Can you think of any blacks' myths about whites? List them and examine which are true and false.

— Part VIII —

Seeing Other Cultures

Culture is often thought of as a quality of refinement. To be cultured means to know which fork to use at a dinner party, to not use double negatives when speaking, and, presumably, to prefer going to a symphonic rather than a rock concert. Social scientists, however, use the term to refer to anything human beings do that does not have a biological basis. You may eat with your fingers rather than the correct fork but you still have culture. As E.B. Tylor stated in 1871, culture is "that complex whole which includes knowledge, belief, art, morals, law, custom, and any other capabilities and habits acquired as a member of society." Culture encompasses, in short, everything—material and nonmaterial—that is socially learned and shared. The significance of culture is that it influences our lives. Box 57 illustrates that being born in one culture rather than another may, in fact, determine questions of life or death. Since such important issues are involved, it is fortunate that Part VIII takes us beyond America to focus on other cultures.

Historian/anthropologist Robert Clarke, in "Lest Ye Be Judged: Ethnocentrism or Cultural Relativism," uses his extensive travel experience to help construct an itinerary that goes all over the world. While he invites us to "jet-set," it is not necessarily going to be all "vacation." Clarke wants us to consider if an "ethnocentric" viewpoint (evaluating our culture as "natural and good" and other cultures as "wrong") should be replaced with "cultural relativism" (seeing "cultural variation within the context of the society where it is observed.") Don't choose sides until after you read the article because the answer may not be as obvious as you think.

The other three articles focus on one specific culture in which people live dramatically different lives than in America. "What Hunters Do for a Living, or, How to Make Out on Scarce Resources" describes a group of people called

---

Box 57

Who Will Live?

The following situations provide an excellent example of contrasting values between American culture and Arab culture. They show that culture even affects chances for survival.

One summer my wife and I became acquainted with an educated, well-to-do Arab named Ahmed in the city of Jerusalem. Following a traditional Arabic dinner one evening, Ahmed decided to test my wisdom. "Moshe," he said, "imagine that you, your mother, your wife, and your child are in a boat, and it capsizes. You can save yourself and only one of the remaining three. Whom will you save?" I said the child.

Ahmed was very surprised. I flunked the test. As he saw it, there was one correct answer and a corresponding rational argument to support it. "You see," he said, "you can have more than one wife in a lifetime, you can have more than one child, but you have only one mother. You must save your mother!"

I told the story to an American class of 100 freshmen and asked for their responses. 60 would save the child and 40 the wife. When I asked who would save the mother, there was a roar of laughter. No one raised their hand. They thought the question was funny.

A group of about 40 American executives responded as follows. More than half would save the child, less than half would save the wife. One reluctantly raised his hand in response to "Who would save the mother?" (I believe he had an accent . . .). I promised the group to send the mothers sympathy cards.

Later, at a large dinner party, the questions again came up. Seated across the table from me sat a husband and wife. Both came from Persia and spent the last seven years in the United States. She came up with a response immediately: "Of course I would save my mother, you have only one mother." Here her values were a perfect match to Ahmed's culture. But then she turned to her husband and added: "I hope you won't do that." The influence of new values in the USA or did she mean specifically her mother-in-law . . .?

Most of our friends reacted as if it was natural to save the child. One said that she would probably drown before she could ever decide what to do . . .

Do you think the responses would have been different if Ahmed had mentioned saving the "husband" instead of the "wife?" If so, for which cultures?

SOURCE: Moshe Rubinstein, *Patterns of Problem Solving* (Englewood, NJ: Prentice-Hall, 1975), pp. 1-2.

the !Kung who survive by hunting wild animals and gathering plants, fruits, and berries. (As mentioned earlier in the book, the exclamation point is pronounced as a click.) While all our human ancestors lived this way of life at some point in the past, increasingly fewer do so today. Anthropologist Richard Lee feels that social scientists may have underestimated the viability of this way of life. "Peoples' lives," he says, "rather than being precarious and arduous, seem surprisingly well adapted." He points to extensive leisure time, less mental illness, respect for the aged, and equality between the sexes.

"Eating Christmas in the Kalahari" is also by Richard Lee. Lee had gone to the Kalahari desert to study the subsistence economy of the !Kung and "to accomplish this it was essential not to provide them with food, share my own food, or interfere in any way with food gathering activities." Not surprisingly, the !Kung accused Lee of stinginess and hard-heartedness. To make amends and to say thank you for !Kung cooperation, Lee decided to hold a Christmas feast serving the largest, meatiest ox that money could buy. The feast almost turns into a disaster!

"The Transformation of the Kalahari !Kung" brings our knowledge of these people to the present day. After centuries of hunting and gathering, the !Kung are abandoning their traditional ways in favor of herding and agriculture. Anthropologist John Yellen indicates that dissatisfaction with foraging is the wrong answer to explain this cultural change. "The impetus," he says, "may well have come largely from internal stresses generated by the desire to have the material goods that had become readily accessible."

Chapter Twenty-Five

Lest Ye Be Judged
Ethnocentrism or Cultural Relativism

Robert H. Clarke

Culture, the "mental map" which we learn from our society, provides us with most of our practical survival knowledge, our technology and much more: our beliefs, values and standards. Our culture implants within us the fundamentals of belief and judgment which we take for granted and seldom hold up to impartial examination. Indeed, one of the functions of social learning or "acculturation" is precisely to teach us that our own group's way of life and of viewing the world is natural and good, a series of guideposts without which we would surely be lost in a chaotic world. This rootedness in a particular group's assumptions and values is what social scientists call "ethnocentrism."

To have absorbed and internalized the lessons of one's culture should hardly be treated as a reason for embarrassment or shame; for it is difficult indeed to stand outside one's culture and to view it with all the detachment a botanist brings to the study of plant parasites or an entomologist to the description of the praying mantis's mating habits. The scientific objectivity which we find relatively easy to bring to bear on the behavior of other species we find daunting indeed to apply to the varieties of human experience.

Nevertheless, most anthropologists *seek* to free their minds of the powerful tug of ethnocentric reactions and try to approach the vast range of variations in the ways of life of different peoples from the alternative perspective of "cultural relativism." The cultural relativist point of view requires the social scientist or student to set aside the standards of his own culture when examining other ways of life; but cultural relativism goes beyond mere neutrality: it assumes that any cultural variation must be interpreted within the context of the society where it is observed. How do the people involved view or understand it? What can we know or speculate concerning how a given cultural form (from physical artifact to article of faith) serves the needs or requirements of the people who embrace it? These are questions of *objective analysis* rather than of moral *judgment*. Although cultural relativists need not be moral idiots, they do feel a duty to analyze first and only later (if ever) to praise or condemn.

In short, the ethnocentric person follows the path of least intellectual and psychological resistance by taking his socialized standards for granted; the cultural relativist sets the goal of regarding *all* standards with the same cool eye, including those of his own culture — perhaps the most problematical task of all.

But what *are* these standards which we learn at our mother's knee (not to mention other low joints) and which cluster to form our cultural heritage? They can be grouped into several pairs of opposites:

1	Good Just	vs.	Evil Unjust	: moral judgments
2.	Natural	vs.	Unnatural	: assumptions concerning "human nature," taught by different cultures
3.	Beautiful Attractive Delicious	vs.	Ugly Repulsive Disgusting	: aesthetic standards
4.	Reasonable Rational Intelligent	vs.	Stupid, Absurd; Ridiculous; Superstitious; Crazy	: intellectual standards
5.	Real	vs.	Unreal, Fantastic	: epistemological standards
6.	Important Significant	vs.	Trivial Meaningless	
7.	Proper	vs.	Improper	

As we contemplate the human comedy, we cannot fail to be impressed by the strong attachments to highly arbitrary group standards which are so often diametrically opposed to those of one's neighbors or more distant "others." For instance, plural marriage or polygamy, approved by most of the world's cultures, is condemned as evil or godless by many others who are firmly attached to monogamy. Yet most monogamists would themselves denounce even monogamous marriages between members of the same sex. The woman whose thick folds of neck fat might make her irresistible to West African suitors would hardly be the ideal of feminine beauty conveyed by American television commercials. Bronislaw Malinowski reported that the Trobriand islanders found the European "missionary position" in sexual intercourse so hilarious, "unpractical and improper" that local comedians entertained their audiences by imitating it. Of course the missionaries considered their mode of lovemaking to be the only natural and divinely approved one. A doctor in Chicago may snicker at her Mexican patient who will not believe he is ill until his grandmother certifies it.

Despite the special training they receive to overcome ethnocentric attitudes, many Peace Corps volunteers, even after two years of close association with villagers in some agricultural-tribal society, may blurt out "I tried with them, but frankly they're just too stupid to learn how to do things better. They just don't make any sense." For example, the villagers believe in the reality of things which outsiders classify as the rankest superstitious fantasies. Do zombies really exist? An agronomist from Nebraska and a Haitian peasant are likely to give different answers to the question.

Thus, the analytical, tolerant, intellectually curious, scientific perspective of cultural relativism stands as an alternative to the more judgmental ethnocentrism bred into everyone. At this point the reader may want to make a mental note answering the question, to which of these two approaches do I feel

---

Box 58

Bob and Ted and Carol and Alice

The Nuer legal fiction is that only men can be the owners of cattle. However, if a man dies without direct male heirs, his cattle will be inherited by a daughter. This cattle-owning daughter is then a sociological male. She can (and should) marry a wife . . . whom she marries with bridecattle in the ordinary way . . .

(In western Egypt) Until quite recently marriages were celebrated between men and boys as well as between men and women. Marriage to a boy was celebrated with great pomp and publicity and the "brideprice" paid for a boy might be as much as fifteen times that paid for a girl.

SOURCE: Edmund Leach, *Social Anthropology* (Fontana Paperbacks, 1982), pp. 187, 210.

Box 59

Voodoo: Reality or Fantasy?

"Well, no . . . personally voodoo does not exist; it is impossible! I don't like it, people will do anything who believe in voodoo—I have seen some of their zombies, flying through the air late at night, with rocket-fire from their feet! No, this voodoo is dangerous; I just ignore it!"
— spoken by a Haitian cab-driver, New York City, 1980

SOURCE: Michelle Anderson, "Authentic Voodoo is Synthetic," *The Drama Review*, Vol. 26, No. 2 (Summer, 1982), p. 89.

---

committed? Most of us prefer the cultural relativist ideal. One way of testing the degree of our abandonment of ethnocentrism is to assess our reactions to some varied customs in two areas of human affairs: (I) eating and dietary preferences; (II) treatment of women.

I. Eating and Diet

A. "Put mine in a doggy bag."
In Southeast Asia some restaurants display chubby puppies in small cages, but not because they operate pet shops as a sideline. Rather, the customers like to select one to be slaughtered and served up fresh for dinner, somewhat like the service from live lobster tanks we see in American seafood restaurants. The French actress Brigitte Bardot recently launched a campaign to compel the Fiji islanders to stop eating dogs, despite the fact that for the local people this dish is a traditional delicacy. In another recent development, Chinese authorities decreed the execution of some 200,000 pet dogs in Peking on the ground that they were a nuisance and a danger to public health; they made an exception for the canine farms that raise dogs for food.

B. "Some people haven't got the brains of a monkey." (But others have.)
As recently as 1949 and perhaps since then, Chinese men with money occasionally sat down to enjoy a special dish which was reputed to serve as both a taste treat and a sexual tonic—i.e., fresh monkey brain, dished up from a live monkey secured to a doughnut-shaped table. In this connection one might note that the traditional Chinese greeting is not "How are you?" but "Have you eaten yet?

Box 60

A Lively Feast

"Do you know what people in China eat when they have the money?" my mother began. "They buy into a monkey feast. The eaters sit around a thick wood table with a hole in the middle. Boys bring in the monkey at the end of a pole. Its neck is in a collar at the end of the pole, and it is screaming. Its hands are tied behind it. They clamp the monkey into the table; the whole table fits like another collar around its neck. Using a surgeon's saw, the cooks cut a clean line in a circle at the top of its head. To loosen the bone, they tap with a tiny hammer and wedge here and there with a silver pick. Then an old woman reaches out her hand to the monkey's face and up to its scalp, where she tufts some hairs and lifts off the lid of the skull. The eaters spoon out the brains."

SOURCE: Maxine Hong Kingston, *The Woman Warrior* (New York: Vintage Books, 1975), pp.107-108.

C. "You look good enough to eat."

Foreign missionaries, appalled by what they found disgusting violations of their standards of decency, have apparently managed to suppress a dining custom among New Guinea highlanders who were accustomed to eating their friends and enemies alike with no ritual or magical involvement. Often they buried corpses for a few days and then dug them up for a feast made all the more delectable because the flesh was decayed and swarming with maggots. Since no one had ever tabooed the eating of human flesh to them and their mothers hadn't told them that worms were filthy and repulsive, they found all this quite natural and requiring no explanation or justification. Considering especially that, at least in the case of eating their friends ("endocannibalism"), these people did not kill for their human flesh meals, is there any difficulty in maintaining one's cultural relativism in the face of this curious custom? Were the missionaries justified in imposing their standards on these cannibals?

II. Treatment of Females

A. "He really burns me up."

In traditional Hindu India, a Brahmin (high-caste) widow was expected to immolate herself on her deceased husband's funeral pyre. The practice was known as *suttee*. No such rule governed the conduct of widowers, who generally

---

Box 61

O Grave, Where Is Thy Victory?

Food and sex (in highland New Guinea) were sometimes neatly combined when the men would copulate with a female corpse before cutting it up for eating. They had one story of a man who got his penis cut off because he dallied too long for the patience of his hungry friends.

SOURCE: Marston Bates, *Gluttons and Libertines* (New York: Random House, 1967), p. 91.

---

remarried. The cultural relativist might investigate links between this custom and its functions; e.g., the symbolic reinforcement of caste distinctions and devaluation of females which served to support the established social order, itself upheld by religious ideology. But the British colonial authorities, representing an alien culture which had brought India under its rule, reacted to *suttee* with revulsion and banned it because it shocked their European Christian minds. Is this an instance where we should side with the ethnocentrics and set aside the detached perspective of the "neutral" anthropologist?

B. Growing pains.

In recent times many voices have been raised against the long-established custom of clitoridectomy, still widely practiced in such places as Kenya and Egypt. This practice involves the removal (often by unsterilized crude instruments) of al! or part of the clitoris of young girls, usually as a rite of passage certifying their emergence into adulthood and marriageable status. Jomo Kenyatta, himself an anthropologist and later president of Kenya, took issue with the efforts of British colonizers to interfere with clitoridectomy, which he viewed as an integral part of Kikuyu culture. The cultural relativist examining how a custom is viewed from *within* might in this instance take special interest in the cosmology of the Dogon of Mali (West Africa), who believe that all people are born hermaphroditic (possessing the characteristics of both sexes); to stimulate procreation, the boy must shed his "female" appendage, the foreskin; and the female must lose her corresponding "male" vestige, the clitoris.

C. "Whatever happened to Baby Jane?"

Female infanticide, the killing of female babies, has long been accepted under certain circumstances by various cultures. By the standards of good and evil prevalent in most industrial societies, this practice is wholly unacceptable.

Box 62

Genital Controversy: Four Views

1. An African Sage:

Provided with its two souls, the child follows its destiny. But the first years are marked by instability. As long as it keeps its foreskin or its clitoris, (which are) foundations of the principle of the sex opposite to the apparent one, masculinity and femininity have the same strength . . . If this indecision were to last, the being would never be inclined toward procreation. Indeed, the clitoris which the girl has received is a symbolic twin, a makeshift male with whom she could not reproduce and which, to the contrary, would prevent her from joining herself with a man.

> Paraphrase of Ogotemmêli, Dogon sage,
> from remarks collected 1946

SOURCE: Marcel Griaule, *Dieu d'Eau* (Paris: Librairie Arthème Fayard, 1966), p. 149. (Translation by R. Clarke)

2. A Viennese doctor:

. . . there can be no doubt that the bisexual disposition which we maintain to be characteristic of human beings manifests itself much more plainly in the female than in the male. The latter has only one principal sexual zone — only one sexual organ — whereas the former has two: the vagina, the true female organ, and the clitoris, which is analogous to the male organ . . . We have long realized that in women the development of sexuality is complicated by the task of renouncing that genital zone which was originally the principal one, namely, the clitoris, in favour of a new zone — the vagina.

SOURCE: Sigmund Freud, "Female Sexuality" (1931), in J. Strachey (ed.), *Freud, Collected Papers*, Vol. 5 (New York: Basic Books, 1959), pp. 255, 252.

3. An African anthropologist:

The missionaries who attack the *irua* (clitoridectomy) of girls are more to be pitied than condemned, for most of their information is derived from Gikuyu converts who have been taught by these same Christians to regard the custom of female circumcision as something savage and barbaric, worthy only of heathens who live in perpetual sin under the influence of the Devil. Because of this prejudiced attitude, the missionaries are at a disadvantage in knowing the true state of affairs. Even the few scientifically minded ones are themselves so obsessed with prejudice against the custom that their objectivity is blurred in trying to unravel the mystery of the *irua*.

SOURCE: Jomo Kenyatta, *Facing Mt. Kenya* (London: Secker and Warburg, 1953), pp. 153-54.

4. Two American feminists:

The White House . . . the various desks of the U.S. State Department, and such agencies as the United Nation's International Children's Fund and the World Health Organization—all in the recent past have expressed reluctance to interfere with "social and cultural attitudes" regarding female genital mutilation. This sensitivity has been markedly absent on other issues—for example, campaigns to disseminate vaccines or vitamins despite resistance from local traditionalists. Clearly, "culture" is that which affects women while "politics" affects men, and human rights statements do not include those needed by the female majority of humanity.

SOURCE: Robin Morgan and Gloria Steinem, "The International Crime of Genital Mutilation," *MS.*, (March 1980), p. 98.

The Central Eskimos (e.g., the Netsilik) of Canada, whose survival during the long winters formerly depended entirely upon the catch of seal by male hunters, often resorted to killing girl babies because of a recognition that given the limited food supply, the potential food-producers must be kept alive lest all the others perish. In other words, as the cultural relativist might observe, the reduced economic value of the female in the Eskimos' ecological niche made female infanticide, in their outlook, both necessary and legitimate. Within the context of their culture, such *triage* choices were regarded as "natural." A similar functional pattern might be discerned to account for the preponderance of girls dropped into the notorious "baby wells" of prerevolutionary China: their traditional system of patrilocal residence, according to which brides left their families to live with the groom's relatives, made boys more valuable than girls. Even today, there are official denunciations of female infanticide in China, arising partly from the recent policy of restricting couples to one child only. Despite vast improvements in social welfare provisions, quite a few rural Chinese still prefer to have boys who will bring daughters-in-law to help aged parents; and a few have resorted to destruction of girl babies so as to be eligible to try again for a boy.

To preserve a dispassionate, observational attitude toward customs or values extremely at variance with one's own is a challenge which most people would rather not meet; the emotional, knee-jerk ethnocentric posture is far more comfortable and comforting. On the other hand, to take up the cultural relativist stance requires a willingness to put first the search for scientific interpretation

---

Box 63

Unintended Consequences

Group marriage occurred among the Todas during the period of British rule in India. In former times the Todas practiced female infanticide, which kept down the female population and thus helped to perpetuate polyandry*. The British took strong measures to discourage infanticide. When the Todas gave it up, the number of women increased, which is said to have led to a rise in group marriages.

* The marriage custom in which one woman marries several husbands (usually brothers).

SOURCE: Victor Barnouw, *An Introduction to Anthropology* (Homewood, IL: The Dorsey Press, 1982), p. 106.

---

and understanding. It does not, however, call for the abandonment of all one's tastes and values: the scientifically disinterested anthropologist need not personally approve all that he observes. But he will not lose sight of the arbitrary and usually nonrational character of his own culture's preferences and institutions. To take a final example, those who find the use of heavy make-up and elaborate jewelry by the contestants in an African male beauty contest to be ludicrous or distasteful might want to consider how the Wodaabe would react to Bert Parks and the Miss America Pageant.

With regard to cultural differences that involve deeper issues than those of taste or propriety, there are several cautions to keep in mind. First, many

---

Box 64

A Mother's Duty

"Frequently an older woman spoke with conviction, and people listened to her. She might be the one to decide on the fate of a newborn infant. Old Nalungiaq told Rasmussen (the anthropologist): 'If my daughter Quertiliq had a girl child I would strangle it at once. If I did not, I think I would be a bad mother.'"

SOURCE: Asen Balikci, *The Netsilik Eskimo* (Prospect Heights, IL: Waveland Press, Inc., 1970, reissued 1989 with changes), pp. 149-150.

Box 65

Let it Be a Son

(An incident from western China in the 1930s:) There was the country-woman who came a long way from Chingsien, eighty *li* or more, to be delivered of her tenth child, because all the others had been daughters; and a neighbor of hers had been to the hospital and had acquired a son; this woman thought she too could obtain a son by coming to be delivered at our hospital. She rode in a rickshaw all the way and this must have cost a good deal; and as she lay on the obstetric table in labour she told Miss Hsu what had happened to her baby daughters: the first was alive, and also the third; but the second had been strangled at birth by the husband and so had the fifth and the sixth; the seventh had been born in a bad year, a year of famine when her belly skin stuck to her spine, and the husband had smashed her skull in with his axe; at the eighth female child the husband had been so angry that he had hurled it against a wall; the ninth was a year old and had been given away to a neighbor and now here was something in her belly . . . oh let it be a son, a male child.

SOURCE: Han Suyin, *Birdless Summer* (Frogmore: Panther Books Ltd., 1972), p. 165.

Box 66

Here He Comes. . .

(The Wodaabe conducted) . . . an exhausting dance marathon highlighted by afternoon and evening performances of the *geerewol*, where the most beautiful men are selected.

Uniformly dressed in tight wrappers bound at the knees, strings of white beads crisscrossing bare chests, and turbans adorned with ostrich feathers, the men line up before their audience.

Resplendent in red ocher face makeup (they). . . replace their ostrich feathers with horsetail plumes . . .

Three unmarried young ladies chosen for their loveliness are brought out by the elders to serve as judges . . .

SOURCE: Carol Beckwith, "Niger's Wodaabe: 'People of the Taboo,'" *National Geographic*, Vol. 164, No. 4 (October 1983), pp. 508-09.

societies are not *internally* fully uniform or homogeneous—what one group or individual adores or craves another may loathe or condemn. The U.S.A., with its many religious, class and ethnic subcultures, is deeply divided over the morality of abortion or the death penalty. Likewise, in North America there are apparently irreconcilable differences over questions of what is real and what is fantasy; for example, approximately half the American population does not accept the scientific view of human evolution.

Second, cultures are not static. Dominant values may reflect the power one group wields over others; and power shifts like revolutions can thus bring important changes in beliefs and customs. Witness the drastic changes in Chinese treatment of women before and after the revolution of 1949. Another example would be Kenya: the first post-independence President, Jomo Kenyatta, defended the custom of clitoridectomy as a legitimate part of the heritage of the Kikuyu people whereas his successor, Daniel Moi, has put through legislation to ban the practice despite its indigenous roots.

Standards of beauty, language, and appropriate dress also often reflect these shifts. Mainstream American men now regularly sport gold earrings, and chic businesswomen partake of power lunches wearing flat athletic shoes that were until recently thought appropriate only for males. The standard of "good looks" conveyed in Mexican soap operas reflects the preference for "Euro-elite" faces and builds not typical of the general population; and in Guatemala the languages and customs of the majority Mayan Indians are not only held in contempt by the dominant "Ladinos" but are frequently ruthlessly suppressed.

The cultural relativist is not obliged to "approve" genocide, patriarchy, homophobia, meat-eating, etc. merely because other cultures accept or practice them. To work from the cultural relativist perspective does not free anyone, scientist or lay person, from the obligation to come to terms with philosophical and moral questions *after* careful comparative study and analysis have been completed. Indeed, one is left with the paradox that scientific rationalism and tolerance, including cultural relativism, are themselves ideals rooted in particular cultures which hesitate to lay claim to any "universal" validity.

Questions

1. Locate the following by reference to the maps in the appendix:
   Niger; New Guinea; Sudan; Kenya

2. Check definitions of the following terms:

patrilocal residence	polyandry
clitoridectomy	infanticide
endocannibalism	

3. If you had the power to do so, would you prohibit or suppress any of the customs described in the article, even if they were accepted and approved by the people practicing them? Which ones? If you are doing this as a classroom exercise, compare the answers from males and females in the class.

4. Which American customs or values do you think might be most shocking or repugnant to observers from other cultures in the areas of (a) eating and diet and (b) standards governing conduct of women?

5. Have you been able to "liberate" yourself from ethnocentric attitudes? Do you want to do so?

6. Provide a definition in your own terms of cultural relativism. What does it require of the observer?

7. Are there any universally valid values which you can apply to different cultures without falling into the net of ethnocentrism? What might they be? Could they provide you with a basis for condemning such things as slavery and institutionalized torture?

Chapter Twenty-Six

What Hunters Do for a Living, or, How to Make Out on Scarce Resources

Richard B. Lee

The current anthropological view of hunter-gatherer subsistence rests on two questionable assumptions. First is the notion that these peoples are primarily dependent on the hunting of game animals, and second is the assumption that their way of life is generally a precarious and arduous struggle for existence.

Recent data on living hunter-gatherers show a radically different picture. We have learned that in many societies, plant and marine resources are far more important than are game animals in the diet. More important, it is becoming clear that the hunter-gatherer subsistence base is at least routine and reliable and at best surprisingly abundant. Anthropologists have consistently tended to underestimate the viability of hunting peoples.

Bushman Subsistence

The !Kung Bushman of Botswana are an apt case for analysis. They inhabit the semi-arid northwest region of the Kalahari Desert. With only six to nine inches of rainfall per year, this is, by any account, a marginal environment

Reprinted by permission from Richard B. Lee and Irven DeVore; copyright © 1968 by the Wenner-Gren Foundation for Anthropological Research, Inc.

for human habitation. In fact, it is precisely the unattractiveness of their homeland that has kept the !Kung isolated from extensive contact with their agricultural and pastoral neighbors.

Field work was carried out in the Dobe area, a line of eight permanent waterholes near the South-West Africa border and 125 miles south of the Okavango River. The population of the Dobe area consists of 466 Bushmen, including 379 permanent residents living in independent camps or associated with Bantu cattle posts, as well as 87 seasonal visitors. The Bushmen share the area with some 340 Bantu pastoralists largely of the Herero and Tswana tribes. The ethnographic present refers to the period of field work: October, 1963—January, 1965.

The Bushmen living in independent camps lack firearms, livestock, and agriculture. Apart from occasional visits to the Herero for milk, these !Kung are entirely dependent upon hunting and gathering for their subsistence. Politically they are under the nominal authority of the Tswana headman, although they pay no taxes and receive very few government services. European presence amounts to one overnight government patrol every six to eight weeks. Although Dobe-area !Kung have had some contact with outsiders since the 1880s, the majority of them continue to hunt and gather because there is no viable alternative locally available to them.

Each of the fourteen independent camps is associated with one of the permanent waterholes. During the dry season (May-October) the entire population is clustered around these wells. . . . Two wells had no camp resident and one large well supported five camps. The number of camps at each well and the size of each camp changed frequently during the course of the year. The "camp" is an open aggregate of cooperating persons which changes in size and composition from day to day. Therefore, I have avoided the term "band" in describing the !Kung Bushman living groups.

Each waterhole has a hinterland lying within a six-mile radius which is regularly exploited for vegetable and animal foods. These areas are not territories in the zoological sense, since they are not defended against outsiders. Rather they constitute the resources that lie within a convenient walking distance of a waterhole. The camp is a self-sufficient subsistence unit. The members move out each day to hunt and gather, and return in the evening to pool the collected foods in such a way that every person present receives an equitable share. Trade in food-stuffs between camps is minimal; personnel do move freely from camp to camp, however. The net effect is of a population constantly in motion. On the average, an individual spends a third of his time living only with close relatives, a third visiting other camps, and a third entertaining visitors from other camps.

Because of the strong emphasis on sharing, and the frequency of movement, surplus accumulation of storable plant foods and dried meat is kept to a minimum. There is rarely more than two or three days' supply of food on hand in a camp at any time. The result of this lack of surplus is that a constant subsistence effort must be maintained throughout the year. Unlike agriculturists who work hard during the planting and harvesting seasons and undergo "seasonal unemployment" for several months, the Bushmen hunter-gatherers collect food every third or fourth day throughout the year.

Vegetable foods comprise from 60-80 per cent of the total diet by weight, and collecting involves two or three days of work per woman per week. The men also collect plants and small animals but their major contribution to the diet is the hunting of medium and large game. The men are conscientious but not particularly successful hunters; although men's and women's work input is roughly equivalent in terms of man-day effort, the women provide two to three times as much food by weight as the men. Box 67 considers why men hunt and women gather.

Box 67

Why Men Hunt; Why Women Gather

Throughout all contemporary gatherer-hunters there is a consistent division of labor between men and women; hunting meat is a male pursuit, whereas gathering plant foods is the responsibility of the women. Why the pursuit of game is principally a male prerogative is not easy to say. Below, anthropologists Leakey and Lewin give their interpretation:

> Gatherer-hunter mothers are usually involved in some stage of child care throughout their adult lives. The burden of carrying infants on food-gathering expeditions is great (!Kung women walk more than fifteen hundred miles a year with a suckling infant on their backs), but they are clearly equal to the task. But, although collecting plant foods is not without the hazard of accidentally disturbing a potential predator, the dangers of hunting are greater. The loss of the child to the hungry jaws of a carnivorous cat would be a serious blow to a woman's reproductive career; to put the child at risk would therefore not be biologically sensible, either for the woman or her mate. What's more, the woman herself is valuable as a future childbearer: in terms of the reproductive potential of a group, the loss of a man's life—either in hunting, or in war—is less of a problem than the loss of a woman's. There would also be the not insubstantial problem of persuading a two-year-old not to make infantile utterings during critical silent stages of stalking prey! For these and other reasons, women only rarely hunt.

SOURCE: Richard Leakey and Roger Lewin, *People of the Lake* (Garden City, NY: Anchor Press, 1978), pp. 245-246.

For the greater part of the year, food is locally abundant and easily collected. It is only during the end of the dry season in September and October, when desirable foods have been eaten out in the immediate vicinity of the waterholes that the people have to plan longer hikes of 10-15 miles and carry their own water to those areas where the mongongo nut is still available. The important point is that food is a constant, but distance required to reach food is a variable; it is short in the summer, fall, and early winter, and reaches its maximum in the spring.

This analysis attempts to provide quantitative measures of subsistence status including data on the following topics: abundance and variety of resources, diet selectivity, range size and population density, the composition of the work force, the ratio of work to leisure time, and the caloric and protein levels in the diet. The value of quantitative data is that they can be used comparatively and also may be useful in archeological reconstruction. In addition, one can avoid the pitfalls of subjective and qualitative impressions; for example, statements about food "anxiety" have proven to be difficult to generalize across cultures.

Abundance and Variety of Resources

It is impossible to define "abundance" of resources absolutely. However, one index of relative abundance is whether or not a population exhausts all the food available from a given area. By this criterion, the habitat of the Dobe-area Bushmen is abundant in naturally occurring foods. By far the most important food is the mongongo (mangetti) nut *Ricinodendron rautaneni* (Schniz). Although tens of thousands of pounds of these nuts are harvested and eaten each year, thousands more rot on the ground each year for want of picking.

The mongongo nut, because of it's abundance and reliability, alone accounts for 50 per cent of the vegetable diet by weight. In this respect it resembles a cultivated staple crop such as maize or rice. Nutritionally it is even more remarkable, for it contains five times the calories and ten times the proteins per cooked unit of the cereal crops. The average daily per-capita consumption of 300 nuts yields about 1,260 calories and 56 grams of protein. This modest portion, weighing only about 7.5 ounces, contains the caloric equivalent of 2.5 pounds of cooked rice and the protein equivalent of 14 ounces of lean beef.

Furthermore the mongongo nut is drought resistant and it will still be abundant in the dry years when cultivated crops may fail. The extremely hard outer shell protects the inner kernel from rot and allows the nuts to be harvested for up to twelve months after they have fallen to the ground. A diet based on mongongo nuts is in fact more reliable than one based on cultivated foods, and it is not surprising, therefore, that when a Bushman was asked why he hadn't taken to agriculture he replied: "Why should we plant, when there are so many mongongo nuts in the world?"

Apart from the mongongo, the Bushmen have available 84 other species of edible food plants, including 29 species of fruits, berries, and melons and 30 species of roots and bulbs. The existence of this variety allows for a wide range of alternatives in subsistence strategy. During the summer months the Bushmen have no problem other than to choose among the tastiest and most easily collected foods. Many species, which are quite edible but less attractive, are bypassed, so that gathering never exhausts *all* the available plant foods of an area. During the dry season the diet becomes much more eclectic and the many species of roots, bulbs, and edible resins make an important contribution. It is this broad base that provides an essential margin of safety during the end of the dry season when the mongongo nut forests are difficult to reach. In addition, it is likely that these rarely utilized species provide important nutritional and mineral trace elements that may be lacking in the more popular foods.

Diet Selectivity

If the Bushmen were living close to the "starvation" level, then one would expect them to exploit every available source of nutrition. That their life is well above this level is indicated by the data in Box 68. Here all the edible plant species are arranged in classes according to the frequency with which they were observed to be eaten. It should he noted, that although there are some 85 species available, about 90 per cent of the vegetable diet by weight is drawn from only 23 species. In other words, 75 per cent of the listed species provide only 10 per cent of the food value.

In their meat-eating habits, the Bushmen show a similar selectivity. Of the 223 local species of animals known and named by the Bushman, 54 species are classified as edible, and of these only 17 species were hunted on a regular basis. Only a handful of the dozens of edible species of small mammals, birds, reptiles, and insects that occur locally are regarded as food. Such animals as rodents, snakes, lizards, termites, and grasshoppers, which in the literature are included in the Bushman dietary, are despised by the Bushmen of the Dobe area.

Range Size and Population Density

The necessity to travel long distances, the high frequency of moves, and the maintenance of populations at low densities are also features commonly associated with the hunting and gathering way of life. Density estimates for hunters in western North America and Australia have ranged from 3 persons/square mile to as low as 1 person/100 square miles. In 1963-65, the resident and visiting Bushmen were observed to utilize an area of about 1,000 square miles during the course of the annual round for an effective population density of 41 persons/100 square miles. Within this area, however, the amount of ground covered by members of an individual camp was surprisingly small. A day's round-trip of twelve miles serves to define a "core" area six miles in radius surrounding each water point. By fanning out in all directions from their well, the members of a camp can gain access to the food resources of well over 100 square miles of territory within a two-hour hike. Except for a few weeks each year, areas lying beyond this six-mile radius are rarely utilized, even though they are no less rich in plants and game than are the core areas.

Although the Bushmen move their camps frequently (five or six times a year) they do not move them very far. A rainy season camp in the nut forests is rarely more than ten or twelve miles from the home waterhole, and often new campsites are occupied only a few hundred yards away from the previous

---

Box 68

!Kung Bushman Plant Foods

	Part Eaten								Totals (Percentages)		
Food Class	Fruit and Nut	Bean and Root	Fruit and Stalk	Root, Bulb	Fruit, Berry, Melon	Resin	Leaves	Seed, Bean	Total Number of Species in Class	Estimated Contribu- tion by Weight to Vegetable Diet	Estimated Contribu- tion of Each Species
I. PRIMARY Eaten daily throughout year (mongongo nut)	1								1	c.50	c.50*
II. MAJOR Eaten daily in season	1	1	1	1	4				8	c.25	c.3
III. MINOR Eaten several times per week in season				7	3	2	2		14	c.15	c.1
IV. SUPPLEMENTARY Eaten when classes I-III locally unavailable				9	12	10	1		32	c.7	c.0.2
V. RARE Eaten several times per year				9	4				13	c.3	c.0.1
VI. PROBLEMATIC Edible but not observed to be eaten				4	6	4	1	2	17	nil	nil
TOTAL SPECIES	2	1	1	30	29	16	4	2	85	100	

* 1 species constitutes 50 percent of the vegetable diet by weight.
† 23 species constitute 90 percent of the vegetable diet by weight.
‡ 62 species constitute the remaining 10 percent of the diet.

one. By these criteria, the Bushmen do not lead a free-ranging nomadic way of life. For example, they do not undertake long marches of 30 to 100 miles to get food, since this task can be readily fulfilled within a day's walk of home base. When such long marches do occur they are invariably for visiting, trading, and marriage arrangements, and should not be confused with the normal routine of subsistence.

Demographic Factors

Another indicator of the harshness of a way of life is the age at which people die. Ever since Hobbes characterized life in the state of nature as "nasty, brutish and short," the assumption has been that hunting and gathering is so rigorous that members of such societies are rapidly worn out and meet an early death. Silberbauer, for example, says of the Gwi Bushmen of the central Kalahari that "life expectancy. . . . is difficult to calculate, but I do not believe that many live beyond 45." And Coon has said. . .

> The practice of abandoning the hopelessly ill and aged has been observed in many parts of the world. It is always done by people living in poor environments where it is necessary to move about frequently to obtain food, where food is scarce, and transportation difficult. . . . Among peoples who are forced to live in this way the oldest generation, the generation of individuals who have passed their physical peak is reduced in numbers and influence. There is no body of elders to hand on tradition and control the affairs of younger men and women, and no formal system of age grading.

The !Kung Bushmen of the Dobe area flatly contradict this view. In a total population of 466, no fewer than 46 individuals (17 men and 29 women) were determined to be over 60 years of age, a proportion that compares favorably to the percentage of elderly in industrialized populations.

The aged hold a respected position in Bushman society and are the effective leaders of the camps. Senilicide is extremely rare. Long after their productive years have passed, the old people are fed and cared for by their children and grandchildren. The blind, the senile, and the crippled are respected for the special ritual and technical skills they possess. For instance, the four elders at !gose waterhole were totally or partially blind, but this handicap did not prevent their active participation in decision-making and ritual curing.

Another significant feature of the composition of the work force is the late assumption of adult responsibility by the adolescents. Young people are not expected to provide food regularly until they are married. Girls typically marry between the age of 15 and 20, and boys about five years later, so that it is not unusual to find healthy, active teenagers visiting from camp to camp while their older relatives provide food for them.

As a result, the people in the age group 20-60 support a surprisingly large percentage of nonproductive young and old people. About 40 per cent of the population in camps contribute little to the food supplies. This allocation of work to young and middle-aged adults allows for a relatively carefree childhood and adolescence and a relatively unstrenuous old age.

Leisure and Work

Another important index of ease or difficulty of subsistence is the amount of time devoted to the food quest. Hunting has usually been regarded by social scientists as a way of life in which merely keeping alive is so formidable a task that members of such societies lack the leisure time necessary to "build culture." The !Kung Bushmen would appear to conform to the rule, for as Lorna Marshall says:

> It is vividly apparent that the !Kung Bushmen ethos, or "the spirit which actuates manners and customs," is survival. Their time and energies are almost wholly given to this task, for life in their environment requires that they spend their days mainly in procuring food.

It is certainly true that getting food is the most important single activity in Bushman life. However this statement would apply equally well to small-scale agricultural and pastoral societies too. How much time is *actually* devoted to the food quest is fortunately an empirical question. And an analysis of the work effort of the Dobe Bushmen shows some unexpected results. From July 6 to August 2, 1964, I recorded all the daily activities of the Bushmen living at the Dobe waterhole. Because of the coming and going of visitors, the camp population fluctuated in size day by day, from a low of 23 to a high of 40, with a mean of 31.8 persons. Each day some of the adult members of the camp went out to hunt and/or gather while others stayed home or went visiting. The daily recording of all personnel on hand made it possible to calculate the number of man-days of work as a percentage of total number of man-days of consumption.

Although the Bushmen do not organize their activities on the basis of a seven-day week, I have divided the data this way to make them more intelligible. The work-week was calculated to show how many days out of seven each adult spent in subsistence activities (Box 69, Column 7). Week II has been eliminated from the totals since the investigator contributed food. In week I, the people spent an average of 2.3 days in subsistence activities, in week III, I .9 days, and week IV, 3.2 days. In all, the adults of the Dobe camp worked about two and a half days a week. Since the average working day was about six hours long, the fact emerges that !Kung Bushmen of Dobe, despite their harsh environment, devote from twelve to nineteen hours a week to getting food.

Box 69

Summary of Dobe Work Diary

Week	(1) Mean Group Size	(2) Adult-Days	(3) Child-Days	(4) Total Man-Days of Consumption	(5) Man-Days of Work	(6) Meat (lbs.)	(7) Average Work Week/Adult	(8) Index of Subsistence Effort
I (July 6-12)	25.6 (23-29)	114	65	179	37	104	2.3	0.21
II (July 13-19)	28.3 (23-27)	125	73	198	22	80	1.2	0.11
III (July 20-26)	34.3 (29-40)	156	84	240	42	177	1.9	0.18
IV (July 27-Aug. 2)	35.6 (32-40)	167	82	249	77	129	3.2	0.31
4-wk. Total	30.9	562	304	866	178	490	2.2	0.21
Adjusted Total*	31.8	437	231	668	156	410	2.5	0.23

* See Text

Key: Column 1: Mean group size $= \dfrac{\text{total man-days of consumption}}{7}$

Column 7: Work week = the number of work days per adult per week.

Column 8: Index of subsistence effort $= \dfrac{\text{man-days of work}}{\text{man-days of consumption}}$ (e.g., in Week 1, the value of "S" = 0.21, i.e.,

21 days of work/100 days of consumption or 1 work day produced food for 5 consumption days.)

Because the Bushmen do not amass a surplus of foods, there are no seasons of exceptionally intensive activities such as planting and harvesting, and no seasons of unemployment. The level of work observed is an accurate reflection of the effort required to meet the immediate caloric needs of the group. This work diary covers the mid-winter dry season, a period when food is neither at its most plentiful nor at its scarcest levels, and the diary documents the transition from better to worse conditions. During the fourth week the gatherers were making overnight trips to camps in the mongongo nut forests seven to ten miles distant from the waterhole. These longer trips account for the rise in the level of work, from twelve or thirteen to nineteen hours per week.

If food getting occupies such a small proportion of a Bushman's waking hours, then how *do* people allocate their time? A woman gathers on one day enough food to feed her family for three days, and spends the rest of her time resting in camp, doing embroidery, visiting other camps, or entertaining visitors from other camps. For each day at home, kitchen routines, such as cooking, nut cracking, collecting firewood, and fetching water, occupy one to three hours of her time. This rhythm of steady work and steady leisure is maintained throughout the year.

The hunters tend to work more frequently than the women, but their schedule is uneven. It is not unusual for a man to hunt avidly for a week and then do no hunting at all for two or three weeks. Since hunting is an unpredictable business and subject to magical control, hunters sometimes experience a run of bad luck and stop hunting for a month or longer. During these periods, visiting, entertaining, and especially dancing are the primary activities of men. (Unlike the Hadza, gambling is only a minor leisure activity.)

The trance-dance is the focus of Bushman ritual life; over 50 per cent of the men have trained as trance-performers and regularly enter trance during the course of the all-night dances. At some camps, trance-dances occur as frequently as two or three times a week and those who have entered trances the night before rarely go out hunting the following day. . . . In a camp with five or more hunters, there are usually two or three who are actively hunting and several others who are inactive. The net effect is to phase the hunting and non-hunting so that a fairly steady supply of meat is brought into a camp.

Caloric Returns

Is the modest work effort of the Bushmen sufficient to provide the calories necessary to maintain the health of the population? Or have the !Kung, in common with some agricultural peoples, adjusted to a permanently substandard nutritional level?

During my field work I did not encounter any cases of kwashiorkor, the most common nutritional disease in the children of African agricultural societies. However, without medical examinations, it is impossible to exclude the possibility that subclinical signs of malnutrition existed.

Another measure of nutritional adequacy is the average consumption of calories and proteins per person per day. The estimate for the Bushmen is based on observations of the weights of foods of known composition that were brought into Dobe camp on each day of the study period. The per-capita figure is obtained by dividing the total weight of foodstuffs by the total number of persons in the camp. . . . During the study period 410 pounds of meat were brought in by the hunters of the Dobe camp, for a daily share of nine ounces of meat per person. About 700 pounds of vegetable foods were gathered and consumed during the same period. Box 70 sets out the calories and proteins available per capita in the !Kung Bushman dietary from meat, mongongo nuts, and other vegetable sources.

This output of 2,140 calories and 93.1 grams of protein per person per day may be compared with the Recommended Daily Allowances (RDA) for persons

---

Box 70

Calorie and Protein Levels in the !Kung Bushman Dietary, July-August, 1964

Class of Food	Percentage Contribution to Diet by Weight	Per Capita Weight in Grams	Consumption Protein in Grams	Calories Per Person Per Day	Percentage Caloric Contribution of Meat and Vegtables
Meat	37	230	34.5	690	33
Mongongo nuts	33	210	56.7	1,260 ⎫	
Other vegetable foods	30	190	1.9	190 ⎭	67
Total All Sources	100	630	93.1	2,140	100

---

of the small size and stature but vigorous activity regime of the !Kung Bushmen. The RDA for Bushmen can be estimated at 1,975 calories and 60 grams of protein per person per day. Thus it is apparent that food output exceeds energy requirements by 165 calories and 33 grams of protein. One can tentatively conclude that even a modest subsistence effort of two or three days work per week is enough to provide an adequate diet for the !Kung Bushmen.

The Security of Bushman Life

I have attempted to evaluate the subsistence base of one contemporary hunter-gatherer society living in a marginal environment. The !Kung Bushmen have available to them some relatively abundant high-quality foods, and they do not have to walk very far or work very hard to get them. Furthermore this modest work effort provides sufficient calories to support not only the active adults, but also a large number of middle-aged and elderly people. The Bushmen do not have to press their youngsters into the service of the food quest, nor do they have to dispose of the oldsters after they have ceased to be productive.

The evidence presented assumes an added significance because this security of life was observed during the third year of one of the most severe droughts in South Africa's history. Most of the 576,000 people of Botswana are pastoralists and agriculturalists. After the crops had failed three years in succession and over 100,000 head of cattle had died on the range for lack of water, the World Food Program of the United Nations instituted a famine relief program which has grown to include 180,000 people, over 30 per cent of the population. This program did not touch the Dobe area in the isolated northwest corner of the country and the Herero and Tswana women there were able to feed their families only by joining the Bushman women to forage for wild foods. Thus the natural plant resources of the Dobe area were carrying a higher proportion of population than would be the case in years when the Bantu harvested crops. Yet this added pressure on the land did not seem to adversely affect the Bushmen.

In one sense it was unfortunate that the period of my field work happened to coincide with the drought, since I was unable to witness a "typical" annual subsistence cycle. However, in another sense, the coincidence was a lucky one, for the drought put the Bushmen and their subsistence system to the acid test and, in terms of adaptation to scarce resources, they passed with flying colors. One can postulate that their subsistence base would be even more substantial during years of higher rain fall.

What are the crucial factors that make this way of life possible? I suggest that the primary factor is the Bushmen's strong emphasis on vegetable food sources. Although hunting involves a great deal of effort and prestige, plant foods provide from 60-80 per cent of the annual diet by weight. Meat has come to be regarded as a special treat; when available, it is welcomed as a break from the routine of vegetable foods, but it is never depended upon as a staple. No one ever goes hungry when hunting fails.

The reason for this emphasis is not hard to find. Vegetable foods are abundant, sedentary, and predictable. They grow in the same place year after year, and the gatherer is guaranteed a day's return of food for a day's expenditure of energy. Game animals, by contrast, are scarce, mobile, unpredictable, and difficult to catch. A hunter has no guarantee of success and may in fact go for days or weeks without killing a large mammal. During the study period, there were eleven men in the Dobe camp, of whom four did no hunting at all. The seven active men spent a total of 78 man-day's hunting, and this work input yielded eighteen animals killed, or one kill for every four man-days of hunting. The probability of any one hunter making a kill on a given day was 0.23. By contrast, the probability of a woman finding plant food on a given day was 1.00. In other words, hunting and gathering are not equally felicitous subsistence alternatives.

Consider the productivity per man-hour of the two kinds of subsistence activities. One man-hour of hunting produces about 100 edible calories, and of gathering, 240 calories. Gathering is thus seen to be 2.4 times more productive than hunting. In short, hunting is a *high-risk, low-return* subsistence activity, while gathering is a *low-risk, high-return* subsistence activity.

It is not at all contradictory that the hunting complex holds a central place in the Bushman ethos and that meat is valued more highly than vegetable foods. Analogously, steak is valued more highly than potatoes in the food preferences in our own society. In both situations the meat is more "costly" than the vegetable food. In the Bushman case, the cost of food can be measured in terms of time and energy expended. By this standard, 1000 calories of meat "costs" ten man-hours, while the "cost" of 1,000 calories of vegetable foods is only four man-hours. Further, it is to be expected that the less predictable, more expensive food source would have a greater accretion of myth and ritual built up around it than would the routine staples of life, which rarely if ever fail.

Eskimo-Bushman Comparisons

Were the Bushmen to be deprived of their vegetable food sources, their life would become much more arduous and precarious. This lack of plant foods, in fact, is precisely the situation among the Netsilik Eskimo. The Netsilik and other Central Arctic peoples are perhaps unique in the almost total absence of vegetable foods in their diet. This factor, in combination with the great cyclical variation in the numbers and distribution of Arctic fauna, makes Eskimo life the most precarious human adaptation on earth. In effect *the kinds of animals that are "luxury goods" to many hunters and gatherers, are to the Eskimos, the absolute necessities of life.* However, even this view should not be exaggerated, since most of the Eskimos in historic times have lived south of the Arctic Circle and many of the Eskimos at all latitudes have depended primarily on fishing, which is a much more reliable source of food than is the hunting of land and sea mammals.

What Hunters Do for a Living: A Comparative Study

I have discussed how the !Kung Bushmen are able to manage on the scarce resources of their inhospitable environment. The essence of their successful strategy seems to be that while they depend primarily on the more stable and abundant food sources (vegetables in their case), they are nevertheless willing to devote considerable energy to the less reliable and more highly valued food sources such as medium and large mammals. The steady but modest input of work by the women provides the former, and the more intensive labors of the men provide the latter. It would be theoretically possible for the Bushmen to survive entirely on vegetable foods, but life would be boring indeed without the excitement of meat feasts. The totality of their subsistence activities thus represents an outcome of two individual goals; the first is the desire to live well with adequate leisure time, and the second is the desire to enjoy the rewards, both social and nutritional, afforded by the killing of game. In short, *the Bushmen of the Dobe area eat as much vegetable food as they need, and as much meat as they can.*

It seems reasonable that a similar kind of subsistence strategy would be characteristic of hunters and gatherers in general. Wherever two or more kinds of natural foods are available, one would predict that the population exploiting them would emphasize the more reliable source. We would also expect, however, that the people would not neglect the alternative means of subsistence. The general view offered here is that gathering activities, for plants and shellfish, should be the most productive of food for hunting and gathering man, followed by fishing, where this source is available. The hunting of mammals is the least reliable source of food and should be generally less important than either gathering or fishing. . . .

Conclusions

Three points ought to be stressed. First, life in the state of nature is not necessarily nasty, brutish, and short. The Dobe-area Bushmen live well today on wild plants and meat, in spite of the fact that they are confined to the least productive portion of the range in which Bushman peoples were formerly found. It is likely that an even more substantial subsistence base would have been characteristic of these hunters and gatherers in the past, when they had the pick of African habitats to choose from.

Second, the basis of Bushman diet is derived from sources other than meat. This emphasis makes good ecological sense to the !Kung Bushmen and appears to be a common feature among hunters and gatherers in general. Since a 30 to 40 per cent input of meat is such a consistent target for modern hunters in a variety of habitats, is iI not reasonable to postulate a similar percentage for prehistoric hunters? Certainly the absence of plant remains on archeological sites is by itself not sufficient evidence for the absence of gathering. Recently-abandoned Bushman campsites show a similar absence of vegetable remains, although this paper has clearly shown that plant foods comprise over 60 per cent of the actual diet.

Finally, one gets the impression that hunting societies have been chosen by ethnologists to illustrate a dominant theme, such as the extreme importance of environment in the molding of certain cultures. Such a theme can be best exemplified by cases in which the technology is simple and/or the environment is harsh. This emphasis on the dramatic may have been pedagogically useful, but unfortunately it has led to the assumption that a precarious hunting subsistence base was characteristic of all cultures in the Pleistocene. This view of both modern and ancient hunters ought to be reconsidered. Specifically

I am suggesting a shift in focus away from the dramatic and unusual cases, and toward a consideration of hunting and gathering as a persistent and well-adapted way of life.

Box 71

!Kung Update

Gathering and hunting will not, most likely, be a viable way of life for future generations of the semi-nomadic !Kung. Changes are accelerating around them. Roads, stores, schools, clinics, government welfare payments, and even high wages paid by the South African army to track nationalist guerrillas are all part of their existence now. While the !Kung are adapting to, and even actively pursuing the positive aspects of this new future, problems like over-grazing of land, alcoholism, violent crime, prostitution, and venereal disease are increasingly in evidence. Even heart disease, high blood pressure, and other stress-related diseases — absent in the past for the !Kung — are now present. It may well be that hunting and gathering, a style of life that has been practiced by the !Kung for thousands of years, will soon disappear.

SOURCE: M. Shostak: *Nisa: The Life and Words of a !Kungwoman* (New York: Vintage Books, 1983), pp. 345-371.

Questions

1. How did Lee gather his information? What was his research design? What was his hypothesis?

2. What assumptions underlie current anthropological views of hunting and gathering societies? Does Lee find them valid?

3. Who are the !Kung? Where and how do they live? Are they nomadic? Does the political situation in southern Africa affect them?

4. How large a food supply do they generally have on hand?

5. Describe their diet. How abundant is it? How varied?

6. What are the differences and similarities in roles of men and women in this society?

7. What is the position of the aged and the young?

8. What is life expectancy?

9. Contrast leisure and work activities. On which do they spend more time?

10. Is the modest work effort of the !Kung sufficient to provide the calories and protein necessary to maintain the health of the population?

11. Compare the !Kung and the Eskimo in terms of way of life.

12. Given the choice, do you prefer Bushmen society or your own?

13. What is the probable future of the !Kung?

Chapter Twenty-Seven

Eating Christmas in the Kalahari

Richard B. Lee

The !Kung Bushmen's knowledge of Christmas is thirdhand. The London Missionary Society brought the holiday to the southern Tswana tribes in the early nineteenth century. Later, native catechists spread the idea far and wide among the Bantu-speaking pastoralists, even in the remotest corners of the Kalahari Desert. The Bushmen's idea of the Christmas story, stripped to its essentials, is "praise the birth of white man's god-chief"; what keeps their interest in the holiday high is the Tswana-Herero custom of slaughtering an ox for his Bushmen neighbors as an annual goodwill gesture. Since the 1930's, part of the Bushmen's annual round of activities has included a December congregation at the cattle posts for trading, marriage brokering, and several days of trance-dance feasting at which the local Tswana headman is host.

As a social anthropologist working with !Kung Bushmen, I found that the Christmas ox custom suited my purposes. I had come to the Kalahari to study the hunting and gathering subsistence economy of the !Kung, and to accomplish this it was essential not to provide them with food, share my own food, or interfere in any way with their food-gathering activities. While liberal handouts of tobacco and medical supplies were appreciated, they were scarcely adequate to erase the glaring disparity in wealth between the anthropologist, who maintained a two-month inventory of canned goods, and the Bushmen, who

Reprinted with permission from *Natural History*, December 1969. Copyright the American Museum of Natural History, 1969.

rarely had a day's supply of food on hand. My approach, while paying off in terms of data, left me open to frequent accusations of stinginess and hard-heartedness. By their lights, I was a miser.

The Christmas ox was to be my way of saying thank you for the cooperation of the past year; and since it was to be our last Christmas in the field, I determined to slaughter the largest, meatiest ox that money could buy, insuring that the feast and trance-dance would be a success.

Through December I kept my eyes open at the wells as the cattle were brought down for watering. Several animals were offered, but none had quite the grossness that I had in mind. Then, ten days before the holiday, a Herero friend led an ox of astonishing size and mass up to our camp. It was solid black, stood five feet high at the shoulder, had a five-foot span of horns, and must have weighed 1,200 pounds on the hoof. Food consumption calculations are my specialty, and I quickly figured that bones and viscera aside, there was enough meat—at least four pounds—for every man, woman, and child of the 150 Bushmen in the vicinity of /ai/ai who were expected at the feast.

Having found the right animal at last, I paid the Herero £20 ($56) and asked him to keep the beast with his herd until Christmas day. The next morning word spread among the people that the big solid black one was the ox chosen by /ontah (my Bushman name; it means, roughly, "whitey") for the Christmas feast. That afternoon I received the first delegation. Ben!a, an outspoken sixty-year-old mother of five, came to the point slowly.

"Where were you planning to eat Christmas?"

"Right here at /ai/ai," I replied.

"Alone or with others?"

"I expect to invite all the people to eat Christmas with me."

"Eat what?"

"I have purchased Yehave's black ox, and I am going to slaughter and cook it."

"That's what we were told at the well but refused to believe it until we heard it from yourself."

"Well, it's the black one," I replied expansively, although wondering what she was driving at.

"Oh, no!" Ben!a groaned, turning to her group. "They were right." Turning back to me she asked, "Do you expect us to eat that bag of bones?"

"Bag of bones! It's the biggest ox at /ai/ai."

"Big, yes, but old. And thin. Everybody knows there's no meat on that old ox. What did you expect us to eat off it, the horns?"

Everybody chuckled at Ban!a's one-line as they walked away, but all I could manage was a weak grin.

That evening it was the turn of the young men. They came to sit at our evening fire. /gaugo, about my age, spoke to me man-to-man.

"/ontah, you have always been square with us," he lied. "What has happened to change your heart? That sack of guts and bones of Yehave's will hardly feed one camp, let alone all the Bushmen around /ai/ai." And he proceeded to enumerate the seven camps in the /ai/ai vicinity, family by family. "Perhaps you have forgotten that we are not few, but many. Or are you too blind to tell the difference between a proper cow and an old wreck? That ox is thin to the point of death."

"Look, you guys," I retorted, "that is a beautiful animal, and I'm sure you will eat it with pleasure at Christmas."

"Of course we will eat it; it's food. But it won't fill us up to the point where we will have enough strength to dance. We will eat and go home to bed with stomachs rumbling."

That night as we turned in, I asked my wife, Nancy: "What did you think of the black ox?"

"It looked enormous to me. Why?"

"Well, about eight different people have told me I got gypped; that the ox is nothing but bones."

"What's the angle?" Nancy asked. "Did they have a better one to sell?"

"No, they just said that it was going to be a grim Christmas because there won't be enough meat to go around. Maybe I'll get an independent judge to look at the beast in the morning."

Bright and early, Halingisi, a Tswana cattle owner, appeared at our camp. But before I could ask him to give me his opinion on Yehave's black ox, he gave me the eye signal that indicated a confidential chat. We left the camp and sat down.

"/ontah, I'm surprised at you: you've lived here for three years and still haven't learned anything about cattle."

"But what else can a person do but choose the biggest, strongest animal one can find?" I retorted.

"Look, just because an animal is big doesn't mean that it has plenty of meat on it. The black one was a beauty when it was younger, but now it is thin to the point of death."

"Well I've already bought it. What can I do at this stage?"

"Bought it already? I thought you were just considering it. Well, you'll have to kill it and serve it, I suppose. But don't expect much of a dance to follow."

My spirits dropped rapidly. I could believe that Ben!a and /gaugo just might be putting me on about the black ox, but Halingisi seemed to be an impartial critic. I went around that day feeling as though I had bought a lemon of a used car.

In the afternoon it was Tomazo's turn. Tomazo is a fine hunter, a top trance performer . . . and one of my most reliable informants. He approached the subject of the Christmas cow as part of my continuing Bushman education.

"My friend, the way it is with us Bushmen," he began, "is that we love meat. And even more than that, we love fat. When we hunt we always search for the fat ones, the ones dripping with layers of white fat: fat that turns into a clear, thick oil in the cooking pot, fat that slides down your gullet, fills your stomach and gives you a roaring diarrhea," he rhapsodized.

"So, feeling as we do," he continued, "it gives us pain to be served such a scrawny thing as Yehave's black ox. It is big, yes, and no doubt its giant bones are good for soup, but fat is what we really crave and so we will eat Christmas this year with a heavy heart."

The prospect of a gloomy Christmas now had me worried, so I asked Tomazo what I could do about it.

"Look for a fat one, a young one . . . smaller, but fat. Fat enough to make us //gom ('evacuate the bowels'), then we will be happy."

My suspicions were aroused when Tomazo said that he happened to know of a young, fat, barren cow that the owner was willing to part with. Was Tomazo working on commission, I wondered? But I dispelled this unworthy thought when we approached the Herero owner of the cow in question and found that he had decided not to sell.

The scrawny wreck of a Christmas ox now became the talk of the /ai /ai water hole and was the first news told to the outlying groups as they began to come in from the bush for the feast. What finally convinced me that real trouble might be brewing was the visit from u!au, an old conservative with a reputation for fierceness. His nickname meant spear and referred to an incident thirty years ago in which he had speared a man to death. He had an intense manner; fixing me with his eyes, he said in clipped tones:

"I have only just heard about the black ox today, or else I would have come here earlier. /ontah, do you honestly think you can serve meat like that to people and avoid a fight?" He paused, letting the implications sink in. "I don't mean fight you, /ontah; you are a white man. I mean a fight between Bushmen. There are many fierce ones here, and with such a small quantity of meat to distribute, how can you give everybody a fair share? Someone is sure to accuse another of taking too much or hogging all the choice pieces. Then you will see what happens when some go hungry while others eat."

The possibility of at least a serious argument struck me as all too real. I had witnessed the tension that surrounds the distribution of meat from a kudu or gemsbok kill, and had documented many arguments that sprang up from a real or imagined slight in meat distribution. The owners of a kill may spend up to two hours arranging and rearranging the piles of meat under the gaze of a circle of recipients before handing them out. And I also knew that the Christmas feast at /ai/ai would be bringing together groups that had feuded in the past.

Convinced now of the gravity of the situation, I went in earnest to search for a second cow; but all my inquiries failed to turn one up.

The Christmas feast was evidently going to be a disaster, and the incessant complaints about the meagerness of the ox had already taken the fun out of it for me. Moreover, I was getting bored with the wisecracks, and after losing my temper a few times, I resolved to serve the beast anyway. If the meat fell short, the hell with it. In the Bushmen idiom, I announced to all who would listen:

"I am a poor man and blind. If I have chosen one that is too old and too thin, we will eat it anyway and see if there is enough meat there to quiet the rumbling of our stomachs."

On hearing this speech, Ben!a offered me a rare word of comfort. "It's thin," she said philosophically, "but the bones will make a good soup."

At dawn Christmas morning, instinct told me to turn over the butchering and cooking to a friend and take off with Nancy to spend Christmas alone in the bush. But curiosity kept me from retreating. I wanted to see what such a scrawny ox looked like on butchering, and if there was going to be a fight, I wanted to catch every word of it. Anthropologists are incurable that way.

The great beast was driven up to our dancing ground, and a shot in the forehead dropped it in its tracks. Then, freshly cut branches were heaped around the fallen carcass to receive the meat. Ten men volunteered to help with the cutting. I asked /gaugo to make the breast bone cut. This cut, which begins the butchering process for most large game, offers easy access for removal of the viscera. But it also allows the hunter to spot-check the amount of fat on the animal. A fat game animal carries a white layer up to an inch thick on the chest, while in a thin one, the knife will quickly cut to bone. All eyes fixed on his hand as /gaugo, dwarfed by the great carcass, knelt to the breast. The first cut opened a pool of solid white in the black skin. The second and third cut widened and deepened the creamy white. Still no bone. It was pure fat; it must have been two inches thick.

"Hey /gau," I burst out, "that ox is loaded with fat. What's this about the ox being too thin to bother eating? Are you out of your mind?"

"Fat?" /gau shot back, "You call that fat? This wreck is thin, sick, dead!" And he broke out laughing. So did everyone else. They rolled on the ground, paralyzed with laughter. Everybody laughed except me; I was thinking.

I ran back to the tent and burst in just as Nancy was getting up. "Hey, the black ox. It's fat as hell! They were kidding about it being too thin to eat. It was a joke or something. A put-on. Everyone is really delighted with it!"

"Some joke," my wife replied. "It was so funny that you were ready to pack up and leave /ai/ai."

If it had indeed been a joke, it had been an extraordinarily convincing one, and tinged, I thought, with more than a touch of malice as many jokes are.

Nevertheless, that it was a joke lifted my spirits considerably, and I returned to the butchering site where the shape of the ox was rapidly disappearing under the axes and knives of the butchers. The atmosphere had become festive. Grinning broadly, their arms covered with blood well past the elbow, men packed chunks of meat into the big cast-iron cooking pots, fifty pounds to the load, and muttered and chuckled all the while about the thinness and worthlessness of the animal and /ontah's poor judgment.

We danced and ate that ox two days and two nights; we cooked and distributed fourteen potfuls of meat and no one went home hungry and no fights broke out.

But the "joke" stayed in my mind. I had a growing feeling that something important had happened in my relationship with the Bushmen and that the clue lay in the meaning of the joke. Several days later, when most of the people had dispersed back to the bush camps, I raised the question with Hakekgose, a Tswana man who had grown up among the !Kung, married a !Kung girl, and who probably knew their culture better than any other non-Bushman.

"With us whites," I began, "Christmas is supposed to be the day of friendship and brotherly love. What I can't figure out is why the Bushmen went to such lengths to criticize and belittle the ox I had bought for the feast. The animal was perfectly good and their jokes and wisecracks practically ruined the holiday for me."

"So it really did bother you," said Hakekgose. "Well, that's the way they always talk. When I take my rifle and go hunting with them, if I miss, they laugh at me for the rest of the day. But even if I hit and bring one down, it's no better. To them, the kill is always too small or too old or too thin; and as we sit down on the kill site to cook and eat the liver, they keep grumbling, even with their mouths full of meat. They say things like, 'Oh this is awful! What a worthless animal! Whatever made me think that this Tswana rascal could hunt!'"

"Is this the way outsiders are treated?" I asked.

"No, it is their custom; they talk that way to each other too. Go and ask them."

/gaugo had been one of the most enthusiastic in making me feel bad about the merit of the Christmas ox. I sought him out first.

"Why did you tell me the black ox was worthless, when you could see that it was loaded with fat and meat?"

"It is our way," he said smiling. "We always like to fool people about that. Say there is a Bushman who has been hunting. He must not come home and announce like a braggard, 'I have killed a big one in the bush!' He must first sit down in silence until I or someone else comes up to his fire and asks, 'What did you see today?' He replies quietly, 'Ah, I'm no good for hunting. I saw nothing at all [pause] just a little tiny one.' Then I smile to myself," /gaugo continued, "because I know he has killed something big.

"In the morning we make up a party of four or five people to cut up and carry the meat back to the camp. When we arrive at the kill we examine it and cry out, 'You mean to say you have dragged us all the way out here in order to make us cart home your pile of bones? Oh, if I had known it was this thin I wouldn't have come.' Another one pipes up, 'People, to think I gave up a nice day in the shade for this. At home we may be hungry but at least we have nice cool water to drink.' If the horns are big, someone says, 'Did you think that somehow you were going to boil down the horns for soup?'

"To all this you must respond in kind. 'I agree,' you say, 'this one is not worth the effort; let's just cook the liver for strength and leave the rest for the hyenas. It is not too late to hunt today and even a duiker or a steenbok would be better than this mess.'

"Then you set to work nevertheless; butcher the animal, carry the meat back to the camp and everyone eats," /gaugo concluded.

Things were beginning to make sense. Next, I went to Tomazo. He corroborated /gaugo's story of the obligatory insults over a kill and added a few details of his own.

"But," I asked, "why insult a man after he has gone to all that trouble to track and kill an animal and when he is going to share the meat with you so that your children will have something to eat?"

"Arrogance," was his cryptic answer.

"Arrogance?"

"Yes, when a young man kills much meat he comes to think of himself as a chief or a big man, and he thinks of the rest of us as his servants or inferiors. We can't accept this. We refuse one who boasts, for someday his pride will make him kill somebody. So we always speak of his meat as worthless. This way we cool his heart and make him gentle."

"But why didn't you tell me this before?" I asked Tomazo with some heat.

"Because you never asked me," said Tomazo, echoing the refrain that has come to haunt every field ethnographer.

The pieces now fell into place. I had known for a long time that in situations of social conflict with Bushmen I held all the cards. I was the only source of tobacco in a thousand square miles, and I was not incapable of cutting an individual off for noncooperation. Though my boycott never lasted longer than a few days, it was an indication of my strength. People resented my presence at the water hole, yet simultaneously dreaded my leaving. In short I was a perfect target for the charge of arrogance and for the Bushmen tactic of enforcing humility.

I had been taught an object lesson by the Bushmen; it had come from an unexpected corner and had hurt me in a vulnerable area. For the big black ox was to be the one totally generous, unstinting act of my year at /ai/ai, and I was quite unprepared for the reaction I received.

As I read it, their message was this: There are no totally generous acts. All "acts" have an element of calculation. One black ox slaughtered at Christmas does not wipe out a year of careful manipulation of gifts given to serve your own ends. After all, to kill an animal and share the meat with people is really no more than Bushmen do for each other every day and with far less fanfare.

In the end, I had to admire how the Bushmen had played out the farce—collectively straight-faced to the end. Curiously, the episode reminded me of the *Good Soldier Schweik* and his marvelous encounters with authority. Like Schweik, the Bushmen had retained a thorough-going skepticism of good intentions. Was it this independence of spirit, I wondered, that had kept them culturally viable in the face of generations of contact with more powerful societies, both black and white? The thought that the Bushmen were alive and well in the Kalahari was strangely comforting. Perhaps, armed with that independence and with their superb knowledge of their environment, they might yet survive the future.

Questions

1. Why hadn't Lee shared his food with the !Kung prior to the Christmas ox?
2. What does arrogance have to do with the joke being played on Lee?

Chapter Twenty-Eight

The Transformation of the Kalahari !Kung

John E. Yellen

We study history to understand the present. Yet sometimes the present can help to clarify the past. So it is with a San-speaking people known as the !Kung—a group of what were once called African Bushmen. Dramatic changes now occurring in the !Kung culture are illuminating a major problem in anthropology: why did most hunting and gathering societies disappear rapidly after coming in contact with societies that kept domesticated animals and plants?

This swift disappearance is puzzling. After all, hunting for animals and gathering wild plants was a robust enough strategy to ensure the survival of anatomically modern human beings from their emergence more than 50,000 years ago until some time after the first animals and plants were domesticated, roughly 10,000 years ago. Conventional wisdom suggests that many traditional societies, recognizing the nutritional advantages of herding and agriculture, simply abandoned their old practices once they learned about newer subsistence strategies. Yet a number of observations indicate that dissatisfaction with foraging is apparently the wrong explanation in many instances.

Archaeologists have shown, for example, that foraging can actually be more beneficial than herding and farming. Detailed analyses of skeletal remains reveal that in parts of North America a shift to agriculture was in fact detrimental to nutrition, health and longevity for certain groups. Similarly, in modern times

From *Scientific American*, April 1990, pp. 96–105. Copyright © 1990 by Scientific American, Inc. Reprinted with permission, all rights reserved.

it has become clear that when droughts strike southern Africa, groups that rely heavily on hunting and gathering tend to be affected less severely than groups that depend primarily on water-hungry herds and crops.

Moreover, foraging probably is not as taxing and unfruitful as it is stereotypically portrayed. Richard B. Lee, when he was a doctoral student at the University of California at Berkeley in the 1960s, found that the !Kung, who at the time were among the few groups in the world still obtaining most of their food by foraging, did not live on the brink of starvation, even though they inhabited the harsh Kalahari Desert. (The !Kung occupy the northwest corner of Botswana and adjacent areas of Namibia and Angola.) Indeed, they spent only several hours each day seeking food.

What, then, accounts for the decline of foraging societies? No one can say definitely, but glimmers of an answer that may have broad application are emerging from studies focusing on the recent changes in the !Kung way of life. Today young boys no longer learn to hunt, and some of the behavioral codes that gave the society cohesion are eroding. One major catalyst of change appears to have been a sudden easy access to goods. Perhaps a similar phenomenon contributed to the demise of past foraging societies.

It is fortunate that a rather detailed portrait of the !Kung's traditional culture was compiled before the onset of dramatic change. Many investigators deserve credit for what is known, including the independent anthropologist Lorna Marshall, who began studying the group in 1951, and Irven DeVore, Lee and other participants in what was called the Harvard Kalahari Project. One aim of the project, which officially ran from the late 1960s into the 1970s (and in which I participated as a doctoral student), was to understand how traditional hunting and gathering societies functioned.

Any description of the !Kung begins most appropriately with a brief history of the peoples in southern Africa. Before the start of the first millennium A.D., Africa south of the Zambezi River was still populated exclusively by foragers who almost certainly were of short stature, had light-brown skin and spoke what are called Khoisan languages (all of which, like those in the San group, include clicks). In the still more distant past, the various groups had apparently shared a common language and culture and then, as they spread out, adapted to the specific conditions of the regions where they settled. Some had adjusted to the seasonal cold of the Drakensberg Mountains, others to the coastal areas (with their wealth of fish), and still others to the drier conditions of the deserts and other inland areas.

The various groups were what archaeologists call late Stone Age peoples; their knife blades and scraping tools were made of stone and specialized for particular tasks. As yet there were none of the hallmarks of so-called Iron Age peoples: domesticated goats, sheep and cattle; cultivated grains such as millet and sorghum; pottery; and smelted and forged iron and copper.

Box 72

Southern Africa

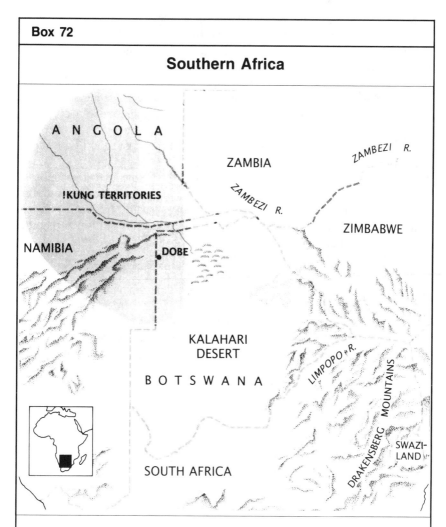

Southern Africa is home to many indigenous groups of San speakers (formerly known as Bushmen), including some who lived essentially as hunters and gatherers, or foragers, well into the 20th century. The !Kung, perhaps the best studied of the San, occupy the Kalahari Desert in parts of Botswana, Namibia and Angola. Much of what is known of the group has been gleaned from anthropological and archaeological studies conducted by a number of investigators in the Dobe region of Botswana.

The first Iron Age influences appeared in southern Africa some time early in the first millennium A.D., when, according to the archaeological record, occasional goods and domesticated animals were introduced, presumably by trade with peoples in more northern territories. The items were soon followed by Iron Age settlers themselves. These newcomers from the north spoke mostly Bantu languages and, compared with the foragers, were taller and darker-skinned. Either directly or indirectly, all of the foraging groups were eventually exposed to the new settlers and technologies and, later, to waves of European intruders: the Dutch and the Portuguese beginning in the 15th and 16th centuries and then the English and Germans as well.

Artifacts as well as journals of European settlers indicate that some of the hunting and gathering groups were exterminated by the intruders. In most other instances, according to clues provided by genetic studies, linguistic analyses and other methods, groups broke up (forcibly or otherwise), often merging with their new neighbors through intermarriage.

In certain cases, foragers were able to maintain a distinct genetic and cultural identity. Some of them, changing many practices, became transformed into new cultures. (For example, the first Dutch settlers, arriving at the southern tip of Africa, met "Hottentots," Khoisan speakers who herded flocks of sheep, goats and cows.) In the Karroo Desert of South Africa and in the northern Kalahari, however, a few hunting and gathering societies—among them, the !Kung—not only stayed intact but also apparently held onto many of their old ways.

Indeed, even as late as 1968, when I first visited the Kalahari as part of the Harvard project, most !Kung men and women in the Dobe region of Botswana still dressed in animal skins and subsisted primarily by hunting and gathering. (Dobe is the site most intensively studied by the project; the people there are, by all indications, quite representative of the !Kung over a broader area.) It is true that iron had long since replaced stone in tools, and plastic and metal containers had supplanted their ceramic counterparts. Yet men still hunted with bows and poisoned arrows, and women set out daily with digging sticks to seek edible plants.

At least it seemed to us that the people we met were behaving much as their ancient ancestors had. Some scholars dissent from that view, contending that the forerunners of 20th-century foragers were probably altered radically by contact with Iron Age peoples. If so, they say, modern foragers, including the !Kung, may reflect but little of the past.

In my view, strong evidence suggests that the !Kung studied in the early years of the Harvard project were very much like their distant forebears. For example, I have determined that the range of stone tools excavated from what is now !Kung territory remained remarkably constant into the late 19th century (when the grandparents of modern !Kung adults would have been born). This finding means that the region was probably populated continuously by one cultural group and that its foraging and manufacturing practices remained essentially unaffected by Iron Age influences.

What were the traditional ways of the !Kung? Observations made back in the 1950s and 1960s reveal that the group's strategy for obtaining food—and in fact its entire social organization—was exquisitely adapted for survival in the Kalahari. There, rainfall can vary dramatically from year to year and region to region, giving rise to profound shifts in the availability of food.

When it came to securing food, the !Kung followed what I call a generalist strategy. Rather than specializing in the pursuit of a limited number of species, as could be done in more predictable environments, they cast their foraging "net" broadly and so could usually find something to eat even if favored foods were in short supply. Remarkably, Lee found that males hunted more than 60 animal species, ranging in size from hare to buffalo. Females recognized more than 100 edible plant species, collecting perhaps a dozen varieties in a single day.

Certain accepted foraging guidelines minimized competition for the desert's limited resources. For example, groups of people were loosely organized into bands, and each band had the right to seek food in specified areas. During the dry season the members of a single band would congregate, setting up camps near a water hole (a year-round source of drinking water) understood to belong to that band. From the camps, individuals or small clusters of people would fan out each day to forage. During the rest of the year, when rainfall was more frequent and rain collected in shallow depressions in the ground known as pans, bands would disperse; small groups foraged in less trafficked areas, staying for as short as a day (and rarely as long as two months) before moving on.

The band system actually made it easy for people to migrate to more desirable places when the territory allotted to a given band was unproductive or becoming depleted. Band membership was rather fluid, and so a family could readily join a different band having more luck.

Consider the options open to a husband and wife, who would have had few possessions to hamper their travels. They could claim the right to join the bands available to both sets of parents, which means that at least four territories were open to them. Moreover, they could join any band in which their brothers or sisters had rights. If the couple also had married children, they might, alternatively, forage anywhere the children's spouses could; indeed, parents frequently arranged their children's marriages with an eye to the accompanying territorial privileges. Individuals could also claim band memberships on the basis of certain less direct kinship ties and on friendship.

The social values of the !Kung complemented this flexible band system, helping to ensure that food was equitably distributed. Most notably, an ethic

Box 73

!Kung Diet Between 1944 and 1975

TIME PERIOD	LARGE MAMMALS GREATER KUDU/CATTLE	MEDIUM MAMMALS STEENBOK/GOAT	SMALL MAMMALS SPRINGHARE/PORCUPINE	REPTILES AND AMPHIBIANS PUFF ADDER/BULLFROG	BIRDS GUINEA FOWL/CHICKEN
1944–1962	1.40	2.40	1.80	0.80	1.20
1963–1968	2.86	2.86	2.14	1.71	1.86
1970–1971	2.33	3.33	2.33	1.67	1.33
1972–1975	2.00	2.75	2.00	1.25	2.25

AVERAGE NUMBER OF SPECIES

!KUNG DIET remained varied between 1944 and 1975, according to an analysis of animal bones excavated from dry-season camps at Dobe. The author identified and counted the number of bones at each camp to learn the relative numbers of the large, medium and small mammalian species and the reptilian, amphibian and bird species consumed at each camp during four periods. (Selected examples are shown.) The balance across categories changed little, indicating that variety was maintained, as was the !Kung's generalist food-securing strategy. The persistence of a diverse diet even after domesticated animals were acquired in the 1970's indicates that the group had not become dependent on their herds, which apparently were viewed as foraging resources like any others. Hence, the popular notion that dissatisfaction with foraging caused hunting and gathering societies of the past to abandon their old way of life does not seem to hold for the Dobe !Kung.

of sharing formed the core of the self-described !Kung system of values. Families were expected to welcome relatives who showed up at their camps. Moreover, etiquette dictated that meat from large kills be shared outside the immediate family, which was obviously a sound survival strategy: a hunter who killed a large antelope or the like would be hard pressed, even with the help of his wife and children, to eat all its meat. By distributing his bounty, the hunter ensured that the recipients of his largess would be obliged to return the favor some time in the future.

Similarly, individuals also established formal relationships with nonrelatives in which two people gave each other gifts such as knives or iron spears at irregular intervals. Reciprocity was delayed, so that one partner would always be in debt to the other. Pauline Weissner, when she was a graduate student at the University of Michigan at Ann Arbor, analyzed those reciprocity relationships and concluded that individuals purposely selected gift-giving partners from distant territories. Presumably it was hoped that a partner would have something to offer when goods were difficult to obtain locally. Hence, in the traditional !Kung view of the world, security was obtained by giving rather than hoarding, that is, by accumulating obligations that could be claimed in times of need.

Clearly, mobility was a critical prerequisite for maintaining reciprocity relationships over long distances and for making it possible to move elsewhere when foraging conditions were unfavorable. The !Kung system of justice had the same requirement of ready movement. Like many other traditional foraging groups, the !Kung society was acephalous, or headless: no one was in charge of adjudicating disputes. When disagreements became serious, individuals or groups of disputants simply put distance between themselves, claiming membership in widely separated bands. As long as everyone could carry their few possessions on their backs, and so could relocate with ease, the approach worked well.

The traditional !Kung, then, were well suited to the Kalahari. They were generalists who lived by the ethic of sharing, ensuring that those who were less successful at finding food could usually be fed nonetheless. Because families owned no more than they could carry, they were able to travel at will whenever resources became scarce or disputes too heated.

By 1975, however, the !Kung were undergoing a cultural transition—at least so it seemed by all appearances at Dobe. I left there in 1970 and returned in the middle of the decade. I found that, in the interim, many families had taken on the ways of the neighboring Bantu. A number had planted fields and acquired herds of goats along with an occasional cow. Fewer of the boys were learning to hunt; traditional bows and arrows were still produced but mostly for eventual sale on a worldwide curio market. The people wore mass-produced clothing instead of animal skins, and traditional grass huts were for the most part replaced by more substantial mud-walled structures, which were now inhabited for longer periods than in the past.

An influx of money and supplies had clearly played a part in many of these changes. Botswana became an independent nation in 1966, after having been the British protectorate Bechuanaland. The new government began to encourage the keeping of livestock and the development of agriculture, such as by giving donkeys to the !Kung for pulling simple plows. And it arranged for the routine purchase of traditional handicrafts (for example, bead necklaces), thereby injecting extraordinary sums of money into the community. Later, when the !Kung in Namibia (then a colony of South Africa) were brought into the South African Army, the !Kung in Botswana received more infusions of cash and goods, mainly via interactions with kin.

Yet the exact meaning of such surface changes remained unclear. To what extent did the livestock and fields, the new clothes and the sturdier huts reflect a weakness in the glue that held !Kung society together? Why had the men and women, who had long been successful as foragers and who were not coerced into changing, decided to take on the burdens of herds and crops and to otherwise allow their mobility to be compromised? Archaeological work I undertook at Dobe between 1975 and 1982 (first as a research associate at the Smithsonian Institution and then as an employee of the National Science Foundation), together with observations made by other workers during the same period, provides some hints.

To be frank, when I returned in 1975, a methodological question preoccupied me. I hoped to learn about what happened to the bones of hunted animals after the carcasses were discarded and became buried naturally in the ground; such information was important for developing archaeological techniques to determine how people in the past killed, butchered and cooked animals. I thought that by locating the remains of old cooking hearths at Dobe, around which families ate, I might gather a good collection of bones—the remains of meals—on which to test a few ideas. Later I realized the data I had collected in the course of this endeavor might also say something about the transformation of the !Kung.

As part of my studies I identified and mapped the locations of huts and their associated hearths dating back to 1944. I then dug up bones that had been dropped in and around the hearths and identified the species to which they belonged (see Box 73). In visits made after 1975, I no longer collected bones, but I continued to map contemporary camps; in the end, I accumulated almost 40 years of settlement data.

The camps were usually occupied by the same extended family and close relatives, such as in-laws, although the specific mix of individuals changed somewhat from year to year. At the older sites, where all visible traces of occupation had disappeared, the huts and the hearths (which were normally

Box 74

Arrangements of Camps

SIMPLE STORAGE STRUCTURE   STORAGE PLATFORM

Legend:
- ⊂ HUT
- × HEARTH
- ▤ STORAGE STRUCTURES
- Y

GOAT KRAAL

DONKEY KRAAL

THORNY FENCE

ARRANGEMENTS of camps changed markedly between 1944 and 1982. The changes, revealed by a series of maps much like these of dry-season camps, seem to reflect a decline in the cohesion of !Kung society. Until the early 1970's the traditional !Kung camp (left) was intimate: closely spaced huts roughly described a circle, and the entryways faced inward so that from a single vantage one could see into many huts. Then the arrangements changed abruptly (center): the average distance between huts increased, and the circular arrangement yielded to linear and other private arrays. The dwellings—which in the past were made of branches and grass (*a*) and now resembled the semipermanent mud-walled huts of the Bantu (*b*)—were sometimes isolated and fenced. Hearths, formerly the focal point of social exchange, were moved inside many huts. Kraals (pens for animals) gained a central place in camp, and private food-storage structures (*c*) joined the landscape.

placed outside a hut's entryway) were identified with the help of family members who actually remembered the placements.

My data supported the conclusion that by the mid-1970s long-standing !Kung values, such as the emphasis on intimacy and interdependence, were no longer guiding behavior as effectively as they once did. The data also indicated that, despite appearances to the contrary, the !Kung had retained their foraging "mentality." These generalists had taken up herding as if their goats and few cows were no different from any other readily accessible foraging resource. This surprising discovery meant that factors other than a failure of the food-securing system were at the root of the !Kung transformation.

My sense that traditional values were losing their influence over behavior came mainly from my analyses of the maps I had drawn (combined with other observations). Traditional !Kung camps, as depicted in the first 25 or so maps, were typically arranged in a circle, and most entrances faced inward. The huts were also set close together, so that from the entrance of one of them it was possible to see into most of the others.

The camp arrangement remained close and intimate until the early 1970s. Then suddenly the distance between huts increased significantly. At the same time, the circular pattern yielded to linear and other arrangements that gave families more privacy; also, in the last two camps I mapped (dating to 1981 and 1982), many of the hearths, which had been central to much social interaction, were located inside the huts instead of in front of them. The changes occurred so abruptly that the pattern of camp design can be said to have been unambiguously transformed from "close" to "distant" within a few years. By implication, such changes in camp design indicate that major changes in social norms for openness and sharing occurred as well in the early to middle 1970s.

This conclusion is consistent with other evidence. In 1976 Diane E. Gelburd, then a graduate student at George Washington University, inventoried the material possessions of individuals at Dobe and compared her data with a survey Lee had conducted in 1963. Whereas Lee found that most people could carry all their worldly belongings with ease, Gelburd found a dramatically different situation. She showed that many !Kung owned large items, such as plows and cast iron pots, which are difficult to transport. With their newfound cash they had also purchased such goods as glass beads, clothing and extra blankets, which they hoarded in metal trunks (often locked) in their huts. Many times the items far exceeded the needs of an individual family and could best be viewed as a form of savings or investment. In other words, the !Kung were behaving in ways that were clearly antithetical to the traditional sharing system.

Yet the people still spoke of the need to share and were embarrassed to open their trunks for Gelburd. Clearly, their stated values no longer directed their activity. Although spoken beliefs and observed behavior do not coincide perfectly in any society, at Dobe in 1976 the disjunction had become extreme.

In what way did my other data set—the animal bones—clarify the causes of the social changes apparent by the 1970s? The presence of domesticated animals and cultivated fields at Dobe caused me to wonder if the changes I saw in the !Kung could be traced through some sequence of events to discontent with foraging. If the bones revealed that by the mid-1970s the !Kung derived meat almost exclusively from domesticated animals, the conclusion could then be entertained that a shift in subsistence strategy had preceded other dramatic social changes and, hence, might have somehow given rise to them.

My data confirmed earlier impressions that through the 1950s the !Kung were almost exclusively hunters and gatherers: in sites dating from that period, the bones of domesticated animals are rare. Then, in the 1960s, the consumption of goat and cattle increased markedly; in fact, by 1974 and 1975 these animals were consumed more than any others. The frequency with which chicken was consumed also increased during that period, although the Dobe !Kung never did eat very much of this Western staple. At the same time—from 1944 to 1975—the once great popularity of certain wild animals waned, including the greater kudu (a large antelope regularly hunted in the dry season) and two smaller antelopes (the steenbok and duiker).

A cursory look at these data might have suggested that the !Kung were indeed abandoning hunting. Yet a closer examination revealed that cattle essentially substituted for kudu, both of which are large animals, and that goats, which approximate steenbok and duiker in size, directly replaced those animals in the diet. It also turns out that the number of species represented at each camp remained essentially the same, as did the mix of small, medium and large species. That is, if the meat diet of the !Kung in the 1940s normally consisted of 10 species, of which 50 percent were small, 30 percent medium and 20 percent large, roughly the same numbers would be found in a 1975 camp, although the species in each category might differ.

These findings show that the !Kung did not reduce the variety in their diet, as would be expected if they had abandoned the traditional, generalist strategy and had committed themselves to becoming herders, who typically are dependent on just a few animal species. Hence, I realized that although anthropologists might view "wild" and "domestic" animals as fundamentally different, the !Kung as late as 1975 did not make such a distinction. From the !Kung perspective, goats were essentially the same as any other medium-size animal (in that they provided a reasonable yield of meat and were relatively easy to carry), and cows were the same as other large creatures. If an animal was easy to obtain, the !Kung ate it, but they apparently did not come to depend on their herd animals to the exclusion of all others.

Anecdotal information supports the assessment that the !Kung of 1975 did not view themselves as herders. For instance, whereas Bantu groups, who depend on their herds for food and prestige, would quickly kill a hyena that preyed on their animals, many !Kung men would not bother to do so. I believe the !Kung would have been less indifferent if they had considered their herds to be all-important sources of meat. Similarly, they seemed to conceive of agriculture and wage labor undertaken for the Bantu and anthropologists— activities they pursued on a part-time, short-term basis—much as they perceived herding: as foraging resources just like any other.

Thus, well into the 1970s, the !Kung retained their generalist strategy, limiting their reliance on any one type of resource. Obviously that approach was adaptable enough to permit the transition from a foraging to a more mixed economy without disrupting social functioning.

If neither empty bellies nor coercion initiated the !Kung's transformation, what did? The impetus may well have come largely from internal stresses generated by the desire to have the material goods that had become readily accessible. The following scenario—based in part on my map data, Gelburd's work and my interactions with the !Kung over the years—is one plausible sequence of events that may have occurred. The scenario does not attempt to be a comprehensive description of how and why the !Kung culture has changed, but it does describe some of the major processes that seem to be driving the society's transformation.

Once the !Kung had ready access to wealth, they chose to acquire objects that had never before been available to them. Soon they started hoarding instead of depending on others to give them gifts, and they retreated from their past interdependence. At the same time, perhaps in part because they were ashamed of not sharing, they sought privacy. Where once social norms called for intimacy, now there was a disjunction between word and action. Huts faced away from one another and were separated, and some hearths were moved inside, making the whole range of social activities that had occurred around them more private. As the old rules began to lose their relevance, boys became less interested in living as their fathers had. They no longer wished to hunt and so no longer tried to learn the traditional skills; instead they preferred the easier task of herding.

Meanwhile the acquisition of goods limited mobility, a change that came to be reflected in the erection of semipermanent mud-walled huts. The lack of mobility fueled still more change, in part because the people could no longer resolve serious arguments in the traditional manner, by joining relatives elsewhere in !Kung territories.

With the traditional means of settling disputes now gone, the !Kung turned to local Bantu chiefs for arbitration. In the process they sacrificed autonomy and, like other San groups, increased their reliance on, and incorporation into, Bantu society. In fact, many !Kung families currently have close relationships with individual Bantu and look on them as protectors.

For their part, the Bantu have accepted the role, often speaking of "my

Bushmen." Marriage of !Kung women to Bantu men is now fairly common, an ominous sign for the cohesion of !Kung society. The children of these unions obtain full rights within the Bantu system, including the right to inherit livestock, and are more likely to think of themselves as Bantu than as !Kung.

Genetic studies of many Bantu-speaking peoples in southern Africa show that Khoisan speakers have been melding into Bantu societies for centuries. Very possibly some of those Khoisan groups and similar ones elsewhere in the world followed a course something like the modern !Kung at Dobe are following now; that is, the acquisition of goods led to a lack of mobility and to societal stresses fatal to the group's cohesion.

Today the issue of whether the !Kung experience is applicable to foraging societies of the past can best be resolved by comparing the forces acting on the !Kung with those acting on the remnants of other foraging societies in Africa, Asia and South America. These groups merit intense and immediate scrutiny. If they are ignored, an important opportunity to understand more about the ways of past foraging groups and about the forces leading to their demise will soon pass forever.

Further Reading

Kalahari Hunter-Gatherers: Studies of the !Kung San and Their Neighbours. Edited by Richard B. Lee and Irven DeVore. Harvard University Press, 1976.
The !Kung of Nyae Nyae. Lorna Marshall. Harvard University Press, 1976.
The !Kung San: Men, Women and Work in a Foraging Society. Richard B. Lee. Cambridge University Press, 1979.
Optimizing and Risk in Human Foraging Strategies. John E. Yellen in *Journal of Human Evolution*, Vol. 15, pages 733–750; 1986.

Questions

1. Is foraging—hunting and gathering—detrimental to nutrition, health, and longevity?
2. What accounts for the decline of foraging societies?
3. Describe the history of the !Kung people.
4. How did the "traditional" !Kung people obtain food?
5. Was there variety in their diet?
6. Did organization into "bands" help them succeed? Who is the head of a band?
7. How do the "present day" !Kung people obtain food?

8. Describe a typical, traditional !Kung camp. How has it changed over time? What does this tell us?

9. Is sharing still important for the !Kung?

10. Why was Yellen interested in what happened to the "bones of hunted animals after the carcasses were discarded and became buried naturally in the ground"?

11. What do you think an anthropologist would find if he were to visit the !Kung in the year 2000?

12. Answer question 2 again.

Part IX

The Elderly in Two Societies

A person born in the United States today can expect to live, on the average, for 75 years. "Why They Live to Be 100 or Even Older, in Abkhasia" looks at longevity on collective farms in the Soviet Union. Anthropologist Sula Benet believes the reason Abkhasians live longer than Americans is because of cultural factors that structure their existence. There is a uniformity and certainty about behavior and an unbroken continuum of life's activities. As the author concludes: "Can Americans learn something from the Abkhasian view of long living people? I think so."

"The Vintage Years" focuses on the "graying of America." Until recently, most accounts of life of the elderly in the United States were negative. Psychologists Jack Horn and Jeff Meer, however, paint a positive picture. They stress the diversity of the aged and point out that most of the elderly have adequate incomes and are fully capable of getting about on their own. While problems such as ageism, ill health, and isolation exist, new research shows that many "older people can maintain and enjoy most of their physical and mental abilities, and even improve in some areas." This is good news since it is predicted that the proportion of the elderly will grow dramatically in the future. The huge baby-boom generation, the one that didn't trust anyone over thirty, will start to retire early in the twenty-first century. The responsibility to care for this group will fall on the shoulders of those of you who are now reading this article!

Chapter Twenty-Nine

Why They Live to Be 100 or Even Older, in Abkhasia

Sula Benet

Not long ago, in the village of Tarnish in the Soviet Republic of Abkhasia, I raised my glass of wine to toast a man who looked no more than 70. "May you live as long as Moses (120 years)," I said. He was not pleased. He was 119.

For centuries, the Abkhasians and other Caucasian peasants have been mentioned in the chronicles of travelers amazed at their longevity and good health. Even now, on occasion, newspaper reports in the United States and elsewhere (never quite concealing bemusement and skepticism) will tell of an Abkhasian who claims to be 120, sometimes 130. When I returned from Abkhasia to New York displaying photographs and statistics, insisting that the tales are true and preoccupied with the question of why, my American friends invariably responded with the mocking question that contained its own answer: "Yogurt?" As a matter of fact, no, not yogurt; but the Abkhasians *do* drink a lot of buttermilk.

Abkhasia is a hard land—the Abkhasians, expressing more pride than resentment, say it was one of God's afterthoughts—but it is a beautiful one; if the Abkhasians are right about its mythical origin, God had a good second thought. It is subtropical on its coast along the Black Sea, alpine if one travels straight back from the sea, through the populated lowlands and valleys, to the main range of the Caucasus Mountains (see Box 75).

The Abkhasians have been there for at least 1,000 years. For centuries they were herdsmen in the infertile land, but now the valleys and foothills are planted

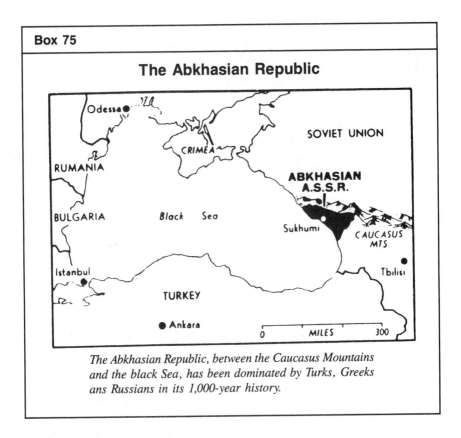

Box 75

The Abkhasian Republic

*The Abkhasian Republic, between the Caucasus Mountains
and the black Sea, has been dominated by Turks, Greeks
ans Russians in its 1,000-year history.*

with tea and tobacco, and they draw their living largely from agriculture. There
are 100,000 Abkhasians, not quite a fifth of the total population of the
autonomous Abkhasian Republic, which is, administratively, part of Georgia,
Joseph Stalin's birthplace; the rest are Russians, Greeks and Georgians.
However, most of the people in government are Abkhasian, and both the official
language and the style of life throughout the region are Abkhasian. The single
city, Sukhumi, is the seat of government and a port of call for ships carrying
foreign tourists. They are often visible in the streets of the city, whose population
includes relatively few Abkhasians. Even those who live and work there tend
to consider the villages of their families their own real homes. It is in the
villages—575 of them between the mountains and the sea, ranging in population
from a few hundred to a few thousand—that most Abkhasians live and work
on collective farms.

   I first went there in the summer of 1970 at the invitation of the Academy
of Sciences of the USSR. The Abkhasians were fascinating: I returned last

summer and will go again next year. It was while interviewing people who had participated in the early efforts at collectivization that I became aware of the unusually large number of people, ranging in age from 80 to 119, who are still very much a part of the collective life they helped organize.

After spending months with them, I still find it impossible to judge the age of older Abkhasians. Their general appearance does not provide a clue: You know they are old because of their gray hair and the lines on their faces, but are they 70 or 107? I would have guessed "70" for all of the old people that I encountered in Abkhasia, and most of the time I would have been wrong.

It is as if the physical and psychological changes which to us signify the aging process had, in the Abkhasians, simply stopped at a certain point. Most work regularly. They are still blessed with good eyesight, and most have their own teeth. Their posture is unusually erect, even into advanced age; many take walks of more than two miles a day and swim in the mountain streams. They look healthy, and they are a handsome people. Men show a fondness for enormous mustaches, and are slim but not frail. There is an old saying that when a man lies on his side, his waist should be so small that a dog can pass beneath it. The women are darkhaired and also slender, with fair complexions and shy smiles.

There are no correct figures for the total number of aged in Abkhasia, though in the village of Dzhgerda, which I visited last summer, there were 71 men and 110 women between 81 and 90 and 19 people over 91 — 15 per cent of the village population of 1,200. And it is worth noting that this extraordinary percentage is not the result of a migration by the young: Abkhasians, young and old, understandably prefer to stay where they are, and rarely travel, let alone migrate. In 1954, the last year for which overall figures are available, 2.58 per cent of the Abkhasians were over 90. The roughly comparable figures for the entire Soviet Union and the United States were 0.1 per cent and 0.4 per cent, respectively.

Since 1932, the longevity of the Abkhasians has been systematically studied on several occasions by Soviet and Abkhasian investigators, and I was given full access to their findings by the Ethnographic Institute in Sukhumi. These studies have shown that, in general, signs of arteriosclerosis, when they occurred at all, were found only in extreme old age. One researcher who examined a group of Abkhasians over 90 found that close to 40 per cent of the men and 30 per cent of the women had vision good enough to read or thread a needle without glasses, and that over 40 per cent had reasonably good hearing. There were no reported cases of either mental illness or cancer in a nine-year study of 123 people over 100.

In that study, begun in 1960 by Dr. G.N. Sichinava of the Institute of Gerontology in Sukhumi, the aged showed extraordinary psychological and neurological stability. Most of them had clear recollection of the distant past, but partially bad recollection for more recent events. Some reversed this pattern, but quite a large number retained a good memory of both the recent and distant past. All correctly oriented themselves in time and place. All showed clear and logical thinking, and most correctly estimated their physical and mental capacities. They showed a lively interest in their families' affairs, in their collective and in social events. All were agile, neat and clean.

Abkhasians are hospitalized only rarely, except for stomach disorders and childbirth. According to doctors who have inspected their work, they are expert at setting broken arms and legs themselves—their centuries of horsemanship have given them both the need and the practice.

The Abkhasian view of the aging process is clear from their vocabulary. They do not have a phrase for "old people"; those over 100 are called "long living people." Death, in the Abkhasian view is not the logical end of life but something irrational. The aged seem to lose strength gradually, wither in size and finally die; when that happens, Abkhasians show their grief fully, even violently.

For the rest of the world, disbelief is the response not to Abkhasians' deaths but to how long they have lived. There really should no longer be any question about their longevity. All of the Soviet medical investigators took great care to cross-check the information they received in interviews. Some of the men studied had served in the army, and military records invariably supported their own accounts. Extensive documentation is lacking only because the Abkhasians had no functioning written language until after the Russian Revolution.

But why *do* they live so long? The absence of a written history, and the relatively recent period in which medical and anthropological studies have taken place, preclude a clear answer. Genetic selectivity is an obvious possibility. Constant hand-to-hand combat during many centuries of Abkhasians existence may have eliminated those with poor eyesight, obesity and other physical shortcomings, producing healthier Abkhasians in each succeeding generation. But documentation for such an evolutionary process is lacking.

When I asked the Abkhasians themselves about their longevity, they told me they live as long as they do because of their practices in sex, work and diet.

The Abkhasians, because they expect to live long and healthy lives, feel it is necessary self-discipline to conserve their energies, including their sexual energy, instead of grasping what sweetness is available to them at the moment. They say it is the norm that regular sexual relations do not begin before the age of 30 for men, the traditional age of marriage; it was once even considered unmanly for a new husband to exercise his sexual rights on his wedding night. (If they are asked what is done to provide substitute gratifications of normal sexual needs before marriage, Abkhasians smile and say, "Nothing," but it is not unreasonable to speculate that they, like everyone else, find substitutes for the satisfaction of healthy, heterosexual sex. Today, some young people marry in their mid-20's instead of waiting for the "proper" age of 30, to the consternation of their elders.)

Postponement of satisfaction may be smiled at, but so is the expectation of prolonged, future enjoyment, perhaps with more reason. One medical team investigating the sex life of the Abkhasians concluded that many men retain their sexual potency long after the age of 70, and 13.6 percent of the women continue to menstruate after the age of 55.

Tarba Sit, 102, confided to me that he had waited until he was 60 to marry because while he was in the army "I had a good time right and left." At present, he said with some sadness, "I have a desire for my wife but no strength." One of his relatives had nine children, the youngest born when he was 100. Doctors obtained sperm from him when he was 119, in 1963, and he still retained his libido and potency. The only occasions on which medical investigators found discrepancies in the claimed ages of Abkhasians was when men insisted they were younger than they actually were. One said he was 95, but his daughter had a birth certificate proving she was 81, and other information indicated he was really 108. When he was confronted with the conflict he became angry and refused to discuss it, since he was about to get married. Makhti Tarkil, 104, with whom I spoke in the village of Duripsh, said the explanation was obvious in view of the impending marriage: "A man is a man until he is 100, you know what I mean. After that, well, he's getting old."

Abkhasian culture provides a dependent and secondary role for women; when they are young, their appearance is stressed, and when they are married, their service in the household is their major role. (As with other aspects of Abkhasian life, the period since the revolution has brought changes, and some women

---

Box 76

Doctoring Themselves

The Abkhasians practice an elaborate folk medicine, using more than 200 indigenous plants to cure a wide variety of ills. They apply plantain leaves to heal severe wounds, take ranunculuses for measles, use poligonaceae as an anticoagulant and asafetida (also known as Devil's Dung) as an antispasmodic. When all else fails, a doctor is called and the aged Abkhasian is taken to the hospital — but always with the expectation, including his own, that he will recover. They never express the fatalistic view, "Well, what do you expect at that age?" Sickness is simply not considered normal and natural.

S.B.

now work in the professions; but, in the main, the traditions are still in force.) In the upbringing of a young woman, great care is taken to make her as beautiful as possible according to Abkhasian standards. In order to narrow her waist and keep her breasts small, she wears a leather corset around her chest and waist; the corset is permanently removed on her wedding night. Her complexion should be fair, her eyebrows thin; because a high forehead is also desireable, the hair over the brow is shaved and further growth is prevented through the application of bleaches and herbs. She should also be a good dancer.

Virginity is an absolute requirement for marriage. If a woman proves to have been previously deflowered, the groom has a perfect right to take her back to her family and have his marriage gifts returned. He always exercises that right, returning the bride and announcing to the family, "Take your dead one." And to him, as well as all other eligible men, she is dead: in Abkhasian society, she has been so dishonored by his rejection that it would be next to impossible to find a man to marry her. (Later on, however, she may be married off to an elderly widower or some other less desirable male from a distant village. When she is discovered, she is expected to name the guilty party. She usually picks the name of a man who has recently died, in order to prevent her family from taking revenge and beginning a blood feud.)

For both married and unmarried Abkhasians, extreme modesty is required at all times. There is an overwhelming feeling of uneasiness and shame over any public manifestation of sex, or even affection. A man may not touch his wife, sit down next to her or even talk to her in the presence of strangers. A woman' s armpits are considered an erogenous zone and are never exposed, except to her husband.

A woman is a stranger, although a fully accepted one, in her husband's household. Her presence always carries the threat that her husband's loyalty to his family may be eroded by his passion for her. In the Abkhasian tradition, a woman may never change her dress nor bathe in the presence of her mother-in-law, and when an Abkhasian couple are alone in a room, they keep their voices low so that the husband's mother will not overhear them.

Despite the elaborate rules — perhaps, in part, because they are universally accepted — sex in Abkhasia is considered a good and pleasurable thing when it is strictly private. And as difficult as it may be for the American mind to grasp, it is guiltless. It is not repressed or sublimated into work, art or religious-mystical passion. It is not an evil to be driven from one's thoughts. It is a pleasure to be regulated for the sake of one's health — like a good wine.

An Abkhasian is never "retired," a status unknown in Abkhasian thinking. From the beginning of life until its end, he does what he is capable of doing because both he and those around him consider work vital to life. He makes the demands on himself that he can meet, and as those demands diminish with age, his status in the community nevertheless increases.

In his nine-year study of aged Abkhasians, Dr. Sichinava made a detailed examination of their work habits. One group included 82 men, most of whom had been working as peasants from the age of 11, and 45 women who, from the time of adolescence, had worked in the home and helped care for farm animals. Sichinava found that the work load had decreased considerably between the ages of 80 and 90 for 48 men, and between 90 and 100 for the rest. Among the women, 27 started doing less work between 80 and 90, and the others slowed down after 90. The few men who had been shepherds stopped following the herds up to the mountain meadow in spring, and instead began tending farm animals, after the age of 90. The farmers began to work less land; many stopped plowing and lifting heavy loads, but continued weeding (despite the bending involved) and doing other tasks. Most of the women stopped helping in the fields and some began to do less housework. Instead of serving the entire family—an Abkhasian family, extended through marriage, may include 50 or more people—they served only themselves and their children. But they also fed the chickens and knitted.

Dr. Sichinava also observed 21 men and 7 women over 100 years old and found that, on the average, they worked a four-hour day on the collective farm—the men weeding and helping with the corn crop, the women stringing tobacco leaves. Under the collective system, members of the community are free to work in their own gardens, but they get paid in what are, in effect, piecework rates for the work they do for the collective. Dr. Sichinava's group of villagers over 100, when they worked for the collective, maintained an hourly output that was not quite a fifth that of the norm for younger workers. But in maintaining their own pace, they worked more evenly and without waste motion, stopping on occasion to rest. By contrast, the younger men worked rapidly, but competitively and tensely. Competitiveness in work is not indigenous to Abkhasian culture but is encouraged by the Soviet Government for the sake of increased production; pictures of the best workers are posted in the offices of the village collectives. It is too soon to predict whether this seemingly fundamental change in work habits will affect Abkhasian longevity.

The persistent Abkhasians have their own workers' heroes: Kelkiliana Khesa, a woman of 109 in the village of Otapi, was paid for 49 workdays (a collective's workday is eight hours) during one summer; Bozba Pash, a man of 94 on the same collective, worked 155 days one year; Minosyan Grigorii of Aragich, often held up as an example to the young, worked 230 days in a year at the age of 90. (Most Americans, with a two-week vacation and several holidays, work between 240 and 250 days, some of them less than eight hours, in a year.)

Both the Soviet medical profession and the Abkhasians agree that their work habits have a great deal to do with their longevity. The doctors say that the way Abkhasians work helps the vital organs function optimally. The Abkhasians say, "Without rest, a man cannot work; without work, the rest does not give you any benefit."

That attitude, though it is not susceptible to medical measurements, may be as important as the work itself. It is part of a consistent life pattern: When they are children, they do what they are capable of doing, progressing from the easiest to the most strenuous tasks, and when they age, the curve descends, but it is unbroken. The aged are never seen sitting in chairs for long periods, passive, like vegetables. They do what they can, and while some consider the piecework system of the collectives a form of exploitation, it does permit them to function at their own pace.

Overeating is considered dangerous in Abkhasia, and fat people are regarded as ill. When the aged see a younger Abkhasian who is even a little overweight, they inquire about his health. "An Abkhasian cannot get fat," they say. "Can you imagine the ridiculous figure one would cut on horseback?" But to the dismay of the elders, the young eat much more than their fathers and grandfathers do: light, muscular and agile horsemen are no longer needed as a first line of defense.

The Abkhasian diet, like the rest of life, is stable: investigators have found that people 100 years and older eat the same foods throughout their lives. They show few idiosyncratic preferences, and they do not significantly change their diet when their economic status improves. Their caloric intake is 23 percent lower than that of the industrial workers in Abkhasia, though they consume twice as much vitamin C; the industrial workers have a much higher rate of coronary insufficiency and a higher level of cholesterol in the blood.

The Abkhasians eat without haste and with decorum. When guests are present, each person in turn is toasted with praise of his real or imaginary virtues. Such meals may last several hours, but nobody minds, since they prefer their food served lukewarm in any case. The food is cut into small pieces, served on platters, and eaten with the fingers. No matter what the occasion, Abkhasians take only small bites of food and chew those very slowly — a habit that stimulates the flow of ptyalin and maltase, insuring proper digestion of the carbohydrates which form the bulk of the diet. And, traditionally, there are no leftovers in Abkhasia; even the poor dispose of uneaten food by giving it to the animals, and no one would think of serving warmed-over food to a guest — even if it had been cooked only two hours earlier. Though some young people, perhaps influenced by Western ideas, consider the practice wasteful, most Abkhasians shun day-old food as unhealthful.

The Abkhasians eat relatively little meat — perhaps once or twice a week — and prefer chicken, beef, young goat and, in the winter, pork. They do not like fish and, despite its availability, rarely eat it. The meat is always freshly slaughtered and either broiled or boiled to the absolute minimum — until the blood stops running freely or, in the case of chicken, until the meat turns white.

It is, not surprisingly, tough in the mouth of a non-Abkhasian, but they have no trouble with it.

At all three meals, the Abkhasians eat *abista*, a corn meal mash cooked in water without salt, which takes the place of bread. *Abista* is eaten warm with pieces of homemade goat cheese tucked into it. They eat cheese daily, and also consume about two glasses of buttermilk a day. When eggs are eaten, which is not very often, they are boiled or fried with pieces of cheese.

The other staples in the Abkhasian diet—staple in Abkhasia means daily or almost so—include fresh fruits, especially grapes; fresh vegetables, including green onions, tomatoes, cucumbers and cabbage; a wide variety of pickled vegetables, and baby lima beans, cooked slowly for hours, mashed and served flavored with a sauce of onions, peppers, garlic, pomegranate juice and pepper. That hot sauce, or a variant of it, is set on the table in a separate dish for anyone who wants it. Large quantities of garlic are also always at hand.

Although they are the main supplier of tobacco for the Soviet Union few Abkhasians smoke. (I did meet one, a woman over 100, who smoked constantly.) They drink neither coffee nor tea. But they do consume a locally produced, dry, red wine of low alcoholic content. Everyone drinks it almost always in small quantities, at lunch and supper, and the Abkhasians call it "life giving." Absent from their diet is sugar, though honey, a local product, is used. Toothaches are rare.

Soviet medical authorities who have examined the Abkhasians and their diet feel it may well add years to their lives: the buttermilk and pickled vegetables; and probably the wine, help destroy certain bacteria and, indirectly, prevent the development of arteriosclerosis, the doctors think. In 1970, a team of Soviet doctors and Dr. Samuel Rosen of New York, a prominent ear surgeon, compared the hearing of Muscovites and Abkhasians, and concluded that the Abkhasians' diet—very little saturated fat, a great deal of fruit and vegetables—also accounted for their markedly better hearing. The hot sauce is the only item most doctors would probably say "no" to, and apparently some Abkhasians feel the same way.

Although the Abkhasians themselves attribute their longevity to their work, sex and dietary habits, there is another, broader aspect of their culture that impresses an outsider in their midst: the high degree of integration in their lives, the sense of group identity that gives each individual an unshaken feeling of personal security and continuity, and permits the Abkhasians as a people to adapt themselves—yet preserve themselves—to the changing conditions imposed by the larger society in which they live. That sense of continuity in both their personal and national lives is what anthropologists would call their spatial and temporal integration.

Their spatial integration is in their kinship structure. It is, literally, the Abkhasians' all-encompassing design for living: It regulates relationships between families, determines where they live, defines the position of women and marriage rules. Through centuries of nonexistent or ineffective centralized authority, kinship was life's frame of reference, and it still is.

Kinship in Abkhasia is an elaborate, complex set of relationships based on patrilineage. At its center is the family, extended through marriage by the sons; it also includes all those families which can be traced to a single progenitor; and finally, to all persons with the same surname, whether the progenitor can be traced or not. As a result, an Abkhasian may be "kin" to several thousand people, many of whom he does not know. I first discovered the pervasiveness of kinship roles when my friend Omar, an Abkhasian who had accompanied me from Sukhumi to the village of Duripsh, introduced me to a number of

---

Box 77

There'll Always Be an Abkhasia

The Abkhasian culture has survived intact despite centuries of warlike raids by, and against, neighboring herdsmen, and domination by the Greeks, Turks and Russians; in Abkhasian history, the rule of the Turks was especially cruel. Many Abkhasians were sold as slaves, but it is a certainty that that depredation left Abkhasian vigor intact. In the 5th century, under Justinian, orthodox Christianity was imposed on the Abkhasians, and in the 15th and 16th centuries, the Sunni sect of Islam. Traces of those religions remain, and some Abkhasians will identify themselves as Christians or Moslems. But they always have been pagans, and their underlying beliefs are pagan, connected to the family structure. They make animal sacrifices at family shrines. Asked to reconcile paganism with the mid-20th century, Abkhasians smile and say, "Oh, we don't believe in it. It's just a tradition."

The years since the Russian Revolution have brought still another wave of change; as usual, the Abkhasians have not been swamped. The economy and political structure have changed greatly: what were once isolated, semipastoral homesteads producing at a subsistence level are now collectives, prospering by comparison to prerevolutionary days. It is the Soviet policy to retain and enhance the national cultures within the U.S.S.R. but after the revolution the shift to collectives produced violent reactions among the peasants in many parts of the Soviet Union. Not in Abkhasia. The village elders opted for collectivism, and the Abkhasians followed. The transition was relatively smooth, and the Abkhasian culture remains intact.

Even the trappings of modernism have been absorbed. Radios are ubiquitous, television sets present but less frequent, and even less frequently watched. Tractors and helicopters please the Abkhasians but an expert horseman and an excellent horse are still prized over a pilot and his plane.

S.B.

people he called his brothers and sisters. When I had met more than 20 "siblings" I asked, "How many brothers and sisters do you have?" "In this village, 30," he said. "Abkhasian reckoning is different from Russian. These people all carry my father's name."

I took his explanation less seriously than I should have. Later, when I expressed admiration for a recording of Abkhasian epic poetry I had heard in the home of one of Omar's "brothers," Omar, without a word, gave the record to me as a gift. "Omar, it isn't yours," I said.

"Oh yes it is. This is the home of my brother," he said.

When I appealed to the "brother," he said, "Of course he can give it to you. He is my brother."

The consanguineal and affinal relationships that make up the foundation of the kinship structure are supplemented by a variety of ritual relationships that involve lifetime obligations and serve to broaden the human environment from which Abkhasians derive their extraordinary sense of security. Although there are no alternative life styles towards which the rebellious may flee, the Abkhasians are ready to absorb others into their own culture. During my visit, for instance, a Christian man was asked to be the godfather of a Moslem child; both prospective godfather and child were Abkhasians. When I expressed surprise, I was told, "It doesn't matter. We want to enlarge our circle of relatives."

The temporal integration of Abkhasian life is expressed in its general continuity, in the absence of limiting, defining conditions of existence like "unemployed," "adolescent," "alienated." Abkhasians are a life-loving, optimistic people, and unlike so many very old "dependent" people in the United States — who feel they are a burden to themselves and their families — they enjoy the prospect of continued life. One 99-year-old Abkhasian, Akhba Sleiman of the village of Achandara, told his doctor, "It isn't time to die yet. I am needed by my children and grandchildren, and it isn't bad in this world — except that I can't turn the earth over and it has become difficult to climb trees."

The old are always active. "It is better to move without purpose than to sit still," they say. Before breakfast, they walk through the homestead's courtyard and orchard, taking care of small tasks that come to their attention. They look for fences and equipment in need of repair and check on the family's animals. At breakfast, their early morning survey completed, they report what has to be done.

Until evening, the old spend their time alternating work and rest. A man may pick up wind-fallen apples, then sit down on a bench, telling stories or making toys for his grandchildren or great-grandchildren. Another chore which is largely attended to by the old is weeding the courtyard, a large green belonging to the homestead, which serves as a center of activity for the kin group. Keeping it in shape requires considerable labor, yet I never saw a courtyard that was not tidy and well-trimmed.

During the summer, many old men spend two or three months high in the mountains, living in shepherds' huts, helping to herd or hunting for themselves and the shepherds (with their arrested aging process, many are excellent marksmen despite their age). They obviously are not fearful of losing their authority during their absence; their time in the mountains is useful and pleasurable.

The extraordinary attitude of the Abkhasians—to feel needed at 99 or 110—is not an artificial, self-protective one; it is the natural expression, in old age, of a consistent outlook that begins in childhood. The stoic upbringing of an Abkhasian child, in which parents and senior relatives participate, instills respect, obedience and endurance. At an early age, children participate in household tasks; when they are not at school, they work in the fields or at home.There are no separate "facts of life" for children and adults: the values given children are the ones adults live by, and there is no hypocritical disparity (as in so many other societies) between adult words and deeds. Since what they are taught is considered important, and the work they are given is considered necessary, children are neither restless nor rebellious. As they mature, there are easy transitions from one status in life to another: a bride, for instance, will stay for a time with her husband's relatives, gradually becoming part of a new clan, before moving into his home. From the beginning, there is no gap between expectation and experience. Abkhasians expect a long and useful life and look forward to old age with good reason: in a culture which so highly values continuity in its traditions, the old are indispensable in their transmission. The elders preside at important ceremonial occasions, they mediate disputes and their knowledge of farming is sought. They feel needed because, in their own minds and everyone else's, they are. They are the opposite of burdens; they are highly valued resources.

The Abkhasians themselves are obviously right in citing their diet and their work habits as contributing factors in their longevity; in my opinion, their postponed, and later prolonged, sex life probably has nothing to do with it. Their climate is exemplary, the air (especially to a New Yorker) refreshing, but it is not significantly different from many other areas of the world, where life spans are shorter. And while some kind of genetic selectivity may well have been at work, there simply is not enough information to evaluate the genetic factor in Abkhasian longevity.My own view is that Abkhasians live as long as they do primarily because of the extraordinary cultural factors that structure their existence: the uniformity and certainty of both individual and group behavior, the unbroken continuum of life's activities—the same games, the same work, the same food, the same self-imposed and socially perceived needs. And the increasing prestige that comes with increasing age.

There is no better way to comprehend the importance of these cultural factors than to consider for a moment some of the prevalent characteristics of American society. Children are sometimes given chores to keep them occupied, but they and their parents know there is no *need* for the work they do; even as adults, only a small percentage of Americans have the privilege of feeling that their work is essential and important. The old, when they do not simply vegetate, out of view and out of mind, keep themselves "busy" with bingo and shuffleboard. Americans are mobile, sometimes frantically so, searching for signs of permanence that will indicate their lives are meaningful.

Can Americans learn something from the Abkhasian view of "long living" people? I think so.

Questions

1. How did Benet gather her information?
2. Where is Abkhasia? Does its geographical location affect the lives of its citizens? How did the Russian Revolution affect it?
3. How long do Abkhasians live? How does this compare to the U.S.A.?
4. Describe the caliber of life of "long-living" Abkhasians.
5. What values are important in the Abkhasian kinship structure?
6. Does diet have anything to do with longevity in Abkhasia? Sexual activity? Work?
7. How do "spatial" and "temporal" integration affect longevity?
8. Why do women live longer than men in Abkhasia? In America?
9. Do cultural or biological factors explain longevity better in Abkhasia? What about in the United States?
10. Can any Abkhasian patterns of behavior be adapted to American culture? Why or why not?
11. What changes would occur in American society if most people lived to be 120?
12. How do you think the Abkhasians reacted to *glasnost*? How do you think they are reacting to the current "break-up" of the former USSR?

Chapter Thirty

The Vintage Years

Jack C. Horn and Jeff Meer

Our society is getting older, but the old are getting younger. As Sylvia Herz told an American Psychological Association (APA) symposium on aging last year, the activities and attitudes of a 70-year-old today "are equivalent to those of a 50-year-old's a decade or two ago."

Our notions of what it means to be old are beginning to catch up with this reality. During the past several decades, three major changes have altered the way we view the years after 65:

- The financial, physical and mental health of older people has improved, making the prospect of a long life something to treasure, not fear.

- The population of older people has grown dramatically, rising from 18 million in 1965 to 28 million today. People older than 65 compose 12 percent of the population, a percentage that is expected to rise to more than 20 percent by the year 2030.

- Researchers have gained a much better understanding of aging and the lives of older people, helping to sort out the inevitable results of biological aging from the effects of illness or social and environmental problems. No one has yet found the fountain of youth, or of immortality. But research has revealed that aging itself is not the thief we once thought it was; healthy older people can maintain and enjoy most of their physical and mental abilities, and even improve in some areas.

Because of better medical care, improved diet and increasing interests in physical fitness, more people are reaching the ages of 65, 75 and older in excellent health. Their functional age—a combination of physical, psychological and social factors that affect their attitudes toward life and the roles they play in the world—is much younger than their chronological age.

Their economic health is better, too, by almost every measure. Over the last three decades, for example, the number of men and women 65 and older who live below the poverty line has dropped steadily from 35 percent in 1959 to 12 percent in 1984, the last year for which figures are available.

On the upper end of the economic scale, many of our biggest companies are headed by what once would have been called senior citizens, and many more of them serve as directors of leading companies. Even on a more modest economic level, a good portion of the United States' retired older people form a new leisure class, one with money to spend and the time to enjoy it. Obviously not all of America's older people share this prosperity. Economic hardship is particularly prevalent among minorities. But as a group, our older people are doing better than ever.

In two other areas of power, politics and the law, people in their sixties and seventies have always played important roles. A higher percentage of people from 65 to 74 register and vote than in any other group. With today's increasing vigor and numbers, their power is likely to increase still further.

Changing attitudes, personal and social, are a major reason for the increasing importance of older people in our society. As psychologist Bernice Neugarten points out, there is no longer a particular age at which someone starts to work or attends school, marries and has children, retires or starts a business. Increasing numbers of older men and women are enrolled in colleges, universities and other institutions of learning. According to the Center for Education Statistics, for example, the number of people 65 and older enrolled in adult education of all kinds increased from 765,000 to 866,000 from 1981 to 1984. Gerontologist Barbara Ober says that this growing interest in education is much more than a way to pass the time. "Older people make excellent students, maybe even better students than the majority of 19- and 20-year-olds. One advantage is that they have settled a lot of the social and sexual issues that preoccupy their younger classmates."

Older people today are not only healthier and more active; they are also increasingly more numerous. "Squaring the pyramid" is how some demographers describe this change in our population structure. It has always been thought of as a pyramid, a broad base of newborns supporting successively smaller tiers of older people as they died from disease, accidents, poor nutrition, war and other causes.

Today, the population structure is becoming more rectangular, as fewer people die during the earlier stages of life. The Census Bureau predicts that by 2030 the structure will be an almost perfect rectangle up to the age of 70.

The aging of America has been going on at least since 1800, when half the people in the country were younger than 16 years old, but two factors have accelerated the trend tremendously. First, the number of old people has increased rapidly. Since 1950 the number of Americans 65 and older has more than doubled to some 28 million—more than the entire current population of Canada. Within the same period, the number of individuals older than 85 has quadrupled to about 2.6 million. (See Box 78 on "the oldest old.")

Box 78

The Oldest Old: The Years After 85

"Every man desires to live long, but no man would be old," or so Jonathan Swift believed. Some people get their wish to live long and become what are termed the "oldest old," those 85 and older. During the past 22 years, this group has increased by 165 percent to 2.5 million and now represents more than 1 percent of the population.

Who are these people and what are their lives like? One of the first to study them intensively is gerontologist Charles Longino of the University of Miami, who uses 1980 census data to examine their lives for the American Association of Retired People.

He found, not surprisingly, that nearly 70 percent are women. Of these, 82 percent are widowed, compared with 44 percent of the men. Because of the conditions that existed when they were growing up, the oldest old are poorly educated compared with young people today, most of whom finish high school. The person now 85 years and older only completed the eighth grade.

Only one-quarter of these older citizens are in hospitals or institutions such as nursing homes, and more than half live in their own homes. Just 30 percent live by themselves. More than a third live with a spouse or with their children. There are certainly those who aren't doing well—one in six have incomes below the poverty level—but many more are relatively well-off. The mean household income for the group, Longino says, was more than $20,000 in 1985.

What of the quality of life? "In studying this group, we have to be aware of youth creep," he says. "The old are getting younger all the time." This feeling is confirmed by a report released late last year by the National Institute on Aging. The NIA report included three studies of people older than 65 conducted in two counties in Iowa, in East Boston, Massachusetts, and in New Haven, Connecticut. There are large regional differences between the groups, of course, and they aren't a cross-section of older people in the nation as a whole. But in all three places, most of those older than 85 seem to be leading fulfilling lives.

Most socialize in a variety of ways. In Iowa, more than half say they go to religious services at least once a week and the same percentage say they belong to some type of professional, social, church-related or recreational group. More than three-quarters see at least one or two children once a month and almost that many see other close relatives that often.

As you would expect, many of the oldest old suffer from disabilities and serious health problems. At least a quarter of those who responded have been in a hospital overnight in the past year and at least 8 percent have had heart attacks or have diabetes. In Iowa and New Haven, more than 13 percent of the oldest old had cancer, while in East Boston the rate was lower (between 7 percent and 8 percent). Significant numbers of the oldest old have suffered serious injury from falls. Other common health problems for this age group are high blood pressure and urinary incontinence. However, epidemiologist Adrian Ostfeld, who directed the survey in New Haven, notes that "most of the disability was temporary."

Longino has found that almost 10 percent of the oldest old live alone with a disability that prevents them from using public transportation. This means that they are "isolated from the daily hands-on care of others," he says. "Even so, there are a surprising number of the oldest old who don't need much in the way of medical care. They're the survivors." "I think we have to agree that the oldest old is, as a group, remarkably diverse," Longino says. "Just as it is unfair to say that those older than 85 are all miserable, it's not fair to say that they all lead wonderful lives, either."

—Jeff Meer

Second, the boom in old people has been paired with a bust in the proportion of youngsters due to a declining birth rate. Today, fewer than one American in four is younger than 16. This drop-off has been steady, with the single exception of the post-World War II baby boom, which added 76 million children to the country between 1945 and 1964. As these baby boomers reach the age of 65, starting in 2010, they are expected to increase the proportion of the population 65 and older from its current 12 percent to 21 percent by 2030.

The growing presence of healthy, vigorous older people has helped overcome some of the stereotypes about aging and the elderly. Research has also played a major part by replacing myths with facts. While there were some studies of aging before World War II, scientific interest increased dramatically during the 1950s and kept growing.

Important early studies of aging included three started in the mid or late 1950s: the Human Aging Study, conducted by the National Institute of Mental Health (NIMH); the Duke Longitudinal Studies, done by the Center for the Study of Aging and Human Development at Duke University; and the Baltimore

Longitudinal Study of Aging, conducted by the Gerontological Institute in Baltimore, now part of the National Institute on Aging (NIA). All three took a multidisciplinary approach to the study of normal aging: what changes take place, how people adapt to them, how biological, genetic, social, psychological and environmental characteristics relate to longevity and what can be done to promote successful aging.

These pioneering studies and hundreds of later ones have benefited from growing federal support. White House Conferences on Aging in 1961 and 1971 helped focus attention on the subject. By 1965 Congress had enacted Medicare and the Older Americans Act. During the 1970s Congress authorized the establishment of the NIA as part of the National Institutes of health and NIMH created a special center to support research on the mental health of older people.

All these efforts have produced a tremendous growth in our knowledge of aging. In the first (1971) edition of the *Handbook of the Psychology of Aging,* it was estimated that as much had been published on the subject in the previous 15 years as in all the years before then. In the second edition, published in 1985, psychologists James Birren and Walter Cunningham wrote that the "period for this rate of doubling has now decreased to 10 years . . . the volume of published research has increased to the almost unmanageable total of over a thousand articles a year."

Psychologist Clifford Swenson of Purdue University explained some of the powerful incentives for this tremendous increase: "I study the topic partly to discover more effective ways of helping old people cope with their problems, but also to load my own armamentarium against that inevitable day. For that is one aspect of aging and its problems that makes it different from the other problems psychologists study: We may not all be schizophrenic or neurotic or overweight, but there is only one alternative to old age and most of us try to avoid that alternative."

One popular misconception disputed by recent research is the idea that aging means inevitable physical and sexual failure. Some changes occur, of course. Reflexes slow, hearing and eyesight dim, stamina decreases. This *primary aging* is a gradual process that begins early in life and affects all body systems.

But many of the problems we associate with old are are *secondary aging*—the results not of age but of disease, abuse and disuse—factors often under our own control. More and more older people are healthy, vigorous men and women who lead enjoyable, active lives. National surveys by the Institute for Social Research and others show that life generally seems less troublesome and freer to older people than it does to younger adults.

In a review of what researchers have learned about subjective well-being—happiness, life satisfaction, positive emotions—University of Illinois psychologist Ed Diener reported that "Most results show a slow rise in satisfaction with age . . . young persons appear to experience higher levels of joy but older persons tend to judge their lives in more positive ways."

Money is often mentioned as the key to a happy retirement, but psychologist Daniel Ogilvie of Rutgers University has found another, much more important, factor. Once we have a certain minimum amount of money, his research shows, life satisfaction depends mainly on how much time we spend doing things we find meaningful. Ogilvie believes retirement-planning workshops and seminars should spend more time helping people decide how to use their skills and interests after they retire.

A thought that comes through clearly when researchers talk about physical and mental fitness is "use it or lose it." People rust out faster from disuse than they wear out from overuse. This advice applies equally to sexual activity. While every study from the time of Kinsey to the present shows that sexual interest and activity diminish with age, the drop varies greatly among individuals. Psychologist Marion Perlmutter and writer Elizabeth Hall have reported that one of the best predictors of continued sexual intercourse "is early sexual activity and past sexual enjoyment and frequency. People who have never had much pleasure from sexuality may regard their age as a good excuse for giving up sex."

They also point out that changing times affect sexual activity. As today's younger adults bring their more liberal sexual attitudes with them into old age, the level of sexual activity among older men and women may rise.

The idea that mental abilities decline steadily with age has also been challenged by many recent and not-so-recent findings (see "The Reason of Age," *Psychology Today,* June 1986). In brief, age doesn't damage abilities as much as was once believed, and in some areas we actually gain; we learn to compensate through experience for much of what we do lose; and we can restore some losses through training. For years, older people didn't do as well as younger people on most tests used to measure mental ability. But psychologist Leonard Poon of the University of Georgia believes that researchers are now taking a new, more appropriate approach to measurement. "Instead of looking at older people's ability to do abstract tasks that have little or no relationship to what they do every day, today's researchers are examining real-life issues."

Psychologist Gisela Labouvie-Vief of Wayne State University has been measuring how people approach everyday problems in logic. She notes that older adults have usually done poorly on such tests, mostly because they fail to think logically all the time. But Labouvie-Vief argues that this is not because they have forgotten how to think logically but because they use a more complex approach unknown to younger thinkers. "The (older) thinker operates within a kind of double reality which is both formal and informal, both logical and psychological," she says.

In other studies, Labouvie-Vief has found that when older people were asked to give concise summaries of fables they read, they did so. But when they were simply asked to recall as much of the fable as possible, they concentrated on the metaphorical, moral or social meaning of the text. They didn't try to duplicate the fable's exact words, the way younger people did. As psychologists Nancy Datan, Dean Rodeheaver and Fergus Hughes of the University of Wisconsin have described their findings, "while (some people assume) that old and young are equally competent, we might better assume that they are differently competent."

John Horn, director of the Adult Development and Aging program at the University of Southern California, suggests that studies of Alzheimer's disease, a devastating progressive mental deterioration experienced by an estimated 5 percent to 15 percent of those older than 65, may eventually help explain some of the differences in thinking abilities of older people. "Alzheimer's, in some ways, may represent the normal process of aging, only speeded up," he says. (To see how your ideas about Alzheimer's square with the facts, take the Alzheimer's quiz in Box 79 and then see how your answers compare to a national sample in Box 80.)

Box 79

Alzheimer's Quiz

Alzheimer's disease, named for German neurologist Alois Alzheimer, is much in the news these days. But how much do you really know about the disorder? Political scientist Neal B. Cutler of the Andrus Gerontology Center gave the following questions to a 1,500-person cross section of people older than 45 in the United States in November 1985. To compare your answers with theirs and with the correct answers, turn to Box 80.

	True	False	Don't know
1. Alzheimer's disease can be contagious.			
2. A person will almost certainly get Alzheimer's if they just live long enough.			
3. Alzheimer's disease is a form of insanity.			
4. Alzheimer's disease is a normal part of getting older, like gray hair or wrinkles.			
5. There is no cure for Alzheimer's disease at present.			
6. A person who has Alzheimer's disease will experience both mental and physical decline.			

7. The primary symptom of Alzheimer's disease is memory loss. _____ _____ _____
8. Among persons older than age 75, forgetfulness most likely indicates the beginning of Alzheimer's disease. _____ _____ _____
9. When the husband or wife of an older person dies, the surviving spouse may suffer from a kind of depression that looks like Alzheimer's disease. _____ _____ _____
10. Stuttering is an inevitable part of Alzheimer's disease. _____ _____ _____
11. An older man is more likely to develop Alzheimer's disease than an older woman. _____ _____ _____
12. Alzheimer's disease is usually fatal. _____ _____ _____
13. The vast majority of persons suffering from Alzheimer's disease live in nursing homes. _____ _____ _____
14. Aluminum has been identified as a significant cause of Alzheimer's disease. _____ _____ _____
15. Alzheimer's disease can be diagnosed by a blood test. _____ _____ _____
16. Nursing-home expenses for Alzheimer's disease patients are covered by Medicare. _____ _____ _____
17. Medicine taken for high blood pressure can cause symptoms that look like Alzheimer's disease. _____ _____ _____

Box 80

Alzheimer's Answers

	True	False	Don't know
1. **False.** There is no evidence that Alzheimer's is contagious, but given the concern and confusion about AIDS, it is encouraging that nearly everyone knows this fact about Alzheimer's.	3%	83%	14%
2. **False.** Alzheimer's is associated with old age, but it is a disease and not the inevitable consequence of aging.	9%	80%	11%
3. **False.** Alzheimer's is a disease of the brain, but it is not a form of insanity. The fact that most people understand the distinction contrasts with the results of public-opinion studies concerning epilepsy that were done 35 years ago. At that time almost half of the public thought that epilepsy, another diesase of the brain, was a form of insanity.	7%	78%	15%

4. False. Again, most of the public knows that Alzheimer's is not an inevitable part of aging. 10%   77%   13%

5. True. Despite announcements of "breakthroughs," biomedical research is in the early laboratory and experimental stages and there is no known cure for the disease. 75%   8%   17%

6. True. Memory and cognitive decline are characteristic of the earlier stages of Alzheimer's disease, but physical decline follow in the later stages. 74%   10%   16%

7. True. Most people know that this is the earliest sign of Alzheimer's disease. 62%   19%   19%

8. False. Most people also know that while Alzheimer's produces memory loss, memory loss may have some other cause. 16%   61%   23%

9. True. This question, like number 8, measures how well people recognize that other problems can mirror Alzheimer's symptoms. This is crucial because many of these other problems are treatable. In particular, depression can cause disorientation that looks like Alzheimer's. 49%   20%   30%

10. False. Stuttering has never been linked to Alzheimer's. The question was designed to measure how willing people were to attribute virtually anything to a devastating disease. 12%   46%   42%

11. False. Apart from age, research has not uncovered any reliable demographic or ethnic patterns. While there are more older women than men, both sexes are equally likely to get Alzheimer's. 15%   45%   40%

12. True. Alzheimer's produces mental and physical decline that is eventually fatal, although the progression varies greatly among individuals. 40%   33%   27%

13. False. The early and middle stages of the disease usually do not require institutional care. Only a small percentage of those with the disease live in nursing homes. 37%   40%   23%

14. False. There is no evidence that using aluminum cooking utensils, pots or foil causes Alzheimer's, although aluminum compounds have been found in the brain tissue of many Alzheimer's patients. They may simply be side effects of the disease. 8%   25%   66%

15. False. At present there is no definitive blood test that can determine with certainty that a patient has Alzheimer's disease. Accurate diagnosis is possible only upon autopsy. Recent studies suggest that genetic or blood testing may be able to identify Alzheimer's, but more research with humans is needed. 12%   24%   64%

16. False. Medicare generally pays only for short-term nursing-home care subsequent to hospitalization and not for long-term care. Medicaid can pay for long-term nursing-home care, but since it is a state-directed program for the medically indigent, coverage for Alzheimer's patients depends upon state regulations and on the income of the patient and family. 16%   23%   61%

17. True. As mentioned earlier, many medical problems have Alzheimer's-like symptoms and most of these other causes are treatable. Considering how much medicine older people take, it is unfortunate that so few people know that medications such as those used to treat high blood pressure can cause these symptoms. 20%   19%   61%

Generalities are always suspect, but one generalization about old age seems solid: It is a different experience for men and women. Longevity is one important reason. Women in the United States live seven to eight years longer, on the average, than do men. This simple fact has many ramifications, as sociologist Gunhild Hagestad explained in *Our Aging Society*. (Box 81 gives some idea of projected life expectancy for men and women.)

For one thing, since the world of the very old is disproportionately a world of women, men and women spend their later years differently. "Most older women are widows living alone; most older men live with their wives . . . among individuals over the age of 75, two-thirds of the men are living with a spouse, while less than one-fifth of the women are."

The difference in longevity also means that among older people remarriage is a male prerogative. After 65, for example, men remarry at a rate eight times that of women. This is partly a matter of the scarcity of men and partly a matter of culture—even late in life, men tend to marry younger women. It is also a matter of education and finances, which, Hagestad explains, "operate quite differently in shaping remarriage probabilities among men and women. The more resources the woman has available (measured in education and income), the less likely she is to remarry. For men, the trend is reversed."

Box 81

Projected Life Expectancy

Boys born in 1990 can expect to live 76.1 years, and girls to the age of 83.4. The trick is to stay alive; life expectancy increases with age.

If you are now. . .	Your life expectancy at birth was. . .		Your life expectancy today is. . .	
	Men	Women	Men	Women
25	72.7	80.6	76.2	83.1
45	70.4	77.9	77.3	82.8
65	64.1	71.9	80.6	84.9
85	54.0	61.4	90.5	91.9

SOURCE: Office of the Actuary, Social Security Administraion

The economic situations of elderly men and women also differ considerably. Lou Glasse, president of the Older Women's League in Washington, D.C., points out that most of these women were housewives who worked at paid jobs sporadically, if at all. "That means their Social Security benefits are lower than men's, they are not likely to have pensions and they are less likely to have been able to save the kind of money that would protect them from poverty during their older years."

Although we often think of elderly men and women as living in nursing homes or retirement communities, the facts are quite different. Only about 5 percent are in nursing homes and perhaps an equal number live in some kind of age-segregated housing. Most people older than 65 live in their own houses or apartments.

We also think of older people as living alone. According to the Census Bureau, this is true of 15 percent of the men and 41 percent of the women. Earlier this year, a survey done by Louis Harris and Associates revealed that 28 percent of elderly people living alone have annual incomes below $5,100, the federal poverty line. Despite this, they were four times as likely to give financial help to their children as to receive it from them.

In addition, fewer than 1 percent of the old people said they would prefer living with their children. Psychiatrist Robert N. Butler, chairman of the Commonwealth Fund's Commission on Elderly People Living Alone, which sponsored the report, noted that these findings dispute the "popular portrait of an elderly, dependent parent financially draining their middle-aged children."

There is often another kind of drain, however, one of time and effort. The Travelers Insurance Company recently surveyed more than 700 of its employees on this issue. Of those at least 30 years old, 28 percent said they directly care for an older relative in some way—taking that person to the doctor, making telephone calls, handling finances or running errands—for an average of 10 hours a week. Women, who are more often caregivers, spent an average of 16 hours, and men five hours, per week. One group, 8 percent of the sample, spent a heroic 35 hours per week, the equivalent of a second job, providing such care. "That adds up to an awful lot of time away from other things," psychologist Beal Lowe says, "and the stresses these people face are enormous."

Lowe, working with Sherman-Lank Communications in Kensington, Maryland, has formed "Caring for Caregivers," a group of professionals devoted to providing services, information and support to those who care for older relatives. "It can be a great shock to some people who have planned the perfect retirement," he says, "only to realize that your chronically ill mother suddenly needs daily attention."

Researchers who have studied the housing needs of older people predictably disagree on many things, but most agree on two points: We need a variety of individual and group living arrangements to meet the varying interests, income and abilities of people older than 65; and the arrangements should be flexible enough that the elderly can stay in the same locale as their needs and abilities change. Many studies have documented the fact that moving itself can be stressful and even fatal to old people, particularly if they have little or no influence over when and where they move.

This matter of control is important, but more complicated than it seemed at first. Psychologist Judith Rodin and others have demonstrated that people in nursing homes are happier, more alert and live longer if they are allowed to take responsibility for their lives in some way, even in something as simple as choosing a plant for their room, taking care of a bird feeder, selecting the night to attend a movie.

Rodin warns that while control is generally beneficial, the effect depends on the individuals involved. For some, personal control brings with it demands in the form of time, effort and the risk of failure. They may blame themselves if they get sick or something else goes wrong. The challenge, Rodin wrote, is to "provide but not impose opportunities. . . . The need for self-determination, it must be remembered, also calls for the opportunity to choose not to exercise control. . . ."

An ancient Greek myth tells how the Goddess of Dawn fell in love with a mortal and convinced Jupiter to grant him immortality. Unfortunately, she forgot to have youth included in the deal, so he gradually grew older and older. "At length," the story concludes, "he lost the power of using his limbs, and then she shut him up in his chamber, whence his feeble voice might at times be heard. Finally she turned him into a grasshopper."

The fears and misunderstandings of age expressed in this 3,000-year-old myth persist today, despite all the positive things we have learned in recent years about life after 65. We don't turn older people into grasshoppers or shut them out of sight, but too often we move them firmly out of the mainstream of life.

In a speech at the celebration of Harvard University's 350th anniversary last September, political scientist Robert Binstock decried what he called The Spectre of the Aging Society: "the economic burdens of population aging; moral dilemmas posed by the allocation of health resources on the basis of age; labor market competition between older and younger workers within the contexts of age discrimination laws; seniority practices, rapid technological change; and a politics of conflict between age groups."

Binstock, a professor at Case Western Reserve School of Medicine, pointed out that these inaccurate perceptions express an underlying ageism, "the attribution of these same characteristics and status to an artificially homogenized group labeled 'the aged.'"

Ironically, much ageism is based on compassion rather than ill will. To protect older workers from layoffs, for example, unions fought hard for job security based on seniority. To win it, they accepted mandatory retirement, a limitation that now penalizes older workers and deprives our society of their experience.

A few companies have taken special steps to utilize this valuable pool of older workers. The Travelers companies, for example, set up a job bank that is open to its own retired employees as well as those of other companies. According to Howard E. Johnson, a senior vice president, the company employs about 175 formerly retired men and women a week. He estimates that the program is saving Travelers $1 million a year in temporary-hire fees alone.

While mandatory retirement is only one example of ageism, it is particularly important because we usually think of contributions to society in economic terms. Malcolm H. Morrison, an authority on retirement and age discrimination in employment for the Social Security Administration, points out that once the idea of retirement at a certain fixed age was accepted, "the old became defined as a dependent group in society, a group whose members could not and should not work, and who needed economic and social assistance that the younger working population was obligated to provide."

We need to replace this stereotype with the more realistic understanding that older people are and should be productive members of society, capable of assuming greater responsibility for themselves and others. What researchers have learned about the strengths and abilities of older people should help us turn this ideal of an active, useful life after 65 into a working reality.

Questions

1. At what age are we old?
2. The opening sentence says "our society is getting older, but the old are getting younger." What does this mean?
3. What three changes have altered the way we view the years after 65?
4. What does "squaring the pyramid" mean?
5. What will happen when the baby boomers reach the age of 65?
6. What is the difference between primary and secondary aging? Over which do we have more control?
7. Discuss the relationship between aging and sexual activity. Between aging and poverty.
8. The article says, "while the old and the young may be equally competent, they are differently competent." What does that mean?
9. Compare the old and the "oldest old" in terms of medical problems, money, housing, recreation, transportation, etc.

10. Does aging affect men and women differently?

11. Do aging parents financially drain their middle-age children? How about emotionally?

12. Did you come across any surprises in the answers to the Alzheimer's quiz? Have there been any new findings regarding the disease since the article was written?

13. Noel Coward said, "The pleasures that once were heaven look silly at sixty-seven." Christopher Isherwood said, "If I had known when I was twenty-one that I should be as happy as I am at seventy, I should have been sincerely shocked." Which point of view does the article support? Which do you think is more accurate?

14. How can ageism be based on "compassion rather than ill will"? Would this be true for racism and sexism as well? Give examples.

15. Will life expectancy be the same for different races? How about different ethnic groups?

16. Are the elderly in America or Abkhasia happier? In which society do they get more respect?

Part X

Research Through Deception
Three Controversial Experiments

Stanley Milgram's government funded research described in "If Hitler Asked You to Electrocute a Stranger, Would You?", the second article in Part X, explores people's willingness to obey irrational commands by leading them to believe they were administering painful shock treatment to their fellow subjects. The experiment, irrespective of its merit or lack of merit, raises a question that is currently being debated in the social sciences: should a social scientist engage in research in which respondents are deceived in order to elicit information needed? While there is no "absolute" answer here, the government has now prescribed regulations for the "protection of human subjects" in research using public funds. In this case, the applicable rule demands that the deception be revealed at the end of the experiment.

Implicit in the above experiment and in Philip Zimbardo's research described in "Pathology of Imprisonment," the first article in Part X, is another question: to what extent is it proper for a social scientist to place his research subjects under strain and pressure in order to get knowledge? After setting up an experiment to explore the respective psychology of "prisoners" and "guards," Zimbardo found it necessary to call off the experiment because the situation had become too unsettling for everyone involved. Both "prisoners" and "guards" could no longer differentiate between the roles they were playing and their "actual" selves. If merely assigning labels to people is sufficient to elicit pathological behavior, researchers certainly must be careful that they design their research in ways that individuals will not be harmed. The federal guidelines here, applicable again only if public funds are used, stress "informed consent'' so that volunteers know what to expect in terms of possible "risk, pain, or harm."

A third controversial experiment is described by freelance writer Morton Hunt in "Research Through Deception." In this study, deafness was hypnotically induced in a naive subject in order to test the hypothesis that the paranoia of many older people is the result of a gradual, undetected loss of hearing. "Even if the experience was genuinely upsetting to subjects," the researcher said, "the stakes were high enough to warrant imposing it on them." Critics of deceptive research, on the other hand, maintain that the risks or costs to the subject outweigh any potential scientific benefits.

Today, professional associations such as the American Psychological Association have begun to police themselves regarding these kinds of issues. They have now established "codes of ethics" so that "morally proper research standards" will be used in both privately and publicly funded studies. Only time will tell how successful they will be. Perhaps now you are beginning to understand why these three experiments are *controversial*!

Chapter Thirty-One

Pathology of Imprisonment

Philip G. Zimbardo

I was recently released from solitary confinement after being held therein for 37 months [months!]. A silent system was imposed upon me and to even whisper to the man in the next cell resulted in being beaten by guards, sprayed with chemical mace, blackjacked, stomped and thrown into a strip-cell naked to sleep on a concrete floor without bedding, covering, wash basin or even a toilet. The floor served as a toilet and bed, and even there the silent system was enforced. To let a moan escape your lips because of the pain and discomfort . . . resulted in another beating. I spent not days, but months there during my 37 months in solitary. . . .I have filed every writ possible against the administrative acts of brutality. The state courts have all denied the petitions. Because of my refusal to let the things die down and forget all that happened during my 37 months in solitary . . . I am the most hated prisoner in [this] penitentiary, and called a "hard core incorrigible."

Maybe I am an incorrigible, but if it's true, it's because I would rather die than to accept being treated as less than a human being. I have never complained of my prison sentence as being unjustified except through legal means of appeals. I have never put a knife on a guard's throat and demanded release. I know that thieves must be punished and I don't justify stealing, even though I am a thief myself. But now I don't think I will be a thief when I am released. No, I'm not rehabilitated. It's just that I no longer think of becoming wealthy by stealing. I now only think of killing—killing those who have beaten me and treated me as if I were a dog. I hope and pray for the sake of my own soul and future life of freedom that I am able to overcome the bitterness and hatred which eats daily at my soul, but I know to overcome it will not be easy.

Published by permission of Transaction Inc. from *Society*, Vol. 9, No. 6. Copyright © 1972 by Transaction Inc.

This eloquent plea for prison reform—for humane treatment of human beings, for the basic dignity that is the right of every American—came to me secretly in a letter from a prisoner who cannot be identified because he is still in a state correctional institution. He sent it to me because he read of an experiment I recently conducted at Stanford University. In an attempt to understand just what it means psychologically to be a prisoner or a prison guard, Craig Haney, Curt Banks, Dave Jaffe and I created our own prison. We carefully screened over 70 volunteers who answered an ad in a Palo Alto city newspaper and ended up with about two dozen young men who were selected to be part of this study. They were mature, emotionally stable, normal, intelligent college students from middle-class homes throughout the United States and Canada. They appeared to represent the cream of the crop of this generation. None had any criminal record and all were relatively homogeneous on many dimensions initially.

Half were arbitrarily designated as prisoners by a flip of a coin, the others as guards. These were the roles they were to play in our simulated prison. The guards were made aware of the potential seriousness and danger of the situation and their own vulnerability. They made up their own formal rules for maintaining law, order and respect, and were generally free to improvise new ones during their eight-hour, three-man shifts. The prisoners were unexpectedly picked up at their homes by a city policeman in a squad car, searched, handcuffed, fingerprinted, booked at the Palo Alto station house and taken blindfolded to our jail. There they were stripped, deloused, put into a uniform, given a number and put into a cell with two other prisoners where they expected to live for the next two weeks. The pay was good (15 dollars a day) and their motivation was to make money.

We observed and recorded on videotape the events that occurred in the prison, and we interviewed and tested the prisoners and guards at various points throughout the study. Some of the videotapes of the actual encounters between the prisoners and guards were seen on the NBC News feature "Chronolog" on November 26, 1971.

At the end of only six days we had to close down our mock prison because what we saw was frightening. It was no longer apparent to most of the subjects (or to us) where reality ended and their roles began. The majority had indeed become prisoners or guards, no longer able to clearly differentiate between role playing and self. There were dramatic changes in virtually every aspect of their behavior, thinking and feeling. In less than a week the experience of imprisonment undid (temporarily) a lifetime of learning; human values were suspended, self-concepts were challenged and the ugliest, most base, pathological side of human nature surfaced. We were horrified because we saw some boys (guards) treat others as if they were despicable animals, taking pleasure in cruelty, while other boys (prisoners) became servile, dehumanized robots who thought only of escape, of their own individual survival and of their mounting hatred for the guards.

We had to release three prisoners in the first four days because they had such acute situational traumatic reactions as hysterical crying, confusion in thinking and severe depression. Others begged to be paroled, and all but three were willing to forfeit all the money they had earned if they could be paroled. By then (the fifth day) they had been so programmed to think of themselves as prisoners that when their request for parole was denied, they returned docilely to their cells. Now, had they been thinking as college students acting in an oppressive experiment, they would have quit once they no longer wanted the $15 a day we used as our only incentive. However, the reality was not quitting an experiment but "being paroled by the parole board from the Stanford County Jail." By the last days, the earlier solidarity among the prisoners (systematically broken by the guards) dissolved into "each man for himself." Finally, when one of their fellows was put in solitary confinement (a small closet) for refusing to eat, the prisoners were given a choice by one of the guards: give up their blankets and the incorrigible prisoner would be let out, or keep their blankets and he would be kept in all night. They voted to keep their blankets and abandon their brother.

About a third of the guards became tyrannical in their arbitrary use of power, in enjoying their control over other people. They were corrupted by the power of their roles and became quite inventive in their techniques of breaking the spirit of the prisoners and making them feel they were worthless. Some of the guards merely did their jobs as tough but fair correctional officers, and several were good guards from the prisoners point of view since they did them small favors and were friendly. However, no good guard ever interfered with a command by any of the bad guards; they never intervened on the side of the prisoners, they never told the others to ease off because it was only an experiment, and they never even came to me as prison superintendent or experimenter in charge to complain. In part, they were good because the others were bad; they needed the others to help establish their own egos in a positive light. In a sense, the good guards perpetuated the prison more than the other guards because their own needs to be liked prevented them from disobeying or violating the implicit guards' code. At the same time, the act of befriending the prisoners created a social reality which made the prisoners less likely to rebel.

By the end of the week the experiment had become a reality, as if it were a Pirandello play directed by Kafka that just keeps going after the audience has left. The consultant for our prison, Carlo Prescott, an ex-convict with 16 years of imprisonment in California's jails, would get so depressed and furious each time he visited our prison, because of its psychological similarity to his experiences, that he would have to leave. A Catholic priest who was

---

Box 82

The Functions of Prisons

Prisons are institutions run by federal and state governments for detaining convicted criminals. They are said to perform four sometimes conflicting purposes: punishment, deterrence, incapacitation, and rehabilitation. The first three are probably obvious: suffering and restricting freedom is "punishment" for causing suffering to others; the threat of imprisonment will "deter" others from committing crimes; locking offenders away "incapacitates" them from committing crimes.

Many Americans believe that rehabilitation—the resocialization of criminals to conform to societies' values and norms and the teaching of work habits and skills—should be prison's most important goal. Yet there can be no doubt that prisons do not come close to achieving this aim. Recidivism refers to the return to prison by those previously imprisoned. According to the FBI, about 70% of all inmates released from prison are arrested again for criminal behavior. The general failure of the corrections system to "correct" has led one harsh critic to conclude that the only things prisons are known to cure is heterosexuality!

SOURCE: S.T. Reid, *Crime and Criminology* (New York: Holt Rinehart, & Winston, 1979).

---

a former prison chaplin in Washington, D.C. talked to our prisoners after four days and said they were just like the other first-timers he had seen.

But in the end, I called off the experiment not because of the horror I saw out there in the prison yard, but because of the horror of realizing that I could have easily traded places with the most brutal guard or become the weakest prisoner full of hatred at being so powerless that I could not eat, sleep or go to the toilet without permission of the authorities. I could have become Calley at My Lai, George Jackson at San Quentin, one of the men at Attica or the prisoner quoted at the beginning of this article.

Individual behavior is largely under the control of social forces and environmental contingencies rather than personality traits, character, will power or other empirically unvalidated constructs. Thus we create an illusion of freedom by attributing more internal control to ourselves, to the individual, than actually exists. We thus underestimate the power and pervasiveness of situational controls over behavior because: (a) they are often non-obvious and subtle, (b) we can often avoid entering situations where we might be so controlled, (c) we label as "weak" or "deviant" people in those situations who do behave differently from how we believe we would.

Each of us carries around in our heads a favorable self-image in which we are essentially just, fair, humane and understanding. For example, we could not imagine inflicting pain on others without much provocation or hurting people who had done nothing to us, who in fact were even liked by us. However, there is a growing body of social psychological research which underscores the conclusion derived from this prison study. Many people, perhaps the majority, can be made to do almost anything when put into psychologically compelling situations—regardless of their morals, ethics, values, attitudes, beliefs or personal convictions. My colleague, Stanley Milgram, has shown that more than 60 percent of the population will deliver what they think is a series of painful electric shocks to another person even after the victim cries for mercy, begs them to stop and then apparently passes out. The subjects complained that they did not want to inflict more pain but blindly obeyed the command of the authority figure (the experimenter) who said that they must go on. In my own research on violence, I have seen mild-mannered co-eds repeatedly give shocks (which they thought were causing pain) to another girl, a stranger whom they had rated very favorably, simply by being made to feel anonymous and put in a situation where they were expected to engage in this activity.

Observers of these and similar experimental situations never predict their outcomes and estimate that it is unlikely that they themselves would behave similarly. They can be so confident only when they were outside the situation. However, since the majority of people in these studies do act in non-rational, non-obvious ways, it follows that the majority of observers would also succumb to the social psychological forces in the situation.

With regard to prisons, we can state that the mere act of assigning labels to people and putting them into a situation where those labels acquire validity and meaning is sufficient to elicit pathological behavior. This pathology is not predictable from any available diagnostic indicators we have in the social sciences, and is extreme enough to modify in very significant ways fundamental attitudes and behavior. The prison situation, as presently arranged, is guaranteed to generate severe enough pathological reactions in both guards and prisoners as to debase their humanity, lower their feelings of self-worth and make it difficult for them to be part of a society outside of their prison.

For years our national leaders have been pointing to the enemies of freedom, to the fascist or communist threat to the American way of life. In so doing they have overlooked the threat of social anarchy that is building within our own country without any outside agitation. As soon as a person comes to the realization that he is being imprisoned by his society or individuals in it, then, in the best American tradition, he demands liberty and rebels, accepting death as an alternative. The third alternative, however, is to allow oneself to become a good prisoner—docile, cooperative, uncomplaining, conforming in thought and complying in deed.

Our prison authorities now point to the militant agitators who are still vaguely referred to as part of some communist plot, as the irresponsible, incorrigible troublemakers. They imply that there would he no trouble, riots, hostages or deaths if it weren't for this small band of bad prisoners. In other words, then, everything would return to "normal" again in the life of our nation's prisons if they could break these men.

The riots in prison are coming from within—from within every man and woman who refuses to let the system turn them into an object, a number, a thing or a nothing. It is not communist inspired, but inspired by the spirit of American freedom. No man wants to be enslaved. To be powerless, to be subject to the arbitrary exercise of power, to not be recognized as a human being is to be a slave.

To be a militant prisoner is to become aware that the physical jails are but more blatant extensions of the forms of social and psychological oppression

---

Box 83

Who Goes to Prison?

Although many studies show that almost all people admit to having committed a crime for which they could be imprisoned, the police are more prone to single out the poor for harsher treatment in our criminal justice system. That is the conclusion of Jeffrey Reimann who has made a detailed review of studies on the relationship between a person's social class and the possibility of his or her arrest, conviction, and sentencing if accused of a crime. For the same criminal behavior the poor are more likely to be arrested; if arrested, they are more likely to be charged; if charged, more likely to be convicted; if convicted, more likely to be sentenced to prison; and if sentenced, more likely to be given longer prison terms than members of the middle and upper classes. At each stage of the criminal justice system, the proportion of poor involved increases.

The end result is a prison system heavily populated by the poor. Only about 10% of the inmates in prisons were at or above the national median income level prior to entering prison. The majority had incomes below the poverty level. How can such inequality of justice exist in a country that prides itself on equality before the law?

SOURCE: Jeffrey Reimann, *Ideology, Class, and Criminal Justice* (New York: John Wiley & Sons, 1979).

Box 84

Prison Experiment Update

In 1983, 95 students at a Westchester, Illinois high school decided to replicate Zimbardo's experiment. They created a schoolhouse prison and spent a weekend either inside the "cells" of the prison or policing them. Even though they followed a regimen modeled after the Stateville Correctional Facility, most expected little more than a fun weekend away from home. Instead they found themselves pulled into their roles with a ferocity they had not anticipated. Guards insulted prisoners and shoved them around; prisoners became angry and resentful. "I couldn't stay here another night," one prisoner said, who escaped by jumping from a 15 foot ladder. (Had he been caught within an hour, he would have flunked. Having successfully escaped, he was given an A-plus and the guards grades were lowered). Other students had to be sent home because, as one said, "I'm scared, I really am." By the time the experiment was over, there seemed to be no doubts that suburban teenagers could truly assume the mind-sets of prisoners and guards. The statuses they occupied did change their behavior.

SOURCE: Barbara Brotman, *Chicago Tribune*, October 17, 1983.

---

experienced daily in the nation's ghettos. They are trying to awaken the conscience of the nation to the ways in which the American ideals are being perverted, apparently in the name of justice but actually under the banner of apathy, fear and hatred. If we do not listen to the pleas of the prisoners at Attica to be treated like human beings, then we have all become brutalized by our priorities for property rights over human rights. The consequence will not only be more prison riots but a loss of all those ideals on which this country was founded.

The public should be aware that they own the prisons and that their business is failing. The 70 percent recidivism rate and the escalation in severity of crimes committed by graduates of our prisons are evidence that current prisons fail to rehabilitate the inmates in any positive way. Rather, they are breeding grounds for hatred of the establishment, a hatred that makes every citizen a target of violent assault. Prisons are a bad investment for us taxpayers. Until now we have not cared, we have turned over to wardens and prison authorities the unpleasant job of keeping people who threaten us out of our sight. Now we are shocked to learn that their management practices have failed to improve the product and instead turn petty thieves into murderers. We must insist upon new management or improved operating procedures.

The cloak of secrecy should be removed from the prisons. Prisoners claim they are brutalized by the guards, guards say it is a lie. Where is the impartial test of the truth in such a situation? Prison officials have forgotten that they work for us, that they are only public servants whose salaries are paid by our taxes. They act as if it is their prison, like a child with a toy he won't share. Neither lawyers, judges, the legislature nor the public is allowed into prisons to ascertain the truth unless the visit is sanctioned by authorities and until all is prepared for their visit. I was shocked to learn that my request to join a congressional investigating committee's tour of San Quentin and Soledad was refused, as was that of the news media.

There should be an ombudsman in every prison, not under the pay or control of the prison authority, and responsible only to the courts, state legislature and the public. Such a person could report on violations of constitutional and human rights.

Guards must be given better training than they now receive for the difficult job society imposes upon them. To be a prison guard as now constituted is to be put in a situation of constant threat from within the prison, with no social recognition from the society at large. As was shown graphically at Attica, prison guards are also prisoners of the system who can be sacrificed to the demands of the public to be punitive and the needs of politicians to preserve an image. Social scientists and business administrators should be called upon to design and help carry out this training.

The relationship between the individual (who is sentenced by the courts to a prison term) and his community must be maintained. How can a prisoner return to a dynamically changing society that most of us cannot cope with after being out of it for a number of years? There should be more community involvement in these rehabilitation centers, more ties encouraged and promoted between the trainees and family and friends, more educational opportunities to prepare them for returning to their communities as more valuable members of it than they were before they left.

Finally, the main ingredient necessary to effect any change at all in prison reform, in the rehabilitation of a single prisoner or even in the optimal development of a child is caring. Reform must start with people — especially people with power — caring about the well-being of others. Underneath the toughest, society-hating convict, rebel or anarchist is a human being who wants his existence to be recognized by his fellows and who wants someone else to care about whether he lives or dies and to grieve if he lives imprisoned rather than lives free.

Questions

1. What was Zimbardo's research design? What was his hypothesis?
2. Does the fact that his sample was small and not chosen randomly affect his findings?
3. Can one generalize from an "artificial" experiment to the larger society? Give examples.
4. What made Zimbardo call off the experiment?
5. Does Zimbardo feel that social environment or will power, character, etc., influence behavior more?
6. How much "internal control" over our behavior do we have?
7. Who goes to prison?
8. What is the purpose of the American prison system? Does it succeed in its purpose?
9. What major changes are needed in American prisons?
10. How can a recidivism rate of 70% be reduced?
11. What happens to persons released from prison? List ways their reintroduction into the society can be made easier.
12. Some prisons are under the control of private firms rather than public authority. Is this a good idea?
13. Would the findings differ if the experiment was replicated in the 1990s?

Chapter Thirty-Two

If Hitler Asked You to Electrocute a Stranger, Would You?

Philip Meyer

In the beginning, Stanley Milgram was worried about the Nazi problem. He doesn't worry much about the Nazis anymore. He worries about you and me, and perhaps, himself a little bit too.

Stanley Milgram is a social psychologist, and when he began his career at Yale University in 1960 he had a plan to prove, scientifically, that Germans are different. The Germans-are-different hypothesis has been used by historians, such as William L. Shirer, to explain the systematic destruction of the Jews by the Third Reich. One madman could decide to destroy the Jews and even create a master plan for getting it done. But to implement it on the scale that Hitler did meant that thousands of other people had to go along with the scheme and help to do the work. The Shirer thesis, which Milgram set out to test, is that Germans have a basic character flaw which explains the whole thing, and this flaw is a readiness to obey authority without question, no matter what outrageous acts the authority commands.

The appealing thing about his theory is that it makes those of us who are not Germans feel better about the whole business. Obviously, you and I are not Hitler, and it seems equally obvious that we would never do Hitler's dirty

Reprinted by permission of *Esquire* Magazine. Copyright © 1970 Esquire, Inc.

work for him. But now, because of Stanley Milgram, we are compelled to wonder. Milgram developed a laboratory experiment which provided a systematic way to measure obedience. His plan was to try it out in New Haven on Americans and then go to Germany and try it out on Germans. He was strongly motivated by scientific curiosity, but there was also some moral content in his decision to pursue this line of research, which was, in turn, colored by his own Jewish background. If he could show that Germans are more obedient than Americans, he could then vary the conditions of the experiment and try to find out just what it is that makes some people more obedient than others. With this understanding, the world might, conceivably, be just a little bit better.

But he never took his experiment to Germany. He never took it any farther than Bridgeport. The first finding, also the most unexpected and disturbing finding, was that we Americans are an obedient people: not blindly obedient, and not blissfully obedient, just obedient. "I found so much obedience," says Milgram softly, a little sadly, "I hardly saw the need for taking the experiment to Germany."

There is something of the theatre director in Milgram, and his technique, which he learned from one of the old masters in experimental psychology, Solomon Asch, is to stage a play with every line rehearsed, every prop carefully selected, and everybody an actor except one person. That one person is the subject of the experiment. The subject of course, does not know he is in a play. He thinks he is in real life. The value of this technique is that the experimenter, as though he were God, can change a prop here, vary a line there, and see how the subject responds. Milgram eventually had to change a lot of the script just to get people to stop obeying. They were obeying so much, the experiment wasn't working—it was like trying to measure oven temperature with a freezer thermometer.

The experiment worked like this: If you were an innocent subject in Milgram's melodrama, you read an ad in the newspaper or received one in the mail asking for volunteers for an educational experiment. The job would take about an hour and pay $4.50. So you make an appointment and go to an old Romanesque stone structure on High Street with the imposing name of The Yale Interaction Laboratory. It looks something like a broadcasting studio. Inside, you meet a young, crew-cut man in a laboratory coat who says he is Jack Williams, the experimenter. There is another citizen, fiftyish, Irish face, an accountant, a little overweight, and very mild and harmless-looking. This other citizen seems nervous and plays with his hat while the two of you sit in chairs side by side and are told that the $4.50 checks are yours no matter what happens. Then you listen to Jack Williams explain the experiment.

It is about learning, says Jack Williams in a quiet, knowledgeable way. Science does not know much about the conditions under which people learn and this experiment is to find out about negative reinforcement. Negative reinforcement is getting punished when you do something wrong, as opposed to positive reinforcement which is getting rewarded when you do something right. The negative reinforcement in this case is electric shock. You notice a book on the table, titled, *The Teaching-Learning Process*, and you assume that this has something to do with the experiment.

Then Jack Williams takes two pieces of paper, puts them in a hat, and shakes them up. One piece of paper is supposed to say, "Teacher" and the other, "Learner." Draw one and you will see which you will be. The mild-looking accountant draws one, holds it close to his vest like a poker player, looks at it, and says, "Learner." You look at yours. It says, "Teacher." You do not know that the drawing is rigged, and both slips say "Teacher." The experimenter beckons to the mild-mannered "learner."

"Want to step right in here and have a seat, please?" he says. "You can leave your coat on the back of that chair . . . roll up your right sleeve, please. Now what I want to do is strap down your arms to avoid excessive movement on your part during the experiment. This electrode is connected to the shock generator in the next room.

"And this electrode paste," he says, squeezing some stuff out of a plastic bottle and putting it on the man's arm, "is to provide a good contact and to avoid a blister or burn. Are there any questions now before we go into the next room?"

You don't have any, but the strapped-in "learner" does.

"I do think I should say this," says the learner. "About two years ago, I was at the veterans' hospital . . . they detected a heart condition. Nothing serious, but as long as I'm having these shocks, how strong are they—how dangerous are they?"

Williams, the experimenter, shakes his head casually. "Oh, no," he says. "Although they may be painful, they're not dangerous. Anything else?"

Nothing else. And so you play the game. The game is for you to read a series of word pairs: for example, blue-girl, nice-day, fat-neck. When you finish the list, you read just the first word in each pair and then a multiple-choice list of four other words, including the second word of the pair. The learner, from his remote, strapped-in position, pushes one of four switches to indicate which of the four answers he thinks is the right one. If he gets it right nothing happens and you go on to the next one. If he gets it wrong, you push a switch that buzzes and gives him an electric shock. And then you go to the next word. You start with 15 volts and increase the number of volts by 15 for each wrong answer. The control board goes from 15 volts on one end to 450 volts on the other. So that you know what you are doing, you get a test shock yourself, at 45 volts. It hurts. To further keep you aware of what you are doing to that man in there, the board has verbal descriptions of the shock levels, ranging from "Slight Shock" at the left-hand side, through "Intense Shock" in the middle, to "Danger: Severe Shock" toward the far right. Finally, at the very end, under 435- and 450-volt switches, there are three ambiguous Xs. If, at any point, you hesitate, Mr. Williams calmly tells you to go on. If you still hesitate, he tells you again.

Except for some terrifying details, which will be explained in a moment, this is the experiment. The object is to find the shock level at which you disobey the experimenter and refuse to pull the switch.

When Stanley Milgram first wrote this script, he took it to fourteen Yale psychology majors and asked them what they thought would happen. He put it this way: Out of one hundred persons in the teacher's predicament, how would their break-off points be distributed along the 15-to-450-volt scale? They thought a few would break off very early, most would quit someplace in the middle and a few would go all the way to the end. The highest estimate of the number out of one hundred who would go all the way to the end was three. Milgram then informally polled some of his fellow scholars in the psychology department. They agreed that very few would go to the end. Milgram thought so too.

"I'll tell you quite frankly," he says, "before I began this experiment, before any shock generator was built, I thought that most people would break off at 'Strong Shock' or 'Very Strong Shock.' You would get only a very, very small proportion of people going out to the end of the shock generator, and they would constitute a pathological fringe."

In his pilot experiments, Milgram used Yale students as subjects. Each of them pushed the shock switches, one by one, all the way to the end of the board.

So he rewrote the script to include some protests from the learner. At first, they were mild, gentlemanly, Yalie protests, but, "it didn't seem to have as much effect as I thought it would or should," Milgram recalls. "So we had more violent protestation on the part of the person getting the shock. All of the time, of course, what we were trying to do was not to create a macabre situation, but simply to generate disobedience. And that was one of the first findings. This was not only a technical deficiency of the experiment, that we didn't get disobedience. It really was the first finding: that obedience would be much greater than we had assumed it would be and disobedience would be much more difficult than we had assumed."

As it turned out, the situation did become rather macabre. The only meaningful way to generate disobedience was to have the victim protest with great anguish, noise, and vehemence. The protests were tape-recorded so that all the teachers ordinarily would hear the same sounds and nuances, and they started with a grunt at 75 volts, proceeded through a "Hey, that really hurts," at 125 volts, got desperate with, "I can't stand the pain, don't do that," at 180 volts, reached complaints of heart trouble at 195, an agonized scream at 285, a refusal to answer at 315, and only heart-rending, ominous silence after that.

Still, sixty-five percent of the subjects, twenty- to fifty-year-old American males, everyday, ordinary people, like you and me, obediently kept pushing those levers in the belief that they were shocking the mild-mannered learner, whose name was Mr. Wallace, and who was chosen for the role because of his innocent appearance, all the way up to 450 volts.

Milgram was now getting enough disobedience so that he had something he could measure. The next step was to vary the circumstances to see what would encourage or discourage obedience. There seemed very little left in the way of discouragement. The victim was already screaming at the top of his lungs and feigning a heart attack. So whatever new impediment to obedience reached the brain of the subject had to travel by some route other than the ear. Milgram thought of one.

He put the learner in the same room with the teacher. He stopped strapping the learners hand down. He rewrote the script so that at 150 volts the learner took his hand off the shock plate and declared that he wanted out of the experiment. He rewrote the script some more so that the experimenter then told the teacher to grasp the learner's hand and physically force it down on the plate to give Mr. Wallace his unwanted electric shock.

"I had the feeling that very few people would go on at that point, if any," Milgram says. "I thought that would be the limit of obedience that you would find in the laboratory."

It wasn't.

Although seven years have now gone by, Milgram still remembers the first person to walk into the laboratory in the newly rewritten script. He was a construction worker, a very short man. "He was so small," says Milgram, "that when he sat on the chair in front of the shock generator, his feet didn't reach the floor. When the experimenter told him to push the victim's hand down and give the shock, he turned to the experimenter, and he turned to the victim, his elbow went up, he fell down on the hand of the victim, his feet kind of tugged to one side and he said, "Like this, boss?" ZZUMPH!

The experiment was played out to its bitter end. Milgram tried it with forty different subjects. And thirty percent of them obeyed the experimenter and kept on obeying.

"The protests of the victim were strong and vehement, he was screaming his guts out, he refused to participate, and you had to physically struggle with him in order to get his hand down on the shock generator," Milgram remembers. But twelve out of forty did it.

Milgram took his experiment out of New Haven. Not to Germany, just twenty miles down the road to Bridgeport. Maybe, he reasoned, the people obeyed because of the prestigious setting of Yale University. If they couldn't trust a center of learning that had been there for two centuries, whom could they trust? So he moved the experiment to an untrustworthy setting.

The new setting was a suite of three rooms in a run-down office building in Bridgeport. The only identification was a sign with a fictitious name: "Research Associates of Bridgeport." Questions about professional connections got only vague answers about "research for industry."

Obedience was less in Bridgeport. Forty-eight percent of the subjects stayed for the maximum shock, compared to sixty-five percent at Yale. But this was enough to prove that far more than Yale's prestige was behind the obedient behavior.

For more than seven years now, Stanley Milgram has been trying to figure out what makes ordinary American citizens so obedient. The most obvious answer—that people are mean, nasty, brutish, and sadistic—won't do. The subjects who gave the shocks to Mr. Wallace to the end of the board did not enjoy it. They groaned, protested, fidgeted, argued, and in some cases, were seized by fits of nervous, agitated giggling.

"They even try to get out of it." says Milgram, "but they are somehow engaged in something from which they cannot liberate themselves. They are locked into a structure, and they do not have the skills or inner resources to disengage themselves."

Milgram, because he mistakenly had assumed that he would have trouble getting people to obey the orders to shock Mr. Wallace, went to a lot of trouble to create a realistic situation.

There was crew-cut Jack Williams and his grey laboratory coat. Not white, which might denote a medical technician, but ambiguously authoritative grey. Then there was the book on the table, and the other appurtenances of the laboratory which emitted the silent message that things were being performed here in the name of science, and were therefore great and good.

But the nicest touch of all was the shock generator. When Milgram started out, he had only a $300 grant from the Higgins Fund of Yale University. Later he got more ample support from the National Science Foundation, but in the beginning he had to create this authentic-looking machine with very scarce resources except for his own imagination. So he went to New York and roamed around the electronic shops until he found some little black switches at Lafayette Radio for a dollar apiece. He bought thirty of them. The generator was a metal box, about the size of a small footlocker, and he drilled the thirty holes for the thirty switches himself in a Yale machine shop. But the fine detail was left to professional industrial engravers. So he ended up with a splendid-looking control panel dominated by the row of switches, each labeled with its voltage, and each having its own red light that flashed on when the switch was pulled. Other things happened when a switch was pushed. Besides the ZZUMPHing noise, a blue light labeled "voltage energizer" went on, and a needle on a dial labeled "voltage" flicked from left to right. Relays inside the box clicked. Finally, in the upper left-hand corner of the control panel was this inscription, engraved in precise block letters:

SHOCK GENERATOR TYPE ZLB
DYSON INSTRUMENT COMPANY
WALTHAM, MASS.
OUTPUT: 15 VOLTS—450 VOLTS

One day a man from the Lehigh Valley Electronics Company of Pennsylvania was passing through the laboratory, and he stopped to admire the shock generator.

"This is a very fine shock generator," he said. "But who is this Dyson Instrument Company?" Milgram felt proud at that, since Dyson Instrument Company existed only in the recesses of his imagination.

When you consider the seeming authenticity of the situation, you can appreciate the agony some of the subjects went through. It was pure conflict. As Milgram explains to his students, "When a parent says, 'Don't strike old ladies,' you are learning two things: the content, and, also, to obey authority. This experiment creates conflicts between the two elements."

Here is a partial transcription from one of the experiments. The naive "teacher" is a heavyset, worried-looking man with prematurely grey hair. He is wearing a polo shirt. He is very polite. He has just pushed the 180-volt lever. A hidden camera is recording the performance.

LEARNER (*who, from the teacher's point of view is heard but not seen, an offstage voice*): Ow, I can't stand the pain. Don't do that. . . .

TEACHER (*Pivoting around in his chair and shaking his head*): I can't stand it. I'm not going to kill that man in there. You hear him hollering?

EXPERIMENTER: As I told you before, the shocks may be painful, but—

TEACHER: But he's hollering. He can't stand it. What's going to happen to him?

EXPERIMENTER (*his voice is patient, matter-of-fact*). The experiment requires that you continue, Teacher.

TEACHER: Aaah, but, unh, I'm not going to get that man sick in there . . . know what I mean?

EXPERIMENTER: Whether the learner likes it or not, we must go on, through all the word pairs.

TEACHER: I refuse to take the responsibility. He's in there hollering!

EXPERIMENTER: It's absolutely essential that you continue, Teacher.

TEACHER (*indicating the unused questions*): There's too many left here, I mean, Geez, if he gets them wrong, there's too many of them left.

I mean who's going to take the responsibility if anything happens to that gentleman?

EXPERIMENTER: I'm responsible for anything that happens to him. Continue please.

TEACHER: All right. (*Consults list of words.*) The next one's "Slow — walk, truck, dance, music." Answer, please. (*A buzzing sound indicates the learner has signaled his answer.*) Wrong. A hundred and ninety-five volts. "Dance."(*Zzumph!*)

LEARNER: Let me out of here. My heart's bothering me! (*Teacher looks at experimenter.*)

EXPERIMENTER: Continue, please.

LEARNER (*screaming*): Let me out of here, you have no right to keep me here. Let me out of here, let me out, my heart's bothering me, let me out! (*Teacher shakes head, pats the table nervously.*)

TEACHER: You see, he's hollering. Hear that? Gee, I don't know.

EXPERIMENTER: The experiment requires. . .

TEACHER (*interrupting*): I know it does, sir, but I mean — hunh! I don't know what he's getting in for. He's up to 195 volts! (*Experiment continues, through 210 volts, 225 volts, 240 volts, 255 volts, 270 volts, delivered to the man in the electric chair, at which point the teacher, with evident relief, runs out of word-pair questions.*)

EXPERIMENTER: You'll have to go back to the beginning of that page and go through them again until he's learned them all correctly.

TEACHER: Aw, no. I'm not going to kill that man. You mean I've got to keep going up with the scale. No sir. He's hollering in there. I'm not going to give him 450 volts.

EXPERIMENTER: The experiment requires that you go on.

TEACHER: I know it does, but that man is hollering in there, sir.

EXPERIMENTER (*same matter-of-fact tone*): As I said before, although the shocks may be painful. . . .

TEACHER (*interrupting*): Awwwww. He-he-he's yelling in there.

EXPERIMENTER: Start with "Blue," please, at the top of the page. Continue, please, Teacher. Just go ahead.

TEACHER (*concentrating intently on list of words in front of him, as if to shut everything else out*): "Blue — boy, girl, grass, hat." (*Buzz indicates answer.*) Correct. "Night — day, sky, job, chair. (*Buzz*) Wrong. The answer is "day." Two hundred and eighty-five volts. (*Zzumph!*)

LEARNER: ohhhuhhoohhh!

EXPERIMENTER: Continue, please.

TEACHER: "Fat — man, lady, tub, neck." Answer, please. (*Buzz*) Wrong. The answer is "neck." Three hundred volts. (*Zzumph!*)

LEARNER: Ohhh. I absolutely refuse to answer any more. (*Shouting urgently, now*) Let me out of here. You can't hold me here. Get me out. Get — me — out — of — here.

EXPERIMENTER: Continue. The next word is "Green," please.

TEACHER: "Green — grass, hat, ink, apple." (*Nothing happens. No answering buzz. Just gloomy silence.*)

TEACHER: I don't think he is going to answer.

EXPERIMENTER: If the learner doesn't answer in a reasonable time, about four or five seconds, consider the answer wrong. And follow the same procedures you have been doing for wrong answers. Say "Wrong," tell him the number of volts, give him the punishment, read him the correct answer. Continue, please.

TEACHER: "Green — grass, hat, ink, apple." Answer, please. (*More silence. Teacher just sits there.*)

EXPERIMENTER: Go on with the procedure, please Teacher.

TEACHER: Three hundred and fifteen volts. The answer is "ink." (*Zzumph!*)

LEARNER: Ohh. Ooohh.

TEACHER (*relieved to hear response*): Next one. . . .

LEARNER: I absolutely refuse to answer.

TEACHER: You got to. You get a shock if you don't answer. (*Experiment continues with learner refusing to answer and, finally, failing even to grunt or groan. At 375 volts, the teacher stands up. Has he had enough? Will he break off the experiment? Will he disobey?*)

TEACHER: I think something's happened to that fellow in there I don't get no answer. He was hollering at less voltage. Can't you check in and see if he's all right, please?

EXPERIMENTER (*same detached calm*): Not once we've started. Please continue, Teacher.

TEACHER (*sits down, sighs deeply*): "Cool — day, shade, water, paint." Answer, please. Are you all right in there? Are you all right?

EXPERIMENTER: Please continue, Teacher. Continue please. (*Teacher pushes lever. Zzumph!*)

TEACHER (*swiveling around in his chair*): Something's happened to that man in there. (*Swiveling back*) Next one. "Low — dollar, necklace, moon, paint." (*Turning around again*) Something's happened to that man in there. You better check on him, sir. He won't answer or nothing.

EXPERIMENTER: Continue. Go on, please.

TEACHER: You accept all responsibility.

EXPERIMENTER: The responsibility is mine. Correct. Please go on. (*Teacher returns to his list, starts running through words as rapidly as he can read them, works through to 450 volts.*)

TEACHER: That's that.

EXPERIMENTER: Continue using the last switch on the board, please. The four-fifty switch for each wrong answer. Continue, please.

TEACHER: But I don't get no anything!

EXPERIMENTER: Please, continue. The next word is "White."

TEACHER: Don't you think you should look in on him, please.

EXPERIMENTER: Not once we've started the experiment.

TEACHER: But what if something has happened to the man?

EXPERIMENTER: The experiment requires that you continue. Go on, please.

TEACHER: Don't the man's health mean anything?

EXPERIMENTER: Whether the learner likes it or not. . . .

TEACHER: What if he's dead in there? (*Gestures toward the room with the electric chair.*) I mean, he told me he can't stand the shock, sir. I don't mean to be rude, but I think you should look in on him. All you have to do is look in the door. I don't get no answer, no noise. Something might have happened to the gentleman in there, sir.

EXPERIMENTER: We must continue. Go on please.

TEACHER: You mean keep giving him what? Four hundred fifty volts, what he's got now?

EXPERIMENTER: That's correct. Continue. The next word is "White."

TEACHER (*now at a furious pace*): "White—cloud, horse, rock, house." Answer, please. The answer is "horse." Four hundred and fifty volts. (Zzumph!) Next word, "Bag—paint, music, clown, girl." The answer is "paint." Four hundred and fifty volts. (Zzumph!) Next word is "Short—sentence, movie. . . .

EXPERIMENTER: Excuse me, Teacher. We'll have to discontinue the experiment.

(*Enter Milgram from camera's left. He has been watching from behind one-way glass.*)

MILGRAM: I'd like to ask you a few questions. (*Slowly, patiently, he dehoaxes the teacher, telling him that the shocks and screams were not real.*)

TEACHER: You mean he wasn't getting nothing? Well, I'm glad to hear that. I was getting upset there. I was getting ready to walk out.

(*Finally, to make sure there are no hard feelings, friendly, harmless Mr. Wallace comes out in coat and tie, gives jovial greeting. Friendly reconciliation takes place. Experiment ends.*)

©Stanley Milgram 1965.

Subjects in the experiment were not asked to give the 450-volt shock more than three times. By that time, it seemed evident that they would go on indefinitely. "No one," says Milgram, "who got within five shocks of the end ever broke off. By that point, he had resolved the conflict."

Why do so many people resolve the conflict in favor of obedience?

Milgram's theory assumes that people behave in two different operating models as different as ice and water. He does not rely on Freud or sex or toilet-training hang-ups for this theory. All he says is that ordinarily we operate in a state of autonomy, which means we pretty much have and assert control over what we do. But in certain circumstances, we operate under what Milgram calls a state of agency (after agent, n . . . one who acts for or in the place of another by authority from him; a substitute; a deputy. — *Webster's Collegiate Dictionary*). A state of agency, to Milgram, is nothing more than a frame of mind.

"There's nothing bad about it, there's nothing good about it," he says. "It's a natural circumstance of living with other people. . . . I think of a state of agency as a real transformation of a person; if a person has different properties when he's in that state, just as water can turn to ice under certain conditions of temperature, a person can move to the state of mind that I call agency . . . the critical thing is that you see yourself as the instrument of the execution of another person's wishes. You do not see yourself as acting on your own. And there's a real transformation, a real change of properties of the person."

To achieve this change, you have to be in a situation where there seems to be a ruling authority whose commands are relevant to some legitimate purpose; the authority's power is not unlimited.

But situations can be and have been structured to make people do unusual things, and not just in Milgram's laboratory. The reason, says Milgram, is that no action, in and of itself, contains meaning.

"The meaning always depends on your definition of the situation. Take an action like killing another person. It sounds bad.

"But then we say the other person was about to destroy a hundred children, and the only way to stop him was to kill him. Well, that sounds good.

"Or, you take destroying your own life, It sounds very bad. Yet, in the Second World War, thousands of persons thought it was a good thing to destroy your own life. It was set in the proper context. You sipped some saki from a whistling cup, recited a few haiku. You said, 'May my death be as clean and as quick as the shattering of crystal.' And it almost seemed like a good, noble thing to do, to crash your kamikaze plane into an aircraft carrier. But the main thing was, the definition of what a kamikaze pilot was doing had been determined by the relevant authority. Now, once you are in a state of agency, you allow the authority to determine, to define what the situation is. The meaning of your action is altered."

So, for most subjects in Milgram's laboratory experiments, the act of giving Mr. Wallace his painful shock was necessary, even though unpleasant, and besides they were doing it on behalf of somebody else and it was for science. There was still strain and conflict, of course, most people resolved it by grimly sticking to their task and obeying. But some broke out. Milgram tried varying the conditions of the experiment to see what would help break people out of their state of agency.

"The results, as seen and felt in the laboratory," he has written, "are disturbing. They raise the possibility that human nature, or more specifically the kind of character produced in American democratic society, cannot be counted on to insulate its citizens from brutality and inhumane treatment at the direction of malevolent authority. A substantial proportion of people do what they are told to do, irrespective of the content of the act and without limitations of conscience, so long as they perceive that the command comes from a legitimate authority. If, in this study, an anonymous experimenter can successfully command adults to subdue a fifty-year-old man and force on him painful electric shocks against his protest, one can only wonder what government, with its vastly greater authority and prestige, can command of its subjects."

This is a nice statement, but it falls short of summing up the full meaning of Milgram's work. It leaves some questions still unanswered.

The first question is this: Should we really be surprised and alarmed that people obey? Wouldn't it be even more alarming if they all refused to obey? Without obedience to a relevant ruling authority there could not be a civil society. And without a civil society, as Thomas Hobbes pointed out in the seventeenth century, we would live in a condition of war, "of every man against every other man," and life would be "solitary, poor, nasty, brutish and short."

In the middle of one of Stanley Milgram's lectures at C.U.N.Y. recently, some mini-skirted undergraduates started whispering and giggling in the back of the room. He told them to cut it out. Since he was the relevant authority in that time and that place, they obeyed, and most people in the room were glad that they obeyed.

This was not, of course, a conflict situation. Nothing in the coeds' social upbringing made it a matter of conscience for them to whisper and giggle. But a case can be made that in a conflict situation it is all the more important to obey. Take the case of war, for example. Would we really want a situation in which every participant in a war, direct or indirect—from front-line soldiers to the people who sell coffee and cigarettes to employees at the Concertina barbed-wire factory in Kansas—stops and consults his conscience before each action. It is asking for an awful lot of mental strain and anguish from an awful lot of people. The value of having civil order is that one can do his duty, or whatever interests him, or whatever seems to benefit him at the moment, and leave the agonizing to others. When Francis Gary Powers was being tried by a Soviet military tribunal after his U-2 spy plane was shot down, the presiding judge asked if he had thought about the possibility that his flight might have provoked a war. Powers replied with Hobbesian clarity: "The people who sent me should think of these things. My job was to carry out orders. I do not think it was my responsibility to make such decisions."

It was not his responsibility. And it is quite possible that if everyone felt responsible for each of the ultimate consequences of his own tiny contributions to complex chains of events, then society simply would not work. Milgram, fully conscious of the moral and social implications of his research, believes that people should feel responsible for their actions. If someone else had invented the experiment, and if he had been the naive subject, he feels certain that he would have been among the disobedient minority.

"There is no very good solution to this," he admits, thoughtfully. "To simply and categorically say that you won't obey authority may resolve your personal conflict, but it creates more problems for society which may be more serious in the long run. But I have no doubt that to disobey is the proper thing to do in this [the laboratory] situation. It is the only reasonable value judgment to make."

The conflict between the need to obey the relevant ruling authority and the need to follow your conscience becomes sharpest if you insist on living by an ethical system based on a rigid code—a code that seeks to answer all questions in advance of their being raised. Code ethics cannot solve the obedience problem. Stanley Milgram seems to be a situation ethicist, and situation ethics does offer a way out: When you feel conflict, you examine the situation and then make a choice among the competing evils. You may act with a presumption in favor of obedience, but reserve the possibility that you will disobey whenever obedience demands a flagrant and outrageous affront to conscience. This, by the way, is the philosophical position of many who resist the draft. In World War II, they would have fought. Vietnam is a different, an outrageously different, situation.

Life can be difficult for the situation ethicist, because he does not see the world in straight lines, while the social system too often assumes such a God-given, squared-off structure. If your moral code includes an injunction against all war, you may be deferred as a conscientious objector. If you merely oppose this particular war, you may not be deferred.

Stanley Milgram has his problems, too. He believes that in the laboratory situation, he would not have shocked Mr. Wallace. His professional critics reply that in his real-life situation he has done the equivalent. He has placed innocent and naive subjects under great emotional strain and pressure in selfish obedience to his quest for knowledge. When you raise this issue with Milgram, he has an answer ready. There is, he explains patiently, a critical difference between his naive subjects and the man in the electric chair. The man in the electric chair (in the mind of the naive subject) is helpless, strapped in. But the naive subject is free to go at any time.

Immediately after he offers this distinction, Milgram anticipates the objection.

"It's quite true," he says, "that this is almost a philosophic position, because we have learned that some people are psychologically incapable of disengaging themselves. But that doesn't relieve them of the moral responsibility."

The parallel is exquisite. "The tension problem was unexpected," says Milgram in his defense. But he went on anyway. The naive subjects didn't expect the screaming protests from the strapped-in learner. But they went on.

"I had to make a judgment," says Milgram. "I had to ask myself, was this harming the person or not? My judgment is that it was not. Even in the extreme cases, I wouldn't say that permanent damage results."

Sound familiar? "The shocks may be painful," the experimenter kept saying, "but they're not dangerous."

After the series of experiments was completed, Milgram sent a report of the results to his subjects and a questionnaire, asking whether they were glad or sorry to have been in the experiment. Eighty-three and seven-tenths percent said they were glad and only 1.3 percent were sorry; 15 percent were neither sorry nor glad. However, Milgram could not be sure at the time of the experiment that only 1.3 percent would be sorry.

Questions

1. Is it valid to ascribe characteristics to an entire nation. Think of examples.

2. What supposedly basic character traits of Germans did Stanley Milgram set out to test? What was his hypothesis?

3. Can we generalize from small group experiments conducted under controlled conditions to larger populations?

4. What is the difference between positive and negative reinforcement? Which do parents use in rearing children? Which does our society use?

5. Why did so many people obey in this experimental situation? Does "state of agency" have something to do with this? What conditions help people break out of a "state of agency?"

6. What was the purpose of moving the experiment from Yale University to a run-down office building in Bridgeport?

7. Milgram says "no action, in and of itself, contains meaning." Can this be true?

8. Can there be a civil society if people disobey most of the time rather than obey? What does this say about the relationship between the individual and society?

9. Do you conceive of yourself as having free will or being determined? How does this affect your responsibility for actions?

10. What is situation ethics?

11. Might not experiments like this be psychologically damaging to subjects? If so, do social scientists have the right to do this kind of research?

12. What does the fact that 83% of the subjects indicated pleasure at having participated in this experiment tell us about the respondents or human nature?

Chapter Thirty-Three

Research Through Deception

Morton Hunt

On a spring evening two years ago, Steve Kaufman, a wiry 18-year-old whose plain-featured intensity reminds one of Dustin Hoffman, hurried across the Stanford University campus to what he thought would be an interesting and enjoyable experience. He was headed for Jordan Hall, where the department of psychology is housed and where he had been receiving training as a hypnotic subject, preparatory to an experiment scheduled for that night.

The experiment was the core of a research project being carried out by Prof. Philip Zimbardo. A social psychologist with a flair for imaginative experimentation, Zimbardo was a campus celebrity and well known in his profession. Steve, a freshman, felt privileged to be working directly with such a notable, but to add to his motivation Zimbardo was rewarding him, and other subjects in the project, with a few dollars and with training in the use of self-hypnosis to increase concentration while studying, fight off fatigue, and control various other mental and physical states.

This night, Steve's final session, would first be devoted to pain control; this interested him because, being a fencer, he thought he might perform better if he could master the pain of physical effort. Later in the evening, he would take part, as a subject, in the experiment, which Zimbardo had said concerned the effect of hypnotism on problem-solving ability.

What Steve expected to take place that evening would take place—but so would much more, for he was wholly unaware of the real but covert goal of the research project. This was to train Steve and other unsuspecting volunteers in becoming good hypnotic subjects until, in the final session, Zimbardo could tell them, while they were in a trance, that afterward they would be partially deaf but would not remember that this had been hypnotically induced. Steve would be a naive subject—and would therefore react to his deafness as if it were genuine.

The morality of research in which human beings may be subjected to unpleasant and possibly harmful experiences that they have not agreed to undergo has long been hotly debated by social psychologists, university officials, ethicists at centers such as the Institute of Society, Ethics and the Life Sciences at Hastings-on-Hudson, N.Y., and administrators of Government agencies funding such work. The debate finally resulted in Federal regulations, put forth in 1971 and 1974, and revised last year; these regulations, setting boundaries on the permissible use of human beings in social-psychological research projects funded by major agencies, have throttled research into many aspects of human psychology without quite killing it off, and limited—but not eliminated—the chances for the stressful use of naive subjects. This compromise between the freedom to inquire and the rights of human beings pleases almost no one, and the debate continues in scientific and governmental circles and in the meetings and publications of institutes of ethics. Many psychologists, disheartened, have given up exploring problems they consider important; others, undeterred, continue to seek knowledge by means that critics label morally unacceptable no matter what the scientific rewards may be.

Zimbardo, convinced that his goal justified what he was doing to his volunteers, had painstakingly worked out a script for the final session, specifying every action and word of those taking part except, of course, the naive member. The entire sting had been thoroughly rehearsed by Zimbardo and his two assistants, and by two confederates—undergraduates who would appear to be Steve's fellow-subjects.

All this, Zimbardo felt, was necessary to put to the test his hypothesis that the paranoia—the demented suspiciousness—of many old people (a common cause of commitment to mental hospitals) was the result not of mental disorder but of a gradual, undetected loss of hearing. Such a change, if unnoticed by the individual, might lead him to wonder why others were whispering or making faces he could not interpret, and to imagine that their behavior was malicious and involved some sort of plot against him.

If Zimbardo was right, paranoia in many elderly persons might be remedied simply by the use of hearing aids rather than treated as an intractable psychosis. Zimbardo hoped, therefore, that when his naive subjects inexplicably had trouble understanding the conversation of the confederates they would attribute it to some dark design on their part. He hoped, in short, to see his subjects suffer an attack of paranoia.

With the possible exception of his small, dark goatee, there is nothing about Zimbardo to suggest a Svengali. A rumpled, paunchy man of 49 who grew up in the brawling southeast Bronx, he is genial, talkative, and concerned—

albeit somewhat sarcastically—about what others think of his research methods. As he said to me when I visited him not long ago: "Imagine someone innocently going into an experiment, perfectly normal, and then this terrible thing happens—they become paranoid! Because essentially I'm making normal people crazy. Now, isn't that an awful thing to do? Who am I to presume to exercise that power over another human being?"

Hostile reactions to his work are nothing new to Zimbardo, for he has a penchant for flamboyant experiments with disturbing consequences. In 1970, for instance, he persuaded 18 Stanford undergraduate men to play the roles of guards and prisoners in a prolonged realistic simulation of prison life. In less than a week, most of the guards had spontaneously become sadistic, while some prisoners had become dangerously hostile and others seriously disturbed. Zimbardo concluded that much of the vile behavior of prisoners and guards stems from the social roles they are cast in. While he regarded this as a valuable finding that should lead to reforms, he was widely criticized for having inflicted suffering on his subjects in the name of science.

Zimbardo planned to limit the deafness-induced paranoia, if any, to no more than half an hour and then to dispel it promptly. But even if the experience was genuinely upsetting to his subjects, he considered the stakes high enough to warrant imposing it on them.

"A fundamental assumption in psychiatry and clinical psychology," he told me, "is that where you see mental illness, there must have been a premorbid personality. But that's a completely unnecessary assumption, based on the study of people who are already disturbed. I hold that that's too late to look for good evidence about how the pathological process began. We should look at normal people and see whether there aren't many kinds of experiences that can transform them, distorting the way they think.

"I hope that the hearing-loss study will be just the first of a series. All sorts of mundane circumstances, I believe, may lead to pathological mental processes of many kinds—phobias, hypochondrias, conversion reactions, and so on. We can investigate all these phenomena by basically the same procedure as in the hearing-loss study—that is, if the work is not prevented." He paused dramatically. "What could prevent it?" he asked, and answered: "A sufficient outcry about the use of deception."

Social psychology, the study of how the individual's mental processes are influenced by interactions with other people, used to be a "soft science," consisting largely of efforts to make wise interpretations of everyday social behavior. But by the 1950s it became scientifically respectable as a result of a shift to the use of laboratory experiments in which social interactions could be controlled and measured.

Unlike laboratory rats, however, human subjects can understand what is going on, and their understanding will often alter and distort their normal responses to the stimulus. If, for instance, they know that the researcher is studying how and when people help strangers in distress, they are quite likely to behave in an admirable—but perhaps not characteristic—fashion.

Accordingly, social psychologists soon saw that they would often have to disguise their real aims. In 1951, for example, in a classic pioneering study of conformity, the social psychologist Solomon E. Asch asked students to participate in "an experiment in perceptual judgment." Several persons took part at a time; they were asked to say which one of three lines on cards in front of them was the same length as a standard line, also on display. In each case, one student—the naive subject—heard the others (who were confederates) choose a line plainly either shorter or longer than the standard. Faced with unanimity among his or her peers, the naive subject would squirm, sweat, feel upset—and, about a third of the time, go along with the majority vote. Deception, here, was obviously crucial; as "The Handbook of Social Psychology," a standard reference work comments, "One cannot imagine an experimenter studying the effects of group pressure . . . by announcing his intentions in advance."

Deception rapidly became the method of choice in investigating many such issues. By the late 1960s and early 1970s, according to several estimates, somewhere between 38 percent and 44 percent of all social-psychological research used deceptive methodology.

From the beginning, deceptive research yielded rich scientific rewards. Deceptive experiments performed in the 1960s, for instance, established the fact that violence seen in a movie increases the likelihood that the viewers will afterward react to provocations with violence.

After the Kitty Genovese murder of 1964, when 38 residents of Kew Gardens, Queens, watched but did nothing as her attacker strangled and stabbed her repeatedly for half an hour, many social critics spoke glumly of the brutish New York character, alienation in contemporary America, and so on. The social psychologists Bibb Latané and John M. Darley conducted a series of experiments in which subjects were fooled into thinking that a stranger was in distress, and found that if the naive subject was alone, he or she would rush to the aid of the stranger, but that if others, especially persons unknown to the subject, were also present, he or she was much less likely to act. (The presence of the others apparently "diffused" the naive subject's sense of responsibility.) The Kitty Genovese incident, Latané and Darley concluded, revealed not a loss of human decency in America but the inhibiting effect on helping behavior of the social interactions typical of big-city life.

Such results gave ingenious deceptive research an aura of glamour and prestige. But some of those who regard it as immoral and who have been fighting its use say that deceptive research came to be prized more for its ingenuity than for the scientific value of its findings. Social psychologists themselves sometimes speak admiringly of the cleverest and trickiest deceptions as "cute." Nonetheless, ingenuity was often required: Human subjects, it turned out, are good at sensing the true goal of an experiment when it is only thinly disguised.

At Jordan Hall, Steve Kaufman went directly to a small room where he had attended previous training sessions. Zimbardo, seated in a chair, greeted him warmly; Steve thought again how lucky he was to be working intimately with a famous scientist. He sank down on a couple of the large pillows scattered around the floor. Another student, whom he did not know, was already sprawled out; he and Steve exchanged hellos. In a moment, a third student, also unknown to Steve, came in, greeted everyone, and then said to the other student, "Say, you were in my Econ One section, weren't you?" The other, nodding, said, "Oh, yeah, right." This interchange established a basis for a spirited later conversation between the two that Steve would misinterpret, if Zimbardo's hypothesis about deafness was correct.

"Today," said Zimbardo, "I'm going to use the first part of this session to help you with pain control. In part two, I'll deepen your hypnotic state even more than before by having you listen to some exotic Oriental music. Then, in part three, I'll ask you to participate, as planned, in our experiment on the effect of hypnosis on creative problem solving."

For half an hour, as the three students several times put themselves into a hypnotic state and came back out of it, Zimbardo taught them how to self-administer suggestions that would counter pain. Then Zimbardo said it was time for the next phase, during which they would listen, separately, to different musical tapes. He handed each a set of earphones and signaled a woman assistant, watching from a control room, to start the tapes. Steve heard Zimbardo's voice slowly and soothingly explaining that by means of the following music he was to induce a deep trance in himself. He then heard a prolonged series of flutelike arpeggios slowly rippling upward. After a few minutes, when Steve was in a profound hypnotic state, Zimbardo's voice returned, saying, "Later on in this experiment, when you see the word 'focus' on the screen in the laboratory, sounds will become very low and difficult to hear. You will not remember having heard this instruction until we put a hand on your shoulder and say, 'That's all for now,' and then your hearing will return and you'll remember everything."

Although Steve's tape was still playing, those of the others seemed to have come to an end. Steve was aware that Susan M. Andersen, Zimbardo's chief assistant, had come in and taken the other students away. As his own tape concluded, she returned and said, "Hi, Steve, are you finished?" Steve said he was. As always, he was entranced by the sight of her. Susan Andersen, a graduate student in her late 20s, was, in Steve's opinion, quite beautiful. She was warm and outgoing, and Steve could easily imagine falling in love with her.

Susan led him to a large laboratory next door. The other two students were seated side by side at a table; nearby, a projector was aimed at a screen, and in one wall was a one-way mirror, beyond which was the observation and control room. As Susan and Steve entered, the other students were talking about what they intended to major in; again, this was meant to set the stage for their later conversations.

Steve took the only available seat, at the end of the table. (This kept the other two together, as planned.) Susan now briefed them: "As you know," she said, "we're interested in the effects of hypnosis on the way people solve problems. We expect that hypnosis may improve these skills." The problems would be a series of slides that they were to interpret in writing. (The slides came from the Thematic Apperception Test, a set of drawings of people in ambiguous situations; the stories an individual makes about them reveal a lot about that person's emotional condition.) Susan added that they were to work by themselves on the first slide but could work together from then on, if they liked, since groups solve certain kinds of problems better than individuals. All other instructions, she said, would appear on the screen.

She turned to the projector and switched it on; apologetically, she said: "It'll take me a few minutes to set this up. We've been having a little trouble with the controls lately. I'll be operating this from the other room. She pushed a button and a test slide came on; the word "focus" appeared on the screen, and she left.

The confederates now talked to each other about whether to work together after the first slide; they decided to do so. One of them then asked Steve, "How about you?" and when Steve made no reply, said, "O.K., fine." Then, with a smile, he said to his partner, "I know where I've seen you since that Econ class. You were at Bob Elder's party, right?—where that guy started heaving all over the television and then looked at everyone like—" and he made a hangdog face and groaned, "Duuuh!" They carried on about the mythical party; laughing and shaking their heads, they glanced at Steve, who, stony-faced, stared at the questionnaires and forms that Susan had left at his place.

He was having a poor time of it. From the moment the word "focus" appeared on the screen, he had been unable to understand what the other two students were saying. He wasn't sure whether he couldn't hear them or couldn't understand them. He had no idea what was wrong, and was fighting to control a wave of panic. When one of the others had spoken to him in what seemed to be either a mumble or doubletalk, Steve had ignored him. "I was getting very upset," Steve recalls, "especially when he and the other guy started talking and laughing and making faces. I was completely in the dark about why they were saying things in a way I couldn't understand. I was very agitated."

At that moment, the projector clicked, and on the screen appeared this message: "As you view the next slide, please write a brief description of what the characters portrayed in the slide are doing, who they are, and what the mood of the scene is." On came a picture of a man standing by a bed, looking down at what seemed to be the figure of a woman. The other two students, still talking, started to write, and Steve, his hands trembling and sweat running down his sides, got to work.

A Supreme Court decision of 1914 established the right of medical patients not to be subjected to treatment without their permission. But since gaining the consent of patients to try new or experimental procedures for research purposes is difficult, many biomedical researchers continued not to ask their patients' permission or to get it through various ruses and deceptions.

To be sure, the aims of these researchers were generally lofty. But in the 1940s the world learned that it could not count on the benevolence of medical researchers: At the Nuremberg trials, 20 Nazi doctors were proved to have conducted atrocious and sadistic experiments on concentration-camp prisoners. As the basis for convicting the doctors of crimes against humanity, the Nuremberg Tribunal formulated a code of ethics governing medical research, the fundamental clause of which read: "The voluntary consent of the human subject is absolutely essential . . . [He] should have sufficient knowledge and comprehension . . . of the subject matter . . . to make an understanding and enlightened decision." This has been known in recent years as the doctrine of "informed consent."

After the Nuremberg trials, world medical opinion officially held that biomedical researchers were morally obliged to obtain the informed consent of their subjects before using them in research; nonetheless, many researchers, unconstrained by law or administrative regulations, continued to take the easier course. In this country, biomedical experiments in which the subjects were ignorant of what was being done to them came to light during the 1950s and 1960s; some proved to be morally repugnant in the extreme, the most notable case being the Tuskegee study in which syphilitic black men were deliberately not treated in order to study the course of the disease. As a result of such disclosures, pressure built up within the Public Health Service (P.H.S.) and in Congress to create controls. During the 1960s, the P.H.S. gradually adopted various rules—including the requirement of informed consent—governing the behavior of biomedical researchers; the rules were binding only on persons supported by P.H.S. grants, but this affected the bulk of those doing such work in America.

Meanwhile, an analogous movement got under way in social research. A number of social psychologists, ethicists, and Government administrators began to attack deceptive methodology as being incompatible with informed consent. They found such research particularly obnoxious when the subjects were made to undergo anxiety, embarrassment, and other stresses.

The experiment that drew the sharpest fire of these critics was conducted by Stanley Milgram at Yale in 1963. In the guise of research into the learning process, Milgram told his naive subjects to administer progressively stronger electrical shocks to an unseen confederate, heard on an intercom, whenever he made a mistake. As the shocks grew stronger (rising to a supposedly dangerous level), the confederate—his voice was actually tape-recorded— would grunt, then cry out, and finally scream in agony. When Milgram's subjects wanted to break off, he would say that the experiment required that they go on. A number of them, he reported, "were observed to sweat, tremble, stutter, bite their lips, groan and dig their fingernails into their flesh"—yet most of them obeyed his orders. Milgram concluded that, when someone else is in authority, perfectly normal people are capable of obediently acting brutally toward others, a finding that might cast light on the behavior of many of the ordinary citizens of Nazi Germany. Milgram's work won the 1964 award for social-psychological research of the American Association for the Advancement of Science.

The opponents of deceptive research, citing such experiments, argue that behavioral research should be subjected to tightened controls. But both the P.H.S., in its rules governing grantees, and the American Psychological Association, in its code of ethics, continued to tolerate deceptive methods in social research—with some reservations—in order not to interfere with the freedom to pursue knowledge. The dilemma, as outlined in "The Handbook of Psychology," stemmed from the coexistence of two incompatible American ideals: "A belief in the value of free scientific inquiry and a belief in the dignity of man and his right to privacy." Researchers could explore certain areas of psychology only by robbing subjects of their right to informed consent; society could protect that right only by depriving researchers of the chance to cast light on important issues through deceptive experimental methods.

While waiting for the second slide to appear, the two confederates chatted animatedly about the chances of getting summer jobs in Palo Alto. One of them, turning to Steve, asked, "Are you staying in Palo Alto in the summer?" Steve, who had understood nothing, stared at him sullenly; the other smiled and said something else, then turned away.

The next slide said they could now work together. Then on came a sketch of a young man, seated, and an older man standing near him, holding a piece of paper in one hand. The confederates, scribbling, showing their papers to each other, and chuckling and talking, decided the scene showed a son, upset at his grades, being comforted by his father. Steve took it to show a Soviet police inspector, seated, to whom a colleague was presenting a report on a civilian suspect. With some difficulty he managed to write this down; the incomprehensible talk and carrying on of the other students was flooding him with anxiety and anger. As he recalls it, "They were talking to each other and laughing and making faces, and I couldn't understand any of it. I kept asking myself, 'Who are these two clowns sitting here and laughing at me? Why are they mumbling or talking in some strange language? How can Susan, who I thought was my friend, be letting this happen to me?' And I was extremely upset that Professor Zimbardo, whom I really admired, was in on it."

After a while the series of slides came to an end and on the screen appeared instructions to fill out the forms and questionnaires in front of each of the students. One questionnaire, listing 12 traits and moods, asked the subject to rate his present status as to each on a scale of 0 to 100. Steve filled in the blanks as follows:

> a. relaxed—0.
> b. agitated—100.
> c. happy—0.
> d. irritated—100.
> e. friendly—0.
> f. hostile—100.
> g. intellectually sharp—20.
> h. confused—100.
> i. vision—0.
> j. hearing—0.
> k. creative—0.
> l. suspicious—100.

The projector clicked again, directing one of the confederates—and in a moment the other—to leave. Steve, filling out a final form, jabbed angrily at the paper and broke his pencil, threw it away, and got up and paced back and forth like a caged animal. He had never in his life felt so peculiar or so agitated.

In 1971 the Department of Health, Education and Welfare tightened the Public Health Service regulations governing biomedical research with human subjects and made them binding on research funded by its other agencies, and in 1974 toughened the policies further. Among other things, informed consent was very strictly construed. For good measure, the regulations covered behavioral research as well. Even minor deceptive methods, in social-psychological experiments, were ruled out unless given special approval by an institutional review board (I.R.B.) — a watchdog committee designated within every university or research foundation to see that research proposals using human subjects obeyed the Federal regulations. Any institution that failed to comply might have all its H.E.W. subsidies cut off.

Social psychologists planning research now had to write detailed explanations, defend their proposals before suspicious I.R.B.'s, and dilute the impact of their experimental situations; even so, their proposals were often turned down. The explicit motive of the I.R.B.'s was to protect human subjects; the implicit one was to safeguard the institutions' grant money. A survey made in 1974 and 1975 for the National Commission for the Protection of Human Subjects (a congressionally created advisory group) asked a large sample of behavioral scientists whether the review procedure had impeded research at their institutions; more than half said it had. As a result of this survey and of many complaints from social scientists, the Department of Health and Human Services (successor to the Department of Health, Education and Welfare) eased the requirements a little in July 1981; among other things, incompletely informed consent was now held acceptable if, in the view of the I.R.B., it involved "minimum risk to the subject" and if the research "could not practicably be carried out" otherwise.

Even in their slightly loosened form, the regulations have made a major change in social-psychological research. Deception is still in common use, but mostly in quite limited form and productive of only trivial experimental stresses. As a result, the scope of research has been significantly narrowed. "You don't even consider experiments that would run into resistance," Prof. Edward E. Jones of Princeton University told me. "Whole lines of research have been nipped in the bud." Obedience experiments like Milgram's are now quite beyond the pale; most helping experiments are considered unacceptably hard on some subjects; and so are research designs which would even briefly frighten or embarrass subjects, or teach them unpleasant truths about themselves.

The case of Prof. Stanley Schachter of Columbia University is instructive. Schachter, for 30 years a leading and innovative researcher, told me that recently he gave up doing experiments. "I simply won't go through all that," he said. "It's a bloody bore and a waste of time."

Nor, if present conditions had prevailed in 1962, would he have made the most seminal discovery of his career. He and Dr. Jerome Singer asked naive subjects for permission to inject them with a vitamin preparation to test its effects on vision. They told their subjects that for some minutes it might make their hearts pound, their faces flush, and their hands shake. The injection was, in fact, adrenalin, which is produced in the body by a variety of emotions. Schachter and Singer sought to show that human beings cannot identify their emotions from bodily sensations alone; they need external cues as to what they are feeling. Accordingly, the researchers had their naive subjects, while feeling the effects of the adrenalin, fill out a form in the company of a confederate (also supposedly injected with vitamins); in some cases, the confederate acted giddy, silly, and happy, while in other cases, the confederate was angered by the questions in the form, eventually tore it up and then stormed out. Naive subjects who had been with euphoric confederates said that they, too, had felt euphoric; those with angry confederates said that they, too, had felt angry. Q.E.D. "That experiment had major consequences," Schachter said, "but I'd hesitate to do it again today. In fact, I couldn't do it."

Susan Anderson came in. "She approached me," Steve recalls, "saying something I couldn't understand, and I dodged away from her and sat down. She came over and put her hand on my shoulder, and I was shaking, not knowing whether to cry or scream or what, but then she said something"— ("That's all for now")— "and I could understand her and she was saying, 'Are you all right?' I was amazed, and all I could say was, 'Would you please tell me what is going on here?'

"She had me relax in a reclining chair and sat next to me and said, 'Do you remember the headphones?' and I did. 'The music?' and I did. And so on, until bit by bit I could remember everything, and it came to me why I had been unable to hear. I was in a state of shock, of total disbelief—but of course total belief, too. I was very bewildered—overjoyed, and yet still extremely upset.

"Then Professor Zimbardo came in with a big smile on his face and said, 'That worked wonderfully! You were terrific!' He sat down and slowly and carefully explained the real purpose of the experiment to me and what he was hoping to show by his research—and had shown in my case. I was absolutely fascinated. He was right—when you're deaf, it seems like they're plotting against you. Even though I still felt shaken, I was really proud that I had played an important part in the work."

Zimbardo asked Steve to come back in a week for a checkup. (When he did, he took a test for paranoia—a retest of one he had taken weeks earlier, which showed him to be normal. The retest showed no residual effects of the experiment.) All in all the debriefing lasted 45 minutes—longer than the experiment; defenders of deceptive research lay great stress on thorough, restorative debriefing. By the time Steve left, he felt in control of himself and calm. But all night his mind was a kaleidoscopic jumble of images and thoughts, and he continued to feel a succession of recalled moods in an emotional reverberation that took days to die away.

Defenders of deceptive research argue that it is morally justified if the risks or costs to the subject—often minor or nil—are outweighed by the benefits to humanity. But how to weigh costs against benefits is far from clear. In what units can one measure embarrassment or anxiety, and how can one compare this to the worth of some piece of new knowledge?

Critics of deceptive research assert that, most of the time, the costs greatly outweigh the benefits. Their evidence, however, is largely anecdotal, consisting of a number of stories of subjects who, despite debriefing, have remained disillusioned, suspicious of authority, or permanently ashamed of something they have learned about themselves, as in the case of people who failed to help a stranger in distress. Diana Baumrind, a psychologist at the University of California at Berkeley, a forceful polemicist against deceptive research, calls the last outcome "inflicted insight," and argues that foisting unsought self-knowledge on another is morally indefensible.

On the other hand, most social psychologists maintain—again on the basis of subjective appraisals—that little, if any, harm is done by deceptive research. And the few follow-up surveys that exist support this sanguine view: Most subjects, looking back on their experiences, say the deception imposed on them, even if stressful, was justified by the scientific knowledge gained. In Milgram's obedience experiment, 84 percent of his subjects said afterward that they were glad they had been in it; only 1.3 percent regretted the experience; and the rest were neutral.

But some of the most articulate enemies of deceptive research reject any justification based on the weighing of costs against benefits. Diana Baumrind, for one, says this is a utilitarian ethic; she rejects it on the grounds that concern for the rights of the human being is morally superior to the freedom to seek knowledge and should take precedence over it. Thomas Murray, a social psychologist at the Hastings Center, says that even if deception does no harm, it does wrong to the person it deprives of free choice; in his view, cost-benefit calculations treat the subjects as useful tools, not as moral agents.

Some critics of deceptive research have said that it is not necessary, that alternative techniques will serve. They have suggested the use of role-playing, for instance, in which subjects are asked to imagine how they would behave in a given experiment if they were naive as to its real purposes. In many cases, they give themselves better marks than when the experiment is run with truly naive subjects. As Dr. Joel W. Goldstein, executive secretary of the Research Scientist Development Review Committee of the Department of Health and Human Services, comments, "We know that what people say or do in role-playing experiments is qualitatively different from what they really do." Much the same, disappointingly, is true of various other suggested alternatives.

Accordingly, both the Federal regulations and the code of ethics of the American Psychological Association reluctantly continue to acknowledge the necessity of deceptive research and to use the cost-benefit ratio as the operative ethical standard by which to judge it. Typically American in its pragmatism, it judges the morality of any case of deceptive research by its results.

By the end of the spring semester, Zimbardo and his assistants had completed the experimental work. Six subjects had been hypnotically made hard of hearing and unaware of why they were; a control group knew why they were experiencing deafness; and another control group was not deafened. Statistical analysis of the test scores plus observations and self-reports showed that the naive deafened subjects had been far more paranoid during the experiment than the control groups; the differences between the groups were "highly significant"—which, in this case, meant that there was only a one-in-a-thousand chance that the results were due to pure accident.

Steve, meanwhile, was feeling disagreeable after effects, but of a kind unrelated to temporary paranoia. He had expected to continue to play a part in Zimbardo's research; indeed, Zimbardo, as part of the cover story, had said as much. "But it didn't turn out that way," Steve says. "I ran into him and said, 'I'd really like to work with you some more,' and he said, 'Sure,' but I never heard from him. I left messages but he never called me back. I felt no resentment about what was done to me in the experiment, but what I did— and still do—resent was being dropped like a cold jellyfish after such a substantial emotional event in my life. That's what made me feel like 'just another subject.' Yet I still greatly admire Professor Zimbardo for the research he's doing and his reasons for doing it. To this day, I feel honored that I was able to work with him and contribute to an important study."

Zimbardo, who is regretful about Steve's feelings but says there is nothing a researcher can do about that, wrote up his results in a journal article in which he concluded that the findings have obvious bearing on the connection between deafness and paranoia among the middle-aged and elderly. The article appeared in the June 26, 1981, issue of the journal Science. Not surprisingly, it was greeted with both approval and criticism—the latter because of its ethics. Zimbardo defended his work, specifying the precautions taken, the need for deception, the lack of harm done, and the value of the findings. He ended by reiterating the cost-benefit ethic: "The risks to the subjects appear to be quite transient while the potential benefits hold substantial promise."

Some social psychologists—the braver ones, or perhaps those in particularly secure positions—continue to use deception, albeit more conservatively than before, to investigate major issues. John M. Darley, now chairman of the psychology department at Princeton, told me why he feels obliged to do so: 'Psychologists have an ethical responsibility to do research about processes that are socially important, and to discover *clearly* what is going on—which means that sometimes they have to keep their subjects in the dark about certain aspects of the study." In a study he recently conducted with a colleague, Princeton undergraduates were asked to help validate a new method by which teachers could judge the potential of pupils. On videotape, some subjects saw a 9-year-old girl playing in shabby, lower-class surroundings; others saw the same girl playing in a manicured suburban setting; each group then saw her giving the same answers aloud as she took an achievement test. Both groups were asked to evaluate her school potential: Those who had seen her in a lower-class milieu rated it below grade level, while those who had seen her in an upper-middle-class milieu rated her well above it. Evidently, knowledge of a person's socioeconomic status can distort perception of his or her performance.

But many other researchers are now turning to topics which can be investigated without deception or, at most, by merely withholding a little information. Some, perhaps many, of those topics are worthy of serious investigation—but so are the topics that require major deception and that are no longer researched except by the few who are able to run the risk. No doubt, the present compromise between freedom of inquiry and the rights of individuals has corrected the occasional flagrant misuses of human subjects, but perhaps the correction has somewhat overshot the mark. Prof. Leon Festinger of the New School for Social Research, a key figure in the history of social psychology, recently deplored the caution that has been forced upon its practitioners. "One can stay far away from ethical questions," he said, 'but it seems to me that steering clear of these difficulties keeps the field away from problems that are important and distinctive to social psychology."

Steve Kaufman is two years older, two inches taller, and rather more realistic than he used to be as a freshman. When he suffered the disappointment of being no longer wanted for further experimental work, its attraction for him dwindled. He has decided to major in German and urban studies. But he still looks back on the period of his participation in Zimbardo's research as one of the high points of his life thus far.

That has not, however, led him to take a simplistic stand on the ethical issues; like all those who find the cost-benefit ethic sensible but difficult to apply, he sees both sides of the issue. "Before I was in the experiment," he says, "I was very much against deceptive research. But then I heard Professor Zimbardo lecture about it, and I could see that you can't get certain kinds of information without deceptive methods. I agree with the people who say it's not right to deceive human beings; it's not right to treat people as if they were mice. But I agree with Professor Zimbardo that he couldn't do his work on deafness and paranoia without deceiving his subjects, because if they knew what was going on, they wouldn't react the same as if they didn't.

"I can see both sides. That's my dilemma, and I don't think there's any simple answer to it, only complicated ones."

Questions

1. What hypothesis was being tested in this study? List the independent and dependent variables. What pay-off is there if the hypothesis is proved true?

2. Describe the research design in detail. In what sense is it a scam?

3. What was the purpose of the Solomon Asch "line" experiment?

4. There are constant references to naive subjects, confederates, etc. What do these terms mean?

5. What factors besides the presence of other people might "diffuse" a person's response to a Kitty Genovese type incident?

6. Zimbardo had deceived subjects in earlier experiments. Why wasn't Steve suspicious of him?

7. Freud, among others, felt hypnosis might have potential use in psychology. Think of areas where it might be useful.

8. Did Steve's "physical seating" or "positioning at the table" affect his reactions?

9. What is informed consent? For what types of research should it be used?

10. Milgram's subjects did not suffer physical pain. In what sense might they have suffered stress?

11. How did Steve feel while going through step three of the experiment? Did he suffer any permanent negative effects?

12. In what sense was Schacter and Singer's experiment with "adrenalin" seminal?

13. What is "role-playing?" Is it a viable alternative technique to deceptive research?

14. Can knowledge of a person's socio-economic status distort one's perception of performance? Give examples.

15. How can one measure if the risks to the subject are outweighed by the benefits to humanity?

Part XI

Poverty,
Two Underclasses,
and Homelessness

If you are easily depressed when confronted by social problems and social pathology, you might consider skipping this part of the book. If you read it closely, however, you might come away with new ideas about such important topics as poverty, the black and Puerto Rican underclasses, and the homeless.

No matter if we measure poverty in absolute or relative terms, the inescapable conclusion is that large numbers of people in the United States are poor. Numbers range from 20 million to 40 million people. Whether we choose the lower range or the higher range, millions of people are still involved. Box 85 indicates the percentage of Americans in various groups who are currently below the poverty level. Sociologist Herbert Gans, in ''The Uses of Poverty: The Poor Pay All,'' has a theory about this that is not often published. He argues that poverty persists because it serves ''useful'' functions in our society. Besides obvious economic functions (for example, how else would we get the ''dirty work'' done?), he sees social, political, and even psychic functions for poverty (for example, who else would be the ''beneficiaries'' of charity affairs?). Our society allows poverty to continue, Gans says, because many of the ''alternatives to poverty would be quite dysfunctional for the affluent members of society.''

Sociologist William Julius Wilson, in ''The Black Underclass,'' offers an equally controversial theory based on ideas from two of his books. *The Declining Significance of Race: Blacks and Changing American Institutions* (1978) argues that economic class had surpassed race in determining African-American access to privilege and power. It is clearly evident, Wilson says,

---

Box 85

Who Are the Poor?

These statistics indicate the percentage of Americans in various groups who are currently living below the poverty level.

Total population	13.1
Husband-wife families	7.1
Families with female heads	33.6
White	10.1
African-American	31.6
Latino	26.8
Over age 65	12.2
Under age 18	20.4

SOURCE: Statistical Abstract of the United States 1990.

"that many talented and educated blacks are now entering positions of prestige and influence at a rate comparable to or, in some situations, exceeding that of whites. It is equally clear that the black underclass is in a hopeless state of economic stagnation." He understands the negative way that racism affects the lives of some African-Americans, of course, but he wants to stress the importance of class. *The Truly Disadvantaged: The Inner City, The Underclass, and Public Policy* (1987) continues this line of thought. Here he stresses that economic and demographic changes in America (for example, the move from the South to the North or the middle class black flight from the inner city) affect the chances of poor African-Americans to escape their conditions. The result is that the underclass has now taken on a life of its own, independent of the reasons for its origins. The selection represented here catches important themes from both books. Read it closely as the ideas presented have important policy implications. (President Clinton reads everything Wilson writes.)

Most people think of inner-city poverty as a black phenomenon. But Nicholas Lemann, a national correspondent for *The Atlantic* and author of *The Promised Land*, points out in "The Other Underclass" that poverty is also alarmingly high among Puerto Ricans. If one considers, for example, that Puerto Rican families are more than twice as likely as black families to be on welfare or are 50 percent more likely to be poor, a case might be made that Puerto Ricans are the most disadvantaged group in the country. All this is true even though Puerto Rico itself has made great progress against poverty and there is a growing Puerto Rican middle class on the mainland.

Sociologist James D. Wright, in "Address Unknown: Homelessness in Contemporary America," pursues another topic that has important policy implications. Not only is homelessness a national disgrace, it is an international embarrassment. We do not even know if we are talking about 600,000 people or three million. All that seems certain is that the numbers are increasing and now include more families, women, and children than was true in the past. Wright does not see long term solutions in the future, but a focus on amelioration. "No problem that is ultimately rooted in the large scale workings of the political economy can be solved easily or cheaply," he says, and "we will not rid ourselves of this national disgrace."

Chapter Thirty-Four

The Uses of Poverty
The Poor Pay All

welfare reform

Herbert Gans

Some twenty years ago Robert K. Merton applied the notion of functional analysis[1] to explain the continuing though maligned existence of the urban political machine: if it continued to exist, perhaps it fulfilled latent—unintended or unrecognized—positive functions. Clearly it did. Merton pointed out how the political machine provided central authority to get things done when a decentralized local government could not act, humanized the services of the impersonal bureaucracy for fearful citizens, offered concrete help (rather than abstract law or justice) to the poor, and otherwise performed services needed or demanded by many people but considered unconventional or even illegal by formal public agencies.

Today, poverty is more maligned than the political machine ever was; yet it too, is a persistent social phenomenon. Consequently, there may be some merit in applying functional analysis to poverty, in asking whether it also has positive functions that explain its persistence.

Merton defined functions as "those observed consequences [of a phenomenon] which make for the adaptation or adjustment of a given [social] system." I shall use a slightly different definition; instead of identifying functions for an entire social system, I shall identify them for the interest groups, socioeconomic classes, and other population aggregates with shared values that "inhabit" a social system. I suspect that in a modern heterogeneous society, few phenomena are functional or dysfunctional for the society as a whole, and that most result in benefits to some groups and costs to others. Nor are any phenomena indispensable; in most instances, one can suggest what Merton calls "functional alternatives" or equivalents for them, i.e., other social patterns or policies that achieve the same positive functions but avoid the dysfunctions.*

Associating poverty with positive functions seems at first glance to be unimaginable. Of course, the slumlord and the loan shark are commonly known to profit from the existence of poverty, but they are viewed as evil men, so their activities are classified among the dysfunctions of poverty. However, what is less often recognized, at least by the conventional wisdom, is that poverty also makes possible the existence or expansion of respectable professions and occupations, for example, penology, criminology, social work, and public health. More recently, the poor have provided jobs for professional and paraprofessional "poverty warriors," and for journalists and social scientists, this author included, who have supplied the information demanded by the revival of public interest in poverty.

Clearly, then, poverty and the poor may well satisfy a number of positive functions for many non-poor groups in American society. I shall describe thirteen such functions—economic, social, and political—that seem to me most significant.

The Functions of Poverty

First, the existence of poverty ensures that society's "dirty work" will be done. Every society has such work: physically dirty or dangerous, temporary, dead-end and underpaid, undignified and menial jobs. Society can fill these jobs by paying higher wages than for "clean" work, or it can force people who have no other choice to do the dirty work—and at low wages. In America, poverty functions to provide a low-wage labor pool that is willing—or, rather, unable to be *un*willing—to perform dirty work at low cost. Indeed, this function of the poor is so important that in some Southern states, welfare payments have been cut off during the summer months when the poor are needed to work in the fields. Moreover, much of the debate about the Negative Income Tax and the Family Assistance Plan has concerned their impact on the work incentive, by which is actually meant the incentive of the poor to do the needed dirty work if the wages therefrom are no larger than the income grant. Many economic activities that involve dirty work depend on the poor for their

---

* I shall henceforth abbreviate positive functions as functions and negative functions as dysfunctions. I shall also describe functions and dysfunctions, in the planners terminology, as benefits and costs.

existence: restaurants, hospitals, parts of the garment industry, and "truck farming," among others, could not persist in their present form without the poor.

Second, because the poor are required to work at low wages, they subsidize a variety of economic activities that benefit the affluent. For example, domestics subsidize the upper middle and upper classes, making life easier for their employers and freeing affluent women for a variety of professional, cultural, civic, and partying activities. Similarly, because the poor pays a higher proportion of their income in property and sales taxes, among others, they subsidize many state and local governmental services that benefit more affluent groups. In addition, the poor support innovation in medical practice as patients in teaching and research hospitals and as guinea pigs in medical experiments.

Third, poverty creates jobs for a number of occupations and professions that serve or "service" the poor, or protect the rest of society from them. As already noted, penology would be minuscule without the poor, as would the police. Other activities and groups that flourish because of the existence of poverty are the numbers game, the sale of heroin and cheap wines and liquors, pentecostal ministers, faith healers, prostitutes, pawn shops, and the peacetime army, which recruits its enlisted men mainly from among the poor.

Fourth, the poor buy goods others do not want and thus prolong the economic usefulness of such goods—day-old bread, fruit and vegetables that would otherwise have to be thrown out, secondhand clothes, and deteriorating automobiles and buildings. They also provide incomes for doctors, lawyers, teachers, and others who are too old, poorly trained, or incompetent to attract more affluent clients.

In addition to economic functions, the poor perform a number of social functions.

Fifth, the poor can be identified and punished as alleged or real deviants in order to uphold the legitimacy of conventional norms. To justify the desirability of hard work, thrift, honesty, and monogamy, for example, the defenders of these norms must be able to find people who can be accused of being lazy, spendthrift, dishonest, and promiscuous. Although there is some evidence that the poor are about as moral and law-abiding as anyone else, they are more likely than middle-class transgressors to be caught and punished when they participate in deviant acts. Moreover, they lack the political and cultural power to correct the stereotypes that other people hold of them and thus continue to be thought of as lazy, spendthrift, etc., by those who need living proof that moral deviance does not pay.

Sixth, and conversely, the poor offer vicarious participation to the rest of the population in the uninhibited sexual, alcoholic, and narcotic behavior in which they are alleged to participate and which, being freed from the constraints of affluence, they are often thought to enjoy more than the middle classes. Thus many people, some social scientists included, believe that the poor not only are more given to uninhibited behavior (which may be true, although it is often motivated by despair more than by lack of inhibition) but derive more pleasure from it than affluent people (which research shows to be patently untrue). However, whether the poor actually have more sex and enjoy it more is irrelevant; so long as middle-class people believe this to be true, they can participate in it vicariously when instances are reported in factual or fictional form.

Seventh, the poor also serve a direct cultural function when culture created by or for them is adopted by the more affluent. The rich often collect artifacts from extinct folk cultures of poor people; and almost all Americans listen to the blues, spirituals, and country music, which originated among the Southern poor. Recently they have enjoyed the rock styles that were born, like the Beatles, in the slums; and in the last year, poetry written by ghetto children has become popular in literary circles. The poor also serve as culture heroes, particularly, of course, to the left; but the hobo, the cowboy, the hipster, and the mythical prostitute with a heart of gold have performed this function for a variety of groups.

Eighth, poverty helps to guarantee the status of those who are not poor. In every hierarchical society someone has to be at the bottom; but in American society, in which social mobility is an important goal for many and people need to know where they stand, the poor function as a reliable and relatively permanent measuring rod for status comparisons. This is particularly true for the working class, whose politics is influenced by the need to maintain status distinctions between themselves and the poor, much as the aristocracy must find ways of distinguishing itself from the *nouveaux riches*.

Ninth, the poor also aid the upward mobility of groups just above them in the class hierarchy. Thus a goodly number of Americans have entered the middle class through the profits earned from the provision of goods and services in the slums, including illegal or nonrespectable ones that upper-class and upper-middle-class businessmen shun because of their low prestige. As a result, members of almost every immigrant group have financed their upward mobility by providing slum housing, entertainment, gambling, narcotics, etc., to later arrivals—most recently to Blacks and Puerto Ricans.

Tenth, the poor help to keep the aristocracy busy, thus justifying its continued existence. "Society" uses the poor as clients of settlement houses and beneficiaries of charity affairs; indeed, the aristocracy must have the poor to demonstrate its superiority over other elites who devote themselves to earning money.

Eleventh, the poor, being powerless, can be made to absorb the costs of change and growth in American society. During the nineteenth century, they did the backbreaking work that built the cities; today, they are pushed out of their neighborhoods to make room for "progress." Urban renewal projects to hold middle-class taxpayers in the city and expressways to enable suburbanites to commute downtown have typically been located in poor neighborhoods, since no other group will allow itself to be displaced. For the same reason, universities, hospitals, and civic centers also expand into land occupied by the poor. The major costs of the industrialization of agriculture have been borne by the poor, who are pushed off the land without recompense; and they have paid a large share of the human cost of the growth of American power overseas, for they have provided many of the foot soldiers for Vietnam and other wars.

Twelfth, the poor facilitate and stabilize the American political process. Because they vote and participate in politics less than other groups, the political system is often free to ignore them. Moreover, since they can rarely support Republicans, they often provide the Democrats with a captive constituency that has no other place to go. As a result, the Democrats can count on their votes, and be more responsive to voters—for example, the white working class—who might otherwise switch to the Republicans.

Thirteenth, the role of the poor in upholding conventional norms (see the *fifth* point, above) also has a significant political function. An economy based on the ideology of laissez-faire requires a deprived population that is allegedly unwilling to work or that can be considered inferior because it must accept charity or welfare in order to survive. Not only does the alleged moral deviancy of the poor reduce the moral pressure on the present political economy to eliminate poverty but socialist alternatives can be made to look quite unattractive if those who will benefit most from them can be described as lazy, spendthrift, dishonest, and promiscuous.

The Alternatives

I have described thirteen of the more important functions poverty and the poor satisfy in American society, enough to support the functionalist thesis that poverty, like any other social phenomenon, survives in part because it is useful to society or some of its parts. This analysis is not intended to suggest that because it is often functional, poverty *should* exist, or that it *must* exist. For one thing, poverty has many more dysfunctions; for another, it is possible to suggest functional alternatives.

For example, society's dirty work could be done without poverty, either by automation or by paying "dirty workers" decent wages. Nor is it necessary for the poor to subsidize the many activities they support through their low-wage jobs. This would, however, drive up the costs of these activities, which would result in higher prices to their customers and clients. Similarly, many of the professionals who flourish because of the poor could be given other roles. Social workers could provide counseling to the affluent, as they prefer to do anyway; and the police could devote themselves to traffic and organized crime. Other roles would have to be found for badly trained or incompetent professionals now relegated to serving the poor, and someone else would have to pay their salaries. Fewer penologists would be employable, however. And pentecostal religion could probably not survive without the poor—nor would parts of the second- and third- hand goods market. And in many cities, "used" housing that no one else wants would then have to be torn down at public expense.

Alternatives for the cultural functions of the poor could be found more easily and cheaply. Indeed, entertainers, hippies, and adolescents are already serving as the deviants needed to uphold traditional morality and as devotees of orgies to "staff" the fantasies of vicarious participation.

The status functions of the poor are another matter. In a hierarchical society, some people must be defined as inferior to everyone else with respect to a variety of attributes, but they need not be poor in the absolute sense. One could conceive of a society in which the "lower class," though last in the pecking order, received 75 percent of the median income, rather than 15-40 percent, as is now the case. Needless to say, this would require considerable income redistribution.

The contribution the poor make to the upward mobility of the groups that provide them with goods and services could also be maintained without the poor's having such low incomes. However, it is true that if the poor were more affluent, they would have access to enough capital to take over the provider role, thus competing with, and perhaps rejecting, the "outsiders." (Indeed, owing in part to antipoverty programs, this is already happening in a number of ghettos, where white store-owners are being replaced by Blacks). Similarly, if the poor were more affluent, they would make less willing clients for upper-class philanthropy, although some would still use settlement houses to achieve upward mobility, as they do now. Thus "Society" could continue to run its philanthropic activities.

The political functions of the poor would be more difficult to replace.With increased affluence the poor would probably obtain more political power and be more active politically. With higher incomes and more political power, the poor would be likely to resist paying the costs of growth and change. Of course, it is possible to imagine urban renewal and highway projects that properly reimbursed the displaced people, but such projects would then become considerably more expensive, and many might never be built. This, in turn, would reduce the comfort and convenience of those who now benefit from urban renewal and expressways. Finally, hippies could serve also as more deviants to justify the existing political economy—as they already do. Presumably, however, if poverty were eliminated, there would be fewer attacks on that economy.

In sum, then, many of the functions served by the poor could be replaced if poverty were eliminated, but almost always at higher costs to others, particularly more affluent others. Consequently, a functional analysis must conclude that poverty persists not only because it fulfills a number of positive functions but also because many of the functional alternatives to poverty would be quite dysfunctional for the affluent members of society. A functional analysis thus ultimately arrives at much the same conclusion as radical sociology, except that radical thinkers treat as manifest what I describe as latent: that social phenomena that are functional for affluent or powerful groups and dysfunctional for poor or powerless ones persist; that when the elimination of such phenomena through functional alternatives would generate dysfunctions for the affluent or powerful, they will continue to persist; and that phenomena like poverty can be eliminated only when they become dysfunctional for the affluent or powerful, or when the powerless can obtain enough power to change society.

Questions

1. What are some "negative" functions of the urban political machine?
2. What economic functions does poverty serve? Social functions? Political functions?
3. Do the poor engage in more uninhibited behavior than the rich?
4. Analyze the current top ten popular songs. Do the lyrics refer to poverty? What is the economic background of the performers?
5. What alternative ways to get "dirty work" done exist?
6. Why will the "status" and "political" functions of poverty be particularly hard to replace?
7. Do you think Mr. Gans is to the right or left politically?
8. Why would some consider this point of view "unorthodox"?

Chapter Thirty-Five

The Black Underclass

William Julius Wilson

It is no secret that the social problems of urban life in the United States are, in great measure, associated with race.

While rising rates of crime, drug addiction, out-of-wedlock births, female-headed families, and welfare dependency have afflicted American society generally in recent years, the increases have been most dramatic among what has become a large and seemingly permanent black underclass inhabiting the cores of the nation's major cities.

And yet, liberal journalists, social scientists, policy-makers, and civil-rights leaders have for almost two decades been reluctant to face this fact. Often, analysts of such issues as violent crime or teenage pregnancy deliberately make no reference to race at all, unless perhaps to emphasize the deleterious consequences of racial discrimination or the institutionalized inequality of American society.

Some scholars, in an effort to avoid the appearance of "blaming the victim," or to protect their work from charges of racism, simply ignore patterns of behavior that might be construed as stigmatizing to particular racial minorities.

Such neglect is a relatively recent phenomenon. Twenty years ago, during the mid-1960s, social scientists such as Kenneth B. Clark (*Dark Ghetto*, 1965), Daniel Patrick Moynihan (*The Negro Family*, 1965), and Lee Rainwater (*Behind Ghetto Walls*, 1970) forthrightly examined the cumulative effects on inner-city blacks of racial isolation and class subordination. They vividly described aspects of ghetto life that, as Rainwater observed, "are usually forgotten or ignored in polite discussions." All of these studies attempted to show the connection between the economic and social environment into which many blacks are born and the creation of patterns of behavior that, in Clark's words, frequently amounted to a "self-perpetuating pathology."

Why have scholars lately shied away from this line of research? One reason has to do with the vitriolic attacks by many black leaders against Moynihan upon publication of his report in 1965 — denunciations that generally focused on the author's unflattering depiction of the black family in the urban ghetto rather than on his proposed remedies or his historical analysis of the black family's special plight. The harsh reception accorded to *The Negro Family* undoubtedly dissuaded many social scientists from following in Moynihan's footsteps.

The "black solidarity" movement was also emerging during the mid-1960s. A new emphasis by young black scholars and intellectuals on the positive aspects of the black experience tended to crowd out older concerns. Indeed, certain forms of ghetto behavior labeled pathological in the studies of Clark et al. were redefined by some during the early 1970s as "functional" because, it was argued, blacks were displaying the ability to survive and in some cases flourish in an economically depressed environment. Scholars such as Andrew Billingsley (*Black Families in White America*, 1968), Joyce Ladner (*Tomorrow's Tomorrow*, 1971), and Robert Hill (*The Strengths of Black Families*, 1971) described the ghetto family as resilient and capable of adapting creatively to an oppressive, racist society.

In the end, the promising efforts of the early 1960s — to distinguish the socioeconomic characteristics of different groups within the black community, and to identify the structural problems of the U.S. economy that affected minorities — were cut short by calls for "reparations" or for "black control of institutions serving the black community." In his 1977 book, *Ethnic Chauvinism*, sociologist Orlando Patterson lamented that black ethnicity had become "a form of mystification, diverting attention from the correct kinds of solutions to the terrible economic conditions of the group."

Meanwhile, throughout the 1970s, ghetto life across the nation continued to deteriorate. The situation is best seen against the backdrop of the family.

In 1965, when Moynihan pointed with alarm to the relative instability of the black family, one-quarter of all such families were headed by women; 15 years later, the figure was a staggering 42 percent. (By contrast, only 12 percent of white families and 22 percent of Hispanic families in 1980 were maintained by women.) Not surprisingly, the proportion of black children living with both their father and their mother declined from nearly two-thirds in 1970 to fewer than half in 1978.

In the inner city, the trend is more pronounced. For example, of the 27,178 families with children living in Chicago Housing Authority projects in 1980, only 2,982, or 11 percent, were husband-and-wife families.

Teenage Mothers

These figures are important because even if a woman is employed full-time, she almost always is paid less than a man. If she is not employed, or employed only part-time, and has children to support, the household's situation may be desperate. In 1980, the median income of families headed by black women ($7,425) was only 40 percent of that of black families with both parents present ($18,593). Today, roughly five out of 10 black children under the age of 18 live below the poverty level; the vast majority of these kids have only a mother to come home to.

The rise in the number of female-headed black families reflects, among other things, the increasing incidence of illegitimate births. Only 15 percent of all births to black women in 1959 were out of wedlock; the proportion today is well over one-half. In the cities, the figure is invariably higher: 67 percent in Chicago in 1978, for example. Black women today bear children out of wedlock at a rate nine times that for whites. In 1982, the number of black babies born out of wedlock (328,879) nearly matched the number of illegitimate white babies (337,050). White or black, the women bearing these children are not always mature adults. Almost half of all illegitimate children born to blacks today will have a teenager for a mother.

The effect on the welfare rolls is not hard to imagine. A 1976 study by Kristin Moore and Steven B. Cardwell of Washington's Urban Institute estimated that, nationwide, about 60 percent of the children who are born outside of marriage and are not adopted receive welfare; furthermore, "more than half of all AFDC (Aid to Families with Dependent Children) assistance in 1975 was paid to women who were or had been teenage mothers." A 1979 study by the Department of City Planning in New York found that 75 percent of all children born out of wedlock in that city during the previous 18 years were recipients of AFDC. (Box 86 explores "what went wrong" as it considers the African-American family's worsening plight.)

Why No Progress?

I have concentrated on young, female-headed families and out-of-wedlock births among blacks because these indices have become inextricably connected with poverty and welfare dependency, as well as with other forms of social dislocation (including joblessness and crime).

Box 86

What Went Wrong?

W. E. B. Du Bois (*The Negro American Family,* 1908) and E. Franklin Frazier (*The Negro Family in the United States,* 1939) were among the first scholars to ask this question about poor black families. Both came up with essentially the same answer — slavery.

Slavery, they noted, often separated man from wife, parent from child. Slave "marriage" had no basis in law. Negroes thus entered Emancipation with a legacy of "sexual irregularity" (Du Bois) that fostered "delinquency, desertions, and broken homes" (Frazier). Discrimination and migration perpetuated such patterns.

The "slavery hypothesis" was challenged during the 1970s by the works of Eugene Genovese (*Roll, Jordan, Roll,* 1974) and Herbert Gutman (*The Black Family in Slavery and Freedom,* 1976). Genovese shows, for example, that blacks *did* establish strong families in slavery. And Gutman notes that as late as 1925, roughly 85 percent of black families in New York City were headed by a married couple.

If slavery did not undermine the black family, what did? Scholars as diverse as Jessie Bernard (*Marriage and Family among Negroes,* 1966), Elliot Liebow (*Tally's Corner,* 1967), William Julius Wilson (*The Declining Significance of Race,* 1978) and Stephen Steinberg (*The Ethnic Myth,* 1981) point the finger at economic hardship and urban unemployment. The rise of a "matriarchal family pattern" in the ghetto, Steinberg writes, was "an inevitable by-product of the inability of men to function as breadwinners for their families." Joblessness, in turn, eroded the black male's sense of manhood and family responsibility.

The disruptive impact of welfare on some black families is generally conceded but not easily quantified. Kristin A. Moore and Martha R. Burt (*Teenage Childbearing and Welfare,* 1981) suggest that Aid to Families with Dependent Children (AFDC) *may* influence a pregnant woman to bear and rear her child (and head up a new household) rather than marry the father, resort to adoption, or submit to abortion. Because AFDC is available only to single-parent families in half of the 50 states, the program may also encourage the break-up of married couples and deter unwed parents from marrying or remarrying.

Whatever its causes, the black family's worsening plight has belatedly been acknowledged by black leaders. So has the need for remedies. A 1983 report by Washington's Joint Center for Political Studies, *A Policy Framework for Racial Justice,* asserted flatly that "family reinforcement constitutes the single most important action the nation can take toward the elimination of black poverty and related social problems."

WJW

As James Q. Wilson observed in *Thinking About Crime* (1975), these problems are also associated with a "critical mass" of young people, often poorly supervised. When that mass is reached, or is increased suddenly and substantially, "a self-sustaining chain reaction is set off that creates an explosive increase in the amount of crime, addiction, and welfare dependency." The effect is magnified in densely populated ghetto neighborhoods, and further magnified in the massive public housing projects.

Consider Robert Taylor Homes, the largest such project in Chicago. In 1980, almost 20,000 people, all black, were officially registered there, but according to one report "there are an additional 5,000 to 7,000 who are not registered with the Housing Authority." Minors made up 72 percent of the population and the mother alone was present in 90 percent of the families with children. The unemployment rate was estimated at 47 percent in 1980, and some 70 percent of the project's 4,200 official households received AFDC. Although less than one-half of one percent of Chicago's population lived in Robert Taylor Homes, 11 percent of all the city's murders, nine percent of its rapes, and 10 percent of its aggravated assaults were committed in the project in 1980.

Why have the social conditions of the black underclass deteriorated so rapidly?

Racial discrimination is the most frequently invoked explanation, and it is undeniable that discrimination continues to aggravate the social and economic problems of poor blacks. But is discrimination really greater today than it was in 1948, when black unemployment was less than half of what it is now, and when the gap between black and white jobless rates was narrower?

As for the black family, it apparently began to fall apart not before but after the mid-20th century. Until publication in 1976 of Herbert Gutman's *The Black Family in Slavery and Freedom*, most scholars had believed otherwise. "Stimulated by the bitter public and academic controversy over the Moynihan report," Gutman produced data demonstrating that the black family was not significantly disrupted during slavery or even during the early years of the first migration to the urban North, beginning after the turn of the century. The problems of the modern black family, he implied, were a product of modern forces.

Those who cite racial discrimination as the root cause of poverty often fail to make a distinction between the effects of *historic* discrimination (that is, discrimination prior to the mid-20th century) and the effects of *contemporary* discrimination. That is why they find it so hard to explain why the economic position of the black underclass started to worsen soon after Congress enacted, and the White House began to enforce, the most sweeping civil-rights legislation since Reconstruction.

Making Comparisons

My own view is that historic discrimination is far more important than contemporary discrimination in understanding the plight of the urban underclass; that, in any event, there is more to the story than discrimination (of whichever kind).

Historic discrimination certainly helped to create an impoverished urban black community in the first place. In his recent *A Piece of the Pie: Black and White Immigrants since 1880* (1980), Stanley Lieberson shows how, in many areas of life, including the labor market, black newcomers from the rural South were far more severely discriminated against in Northern cities than were the new white immigrants from southern, central, and eastern Europe. Skin color was part of the problem, but it was not all of it.

The disadvantage of skin color—the fact that the dominant whites preferred whites over nonwhites—is one that blacks shared with Japanese, Chinese, and others. Yet the experience of the Asians, whose treatment by whites "was of the same violent and savage character in areas where they were concentrated," but who went on to prosper in their adopted land, suggests that skin color *per se* was not an "insurmountable obstacle." Indeed, Lieberson argues that the greater success enjoyed by Asians may well be explained largely by the different context of their contact with whites. Because changes in immigration policy cut off Asian migration to America in the late nineteenth century, the Japanese and Chinese populations did not reach large numbers and therefore did not pose as great a threat as did blacks.

Furthermore, the discontinuation of large-scale immigration from Japan and China enabled Chinese and Japanese to solidify networks of ethnic contacts and to occupy particular occupational niches in small, relatively stable communities. For blacks, the situation was different. The 1970 census recorded 22,580,000 blacks in the United States but only 435,000 Chinese and 591,000 Japanese. "Imagine," Lieberson exclaims, "22 million Japanese Americans trying to carve out initial niches through truck farming."

The Youth Explosion

If different population sizes accounted for a good deal of the difference in the economic success of blacks and Asians, they also helped determine the dissimilar rates of progress of urban blacks and the new *European* arrivals. European immigration was curtailed during the 1920s, but black migration to the urban North continued through the 1960s. With each passing decade, Lieberson writes, there were many more blacks who were recent migrants to the North, whereas the immigrant component of the new Europeans dropped off over time. Eventually, other whites muffled their dislike of the Poles and Italians and Jews and saved their antagonism for blacks. As Lieberson notes, "The presence of blacks made it harder to discriminate against the new Europeans because the alternative was viewed less favorably."

The black migration to New York, Philadelphia, Chicago, and other Northern cities—the continual replenishment of black populations there by poor newcomers—predictably skewed the age profile of the urban black community and kept it relatively young. The number of central-city black youths aged 16-19 increased by almost 75 percent from 1960 to 1969. Young black adults (ages 20-24) increased in number by two-thirds during the same period, three times the increase for young white adults. In the nation's inner cities in 1977, the median age for whites was 30.3, for blacks 23.9. The importance of this jump in the number of young minorities in the ghetto, many of them lacking one or more parent, cannot be overemphasized.

Age correlates with many things. For example, the higher the median age of a group, the higher its income; the lower the median age, the higher the unemployment rate and the higher the crime rate. (More than half of those arrested in 1980 for violent and property crimes in American cities were under 21.) The younger a woman is, the more likely she is to bear a child out of wedlock, head up a new household, and depend on welfare. In short, much of what has gone awry in the ghetto is due in part to the sheer increase in the number of black youths. As James Q. Wilson has argued, an abrupt rise in the proportion of young people in *any* community will have an "exponential effect on the rate of certain social problems."

The population explosion among minority youths occurred at a time when changes in the economy were beginning to pose serious problems for unskilled workers. Urban minorities have been particularly vulnerable to the structural economic changes of the past two decades: the shift from goods-producing to service-providing industries, the increasing polarization of the labor market into low-wage and high-wage sectors, technological innovations, and the relocation of manufacturing industries out of the central cities. During the 1970s, Chicago lost more than 200,000 jobs, mostly in manufacturing, where many inner-city blacks had traditionally found employment. New York City lost 600,000 jobs during the same period, even though the number of white-collar professional, managerial, and clerical jobs increased in Manhattan. Today, as John D. Kasarda has noted, the nation's cities are being transformed into "centers of administration, information exchange, and service provision." Finding work now requires more than a willing spirit and a strong back. (Box 87 suggests the changing class structure of ghetto neighborhoods is another factor to consider if one is to understand the black underclass.)

Box 87

Changing Neighborhoods

In the 1940s, 1950s, and even the 1960s, lower-class, working-class, and middle-class black urban families all resided more or less in the same ghetto areas, albeit on different streets. A perceptive ghetto youngster may observe increasing joblessness and idleness, but will also witness many individuals regularly going to and from work. He may sense an increase in school dropouts, but can also see a connection between education and meaningful employment. He may detect a growth in single-parent families, but will also be aware of the presence of many married-couple families. He may notice an increase in welfare dependency, but can also see a significant number of families who are not on welfare. He may be cognizant of an increase in crime, but can recognize that many residents in his neighborhood are not involved in criminal activity. However, in contrast to previous years, today's ghetto residents represent almost exclusively the most disadvantaged segments of the urban black community.

The exodus of non-poor working and middle-class families from many ghetto neighborhoods removes an important "social buffer" that could deflect the impact of joblessness created by uneven economic growth and periodic recessions. The basic institutions in that area (churches, schools, stores, recreational facilities, etc.) would remain viable if much of the base of their support comes from the more economically stable and secure families.

Moreover, the very presence of these families during such periods provides mainstream role models that help keep alive the perception that education is meaningful, that steady employment is a viable alternative to welfare, and that family stability is the norm, not the exception.

SOURCE: Adapted from William Julius Wilson, *The Truly Disadvantaged: The Inner City, The Underclass, and Public Policy* (Chicago: University of Chicago Press, 1987) and William Julius Wilson, "The Ghetto," in *The Black Scholar*, Vol. 19, No. 3, (May/June 1988).

Beyond Race

Roughly 60 percent of the unemployed blacks in the United States reside within the central cities. Their situation, already more difficult than that of any other major ethnic group in the country, continues to worsen. Not only are there more blacks without jobs every year; many, especially young males, are dropping out of the labor force entirely. The percentage of blacks who were in the labor force fell from 45.6 in 1960 to 30.8 in 1977 for those aged

16-17 and from 90.4 to 78.2 for those aged 20-24. (During the same period, the proportion of white teenagers in the labor force actually *increased*.)

More and more black youths, including many who are no longer in school, are obtaining no job experience at all. The proportion of black teenage males who have *never* held a job increased from 32.7 to 52.8 percent between 1966 and 1977; for black males under 24, the percentage grew from 9.9 to 23.3. Research shows, not surprisingly, that joblessness during youth has a harmful impact on one's future success in the job market.

There have been recent signs, though not many, that some of the inner city's ills may have begun to abate. For one, black migration to urban areas has been minimal in recent years; many cities have experienced net migration of blacks *to* the suburbs. For the first time in the twentieth century, a heavy influx from the countryside no longer swells the ranks of blacks in the cities. Increases in the urban black population during the 1970s, as demographer Philip Hauser has pointed out, were mainly due to births. This means that one of the major obstacles to black advancement in the cities has been removed. Just as the Asian and European immigrants benefited from a cessation of migration, so too should the economic prospects of urban blacks improve now that the great migration from the rural South is over.

Even more significant is the slowing growth in the number of *young* blacks inhabiting the central cities. In metropolitan areas generally, there were six percent fewer blacks aged 13 or under in 1977 than there were in 1970; in the inner city, the figure was 13 percent. As the average age of the urban black community begins to rise, lawlessness, illegitimacy, and unemployment should begin to decline. (Box 88 suggests that the schools might be useful for blacks trying to catch up.)

Even so, the problems of the urban black underclass will remain crippling for years to come. And I suspect that any significant reduction of joblessness, crime, welfare dependency, single-parent homes, and out-of-wedlock pregnancies would require far more comprehensive social and economic change than Americans have generally deemed appropriate or desirable.· It would require a radicalism that neither the Republican nor the Democratic Party has been bold enough to espouse.

The existence of a black underclass, as I have suggested, is due far more to historic discrimination and to broad demographic and economic trends than it is to racial discrimination in the present day. For that reason, the underclass has not benefited significantly from "race specific" antidiscrimination policies, such as affirmative action, that have aided so many trained and educated blacks. If inner-city blacks are to be helped, they will be helped not by policies addressed primarily to inner-city minorities but by policies designed to benefit all of the nation's poor.

Box 88

Blacks in School:
Trying to Catch Up

When black children finally gained access to "mainstream" public schools, they arrived during the turmoil of the late 1960s. Schools were beset by falling standards, lax discipline, and rising rates of crime and vandalism, not to mention repeated efforts to achieve greater racial balance. The big-city public schools, in particular, were in poor condition to help an influx of black underclass youths overcome the cumulative effects of family instability, poverty, and generations of inferior education. When family finances permitted, blacks, like whites, often put their offspring in private schools or moved to the suburbs.

Blacks have nevertheless made some gains through public education. At the grade school level, the gap in school attendance rates between whites and blacks has been closed. Between 1970 and 1982, the proportion of blacks graduating from high school (now 76.5 percent) grew twice as fast as that of whites. The National Assessment of Educational Progress (NAEP) reveals that blacks in grade school and junior high are improving their skills more quickly than are whites, though they still lag behind.

But high school students of neither race are doing better now than their counterparts were 10 years ago. Indeed, the NAEP reports that the proportion of 17-year-old blacks scoring in the "highest achievement group" in reading tests actually declined from 5.7 to 3.9 percent between 1971 and 1980. In the Age of Technology, blacks are still less likely than whites to take science and math courses. The modest gains by blacks during the past decade on the Scholastic Aptitude Test (SAT) still produced an average combined (math and verbal) score in 1983 of only 708 out of a possible 1600. The National Assault on Illiteracy Program estimates that 47 percent of all black Americans still read at a fourth-grade level or lower. As more blacks finish high school and college, such "functional illiteracy" will decline.

WJW

I am reminded in this connection of Bayard Rustin's plea during the early 1960s that blacks recognize the importance of *fundamental* economic reform (including a system of national economic planning along with new education, manpower, and public works programs to help achieve full employment) and the need for a broad-based coalition to achieve it. Politicians and civil-rights leaders should, of course, continue to fight for an end to racial discrimination. But they must also recognize that poor minorities are profoundly affected by problems that affect other people in America as well, and that go beyond racial considerations. Unless those problems are addressed, the underclass will remain a reality of urban life. (Box 89 suggests that Wilson might have changed his mind of the causes and solutions of some inner-city problems.)

Box 89

He's Changed His Mind:
The Rising Significance of Race

William Julius Wilson has recently headed and completed a five year major research information gathering project in which 2,500 Chicagoans, mostly black and Latino, were interviewed, reinterviewed, and observed. Preliminary findings of this new study support most of the ideas in this article, that is, impoverishment is due to the loss of blue collar jobs and the concentration of the unemployed in problem plagued low-income neighborhoods. The unexpected finding was that contemporary institutional racism, thought to be on the wane, was actually increasing. "It's fair to say, yes, my thinking has evolved," says Wilson. He now stresses local race-specific programs to combat the destructive dynamics of inner-city poverty: privately financed car pools to get the poor to the suburbs where the jobs are; create job-information centers in the poor neighborhoods to take the place of referrals from friends; work with employers to improve the city's job-training programs and thereby mitigate the perception of black males as undesirable employees; find ways to provide reliable child care. "None of these are too costly, in fiscal or political terms, although they're targeted directly at minority, inner-city poor. They could be put in place immediately. I'd like to see that happen."

SOURCE: Gretchen Reynolds, "The Rising Significance of Race," in *Chicago*, (December, 1992).

Questions

1. Why have social scientists, policy makers, and even civil rights leaders since the 1960s shied away from research that might show African-Americans in a negative light?

2. How does a "critical mass" of unsupervised young people set off a "self-sustaining chain reaction?" Describe the chain reaction.

3. Is racial discrimination responsible for the underclass. Compare racial discrimination in 1948 and the present.

4. Distinguish between historic and contemporary discrimination and between individual and institutional racism. Which are declining or increasing?

5. What "went wrong" with the black family? Compare family patterns in Africa, during slavery, and in the present.

6. The Chinese, Japanese, and other Asian groups suffered racial discrimination and yet went on to prosper. Why?

7. Compare European-American and African-American discrimination from the 1920s to the present.

8. How do structural changes in the economy affect urban minorities?

9. How does joblessness during youth impact on future success in the job market? Does the fact that the black underclass is relatively young have other implications?

10. Will education help the underclass?

11. Why hasn't affirmative action been more beneficial?

12. Are there any positive signs on the horizon for the black underclass? An Asian one?

13. Latinos will become the largest minority in the 21st century. Is there a Latino underclass? How about a white underclass?

14. A 1990 statistical study by Douglas Massey suggests that the black flight theory is overestimated. He believes better off African-Americans live next to poor ones in inner city neighborhoods as much today as they ever did. Can this be?

15. Has Wilson changed his mind regarding racism?

Chapter 36

The Other Underclass

Nicholas Lemann

The term "Hispanic," which is used to describe Spanish-speaking American ethnic groups—mainly Mexican-Americans, but also Cubans, Puerto Ricans, Dominicans, Colombians, Salvadorans, Nicaraguans, and immigrants from other Latin American countries—may wind up having only a brief run in common parlance. It has been in official governmental use for only a few years; the Census Bureau did not extensively use the term "Hispanic" until the 1980 census. Now it faces two threats: First, although most Hispanic groups are comfortable with the term, another name, "Latino," is gaining favor, especially on campuses, because it implies that Latin America has a distinctive indigenous culture, rather than being just a step-child of Spain. Second, the very idea that it is useful to try to understand all Americans with Spanish-speaking backgrounds as members of a single group tends to crumble on examination.

Cubans, who are much more prosperous than the other Hispanic subgroups, have now risen above the national mean in family income. They are concentrated in Florida. Mexican-Americans, who make up about two thirds of the country's 22.4 million Hispanics, live mainly in the Southwest, especially California and Texas. Puerto Ricans are the second-largest Hispanic group—2.75 million people in the mainland United States. A third of them live in one city—New York.

As soon as the Hispanic category is broken down by group, what leaps out at anyone who takes even a casual look at the census data is that Puerto Ricans are the worst-off ethnic group in the United States. For a period in

From *The Atlantic*, December 1991, pp. 96-102, 104, 107-108, 110. Copyright © 1991 by Nicholas Lemann. Reprinted by permission of the author.

the mid-1980s nearly half of all Puerto Rican families were living in poverty. It seems commonsensical that for Hispanics poverty would be a function of their unfamiliarity with the mainland United States, inability to speak English, and lack of education. But Mexican-Americans, who are no more proficient in English than Puerto Ricans, less likely to have finished high school, and more likely to have arrived here very recently, have a much lower poverty rate. The *Journal of the American Mexican Association* reported earlier this year that, as the newsletter of a leading Puerto Rican organization put it, "On almost every health indicator. . . Puerto Ricans fared worse" than Mexican-Americans or Cubans. Infant mortality was 50 percent higher than among Mexican-Americans, and nearly three times as high as among Cubans.

The statistics also show Puerto Ricans to be much more severely afflicted than Mexican-Americans by what might be called the secondary effects of poverty, such as family breakups, and not trying to find employment—which work to ensure that poverty will continue beyond one generation. In 1988 females headed 44 percent of Puerto Rican families, as opposed to 18 percent of Mexican-American families. Mexican-Americans had a slightly higher unemployment rate, but Puerto Ricans had a substantially higher rate in the sociologically ominous category "labor force non-participation," meaning the percentage of people who haven't looked for a job in the previous month.

Practically everybody in America feels some kind of emotion about blacks, but Puerto Rican leaders are the only people I've ever run across for whom the emotion is pure envy. In New York City, black median family income is substantially higher than Puerto Rican, and is rising more rapidly. The black home-ownership rate is more than double the Puerto Rican rate. Puerto Rican families are more than twice as likely as black families to be on welfare, and are about 50 percent more likely to be poor. In the mainland United States, Puerto Ricans have nothing like the black institutional network of colleges, churches, and civil-rights organizations; there isn't a large cadre of visible Puerto Rican successes in nearly every field; black politicians are more powerful than Puerto Rican politicians in all the cities with big Puerto Rican populations; and there is a feeling that blacks have America's attention, whereas Puerto Ricans, after a brief flurry of publicity back in *West Side Story* days, have become invisible.

The question of why poverty is so widespread, and so persistent, among Puerto Ricans is an urgent one, not only for its own sake but also because the answer to it might prove to be a key to understanding the broader problem of the urban underclass. "Underclass" is a supposedly nonracial term, but by most definitions the underclass is mostly black, and discussions of it are full of racial undercurrents. Given the history of American race relations, it is nearly impossible for people to consider issues like street crime, unemployment, the high school dropout rate, and out-of-wedlock pregnancy without reopening a lot of ancient wounds. To seek an explanation for poverty among Puerto Ricans rather than blacks may make possible a truly deracialized grasp of what most experts agree is a nonrace-specific problem. Although there is no clear or agreed-upon answer, the case of Puerto Ricans supports the view that being part of the underclass in the United States is the result of a one-two punch of economic factors, such as unemployment and welfare, and cultural ones, such as neighborhood ambience and ethnic history.

The First Emigration

Puerto Rico was inhabited solely by Arawak Indians until 1493, when Christopher Columbus visited it on his second voyage to the New World. The island became a Spanish colony, and it remained one until 1898. In that year an autonomous Puerto Rican government was set up, with Spain's blessing, but it functioned for only a few days; American troops invaded during the Spanish-American War and the island became a possession of the United States shortly thereafter. The U.S. conquest of Puerto Rico was not the bloody kind that resonates psychologically through the generations; there was little resistance, and the arrival of the troops was cheered in many places. In 1917 all Puerto Ricans were granted U.S. citizenship and allowed to elect a senate, but until after the Second World War the island was run by a series of colonial governors sent from Washington.

During this period Puerto Rico underwent an economic transformation, as big U.S. sugar companies came in and established plantations. Previously the island's main crops had been grown on small subsistence farms up in the hills. The sugar plantations induced thousands of people to move down to the coastal lowlands, where they became what the anthropologist Sidney Mintz calls a "rural proletariat," living in hastily constructed shantytowns and often paid in company scrip. The most salient feature of Puerto Rico throughout the first half of the twentieth century, at least in the minds of non-Puerto Ricans, was its extreme poverty and overpopulation. "What I found appalled me," John Gunther wrote, in *Inside Latin America* (1941), about his visit to Puerto Rico. "I saw native villages steaming with filth—villages dirtier than any I ever saw in the most squalid parts of China. . . . I saw children bitten by disease and on the verge of starvation, in slum dwellings—if you can call them dwellings— that make the hovels of Calcutta look healthy by comparison." Gunther reported that more than half of Puerto Rican children of school age didn't go to school, that the island had the highest infant-mortality rate in the world, and that it was the second most densely populated place on earth, after Java.

From such beginnings Puerto Rico became, after the Second World War, one of the great economic and political successes of the Latin American Third

World. The hero of the story is Luis Muñoz Marín (the son of the most important Puerto Rican political leader of the early twentieth century), who founded the biggest Puerto Rican political party and, after the United States decided to allow the island to elect its own governor, was the first Puerto Rican to rule Puerto Rico, which he did from 1949 to 1964. Muñoz was the leading proponent of the idea of commonwealth status, as opposed to statehood or independence, for Puerto Rico. Under the system he helped to institute, Puerto Ricans forfeited some rights of U.S. citizenship, such as eligibility for certain federal social-welfare programs and the right to participate in national politics, and in return remained free of certain responsibilities, mainly that of paying federal income taxes. (Local taxes have always been high.)

Muñoz's main goal was the economic development of the island. He accomplished it by building up the educational system tremendously at all levels, by using the tax breaks to induce U.S. companies to locate manufacturing plants in Puerto Rico, and perhaps (here we enter a realm where the absolute truth is hard to know) by encouraging mass emigration. Michael Lapp, a professor at the College of New Rochelle, unearthed memoranda from several members of Muñoz's circle of advisers during the 1940s in which they discuss schemes to foster large-scale emigration from Puerto Rico as a way of alleviating the overpopulation problem. "They speculated about the possibility of resettling a breathtakingly large number of people," Lapp wrote in his doctoral dissertation, and described several never-realized plans to create agricultural colonies for hundreds of thousands of Puerto Ricans elsewhere in Latin America.

It's doubtful that the Muñoz government would ever have been able to export Puerto Ricans en masse to Brazil or the Dominican Republic, but in any case the issue became moot, because heavy voluntary emigration to an extremely nonagricultural venue—New York City—was soon under way. In 1940 New York had 70,000 Puerto Rican residents, in 1950 it had 250,000, and in 1960 it had 613,000. In general, what brought people there was economic prospects vastly less dismal than those in Puerto Rico. Back home, at the outset of the migration, industrialization was still in its very early stages, sugar prices were depressed, and thousands of people who had moved from the hills to the lowlands a generation earlier now had to move again, to notorious slums on the outskirts of urban areas, such as La Perla ("the pearl") and El Fanguito ("the little mudhole"). "The whole peasantry of Puerto Rico was displaced," says Ramón Daubón, a former vice-president of the National Puerto Rican Coalition. Among Muñoz's many works was the construction of high-rise housing projects to replace the slums, but during the peak years of Puerto Rican emigration little decent housing for the poor was available locally.

In particular what set off the migration was the institution of cheap air travel between San Juan and New York. During the 1940s and 1950s a one-way ticket from San Juan to New York could be bought for less than $50, and installment plans were available for those without enough cash on hand. Muñoz's government may not have invented the emigration, but it did do what it could to help it along—first by allowing small local airlines to drive down air fares, and second by opening, in 1948, a Migration Division in New York, which was supposed to help Puerto Ricans find jobs and calm any mainland fears about the migration which might lead to its being restricted, as had been every previous large-scale migration of an ethnic group in the twentieth century.

The South Bronx Becomes the South Bronx

At first the center of Puerto Rican New York was 116th Street and Third Avenue, in East Harlem. This was part of the congressional district of Vito Marcantonio, the furthest-to-the-left member of the House of Representatives and a staunch friend of the Puerto Ricans. A rumor of the time was that he was "bringing them up" because Italian-Americans were moving out of Harlem and he needed a new group of loyal constituents. But the migration increased after Marcantonio lost his seat in the 1950 election. By the end of the 1950s the Puerto Rican center had begun to shift two miles to the north, to 149th Street and Third Avenue, in the Bronx, which is where it is today.

At the time, the South Bronx was not a recognized district. A series of neighborhoods at the southern tip of the Bronx—Mott Haven, Hunts Point, Melrose—were home to white ethnics who had moved there from the slums of Manhattan, as a step up the ladder. These neighborhoods were mostly Jewish, Italian, and Irish. Most of the housing stock consisted of tenement houses, but they were nicer tenements than the ones on the Lower East Side and in Hell's Kitchen. From there the next move was usually to the lower-middle-class northern and eastern Bronx, or to Queens. During the boom years after the Second World War whites were leaving the South Bronx in substantial numbers. Meanwhile, urban renewal was displacing many blacks and Puerto Ricans from Manhattan, and the city was building new high-rise public housing—much of it in the South Bronx. During the mid-1960s another persistent rumor was that Herman Badillo, who had been appointed the city's relocation commissioner in 1961, tried to engineer the placement of as many Puerto Ricans as possible in the South Bronx, so that he would have a base from which to run for office. (Badillo was elected borough president of the Bronx in 1965, and in 1970 he became the first Puerto Rican elected to the U.S. Congress.)

For most of the Puerto Ricans moving to the South Bronx, though, the neighborhood was just what it had been for the area's earlier occupants—a step up (usually from East Harlem). All through the 1950s and 1960s it was possible to see Puerto Ricans as a typical rising American immigrant group (rising more slowly than most, perhaps), and their relocation to the South Bronx was part of the evidence. The idea that New York was going to be continually inundated by starving Puerto Rican peasants for whom there was no livelihood at home had faded, because spectacular progress was being made back on the island: per capita income increased sixfold from 1940 to 1963; the percentage of children attending school rose to 90.

In a new preface for the 1970 edition of *Beyond the Melting Pot*, Nathan Glazer and Daniel Patrick Moynihan wrote, "Puerto Ricans are economically and occupationally worse off than Negroes, but one does find a substantial move in the second generation that seems to correspond to what we expected for new groups in the city." In keeping with the standard pattern for immigrants, Puerto Ricans were beginning to achieve political power commensurate with their numbers in the city. And the War on Poverty and the Model Cities program created small but important new cache of jobs for Puerto Ricans which were more dignified and better-paying than jobs in the garment district and hotel dining rooms and on loading docks and vegetable farms.

But the 1970s were a nightmare decade in the South Bronx. The statistical evidence of Puerto Rican progress out of poverty evaporated. After rising in the 1960s, Puerto Rican median family income dropped during the 1970s. Family structure changed dramatically: the percentage of Puerto Ricans living in families headed by a single, unemployed parent went from 9.9 in 1960 and 10.1 in 1970 to 26.9 in 1980. The visible accompaniment to these numbers was the extraordinary physical deterioration of the South Bronx, mainly through arson. Jill Jonnes, in *We're Still Here: The Rise, Fall, and Resurrection of the South Bronx*, wrote:

> There was arson commissioned by landlords out for their insurance. . . . Arson was set by welfare recipients who wanted out of their apartments. . . . Many fires were deliberately set by junkies—and by that new breed of professional, the strippers of buildings, who wanted to clear a building so they could ransack the valuable copper and brass pipes, fixtures, and hardware. . . . Fires were set by firebugs who enjoyed a good blaze and by kids out for kicks. And some were set by those who got their revenge with fire, jilted lovers returning with a can of gasoline and a match. . . .

Exact numbers are difficult to come by, but it seems safe to say that the South Bronx lost somewhere between 50,000 and 100,000 housing units during the 1970s, and this produced the vistas of vacant, rubble-strewn city blocks by which the outside world knows the South Bronx. Two Presidents, Jimmy Carter and Ronald Reagan, paid well-publicized visits to burned-out Charlotte Street. Theories abound about why, exactly, the South Bronx burned: the excessive strictness of rent control in New York, the dispiriting effects of welfare and unemployment, the depredations of drugs. It is not necessary to choose among them to be able to say that the burning took place because most parties had abandoned any commitment to maintaining a functional society there. It is rare for the veneer of civilization to be eroded so rapidly anywhere during peacetime. Fernando Ferrer, the Bronx's borough president, says, "I remember in 1974 walking around Jennings Street. One weekend everything's going, stores, et cetera. The next week, boom, it's gone. It hit with the power of a locomotive. In '79, '80, it seemed like *every* goddamn thing was burning."

By virtue of the presidential visits and its location in New York City (and its prominence in *Bonfire of the Vanities*), the South Bronx has become the most famous slum in America. To visit it today is to be amazed by how much less completely devastated it is than we've been led to expect. The area around 149th Street and Third Avenue, which is known as the Hub, is a thriving retail district, complete with department stores and the usual *bodegas* (corner stores) and *botánicas* (shops selling religious items and magic potions). A neighborhood like Lawndale in Chicago, in contrast, hasn't had any substantial commercial establishments for more than twenty years. During the daytime the Hub area feels lively and safe. Also, there is new and rehabilitated housing all over the South Bronx, including incongruous ranch-style suburban houses lining Charlotte Street, row houses on Fox Street, and fixed-up apartment houses all over the old tenement districts from Hunts Point to Mott Haven.

What accounts for the signs of progress is, first, a decision during the prosperous 1980s by the administration of Mayor Ed Koch ("kicking and screaming," Ferrer says) to commit a sum in the low billions to the construction and rehabilitation of housing in the South Bronx. This has led to the opening of many thousands of new housing units. Some of them are very unpopular in the neighborhood, because they are earmarked to house homeless people who are being moved out of welfare hotels in Manhattan. Community leaders in the Bronx grumble that there's a master plan to export Manhattan's problems to their neighborhood.

Several impressive community-development groups, including the Mid-Bronx Desperadoes, Bronx Venture Corporation, and Banana Kelly, have played a part in the rehabilitation of the neighborhood, by using funds from the city and foundations to fix up and then manage apartment buildings. Nationally, a generation's worth of efforts to redevelop urban slums haven't worked well on the whole. The lesson of the community groups' success in the Bronx seems to be that if the focus of redevelopment is on housing rather than job creation, and if there is money available to renovate the housing, and if the groups are permitted to function as tough-minded landlords, then living conditions in poor neighborhoods can be made much more decent.

The biggest community-development organization in the South Bronx is the South East Bronx Community Organization, which is run by Father Louis

Gigante. Gigante, a Catholic priest, is a legendary figure in the Bronx. He is the brother of Vincent "The Chin" Gigante, the reputed head of the Genovese organized-crime family. He has been associated with St. Athanasius Church in Hunts Point since 1962, but he is an atypical priest: he is tough, combative, politically active (he served on the New York city council, and once ran for Congress), and immodest. The area surrounding St. Athanasius is an oasis of clean streets and well-kept housing, which Gigante runs in the manner of a benevolent dictator. He is known for his tough tenant-screening policy. "You've got to house a base of people with economic strength," he told me recently. "We look at family structure—how do they live? We visit everyone. We look in their background and see if there are extensive social problems, like drugs or a criminal record. Back in the late seventies, I'd only take ten or twelve percent of people on some government subsidy—including pensions. I was looking for working-class people. You cannot put a whole massive group of social problems all together in one place. They're going to kill you. They're going to destroy you. They're going to eat you up with their problems."

For many years the politics of Hunts Point was dominated by a rivalry between Gigante and Ramon Velez, another legendary figure who was also a New York city councilman. Velez ran the Hunts Point Multi-Service Center, a large, government-funded social-services dispensary that provided him with a base of political-patronage jobs. Born in Puerto Rico, Velez came to the South Bronx as a welfare caseworker in 1961, the year before Gigante arrived. A fiery street-corner speaker, he quickly became the kind of up-from-the-streets community leader that the War on Poverty liked to fund. He made the multi-service center into a big organization, ran for Congress once, registered hundreds of thousands of Puerto Rican voters, became a power in the Puerto Rican Day parade, and led demonstrations that helped induce the city to rebuild a large South Bronx hospital, which has been by far the most significant new source of jobs in the area. He was investigated and audited many times because of government money unaccounted for at his organizations. His aides were rumored to carry weapons and to threaten political rivals with violence. (Velez says this isn't true.) Once Velez and Gigante got into a fistfight after Velez called Gigante a *maricón* ("queer"). (Velez insists that this never happened.)

Today Gigante and Velez are both in their late fifties, gray-haired (at least they were until recently, when Velez dyed his hair black), and mellowed. Each professes to have developed a grudging respect for the other. No doubt they will soon be representatives of a certain period in the past—the rough-and-tumble period when the Bronx was just becoming Puerto Rican. Fernando Ferrer, on the other hand, is part of the first generation of Puerto Ricans born and raised in the Bronx to come to power. He has been groomed for leadership ever since, as a teenager, he joined a program for promising Puerto Rican kids called ASPIRA.

A different group—Dominicans—is now streaming into New York (mainly Washington Heights, in Manhattan, but also the South Bronx) but is too recently arrived to have produced the kind of leaders whose names are widely recognized. A common Dominican route to the United States is to pay a smuggler $800 or $1,000 for boat passage from the Dominican Republic to Puerto Rico, and then to buy a plane ticket from San Juan to New York. Estimates of the number of Dominicans who have moved to New York City in the past decade run between a half million and a million. Dominicans are known for their industriousness, and many of them are illegal aliens ineligible for any kind of social-welfare program; they have gone into the undesirable, illegal, or disorganized end of the labor market, working in sweatshops, driving gypsy cabs, dealing drugs, and operating nightclubs and other perilous small businesses. In New York City, according to Ramon Velez, 6,500 "Puerto Rican Judases" have sold their *bodegas* to Dominicans. Gigante says that many of his tenants are now Dominican. Partly because the Dominican migration is predominantly male and the Puerto Rican family in the South Bronx is predominantly female-headed, Dominican-Puerto Rican marriages and liaisons are becoming common. Surely the Dominican migration is partly responsible for the increased vitality that the South Bronx has begun to display.

I don't mean to make the South Bronx sound happier than it is. Only a block and a half from the Hub, at the corner of 148th Street and Bergen Avenue, is an outdoor drug market, one of many in the area. There is still a great deal of deteriorated housing and vacant land where housing used to be. I spent a couple of mornings recently at Bronx Venture Corporation, a job-placement and community-development organization in the Hub, talking to Puerto Ricans who had come in to get help finding work. Without exception they wanted to leave the South Bronx. They complained about absent fathers, angry mothers, brothers in jail, sisters on welfare; about ruthless competition with the Dominicans for jobs, shoot-outs between drug dealers, high schools where nobody learns, domestic violence, alcoholism, a constant sense of danger. Something is badly wrong there.

Why Is There a Puerto Rican Underclass?

There is no one-factor explanation of exactly what it is that's wrong. In fact, most of the leading theorists of the underclass could find support for their divergent positions in the Puerto Rican experience.

One theory, which fits well with William Julius Wilson's argument that the underclass was created by the severe contraction of the unskilled-labor market in the big northeastern and midwestern cities, is that Puerto Ricans who moved to the mainland during the peak years of the migration were unlucky in where they went. New York City lost hundreds of thousands of jobs during the 1970s. Particularly unfortunate for Puerto Ricans was the exodus of much of the garment industry to the South. "What I see is a community that came here and put all its eggs in one basket, namely the garment industry and manufacturing," says Angelo Falcón, the president of the Institute for Puerto Rican Policy. When the unskilled jobs in New York began to disappear, Puerto Ricans, who had little education and so were not well prepared to find other kinds of work, began to fall into drugs, street crime, and family dissolution.

The ill effects of unemployment have been exacerbated by the nature of Puerto Rican sex roles and family life. The tradition on the island is one of strong extended-family networks. These deteriorated in New York. "You find the extended family in Puerto Rico and the nuclear family here," says Olga Mendez, a Puerto Rican state senator in New York. The presence of relatives in the home would make it easier for Puerto Rican mothers to work; their absence tends to keep mothers at home, and so does the island ethic that women shouldn't work. In 1980 in New York City, 49 percent of black women and 53 percent of white women were out of the labor force—and 66 percent of Puerto Rican women. Even this low rate of labor-force participation is much higher than the rate for Puerto Rican women on the island. In the United States today the two-income family is a great generator of economic upward mobility, but it is a rare institution among poor Puerto Ricans, whose men are often casualties of the streets, addicted or imprisoned or drifting or dead. Also rare is the female-headed family in which the woman works. "That poverty rates soared for Puerto Rican families while they have declined for black families largely can be traced to the greater success of black women in the labor market," says a 1987 paper by Marta Tienda and Leif Jensen, two of the leading experts on Puerto Ricans.

Conservatives who emphasize the role of the welfare system in creating the underclass would say that since other Hispanic groups have labor-force participation rates and family structures markedly different from those of Puerto Ricans, the real issue must be the availability of government checks, not jobs. Other than Cubans, Puerto Ricans are the only Spanish-speaking ethnic group for whom full U.S. citizenship (and therefore welfare eligibility) in the immigrant generation is the rule rather than the exception. "What should be an advantage for Puerto Ricans—namely, citizenship—has turned into a liability in the welfare state," Linda Chavez writes in *Out of the Barrio: Toward a New Politics of Hispanic Assimilation*. "They have been smothered by entitlements."

In the community of underclass experts the role of pure skin-color prejudice is not much stressed these days, but the case can be made that it has contributed to the woes of poor Puerto Ricans. A staple of Puerto Rican reminiscence, written and oral, is the shock and hurt that dark-skinned Puerto Ricans feel when they come here and experience color prejudice for the first time. Blacks were enslaved on Puerto Rico for centuries—emancipation took place later there than here—but the structure of race relations was different from what it was in the American South. Plantations were relatively unimportant in pre-emancipation Puerto Rico, blacks were always a minority of the island's population, and there was a much higher proportion of free blacks than in the United States. Puerto Rico never developed the kind of rigid racial caste system that characterized places with plantation economies and black majorities. Intermarriage was common, and there was no bright legal and social line between those having African blood and whites. (The U.S. Census Bureau no longer asks Puerto Ricans to identify themselves by race.) In Puerto Rico the prosperous classes tend to be lighter-skinned, but dark-skinned people who acquire money don't find the same difficulty in being accepted in neighborhoods and social clubs that they do here.

On the mainland racial prejudice may play a role in shutting Puerto Ricans out of jobs, in ensuring that they live in ghettos, and in instilling an internalized, defeatist version of the wider society's racial judgments. But what's striking about the racial consciousness of Puerto Ricans as against that of African-Americans is the much lower quotient of anger at society. The whole question of who is at fault for the widespread poverty—the poor people or the United States—seems to preoccupy people much less when the subject is Puerto Ricans. For example, conservatives now commonly attribute the persistent poverty of the black underclass to the "victim mentality" expressed by black professors and leadership organizations. I think that the victim mentality among blacks is much more a part of the life of the upper-middle class than of the poor. But even if we grant the premise that ethnic groups are ideologically monolithic, the Puerto Rican case would indicate that the victim mentality doesn't have anything to do with persistent poverty: the Puerto Rican leadership does not have a victim mentality, but persistent poverty is much more severe among Puerto Ricans than among blacks. The National Puerto Rican Coalition publishes first-rate studies about Puerto Rican poverty that take different sides on the question of whether or not it's completely society's fault—something it's difficult to imagine of the NAACP.

Va y Ven

A final theory about why Puerto Ricans are so poor as a group has to do with migration patterns. During the peak years of migration from Puerto Rico to the mainland, the people who migrated were apparently worse off than the people who didn't. A paper by Vilma Ortiz, of the Educational Testing Service, cites figures showing that in 1960 a group of recent Puerto Rican immigrants had a lower percentage of high school and college graduates than a control group on the island. Ortiz's view that it was not a migration of the most ambitious and capable—that people with less education and lower-status occupations were likelier to move—fits with the idea that for Muñoz emigration was a way to reduce the crush of destitute former peasants on the island. Since about 1970, most experts believe, the pattern has been changing and better-educated Puerto Ricans have become more likely to leave the island, because of a shortage of middle-class jobs there. Oscar Lewis wrote in *La Vida*, his 1965 book about Puerto Rican poverty, "The majority of migrants in the New York sample had made a three-step migration—from a rural birthplace in Puerto Rico to a San Juan slum to New York." (Lewis did a lifetime of work on Latin American poverty which contains a great deal of interesting material, but he is rarely quoted anymore; his reputation is in total eclipse in academic circles because he invented the phrase "culture of poverty," which is now seen as a form of blaming the victim.)

Social critics commonly complain that Puerto Ricans lack a true immigrant mentality—that they aren't fully committed to making it on the mainland, so they don't put down deep neighborhood and associational roots, as other immigrants do, and they are constantly moving back and forth from Puerto Rico. Glazer and Moynihan wrote,

> In 1958-1959, 10,600 children were transferred from Puerto Rican schools, and 6,500 were released to go to school in Puerto Rico. . . . Something new perhaps has been added to the New York scene—an ethnic group that will not assimilate to the same degree as others do.

This is known as the *va y ven* syndrome; those who dispute its existence say that the heavy air traffic back and forth between New York and San Juan is evidence that Puerto Ricans visit their relatives a lot, not that they relocate constantly. "Where's your data [about constant relocation]?" Clara Rodriguez, a sociologist at Fordham University asks. "There's nothing but travel data."

The migration patterns of middle-class, as well as poor, Puerto Ricans have become an issue in recent years. As has been the case with other ethnic groups, the well-educated and employed Puerto Ricans leave the slums. For Puerto Ricans who came to New York during the 1940s and 1950s—in slang, "Nuyoricans"—the most common sequence of moves was from the island to East Harlem to the South Bronx to Soundview, a blue-collar neighborhood just across the Bronx River from Hunt's Point, and then to the middle-class North Bronx, Queens, New Jersey, or Connecticut.

The consequent isolation of the Puerto Rican poor seems to be even more pronounced than the isolation of the black poor. Churches in black ghettos are all-black institutions often dominated by middle-class blacks; the major churches in the South Bronx are Catholic and aren't run by Puerto Ricans. The work force of the New York City government is a third black and only a tenth Puerto Rican, meaning that middle-class blacks are much more likely than middle-class Puerto Ricans to return to the slums during the workday to perform professional social-service functions. The most common form of upward mobility in the South Bronx is supposed to be military service (South Bronx soldiers were often in the news during the Gulf War), but that makes people more successful by taking them thousands of miles away from the neighborhood.

The leaders of the South Bronx often don't live there. Ramon Velez has a residence in the Bronx but also ones in Manhattan and Puerto Rico; Ferrer and Badillo live in more prosperous sections of the Bronx; Robert Garcia, Badillo's much-loved successor in Congress, who resigned in a scandal, owned a house north of the New York City suburbs during the time he was in Congress; Yolanda Rivera, who as the head of Banana Kelly is one of the most promising young community leaders in the South Bronx, keeps a house in Old Saybrook, Connecticut. The Reverend Earl Kooperkamp, an Episcopal minister who was recently transferred to a South Bronx church after tours of duty in several poor black neighborhoods in New York City, says, "Anybody who was living here before and making anything got the hell out. In Harlem, East New York, Bushwick, Bedford Stuyvesant, you had the occasional professional. There are no lawyers and doctors in this community."

When middle-class blacks move out of black ghettos, they usually relocate to more prosperous black neighborhoods, which form a nonblighted locus of the ethnic culture. Puerto Ricans who leave the South Bronx for other parts of the New York area tend to melt into more integrated neighborhoods, where it's much harder to maintain the fierce concern with "the race" that has historically existed in the black middle class. Ramón Daubón, of the National Puerto Rican Coalition, goes so far as to say, "There is no distinctive middle-class Puerto Rican neighborhood in the United States."

There *is* a Levittown for Puerto Ricans who are pursuing the standard dream of escape to suburban comfort—just outside San Juan. "If a Puerto Rican makes fifty or sixty thousand a year here, he wants to move back," says Ramon Velez. "He wants to buy land, build a house." Black middle-class emigrants from ghettos tend to remain in the same metropolitan area. Middle-class Puerto Ricans who move back to Puerto Rico can hardly function as role models, political leaders, counselors, or enlargers of the economic pie for the people in the South Bronx. "Look around in Puerto Rico," Velez says. "The legislature, all the influential people—they're all from New York. Two of my former employees are in the state senate. Those who are able to achieve something here and make money, they go back."

When young middle-class Puerto Ricans leave the island for the mainland because they can't find work as doctors or engineers at home, they often gravitate not to New York but to Sun Belt destinations like Orlando and Houston. The

Puerto Rican population of Florida rose by 160 percent in the 1980s. New York now has a reputation on the island as the place that poor people move to, and later leave if they make any money. The percentage of mainland Puerto Ricans who live in New York has dropped steadily over the years, and if you exclude Nuyoricans from the social and economic statistics, Puerto Ricans look much less like an underclass.

Douglas Gurak and Luis Falcón, in a 1990 paper on Puerto Rican migration patterns, argue that poverty, nonparticipation in the labor force, and unstable marriages were often characteristic of the Puerto Ricans who are now poor here, rather than resulting from the economic and social conditions of New York. They write,

> It is clear that the selectivity of the migration process . . . results in an overrepresentation of women in the New York region who are characterized by traits associated with poverty. Those with less labor force experience, less education, more children, and more marital instability are the ones most likely to migrate to the mainland. Those with more stable unions, fewer children and more education are more likely to return to the island.

In Puerto Rico, especially rural Puerto Rico, commonlaw marriage and out-of-wedlock childbearing are long-established customs. Before Muñoz's modernization efforts brought the rates down, a quarter of all marriages on the island were consensual, and one-third of all births were out of wedlock. (Muñoz himself had two daughters out of wedlock, and married their mother only when he was about to assume the governorship of Puerto Rico.) Female immigrants to New York, Gurak and Falcón say, tend to come out of this tradition, and they are more likely than those who don't emigrate to have recently gone through the breakup of a marriage or a serious relationship. Other Hispanic emigrants, such as Dominicans and Colombians, tend to rank higher than non-emigrants on "human capital" measures like education, family structure, and work history; and Puerto Rican immigrants who settle outside New York aren't generally more disadvantaged than people who remain in Puerto Rico. The overall picture is one of entrenched Puerto Rican poverty becoming increasingly a problem in New York City rather than nationwide.

Although their explanations vary, experts on Puerto Rican poverty tend to agree on how to ameliorate it: both Marta Tienda and Douglas Gurak, for example, call for special educational and job-training efforts. There is something about black-white race relations in America that leads people in all camps to dismiss those kinds of anti-poverty efforts in behalf of blacks as unimaginative, old-fashioned, vague, unworkable, or doomed to failure. The self-defeating view that the problem is so severe that it could be solved only through some step too radical for the political system ever to take seems to evaporate when the subject is Puerto Ricans rather than blacks.

The Status Question

Or it may be that the reason for the relatively calm and undramatic quality of discussions of Puerto Rican poverty is that the whole issue is really only a sideshow. The consuming policy matter for Puerto Ricans, including mainland Puerto Ricans, is what's known as the status question: the issue of whether Puerto Rico should become a state, become independent, or remain a commonwealth. "It affects our psyche, our opportunity, our identity, our families," says Jorge Batista, a Puerto Rican lawyer who is a former deputy borough president of the Bronx. "The only analogy for you is the Civil War. It permeates all our lives."

Puerto Rico occupies an unusual economic middle ground—worse off than the United States, better off than most of the rest of Latin America. Progress is now coming much more slowly than it did in the Muñoz years. Muñoz retired in 1964, after handpicking his successor. During the next four years, however, Muñoz's commonwealth party split into factions, and in 1968 Luis Ferré, the head of the archrival statehood party, won the governorship. Muñoz, then in retirement in Spain but still a god in Puerto Rico, handpicked another successor, Rafael Hernández Colón. Hernández unseated Ferré in the 1972 election, and the statehood party passed into the hands of Carlos Romero Barceló. The next few gubernatorial elections pitted Hernández against Romero: Romero won in 1976 and 1980, and Hernández won in 1984, and was re-elected against a different opponent in 1988.

The essential features of commonwealth are federal-income-tax exemption, only partial participation in the U.S. welfare system, and a lack of voting representation in Congress. Psychically, commonwealth status implies a certain distance from the United States—a commitment to the preservation of the Spanish language and of Puerto Rican culture. Like other liberal parties of long standing around the world, the commonwealth party is perceived as both the party of the establishment—of the way things are done in Puerto Rico— and the party of the common man. The party's symbol is the *jíbaro*, the agrarian peasant from the mountains, the closest thing there is to an emblematic national figure. The typical Puerto Rican is no longer a *jíbaro*, but that doesn't matter— the typical Texan is no longer a pickup-driving country boy named Bubba, either. Puerto Rico's idea of itself is as an island of earthy, unpretentious, good-hearted people who treat each other with *dulce cariño*, "sweet caring." It's easy to see how American culture could be perceived as a threat to this ethos, and thus something that should be kept at arm's length.

The statehood party is prepared to take the plunge into American life, although it promises, by way of soothing people's fears, to establish an *estatidad jíbara*. Politically, the statehood party is to the right of the commonwealth party (and far to the right of the small, left-wing independence party) on the classic Latin

American issue of whether or not to view the United States as a benign force in the hemisphere.

In terms of what would actually happen under statehood, though, the party, conservative though it may be, would bring into being a conservative counter-utopia. As a state, Puerto Rico would have two U.S. senators and five or six congressmen, all of whom might well be Democrats. And if Puerto Rico became a state, Republicans would find it more difficult to maintain their opposition to making the District of Columbia, even more solidly Democratic, a state too. Taxes on the island might rise significantly, because Section 936 of the Internal Revenue Code, the big Puerto Rican tax break, would be abolished; businesses would presumably relocate elsewhere. Puerto Rico is now given parts of the U.S. social-welfare benefits package, and 1.4 million people, nearly half the island's population, receive food assistance. Statehood would bring full benefits and the welfare rolls of the new state might swell tremendously, not just with islanders but possibly also with mainland Puerto Ricans who would move back. A bitter controversy could be expected to emerge over whether to make English the island's official language.

Robert L. Bartley, the editorial-page editor of *The Wall Street Journal*, who in conservative battles can usually be relied on to side with the ideologues against the pragmatists, recently concluded after a visit to Puerto Rico that "what the statehood issue really needs is a good vacation." Advocates of statehood—a mixture of business interests and the rising lower and middle classes, like Margaret Thatcher's coalition in Britain—acknowledge that it would be worse in the short term, and stress the overriding historical importance of the island's becoming fully American.

The last time the status question was put to a vote in Puerto Rico was in 1967; commonwealth won. There the matter rested until 1989, when Governor Hernández, at his inauguration, issued a surprise call for resolution of the status question—and then, even more surprising, President Bush announced that he favors Puerto Rican statehood in his first address to Congress. Bush's Puerto Rico policy is usually explained as an example of his tendency to make decisions more on the basis of personal loyalty than of political analysis. Luis Ferré, the first statehood-party governor, now an eighty-seven-year-old patriarch, is an old friend of Bush's, and endorsed him for President in 1980. Soon after the 1988 election Don Luis came to Washington and stayed as a guest in the Bush home. There, the rumor goes, Bush asked him what he wanted as his reward now that the long crusade for the White House was over, and Ferré said, "Before I die, I would like to hear a President of the United States say before a joint session of Congress that he wants statehood for Puerto Rico."

Bush's remarks in favor of statehood set off a two-year process in Congress to arrange another plebiscite in Puerto Rico. It was supposed to take place this year, but negotiations fell apart over such issues as whether the results would be binding on Congress and whether mainland Puerto Ricans would be allowed to vote. Now the plebiscite is sure to be put off until a year or two after the 1992 election. In the meantime, the commonwealth party's dream is that the U.S. Congress will allow it to be represented on the ballot by an option called "enhanced commonwealth," which would give Puerto Rico greater political autonomy, including the right to negotiate with foreign governments; even if this happens, it is not a foregone conclusion that the commonwealth option will win the plebiscite.

Every possible outcome of the status question would have some effect on Puerto Rican poverty on the mainland. In the almost completely unlikely event of independence, the new Puerto Rican nation would be unable to offer anything like the current level of food-stamp benefits, and presumably there would be another mass emigration of the poor to the United States, motivated by fear of privation; when independence took effect, islanders would lose the right of free immigration to the mainland that they now have as U.S. citizens. Statehood would raise food assistance and other benefits on the island to their mainland levels, and so would engender some migration of the poor from the mainland to the island, thus making the problem of Puerto Rican poverty less severe in New York and other big eastern cities.

Enhanced commonwealth is the only one of the three status options that holds any real promise of spurring economic development on the island in the near future. Even a muted reprise of Muñoz's economic miracle could surely be expected to help alleviate Puerto Rican poverty in New York, by drawing people back to the island to find the unskilled jobs that they can no longer find on the mainland.

Obviously, a great deal could be done on the mainland to reduce Puerto Rican poverty. That it can even be discussed as an island problem, susceptible to island solutions, may be the most important of all the differences between the situations of Puerto Ricans and blacks. For many blacks there is, psychologically, a homeland off-stage, in the South or in Africa, but nobody can really think of it as a place where the wrenching difficulties of the present might be worked out.

Questions

1. Why might Latino be a more appropriate name than Hispanic when referring to the Spanish-speaking population in the United States?

2. How many people live in Puerto Rico? Describe the history of Puerto Rico.

3. How many Puerto Ricans are there in the mainland United States? Where do they live?

4. In what sense are Puerto Ricans the worst-off ethnic group?

5. Why might an explanation for Puerto Rican poverty "make possible a truly deracialized grasp of what most experts agree is a nonrace-specific problem"?

6. Do economic, cultural, or historical theories best explain the persistence of the Puerto Rican underclass?

7. Do migration patterns have anything to do with this?

8. What is the *va y ven* syndrome? Does this affect underclass position?

9. How do institutions like churches affect black and/or Puerto Rican poverty?

10. Why are there fewer Puerto Rican role models than black role models?

11. Why must a different strategy be used to alleviate Puerto Rican poverty than that which would be used for African-Americans?

12. How does the "status question" in Puerto Rico affect all this?

13. Distinguish between commonwealth, statehood, and independence parties in Puerto Rico.

14. Predict the future for Puerto Ricans living on the mainland and in Puerto Rico itself.

Chapter Thirty-Seven

Address Unknown
Homelessness in Contemporary America

James D. Wright

The past decade has witnessed the growth of a disturbing and largely unexpected new problem in American cities: the rise of what has been called the "new homeless." Homeless derelicts, broken-down alcoholics, and skid row bums have existed in most times and places throughout our history. But the seemingly sudden appearance of homeless young men, women, children, and whole families on the streets and in the shelters was, in retrospect, a clear signal that something had gone very seriously wrong.

The sudden intensity and new visibility of the homelessness problem took most observers by surprise. Ten or fifteen years ago, a walk along the twenty-odd blocks from Madison Square Gardens to Greenwich Village would have been largely uneventful, a pleasant outing in an interesting part of New York City. The same walk today brings one across an assortment of derelict and indigent people—old women rummaging in the trash for bottles and cans, young kids swilling cheap wine from paper bags, seedy men ranting meaninglessly at all who venture near. Who are these people? Where did they come from? What, if anything, can or should be done to help?

Published by permission of Transaction Publishers, from *Society*. Vol. 26, No. 6. Copyright © 1989 by Transaction Publishers.

Many stereotypes about the homeless have sprung up in the last decade. One of the most popular is that they are all crazy people who have been let loose from mental hospitals. A variation is that they are all broken-down old drunks. One writer had described them as the "drunk, the addicted, and the just plain shiftless"; the implication is that most of the homeless could do better for themselves if they really wanted to. Still another view is that they are welfare leeches, living off the dole. A particularly popular view that sprang up during the Reagan years was that most of the homeless are, as Reagan put it, "well, we might say, homeless by choice," people who have chosen to give up on the rat race of modern society and to live unfettered by bills, taxes, mortgage payments, and related worries. In truth, all of these stereotypes are true of some homeless people, and none of them are true of all homeless people. As with any other large group in the American population, the homeless are a diverse, heterogeneous lot. No single catch phrase or easy myth can possibly describe them all.

As in times past, most homeless people in America today are men, but a sizable fraction are women and a smaller but still significant fraction are the children of homeless adults. All told, the women and children add up to between one-third and two-fifths of the homeless population. Indifference to the plight of homeless adult men comes easily in an illiberal era, but indifference to the plight of homeless women and children, groups society has traditionally obligated itself to protect, comes easily only to the coldhearted.

Likewise, alcohol abuse and homelessness are tightly linked in the popular stereotype, but recent studies confirm that less than 40 percent of the homeless population abuses alcohol to excess; the majority, the remaining 60 percent, do not. Focusing just on the adult men, the studies show that alcohol abuse still runs only to about 50 percent: about half the men are chronic alcoholics, but then, the other half are not.

In like fashion, mental illness is certainly a significant problem within the homeless population, but severe chronic psychiatric disorder characterizes only about a third; the remaining two-thirds are not mentally ill, at least not according to any meaningful clinical standard.

Being among the poorest of the poor, it is also true that many homeless people receive governmental assistance in the form of general assistance (welfare), food stamps, disability pensions, and the like. Yet, nationwide, the studies show that only about half the homeless receive any form of social welfare assistance; the remaining half survive on their own devices, without government aid of any sort.

And so: Some of the homeless *are* broken-down alcoholics, but most are not. Some *are* mentally impaired, but most are not. Some *are* living off the benefit programs made available through the social welfare system, but most are not. Clearly, the popular mythologies do not provide an adequate portrait of the homeless in America today.

On Definitions and Numbers

Defining homelessness for either research or operational purposes has proven to be a rather sticky business. It is easy to agree on the extremes of a definition: an old man who sleeps under a bridge down by the river and has nowhere else to go would obviously be considered homeless in any conceivable definition of the term. But there are also many ambiguous cases. What of persons who live in rooming houses or flophouses? Even if they have lived in the same room for years, we might still want to consider them homeless in at least some senses of the term. What of persons who live in abandoned buildings? In tents or shacks made from scrap materials? In cars and vans? What of a divorced woman with children who can no longer afford rent on the apartment and who has an offer from her family "to live with us for as long as you need"? What of people who would be homeless except that they have temporarily secured shelter in the homes of their families or friends? Or those that would be homeless except that they are temporarily "housed" in jails, prisons, hospitals, or other institutions? What of the person on a fixed income who rents a cheap hotel room three weeks a month and lives on the streets or in the shelters for the fourth week because the pension is adequate to cover only three-quarters of the monthly room rent?

Clearly, to be homeless is to lack regular and customary access to a conventional dwelling unit. The ambiguities arise in trying to define "regular and customary access" and "conventional dwelling unit."

These examples demonstrate that *homelessness is not and cannot be a precisely defined condition.* A family who sleeps in its pickup truck and has nowhere else to go would be considered homeless by almost everyone. A long-distance trucker who sleeps regularly — perhaps three or four nights a week — in the cab of his $100,000 rig, who earns $30,000 or $40,000 a year, and who has a nice home where he sleeps when he is not on the road, would not be considered "homeless" by anyone. Our long-distance trucker has options; our homeless family living in its pickup does not.

Thus, choice is implied in any definition of homelessness. In general, people who choose to live the way they do are not to be considered homeless, however inadequate their housing may appear to be, while those who live in objectively inadequate housing — in makeshift quarters or cheap flophouses or in the shelters and missions — because they do not have the resources to do otherwise *would* be considered homeless in most definitions, clearly in mine.

"The resources to do otherwise" implies yet another aspect of my definition of homelessness: that true homelessness results from extreme poverty. One hears from time to time of "street people" who are found to have a locker in the bus station stuffed with cash, or of vagabonds who, in a former life, traded stock on Wall Street but cashed in for the unfettered romance of life on the road. In some sense, these people are "homeless," but they are homeless by choice. Ronald Reagan notwithstanding, they comprise no important part of the homeless problem in this nation and I shall say nothing further about them.

Poor people living in objectively inadequate housing because they lack the means to do otherwise number in the tens of millions. Indeed, if we adopt a sufficiently inclusive definition of "objectively inadequate housing," we would capture virtually the entire poverty population of the country, some 35 million people, within the homeless category. And yet, surely, being homeless is more than just being poor, although, just as surely, being poor has a lot to do with it.

My colleagues and I have therefore found it useful to distinguish between the *literally homeless* and the *marginally housed*. By "literally homeless" I mean those who, on a given night, have nowhere to go—no rented room, no friend's apartment, no flophouse—people who sleep out on the streets or who *would* sleep out on the streets except that they avail themselves of beds in shelters, missions, and other facilities set up to provide space for otherwise homeless people. And by "marginally housed" I mean those who have a more or less reasonable claim to more or less stable housing of more or less minimal adequacy, being closer to the "less" than the "more" on one or all criteria. This distinction certainly does not solve the definitional problem, but it does specify more clearly the subgroups of interest.

This discussion should be adequate to confirm that there is no single, best, correct, easily agreed upon definition of "homelessness," and thus, no single correct answer to the question: "How many homeless people are there?" There is, rather, a continuum of housing adequacy or housing stability, with actual cases to be found everywhere along the continuum. Just where in the continuum one draws the line, defining those above as adequately if marginally housed and those below as homeless, is of necessity a somewhat arbitrary and therefore disputable decision.

Nonetheless, despite the unavoidable arbitrariness, the discussion calls attention to three pertinent groups: (1) the poverty population as a whole, (2) the subset of the poverty population that is marginally housed, and (3) the subset of the poverty population that is literally homeless. It is useful to get some feel for the relative sizes of these three groups.

I focus in this brief discussion on the city of Chicago. According to U.S. government statistics and definitions, the poverty population of the city of Chicago amounts to about 600,000 persons. Of these, approximately 100,000 are poor enough to qualify for General Assistance under the rather strict Illinois guidelines. A recent study of General Assistance recipients in Chicago found that fully half resided with relatives and friends—that is, were not literally homeless (mainly because of the largess of their social networks) but who were at high risk of literal homelessness in the face of the merest misfortune. Certainly, we shall not be too far off if we let this group, some 50,000 persons, represent the "marginally housed."

The most recent, systematic, and sophisticated attempt to tally the literally homeless population of Chicago reports about 3,000 literally homeless persons on any given night. Taking these numbers at face value, the ratio of poor persons to marginally housed persons to literally homeless persons, at least in one large American city, is on the order of 600 to 50 to 3.

It is transparent that homelessness is only a small part, indeed, a very small part, of the larger poverty problem in the nation. Most poor people, even most of the very poor, manage to avoid literal homelessness and secure for themselves some sort of reasonably stable housing. Just how they manage to do this given recent trends in the housing economy is an important question that is yet to be successfully answered.

Also, the number of literally homeless at any one time is much lower than the number of potentially homeless (or marginally housed) people. The evidence from Chicago suggests a pool of 50,000 persons who might easily become homeless on any given day; the actual pool at risk is no doubt even larger. Even with a literally homeless count of 3,000, Chicago is hard-pressed to come up with sufficient shelter space. The point is that however bad the homelessness problem has become, it could easily be worse by one or two orders of magnitude. The *potential* homelessness problem in contemporary America, in short, is many times worse than the *actual* problem being confronted today.

It is also worth stressing that the number of literally homeless *on any given night* is not a true indication of the magnitude of the problem since that number is by definition smaller than the number of homeless *in any given month* or over the span of *any given year.* To illustrate, in the Chicago census of the literally homeless, 31 percent were found to have been homeless less than two months, whereas 25 percent had been homeless for more than two years. Homelessness, that is, is a heterogeneous mixture of transitory short-term and chronic long-term housing problems. Some people become homeless only to reclaim a stable housing arrangement in a matter of days, weeks, or months; some become homeless and remain homeless for the rest of their lives.

The transitory or situational component adds even more ambiguity to the numbers question. The estimate in Chicago, to illustrate, is that the number ever homeless in the span of a year exceeds the number homeless on any given night approximately by a factor of three. A recent study by the Rand Corporation in California gives similar results. Three separate counties were included in that study; the estimated ratios of annual to nighttime homeless in the three counties were about 2 to 1, 3 to 1, and 4 to 1.

Nevertheless, it is still important to have some sense of the approximate dimensions of the homeless problem in America today. Unfortunately, there is no national study that provides this information. (Box 90 calls to our attention that the 1990 Census is making an attempt to do so.) However, Martha Burt has published results from a national probability sample of shelter and soup kitchen users suggesting that roughly 200,000 homeless adults used shelters and soup kitchens in the large U.S. cities in a typical week in March, 1987. To provide a *complete* estimate of the "single point in time" number of homeless, one would need to add to this figure all homeless children (who comprise perhaps a tenth of the total), all homeless adults who did not use shelters or soup kitchens during the week in question (an unknown number), and all homeless persons living outside cities with populations of 100,000 or more (also an unknown number). These additions, I think, would bring the final estimate somewhere respectably close to the "best guess" figure given later.

Box 90

People Who Count

In the belief that a bad estimate is better than none, the Census Bureau dispatched 15,000 head counters on a 14-hour manhunt. Clipboards in hand, maps at the ready, the enumerators peered under bridges, down subway platforms, and through alleys to figure out whether there are 600,000 homeless people, as some researchers estimate, or 3 million, as advocacy groups maintain.

The resultant "snapshot" of the homeless, critics warn, may not be of much use in identifying either their numbers or their needs. Too few counters had too little time to cover too much territory. Among places they skipped: subway tunnels, rooftops, and the many dangerous corners where the homeless may hide. Their caution was probably well advised. Shots rang out as census takers approached one building in Brooklyn, and two counters were robbed at knifepoint in Florida.

Since the count determines who gets federal and state aid, and how much, some advocates of the homeless fear that an underestimate could give officials an excuse to cut programs that already suffer from a lack of funds.

SOURCE: *Time*, April 2, 1990, p. 25.

I have reviewed the results from a number of studies done in single cities, discarding those that I felt were obviously deficient and giving the greatest weight to those that I felt had been the most scientifically respectable. Based on these studies and the usual simplifying assumptions, my conclusion is that the total literally homeless population of the nation on any given night numbers in the hundreds of thousands, although probably not in the millions. As a rule of thumb, we can speak of a half million homeless people in America at any one time. And if the ratio of one-night to annual homelessness estimated for the city of Chicago (about 3 to 1) is generally true, then the *annual* homeless population of the nation is on the order of one-and-a-half millions.

"Reasoned guesses" by advocacy groups invariably posit much larger numbers than these. None of the studies that go into my estimates could be considered definitive, and so it is certainly possible that the true numbers are very much larger than the numbers I have cited. Most of the researchers whose results I have summarized above, however, began their studies expecting to find many more homeless people than they actually found, and almost all of them would have been more satisfied with their results had they done so. In any case, I am aware of no compelling *evidence* that implies numbers of literally homeless people substantially larger than those I have cited.

Worthy and Unworthy Homeless

What have we learned in the research of the past decade about these half-million or so Americans who are homeless on any given night? We have learned, first of all, that they are a very diverse group of unfortunates: men and women, adults and children, young and old, black and white. We have also learned that relatively few of them are chronically homeless. Indeed, only a quarter to a third would be considered chronically or permanently homeless. The majority are *episodically* homeless; that is, they become homeless now and again, with the episodes of literal homelessness punctuated by periods of more or less stable housing situations. And of course, many homeless people on any given night are recently homeless for the first time, so that no pattern is yet established.

Let me digress briefly to a personal reminiscence. A few years ago, I was having dinner with my mother. In the course of our conversation, the subject of my research on the homeless came up, and my mother asked me, "Who are these homeless people anyway?" I began to respond with my standard litany — the average age, the proportion white, the proportion of women, and such — when I was stopped short. "That is not what I want to know," Mother said. "What I want to know is, how many of these people should I really feel sorry for and how many are just bums who could do better for themselves if they tried?" This abrupt question got directly to the heart of the matter.

At the time of the conversation, I was engaged in the national evaluation of the Health Care for the Homeless (HCH) program, a demonstration project that had established clinics to provide health care for the homeless in nineteen large U.S. cities. At the time, we had data on nearly thirty thousand people who had received health care services through this program, and so I tried to tease an answer to my mother's question from these data.

I began with the homeless families, the lone homeless women, and the homeless adolescents already out on their own, figuring that anybody, even Mother, would find it easy to sympathize with these people. It took her aback to learn that about 15 percent of the HCH clients were children or adolescents aged nineteen or less, and that an additional 23 percent were adult women; the women and children, that is, added up to three eighths of the total. She allowed as how all of these were to be counted among the "deserving homeless." And so I then turned to the lone adult men.

Among the remaining five-eighths of the clients who are adult men, some 3 percent are elderly persons over sixty-five. Being close to sixty-five herself, Mother had no difficulty in adding these to the "deserving" group. Of the remaining non-elderly adult men—and we were now down to about 56 or 57 percent of the client base—fully a third turn out to be veterans of the U.S. armed services. Mother served in the Navy in World War II and found this to be a shocking figure; she just *assumed* that the Veterans' Administration took care of the people who had served their country. And so these too went into the pile of "deserving homeless."

Without the veterans, the elderly, the homeless families, the women, and the children, we were only left with about three-eighths of the client base. Among this three-eighths, I pointed out, fully a third are disabled by psychiatric impairments ranging from the moderate to the profound, and among those without disabling psychiatric impairments, more than a tenth are *physically* disabled and incapable of work. Mother readily agreed that the disabled, either physically or mentally, also deserved our compassion; and we were thus left with fewer than a quarter of the original client base, 22 percent to be precise.

I then pointed out that among this 22 percent—the nonelderly, nonveteran, nondisabled lone adult men—more than half had some sort of job—full-time employment in a few cases, part-time or sporadic employment in most cases, but in all cases jobs whose earnings were not adequate to sustain a stable housing situation. And of those not currently employed, more than half were in fact looking for work. Thus, of the 22 percent of clients remaining at this point, more than 80 percent either had work or were at least looking for work, and Mother, living in a section of Indiana that has been hard hit by the economic developments of the last decade, found it within herself to be sympathetic to these men as well.

We were then left with what she and I both agreed were the "undeserving" or "unworthy" homeless—not members of homeless families, not women or children or youth, not elderly, not veterans, not mentally or physically disabled, not currently working, and not looking for work. My mother's attitude about homelessness in America was altered dramaticallly when she realized that this group comprised less than 5 percent of the total, barely one homeless person in twenty.

Is Homelessness a "New" Problem?

I began this article by referring to "the growth of a disturbing and largely unexpected new problem." But it is worth asking whether this is a new problem, and whether this is a growing problem.

Strictly speaking, homelessness is definitely *not* a "new problem," in that homeless people have always existed in American society (and, for that matter, in most other societies as well). In the recent past, the homeless were seen to consist mainly of "hobos" (transient men who "rode the rails" and whose style of life was frequently romanticized in the pulp novels of an earlier era) and "skid row bums" (older, usually white, men whose capacity for independent existence had been compromised by the ravages of chronic alcoholism). Scholarly interest in skid row spawned a large academic literature on the topic, but the homeless received no sustained policy attention; they and their problems were largely invisible to social-policy makers and to the American public at large.

Rather surprisingly, even during the War on Poverty of the middle 1960s, little or nothing was written about the *homeless* poor, although one must assumed they existed even then. The most influential book ever written about poverty is probably Michael Harrington's *The Other America,* published initially in 1962. Despite several readings of that fine, sensitive volume, I am unable to find a single word about the homeless poor. Many of the processes that I think have contributed directly to today's homelessness problem, particularly the displacement of the poor to make way for urban renewal and the revitalization of downtown, are taken up by Harrington in considerable detail, but the apparent implication, that some of the displaced would become *permanently* displaced, and therefore *homeless,* goes unstated.

Recent historical research on homelessness confirms that the problem dates back at least to the colonial era, when there were sufficient numbers of "wandering poor" at least to raise popular alarms and enact legal measures to deal with them. In Massachusetts, the chosen mechanism was the process of "warning out." Names of transients, along with information on their former residences, were presented to the colonial courts. Upon judicial review, the person or family could then be "warned out" (that is, told to leave town). Some of the more populous towns actually hired persons to go door-to-door seeking out strangers.

These methods were to the end of controlling the relief rolls; up until 1739, a person was eligible for poor relief in Massachusetts if he or she had not been warned out within the first three months of residency. The modern-day equivalent has come to be known as "Greyhound therapy," whereby transients and derelicts are given a bus ticket that will take them and their problems elsewhere. Transients could also be "bound out," in essence, indentured to families needing laborers or servants: a colonial-era version, perhaps, of what we call "workfare." These methods were used to control homelessness in Massachusetts until they were ended by law in 1794.

As in the present day, the wandering poor of colonial times were largely single men and women, although two-parent families were surprisingly common (comprising between 28 and 68 percent of those warned out across the towns and years covered in these studies). Also as in the present day, the wandering poor were drawn from the bottom of the social hierarchy: the men were artisans, mariners, or laborers, and the women were domestic servants for the most part. Except for the overseas immigrants (mostly Irish), they came from towns within a ten-mile radius. Interestingly, there were as many women as men among those warned out. Similar findings appear in several historical studies of indigent and homeless populations throughout the nineteenth and early twentieth centuries.

The Great Depression marked the last great wave of homelessness in this country. Peter Rossi has pointed out that in 1933, the Federal Emergency Relief Administration housed something like 125,000 people in its transient camps around the country. Another survey of the time, also cited by Rossi, estimated that the homeless population of 765 select cities and towns was on the order of 200,000 with estimates for the entire nation ranging upward to perhaps one-and-a-half million (much as the estimates of today). Most of the homeless of the Depression were younger men and women moving from place to place in search of jobs.

The outbreak of World War II in essence ended the Depression and created immense employment opportunities for men and women alike, an economic boom that continued throughout the postwar decades, certainly well into the middle of the 1960s, and that caused the virtual extinction of homelessness. Certainly, residual pockets of homelessness remained in the skid row areas, but the residents of skid row came less and less to be the economically down-and-out and more and more to be debilitated alcoholic males. Based on the urban renewal efforts of the 1960s and the obvious aging of the residual skid row population, the impending demise of skid row was widely and confidently predicted.

The postwar real growth in personal income ended in 1966, as the Vietnam war heated up. Between the war-related inflation and decay of living standards, the 1973 Arab oil embargo, and other related developments in the world economy, the country entered an economic slump that was to last until 1980. During this period, double-digit inflation *and* double-digit unemployment were not uncommon, and the national poverty rate, which had been steadily declining, began, just as steadily, to climb back up. By 1983, the poverty level was the highest recorded in any year since 1966, and while the rate has dipped back down again slightly since 1983, it is still very much higher than anything witnessed in the 1970s. And thus, by the late 1970s and certainly by the early 1980s, homelessness—the most extreme manifestation of poverty—reappeared as a problem on the national scene.

Homelessness, in short, is not a new problem in the larger historical sweep of things, but the current rash of homelessness certainly exceeds anything witnessed in this country in the last half-century. More to the point, the last major outbreak occurred as a consequence of the worst economic crisis in American history; the current situation exists in the midst of national prosperity literally unparalleled in the entire history of the world.

Not only did homelessness make a "comeback" in the early 1980s, but the character of homelessness also changed; this is another sense in which today's problem could be described as "new." In 1985, my colleagues and I had occasion to review medical records of men seen in a health clinic at the New York City Men's Shelter, in the very heart of the Bowery, for the period 1969-1984. Among the men seen in the early years of this period (1969-1972), almost half (49 percent) were white, 49 percent were documented alcohol or drug abusers, and the average age was forty-four. Among men seen at the end of the period (1981-1984), only 15 percent were white, only 28 percent were documented alcohol or drug abusers, and the average age was thirty-six. Thus, during the 1970s and early 1980s, the homeless population changed from largely white, older, and alcohol-abusive, into a population dominated by younger, non-substance-abusive, nonwhite men. Between the Great Depression and the 1980s, the road to homelessness was paved with alcohol abuse; today, quite clearly, many alternative routes have been opened.

In *Without Shelter* Peter Rossi presents a detailed comparison of results from studies of the homeless done in the 1950s and early 1960s with those undertaken in the 1980s, thus contrasting the "old" homeless and the "new." The first point of contrast is that the homeless of today suffer a more severe form of housing deprivation than did the homeless of twenty or thirty years past. Bogue's 1958 study in Chicago found only about a hundred homeless men sleeping, literally, out on the streets, out of a total homeless population estimated at twelve thousand. Rossi's 1986 survey found nearly fourteen hundred homeless persons sleeping out of doors in a total population estimated at about three thousand. Nearly all of the old homeless somehow found nightly shelter indoors (usually in flophouses and cubicle hotels, most of which have disappeared), unlike the new homeless, sizable fractions of whom sleep in the streets.

A second major difference is the presence of sizable numbers of women among today's homeless. Bogue's estimate in 1958 was that women comprised no more than 3 percent of the city's skid row population; in the middle 1980s, one homeless person in four is a woman. A third important contrast concerns the age distribution, the elderly having disappeared almost entirely from the ranks of the new homeless. Studies of the 1950s and 1960s routinely reported the average age of homeless persons to be somewhere in the middle fifties. Today, it is in the middle thirties.

Rossi points out two further differences: the substantially more straitened economic circumstances and the changing racial and ethnic composition of the new homeless. In 1958, Bogue estimated the average annual income of Chicago's homeless to be $1,058; Rossi's estimate for 1986 is $1,198. Converted to constant dollars, the average income of today's homeless is barely a third of the income of the homeless in 1958. Thus, the new homeless suffer a much more profound degree of economic destitution, often surviving on 40 percent or less of a poverty-level income.

Finally, the old homeless were mostly white—70 percent in Bahr and Caplow's well-known study of the Bowery, 82 percent in Bogue's study of Chicago. Among the new homeless, racial and ethnic minorities are heavily overrepresented.

We speak, then, of the "new face of homelessness" and of the "new homeless" to signify the very dramatic transformation of the nature of the homeless population that has occurred in the past decade.

Is Homelessness a Growing Problem?

Granted that the character of homelessness has changed, what evidence is there that the magnitude of the problem has in fact been increasing? Certainly, the amount of attention being devoted to the topic has grown, but what of the problem itself?

Since, as I have already stressed, we do not know very precisely just how many homeless people there are in America today, it is very difficult to say whether that number is higher, lower, or the same as the number of homeless five or ten or twenty years ago. The case that homelessness is in fact a growing problem is therefore largely inferential. The pertinent evidence has been reviewed in some detail by the U.S. General Accounting Office (GAO). Rather than cover the same ground here, let me simply quote GAO's conclusions:

> In summary, no one knows how many homeless people there are in America because of the many difficulties (in) locating and counting them. As a result, there is considerable disagreement over the size of the homeless population. However, there is agreement in the studies we reviewed and among shelter providers, researchers, and agency officials we interviewed that the homeless population is growing. Current estimates of annual increases in the growth of homelessness vary between 10 and 38 percent.

The most recent evidence on the upward trend in homelessness in the 1980s has been reviewed by economists Richard Freeman and Brian Hall. Between 1983 and 1985, they report, the shelter population of new York City increased by 28 percent, and that of Boston by 20 percent. Early in 1986, the U.S. Conference of Mayors released a study of twenty-five major U.S. cities, concluding that in twenty-two of the twenty-five, homelessness had indeed increased. There has also been a parallel increase in the numbers seeking food from soup kitchens, food banks, and the like. Thus, while all indicators are indirect and inferential, none suggest that the size of the homeless population is stable or declining; to the contrary, all suggest that the problem is growing rapidly.

How Did It Come To Be?

To ask how it came to be is to ask of the causes of homelessness, a topic about which everyone seems to have some opinion. *My* opinion is that many of the most commonly cited and much-discussed "causes" of contemporary homelessness are, in fact, not very important after all.

Chief among these not-very-important factors is the ongoing movement to deinstitutionalize the mentally ill. I do not mean to make light of the very serious mental health problems faced by many homeless people, but it is simply wrong to suggest that most, or even many, people are homeless because they have recently been released from a mental hospital.

What is sometimes overlooked in discussions of homelessness and deinstitutionalization is that we began deinstitutionalizing the mentally ill in the 1950s. The movement accelerated in the 1960s, owing largely to some favorable court orders concerning less restrictive treatments. By the late 1970s, most of the people destined ever to be "deinstitutionalized" already had been. So as a direct contributing factor to the rise of homelessness in the 1980s, deinstitutionalization cannot be that important.

Many also seem to think that the rise of homelessness in the 1980s was the direct responsibility of Ronald Reagan, particularly the result of the many cutbacks that Reagan engineered in human-services spending. This, like the deinstitutionalization theme, is at best a half-truth. Certainly, the Reagan years were not kind or gentle to the nation's poor, destitute, and homeless. A particular problem has been the federal government's absolute bail-out from its commitment to the subsidized construction of low-income housing units, a point that I will return to shortly. But at the same time, many of the factors that have worked to increase or exacerbate the problem of homelessness in the 1980s are rooted in the larger workings of the political economy, not in specific political decisions made by the Reagan administration.

What, then, *has* been the cause of this growing problem? Like most other social problems, homelessness has many complex causes that are sometimes difficult to disentangle. We can begin to get a handle on the complexity, however, by stating an obvious although often overlooked point: homeless people are people without housing, and thus, the *ultimate* cause of the problem is an insufficient supply of housing suitable to the needs of homeless people. Although this means, principally, an inadequate supply of low-income housing suitable to single individuals, the housing problem cuts even more deeply.

In twelve large U.S. cities, between the late 1970s and the early 1980s, the number of low-income housing units dropped from 1.6 million units to 1.1 million units, a decline of about 30 percent. Many of these "lost" units have been taken from the single room occupancy hotels or flophouse hotels and rooming houses, those that have always served as the "housing of last resort" for the socially and economically marginal segments of the urban poverty population. Many likewise have been lost through arson or abandonment. And many have disappeared as low-income housing only to reappear as housing for the affluent upper-middle class, in a process that has come to be known as gentrification. (Box 91 pursues this further.)

Saying that the homeless lack housing, however, is like saying that the poor lack money: the point is a correct one, even a valuable one, but it is by no means the whole story. A second critical factor has been the recent increase in the poverty rate and the growing size of the "population at risk" for homelessness, the urban poor. In the same twelve cities mentioned above, over the same time frame, the poverty population increased from about 2.5 million poor people to 3.4 million, an increase of 36 percent. Dividing poor people into low-income units, these twelve cities averaged 1.6 poor people per unit in the late 1970s, and 3.1 poor people per unit in the early 1980s. In a five-year span, in short, the low-income housing "squeeze" tightened by a factor of two. Less low-income housing for more low-income persons necessarily predestines a rise in the numbers without housing, as indeed we have dramatically witnessed in the early years of the decade.

My argument is that these large scale housing and economic trends have conspired to create a housing "game" that increasingly large numbers are destined to lose. Who, specifically, will in fact lose at the housing game is a separate question, and on this point, attention turns to various personal characteristics of the homeless population that cause them to compete poorly in this game. Their extreme poverty, social disaffiliation, and high levels of personal disability are, of course, the principal problems. Thus, it is not entirely *wrong* to say that people are homeless because they are alcoholic or mentally ill or socially estranged—just as it is not entirely wrong to blame "bad luck" for losing at cards. Given a game that some are destined to lose, it is appropriate

---

Box 91

Changing Cities and the Homeless

It is important to remember the immensity of the changes that have occurred in cities in the past twenty or thirty years. Whole sections of many cities — the Bowery of New York, the Tenderloin in San Francisco — were once ceded to the transient. In every skid-row area in America you could find what you needed to survive: hash houses, saloons offering free lunches, pawnshops, surplus-clothing stores, and, most important of all, cheap hotels and flophouses and two-bit employment agencies specializing in the kinds of labor transients have always done.

But things have changed. There began to pour into the transient world more and more people who neither belonged nor knew how to survive there. At the same time the transient world was being inundated by new inhabitants, its landscape, its economy, was shrinking radically. Jobs became harder to find. Modernization had something to do with it; machines took the place of men and women. And the influx of workers from Mexico and points farther south created a class of semipermanent workers who took the place of casual transient labor. More important, perhaps, was the fact that the forgotten parts of many cities began to attract attention. Downtown areas were redeveloped, reclaimed. The skid-row sections of smaller cities were turned into "Old Townes." The old hotels that once catered to transients were upgraded or torn down or became warehouses for welfare families — an arrangement far more profitable to the owners. The price of housing increased; evictions increased.

Nor was it only cheap shelter that disappeared. It was also those "open" spaces that had once been available to those without other shelter. As property rose in value, the nooks and crannies in which the homeless had been able to hide became more visible. Doorways, alleys, abandoned buildings, vacant lots — these holes in the cityscape, these gaps in public consciousness, became *real estate.*

SOURCE: Peter Marin, "Helping and Hating the Homeless," *Harper's Magazine,* January, 1987, pp. 39-44, 46-49.

to ask who the losers turn out to be. But it is wrong, I think, to mistake an analysis of the losers for an analysis of the game itself.

Another important factor that is often overlooked in discussions of the homeless is the seemingly endless deterioration of the purchasing power of welfare and related benefits. Converted to constant dollars, the value of welfare, aid to families with dependent children (AFDC), and most other social benefit payments today is about half that of twenty years ago. Twenty years ago, or so it would seem, these payments were at least adequate to maintain persons and families in stable housing situations, even in the face of the loss of other income. Today, clearly, they are not. To cite one recent example, the state of Massachusetts has one of the more generous AFDC programs of any state in the country, and yet the state has been ordered by the courts twice in the past few years to increase AFDC payments. Why? The court compared the average AFDC payment in the state to the average cost of rental housing in the Boston area and concluded that the payment levels, although already generous by national standards, could only be contributing to the homelessness problem among AFDC recipients.

What we witness in the rise of the new homeless is a new form of class conflict—a conflict over housing in the urban areas between that class in the population whose income is adequate to cover its housing costs, and that class whose income is not. In the past, this conflict was held largely in check by the aversion of the middle class to downtown living and by the federal government's commitment to subsidized housing for the poor. As the cities are made more attractive to the middle class, as revitalization and gentrification lure the urban tax base back to the central cities, and as the federal commitment to subsidized housing fades, the intensity of this conflict grows—and with it, the roster of casualties, the urban homeless.

No problem that is ultimately rooted in the large-scale workings of the political economy can be solved easily or cheaply, and this problem is no exception. Based on my analysis, the solution has two essential steps: the federal government must massively intervene in the private housing market, to halt the loss of additional low-income units and to underwrite the construction of many more; and the benefits paid to the welfare-dependent population—AFDC, general assistance, Veterans Administration income benefits, Social Security, and so on—must approximately double.

Either of the above will easily add a few tens of billions to the annual federal expenditure, and thus, neither is the least bit likely to happen in the current political environment, where lowering the federal deficit and reducing federal spending are seen as a Doxology of Political Faith, widely subscribed to by politicians of all ideological persuasions. Thus, in the short run, which is probably to say for the rest of this century, the focus will be on amelioration, not on solutions. We will do what we can to improve the lives of homeless people—more and better temporary shelters, more adequate nutrition, better and more accessible health care, and so on. In the process, we will make the lives of many homeless people more comfortable, perhaps, but we will not rid ourselves of this national disgrace.

Questions

1. How true are statements that the homeless are crazy, lazy, drugged, drunken welfare leeches?
2. Why is it difficult to define homelessness precisely?
3. What is the relationship between poverty and homelessness?
4. What is the ratio of poor people to marginally housed people to literally homeless people in a city like Chicago? What do we know about this nationally?
5. In what sense is the potential homelessness problem worse than the actual problem?
6. The 1990 census attempted to count the homeless on *one* night. Why does the author feel it would be more accurate to have monthly or yearly figures?
7. Why is it important to distinguish between the chronically and episodically homeless?
8. As the author's mother said, "How many of these people should I really feel sorry for and how many are just bums?"
9. If we exclude from our count of the homeless all children, women, elderly, veterans, those working, those looking for work, those psychologically impaired, and those physically disabled, how many are left? Who are they?
10. How can homelessness be both a "new" problem and not a "new" problem?
11. Has there ever been a period in American history when homelessness was not a problem?
12. Describe characteristics of the homeless in the 1930s, 1940s, 1950s, 1960s, 1970s, 1980s, and the 1990s. How have things changed?
13. Is homelessness growing or is it just that the media is paying more attention to it?
14. The author says the problems of homelessness are rooted in the larger workings of the political economy and not in specific political decisions. What does this mean?
15. What is gentrification? How does homelessness relate to it?
16. What other changes are occurring in cities that affect the homeless?

17. Would a good public housing policy help the homeless? What would be a good public housing policy? High rise? Dispersed? Mixed income groups?

18. What specific suggestions does the author make to rid America of the homeless? What are the chances they will be implemented?

Part XII

Seeing Ourselves
Nature and/or Nurture

The articles in this section of the book deal with various aspects of the question as to whether heredity or environment is more important in shaping human behavior. The first selection, "Why Do We Do What We Do? A Freudian and Skinnerian Overview," attempts to put the debate into a broad framework by considering the theories of two giants in social science. It would probably be safe to conclude that a "nature versus nurture" debate may be pointless. Biology may set broad outlines and limits of our potential, but how or whether we use that potential depends on the environment in which we live.

The second selection examines the work of psychoanalyst Erik Erikson. Erikson, one of Freud's students, expands on the scope and content of his teacher's theory of human development. Whereas Freud saw the personality as being determined in the period from infancy to adolescence, Erikson views self-development as a never ending process. We continually change, he would say, to respond to changing demands in our environment. He outlines eight stages we all go through.

Further evidence of the importance of the cultural environment in shaping us is found in sociologist Kingsley Davis' "Final Note on a Case of Extreme Isolation." This heart-rending third reading raises the question to what extent biological equipment alone contributes to the creation of personality. The report on Anna and Isabelle, two socially isolated female children, suggests that qualities assumed to be human — walking, loving — do not appear in the absence of social interaction. Of crucial importance for human development, according to Davis, is language.

In the fourth selection, "Shattered Innocence", psychologist Alfie Kohn summarizes current research on childhood sexual abuse. She calls to our attention that one in six Americans may have been sexually victimized as children. As if this were not bad enough, boys who are abused, it seems, turn into offenders and girls who are abused tend to produce children who are abused. To what extent heredity and/or environment shape this aberrant behavior is obviously a question of importance. The last article brings in an anthropological perspective. Edward and Mildred Hall pursue the effect language has on us, but with a twist. They believe nonverbal communication — the "sounds of silence" — may be most important in the "warp and woof of daily interactions with others."

Chapter Thirty-Eight

Why Do We Do What We Do?
A Freudian and Skinnerian Overview

Frank Zulke

Why do we do what we do? This short essay will consider how Sigmund Freud (the Viennese father of psychoanalysis) and B.F. Skinner (a contemporary American behavioral psychologist) would answer the question. Freud and Skinner were chosen because their theories exemplify opposing sides of the question whether heredity or environment is more important in shaping behavior.

Before dealing with the ideas of either of these men, it is important that we know something about a third person: Charles Darwin. The impact of his *Origin of the Species* (1859) and *The Descent of Man* (1871) was immense. The theory of evolution espoused in the books—that all mammals have a common ancestry and have evolved according to a principle of natural selection in which the fittest survive—meant that we, being mammals, had to see ourselves as "evolving biological organisms." Before Darwin, humans were thought of as having a soul; after Darwin, they were merely a part of nature, an animal among other animals. This was hard for people in Darwin's time to accept because it necessitated a revision of the biblical account of creation. Even today, as Box 92 on "evolution versus creationism" indicates, the controversy still rages.

Acceptance of this radical evolutionary doctrine—and scientific evidence seems to be on its side—meant that humans, not substantially different from less complex forms of life, could become objects of scientific study.

Box 92

Evolution Versus Creationism

In 1981, Arkansas enacted a law to require the teaching of scientific creationism in public schools where evolution is taught. In 1982, a U.S. District Court declared the law unconstitutional because to teach a literal interpretation as presented in Genesis would require religious beliefs; thus, it is religious teaching and would violate that First Amendment which prohibits establishment of a state religion. Robert Perruci and Dean Knudsen summarize the two positions below.

Evolutionists argue: (I) the concept of creation requires the concept of a supernatural creator, an inherently religious belief; (2) the theory of creation has no support and that the "fit" of the explanation of change as an evolutionary process is the best possible explanation of observed facts; (3) the idea of creation requires a belief in the creation myth of the Bible; such religion is not compatible with science, which rests on facts, not myths, and is subject to testing and changing interpretations.

Creationists argue: (1) evolution essentially has become a religion that seeks to explain origins of man and life, but is unable to give adequate answers; (2) the theory of evolution requires a major jump in faith as well, and the many gaps or "missing links" of evolution are evidence of its inadequacy to explain life; (3) science cannot deal with the important question of "why" things exist; only religion can and only by adding creation to science is the full explanation of life possible.

Do you think we have heard the end of this controversy?

SOURCE: Robert Perrucci and Dean Knudsen, *Sociology* (St. Paul, Minn.: West, 1983), p. 517.

Conceived of as evolving biological organisms, some believed that explanations for behavior should focus on instincts, i.e., behavior patterns biologically fixed for a species. Just as, for example, nest building techniques among birds of the same species do not differ, our behavior, too, might be explained on the basis of instincts.

Sigmund Freud (1856-1939)

One towering figure profoundly influenced by Darwinian ideas was Sigmund Freud. He knew human instincts would be more complex than those of "birds building nests" and, in exploring this complexity, eventually put forth the idea that our biological instincts could be molded into a variety of behaviors, some conscious and some unconscious. Indeed, Freud's "discovery" of the unconscious is regarded by many as one of the great achievements of modern times for it opened up a whole new realm of human existence that was previously concealed. His theory of personality has influenced, if not dominated Western ideas for the last half century. As Box 93 indicates, Freud brought together a diverse background to answer the question of why we behave as we do.

Freud saw humans as propelled by powerful biological drives or urges which need to be satisfied. There is a battle within us between "eros" (urges toward both sexual and asexual love referred to as the life instincts) and "thanatos" (urges to become inorganic referred to as the death instincts). While the former is certainly easier to understand than the latter, Freud believes the interplay between the two explains our behavior. Because Freud believed that the first five years of life set the stage for and determine a life style which is then manifested continuously throughout the individual's life time, it might be useful to look deeper into his ideas regarding the human personality and how it is formed. In essence, Freud sees three main components to our psyche: id, ego, and superego.

The infant is an instinctive, pleasure-seeking creature who is totally absorbed in obtaining bodily gratification. Pleasure comes from satisfying both the life

---

Box 93

Who Was Freud?

By profession Freud was a physician. He treated sick people, particularly those suffering from nervous or mental disorders, with methods he himself had devised (psychoanalysis). But, as Calvin Hall tells us below, it is not easy to pigeonhole him.

What then was Freud? Physician, psychiatrist, psychoanalyst, philosopher, and critic — these were his several vocations. Yet, taken separately or together, they do not really convey Freud's importance to the world. Although the word "genius" is used indiscriminately to describe a number of people, there is no single word that fits Freud as well as this word does. He was a genius. One may prefer to think of him, as I do, as one of the few men in history who possessed a universal mind. . . . Whatever he touched he illuminated. He was a very wise man.

SOURCE: Calvin S. Hall, *A Primer of Freudian Psychology* (New York: The New American Library, 1954), p. 21.

instincts (for example, thumb sucking) and the death instincts (for example, aggressive behavior). Freud calls this part of the psyche the *id* and states that it operates irrationally and unconsciously. It is amoral. As the child grows, it begins to discover that the world will not always satisfy its desires. People have rules and the child must play by the rules to get what it wants. Gradually, as the child develops the ability to reason, it learns to gratify needs in socially approved ways. Freud calls this rational, conscious part of personality the *ego*. As the child begins to learn the norms of society, there develops what Freud called a *superego*, or conscience which, although unconscious, imposes morality on the id. In effect, the superego is an internalization of others' ideas — the culture's and the parents, for example — about right and wrong. The id is a biological given that the child is born with; the ego begins to form from the moment of birth; the super-ego forms roughly around the fifth year of life.

Although oversimplified already, think of it this way: 1) the id desires pleasure; 2) the ego operates according to reality; 3) the superego wants perfection. It is probable that the id, being propelled by incompatible "eros" and "thanatos," will be at odds with the superego (and the reality demands of the ego). It will then be the role of the ego in the mentally healthy person to reconcile these forces by redirecting impulses from the id into realistic channels the superego finds acceptable. Or, in other words, 4) the ego mediates between the id and superego.

Freud enumerated a series of "psychosexual stages of development" that children pass through on their way to maturity. One stage in particular might illuminate why the superego may conflict with the id and needs the ego to mediate. It also offers a vivid example of "eros" and "thanatos" at work. The "phallic stage of development" occurs from three to six. During this stage, the child experiences pleasurable and conflicting feelings associated with the genital organs. These culminate, according to Freud, in the *Oedipal complex*, i.e., the child's desire to possess the opposite-sex parent and do away with the same-sex parent. (Some say the term Oedipal complex applies only to the male and a feminine version of this is sometimes referred to as the *Electra complex*.) Note that Freud is not saying that children actually desire to perform sexual intercourse and commit murder. While absurd as a literal depiction, however, he believes it to be true on an unconscious level for *all* people. Keep in mind too that the child goes through this Oedipal or Electra complex at approximately the same time the superego is formed. Some say it is the reason the superego *must* form and why it must be so relentless and cruel in its insistence on perfection.

We behave as we do, according to Freud, because of biological instincts; at the same time, the demands of society set certain limits on behavior patterns that will be tolerated. Therefore, the individual is constantly in conflict: even though the individual needs society, society's restrictive norms and values are a source of ongoing unhappiness. The title of Freud's last book was *Civilization and Its Discontents* and in it he suggests that society and the individual are enemies, with the latter yielding to the former reluctantly and only out of compulsion.

While most social scientists accept Freud's idea of an interplay between our instinctual urges and the society in which we live, some feel his theory is too pessimistic. They feel, furthermore, that it is not, strictly speaking, scientific. How, for example, does one measure unconscious mental processes? Moreover, even if it is true that humans possess instincts at birth, they are too quickly modified by culture to be detected in their purity. Such critics say we must have a science of behavior which deals with that which can be observed and not with intuition and guesswork.

B.F. Skinner (1904-1990)

Behaviorist B.F. Skinner is a leading proponent of this school of thought. Behaviorists, as the name implies, concentrate on behavior with minimal attention to such subjective factors as unconscious instincts, internal motivations, or emotions. Skinner emphasizes that we should limit ourselves to two things: 1) the study of overt behavior that can be objectively observed, and 2) the effects of the environment on behavior. He bases his theory on empirical evidence collected through laboratory experimentation with humans and animals.

Skinner's basic idea is that the individual is a product of his or her environment. The environment, in other words, molds the behavior of the individual. At birth the child may almost be thought of as a *tabula rasa*, a blank slate. He or she has no personality, no characteristic way of thinking, feeling, and acting. And, Skinner would say, it doesn't make any difference if these things might be unconscious: causality of behavior does not depend upon awareness.

Crucial to understanding how the child ultimately does acquire a personality is Skinner's belief that the child is "conditioned" to behave through "rewards" and "punishments," that is, the child learns to think, feel, and act because he or she is rewarded for good behavior and punished for bad behavior. Responses that are rewarded are repeated and become part of the individual's behavioral repertoire. Responses that are punished, or perhaps ignored, are discontinued.

Skinner feels we are generally controlled by the less effective negative or aversive reinforcement in contemporary society rather than by the more effective positive reinforcement. Applying this, for example, to our school system, one might say that the process of education for the child is more likely to proceed because of the threat of failure or punishment to which the child is exposed rather than in terms of the promise of success or reward. As Box 94 indicates, however, Skinner is optimistic about the future. He believes the long-term historical evidence shows a movement away from aversive control toward a more positive control.

What is fascinating—and controversial—about Skinner's theory is the belief that we can be conditioned to behave in ethical ways through rewards and punishments. The problem that arises, of course, is that what is ethical to one person may not be ethical to another. We may have developed a "technology of behavior" but, Skinner says, "Who will use a technology and to what ends? Until these issues are resolved, a technology of behavior will continue to be rejected, and with it possibly the only way to solve our problems."

Skinner's novel, *Walden Two*, was a masterful vehicle for bringing these ideas to the attention of the general public. Using "behavioral engineering," the characters in the book fashioned a utopian society based on a planned order that eliminated aversive controls. *Beyond Freedom and Dignity*, a non fictional book, continued to press home these ideas. Skinner tells us again that a viable

---

Box 94

Toward Positive Reinforcement

Richard Evans interviewed B.F. Skinner and asked for some predictions for the future. While Skinner was hesitant to be specific, he was willing to tell us the following:

> Civilization has moved from an aversive control toward a positive approach. There are only a few places in the world today where slavery is practiced, where labor is coerced by the whip. We have substituted the payment of wages for physical punishment, and are even concerned with finding other reinforcers. We should like to have a man work productively for the sheer love of it, and we reflect back on the old craft system as an example. . . . In religion, there is less emphasis on hell-fire and the threat of damnation; people are to be good for positive reasons, for the love of God or their fellowmen. . . . And on a more intimate level, we prefer to have people get along well with each other because their outgoing, positive behavior is richly reinforcing rather than because they are afraid of being criticized. . . . A punitive society is not supported by the people under it, whereas a society which is full of good things is likely to be strong.

Do you think Skinner is correct about the future?

SOURCE: Richard I Evans. *B.F. Skinner: The Man and His Ideas* (New York: E. P. Dutton, 1968) pp. 32-33.

society is possible if we condition people positively for changes. That this is not merely an academic exercise is indicated in the fact that a commune called Twin Oaks exists in Virginia where 100 people live their lives according to Skinnerian principles. Or in the fact, as Skinner says, that we can be "programmed" for peace or war.

The rub in both books, however, is that we may have to give up cherished and sacred ideals to attain desired ends. Freedom, for example, is almost casually brushed aside. "I deny that freedom exists at all or my program would be absurd. . . The increasing success of a science of behavior makes it more and more plausible that man is not free." For Skinner, behavior is determined by the environment and that's that.

Skinner achieved some notoriety thirty years ago by tending his infant daughter for part of the day in a completely controlled environment that became known as a *Skinner box*. The child not only survived but thrived, contrary to the expectations of many. Since then, Skinner and his followers have invented "teaching machines" for use in the schools and "behavior modification," i.e., the withholding of rewards in exchange for desired behavior, is standard practice in many offices, mental hospitals, and even prisons. It works particularly well in the latter two as these are environments which can be controlled for twenty four hours a day. In fact, Skinner's importance may be gauged by a recent survey of the membership of the American Psychological Association which rated him as perhaps the most influential contemporary psychologist. Not all, of course, agree. Some are quick to criticize Skinner as an environmental determinist who ignores other relevant factors. Others feel it is invalid to see the world as a laboratory and dehumanizing to see us as subjects in an experiment in that laboratory. These critics point to the immorality of manipulating human beings. Whichever position one takes regarding Skinner, one must note that his theory has affected the way we understand behavior.

Today, most social scientists would say the key to understanding "why we do what we do?" probably lies somewhere between the Freudian and Skinnerian schools of thought. After all, people are born with certain biologically determined needs and potentials, but they learn ways to satisfy their needs and develop their potentials in a social setting. The current approach has finally evolved into an investigation as to which constellation of factors is more important — heredity or environment, or a combination of both.

Questions

1. Why are Freud and Skinner chosen to explain "why we do what we do"?
2. Where does Darwin fit into this?

3. Will evolution or creationism be the ultimate winner?

4. What were Freud's vocations?

5. What are the life and death instincts? Give examples.

6. Define id, ego, and superego. How do they interact?

7. What is the difference between the Oedipal and Electra complexes? Are they conscious or unconscious? Why do you think they are named as they are?

8. Will children raised without both parents, or in societies without nuclear families, exhibit the Oedipal and Electra complexes?

9. Are both Freud and Skinner determinists?

10. Why is Skinner a behaviorist?

11. In what sense are we "blank slates"?

12. Distinguish between positive and negative reinforcement? Which is better? Which will be more important in the future?

13. Can morality be conditioned?

14. What value beside freedom might we have to give up if a Skinnerian society comes about?

15. If you wanted to design a utopian society, how would you organize the family, religion, politics, education, economics, etc. Pretend you are starting from scratch.

16. Do you think the theories of Freud or Skinner will be considered more important in the future?

Chapter Thirty-Nine

Erik Erikson's
Eight Ages of Man

David Elkind

At a recent faculty reception I happened to join a small group in which a young mother was talking about her "identity crisis." She and her husband, she said, had decided not to have any more children and she was depressed at the thought of being past the childbearing stage. It was as if, she continued, she had been robbed of some part of herself and now needed to find a new function to replace the old one.

When I remarked that her story sounded like a case history from a book by Erik Erikson, she replied, "Who's Erikson?" It is a reflection on the intellectual modesty and literary decorum of Erik H. Erikson, psychoanalyst and professor of developmental psychology at Harvard that so few of the many people who today talk about the "identity crisis" know anything of the man who pointed out its pervasiveness as a problem in contemporary society two decades ago.

Erikson has, however, contributed more to social science than his delineation of identity problems in modern man. His descriptions of the stages of the life cycle, for example, have advanced psychoanalytic theory to the point where it can now describe the development of the healthy personality on its own terms and not merely as the opposite of a sick one. Likewise, Erikson's emphasis upon the problems unique to adolescents and adults living in today's society has helped to rectify the one-sided emphasis on childhood as the beginning and end of personality development.

Finally, in his biographical studies, such as "Young Man Luther" and "Gandhi's Truth" (which has just won a National Book Award in philosophy and religion), Erikson emphasizes the inherent strengths of the human personality by showing how individuals can use their neurotic symptoms and conflicts for creative and constructive social purposes while healing themselves in the process.

It is important to emphasize that Erikson's contributions are genuine advances in psychoanalysis in the sense that Erikson accepts and builds upon many of the basic tenets of Freudian theory. In this regard, Erikson differs from Freud's early co-workers such as Jung and Adler who, when they broke with Freud, rejected his theories and substituted their own.

Likewise, Erikson also differs from the so-called neo-Freudians such as Horney, Kardiner and Sullivan who (mistakenly, as it turned out) assumed that Freudian theory had nothing to say about man's relation to reality and to his culture. While it is true that Freud emphasized, even mythologized, sexuality, he did so to counteract the rigid sexual taboos of his time, which, at that point in history, were frequently the cause of neuroses. In his later writings, however, Freud began to concern himself with the executive agency of the personality, namely the ego, which is also the repository of the individual's attitudes and concepts about himself and his world.

It is with the psychosocial development of the ego that Erikson's observations and theoretical constructions are primarily concerned. Erikson has thus been able to introduce innovations into psychoanalytic theory without either rejecting or ignoring Freud's monumental contribution.

The man who has accomplished this notable feat is a handsome Dane, whose white hair, mustache, resonant accent and gentle manner are reminiscent of actors like Jean Hersholt and Paul Muni. Although he is warm and outgoing with friends, Erikson is a rather shy man who is uncomfortable in the spotlight of public recognition. This trait, together with his ethical reservations about making public even disguised case material, may help to account for Erikson's reluctance to publish his observations and conceptions (his first book appeared in 1950, when he was 48).

In recent years this reluctance to publish has diminished and he has been appearing in print at an increasing pace. Since 1960 he has published three books, "Insight and Responsibility," "Identity: Youth and Crisis" and "Gandhi's Truth," as well as editing a fourth, "Youth: Change and Challenge." Despite the accolades and recognition these books have won for him, both in America and abroad, Erikson is still surprised at the popular interest they have generated and is a little troubled about the possibility of being misunderstood and misinterpreted. While he would prefer that his books spoke for themselves and that he was left out of the picture, he has had to accede to popular demand for more information about himself and his work.

The course of Erikson's professional career has been as diverse as it has been unconventional. He was born in Frankfurt, Germany, in 1902 of Danish parents. Not long after his birth his father died, and his mother later married the pediatrician who had cured her son of a childhood illness. Erikson's stepfather urged him to become a physician, but the boy declined and became an artist instead—an artist who did portraits of children. Erikson says of his post-adolescent years, "I was an artist then, which in Europe is a euphemism for a young man with some talent and nowhere to go." During this period he settled in Vienna and worked as a tutor in a family friendly with Freud's. He met Freud on informal occasions when the families went on outings together.

These encounters may have been the impetus to accept a teaching appointment at an American school in Vienna founded by Dorothy Burlingham and directed by Peter Blos (both now well known on the American psychiatric scene). During these years (the late nineteen twenties) he also undertook and completed psychoanalytic training with Anna Freud and August Aichhorn. Even at the outset of his career, Erikson gave evidence of the breadth of his interests and activities by being trained and certified as a Montessori teacher. Not surprisingly, in view of that training, Erikson's first articles dealt with psychoanalysis and education.

It was while in Vienna that Erikson met and married Joan Mowat Serson, an American artist of Canadian descent. They came to America in 1933, when Erikson was invited to practice and teach in Boston. Erikson was, in fact, one of the first if not the first child-analyst in the Boston area. During the next two decades he held clinical and academic appointments at Harvard, Yale and Berkeley. In 1951 he joined a group of psychiatrists and psychologists who moved to Stockbridge, Massachusetts, to start a new program at the Austen Riggs Center, a private residential treatment center for disturbed young people. Erikson remained at Riggs until 1961, when he was appointed professor of human development and lecturer on psychiatry at Harvard. Throughout his career he has always held two or three appointments simultaneously and has traveled extensively.

Perhaps because he had been an artist first, Erikson has never been a conventional psychoanalyst. When he was treating children, for example, he always insisted on visiting his young patients' homes and on having dinner with the families. Likewise in the nineteen thirties, when anthropological investigation was described to him by his friends Scudder McKeel, Alfred Kroeber and Margaret Mead, he decided to do field work on an Indian reservation. "When I realized that Sioux is the name which we (in Europe) pronounced 'See us' and which for us was *the* American Indian, I could not resist." Erikson thus antedated the anthropologists who swept over the Indian reservations in the post-Depression years. (So numerous were the field workers at that time that the stock joke was that an Indian family could be defined as a mother, a father, children and an anthropologist.)

Erikson did field work not only with the Oglala Sioux of Pine Ridge, South Dakota (the tribe that slew Custer and was in turn slaughtered at the Battle of Wounded Knee), but also with the salmon-fishing Yurok of Northern California. His reports on these experiences revealed his special gift for sensing and entering into the world views and modes of thinking of cultures other than his own.

It was while he was working with the Indians that Erikson began to note syndromes which he could not explain within the confines of traditional psychoanalytic theory. Central to many an adult Indian's emotional problems seemed to be his sense of uprootedness and lack of continuity between his present lifestyle and that portrayed in tribal history. Not only did the Indian sense a break with the past, but he could not identify with a future requiring assimilation of the white culture's values. The problems faced by such men, Erikson recognized, had to do with the ego and with culture and only incidentally with sexual drives.

The impressions Erikson gained on the reservations were reinforced during World War II when he worked at a veterans' rehabilitation center at Mount Zion Hospital in San Francisco. Many of the soldiers he and his colleagues saw seemed not to fit the traditional "shell shock" or "malingerer" cases of World War I. Rather, it seemed to Erikson that many of these men had lost the sense of who and what they were. They were having trouble reconciling their activities, attitudes and feelings they had known before the war. Accordingly, while these men may well have had difficulties with repressed or conflicted drives, their main problem seemed to be, as Erikson came to speak of it at the time, "identity confusion."

It was almost a decade before Erikson set forth the implications of his clinical observations in "Childhood and Society." In that book, the summation and integration of 15 years of research, he made three major contributions to the study of the human ego. He posited (1) that, side by side with the stages of psychosexual development described by Freud (the oral, anal, phallic, Oedipal, latency, and pubertal), were psychosocial stages of ego development, in which the individual had to establish new basic orientations to himself and his social world; (2) that personality development continued throughout the whole life cycle; and (3) that each stage had a positive *as well* as a negative component.

Much about these contributions—and about Erikson's way of thinking—can be understood by looking at his scheme of life stages. Erikson identifies eight stages in the human cycle, in each of which a new dimension of "social interaction" becomes possible—that is, a new dimension in a person's interaction with himself, and with his social environment.

Box 95

Freud's "Ages of Man"

Erik Erikson's definition of the "eight ages of man" is a work of synthesis and insight by a psychoanalytically trained and worldly mind. Sigmund Freud's description of human phases stems from his epic psychological discoveries and centers almost exclusively on the early years of life. A brief summary of the phases posited by Freud:

Oral stage — roughly the first year of life, the period during which the mouth region provides the greatest sensual satisfaction. Some derivative behavioral traits which may be seen at this time are *incorporativeness* (first six months of life) and *aggressiveness* (second six months of life).

Anal stage — roughly the second and third years of life. During this period the site of greatest sensual pleasure shifts to the anal and urethral areas. Derivative behavioral traits are *retentiveness* and *expulsiveness*.

Phallic stage — roughly the third and fourth years of life. The site of greatest sensual pleasure during this stage is the genital region. Behavior traits derived from this period include *intrusiveness* (male) and *receptiveness* (female).

Oedipal stage — roughly the fourth and fifth years of life. At this stage the young person takes the parent of the opposite sex as the object or provider of sensual satisfaction and regards the same-sex parent as a rival. (The "family romance.") Behavior traits originating in this period are *seductiveness* and *competitiveness*.

Latency stage — roughly the years from age 6 to 11. The child resolves the Oedipus conflict by identifying with the parent of the opposite sex and by so doing satisfies sensual needs vicariously. Behavior traits developed during this period include *conscience* (or the internalization of parental moral and ethical demands.)

Puberty stage — roughly 11 to 14. During this period there is an integration and subordination of oral, anal and phallic sensuality to an overriding and unitary genital *sexuality*. The genital sexuality of puberty has another young person of the opposite sex as its object and discharge (at least for boys) as its aim. Derivative behavior traits (associated with the control and regulation of genital sexuality) are *intellectualization* and *estheticism*.

Trust vs. Mistrust

The first stage corresponds to the oral stage in classical psychoanalytic theory and usually extends through the first year of life. In Erikson's view, the new dimension of social interaction that emerges during this period involves basic *trust* at the one extreme, and *mistrust* at the other. The degree to which the child comes to trust the world, other people and himself depends to a considerable extent upon the quality of the care that he receives. The infant whose needs are met when they arise, whose discomforts are quickly removed, who is cuddled, fondled, played with and talked to, develops a sense of the world as a safe place to be and of people as helpful and dependable. When, however, the care is inconsistent, inadequate and rejecting, it fosters a basic mistrust, an attitude of fear and suspicion on the part of the infant toward the world in general and people in particular that will carry through to later stages of development.

It should be said at this point that the problem of basic trust-versus-mistrust (as is true for all the later dimensions) is not resolved once and for all during the first year of life; it arises again at each successive stage of development. There is both hope and danger in this. The child who enters school with a sense of mistrust may come to trust a particular teacher who has taken the trouble to make herself trustworthy; with this second chance, he overcomes his early mistrust. On the other hand, the child who comes through infancy with a vital sense of trust can still have his sense of mistrust activated at a later stage if, say, his parents are divorced and separated under acrimonious circumstances.

This point was brought home to me in a very direct way by a 4-year-old patient I saw in a court clinic. He was being seen at the court clinic because his adoptive parents, who had had him for six months, now wanted to give him back to the agency. They claimed that he was cold and unloving, took things and could not be trusted. He was indeed a cold and apathetic boy, but with good reason. About a year after his illegitimate birth, he was taken away from his mother, who had a drinking problem, and was shunted back and forth among several foster homes. Initially he had tried to relate to the persons in the foster homes, but the relationships never had a chance to develop because he was moved at just the wrong times. In the end he gave up trying to reach out to others, because the inevitable separations hurt too much.

Like the burned child who dreads the flame, this emotionally burned child shunned the pain of emotional involvement. He had trusted his mother, but now he trusted no one. Only years of devoted care and patience could now undo the damage that had been done to this child's sense of trust.

Autonomy vs. Doubt

Stage Two spans the second and third years of life, the period which Freudian theory calls the anal stage. Erikson sees here the emergence of *autonomy*. This autonomy dimension builds upon the child's new motor and mental abilities.

At this stage the child can not only walk but also climb, open and close, drop, push and pull, hold and let go. The child takes pride in these new accomplishments and wants to do everything himself, whether it be pulling the wrapper off a piece of candy, selecting the vitamin out of the bottle or flushing the toilet. If parents recognize the young child's need to do what he is capable of doing at his own pace and in his own time, then he develops a sense that he is able to control his muscles, his impulses, himself and, not insignificantly, his environment—the sense of autonomy.

When, however, his caretakers are impatient and do for him what he is capable of doing himself, they reinforce a sense of shame and doubt. To be sure, every parent has rushed a child at times and children are hardy enough to endure such lapses. It is only when caretaking is consistently overprotective and criticism of "accidents" (whether these be wetting, soiling, spilling or breaking things) is harsh and unthinking that the child develops an excessive sense of shame with respect to other people and an excessive sense of doubt about own abilities to control his world and himself.

If the child leaves this stage with less autonomy than shame or doubt, he will be handicapped in his attempts to achieve autonomy in adolescence and adulthood. Contrariwise, the child who moves through this stage with his sense of autonomy buoyantly outbalancing his feelings of shame and doubt is well prepared to be autonomous at later phases in the life cycle. Again, however, the balance of autonomy to shame and doubt set up during this period can be changed in either positive or negative directions by later events.

It might be well to note, in addition, that too much autonomy can be as harmful as too little. I have in mind a patient of 7 who had a heart condition. He had learned very quickly how terrified his parents were of any signs in him of cardiac difficulty. With the psychological acuity given to children, he soon ruled the household. The family could not go shopping, or for a drive, or on a holiday if he did not approve. On those rare occasions when the parents had had enough and defied him, he would get angry and his purple hue and gagging would frighten them into submission.

Actually, this boy was frightened of this power (as all children would be) and was really eager to give it up. When the parents and the boy came to realize this, and to recognize that a little shame and doubt were a healthy counterpoise to an inflated sense of autonomy, the three of them could once again assume their normal roles.

Initiative vs. Guilt

In this stage (the phallic stage of classical psychoanalysis) the child, age 4 to 5, is pretty much master of his body and can ride a tricycle, run, cut and hit. He can thus initiate motor activities of various sorts on his own and no longer merely responds to or imitates the actions of other children. The same holds true for his language and fantasy activities. Accordingly, Erikson argues that the social dimension that appears at this stage has *initiative* as one of its poles and *guilt* at the other.

Whether the child will leave this stage with his sense of initiative far out balancing his sense of guilt depends to a considerable extent upon how parents respond to his self-initiated activities. Children who are given much freedom and opportunity to initiate motor play such as running, bike riding, sliding, skating, tussling and wrestling have their sense of initiative reinforced. Initiative is also reinforced when parents answer their children's questions (intellectual initiative) and do not deride or inhibit fantasy or play activity. On the other hand, if the child is made to feel that his motor activity is bad, that his questions are a nuisance and that his play is silly and stupid, then he may develop a sense of guilt over self-initiated activities in general that will persist through later life stages.

Industry vs. Inferiority

Stage Four is the age period from 6 to 11, the elementary school years (described by classical psychoanalysis as the latency phase). It is a time during which the child's love for the parent of the opposite sex and rivalry with the same sexed parent (elements in the so-called family romance) are quiescent. It is also a period during which the child becomes capable of deductive reasoning, and of playing and learning by rules. It is not until this period, for example, that children can really play marbles, checkers and other "take turn" games that require obedience to rules. Erikson argues that the psychosocial dimension that emerges during this period has a sense of *industry* at one extreme and a sense of *inferiority* at the other.

The term industry nicely captures a dominant theme of this period during which the concern with how things are made, how they work and what they do predominates. It is the Robinson Crusoe age in the sense that the enthusiasm and minute detail with which Crusoe describes his activities appeals to the child's own budding sense of industry. When children are encouraged in their efforts to make, do, or build practical things (whether it be to construct creepy crawlers, tree houses, or airplane models or to cook, bake or sew), are allowed to finish their products, and are praised and rewarded for the results, then the sense of industry is enhanced. But parents who see their children's efforts at making and doing as "mischief," and as simply "making a mess," help to encourage in children a sense of inferiority.

During these elementary school years, however, the child's world includes more than the home. Now social institutions other than the family come to play a central role in the development of the individual. (Here Erikson introduced still another advance in psychoanalytic theory, which heretofore concerned itself only with the effects of the parents' behavior upon the child's development.)

A child's school experiences affect his industry-inferiority balance. The child, for example, with an I.Q. of 80 to 90 has a particularly traumatic school experience, even when his sense of industry is rewarded and encouraged at home. He is "too bright" to be in special classes, but "too slow" to compete with children of average ability. Consequently he experiences constant failures in his academic efforts that reinforces a sense of inferiority.

On the other hand, the child who had his sense of industry derogated at home can have it revitalized at school through the offices of a sensitive and committed teacher. Whether the child develops a sense of industry or inferiority, therefore, no longer depends solely on the caretaking efforts of the parents but on the actions and offices of other adults as well.

Identity vs. Role Confusion

When the child moves into adolescence (Stage Five — roughly the ages 12-18), he encounters, according to traditional psychoanalytic theory, a reawakening of the family-romance problem of early childhood. His means of resolving the problem is to seek and find a romantic partner of his own generation. While Erikson does not deny this aspect of adolescence, he points out that there are other problems as well. The adolescent matures mentally as well as physiologically, and in addition to the new feelings, sensations and desires he experiences as a result of changes in his body, he develops a multitude of new ways of looking at and thinking about the world. Among other things, those in adolescence can now think about other people's thinking and wonder about what other people think of them. They can also conceive of ideal families, religions and societies which they then compare with the imperfect families, religions and societies of their own experience. Finally, adolescents become capable of constructing theories and philosophies designed to bring all the varied and conflicting aspects of society into a working, harmonious and peaceful whole. The adolescent, in a word, is an impatient idealist who believes that it is as easy to realize an ideal as it is to imagine it.

Erikson believes that the new interpersonal dimension which emerges during this period has to do with a sense of *ego identity* at the positive end and a sense of *role confusion* at the negative end. That is to say, given the adolescent's newfound integrative abilities, his task is to bring together all of the things he has learned about himself as a son, student, athlete, friend, Scout, newspaper boy, and so on, and integrate these different images of himself into a whole that makes sense and that shows continuity with the past while preparing for the future. To the extent that the young person succeeds in this endeavor, he arrives at a sense of psychosocial identity, a sense of who he is, where he has been and where he is going.

In contrast to the earlier stages, where parents play a more or less direct role in the determination of the result of the developmental crises, the influence of parents during this stage is much more indirect. If the young person reaches adolescence with, thanks to his parents, a vital sense of trust, autonomy, initiative and industry, then his chances of arriving at a meaningful sense of ego identity are much enhanced. The reverse, of course, holds true for the young person who enters adolescence with considerable mistrust, shame, doubt, guilt and inferiority. Preparation for a successful adolescence, and the attainment of an integrated psychosocial identity must, therefore, begin in the cradle.

Over and above what the individual brings with him from his childhood, the attainment of a sense of personal identity depends upon the social milieu in which he or she grows up. For example, in a society where women are to some extent second-class citizens, it may be harder for females to arrive at a sense of psychosocial identity. Likewise at times, such as the present, when rapid social and technological change breaks down many traditional values, it may be more difficult for young people to find continuity between what they learned and experience as adolescents. At such times young people often seek causes that give their lives meaning and direction. The activism of the current generation of young people may well stem, in part at least, from this search.

When the young person cannot attain a sense of personal identity, either because of an unfortunate childhood or difficult social circumstances, he shows a certain amount of *role confusion* — a sense of not knowing what he is, where he belongs or whom he belongs to. Such confusion is a frequent symptom in delinquent young people. Promiscuous adolescent girls, for example, often seem to have a fragmented sense of ego identity. Some young people seek a "negative identity," an identity opposite to the one prescribed for them by their family and friends. Having an identity as a "delinquent," or as a "hippie," or even as an "acid head," may sometimes be preferable to having no identity at all.

In some cases young people do not seek a negative identity so much as they have it thrust upon them. I remember another court case in which the defendant was an attractive 16-year-old girl who had been found "tricking it" in a trailer located just outside the grounds of an Air Force base. From about the age of 12, her mother had encouraged her to dress seductively and to go out with boys. When she returned from dates, her sexually frustrated mother demanded a kiss-by-kiss, caress-by-caress description of the evening's activities. After the mother had vicariously satisfied her sexual needs, she proceeded to call her daughter a "whore" and a "dirty tramp." As the girl told me, "Hell, I have the name, so I might as well play the role."

Failure to establish a clear sense of personal identity at adolescence does not guarantee perpetual failure. And the person who attains a working sense of ego identity in adolescence will of necessity encounter challenges and threats to that identity as he moves through life. Erikson, perhaps more than any other personality theorist, has emphasized that life is constant change and that confronting problems at one stage in life is not a guarantee against the reappearance of these problems at later stages, or against the finding of new solutions to them.

Intimacy vs. Isolation

Stage Six in the life cycle is young adulthood; roughly the period of courtship and early family life that extends from late adolescence till early middle age. For this stage, and the stages described hereafter, classical psychoanalysis has nothing new or major to say. For Erikson, however, the previous attainment of a sense of personal identity and the engagement in productive work that marks this period gives rise to a new interpersonal dimension of *intimacy* at the one extreme and *isolation* at the other.

When Erikson speaks of intimacy he means much more than lovemaking alone; he means the ability to share with and care about another person without fear of losing oneself in the process. In the case of intimacy, as in the case of identity, success or failure no longer depends directly upon the parents but only indirectly as they have contributed to the individual's success or failure at the earlier stages. Here, too, as in the case of identity, social conditions may help or hinder the establishment of a sense of intimacy. Likewise, intimacy need not involve sexuality; it includes the relationship between friends. Soldiers who have served together under the most dangerous circumstances often develop a sense of commitment to one another that exemplifies intimacy in its broadest sense. If a sense of intimacy is not established with friends or a marriage partner, the result, in Erikson's view, is a sense of isolation—of being alone without anyone to share with or care for.

Generativity vs. Self-Absorption

This stage—middle age—brings with it what Erikson speaks of as either *generativity* or *self-absorption*, and stagnation. What Erikson means by generativity is that the person begins to be concerned with others beyond his immediate family, with future generations and the nature of the society and world in which those generations will live. Generativity does not reside only in parents; it can be found in any individual who actively concerns himself with the welfare of young people and with making the world a better place for them to live and to work.

Those who fail to establish a sense of generativity fall into a state of self-absorption in which their personal needs and comforts are of predominate concern. A fictional case of self-absorption is Dickens's Scrooge in "A Christmas Carol." In his one-sided concern with money and in his disregard for the interests and welfare of his young employee, Bob Cratchit, Scrooge exemplifies the self-absorbed, embittered (the two often go together) old man. Dickens also illustrated, however, what Erikson points out: namely, that unhappy solutions to life's crises are not irreversible. Scrooge, at the end of the tale, manifested both a sense of generativity and of intimacy which he had not experienced before.

Integrity vs. Despair

Stage Eight in the Eriksonian scheme corresponds roughly to the period when the individual's major efforts are nearing completion and when there is time for reflection — and for the enjoyment of grandchildren, if any. The psychosocial dimension that comes into prominence now has *integrity* on one hand and *despair* on the other.

The sense of integrity arises from the individual's ability to look back on his life with satisfaction. At the other extreme is the individual who looks back upon his life as a series of missed opportunities and missed directions; now in the twilight years he realizes that it is too late to start again. For such a person the inevitable result is a sense of despair at what might have been. (Box 96 pinpoints Erikson's most recent ideas regarding Stage Eight).

These, then, are the major stages in the life cycle as described by Erikson. Their presentation, for one thing, frees the clinician to treat adult emotional problems as failures (in part at least) to solve genuinely adult personality crises and not, as heretofore, as mere residuals of infantile frustrations and conflicts. This view of personality growth, moreover, takes some of the onus off parents and takes account of the role which society and the person himself play in the formation of an individual personality. Finally, Erikson has offered hope for us all by demonstrating that each phase of growth has its strengths as well as its weaknesses and that failures at one stage of development can be rectified by successes at later stages.

Box 96

Erikson Expands His View of Life

Mr. Erikson died in 1994. In the ninth decade of his life, he and his wife Joan put forth some new ideas about his eight stage model of the life cycle. In their new amplification, they point out that a positive resolution of the conflicts involved in each of the earlier stages of life adds to and matures into "full" wisdom in old age. The many facets of wisdom are presented below along with illustrative quotations.

Conflict and Resolution	Culminates in Old Age As:
Infancy: Trust vs. mistrust: hope	Appreciation of interdependence. "We need each other and the sooner we learn that the better for us all."
Early Childhood Autonomy vs. shame: will	Acceptance of the cycle of life. "The body deteriorates and one needs to learn to accept it."
Play Age Initiative vs. guilt: purpose	Humor and empathy. "I can't imagine a wise old person who can't laugh. The more you know yourself, the more patience you have for others."
School Age Industry vs. inferiority: competence	Humility. "Humility is a realistic appreciation of one's limits and competencies."
Adolescence Identity vs. role confusion: fidelity	Sense of complexity of life. "This leads to a new way of perceiving that merges sensory, logical, and esthetic perceptions. Too often people overemphasize logic."
Early Adulthood Intimacy vs. isolation: love	Love and sense of complexity of relationships. "You learn to love freely, in the sense of wanting nothing in return."
Adulthood Generativity vs. stagnation: care	Caring and concern for others. "The only thing that can save us as a species is seeing how we're not thinking about future generations in the way we live."
Old Age Integrity vs. despair: wisdom	*Full* wisdom. "If everything has gone well, one achieves a sense of completeness . . . strong enough to withstand physical disintegration. Real wisdom comes from life experience. It's not what comes from reading great books.

SOURCE: Daniel Goleman, "Erikson, In His Old Age, Expands His View of Life," *The New York Times*, June 14, 1988.

The reason that these ideas, which sound so agreeable to "common sense," are in fact so revolutionary has a lot to do with the state of psychoanalysis in America. As formulated by Freud, psychoanalysis encompassed a theory of personality development, a method of studying the human mind and, finally, procedures for treating troubled and unhappy people. Freud viewed this system as a scientific one, open to revision as new facts and observations accumulated.

The system was, however, so vehemently attacked that Freud's followers were constantly in the position of having to defend Freud's views. Perhaps because of this situation, Freud's system became, in the hands of some of his followers and defenders, a dogma upon which all theoretical innovation, clinical observation and therapeutic practice had to be grounded. That this attitude persists is evidenced in the recent remark by a psychoanalyst that he believed psychotic patients could not be treated by psychoanalysis because "Freud said so." Such attitudes, in which Freud's authority rather than observation and data is the basis of deciding what is true and what is false has contributed to the disrepute in which psychoanalysis is widely held today.

Erik Erikson has broken out of this scholasticism and has had the courage to say that Freud's discoveries and practices were the start and not the end of the study and treatment of the human personality. In addition to advocating the modifications of psychoanalytic theory outlined above, Erikson has also suggested modifications in the therapeutic practice, particularly in the treatment of young patients. "Young people in severe trouble are not fit for the couch," he writes. "They want to face you, and they want you to face them, not a facsimile of a parent or wearing the mask of a professional helper, but as a kind of over-all individual a young person can live with or despair of."

Erikson has had the boldness to remark on some of the negative effects that distorted notions of psychoanalysis have had on society at large. Psychoanalysis, he says, has contributed to a widespread fatalism—"even as we are trying to devise, with scientific determinism, a therapy for the few, we were led to promote an ethical disease among the many."

Perhaps Erikson's innovations in psychoanalytic theory are best exemplified in his psycho-historical writings, in which he combines psychoanalytic insight with a true historical imagination. After the publication of "Childhood and Society," Erikson undertook the application of his scheme of the human life cycle to the study of historical persons. He wrote a series of brilliant essays on men as varied as Maxim Gorky, George Bernard Shaw and Freud himself. These studies were not narrow case histories but rather reflected Erikson's remarkable grasp of Europe's social and political history, as well as of its literature. (His mastery of American folklore, history and literature is equally remarkable.)

While Erikson's major biographical studies were yet to come, these early essays already revealed his unique psycho-history method. For one thing,

Erikson always chose men whose lives fascinated him in one way or another, perhaps because of some conscious or unconscious affinity with them. Erikson thus had a sense of community with his subjects which he adroitly used (he calls it *disciplined subjectivity*) to take his subject's point of view and to experience the world as that person might.

Secondly, Erikson chose to elaborate a particular crisis or episode in the individual's life which seemed to crystallize a life-theme that united the activities of his past and gave direction to his activities for the future. Then, much as an artist might, Erikson proceeded to fill in the background of the episode and add social and historical perspective. In a very real sense Erikson's biographical sketches are like paintings which direct the viewer's gaze from a focal point of attention to background and back again, so that one's appreciation of the focal area is enriched by having pursued the picture in its entirety.

This method was given its first major test in Erikson's study of "Young Man Luther." Originally, Erikson planned only a brief study of Luther, but "Luther proved too bulky a man to be merely a chapter in a book." Erikson's involvement with Luther dated from his youth when, as a wandering artist, he happened to hear the Lord's Prayer in Luther's German. "Never knowingly having heard it, I had the experience, as seldom before or after, of a wholesomeness captured in a few simple words, of poetry fusing the esthetic and the moral; those who have suddenly 'heard' the Gettysburg Address will know what I mean."

Erikson's interest in Luther may have had other roots as well. In some ways, Luther's unhappiness with the papal intermediaries of Christianity resembled on a grand scale Erikson's own dissatisfaction with the intermediaries of Freud's system. In both cases some of the intermediaries had so distorted the original teachings that what was being preached in the name of the master came close to being the opposite of what he had himself proclaimed. While it is not possible to describe Erikson's treatment of Luther here, one can get some feeling for Erikson's brand of historical analysis from his sketch of Luther:

> Luther was a very troubled and a very gifted young man who had to create his own cause on which to focus his fidelity in the Roman Catholic world as it was then . . . He first became a monk and tried to solve his scruples by being an exceptionally good monk. But even his superiors thought that he tried much too hard. He felt himself to be such a sinner that he began to lose faith in the charity of God and his superiors told him,"Look, God doesn't hate you, you hate God or else you would trust Him to accept your prayers." But I would like to make it clear that someone like Luther becomes a historical person only because he also has an acute understanding of historical actuality and knows how to 'speak to the condition' of his times. Only then do inner struggles become representative

of those of a large number of vigorous and sincere young people — and begin to interest some troublemakers and hangers-on.

After Erikson's study of "Young Man Luther" (1958), he turned his attention to "middle-aged" Gandhi. As did Luther, Gandhi evoked for Erikson childhood memories. Gandhi led his first nonviolent protest in India in 1918 on behalf of some mill workers, and Erikson, then a young man of 16, had read glowing accounts of the event. Almost a half a century later Erikson was invited to Ahmedabad, an industrial city in western India, to give a seminar on the human life cycle. Erikson discovered that Ahmedabad was the city in which Gandhi had led the demonstration about which Erikson had read as a youth. Indeed, Erikson's host was none other than Ambalal Sarabahai, the benevolent industrialist who had been Gandhi's host — as well as antagonist — in the 1918 wage dispute. Throughout his stay in Ahmedabad, Erikson continued to encounter people and places that were related to Gandhi's initial experiments with nonviolent techniques.

The more Erikson learned about the event at Ahmedabad, the more intrigued he became with its pivotal importance in Gandhi's career. It seemed to be the historical moment upon which all the earlier events of Gandhi's life converged and from which diverged all of his later endeavors. So captured was Erikson by the event at Ahmedabad, that he returned the following year to research a book on Gandhi in which the event would serve as a fulcrum.

At least part of Erikson's interest in Gandhi may have stemmed from certain parallels in their lives. The 1918 event marked Gandhi's emergence as a national political leader. He was 48 at the time, and had become involved reluctantly, not so much out of a need for power or fame as out of a genuine conviction that something had to be done about the disintegration of Indian culture. Coincidentally, Erikson's book "Childhood and Society," appeared in 1950 when Erikson was 48, and it is that book which brought him national prominence in the mental health field. Like Gandhi, too, Erikson reluctantly did what he felt he had to do (namely, publish his observations and conclusions) for the benefit of his ailing profession and for the patients treated by its practitioners. So while Erikson's affinity with Luther seemed to derive from comparable professional identity crises, his affinity for Gandhi appears to derive from a parallel crisis of generativity. A passage from "Gandhi's Truth" (from a chapter wherein Erikson addresses himself directly to his subject) helps to convey Erikson's feeling for his subject.

> So far, I have followed you through the loneliness of your childhood and through the experiments and the scruples of your youth. I have affirmed my belief in your ceaseless endeavor to perfect yourself as a man who came to feel that he was the only one available to reverse India's fate. You experimented with what to you were debilitating temptations and you

did gain vigor and agility from your victories over yourself. Your identity could be no less than that of universal man, although you had to become an Indian — and one close to the masses — first.

The following passage speaks to Erikson's belief in the general significance of Gandhi's efforts:

> We have seen in Gandhi's development the strong attraction of one of those more inclusive identities: that of an enlightened citizen of the British Empire. In proving himself willing neither to abandon vital ties to his native tradition nor to sacrifice lightly a Western education which eventually contributed to his ability to help defeat British hegemony — in all of these seeming contradictions Gandhi showed himself on intimate terms with the actualities of his era. For in all parts of the world, the struggle now is for *the anticipatory development of more inclusive identities* . . . I submit then, that Gandhi, in his immense intuition for historical actuality and his capacity to assume leadership in "truth in action" may have created a ritualization through which men, equipped with both realism and strength, can face each other with mutual confidence.

There is now more and more teaching of Erikson's concepts in psychiatry, psychology, education and social work in America and in other parts of the world. His description of the stages of the life cycle are summarized in major textbooks in all of these fields, and clinicians are increasingly looking at their cases in Eriksonian terms.

Research investigators have, however, found Erikson's formulations somewhat difficult to test. This is not surprising, inasmuch as Erikson's conceptions, like Freud's, take into account the infinite complexity of the human personality. Current research methodologies are, by and large, still not able to deal with these complexities at their own level, and distortions are inevitable when such concepts as "identity" come to be defined in terms of responses to a questionnaire.

Likewise, although Erikson's life-stages have an intuitive "rightness" about them, not everyone agrees with his formulations. Douvan and Adelson in their book, "The Adolescent Experience," argue that while his identity theory may hold true for boys, it doesn't for girls. This argument is based on findings which suggest that girls postpone identity consolidation until after marriage (and intimacy) have been established. Such postponement occurs, says Douvan and Adelson, because a woman's identity is partially defined by the identity of the man whom she marries. This view does not really contradict Erikson's, since he recognizes that later events, such as marriage, can help to resolve both current and past developmental crises. For the woman, but not for the man, the problems of identity and intimacy may be solved concurrently.

Objections to Erikson's formulations have come from, other directions as well. Robert W. White, Erikson's good friend and colleague at Harvard, has a long standing (and warm-hearted) debate with Erikson over his life-stages. White believes that his own theory of "competence motivation," a theory which has received wide recognition, can account for the phenomena of ego development much more economically than can Erikson's stages. Erikson has, however, little interest in debating the validity of the stages he has described. As an artist he recognizes that there are many different ways to view one and the same phenomenon and that a perspective that is congenial to one person will be repugnant to another. He offers his stage-wise description of the life cycle for those who find such perspectives congenial and not as a world view that everyone should adopt.

It is this lack of dogmatism and sensitivity to the diversity and complexity of the human personality which help to account for the growing recognition of Erikson's contribution within as well as without the helping professions. Indeed, his psycho-historical investigations have originated a whole new field of study which has caught the interest of historians and political scientists alike. (It has also intrigued his wife, Joan, who has published pieces on Eleanor Roosevelt and who has a book on Saint Francis in press.) A recent issue of Daedalus, the journal for the American Academy of Arts and Sciences, was entirely devoted to psycho-historical and psycho-political investigations of creative leaders by authors from diverse disciplines who have been stimulated by Erikson's work.

Now in his 68th year, Erikson maintains the pattern of multiple activities and appointments which has characterized his entire career. He spends the fall in Cambridge, Mass., where he teaches a large course on "the human life cycle" for Harvard seniors. The spring semester is spent at his home in Stockbridge, Mass., where he participates in case conferences and staff seminars at the Austen Riggs Center. His summers are spent on Cape Cod. Although Erikson's major commitment these days is to his psycho-historical investigation, he is embarking on a study of preschool children's play constructions in different settings and countries, a follow-up of some research he conducted with preadolescents more than a quarter-century ago. He is also planning to review other early observations in the light of contemporary change. In his approach to his work, Erikson appears neither drawn nor driven, but rather to be following an inner schedule as natural as the life cycle itself.

Although Erikson, during his decade of college teaching, has not seen any patients or taught at psychoanalytic institutes, he maintains his dedication to psychoanalysis and his psycho-historical investigations as an applied branch of that discipline. While some older analysts continue to ignore Erikson's work, there is increasing evidence (including a recent poll of psychiatrists and psychoanalysts) that he is having a rejuvenating influence upon a discipline which many regard as dead or dying. Young analysts are today proclaiming a "new freedom" to see Freud in historical perspective—which reflects the Eriksonian view that one can recognize Freud's greatness without bowing to conceptual precedent.

Accordingly, the reports of the demise of psychoanalysis may have been somewhat premature. In the work of Erik Erikson, at any rate, psychoanalysis lives and continues to beget life.

Questions

1. What is an "identity crisis"?
2. How did Erikson's field work with the Sioux and the veterans of World War II affect his ideas?
3. What other factors in his background may have affected his ideas?
4. Give examples of the eight stages of development.
5. Are some stages more important than others?
6. Why does each stage have both a positive and a negative component?
7. To what extent can a failure at one stage of development be rectified by success at a later stage? Give examples.
8. Why do some critics say that Erikson's identity theory is true for boys and not girls?
9. What do the earlier stages contribute to the *full* wisdom that comes about in old age?
10. Someone said that "stage theories" are a little like horoscopes—vague enough to let everyone see something of themselves in them. Is this true?
11. In what ways are Freud and Erikson compatible? In what ways do their theories differ?
12. What is "psycho-history?" How did Erikson apply this methodology to Luther and Gandhi?

Chapter Forty

Final Note on a Case of Extreme Isolation

Kingsley Davis

Early in 1940 there appeared . . . an account of a girl called Anna.[1] She had been deprived of normal contact and had received a minimum of human care for almost the whole of her first six years of life. At that time observations were not complete and the report had a tentative character. Now, however, the girl is dead, and, with more information available,[2] it is possible to give a fuller and more definitive description of the case from a sociological point of view.

Anna's death, caused by hemorrhagic jaundice, occurred on August 6, 1942. Having been born on March 1 or 6,[3] 1932, she was approximately ten and a half years of age when she died. The previous report covered her development up to the age of almost eight years; the present one recapitulates the earlier period on the basis of new evidence and then covers the last two and a half years of her life.

Early History

The first few days and weeks of Anna's life were complicated by frequent changes of domicile. It will be recalled that she was an illegitimate child, the

"Final Note on a Case of Extreme Isolation" by Kingsley Davis. Reprinted from the *American Journal of Sociology,* 52: 5, 1947, pp. 432-437, with the permission of the author.

second such child born to her mother, and that her grandfather, a widowed farmer in whose house her mother lived, strongly disapproved of this new evidence of the mother's indiscretion. This fact led to the baby's being shifted about.

Two weeks after being born in a nurse's private home, Anna was brought to the family farm, but the grandfather's antagonism was so great that she was shortly taken to the house of one of her mother's friends. At this time a local minister became interested in her and took her to his house with an idea of possible adoption. He decided against adoption, however, when he discovered that she had vaginitis. The infant was then taken to a children's home in the nearest large city. This agency found that at the age of only three weeks she was already in a miserable condition, being "terribly galled and otherwise in very bad shape." It did not regard her as a likely subject for adoption but took her in for a while anyway, hoping to benefit her. After Anna had spent eight weeks in this place, the agency notified her mother to come to get her. The mother responded by sending a man and his wife to the children's home with a view to their adopting Anna, but they made such a poor impression on the agency that permission was refused. Later the mother came herself and took the child out of the home and then gave her to this couple. It was in the home of this pair that a social worker found the girl a short time thereafter. The social worker went to the mother's home and pleaded with Anna's grandfather to allow the mother to bring the child home. In spite of threats, he refused. The child by then more than four months old, was next taken to another children's home in a nearby town. A medical examination at this time revealed that she had impetigo, vaginitis, umbilical hernia, and skin rash.

Anna remained in this second children's home for nearly three weeks, at the end of which time she was transferred to a private foster-home Since, however, the grandfather would not, and the mother could not, pay for child's care, she was finally taken back as a last resort to the grandfather's house (at the age of five and a half months). There she remained, kept on the second floor in an attic-like room because her mother hesitated to incur the grandfather's wrath by bringing her downstairs.

The mother, a sturdy woman weighing about 180 pounds, did a man's work on the farm. She engaged in heavy work such as milking cows and tending hogs and had little time for her children. Sometimes she went out at night, in which case Anna was left entirely without attention. Ordinarily, it seems, Anna received only enough care to keep her barely alive. She appears to have been seldom moved from one position to another. Her clothing and bedding were filthy. She apparently had no instruction, no friendly attention. It is little wonder that, when finally found and removed from the room in the grandfather's house at the age of six years, the child could not talk, walk, or do anything that showed intelligence. She was in an extremely emaciated and undernourished condition, with skeleton-like legs and a bloated abdomen. She had been fed on virtually nothing except cow's milk during the years under her mother's care.

Anna's condition when found, and her subsequent improvement, have been described in the previous report. It now remains to say what happened to her after that.

Later History

In 1939, nearly two years after being discovered, Anna had progressed, as previously reported, to the point where she could walk, understand simple commands, feed herself, achieve some neatness, remember people, etc. But she still did not speak, and, though she was much more like a normal infant of something over one year of age in mentality, she was far from normal for her age.

On August 30, 1939, she was taken to a private home for retarded children, leaving the county home where she had been for more than a year and a half. In her new setting she made some further progress, but not a great deal. In a report of an examination made November 6 of the same year, the head of the institution pictured the child as follows:

> Anna walks about aimlessly, makes periodic rhythmic motions of her hands, and, at intervals, makes guttural and sucking noises. She regards her hands as if she had seen them for the first time. It was impossible to hold her attention for more than a few seconds at a time — not because of distraction due to external stimuli but because of her inability to concentrate. She ignored the task in hand to gaze vacantly about the room. Speech is entirely lacking. Numerous unsuccessful attempts have been made with her in the hope of developing initial sounds. I do not believe that this failure is due to negativism or deafness but that she is not sufficiently developed to accept speech at this time. . . .The prognosis is not favorable. . . .

More than five months later, on April 25, 1940, a clinical psychologist, the late Professor Francis N. Maxfield, examined Anna and reported the following: large for her age; hearing "entirely normal;" vision apparently normal; able to climb stairs; speech in the "babbling stage" and "promise for developing intelligible speech later seems to be good." He said further that "on the Merrill-Palmer scale she made a mental score of 19 months. On the Vineland social maturity scale she made a score of 23 months."[4]

Professor Maxfield very sensibly pointed out that prognosis is difficult in such cases of isolation. "It is very difficult to make scores on tests standardized under average conditions of environment and experience," he wrote, "and interpret them in a case where environment and experience have been so unusual." With this warning he gave it as his opinion at that time that Anna would eventually "attain an adult mental level of six or seven years."[5]

The school for retarded children, on July 1, 1941, reported that Anna had reached 46 inches in height and weighed 60 pounds. She could bounce and catch a ball and was said to conform to group socialization, though as a follower rather than a leader. Toilet habits were firmly established. Food habits were normal, except that she still used a spoon as her sole implement. She could dress herself except for fastening her clothes. Most remarkable of all, she had finally begun to develop speech. She was characterized as being at about the two-year level in this regard. She could call attendants by name and bring in one when she was asked to. She had a few complete sentences to express her wants. The report concluded that there was nothing peculiar about her, except that she was feeble-minded—"probably congenital in type."[6]

A final report from the school, made on June 22, 1942, and evidently the last report before the girl's death, pictured only a slight advance over that given above. It said that Anna could follow directions, string beads, identify a few colors, build with blocks, and differentiate between attractive and unattractive pictures. She had a good sense of rhythm and loved a doll. She talked mainly in phrases but would repeat words and try to carry on a conversation. She was clean about clothing. She habitually washed her hands and brushed her teeth. She would try to help other children. She walked well and could run fairly well, though clumsily. Although easily excited, she had a pleasant disposition.

Interpretation

Such was Anna's condition just before her death. It may seem as if she had not made much progress, but one must remember the condition in which she had been found. One must recall that she had no glimmering of speech, absolutely no ability to walk, no sense of gesture, not the least capacity to feed herself even when the food was put in front of her, and no comprehension of cleanliness. She was so apathetic that it was hard to tell whether or not she could hear. And all this at the age of nearly six years. Compared with this condition, her capacities at the time of her death seem striking indeed, though they do not amount to much more than a two-and-a-half-year mental level. One conclusion therefore seems safe, namely, that her isolation prevented a considerable amount of mental development that was undoubtedly part of her capacity. Just what her original capacity was, of course, is hard to say: but her development after her period of confinement (including the ability to walk and run, to play, dress, fit into a social situation, and, above all, to speak) shows that she had at least this much capacity—capacity that never could have been realized in her original condition of isolation.

A further question is this: What would she have been like if she had received a normal upbringing from the moment of birth? A definitive answer would have been impossible in any case, but even an approximate answer is made difficult by her early death. If one assumes, as was tentatively surmised in the previous report, that it is "almost impossible for any child to learn to speak, think, and act like a normal person after a long period of early isolation," it seems likely that Anna might have had a normal or near-normal capacity, genetically speaking. On the other hand, it was pointed out that Anna represented "a marginal case, [because] she was discovered before she had reached six years of age," an age "young enough to allow for some plasticity." [7] While admitting, then, that Anna's isolation *may* have been the major cause (and was certainly a minor cause) of her lack of rapid mental progress during the four and a half years following her rescue from neglect, it is necessary to entertain the hypothesis that she was congenitally deficient.

In connection with this hypothesis, one suggestive though by no means conclusive circumstance needs consideration, namely, the mentality of Anna's forebears. Information on this subject is easier to obtain, as one might guess, on the mother's than on the father's side. Anna's maternal grandmother, for example, is said to have been college educated and wished to have her children receive a good education, but her husband, Anna's stern grandfather, apparently a shrewd, hard-driving, calculating farm-owner, was so penurious that her ambitions in this direction were thwarted. Under the circumstances her daughter (Anna's mother) managed, despite having to do hard work on the farm, to complete the eighth grade in a country school. Even so, however, the daughter was evidently not very smart. "A schoolmate of [Anna's mother] stated that she was retarded in schoolwork; was very gullible at this age; and that her morals even at this time were discussed by other students." Two tests administered to her on March 4, 1938, when she was thirty-two years of age, showed that she was mentally deficient. On the Stanford Revision on the Binet-Simon Scale her performance was equivalent to that of a child of eight years, giving her an I.Q. of 50 and indicating mental deficiency of "middle-grade moron type." [8]

As to the identity of Anna's father, the most persistent theory holds that he was an old man about seventy-four years of age at the time of the girl's birth. If he was the one, there is no indication of mental or other biological deficiency, whatever one may think of his morals. However, someone else may actually have been the father.

To sum up: Anna's heredity is the kind that *might* have given rise to innate mental deficiency, though not necessarily.

Comparison with Another Case

Perhaps more to the point than speculations about Anna's ancestry would be a case for comparison. If a child could be discovered who had been isolated about the same length of time as Anna but had achieved a much quicker recovery and a greater mental development, it would be a stronger indication that Anna was deficient to start with.

Such a case does exist. It is the case of a girl at about the same time as Anna and under strikingly similar circumstances. A full description of the details of this case has not been published, but, in addition to newspaper reports, an excellent preliminary account by a speech specialist, Dr. Marie K. Mason, who played an important role in the handling of the child, has appeared.[9] Also the late Dr. Francis N. Maxfield, clinical psychologist at Ohio State University, as was Dr. Mason, has written an as yet unpublished but penetrating analysis of the case.[10] Some of her observations have been included in Professor Zingg's book on feral man.[11] The following discussion is drawn mainly from these enlightening materials. The writer, through the kindness of Professors Mason and Maxfield, did have a chance to observe the girl in April, 1940, and to discuss the features of her case with them.

Born apparently one month later than Anna, the girl in question, who has been given the pseudonym Isabelle, was discovered in November, 1938 nine months after the discovery of Anna. At the time she was found she was approximately six and a half years of age. Like Anna, she was an illegitimate child and had been kept in seclusion for that reason. Her mother was a deaf-mute, having become so at the age of two, and it appears that she and Isabelle had spent most of their time together in a dark room shut off from the rest of the mother's family. As a result Isabelle had no chance to develop speech; when she communicated with her mother, it was by means of gestures. Lack of sunshine and inadequacy of diet had caused Isabelle to become rachitic. Her legs in particular were affected; "they were so bowed that as she stood erect the soles of her shoes came nearly flat together, and she got about with a skittering gait."[12] Her behavior toward strangers, especially men, was almost that of a wild animal, manifesting much fear and hostility. In lieu of speech she made only a strange croaking sound. In many ways she acted like an infant. "She was apparently utterly unaware of relationships of any kind. When presented with a ball for the first time, she held it in the palm of her hand, then reached out and stroked my face with it. Such behavior is comparable to that of a child of six months."[13] At first it was even hard to tell whether or not she could hear, so unused were her senses. Many of her actions resembled those of deaf children.

It is small wonder that, once it was established that she could hear, specialists working with her believed her to be feeble-minded. Even on nonverbal tests her performance was so low as to promise little for the future. Her first score on the Stanford-Binet was 19 months, practically at the zero point of the scale. On the Vineland social maturity scale her first score was 39, representing an age level of two and a half years.[14] "The general impression was that she was wholly uneducable and that any attempt to teach her to speak, after so long a period of silence, would meet with failure."[15]

In spite of this interpretation, the individuals in charge of Isabelle launched a systematic and skillful program of training. It seemed hopeless at first. The approach had to be through pantomime and dramatization, suitable to an infant. It required one week of intensive effort before she even made her first attempt at vocalization. Gradually she began to respond, however, and, after the first hurdles had at last been overcome, a curious thing happened. She went through the usual stages of learning characteristic of the years from one to six not only in proper succession but far more rapidly than normal. In a little over two months after her first vocalization she was putting sentences together. Nine months after that she could identify words and sentences on the printed page, could write well, could add to ten, and could retell a story after hearing it. Seven months beyond this point she had a vocabulary of 1,500-2,000 words and was asking complicated questions. Starting from an educational level of between one and three years (depending on what aspect one considers), she had reached a normal level by the time she was eight and a half years old. In short, she covered in two years the stages of learning that ordinarily require six.[16] Or, to put it another way, her I.Q. trebled in a year and a half.[17] The speed with which she reached the normal level of mental development seems analogous to the recovery of body weight in a growing child after an illness, the recovery being achieved by an extra fast rate of growth for a period after the illness until normal weight for the given age is again attained.

When the writer saw Isabelle a year and a half after her discovery, she gave him the impression of being a very bright, cheerful, energetic little girl. She spoke well, walked and ran without trouble, and sang with gusto and accuracy. Today she is over fourteen years old and has passed the sixth grade in a public school. Her teachers say that she participates in all school activities as normally as other children. Though older than her classmates, she has fortunately not physically matured too far beyond their level.[18]

Clearly the history of Isabelle's development is different from that of Anna's. In both cases there was an exceedingly low, or rather blank, intellectual level to begin with. In both cases it seemed that the girl might be congenitally feeble-minded. In both a considerably higher level was reached later on. But the Ohio girl achieved a normal mentality within two years, whereas Anna was still marked inadequate at the end of four and a half years. This difference in achievement may suggest that Anna had less initial capacity. But an alternative hypothesis is possible.

One should remember that Anna never received the prolonged and expert attention that Isabelle received. The result of such attention, in the case of the Ohio girl, was to give her speech at an early stage, and her subsequent rapid development seems to have been a consequence of that. "Until Isabelle's speech and language development, she had all the characteristics of a feeble-minded child." Had Anna, who, from the standpoint of psychometric tests and early history, closely resembled this girl at the start, been given a mastery of speech at an earlier point by intensive training, her subsequent development might have been much more rapid.[19] (Box 97 calls to our attention that there may be "critical" or "sensitive" periods which affect our language development.)

Box 97

Critical or Sensitive Periods and Language

When asking what is essential to being a human being, the answer that often comes to mind is the ability to think, reason, and anticipate future events. In a sense, this is the right answer, but the question still remains: what makes it possible to think, reason, and anticipate? The answer is language — verbal and nonverbal. Language is more than words: it is a system of arbitrary symbols (or signs) which stand for or represent something else, be it a physical object or an idea or feeling. Language is crucial because it not only enables human beings to communicate with other human beings, but it also structures their thinking, their activities, and even their feelings. Without language, socialization would not be possible. Language gives humans a flexibility that no other animal has. Free from the world of direct and immediate experience, humans can solve problems, imagine, create, and recreate experience internally.

It may be that there are "critical" or "sensitive" periods when humans are most open to experiences which will affect learning abilities. Certainly this is true for emotional development. If a child does not have a warm, secure, positive emotional relationship during the first year of life, the child may forever be hampered in later development. If children do not learn language before puberty, can they *ever* learn language or learn it well? Data gathered about people who are learning a new language, as well as people who have had some kind of brain injury, indicate that puberty may be a cut-off point for easy recovery. We know that immigrants to this country are amazed as their pre-school children become quickly fluent in English as well as their parents' language, while the parents are slogging through the English as a Second Language Program. Before puberty, learning a new language comes easily and the person comes to speak it without any accent derived from their original language; after puberty, it is difficult to learn another language without retraining an accent from one's mother tongue. Another example of sensitivity before puberty comes from the study of aphasias. Aphasias are the loss of one or more language functions due to an injury to the brain. As with learning a new language, researchers have found that if the injury to the brain occurred before puberty, children will recover almost all of their language functions without therapy. After puberty, it is a much longer and more difficult process.

SOURCE: Frank Zulke and Jacqueline Kirley

The hypothesis that Anna began with a sharply inferior mental capacity is therefore not established. Even if she were deficient to start with, we have no way of knowing how much so. Under ordinary conditions she might have been a dull normal or, like her mother, a moron. Even after the blight of her isolation, if she had lived to maturity, she might have finally reached virtually the full level of her capacity, whatever it may have been. That her isolation did have a profound effect upon her mentality, there can be no doubt. This is proved by the substantial degree of change during the four and a half years following her rescue.

Consideration of Isabelle's case serves to show, as Anna's case does not clearly show, that isolation up to the age of six, with failure to acquire any form of speech and hence failure to grasp nearly the whole world of cultural meaning, does not preclude the subsequent acquisitions of these. Indeed, there seems to be a process of accelerated recovery in which the child goes through the mental stages at a more rapid rate than would be the case in normal development. Just what would be the maximum age at which a person could remain isolated and still retain the capacity for full cultural acquisition is hard to say. Almost certainly it would not be as high as age fifteen; it might possibly be as low as age ten. (Box 98 describes a more recent case of childhood isolation which suggests that age thirteen may already be too late.) Undoubtedly various individuals would differ considerably as to the exact age.

Box 98

Genie

Genie was a thirteen and a half year old girl who was found in California in 1970. She had been deprived of socialization for about twelve years — twice as long as Anna or Isabelle. She was strapped to a potty chair or caged in a crib throughout most of her childhood. Her father would beat her if she made any noise. Her terrified mother, forbidden to speak to her, fed her in silence and haste. Upon discovery, she weighed 59 pounds and had the mental development and social maturity of a one-year-old child. She was incontinent, masturbated excessively, and did not vocalize in any way. For the next eight years, social workers, psycholinguists, speech therapists, and special education teachers worked intensively with her. Her ability to use language, however, never became better than that of a four-year-old child. She was finally placed in an institution. There may be a point at which isolation in infancy results in damage that cannot be repaired. Some hypothesize that without social experience leading to the development of language in early childhood, the human brain loses much of its capacity for subsequent development.

SOURCE: Maya Pines, "The Civilization of Genie" in *Psychology Today* 15, (1981)

Anna's is not an ideal case for showing the effects of extreme isolation, partly because she was possibly deficient to begin with, partly because she did not receive the best training available, and partly because she did not live long enough. Nevertheless, her case is instructive when placed in the record with numerous other cases of extreme isolation. This and the previous article about her are meant to place her in the record. It is to be hoped that other cases will be described in the scientific literature as they are discovered (as unfortunately they will be), for only in these rare cases of extreme iosolation is it possible "to observe *concretely separated* two factors in the development of human personality which are always otherwise only analytically separated, the biogenic and the sociogenic factors."[20] (Box 99 tackles this issue in a different way.)

Box 99

Feral Children, Institutionalized Children, and Monkeys

The cases of Anna and Isabelle provide evidence that "human" development is acquired through social contact with other humans. Additional evidence from three other sources—studies of feral children, studies of institutionalized children, and studies of monkeys raised in isolation—lend further support for this idea.

1. Studies of feral children

    History is replete with tales of lost or deserted feral children, who were raised by animals. Tarzan was raised by apes. Rome was supposedly founded by Romulus and Remus, two children who had been raised by a wolf. One of the most famous "documented" cases is the "wild boy of Aveyron." In 1797, three hunters found a naked eleven year old boy in a forest in southern France. He shuffled about on all fours, could only make animal-like noises, and bit and scratched anyone who approached him. At first he was paraded around Paris as a freak who had been raised by animals. But a physician named Jean Itard felt that he could train the child and make him normal. Even after five years of devoted effort, the boy did not become fully human. He never learned to speak nor to interact with anyone. Dr. Itard concluded that lack of early human contact was the reason. If certain things are not learned early, he said, they may never be learned.

SOURCE: Harlan Lane, *The Wild Boy of Aveyron* (Cambridge: Harvard University Press, 1976).

2. Studies of Institutionalized Children

Studies of institutionalized children indicate that isolation need not be as extreme as it was for Anna and Isabelle to affect a child's personal and social development. They indicate that children may be affected adversely when the degree of contact is simply limited or when emotional attachments cannot be formed. Casler, for example, found that the developmental growth rate of institutionalized children can be affected by only 20 minutes of "touching" a day. Spitz examined comparable groups of children in orphanages and in women's prison nurseries and found children in orphanages to be retarded and psychologically underdeveloped. He traced this to the small amount of emotional and mental stimulation available in the orphanages. Goldfarb compared institutionalized children with those in foster homes and found the institutionalized children had difficulty caring for others and were immature and passive. This persisted even after the children had been placed in foster homes. It does indeed seem that isolation need not be as extreme as it was for Anna and Isabelle before there are adverse effects.

SOURCES: Lawrence Casler, "The Effect of Extra Tactile Stimulation on a Group of Institutionalized Infants" in *Genetic Psychology Monographs* 71 (1965); Rene Spitz, "Hospitalism" in Anna Freud, et al. (eds.) the *Psychoanalytic Study of the Child* (New York: International Universities Press, 1965); William Goldfarb, "Psychological Privation in Infancy and Subsequent Privation" in *American Journal of Orthopsychiatry* 15 (1945).

3. Studies of Monkeys Raised in Isolation

A series of experiments on the effect of isolation on rhesus monkeys showed that even in monkeys, social behavior is learned, not inherited. Monkeys isolated for as little as six months grew up to be fearful of, and/or hostile to, other monkeys. They did not know how to mate and could not be taught to do so. Artificially impregnated mothers turned out to be abusive mothers. One experiment offered monkey infants two

substitute mothers, one made of wire with a feeding bottle and one made
of terry cloth without a bottle. The monkey infants preferred the cuddly
"mother" to the one that fed them.

SOURCES: Harry Harlow and Margaret Harlow, "Social Deprivation in Monkeys"
in *Scientific American* 207 (1962); Harry Harlow and R.R. Zimmerman, "Affectional
Responses in the Infant Monkey" in *Science* 130 (1959).

Questions

1. Why is the social scientist interested in isolated children?
2. Contrast the development of Anna and Isabelle. In what ways is it alike and in what ways different?
3. Why is language so important to socialization?
4. Is there a critical period that affects language development?
5. Why do you think that most cultures throughout the world have tales and legends about feral children? Why is it so hard to document them?
6. Would abandoned animals develop abnormalities?
7. Humans are not monkeys. Of what use, then, are experiments like those conducted by Harry Harlow and his associates?
8. What do you think is the maximum age to which a person can remain isolated and still retain the capacity for full cultural acquisition?
9. Does the case of Genie add any new information about the effects of isolation on children?
10. Discuss this statement: "You can't be human all by yourself."
11. Davis closes by saying that only in cases of isolation is it possible "to observe *concretely separated* two factors in the development of human personality which are always otherwise only analytically separated, the biogenic and the sociogenic factors." What does this mean?
12. Is it reasonable to conclude that the largest part of what we usually consider human is acquired through social contact with other humans? What kinds of empirical evidence support this idea?

Chapter Forty-One

Shattered Innocence

Alfie Kohn

No one would claim today that child sexual abuse happens in only one family in a million. Yet that preposterous estimate, based on statistics from 1930, was published in a psychiatric textbook as recently as 1975. Sensational newspaper headlines about day-care center scandals seem to appear almost daily and, together with feminist protests against sexist exploitation, these reports have greatly increased public awareness of what we now know is a widespread problem.

Even so, the most recent scientific findings about child sexual abuse—how often it happens and how it affects victims in the short and long term—have received comparatively little attention. These findings suggest that as many as 40 million people, about one in six Americans, may have been sexually victimized as children. As many as a quarter of these people may be suffering from a variety of psychological problems, ranging from guilt and poor self-esteem to sexual difficulties and a tendency to raise children who are themselves abused.

The startling figure of 40 million is derived from several studies indicating that 25 to 35 percent of all women and 10 to 16 percent of all men in this country experienced some form of abuse as children, ranging from sexual fondling to intercourse. In August 1985, *The Los Angeles Times* published the results of a national telephone poll of 2,627 randomly selected adults. Overall, 22 percent of respondents (27 percent of the women and 16 percent of the

From *Psychology Today,* February 1987, pp. 54-58. Copyright © 1987 by Alfie Kohn. Reprinted with permission of the author.

men) confided that they had experienced as children what they now identify as sexual abuse.

Some victims of abuse may be reluctant to tell a stranger on the telephone about something as traumatic and embarrassing as sexual abuse, which suggests that even the *Times* poll may have understated the problem. When sociologist Diana Russell of Mills College sent trained interviewers around San Francisco to interview 930 randomly selected women face-to-face, she found that 357, or 38 percent, reported at least one instance of having been sexually abused in childhood. When the definition of abuse was widened to include sexual advances that never reached the stage of physical contact, more than half of those interviewed said they had had such an experience before the age of 18.

Confirming the *Times* and Russell studies is a carefully designed Gallup Poll of more than 2,000 men and women from 210 Canadian communities. The results, published in 1984, show that 22 percent of the respondents were sexually abused as children. As with Russell's study, that number increases dramatically, to 39 percent, when noncontact abuse is included.

John Briere, a postdoctoral fellow at Harbor-University of California, Los Angeles Medical Center, has reviewed dozens of studies of child abuse in addition to conducting several of his own. "It is probable," he says, "that at least a quarter to a third of adult women and perhaps half as many men have been sexually victimized as children."

One reason these numbers are so surprising, and the reason estimates of one family in a million could be taken seriously for so long, is that many children who are sexually abused understandably keep this painful experience to themselves. In the *Times* poll, one-third of those who said they had been victimized also reported that they had never before told anyone. Many therapists still do not bother to ask their clients whether abuse has taken place, even when there is good reason to suspect that it has.

Studies demonstrate that most child sexual abuse happens to those between the ages of 9 and 12 (although abuse of 2- and 3-year-olds is by no means unusual), that the abuser is almost always a man and that he is typically known to the child—often a relative. In many cases, the abuse is not limited to a single episode, nor does the abuser usually use force. No race, ethnic group or economic class is immune.

All children do not react identically to sexual abuse. But most therapists would agree that certain kinds of behavior and feelings occur regularly among victims. The immediate effects of sexual abuse include sleeping and eating disturbances, anger, withdrawal and guilt. The children typically appear to be either afraid or anxious.

Two additional signs show up so frequently that experts rely upon them as indicators of possible abuse when they occur together. The first is sexual preoccupation: excessive or public masturbation and an unusual interest in sexual organs, sex play and nudity. According to William Friedrich, associate professor of psychology at the Mayo Medical School in Rochester, Minnesota, "What seems to happen is the socialization process toward propriety goes awry in these kids."

The second sign consists of a host of physical complaints or problems, such as rashes, vomiting and headaches, all without medical explanation. Once it is discovered that children have been abused, a check of their medical records often reveals years of such mysterious ailments, says psychologist Pamela Langelier, director of the Vermont Family Forensic Institute in South Burlington, Vermont. Langelier emphasizes that children who have been sexually abused should be reassessed every few years because they may develop new problems each time they reach a different developmental stage. "Sometimes it looks like the kids have recovered," she says, "and then at puberty the issues come back again."

While there are clear patterns in the immediate effects of child sexual abuse, it is far more difficult to draw a definitive connection between such abuse and later psychological problems. "We can't say every child who is abused has this or that consequence, and we are nowhere near producing a validated profile of a child-abuse victim," says Mariz Sauzier, a psychiatrist who used to direct the Family Crisis Program for Sexually Abused Children at the New England Medical Center in Boston. In fact, some experts emphasize that many sexual abuse victims emerge relatively unscathed as adults. Indeed, David Finkelhor, associate director of the Family Violence Research Program at the University of New Hampshire, has warned his colleagues against "exaggerating the degree and inevitability of the long-term negative effects of sexual abuse." For example, Finkelhor and others point out that studies of disturbed, atypical groups, such as prostitutes, runaways, and drug addicts, often find that they show higher rates of childhood sexual abuse than in the general population. Yet according to the estimate of Chris Bagley, a professor of social welfare at the University of Calgary, "At least 50 percent of women who were abused do not suffer long-term ill effects."

If 50 percent survive abuse without problems, of course it follows that 50 percent do not. And Bagley, in fact, has conducted a study indicating that a quarter of all women who are sexually abused develop serious psychological problems as a result. Given the epidemic proportions of sexual abuse, that means that millions are suffering.

Briere, for example, has found a significant degree of overlap between abuse victims and those who suffer from "borderline personality disorder," people whose relationships, emotions and sense of self are all unstable and who often become inappropriately angry or injure themselves. "Not all borderlines have been sexually abused, but many have been," Briere says.

Briere, working with graduate student Marsha Runtz, has also noticed that some female abuse victims "space out" or feel as if they are outside of their own bodies at times. And he has observed that these women sometimes have physical complaints without any apparent medical cause. Briere points out that these two tendencies, known as "dissociation" and "somatization," add up to something very much like hysteria, as Freud used the term.

Other therapists believe the label Post-Traumatic Stress Disorder (PTSD), which has most often been applied to veterans of combat, may also be an appropriate diagnosis for some of those who have been abused. Symptoms of the disorder include flashbacks to the traumatic events, recurrent dreams about them, a feeling of estrangement from others and a general sense of numbness. "It feels to me like the fit is very direct to what we see with (victims of) child sexual abuse," says Christine Courtois, a psychologist from Washington D.C. "Many victims . . . experience the symptoms of acute PTSD." She describes an 18-year-old client, abused by her father for nine years, who carved the words "help me" in her arm. In the course of dealing with what had happened, she would sometimes pass out, an occasional response to extreme trauma.

Even when no such serious psychological problems develop, those who were sexually abused often display a pattern of personal and social problems. Abused individuals in psychotherapy have more difficulties with sexuality and relationships than do others in psychotherapy, for instance. And women who have been victimized often have difficulty becoming sexually aroused. Ironically, others engage in sex compulsively.

Abused women often feel isolated, remain distrustful of men and see themselves as unattractive. "Some (victims) become phobic about intimacy. They can't be touched," says Gail Ericson, a social worker at the Branford Counseling Center in Connecticut. "These women feel rotten about themselves—especially their bodies." As a group, adults who were sexually abused as children consistently have lower self-esteem than others. Other studies have found abuse victims to be more anxious, depressed and guilt-ridden.

Might there be a connection between the high incidence of child sexual abuse among girls and the fact that women tend, in general, to score lower on measures of self-esteem than men? Bagley believes that this disparity may simply reflect the fact that in our society, more women are abused: Seven of ten victims are girls, so any random sampling of men and women will pick up more abused women than men, perhaps enough of a difference to account for the gender gap in self-esteem.

In one study, Bagley discovered that half of all women with psychological problems had been abused. "The reason for the higher rate (of psychopathology) for women is the higher rate of sexual abuse in women," he says. Other researchers might not support so sweeping a conclusion, but Bagley points to a study of his that showed that nonabused men and women have comparable self-esteem.

One of the most disturbing findings about child abuse is its strong intergenerational pattern: Boys who are abused are far more likely to turn into offenders, molesting the next generation of children; girls are more likely to produce children who are abused. Two of five abused children in a study conducted by Sauzier, psychologist Beverly Gomes-Schwartz and psychiatrist Jonathan Horowitz had mothers who were themselves abused.

In addition, victimization can lead to revictimization. Nearly two-thirds of those in Russell's survey who had been abused as children reported that they were later victims of rape or attempted rape. Abuse victims "don't know how to take care of themselves," Courtois says. "They're easy targets for somebody, waiting for victimization to happen." This may be due to poor self-image, lack of assertiveness or the feeling that they deserve to be punished.

Women, of course, are not to blame for being victims. "In a society that raises males to behave in a predatory fashion toward females, undermining a young girl's defenses is likely to be exceedingly perilous for her," Russell says, since childhood abuse "could have stripped away some of (her) potential ability to protect" herself.

Men who were abused, meanwhile, are likely to be confused about their sexual identity, deeply ashamed, unwilling to report the experience and apt to respond aggressively. Says Jack Rusinoff, a counselor in Minneapolis who works with male victims, "I have one five-year-old boy who's already on the road to being an abuser." This boy, like many others, has displayed sexual aggression, even at this age. Langelier, who has seen more than 200 victims over the last three years, notes that her young male clients are sometimes caught reaching for others' genitals or "making demands for sexual stimulation."

Is there any indication, given this variation in psychological outcome, why one case of childhood sexual abuse leads to serious adult problems while another does not? So far, only two characteristics of abuse have consistently been linked with major difficulties later on. For one, studies by Bagley, Briere and others have shown that the prognosis is particularly bad for those who have been abused by more than one person. Counselor Claire Walsh, director of the Sexual Assault Recovery Service at the University of Florida, has paid special attention to this subgroup. She studied thirty women who were in psychotherapy and who had been abused by their fathers, eighteen of whom had also been abused by at least one other person. Walsh found a different psychological profile for those who had been molested by more than one person, which included more anxiety, fear and flashbacks. She also believes that PTSD may show up more often when there is more than one abuser.

Another important variable is the age of the abuser. Russell found that victims are most traumatized if their abuser was between the ages of 26 and 50.

Victims seem to experience more serious problems if force is used during the abuse and if the abuser is a close relative, but evidence for these claims is not conclusive.

Obviously, large gaps remain in the research on the long-term effects of child sexual abuse. This is not very surprising given how new the field is. Most of the studies reported here have been conducted since 1980, and the five scholarly journals devoted to the subject have all been launched within the last two years. Only in 1986 was the groundwork finally laid for an American professional society dealing with sexual child abuse.

There is no question that the field already has produced striking findings. "We now clearly know that sexual abuse is a major risk factor for a lot of later mental-health problems," Finkelhor says. "What we don't yet know is who is most susceptible to these problems, how other experiences interact with abuse or what can be done."

Box 100

Childhood Through the Ages

Were things better for children in the past? While no figures for sexual abuse are available, historical research in other areas indicates that childhood in earlier ages was often a nightmare.

1. Infanticide was common from antiquity to medieval times. Ratios of boys to girls ran as high as four to one since it was uncommon for more than one girl in a family to be spared.

2. Infants were "swaddled" in tightly bound clothes their first year. They might be thrown about like a ball for amusement. A brother of King Henri IV of France was dropped and killed while being tossed from one window to another.

3. Regular beatings and batterings occurred at home and in school even for such behavior as crying or wanting to play. Parents believed that "If you spare the rod, you spoil the child."

4. Wealthy parents would send their infants to breast-feed in the home of a wet nurse and to be returned at age three or four.

5. Children would work as soon as they were physically able to do so. This was true in the U.S. until 1900 and is probably still true in third world countries today.

SOURCE: Lloyd DeMause, *The History of Childhood* (New York: Psychohistory Press, 1974).

Finkelhor adds that research on child sexual abuse "should teach all social scientists and mental-health practitioners some humility. Despite several generations of clinical expertise and knowledge of childhood development, it was only very recently that we came to see how incredibly widespread this childhood trauma is.

"It may make us realize that there are other things about childhood that we don't have a clear perspective on as well," he says.

Questions

1. How accurate is the claim that childhood abuse happens in only one family in a million?

2. Why has the public only recently become aware of childhood sex abuse?

3. How does sex abuse affect victims in the short run?

4. How does sex abuse affect victims in the long run?

5. Is there a connection between the high incidence of sexual abuse among girls and the fact that women tend to score lower on measures of self-esteem than men?

6. Does research into child abuse indicate any intergenerational patterns?

7. The article says "victimization can lead to revictimization." What does this mean?

8. Some cases of childhood sexual abuse lead to serious adult problems and some do not. Why is that?

9. Why might research on childhood sexual abuse teach social scientists and mental health practitioners humility?

10. Did our forebears treat children better or worse in ages past?

11. In 1994, a 34 year-old man filed a $10 million lawsuite against Joseph Cardinal Bernardin of Chicago, charging that he sexually abused him when he was 17 years old. He said he had remembered the abuse a month before under hypnosis, while he was in therapy. Three months later, the man dropped the charges, saying, "I now realize that the memories which arose during and after hypnosis are unreliable." How can it be determined which recovered memories of sexual abuse that suddenly come to consciousness represent full and accurate renditions of past events and which don't?

Chapter Forty-Two

The Sounds of Silence

Edward T. Hall and Mildred R. Hall

Bob leaves his apartment at 8:15 A.M. and stops at the corner drugstore for breakfast. Before he can speak, the counterman says, "The usual?" Bob nods yes. While he savors his Danish, a fat man pushes onto the adjoining stool and overflows into his space. Bob scowls, and the man pulls himself in as much as he can. Bob has sent two messages without speaking a syllable.

Henry has an appointment to meet Arthur at 11:00 A.M.; he arrives at 11:30. Their conversation is friendly, but Arthur retains a lingering hostility. Henry has unconsciously communicated that he doesn't think the appointment is very important or that Arthur is a person who needs to be treated with respect.

George is talking to Charley's wife at a party. Their conversation is entirely trivial, yet Charley glares at them suspiciously. Their physical proximity and the movements of their eyes reveal that they are powerfully attracted to each other.

José Ybarra and Sir Edmund Jones are at the same party, and it is important for them to establish a cordial relationship for business reasons. Each is trying to be warm and friendly, yet they will part with mutual distrust, and their business transaction will probably fall through. José, in Latin fashion moves closer and closer to Sir Edmund as they speak, and his movement is being miscommunicated as pushiness to Sir Edmund, who keeps backing away from this intimacy, which in turn is being miscommunicated to José as coldness.

Edward T. Hall and Mildred R. Hall. "The Sounds of Silence." *Playboy*, 1971.

The silent languages of Latin and English cultures are more difficult to learn than their spoken languages.

In each of these cases, we see the subtle power of nonverbal communication. The only language used throughout most of the history of humanity (in evolutionary terms, vocal communication is relatively recent), it is the first form of communication you learn. You use this preverbal language, consciously and unconsciously, every day to tell other people how you feel about yourself and them. This language includes your posture, gestures, facial expressions, costume, the way you walk, even your treatment of time and space and material things. All people communicate on several different levels at the same time but are usually aware of only the verbal dialogue and don't realize that they respond to nonverbal messages. But when a person says one thing and really believes something else, the discrepancy between the two can usually be sensed. Nonverbal communication systems are much less subject to the conscious deception that often occurs in verbal systems. When we find ourselves thinking, "I don't know what it is about him, but he doesn't seem sincere," it's usually this lack of congruity between a person's words and his behavior that makes us anxious and uncomfortable.

Few of us realize how much we all depend on body movement in our conversation or are aware of the hidden rules that govern listening behavior. But we know instantly whether or not the person we're talking to is "tuned in," and we're very sensitive to any breach in listening etiquette. In white middle-class American culture, when someone wants to show he is listening to someone else, he looks either at the other person's face or, specifically, at his eyes, shifting his gaze from one eye to the other.

If you observe a person conversing, you'll notice that he indicates he's listening by nodding his head. He also makes little "Hmm" noises. If he agrees 'with what's being said, he may give a vigorous nod. To show pleasure or affirmation, he smiles; if he has some reservations, he looks skeptical by raising an eyebrow or pulling down the corners of his mouth. If a participant wants to terminate the conversation, he may start shifting his body position, stretching his legs, crossing or uncrossing them, bobbing his foot, or diverting his gaze from the speaker. The more he fidgets, the more the speaker becomes aware that he has lost his audience. As a last measure, the listener may look at his watch to indicate the imminent end of the conversation.

Talking and listening are so intricately intertwined that a person cannot do one without the other. Even when one is alone and talking to oneself, there is part of the brain that speaks while another part listens. In all conversations, the listener is positively or negatively enforcing the speaker all the time. He may even guide the conversation without knowing it, by laughing or frowning or dismissing the argument with a wave of his hand.

The language of the eyes — another age-old way of exchanging feelings — is both subtle and complex. Not only do men and women use their eyes differently, but there are class, generation, regional, ethnic, and national cultural differences. Americans often complain about the way foreigners stare at people or hold a glance too long. Most Americans look away from someone who is using his eyes in an unfamiliar way because it makes them self-conscious. If a man looks at another man's wife in a certain way, he's asking for trouble, as indicated earlier. But he might not be ill-mannered or seeking to challenge the husband. He might be a European in this country who hasn't learned our visual mores. Many American women visiting France or Italy are acutely embarrassed because, for the first time in their lives, men really look at them — their eyes, hair, nose, lips, breasts, hips, legs, thighs, knees, ankles, feet, clothes, hairdo, even their walk. These same women, once they have become used to being looked at, often return to the United States and are overcome with the feeling that "No one ever really looks at me anymore."

Analyzing the mass of data on the eyes, it is possible to sort out at least three ways in which the eyes are used to communicate: dominance vs. submission, involvement vs. detachment, and positive vs. negative attitude. In addition, there are three levels of consciousness and control, which can be categorized as follows: (1) conscious use of the eyes to communicate, such as the flirting blink and the intimate nosewrinkling squint; (2) the very extensive category of unconscious but learned behavior governing where the eyes are directed and when (this unwritten set of rules dictates how and under what circumstances the sexes, as well as people of all status categories, look at each other); and (3) the response of the eye itself; which is completely outside both awareness and control — changes in the cast (sparkle) of the eye and the pupillary reflex.

The eye is unlike any other organ of the body, for it is an extension of the brain. The unconscious pupillary reflex and the cast of the eye have been known by people of Middle Eastern origin for years — although most are unaware of their knowledge. Depending on the context, Arabs and others look either directly at the eyes or deeply into the eyes of their interlocutor. We became aware of this in the Middle East several years ago while looking at jewelry. The merchant suddenly started to push a particular bracelet at a customer and said, "You buy this one." What interested us was that the bracelet was not the one that had been consciously selected by the purchaser. But the merchant, watching the pupils of the eyes, knew what the purchaser really wanted to buy. Whether he specifically knew how he knew is debatable.

A psychologist at the University of Chicago, Eckhard Hess, was the first to conduct systematic studies of the pupillary reflex. His wife remarked one evening, while watching him reading in bed, that he must be very interested in the text because his pupils were dilated. Following up on this, Hess slipped some pictures of nudes into a stack of photographs that he gave to his male assistant. Not looking at the photographs but watching his assistant's pupils, Hess was able to tell precisely when the assistant came to the nudes. In further experiments, Hess retouched the eyes in a photograph of a woman. In one print, he made the pupils small, in another, large; nothing else was changed. Subjects who were given the photographs found the woman with the dilated pupils much more attractive. Any man who has had the experience of seeing a woman look at him as her pupils widen with reflex speed knows that she's flashing him a message.

The eye-sparkle phenomenon frequently turns up in our interviews of couples in love. It's apparently one of the first reliable clues in the other person that love is genuine. To date, there is no scientific data to explain eye sparkle; no investigation of the pupil, the cornea, or even the white sclera of the eye shows how the sparkle originates. Yet we all know it when we see it.

One common situation for most people involves the use of the eyes in the street and in public. Although eye behavior allows a definite set of rules, the rules vary according to the place, the needs and feelings of the people, and their ethnic background. For urban whites, once they're within definite recognition distance (sixteen to thirty-two feet for people with average eyesight), there is mutual avoidance of eye contact — unless they want something specific: a pickup, a handout, or information of some kind. In the West and in small towns generally, however, people are much more likely to look and greet one another, even it they are strangers.

It's permissible to look at people if they're beyond recognition distance, but once inside this sacred zone, you can only steal a glance at strangers. You *must* greet friends, however; to fail to do so is insulting. Yet, to stare too fixedly even at them is considered rude and hostile. Of course, all of these rules are variable.

A great many blacks, for example, greet each other in public even if they don't know each other. To blacks, most eye behavior of whites has the effect of giving the impression that they aren't there, but this is due to white avoidance of eye contact with anyone in the street.

Another very basic difference between people of different ethnic backgrounds is their sense of territoriality and how they handle space. This is the silent communication, or miscommunication, that caused friction between Mr. Ybarra and Sir Edmund Jones in our earlier example. We know from the research that everyone has around himself an invisible bubble of space that contracts and expands depending on several factors: his emotional state, the activity he's performing at the time, and his cultural background. This bubble is a kind of mobile territory that he will defend against intrusion. If he is accustomed to close personal distance between himself and others, his bubble will be smaller than that of someone who's accustomed to greater personal distance. People of northern European heritage—English, Scandinavian, Swiss, and German—tend to avoid contact. Those whose heritage is Italian, French, Spanish, Russian, Latin American, or Middle Eastern like close personal contact.

People are very sensitive to any intrusion into their spatial bubble. If someone stands too close to you, your first instinct is to back up. If that's not possible, you lean away and pull yourself in, tensing your muscles. If the intruder doesn't respond to these body signals, you may then try to protect yourself, using a briefcase, umbrella, or raincoat. Women—especially when traveling alone—often plant their pocketbooks in such a way that no one can get very close to them. As a last resort, you may move to another spot and position yourself behind a desk or a chair that provides screening. Everyone tries to adjust the space around himself in a way that's comfortable for him; most often, he does this unconsciously.

Emotions also have a direct effect on the size of a person's territory. When you're angry or under stress, your bubble expands and you require more space. New York psychiatrist Augustus Kinzel found a difference in what he calls body buffer zones between violent and nonviolent prison in-mates. Dr. Kinzel conducted experiments in which each prisoner was placed in the center of a small room, and then Dr. Kinzel slowly walked toward him. Nonviolent prisoners allowed him to come quite close, while prisoners with a history of violent behavior couldn't tolerate his proximity and reacted with some vehemence.

Apparently, people under stress experience other people as looming larger and closer than they actually are. Studies of schizophrenic patients have indicted that they sometimes have a distorted perception of space, and several psychiatrists have reported patients who experience their body boundaries as filling up an entire room. For these patients, anyone who comes into the room is actually inside their body, and such an intrusion may trigger a violent outburst.

Unfortunately, there is little detailed information about normal people who live in highly congested urban areas. We do know, of course, that the noise, pollution, dirt, crowding, and confusion of our cities induce feelings of stress in most of us, and stress leads to a need for greater space. The man who's packed into a subway, jostled in the street, crowded into an elevator, and forced to work all day in a bull pen or in a small office without auditory or visual privacy is going to be very stressed at the end of his day. He needs places that provide relief from constant overstimulation of his nervous system. Stress from overcrowding is cumulative, and people can tolerate more crowding early in the day than later; note the increased bad temper during the evening rush hour as compared with the morning melee. Certainly one factor in people's desire to commute by car is the need for privacy and relief from crowding (except, often, from other cars); it may be the only time of the day when nobody can intrude.

In crowded public places, we tense our muscles and hold ourselves stiff, and thereby communicate to others our desire not to intrude on their space and, above all, not to touch them. We also avoid eye contact, and the total effect is that of someone who has "tuned out." Walking along the street, our bubble expands slightly as we move in a stream of strangers, taking care not to bump into them. In the office, at meetings, in restaurants, our bubble keeps changing as it adjusts to the activity at hand.

Most white middle-class Americans use four main distances in their business and social relations: intimate, personal, social, and public. Each of these distances has a near and a far phase and is accompanied by changes in the volume of the voice. Intimate distance varies from direct physical contact with another person to a distance of six to eighteen inches and is used for our most private activities—caressing another person or making love. At this distance, you are overwhelmed by sensory inputs from the other person—heat from the body, tactile stimulation from the skin, the fragrance of perfume, even the sound of breathing—all of which literally envelop you. Even at the far phase, you're still within easy touching distance. In general, the use of intimate distance in public between adults is frowned on. It's also much too close for strangers, except under conditions of extreme crowding.

In the second zone—personal distance—the close phase is one and a half to two and a half feet; it's at this distance that wives usually stand from their husbands in public. If another woman moves into this zone, the wife will most likely be disturbed. The far phase—two and a half to four feet—is the distance used to "keep someone at arm's length" and is the most common spacing used by people in conversation.

The third zone—social distance—is employed during business transactions or exchanges with a clerk or repairman. People who work together tend to use close social distance—four to seven feet. This is also the distance for conversation at social gatherings. To stand at this distance from someone who is seated has a dominating effect (e.g., teacher to pupil, boss to secretary). The far phase of the third zone—seven to twelve feet—is where people stand when someone says, "Stand back so I can look at you." This distance lends a formal tone to business or social discourse. In an executive office, the desk serves to keep people at this distance.

The fourth zone—public distance—is used by teachers in classrooms or speakers at public gatherings. At its farthest phase—twenty-five feet and beyond—it is used for important public figures. Violations of this distance can lead to serious complications. During his 1970 U.S. visit, the president of France, Georges Pompidou, was harassed by pickets in Chicago, who were permitted to get within touching distance. Since pickets in France are kept behind barricades a block or more away, the president was outraged by this insult to his person, and President Nixon was obliged to communicate his concern as well as offer his personal apologies.

It is interesting to note how American pitchmen and panhandlers exploit the unwritten, unspoken conventions of eye and distance. Both take advantage of the fact that once explicit eye contact is established, it is rude to look away, because to do so means to brusquely dismiss the other person and his needs. Once having caught the eye of his mark, the panhandler then locks on, not letting go until he moves through the public zone, the social zone, the personal zone and, finally, into the intimate sphere, where people are most vulnerable.

Touch also is an important part of the constant stream of communication that takes place between people. A light touch, a firm touch, a blow, a caress are all communications. In an effort to break down barriers among people there's been a recent upsurge in group-encounter activities, in which strangers are encouraged to touch one another. In special situations such as these, the rules for not touching are broken with group approval, and people gradually lose some of their inhibitions.

Although most people don't realize it, space is perceived and distances are set not by vision alone but with all the senses. Auditory space is perceived with the ears, thermal space with the skin, kinesthetic space with the muscles of the body, and olfactory space with the nose. And, once again, it's one's culture that determines how his senses are programmed—which sensory information ranks highest and lowest. The important thing to remember is that culture is very persistent. In this country, we've noted the existence of culture patterns that determine distance between people in the third and fourth generations of some families, despite their prolonged contact with people of very different cultural heritages.

Whenever there is great cultural distance between two people, there are bound to be problems arising from differences in behavior and expectations. An example is the American couple who consulted a psychiatrist about their marital problems. The husband was from New England and had been brought up by reserved parents who taught him to control his emotions and to respect the need for privacy. His wife was from an Italian family and had been brought up in close contact with all the members of her large family, who were extremely warm, volatile, and demonstrative.

When the husband came home after a hard day at the office, dragging his feet and longing for peace and quiet, his wife would rush to him and smother him. Clasping his hands, rubbing his brow, crooning over his weary head, she never left him alone. But when the wife was upset or anxious about her day, the husband's response was to withdraw completely and leave her alone. No comforting, no affectionate embrace, no attention—just solitude. The woman became convinced her husband didn't love her, and in desperation she consulted a psychiatrist. Their problem wasn't basically psychological but cultural.

Why has man developed all these different ways of communicating messages without words? One reason is that people don't like to spell out certain kinds of messages. We prefer to find other ways of showing our feelings. This is especially true in relationships as sensitive as courtship. Men don't like to be rejected, and most women don't want to turn a man down bluntly. Instead, we work out subtle ways of encouraging or discouraging each other that save face and avoid confrontations.

How a person handles space in dating others is an obvious and very sensitive indicator of how he or she feels about the other person. On a first date, if a woman sits or stands so close to a man that he is acutely conscious of her physical presence—inside the intimate-distance zone—the man usually construes it to mean that she is encouraging him. However, before the man starts moving in on the woman, he should be sure what message she's really sending; otherwise, he risks bruising his ego. What is close to someone of northern European background may be neutral or distant to someone of Italian heritage. Also, a woman sometimes use space as a way of misleading a man, and there are few things that put men off more than women who communicate contradictory messages, such as women who cuddle up and then act insulted when a man takes the next step.

How does a woman communicate interest in a man? In addition to such familiar gambits as smiling at him, she may glance shyly at him, blush, and then look away. Or she may give him a real come-on look and move in very close when he approaches. She may touch his arm and ask for a light. As she leans forward to light her cigarette, she may brush him lightly, enveloping him in her perfume. She'll probably continue to smile at him, and she may use what ethologists call preening gestures—touching the back of her hair, thrusting her breasts forward, tilting her hips as she stands, or crossing her legs if she's seated, perhaps even exposing one thigh or putting a hand on her thigh and stroking it. She may also stroke her wrists as she converses or show the palm of her hand as a way of gaining his attention. Her skin may be unusually flushed or quite pale, her eyes brighter, the pupils larger.

If a man sees a woman whom he wants to attract, he tries to present himself by his posture and stance as someone who is self-assured. He moves briskly and confidently. When he catches the eye of the woman, he may hold her glance a little longer than normal. If he gets an encouraging smile, he'll move in close and engage her in small talk. As they converse, his glance shifts over her face and body. He, too, may make preening gestures—straightening his tie, smoothing his hair, or shooting his cuffs.

How do people learn body language? The same way they learn spoken language—by observing and imitating people around them as they're growing up. Little girls imitate their mothers or an older female. Little boys imitate their fathers or a respected uncle or a character on television. In this way, they learn the gender signals appropriate for their sex. Regional, class, and ethnic patterns of body behavior are also learned in childhood and persist throughout life.

Such patterns of masculine and feminine body behavior vary widely from one culture to another. In America, for example, women stand with their thighs together. Many walk with their pelvis tipped slightly forward and their upper arms close to their body. When they sit, they cross their ankles. American men hold their arms away from their body, often swinging them as they walk. They stand with their legs apart (an extreme example is the cowboy, with legs apart and thumb tucked into his belt.) When they sit, they put their feet on the floor with legs apart, and, in some parts of the country, they cross their legs by putting one ankle on the other knee.

Leg behavior indicates sex, status, and personality. It also indicates whether or not one is at ease or is showing respect or disrespect for the other person. Young Latin American males avoid crossing their legs. In their world of machismo, the preferred position for young males when with one another (if there is no older dominant male present to whom they must show respect) is to sit on the base of their spine with their leg muscles relaxed and their feet wide apart. Their respect position is like our military equivalent: spine straight, heels and ankles together—almost identical to that displayed by properly brought up young women in New England in the early part of this century.

American women who sit with their legs spread apart in the presence of males are not normally signaling a come-on—they are simply (and often unconsciously) sitting like men. Middle-class women in the presence of other women to whom they are very close may on occasion throw themselves down on a soft chair or sofa and let themselves go. This is a signal that nothing serious will be taken up. Males, on the other hand, lean back and prop their legs up on the nearest object.

The way we walk similarly indicates status, respect, mood, and ethnic or cultural affiliation. The many variants of the female walk are too well known to go into here, except to say that a man would have to be blind not to be turned on by the way some women walk—a fact that made Mae West rich before scientists ever studied these matters. To white Americans, some French middle-class males walk in a way that is both humorous and suspect. There is a bounce and looseness to the French walk, as though the parts of the body were somehow unrelated. Jacques Tati, the French movie actor, walks this way; so does the great mime, Marcel Marceau.

Blacks and whites in America—with the exception of middle- and upper-middle-class professions of both groups—move and walk very differently from each other. To the blacks, whites often seem incredibly stiff, almost mechanical in their movements. Black males, on the other hand, have a looseness and coordination that frequently makes whites a little uneasy; it's too different, too integrated, too alive, too male. Norman Mailer has said that squares walk from the shoulders, like bears, but blacks and hippies walk from the hips, like cats.

All over the world, people walk not only in their own characteristic way but have walks that communicate the nature of their involvement with whatever it is they're doing. The purposeful walk of northern Europeans is an important component of proper behavior on the job. Any male who has been in the military knows how essential it is to walk properly (which makes for a continuing source of tension between blacks and whites in the service). The quick shuffle of servants in the Far East in the old days was a show of respect. On the island of Truk, when we last visited, the inhabitants even had a name for the respectful walk that one used when in the presence of a chief or when walking past a chief's house. The term was *sufan*, which meant to be humble and respectful.

The notion that people communicate volumes by their gestures, facial expressions, posture, and walk is not new; actors, dancers, writers, and psychiatrists have long been aware of it. Only in recent years, however, have scientists begun to make systematic observations of body motions. Ray L. Birdwhistell of the University of Pennsylvania is one of the pioneers in body-motion research and coined the term kinesics to describe this field. He developed an elaborate notation system to record both facial and body movements, using an approach similar to that of the linguist, who studies the basic elements of speech. Birdwhistell and other kinesicists such as Albert Sheflen, Adam Kendon, and William Condon take movies of people interacting. They run the film over and over again, often at reduced speed for frame-by-frame analysis, so that they can observe even the slightest body movements not perceptible at normal interaction speeds. These movements are then recorded in notebooks for later analysis.

To appreciate the importance of nonverbal communication systems, consider the unskilled inner-city black looking for a job. His handling of time and space alone is sufficiently different from the white middle-class pattern to create great misunderstandings on both sides. The black is told to appear for a job interview at a certain time. He arrives late. The white interviewer concludes from his tardy arrival that the black is irresponsible and not really interested in the job. What the interviewer doesn't know is that the black time system (often referred to by blacks as C.P.T. — colored people's time) isn't the same as that of whites. In the words of a black student who had been told to make an appointment to see his professor: "Man, you must be putting me on. I never had an appointment in my life."

The black job applicant, having arrived late for his interview, may further antagonize the white interviewer by his posture and his eye behavior. Perhaps he slouches and avoids looking at the interviewer; to him, this is playing it cool. To the interviewer, however, he may well look shifty and sound uninterested. The interviewer has failed to notice the actual signs of interest and eagerness in the black's behavior, such as the subtle shift in the quality of the voice — a gentle and tentative excitement — an almost imperceptible change in the cast of the eyes and a relaxing of the jaw muscles.

Moreover, correct reading of black-white behavior is continually complicated by the fact that both groups are comprised of individuals — some of whom try to accommodate and some of whom make it a point of pride *not* to accommodate. At present, this means that many Americans, when thrown into contact with one another, are in the precarious position of not knowing which pattern applies. Once identified and analyzed, nonverbal communications systems can be taught, like a foreign language. Without this training, we respond to nonverbal communications in terms of our own culture; we read everyone's behavior as if it were our own, and thus we often misunderstand it.

Several years ago in New York City, there was a program for sending children from predominantly black and Puerto Rican low-income neighborhoods to summer school in a white upper-class neighborhood on the East Side. One morning, a group of young black and Puerto Rican boys raced down the street, shouting and screaming and overturning garbage cans on their way to school. A doorman from an apartment building nearby chased them and cornered one of them inside a building. The boy drew a knife and attacked the doorman. This tragedy would not have occurred if the doorman had been familiar with the behavior of boys from low-income neighborhoods, where such antics are routine and socially acceptable and where pursuit would be expected to invite a violent response.

The language of behavior is extremely complex. Most of us are lucky to have under control one subcultural system — the one that reflects our sex, class, generation, and geographic region within the United States. Because of its complexity, efforts to isolate bits of nonverbal communication and generalize from them are in vain; you don't become an instant expert on people's behavior by watching them at cocktail parties. Body language isn't something that independent of the person, something that can be donned and doffed like a suit of clothes.

Our research and that of our colleagues has shown that, far from being a superficial form of communication that can be consciously manipulated, nonverbal communication systems are interwoven into the fabric of the personality and, as sociologist Erving Goffman has demonstrated, into society itself. They are the warp and woof of daily interactions with others, and they influence how one expresses oneself, how one experiences oneself as a man or a woman.

Nonverbal communications signal to members of your own group what kind of person you are, how you feel about others, how you'll fit into and work in a group, whether you' re assured or anxious, the degree to which you feel comfortable with the standards of your own culture, as well as deeply significant feelings about the self, including the state of your own psyche. For most of us, it's difficult to accept the reality of another behavioral system. And, of course, none of us will ever become fully knowledgeable of the importance of every nonverbal signal. But as long as each of us realizes the power of these signals, this society's diversity can be a source of great strength rather than a further—and subtly powerful—source of division.

Questions

1. What is "nonverbal communication?" How conscious is it?
2. How does the "language of the eyes" differ for social classes, generations, regions, ethnic groups, etc.?
3. What do Hess' studies of pupillary reflex show?
4. What is territoriality? How do spatial bubbles expand and contract?
5. Distinguish between intimate, personal, social, and public "distance." Which do pitchmen use?
6. In what ways is "touch" a form of nonverbal communication? Describe differences between men and women.
7. How does "leg behavior" or the "way we walk" indicate sex, status, personality, mood, cultural affiliation, etc.?
8. What is kinesics? Give examples.
9. Is nonverbal communication a "superficial form of communication that can be consciously manipulated: or is it "interwoven into the fabric of the personality and society itself?"
10. Is there any practical benefit to knowing about the "sounds of silence"?

Part XIII

Seeing the Future
Cities, Families, the Schools, and Overpopulation

The last four selections in this volume are concerned with the future. In the first selection, political scientist/economist Edward Banfield focuses on important changes now taking place in big cities that will determine the nature of urban problems in the year 2000. "Like it or not," he says, "the big cities always have been—and will continue to be—the center of. . . activity for our whole society." While he predicts "neighborhood decay" and further "decline of older, northern, industrial cities," he also sees "prospering downtowns" and a "reduction in prejudice."

Sociologists Andrew Cherlin and Frank Furstenberg, Jr., in the second selection, offer predictions for the American family in the year 2000. "Diversity" is the word for what they see happening. While there will be more divorces and single-parent families, the "ideal" of marrying and having children will still be very much a part of the American experience. It is nice to hear that dire warnings about the "demise" of the family are exaggerated.

In the third selection, futurologist Marvin Cetron offers his views on the schools. The high school class of 2000 will graduate into a different society than the kind we know today, he says, and "simply living in modern society will raise the level of education we all need." Though "the school system is clearly overburdened," he believes some embarrassingly simple measures such as smaller classes, use of computers, school-business partnerships, etc. can insure high quality education in the future. Since one American in five currently participates in the educational institution, let us hope he is right.

Ralph Hamil, in the concluding selection, asks us to consider the socioeconomic implications of having a world population of 5 billion—with another 5 billion en route. As he says, how do we "dampen the population boom that so far defies all controls?"

483

Chapter Forty-Three

America's Cities Enter a Crucial Decade

Edward C. Banfield

Dramatic change is taking place in the big cities of America. Although only 10 per cent of us live in the nation's 20 largest cities, what happens there affects us all.

Like it or not, the big cities always have been—and will continue to be—the center of economic, political, and cultural activity for our whole society.

With the exception of a few urban centers like Los Angeles that were born after the automobile, the cities have always grown from the inside out. As population increased and transportation improved, the people who could afford them sought more space and newer housing. This meant moving to the fringes of the cities where there was vacant land.

The relatively poor remained in the inner districts, close to their places of work. As their incomes rose they followed the "tenement trail" to the outlying neighborhoods and beyond to the suburbs. This historic process was interrupted by the Depression and the Second World War. But in the 1950s and 1960s the accumulated backlog of demand for more space and better housing was suddenly released.

The wholesale exodus to the suburbs produced a huge stock of structurally sound housing in the inner cities. This in turn made possible a mass movement of blacks, Puerto Ricans, and others from the rural South and other places where educational and job opportunities had always been poor and incomes low.

Used by permission of the author.

485

Unfortunately for the unskilled people moving into the cities, manufacturing — the chief source of jobs for the low-skilled — was at the same time moving out. It had become more efficient to build new plants on major highways outside of the city, shifting from rail to truck transportation.

The advantage to the poor of cheap housing in the city, many soon discovered, was more than offset by a shortage of jobs.

That the newcomers to the inner city were mostly black complicated matters. Finding they were welcome only in neighborhoods that whites had abandoned and that the quality of schools and other public services in these neighborhoods declined rapidly when they arrived, they concluded they were being victimized by white prejudice. All too often this was indeed the case.

Profound changes were occurring, however, in the attitudes of whites, especially of young people finishing high school and going to college. To most blacks and to many whites in the 1960s, the "urban crisis" was a racial problem, which is to say a moral one. To others — myself included — it appeared to be what it had always been, *essentially* an economic problem: As had happened many times before, a wave of unskilled and therefore poor people had come to the city. The difference was that this time they had moved into the city when jobs were moving out.

That they were mostly black made a difference: racial prejudice was still widespread. But if they had all turned white overnight the crucial facts — lack of skills and lack of jobs — would not have changed.

So much for the background. Now let's identify what I think are the important changes now taking place in the big cities.

Most were not anticipated even 10 years ago. In my opinion they will determine the nature of the urban problem — some may want to call it the urban "crisis" — that will face us in the year 2000. There are eight items on my list:

1. Loss of population

Whereas until recently the cities were losing population slowly or not at all, now they are losing it at a rapid rate. Of the 20 cities that were largest in 1970, all but one lost population in the ensuing decade. Nine lost more than 10 per cent. Even more surprising is the net out-migration from many metropolitan areas (city and suburbs taken together).

In some of these metropolitan areas the losses from migration are not being — and will not be — offset by an excess of births over deaths. According to the best available estimates, some whole states in the most industrialized part of the country — New York, New Jersey, and Rhode Island — are losing population.

Beginning in 1960 the birthrate began dropping rapidly. We are now close to a zero rate of population growth. In the whole country there were only 2,000 more births in 1978 than in 1977.

A second fundamental fact is that more and more people are choosing to live in small towns and rural places beyond the rather arbitrarily defined limits of the metropolitan areas.

A third fundamental fact is that the movement of population to the so-called Sunbelt, which attracted little notice even 10 years ago, is now substantial: The only large cities in America to gain population in the 1970s were in the Southwest.

2. Changes in lifestyles

The drop in the birthrate is only one of many "style of life" changes affecting the cities. It has suddenly become commonplace for young adults to remain unmarried (20 percent of U.S. households are estimated to consist of one person) or to live together without being married (the number of such couples is thought to have more than doubled in the 1970s). Or, if they do marry, they remain married briefly (seven years on the average) and very often have no children. Women, including those with small children, have entered the labor market on a mass scale.

One consequence of these changes is a sharp increase in the number of households with high per capita incomes. In the "old" days the husband worked, earning, say, $12,000. Meanwhile, his wife looked after the children—two, let's say. That was a per capita income of $3,000.

Now, frequently, the husband and wife both work and there are no children. The per capita income is therefore three or four times what it was. According to a recent census report, the median income of two-income families—not all of them childless of course—was $18,704 in 1977.

These changes in lifestyle and income have stimulated a movement by young professionals and others to re-occupy and rehabilitate parts of the inner city. For many, the old incentives to live in the suburbs—ample yards and good schools for the children—no longer exist. What the "swinging single" or the two-income couple wants is to be near restaurants, bars, shops, theatres and, in the case of the couples, transportation to jobs that may be in opposite directions. With high per capita incomes they can afford to buy and renovate housing in some conveniently located neighborhoods that were badly run-down.

3. The vitality of downtowns

Until a few years ago there were many who thought that the city's business and cultural center—its "downtown"—could not prosper and might not even survive the movement of the middle class to the suburbs and the deterioration of what had once been the manufacturing districts.

As it has turned out, service and office industries have flourished in the central business districts of most of the large cities. Los Angeles, which until a few years ago had no real downtown, is perhaps the most conspicuous example of growth. Even Manhattan, with the city in near bankruptcy, has been building hotels and offices at an unprecedented rate.

The evidence in these and other cities shows that a downtown may prosper and grow in the midst of a general decline, indeed of a wasteland.

4. A permanent underclass

The future city will be profoundly affected by the continued polarization of the black population into an upper and a lower class.

First the good news: Those blacks who have acquired job skills have been moving upward in income and education at a rapid pace. A dozen years ago only 9 per cent of black employees were in professional or managerial positions. Now 17 percent are. (The comparable numbers for whites is 26 per cent). The bad news is that this upward movement on the part of some has been more than matched by a downward movement on the part of others. The figures bearing on family disorganization that shocked and angered so many people when the so-called Moynihan Report appeared a dozen years ago would have to be doubled in most instances to describe matters as they are now.

Moreover, the official unemployment rate takes no account of those who for one reason or another are not trying to find a job. If these "drop-outs" are counted, more than half of all black teenagers might be jobless.

Persistent and large-scale efforts to train youths and fit them into jobs have largely failed. It now appears that the big cities are going to have substantial populations of people who have never had a job and have no expectation of ever having one. They may become America's permanent underclass.

5. Neighborhood decay

The presence in the city of this apparently permanent class of persons who are more or less reconciled to a life of joblessness and poverty and whose attachment to family, neighborhood, and community is weak or non-existent is both cause and effect of the deterioration of housing and of the physical environment in general. In some places — the South Bronx of New York is only one example — this decay is absolutely alarming.

In several cities, most notably New York, Philadelphia, St. Louis, and Baltimore, useful housing is being abandoned block by block because of vandalism and because rent-control and other ordinances intended to protect tenants have made it impossible for the owners of rental housing to get what they consider a reasonable return on their investment.

City planners propose "targeting" public funds to preserve neighborhoods threatened with decline. They hope to avoid wasting money on those areas past the point of no return. Some urge the city to follow a policy of "planned shrinkage" by scheduling well in advance a cut-off of services to areas manifestly doomed to depopulation and impossible to police or to serve adequately with schools, hospitals and other public facilities. Politically, however, such a policy is—and doubtless will remain—well beyond the bounds of possibility.

6. Illegal immigration

Historically, the city has been a place of opportunity for the low-skilled and the poor. After a generation or two in the city they have acquired skills and savings sufficient to enable them to move off to better things in the suburbs. This, in turn, has made way for a fresh wave of migration to the city by a new and ethnically different set of the low-skilled and poor.

Now and in the future, however, this movement may not operate normally. A large new wave of immigration to the city is already under way even though a considerable proportion of the previous wave remains in the city, apparently permanently stuck in rapidly deteriorating slums.

Illegal immigration, most of it from Mexico, has increased greatly during the last few years and seems bound to increase even more rapidly in the years ahead. Mexico has one of the fastest-growing populations in the world. No matter how much oil it may have, there will be many more poor people crossing the border, a border 2,000 miles long and impossible to police by any methods that the American public would tolerate.

No one really knows how many illegal entries there are now (estimates vary from 500,000 to 2 million a year) or how many of these are "settlers" rather than "migrants."

It would not be surprising, however, if by the year 2000 the cities had as many poor people of Mexican origin as they now do poor blacks and Puerto Ricans.

Whether or in what sense the large influx of illegal aliens constitutes a "problem" is, of course, a matter of opinion. At present almost all of the aliens are employed, about half of them at jobs that pay the minimum wage or more. There is little doubt, however, that before long their presence will be legalized. They will then be eligible to receive welfare, public housing, and other such benefits. When that happens many who now feel compelled to work might stop working and join the already sizeable class of the permanently unskilled and unemployed.

However this may turn out, there will be sharp antagonism between Mexicans and blacks who compete for the same jobs and housing.

Political separatism is also a possibility. Until recently the public and parochial schools, by teaching in English, made the "melting pot" work. Now, however, much teaching is in the child's native language with the result that he may learn very little English and, what may be more important, think of himself thereafter as belonging to the Hispanic, not the American, community.

7. Black-white relations

This brings me to consider the changes that seem to be occurring in the relations between blacks and whites. For many years public opinion polls have shown a reduction in white prejudice against blacks. More and more respondents say, for example, that they would not mind having black neighbors. Talk is cheap, to be sure, but it is rare nowadays for whites to make a fuss when a black family does move into the neighborhood. (Incidentally, between 1970 and 1977 the number of blacks living in suburbs increased by one-third. But most of the suburbs into which most of them moved were already predominantly or wholly black).

Several of the largest cities, notably Chicago, Los Angeles, Detroit, and Atlanta, have elected black mayors when whites were a substantial majority of the electorate. Finally — and what is perhaps the most telling indicator of the trend of white opinion — no politician of consequence has made any effort to develop a racist constituency.

Black leaders generally, however, do not share this optimistic view of the trend in white opinion. Few are now prepared to say, as many did a decade ago, that white America contemplates a policy of genocide.

But many do seem to think that the civil rights revolution has run its course and a reaction has set in. The closer collaboration between black and white civic leaders that one would expect is conspicuous by its absence in some of the large cities.

8. Growth of bureaucracy

A development of great importance since 1960 has been the doubling — from about 6 to 12 million — of the number of public employees in state and local government.

Because of their increase in numbers and because nearly two-thirds of them (in the largest cities almost 100 per cent) have joined unions or professional associations, city employees are now — and will surely be in the future — the single most powerful interest group on the local scene. Almost everywhere it is illegal for them to strike. But it has become clear in city after city that in even the most essential services (fire, police, and sanitation) public employee unions are willing to defy the law. Furthermore, as a practical matter, there appears to be no effective way of punishing them when they do so.

One may safely predict, therefore, both that the wages of public employees will continue to rise relative to those doing comparable work and that there will be no corresponding increase in their productivity. By the year 2000 the cost and behavior of the big-city bureaucracy may be the principal component of "the urban crisis."

In view of the current alarm about energy supplies, perhaps I should mention a trend I believe will *not* occur. And that is the wholesale movement of suburbanites and exurbanites back to the central city because of the high price of gasoline or a massive shift from private to mass transit.

In my opinion, no fuel problem will ever spoil the love affair between Americans and their cars. Between 1960 and 1975 the number of urban auto passenger miles more than doubled—from 627 billion to 1,341 billion. I would not be surprised if there were another doubling before the year 2000.

Box 101

Banfield Update

The "crucial decade" referred to by Banfield has arrived. Therefore, it is possible to consider if his projections have proved to be valid.

According to current statistics, 7 of the 20 largest cities continued to lose population—all in the Northeast or Midwest. Four cities in these regions increased in population: New York 3.5 percent, Boston 2.0 percent, Columbus, Ohio 12.0 percent, Indianapolis 4.3 percent. None of these are traditional manufacturing centers but are now cities of high-tech industries. Indeed, 18 traditional manufacturing cities in the Northeast and Midwest not included in the top 20 show population losses. With the exception of the 4 cities above, all of the largest 20 cities gaining populations were in the South, Southwest and West "sunbelts."

Loss of population usually reflects loss of job opportunities. As Banfield mentions, this has hit later groups migrating to cities hardest, especially minorities. The 7 top 20 cities losing population all have large African-American populations, and 14 of the additional 18 Northeast-Midwest manufacturing cities have African-American populations in excess of 25 percent.

One indicator of changing lifestyles is the increase in number of persons who never marry. Unmarried males increased from 18.9 percent in 1972 to 26.2 percent in 1992 and unmarried females from 13.7 percent in 1972 to 19.2 percent in 1992. Another indicator is the increase in later ages of marriage for both males and females measured in terms of percentage still single at various ages. Single males age 25-29, for example, comprised 48.7 percent of the population in 1992 compared to 19.1 percent in 1970. Single females age 25-29 were 33.2 percent in 1992 compared to 10.5 percent in 1970. Such statistics as these probably indicate smaller families, more nonmarried living arrangements and emphasis on careers.

SOURCE: Statistical Abstract of the United States, 1993.

Questions

1. What percentage of America is urban? How does the census define urban? What are the nation's 20 largest cities?

2. Is the urban crisis a racial or an economic problem?

3. Are the majority of city dwellers living better or worse than in the past? In what ways?

4. What additional "style of life" changes besides "swinging singles" and "two income families" affect cities?

5. What future do "downtowns" have in America?

6. In what ways can neighborhood decay be stopped?

7. Why will migration into the cities be different in the future than it was in the past?

8. What are the positive and negative consequences of the growth of bureaucracy in our cities?

9. How well do Banfield's predictions hold up in the 1990s?

Chapter Forty-Four

The American Family in the Year 2000

Andrew Cherlin
Frank F. Furstenberg, Jr.

- At current rates, half of all American marriages begun in the early 1980s will end in divorce.
- The number of unmarried couples living together has more than tripled since 1970.
- One out of four children is not living with both parents.

The list could go on and on. Teenage pregnancies: up. Adolescent suicides: up. The birthrate: down. Over the past decade, popular and scholarly commentators have cited a seemingly endless wave of grim statistics about the shape of the American family. The trends have caused a number of the concerned Americans to wonder if the family, as we know it, will survive the twentieth century.

And yet, other observers ask us to consider more positive developments:

- Seventy-eight percent of all adults in a recent national survey said they get "a great deal" of satisfaction from their family lives; only 3% said "a little" or "none."
- Two-thirds of the married adults in the same survey said they were "very happy" with their marriages; only 3% said "not too happy."

Reprinted with permission from *The Futurist,* Vol. XVII, No. 3, June 1983, pp. 7-14.

- In another recent survey of parents of children in their middle years, 88% said that if they had to do it over, they would choose to have children again.
- The vast majority of the children (71%) characterized their family life as "close and intimate."

Family ties are still important and strong, the optimists argue, and the predictions of the demise of the family are greatly exaggerated.

Neither the dire pessimists who believe that the family is falling apart nor the unbridled optimists who claim that the family has never been in better shape provide an accurate picture of family life in the near future. But these trends indicate that what we have come to view as the "traditional" family will no longer predominate. (Box 102 describes the findings of two sociologists who did a study of traditional and nontraditional couples in America.)

Box 102

American Couples

Sociologists Philip Blumstein and Pepper Schwartz did an in-depth study of American couples, defined as two individuals who live together and who have or have had a sexual relationship. They concentrated on four types of couples: Heterosexual married couples, cohabiting heterosexual couples, gay male couples, and lesbian couples. A 38-page questionnaire was completed by over 6,000 couples. Blumstein and Schwartz personally interviewed 300 couples and did follow-up interviews after two years to find out if couples were still together and why. Listed below are some of their specific findings grouped around the areas of money, work, and sex.

With Respect to Money:
1. Few couples believe there should be only one breadwinner.
2. Couples argue more about the way money is managed than about how much they have.
3. Married couples fight more about money management than all other couples.
4. Gay male and lesbian couples are relatively egalitarian because members of the couple generally have similar incomes.
5. Nonmarried couples do not pool their finances if they doubt the durability of the relationship.

With Regard to Work:
1. Heterosexual women do most of the housework whether they have full-time jobs or not; when heterosexual males do a lot of housework, the couple argues more.

2. Same sex couples "share" household chores more.
3. Wives want to work more than husbands want them to.
4. Wives of successful husbands are happier with their marriages, as are husbands of successful women.
5. Few men and women judge their success by comparing it with their partner's success.

With Regard to Sex:

1. The frequency of "sex" tends to decline over the years.
2. Equality in sexual initiation and refusal goes with a happier sex life.
3. Women, more than men, need to be in love to have sex.
4. Most suspicions about infidelity are justified.
5. Gay male couples have the highest rate of sexual involvement outside the relationship; lesbian couples have the lowest rate.

The researchers conclude that when Americans are "coupled," they hope they are making a lifetime commitment. If this fails, "the desire to be part of a couple is so strong that most try again."

SOURCE: Philip Blumstein and Pepper Schwartz: *American Couples: Money, Work, and Sex* (New York: William Morrow, 1983).

Diverse Family Forms

In the future, we should expect to see a growing amount of diversity in family forms, with fewer Americans spending most of their life in a simple "nuclear" family consisting of husband, wife, and children. By the year 2000, three kinds of families will dominate the personal lives of most Americans: families of first marriages, single-parent families, and families of remarriages.

In first-marriage families, both spouses will be in a first marriage, frequently begun after living alone for a time or following a period of cohabitation. Most of these couples will have one, two, or less, frequently, three children.

A sizable minority, however, will remain childless. Demographer Charles F. Westoff predicts that about one-fourth of all women currently in their childbearing years will never bear children, a greater number of childless women than at any time in U.S. history.

One other important shift: in a large majority of these families, both the husband and the wife will be employed outside the home. In 1940, only about one out of seven married women worked outside the home; today the proportion is one out of two. We expect this proportion to continue to rise, although not as fast as it did in the past decade or two.

Single-Parent Families

The second major type of family can be formed in two ways. Most are formed by a marital separation, and the rest by births to unmarried women. About half of all marriages will end in divorce at current rates, and we doubt that the rates will fall substantially in the near future.

When the couple is childless, the formerly married partners are likely to set up independent households and resume life as singles. The high rate of divorce is one of the reasons why more men and women are living in single-person households than ever before.

But three-fifths of all divorces involve couples with children living at home. In at least nine out of ten cases, the wife retains custody of the children after a separation.

Although joint custody has received a lot of attention in the press and in legal circles, national data show that it is still uncommon. Moreover, it is likely to remain the exception rather than the rule because most ex-spouses can't get along well enough to manage raising their children together. In fact, a national survey of children aged 11 to 16 conducted by one of the authors demonstrated that fathers have little contact with their children after a divorce. About half of the children whose parents had divorced hadn't seen their father in the last year; only one out of six had managed to see their father an average of once a week. If the current rate of divorce persists, about half of all children will spend some time in a single-parent family before they reach 18.

Much has been written about the psychological effects on children of living with one parent, but the literature has not yet proven that any lasting negative effects occur. (Box 103 describes research findings on this topic.) One effect, however, does occur with regularity: women who head single-parent families typically experience a sharp decline in their income relative to before their divorce. Husbands usually do not experience a decline. Many divorced women have difficulty reentering the job market after a long absence; others find that their low-paying clerical or service-worker jobs aren't adequate to support a family.

Of course, absent fathers are supposed to make child-support payments, but only a minority do. In a 1979 U.S. Bureau of the Census survey, 43% of all divorced and separated women with children present reported receiving child-support payments during the previous year, and the average annual payment was about $1,900. Thus, the most detrimental effect for children living in a single-parent family is not the lack of a male presence but the lack of a male income.

Families of Remarriages

The experience of living as a single parent is temporary for many divorced women, especially in the middle class. Three out of four divorced people

---

Box 103

Children's Adjustment to Divorce

An issue of importance today is the effects of divorce on children. One study that interviewed 101 children over a five-year period found at least three different types of responses for children. Approximately 34 percent reacted to the divorce by adjusting quite well and were happy and healthy five years later. An additional 29 percent adjusted reasonably well, but continued to have some problems with anger or diminished self-esteem. The remaining 37 percent became depressed and remained lonely, unhappy, and maladjusted five years after the divorce.

The major factors which determined how the children reacted were: how well adjusted children were prior to the divorce; the type of relationship children had with the mother after the divorce; and, most important, the type of relationship the children had with the father after the divorce. Those children whose fathers remained active and involved as fathers tended to adapt quite well.

Because 63 percent of the children adjusted reasonably well, it is probably safe to conclude that unhappily married parents should not remain married "for the sake of the children."

Source: Judith Wallerstein and Joan Kelly: *Surviving the Break-Up: How Children Actually Cope With Divorce* (New York: Basic Books, 1980).

---

remarry, and about half of these marriages occur within three years of the divorce.

Remarriage does much to solve the economic problems that many single-parent families face because it typically adds a male income. Remarriage also relieves a single parent of the multiple burdens of running and supporting a household by herself.

But remarriage also frequently involves blending together two families into one, a difficult process that is complicated by the absence of clear-cut ground rules for how to accomplish the merger. Families formed by remarriages can become quite complex, with children from either spouse's previous marriage or from the new marriage and with numerous sets of grandparents, step-grandparents, and other kin and quasi-kin.

The divorce rate for remarriages is modestly higher than for first marriages, but many couples and their children adjust successfully to their remarriage and, when asked, consider their new marriage to be a big improvement over their previous one.

The Life Course: A Scenario for the Next Two Decades

Because of the recent sharp changes in marriage and family life, the life course of children and young adults today is likely to be far different from what a person growing up earlier in this century experienced. It will not be uncommon, for instance, for children born in the 1980s to follow this sequence of living arrangements: live with both parents for several years, live with their mothers after their parents divorce, live with their mothers and stepfathers, live alone for a time when in their early twenties, live with someone of the opposite sex without getting married, and end up living alone once more following the death of their spouses.

Not everyone will have a family history this complex, but it is likely that a substantial minority of the population will. And many more will have family histories only slightly less complex.

Overall, we estimate that about half of the young children alive today will spend some time in a single-parent family before they reach 18; about nine out of ten will eventually marry; about one out of two will marry and then divorce; and about one out of three will marry, divorce, and then remarry. In contrast, only about one out of six women born in the period 1910 to 1914 married and divorced and only about one in eight married, divorced, and remarried.

Without doubt, Americans today are living in a much larger number of family settings during their lives than was the case a few generations ago.

The life-course changes have been even greater for women than for men because of the far greater likelihood of employment during the childbearing years for middle-class women today compared with their mothers and grandmothers. Moreover, the increase in life expectancy has increased the difference between men's and women's family lives. Women now tend to outlive men by a wide margin, a development that is new in this century. Consequently, many more women face a long period of living without a spouse at the end of their lives, either as a widow or as a divorced person who never remarried.

Long-lived men, in contrast, often find that their position in the marriage market is excellent, and they are much more likely to remain married (or remarried) until they die.

Convergence and Divergence

The family lives of Americans vary according to such factors as class, ethnicity, religion, and region. But recent evidence suggests a convergence among these groups in many features of family life. The clearest example is in childbearing, where the differences between Catholics and non-Catholics or between Southerners and Northerners are much smaller than they were

20 years ago. We expect this process of convergence to continue, although it will fall far short of eliminating all social class and subcultural differences.

The experiences of blacks and whites also have converged in many respects, such as in fertility and in patterns of premarital sexual behavior, over the past few decades. But with respect to marriage, blacks and whites have diverged markedly since about 1960.

Black families in the United States always have had strong ties to a large network of extended kin. But in addition, blacks, like whites, relied on a relatively stable bond between husbands and wives. But over the past several decades—and especially since 1960—the proportion of black families maintained by a woman has increased sharply; currently, the proportion exceeds four in ten. In addition, more young black women are having children out of wedlock; in the late 1970s, about two out of three black women who gave birth to a first child were unmarried.

These trends mean that we must qualify our previously stated conclusion that marriage will remain central to family life. This conclusion holds for Americans in general. For many low-income blacks, however, marriage is likely to be less important than the continuing ties to a larger network of kin.

Marriage is simply less attractive to a young black woman from a low-income family because of the poor prospects many young black men have for steady employment and because of the availability of alternative sources of support from public-assistance payments and kin. Even though most black women eventually marry, their marriages have a very high probability of ending in separation or divorce. Moreover, they have a lower likelihood of remarrying.

Black single-parent families sometimes have been criticized as being "disorganized" or even "pathological." What the critics fail to note is that black single mothers usually are embedded in stable, functioning kin networks. These networks tend to center around female kin—mothers, grandmothers, aunts—but brothers, fathers, and other male kin also may be active. The members of these networks share and exchange goods and services, thus helping to share the burdens of poverty. The lower-class black extended family, then, is characterized by strong ties among a network of kin but fragile ties between husband and wife. The negative aspects of this family system have been exaggerated greatly; yet it need not be romanticized, either. It can be difficult and risky for individuals to leave the network in order to try to make it on their own; thus, it may be hard for individuals to raise themselves out of poverty until the whole network is raised.

The Disintegrating Family?

By now, predictions of the demise of the family are familiar to everyone. Yet the family is a resilient institution that still retains more strength than its harshest critics maintain. There is, for example, no evidence of a large-scale rejection of marriage among Americans. To be sure, many young adults are living together outside of marriage, but the evidence we have about cohabitation suggests that it is not a life-long alternative to marriage; rather it appears to be either another stage in the process of courtship and marriage or a transition between first and second marriages.

The so-called "alternative lifestyles" that received so much attention in the late 1960s, such as communes and lifelong singlehood, are still very uncommon when we look at the nation as a whole.

Young adults today do marry at a somewhat older age, on average, than their parents did. But the average age at marriage today is very similar to what it was throughout the period from 1890 to 1940.

To be sure, many of these marriages will end in divorce, but three out of four people who divorce eventually remarry. (Box 104 suggests that some marriages are more prone to divorce than others.) Americans still seem to desire the intimacy and security that a marital relationship provides.

Box 104

Who Gets Divorced?

Sociological research suggests that some marriages are more prone to divorce than others. The likelihood of divorce is highest when:

The husband and wife live in an urban area.

They both work, but their incomes are not high.

They married early.

They have not been married long.

They have different views regarding egalitarian attitudes about labor in the home.

Neither husband nor wife has strong religious convictions.

Both husband and wife are liberal in their attitudes.

Both husband and wife are pessimistic about life.

One or both have parents who are divorced.

If have children, the children are older.

If have children, the children were born before parents got married.

None of these factors alone, nor even all of them together, make divorce inevitable. As they accumulate, however, the statistical likelihood increases that the marriage will eventually be dissolved.

SOURCE: Lynn K. White, "Determinants of Divorce: A Review of Research in the Eighties," *Journal of Marriage and the Family*, November 1990, pp. 904-912.

Much of the alarm about the family comes from reactions to the sheer speed at which the institution changed in the last two decades. Between the early 1960s and the mid-1970s, the divorce rate doubled, the marriage rate plunged, the birthrate dropped from a twentieth-century high to an all-time low, premarital sex became accepted, and married women poured into the labor force. But since the mid-1970s, the pace of change has slowed. The divorce rate has risen modestly and the birthrate even has increased a bit. We may have entered a period in which American families can adjust to the sharp changes that occurred in the 1960s and early 1970s. We think that, by and large, accommodations will be made as expectations change and institutions are redesigned to take account of changing family practices.

Despite the recent difficulties, family ties remain a central part of American life. Many of the changes in family life in the 1960s and 1970s were simply a continuation of long-term trends that have been with us for generations.

The birthrate has been declining since the 1820s, the divorce rate has been climbing since at least the Civil War, and over the last half century a growing number of married women have taken paying jobs. Employment outside the home has been gradually eroding the patriarchal system of values that was a part of our early history, replacing it with a more egalitarian set of values.

The only exception occurred during the late 1940s and the 1950s. After World War II, Americans raised during the austerity of depression and war entered adulthood at a time of sustained prosperity. The sudden turnabout in their fortunes led them to marry earlier and have more children than any generation before or since in this century. Because many of us were either parents or children in the baby-boom years following the war, we tend to think that the 1950s typify the way twentieth-century families used to be. But the patterns of marriage and childbearing in the 1950s were an aberration resulting from special historical circumstances; the patterns of the 1960s and 1970s better fit the long-term trends. Barring unforeseen major disruptions, small families, working wives, and impermanent marital ties are likely to remain with us indefinitely.

A range of possible developments could throw our forecasts off the mark. We do not know, for example, how the economy will behave over the next 20 years, or how the family will be affected by technological innovations still at the conception stage. But, we do not envision any dramatic changes in family life resulting solely from technological innovations in the next two decades.

Having sketched our view of the most probable future, we will consider three of the most important implications of the kind of future we see.

Growing Up in Changing Families

Children growing up in the past two decades have faced a maelstrom of social change. As we have pointed out, family life is likely to become even more complex, diverse, unpredictable, and uncertain in the next two decades.

Even children who grow up in stable family environments will probably have to get along with a lot less care from parents (mothers in particular) than children received early in this century. Ever since the 1950s, there has been a marked and continuous increase in the proportion of working mothers whose preschool children are cared for outside the home, rising from 31% in 1958 to 62% in 1977. The upward trend is likely to continue until it becomes standard practice for very young children to receive care either in someone else's home or in a group setting. There has been a distinct drop in the care of children by relatives, as fewer aunts, grandmothers, or adult children are available to supplement the care provided by parents. Increasingly, the government at all levels will be pressured to provide more support for out-of-home daycare.

How are children responding to the shifting circumstances of family life today? Are we raising a generation of young people who, by virtue of their own family experiences, lack the desire and skill to raise the next generation? As we indicated earlier, existing evidence has not demonstrated that marital disruption creates lasting personality damage or instills a distinctly different set of values about family life.

Similarly, a recent review on children of working mothers conducted by the National Research Council of the National Academy of Sciences concludes:

> If there is only one message that emerges from this study, it is that parental employment in and of itself—mother's employment or fathers' or both parents'—is not necessarily good or bad for children.

The fact that both parents work *per se* does not adversely affect the well-being of children.

Currently, most fathers whose wives are employed do little childcare. Today, most working mothers have two jobs: they work for pay and then come home to do most of the childcare and housework. Pressure from a growing number of harried working wives could prod fathers to watch less television and change more diapers. But this change in fathers' roles is proceeding much more slowly than the recent spate of articles about the "new father" would lead one to expect. The strain that working while raising a family places on working couples, and especially on working mothers, will likely make childcare and a more equitable sharing of housework prominent issues in the 1980s and 1990s.

Family Obligations

Many of the one out of three Americans who, we estimate, will enter a second marriage will do so after having children in a first marriage. Others may enter into a first marriage with a partner who has a family from a previous marriage. It is not clear in these families what obligations remain after divorce or are created after remarriage. For one thing, no clear set of norms exists specifying how people in remarriages are supposed to act toward each other. Stepfathers don't know how to discipline their stepchildren; second wives don't know what they're supposed to say when they meet their husbands' first wives; stepchildren don't know what to call their absent father's new wife.

The ambiguity about family relations after divorce and remarriage also extends to economic support. There are no clear-cut guidelines to tell adults how to balance the claims of children from previous marriages versus children from their current marriages. Suppose a divorced man who has been making regular payments to support his two small children from a previous marriage marries a woman with children from her previous marriage. Suppose her husband isn't paying any child support. Suppose further that the remarried couple have a child of their own. Which children should have first claim on the husband's income? Legally, he is obligated to pay child support to his ex-wife, but in practice he is likely to feel that his primary obligation is to his stepchildren, whose father isn't helping, and to his own children from his remarriage.

Our guess, supported by some preliminary evidence from national studies, is that remarriage will tend to further reduce the amount of child support that a man pays, particularly if the man's new family includes children from his new wife's previous marriage or from the current marriage. What appears to be occurring in many cases is a form of "child-swapping," with men exchanging an old set of children from a prior marriage for a new set from their new wife's prior marriage and from the remarriage.

Sociologist Lenore I. Weitzman provides a related example in her book *The Marriage Contract*. Suppose, she writes, a 58-year-old corporate vice president with two grown children divorces his wife to marry his young secretary. He agrees to adopt the secretary's two young children. If he dies of a heart attack the following year:

> In most states, a third to half of his estate would go to his new wife, with the remainder divided among the four children (two from his last marriage, and his new wife's two children). His first wife will receive nothing — neither survivors' insurance nor a survivors' pension nor a share of the estate — and both she and his natural children are likely to feel that they have been treated unjustly.

Since the rate of mid-life divorce has been increasing nearly as rapidly as that of divorce at younger ages, this type of financial problem will become increasingly common. It would seem likely that there will be substantial pressure for changes in family law and in income security systems to provide more to the ex-wife and natural children in such circumstances.

Intergenerational Relations

A similar lack of clarity about who should support whom may affect an increasing number of elderly persons. Let us consider the case of an elderly man who long ago divorced his first wife and, as is fairly typical, retained only sporadic contact with his children. If his health deteriorates in old age and he needs help, will his children provide it? In many cases, the relationship would seem so distant that the children would not be willing to provide major assistance. To be sure, in most instances the elderly man would have remarried, possibly acquiring stepchildren, and it may be these stepchildren who feel the responsibility to provide assistance. Possibly the two sets of children may be called upon to cooperate in lending support, even when they have had little or no contact while growing up. Currently, there are no clear guidelines for assigning kinship responsibilities in this new type of extended family.

Even without considering divorce, the issue of support to the elderly is likely to bring problems that are new and widespread. As is well known, the low fertility in the United States, which we think will continue to be low, means that the population is becoming older. The difficulties that this change in age structure poses for the Social Security system are so well known that we need not discuss them here. Let us merely note than any substantial weakening of the Social Security system would put the elderly at a great disadvantage with regard to their families, for older Americans increasingly rely on Social Security and other pensions and insurance plans to provide support. A collapse of Social Security would result in a large decrease in the standard of living among older Americans and a return to the situation prevailing a few decades ago in which the elderly were disproportionately poor.

The relations between older people and their children and grandchildren are typically close, intimate, and warm. Most people live apart from their children, but they generally live close by one or more of them. Both generations prefer the autonomy that the increased affluence of the older generation has recently made possible. Older people see family members quite often, and they report that family members are their major source of support. A survey by Louis Harris of older Americans revealed that more than half of those with children had seen them in the past day, and close to half had seen a grandchild. We expect close family ties between the elderly and their kin to continue to be widespread. If, however, the economic autonomy of the elderly is weakened, say, by a drop in Social Security, the kind of friendly equality that now characterizes intergenerational relations could be threatened.

One additional comment about the elderly: Almost everyone is aware that the declining birthrate means that the elderly will have fewer children in the future on whom they can rely for support. But although this is true in the long run, it will not be true in the next few decades. In fact, beginning soon, the elderly will have more children, on average, than they do today. The reason is the postwar baby boom of the late 1940s and 1950s. As the parents of these large families begin to reach retirement age near the end of this century, more children will be available to help their elderly parents. Once the next generation—the baby-boom children—begins to reach retirement age after about 2010, the long-term trend toward fewer available children will sharply reassert itself.

Were we to be transported suddenly to the year 2000, the families we would see would look very recognizable. There would be few unfamiliar forms— not many communes or group marriages, and probably not a large proportion of lifelong singles. Instead, families by and large would continue to center around the bonds between husbands and wives and between parents and children. One could say the same about today's families relative to the 1960s: the forms are not new. What is quite different, comparing the 1960s with the 1980s, or the 1980s with a hypothetical 2000, is the distribution of these forms.

In the early 1960s, there were far fewer single-parent families and families formed by remarriages after divorce than is the case today; and in the year 2000 there are likely to be far more single-parent families and families of remarriage than we see now. Moreover, in the early 1960s both spouses were employed in a much smaller percentage of two-parent families; in the year 2000, the percentage with two earners will be greater still. Cohabitation before marriage existed in the 1960s, but it was a frowned-upon, bohemian style of life. Today, it has become widely accepted; it will likely become more common in the future. Yet we have argued that cohabitation is less an alternative to marriage than a precursor to marriage, though we expect to see a modest rise in the number of people who never marry.

Questions

1. How accurate are predictions for the demise of the family?
2. What kinds of families will predominate in the year 2000? 2010?
3. How does this compare to 1910? 1932? 1959? 1975?
4. What other findings do you think Blumstein and Schwartz came up with besides those listed in Box 102?
5. What types of marriages might be more prone to divorce than others?
6. Are single-parent families "bad" for children?
7. How do most children adjust psychologically to divorce?
8. What problems do "families of remarriages" have that "families of first marriages" do not?
9. Will males or females have more advantages in families of the future?
10. Compare black and white family structure in the present and future.
11. What legal complications will arise for future families?
12. How will future families affect the elderly?
13. Answer question 1 again.

Chapter Forty-Five

Class of 2000
The Good News and the Bad News

Marvin J. Cetron

The year 2000 is still in the future, but the high-school graduating class of 2000 is with us already; its members entered kindergarten in September 1987. The best of them are bright, inquiring, and blessed with all the benefits that caring, attentive parents can provide. They will need all those advantages and more. The class of 2000, and their schools, face educational demands far beyond those of their parents' generation. And unless they can meet those demands successfully, the United States could be nearing its last days as a world power.

No one had to tell Ben Franklin or Thomas Jefferson that their new country would live or die with its school system. In a democracy, citizens must be able to read, so they can learn about the issues on which they are voting. (No, television and radio have not made reading unnecessary.) They must know history so that they can develop political judgments and not be taken in by the false promises of unscrupulous candidates. Today, they must also understand basic science so that they can make informed decisions about such issues as the space program, nuclear power, computer technology, and genetic engineering.

Preparing for 2000

The class of 2000 will need a far better education simply to get a decent job. In part, this is because today's fast-growing employment areas—the ones

Reproduced with permission from *The Futurist* (July/August, 1987), published by the World Future Society, 7910 Woodmont Avenue, Suite 450, Bethesda, Maryland 20814.

where good jobs can be found—are fields such as computer programming, health care, and law. They require not only a high-school diploma, but advanced schooling or job-specific training.

By contrast, less than 6 percent of workers will find a place on the assembly lines that once gave high-school graduates a good income; the rest will have been replaced by robots. Instead, service jobs will form nearly 90 percent of the economy. A decade ago, about 77 percent of jobs involved at least some time spent in generating, processing, retrieving, or distributing information. By the year 2000, that figure will be 95 percent, and that information processing will be heavily computerized.

Traditional jobs also call for more familiarity with technology; even a department store sales clerk must be "computer literate" enough to use a computerized inventory system. Approximately 60 percent of today's jobs are open to applicants with a high-school diploma; among new jobs, more than half require at least some college. By the year 2010, virtually every job in the country will require some skill with information-processing technology.

Beyond that, simply living in modern society will raise the level of education we all need. By the year 2000, new technology will be changing our working lives so fast that we will need constant retraining, either to keep our existing jobs or to find new ones. Even today, engineers find that half of their professional knowledge is obsolete within five years and must go back to school to keep up; the rest of us will soon join them in the classroom. Knowledge itself will double not once, not twice, but four times by the year 2000! In that single year, the class of 2000 will be exposed to more information and knowledge than their grandparents experienced in a lifetime. (Box 105 gives additional information about what it will be like on Graduation Day, 2000.)

The Challenge for Schools

Schools will have to meet these new demands. Today, schools offer adult education as a community service or in hope of earning sorely needed revenue. In the future, they will be teaching adults because they haven't any choice. Many public schools will be open 24 hours a day, retraining adults from 4 p.m. to midnight and renting out their costly computer and communications systems to local businesses during the graveyard shift.

Fortunately, American schools can provide top-quality education when they make the effort to do so. The proof can be seen not only in affluent suburbs, but in some cities. In Fairfax, a community of about 350,000, Mantua Elementary School principal Joe Ross has made this effort. His "school for all reasons, school for all seasons" seems quite ordinary on the outside. But enter its tiled halls and you will find yourself surrounded by multicolored posters

---

Box 105

Graduation Day, 2000

When the class of 200 graduates:

- The body of knowledge will have doubled four times since 1988.
- Graduates will have been exposed that year to more information than their grandparents were in a lifetime.
- Only about 15 percent of jobs will require a college education, but nearly all will require job-specific training after high school.
- Women's salaries will have grown to within 10 percent of men's.
- Ninety percent of the labor force will work for companies employing fewer than 200 people.
- Children born in 2000 will live to be 81 years old on average (83.5 for women and 78.5 for men), compared with 74.9 years for children born in 1986 (78.5 years for women and 71.5 for men).
- Minorities will be the majorities in 53 of the 100 largest U.S. cities.

M.C.

---

depicting cultural highlights of Kuwait—all written in Arabic. Other posters appear in languages ranging from German to Vietnamese—and all are readily understood by children who are eight or nine years old. Children learn sign language as early as kindergarten, when basic consonants are taught. The school is stocked with desktop computers, and there is video equipment for every room.

Specialized classes are a major feature of Mantua's educational program. There are classrooms filled with high-technology devices to aid handicapped students. Advanced students hone their thinking skills in programs designed for the gifted and talented. At one end of the building, a school-age-child-care center continues the educational process long after traditional school hours have ended. There are also programs for the hearing impaired, the learning disabled, preschool handicapped, and English as a Second Language students.

Mantua's educational system works. Its average students rank far higher than the national average, and all the specialized programs manage to extract top grades from students who in many cases might be expected to fail. Perhaps more importantly, the Mantua Elementary children are exposed to and work with the students in the special programs mentioned above and know they are an integral part of a pluralistic society. These children will better accept each person, whatever his or her gift or handicap, as an individual and not as someone to be stared at.

Parental Guidance Suggested

Parental involvement is the key to making the system work. At Mantua, teachers have long emphasized this need. According to my wife, Gloria, who teaches kindergarten at the school, it is very simple: "When the parents get involved, the kids do better." In an effort to get the parents involved, Gloria and her aide, Lynn Curran, asked parents of the kindergartners in the class of 2000 what they are doing to prepare their children for the year 2000. Jason Hovell's parents answered, "To prepare a child for the year 2000, we think a child needs a first-rate education and strong family relationships." The parents of Sarah Crutchfield believe that "exposing (her) to the avenues of learning . . . (through) library trips, museums, nature walks, and the theater" will be the best preparation.

Many of the parents expressed concern about the moral fabric of America. Heather Goodwin's parents are "trying to rear her in a manner that leads to upright moral conduct and ethical practices, to teach her to believe in herself and stand up for what is right, and to respect the views and beliefs of others." The parents go to the head of the class. They are at the first critical stage of awareness. (Box 106 lists additional specific comments of parents of the class of 2000.)

Box 106

Parents of Kindergartners in the Class of 2000 Have Their Say

1. We must reemphasize foreign-language education and study of foreign culture to understand other customs and traditions. Perhaps a better understanding of our neighbors will help us avoid future conflicts and tensions among countries.

2. The curriculum should emphasize hands-on experiences and the child following his own interests — and deemphasize workbooks with a simplistic, "one-right-answer" approach.

3. I still think socialization is important in the curriculum. Children like to role-play real-life situations and to solve problems by play-acting.

4. Kindergarten has started this journey to the year 2000. It provides young children the opportunity of learning and participation, to love and care for everyone at school.

M.C.

The State of Education Today

Programs similar to those at Mantua Elementary are available—and successful—all over the country. Unfortunately, these remain rare bright spots in a bleak educational picture. There is all too much evidence that American schools are failing many students. In 1982, American eighth-graders taking a standardized math test answered only 46 percent of the questions correctly, which put them in the bottom half of the eleven nations participating. (Japanese children got 64 percent correct.) That same year, the top 5 percent of twelfth-graders from nine developed countries, the ones who had taken advanced math courses, took standardized tests of algebra and calculus. America's best and brightest came in dead last.

The failure is not limited to tough subjects like math. Other studies have shown that only one high-school junior in five can write a comprehensible note applying for a summer job; that among high-school seniors, fewer than one-third know to within 50 years when the Civil War took place, and one in three does not know that Columbus discovered America before 1750. (Box 107 offers a quiz to see how knowledgeable you are.)

More than 500,000 children drop out of school each year; in some school districts, the dropout rate exceeds 50 percent. Perhaps 700,000 more students in each class finish out their twelve years hardly able to read their own diplomas. Among young adults, one government-sponsored study found, well under 40 percent can understand an average *New York Times* article or figure out their change when paying for lunch, and only 20 percent have mastered the weighty intellectual challenge of reading a bus schedule.

The results of this endemic ignorance can already be seen throughout American society. The sad condition of America's once-great space program is a heartrending comment on the state of science education in the country; as a nation, we simply are not qualified to manage large, demanding technological problems. And listen to the National Restaurant Association, which estimates that by the year 1995 a million jobs in their industry will go unfilled because too many entry-level job hunters are too poorly educated to succeed even as waiters, cashiers, and hamburger flippers. By the year 2000, according to one estimate, the literacy rate in America will be only 30 percent.

Training for the Future

Solving the problems of conventional education is only one half of the task. America will also need a much stronger system of vocational education if it is to meet the challenge of the years to come. On average, the next generation of workers will have to make no fewer than five complete job changes in a

---

Box 107

A Cultural Literacy Quiz

Newspapers, magazine articles, and television news reports take for granted that their audiences have prior knowledge of most events, people, and places to which they refer. Teachers assume they share a body of facts with their students. Yet recent surveys document large gaps in American's basic knowledge. E. D. Hirsch, a professor of English at the University of Virginia, has compiled a list of 4,500 pieces of information that Americans need to know to be "culturally literate." Without this background knowledge, he says, you will not be able to make sense of what you read or hear on television. Below is a random sample of items from Hirsch's list. As you test yourself, keep in mind that basic recognition, not in-depth knowledge, is sufficient to make an item quality as part of your background knowledge. If you couldn't identify all the items, look up the answers under "Notes" in the Appendix.

1. Achilles' heel	16. yellow press	31. Icarus
2. as rich as Croesus	17. Joseph Stalin	32. Jim Crow laws
3. Benedict Arnold	18. Elvis Presley	33. I,V,X,L,C,D,M
4. Romulus and Remus	19. n.b.	34. Jane Addams
5. *carte blanche*	20. DNA	35. hypothesis
6. Davy Jones' locker	21. Brisbane	36. WASP
7. Booker T. Washington	22. featherbedding	37. Nisei
8. *hoi polloi*	23. witch hunt	38. Saturn
9. A Streetcar Named Desire	24. WCTU	39. Pompeii
10. Brown v. Board of Education	25. Chicanos	40. jeremiad
11. lip service	26. *tabula rasa*	41. Parsifal
12. Ferdinand Magellan	27. Notre Dame	42. yellow peril
13. mare's nest	28. 1939-1945	43. Salvador Dali
14. Monroe Doctrine	29. AFL-CIO	44. Tchaikovsky
15. sociobiology	30. Bard of Avon	45. Virgin Mary

Source: E. D. Hirsch, *Cultural Literacy* (Boston: Houghton Mifflin, 1987).

---

lifetime, not counting the multiple tasks (which will also be changing) associated with each respective job. This is a mandate for continuous retraining.

In the future, vocational training will be just as crucial as traditional education. If schools fail to turn out well-educated high-school and college graduates, more and more young people will find themselves unqualified for any meaningful career, while millions of jobs go begging for trained people to fill them. If schools and businesses fail to retrain adults for the growing technical demands of their jobs, millions of conscientious workers will find their careers cut short, and the skilled work they should have done will be exported to countries like Japan and Taiwan, where educational systems definitely are up to the task.

Education for the Class of 2000

America's school system today is clearly overburdened, even by the traditional demands placed on it. How can the school system be strengthened to bring high-quality education to all members of the class of 2000? And what can be done about the growing demand for adult education in the years to come? Over half a dozen measures come to mind, most of them embarrassingly simple:

- Lengthen the school day and year. In any field, you can get more work done in eight hours than in six, in ten days than in seven. Japan's school year consists of 240 eight-hour days. America's averages 180 days of about 6.5 hours. So let's split the difference: Give us 210 seven-hour school days a year.

- Cut the median class size down from 17.8 to 10 students. Naturally, this means hiring more teachers. This will give teachers more time to focus on the *average* student.

  Not too long ago, schools were just beginning to recognize the needs of special students with learning disabilities or exceptional talents. Now there are programs for the learning disabled and the gifted and talented, as there should be. But, in focusing attention and resources on the needs of the minority at the extremes, the nation's schools have neglected the needs of the majority in the middle. American students' dismal performance on standardized tests attests to this.

  Inadequate attention at school is exacerbated by inadequate attention at home for the average student. The big advantage that schools like Mantua enjoy over less successful institutions is not their specialized programs, but the fact that their students are drawn largely from traditional families where parents are available and are actively interested in the child's education. Where one-parent homes are the rule, teachers must provide the individual attention that parents cannot. In crowded classrooms, they simply can't do it. The answer is to cut class size.

- Computerize. Computer-aided learning programs are already replacing drill books; as software improves, they will begin to replace some kinds of textbooks as well. More teachers should be actively involved in writing the software. The best computerized learning programs already include primitive forms of artificial intelligence that can diagnose the student's learning problems and tailor instruction to compensate for them.

"We can put 30 computers in a room, and they will go as fast or as slow as each child needs; the child controls it," observes Representative James Scheuer (Democrat, New York). "He has an equal and comfortable relationship, building his morale and self-esteem, which can only enhance the learning process."

The result may not be as good as having highly skilled, caring teachers give hours of personal attention to each student, but computerization is a lot easier to achieve, and it's a big improvement over today's situation. This should be an easy notion to sell to taxpayers; in a survey of parents of Mantua kindergartners, fully two-thirds cited computers as one of the most important topics their children should learn in school.

But making this transition won't be cheap. By 1990, the United States will already have spent $1 billion on computerized learning, but two-thirds of that will have been spent by affluent parents for their own children. If public school systems fail to develop their own programs, the less-affluent students could suffer an irreparable educational disadvantage.

- Tailor courses to the needs of individual students. Individualized education programs (IEPs) are already used in many schools; they suggest which skills the student should practice and recommend ways of testing to make sure they have been learned. But far more is possible.

In the future, IEPs will look at the students' learning style: whether they learn best in small groups or large classes; whether they learn best from reading, lectures, or computer programs; how much supervisions they need; and so on. Teachers will be evaluated in the same way and assigned to large or small classes, good readers or good listeners, as best suits them. These programs may not be adopted in time to help the class of 2000, but the sooner the better.

- Promote students based on performance, not on time served in class. Students starting school in 2000 will move up not by conventional grade levels, but by development levels, ensuring that each child can work on each topic until it's mastered.

- Recruit teachers from business and industry, not just university educational programs. Get chemists to teach chemistry, accountants to teach arithmetic, and so on. These specialists could become teachers in areas where teachers are scarce. Give them the required courses in education necessary to meet teaching standards. But start by making sure that would-be teachers actually know something worth teaching.

- Set new priorities for school systems that today are overregulated and underaccountable. In many communities, the curriculum is so standardized that teachers in any given course on any given day will be covering the same material. It's time to cut through that kind of red tape and give teachers the right to do the job they supposedly were trained for. Then make teachers and their supervisors responsible for the performance of their students. Teachers who turn out well-educated students should be paid and promoted accordingly. If students don't advance, neither should their would-be educators.

- Bring business and industry into the public school system. Corporations must train and retrain workers constantly, and that requirement will grow ever more pressing. The obvious answer is for them to contract with schools to do the teaching. The money earned from such services can go toward teachers' salaries and investments in computers, software, and such things as air conditioning needed to keep schools open all year.

  For students not headed toward college, businesses may also provide internships that give high-school students practical experience in the working world they are about to enter. When public schools turn out graduates who haven't mastered reading, writing, or math, business suffers. (Box 108 pursues this school-business partnership further.)

- Finally, if Americans really want quality education, they must be willing to pay for it. Since the National Commission on Excellence in Education published its landmark report, *A Nation at Risk,* in 1983, the Reagan administration has never asked for a significant increase in federal aid to education. In fact, since 1984, the White House has attempted to cut the national education budget by more than $10 billion. Though Congress has always restored most of those proposed cuts, the federal government is actually spending, after inflation, about 14 percent less for education than it did five years ago. (Thus far, this is true for the Bush administration as well.)

  Teachers are still dramaticallly underpaid compared with other professions that require a college education. In 1987, the average starting salary for an accountant was $21,200, new computer specialists received $26,170, and engineers began at $28,500. The average starting salary for teachers was only $17,500.

Today's education system cannot begin to prepare students for the world they will enter on graduation from high school. By 2030, when the class of 2000 will still be working, they will have had to assimilate more inventions and more new information than have appeared in the last 150 years. By 2010,

---

Box 108

School—Business Partnership

The future of business depends on education. Future prosperity turns upon the quality of a nation's workers. As the United States approaches the twenty-first century, there will be even stiffer competition in world markets than there is today. Businesses will be beating down the doors of the little red schoolhouse for bright, inquiring students to fill a growing number of knowledge-intensive positions. The only problem is that, at a time when jobs requiring higher skills and education are increasing, schools are churning out virtually unemployable grads.

Quite simply, the business community is alarmed and appalled at the quality of new workers. Education was ranked the top concern of 2,000 businesses and other organizations in a 1987 survey by the Conference Board. The situation is so bad that the National Alliance of Business recently called upon the business community to "view education from a perspective of a company in trouble," urging its members to become more actively involved in education.

The "company" is in trouble because of an education system characterized by fewer course requirements, lower academic standards, and fewer homework assignments than in the past, and these are just a few of the things that the business community would like to see changed.

The situation is not only sad, but expensive. Some $240 billion a year is sacrificed in lost earnings and forgone taxes by each year's crop of dropouts. Businesses spend another $25 billion a year teaching workers basic skills that should have been taught at school. A large financial contributor to education in the past, the business community is now starting to demand a return on its investment. It is calling for significant reforms.

No less than "complete restructuring is in order," asserts David Kearns, chairman and chief executive officer of the Xerox Corporation. Businesses are demanding: higher pay for teachers, better teacher training, more decision-making authority for teachers and principals at individual schools, higher academic standards, early childhood education, support for magnet schools, teaching of "higher-order thinking" skills, and, finally, choice and competition within and from outside school districts. Only if such changes are instituted will businesses support schools financially.

The business community is a powerful force, and, marshaled to fight for education, should get results. Business has a lot to gain if it plays this more active role, and it has a lot to lose if it doesn't.

M.C.

there will be hardly a job in the country that does not require skill in using powerful computers and telecommunications systems.

America needs to enact all the reforms outlined above, and many others as well. It is up to concerned citizens, parents, and teachers to equip our children with the knowledge and skills necessary to survive and thrive in the twenty-first century. Education should be a major political issue, for time is running out: The class of 2000 is already with us.

Questions

1. Why is the educational system especially important in democratic societies?

2. Obviously the three R's are important subjects. The article mentions knowledge of history, science, the computer, and foreign languages as well. Can you think of any additional subjects that would be important?

3. It used to be that a person graduated from school and got a job. Now it seems humans will be in and out of the classroom all their lives. Is this good or bad?

4. What does the "school for all reasons, school for all seasons" do that allows it to provide top-quality education?

5. How important is "high tech" equipment (videos, computers, etc.) to making our schools better?

6. Should we require students to learn a foreign language? What should it be? At what age should the child begin study of it?

7. Parental involvement is said to be the key to making the educational system work. How do we get parents involved? How much authority should parents have about textbook selection, teacher hiring and firing, etc.? Have local parent councils worked in those cities and towns that have tried them?

8. Alan Bloom's *The Closing of the American Mind* was a best seller that blasted American colleges for focusing on trendy, "relevant," career-oriented courses. Is this true of the high school curriculum?

9. What additional items come immediately to mind that should be added to Hirsch's list?

10. Functional illiteracy is estimated at 15 to 20 percent. What can we do about it?

11. Cetron's suggestions for improving schools are geared to elementary and high schools. Can any of them be applied to colleges and universities?

12. Will smaller classes make a difference? Would the class you are in right now be better worse with ten students?

13. Aren't such suggestions as "IEPs," unconventional grade levels, teachers from business, etc., totally unrealistic?

14. Should teachers get higher salaries? Isn't it true that "those who can, do, and those who can't, teach"?

Chapter Forty-Six

The Arrival of the 5-Billionth Human

Ralph E. Hamil

July 11, 1987, according to United Nations demographers, saw the world's population pass the 5-billion mark.

This billion was added in only 12 years. The 6-billionth person should arrive by century's end. (This refers to population size at a particular time, *not* population ever living.) Every day, some 220,000 people are added to the world's population, or 80 million per year. Ninety percent of this expansion is in developing countries.

The rate of growth is gradually slowing, but before world population reaches stability—perhaps a hundred years from now—there may be twice as many people on the planet as there are at present. The socioeconomic implications of having a world population of 5 billion—with another 5 billion en route— are enormous.

Distinguished Predecessors

The rate of population growth in the twentieth century is unprecedented. The world's population did not reach 5 million until the end of the Neolithic period (c. 8000-5000 B.C.), before the spread of agriculture permitted higher population densities. The 50-millionth human lived about 2000 B.C., probably

Reproduced with permission from *The Futurist* (July/August, 1987), published by the World Future Society, 7910 Woodmont Avenue, Suite 450, Bethesda, Maryland 20814.

in Asia, although he or she may have been a subject of a Theban Dynasty pharaoh.

As civilization expanded, cities were built that could support a million souls: Rome, Angkor, Hangchow, and Beijing in their heydays are examples. There were setbacks during the Dark Ages, the Black Death, and chronic wars, but human numbers recovered. The 500-millionth human arrived around 1575 A.D.

The Americas were settled, life expectancy grew, and the billion mark was reached around 1830. Ten million people died in World War I and more in the civil wars that followed. Twenty million died in the Spanish Flu pandemic. Nonetheless, the 2-billionth human arrived around 1930. By then, most countries had censuses, and the League of Nations began to compile world population estimates.

Fifty million died in World War II (and there have been 20 million more war-related deaths in the years since), but planetary population growth continued to accelerate. Demographers noted the arrival of number 3 billion in 1959-1960 and number 4 billion in 1974-1975.

Wide variations in world population estimates remained, in large part because of disputes over the long-uncounted Chinese population. In 1982, China completed a widely admired census and announced a total population of just over 1 billion. Question marks still remain as to the actual population of such large nations as Nigeria, Mexico, and Zaire, but the bottom-line numbers are converging. The world's main gatherers of data—the U.N., the World Bank, and the U.S. Census Bureau—agree that the world's population reached 5 billion in or about mid-1987.

Welcome, Mohammed Wang

Let us call this newborn 5-billionth human Mohammed Wang, using the worlds most popular given and family names. Assuming Mohammed is in other ways typical, one can make a number of statements about him.

Mohammed is male. There are more boys born than girls, and men have usually outnumbered women throughout history. An exception is after major wars; it took 15 years before males regained equivalence after World War II. Because of declining infant mortality, the worldwide ratio of men to women will increase until 2000, then slide back to equivalence around 2035. By 2100, when world zero population growth is expected, there will be 175 million more women than men. The typical human might then be known as Maria Wang.

Mohammed is Asian. Long ago, Asia surpassed Africa as the continent with the most people and has since been home to more than half of humanity. Six Asian nations today have populations in excess of 100 million.

Mohammed enjoys certain advantages not shared by his ancestors. He will drink potable water, will be vaccinated, will receive some schooling, will perhaps marry for love rather than through parental arrangement, will someday live in a home with electricity if he does not already do so, will vote (although it may lack meaning), and will live into his 60s. Through his transistor radio and access to television, Mohammed will be a part of the communications complex of the global village. He will cheer his country's prowess in the Olympics and the World Cup. The coronations, marriages, and funerals of celebrities will be available to him with all their pageantry.

AIDS could jeopardize Mohammed's hopes of a long and prosperous life. The World Health Organization and ministries of health everywhere are fearful that the AIDS pandemic will spread and cause up to 100 million deaths by 2000. Perhaps double that number might go unborn because of reduced sexual activity and increased use of condoms. In Africa, the fastest growing continent by far, the disease has already affected millions. After Africa, the demographic effect would probably be greatest in Latin America, North America, Europe, and Asia, in that order.

Some chilly December day in Stockholm, the discoverer(s) of a cure or vaccine for AIDS will, no doubt, rightfully receive the Nobel Prize for medicine. But meanwhile, AIDS may shape the 1990s in the same way that the Depression and World Wars dominated their decades.

Countercolonization

The world of 5 billion offers strange contrasts. Central Europe has achieved zero population growth, whereas Kenya's numbers increased 4 percent per year. Third World nations are sending their surplus sons and daughters to North America and Europe. Latins, Arabs, Africans, and Asians are colonizing their former mother countries. Among violence-stimulating situations are those where political and economic power does not reflect disparate population growth rates (Lebanon) or where a massive influx of immigrants causes problems of assimilation (Miami and the Arab Gulf states).

While a number of nations will witness considerable change in ethnic makeup, some—such as Japan—can be expected to protect their homogeneous character through tight immigration regulations. Though their efficacy is questioned, border controls are being tightened in order to forestall AIDS. The perceived need for health measures may make politically palatable more chauvinistic immigration policies in the United States, Canada, and France, among others— countries viewed as quite liberal at present.

Still Counting

The days for the 6-billionth, 7-billionth, and 8-billionth human beings are anticipated for 1998, 2010, and 2023 respectively, according to U.N. forecasts. By the later date, the human exodus from the earth may have begun, with small but growing numbers of people living and working in space on the moon and Mars.

After the next generation, demographers differ on where and when human numbers will reach zero growth. None, however, predicts another tenfold increase to 50 billion, and only a handful would prognosticate even a fivefold increase.

Ten billion people, crammed into super-cities and intra-urban strip cities of highrise apartment complexes, will occupy land that has, at some point, been taken out of food production. Demand for fuel and non-fuel minerals will rise with burgeoning population. There are no guarantees that a continuously improving standard of living can be maintained with such strains on the biosphere and geosphere. And, without such improvements, social and, perhaps, international strife may be inevitable. (Box 109 predicts a very optimistic future.)

Box 109

Can This Be?
Optimistic Long Term Trends in Population

Until the 18th century, there was slow growth in population, almost no increase in health, no decrease in mortality, slow growth in the availability of natural resources, increase in wealth for a few, and mixed effects on the environment. Since the 18th century, there has been rapid growth in population due to spectacular decreases in the death rate, rapid growth in resources, widespread increases in wealth, and an unprecedented clean and beautiful living environment in many parts of the world (along with a poor and degraded environment in the poor and socialist parts of the world).

This is the opposite of what the press and antinatilist environmental organizations have led us to believe. Yet it is true. The key to understanding this is that almost every economic or social change or trend points in a positive direction as long as we view the matter over a reasonably long period of time. "We should look at long-term trends. But the short-run comparisons— between the sexes, age groups, races, political groups, which are usually purely relative—make more news. To repeat, just about every important long-run measure of human welfare shows improvement over the decades and centuries, in the United States as well as in the rest of the world. And there is no persuasive reason to believe that these trends will not continue indefinitely."

SOURCE: Julian L. Simon, "More People, Greater Wealth, More Resources, Healthier Environment," in Kurt Finsterbusch and George McKenna (eds.), *Taking Sides: Clashing Views on Controversial Social Issues*, Eighth Edition (Guilford, Connecticut: Dushkin, 1994).

Science and technology have, thus far, allowed human numbers to grow without quite overloading the planet's carrying capacity. Near-term technological innovation will allow extraction of the resources of the oceans, polar regions, and marginal deposits of minerals and fossil fuels elsewhere. The next century should see the beginnings of off-planet resource extraction. The twenty-second century may witness the first demographically significant emigration into space.

In the meantime, the 5 billion people now on earth must dampen the population boom that so far defies all controls.

Questions

1. How many people are there in the world? How do we know?
2. Is there a typical 5-billionth human? Describe him. Or is it her?
3. Describe population growth prior to and after the agricultural revolution.
4. Describe population growth prior to and after the industrial revolution.
5. Constrast colonization and countercolonization.
6. Does population growth affect the environment?
7. Should we be optimistic or pessimistic about future population growth?

Appendix

Notes

Chapter 3: Science, the Scientific Method, and Research Designs in the Social Sciences

(Scoring for the experiment described on page 23.)

NASA ranks the items this way:

A. 15	F. 11	K. 14
B. 4	G. 12	L. 2
C. 6	H. 1	M. 10
D. 8	I. 3	N. 7
E. 13	J. 9	O. 5

To compute either individual or group scores, subtract the ranking "choice" for a specific item from NASA's ranking for that item. (Disregard positive or negative numbers and always subtract the lower number from the higher number.) When you have completed this, add up the differences. The lower the total score, the more the score conforms to NASA's judgment. In the many times I have tried this experiment, the range for individual scores has gone from a low of 20 to a high in the 80s. Group scores have averaged in the 30s.

Chapter 5: Sociology

Answers for "true-false quiz on sociological research" are all false.

Chapter 18: Body Ritual Among the Nacirema (References Cited)

Linton, Ralph, *The Study of Man*, New York: D. Appleton-Century Co., 1936.
Malinowski, Bronislaw, *Magic, Science, and Religion*, Prospect Heights, IL: Waveland Press (copyright 1948), reissued 1992.
Murdock, George P., *Social Structure*, New York: The Macmillan Co., 1949.

525

Chapter 34: The Uses of Poverty: The Poor Pay All

1. "Manifest and Latent Functions," in *Social Theory and Social Culture*, (Glencoe, IL: The Free Press, 1949), p. 71.

Chapter 40: Final Note on a Case of Extreme Isolation

1. Kingsley Davis, "Extreme Social Isolation of a Child," *American Journal of Sociology*, XLV (January, 1940), pp. 554-65.
2. Sincere appreciation is due to the officials in the Department of Welfare, Commonwealth of Pennsylvania, for their kind cooperation in making available the records concerning Anna and discussing the case frankly with the writer. Helen C. Hubbell, Florentine Hackbusch, and Eleanor Meckelnburg were particularly helpful, as was Fanny L. Matchette. Without their aid neither of the reports on Anna could have been written.
3. The records are not clear as to which day.
4. Letter to one of the state officials in charge of the case.
5. *Ibid.*
6. Progress report of the school.
7. Davis, *op. cit.*, p. 564.
8. The facts set forth here as to Anna's ancestry are taken chiefly from a report of mental tests administered to Anna's mother by psychologists at a state hospital where she was taken for this purpose after the discovery of Anna's seclusion. This excellent report was not available to the writer when the previous paper on Anna was published.
9. Marie K. Mason, "Learning To Speak After Six and One-Half Years of Silence," *Journal of Speech Disorder*, VII (1942), pp. 295-304.
10. Francis N. Maxfield, "What Happens When the Social Environment of a Child Approaches Zero." The writer is greatly indebted to Mrs. Maxfield and to Professor Horace B. English, a colleague of Professor Maxfield, for the privilege of seeing this manuscript and other materials collected on isolated and feral individuals.
11. J.A.L. Singh and Robert M. Zingg, *Wolf-Children and Feral Man* (New York: Harper & Bros., 1941), pp. 248-51.
12. Maxfield, unpublished manuscript cited above.
13. Mason, *op. cit.* p. 299.
14. Maxfield, unpublished manuscript.
15. Mason, *op. cit.*, p. 299.
16. *Ibid.*, pp. 300-304.
17. Maxfield, unpublished manuscript.
18. Based on a personal letter from Dr. Mason to the writer, May 13, 1946.
19. This point is suggested in a personal letter from Dr. Mason to the writer, October 22, 1946.
20. Singh and Zingg, *op. cit.*, pp. xxi-xxii, in a foreword by the writer.

Chapter 45: Class of 2000

Answers to Cultural Literacy Quiz

1. A small but mortal weakness. Achilles was invulnerable except in the heel. An arrow struck him there and killed him.
2. Ancient King of Lydia noted for his wealth.
3. American Revolutionary War general who turned traitor.
4. Mythical twin brothers who founded Rome.
5. French for blank card. Freedom to do what one wants.
6. Bottom of the sea. Graves of those who perish there.
7. Black educator, 1856-1915, who said blacks should work for advances in education and employment instead of social equality.
8. Greek for people. Refers to common people, usually derogatory.
9. Contemporary drama by Tennessee Williams.
10. Supreme Court decision which outlawed segregated schools.
11. Insincere expression of support.
12. Portuguese navigator, 1480-1521, who circumnavigated the world.
13. Extremely complex situation. Possibly a hoax or delusion.
14. President's policy that U.S. will not brook interference in the Americas by outside powers.
15. Academic discipline that combines findings of sociology and biology.
16. Sensational journalism.
17. Authoritarian premier of U.S.S.R. from 1941 to 1953.
18. King of rock and roll.
19. *Nota bene* Latin for note well.
20. Deoxyribonucleic acid. Chemical material that makes up the genes.
21. Capital of Queensland, Australia.
22. Limiting output or using more workers than needed.
23. Investigation supposedly to uncover wrongdoing but really to harass political opposition.
24. Women's Christian Temperance Union. Organization to ban use of alcohol.
25. Mexican-Americans
26. Latin for a clean or empty slate. The mind at birth.
27. Cathedral in Paris or university in Indiana
28. Dates of World War II.
29. Important industrial unions.
30. William Shakespeare
31. Legendary son of Daedalus who flew too close to the Sun and fell to his death.
32. Laws used to maintain caste system after American Civil War.
33. Roman numerals.
34. Chicago social worker and reformer at turn of the century.
35. Hunch or educated guess.
36. White, Anglo-Saxon, Protestant
37. American born children of Japanese parentage.
38. Planet
39. Roman city destroyed by volcano.

40. Tale of woe, from Jeremiah's biblical lamentations
41. German opera by Richard Wagner.
42. Fear of Chinese immigrants at time of California gold rush.
43. Contemporary Spanish painter
44. Russian classical music composer
45. Mother of Christ

Maps

EUROPE

| 0 | 200 | 400 | 600 km |

| 0 | 200 | 400 mi |

1 THE FORMER YUGOSLAV REP. OF MACEDONIA   The boundaries and names shown on this map do not imply
official endorsement or acceptance by the United Nations.

MAP NO. 3694 Rev.2 UNITED NATIONS
JULY 1994

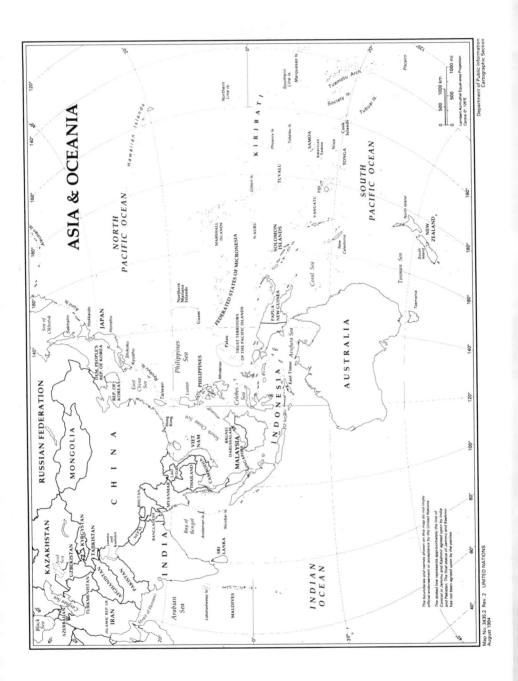

ASIA & OCEANIA

Department of Public Information
Cartographic Section

Map No. 3435.2 Rev. 2 UNITED NATIONS
August 1994

Lambert Azimuthal Equal-area Projection
Centre: 0°, 120°E

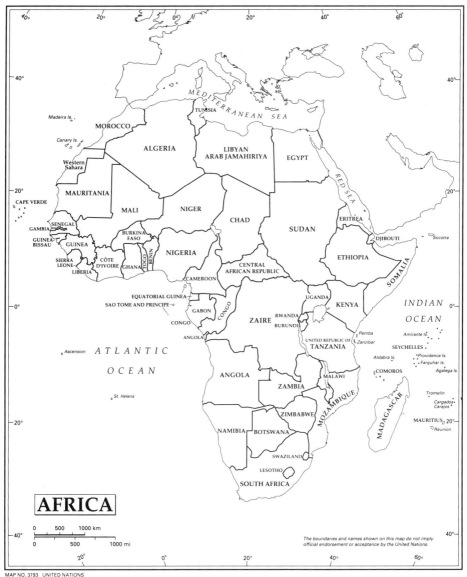

AFRICA

0   500   1000 km
0   500   1000 mi

The boundaries and names shown on this map do not imply
official endorsement or acceptance by the United Nations.

MAP NO. 3793 UNITED NATIONS
JULY 1993

531

The boundaries shown on this map do not imply official endorsement or acceptance by the United Nations.

SOUTH AMERICA

CARIBBEAN SEA

BELIZE
GUATEMALA
HONDURAS
EL SALVADOR
NICARAGUA
COSTA RICA
PANAMA

Monserrat
Aves
Guadeloupe
DOMINICA
Martinique
ST LUCIA
BARBADOS
ST VINCENT AND THE GRENADINES
GRENADA
TRINIDAD AND TOBAGO

Providencia
San Andres

Aruba Curaçao
Bonaire
Margarita

VENEZUELA

COLOMBIA

GUYANA
SURINAME
French
Guiana

Malpelo

Marajo

S Pedro e S Paulo

ECUADOR

Isabela
San Salvador
San Cristobal
Santa Cruz
Galapagos Is
(Archipelago de Colon)

Rocas
Fernando
de Noronha

P E R U

B R A Z I L

BOLIVIA

PACIFIC

PARAGUAY

Trindade
Martin Vaz

San Felix
San Ambrosio

O C E A N

Juan Fernandez Is

C H I L E

A R G E N T I N A

URUGUAY

ATLANTIC

OCEAN

Chiloe

Wellington

Falkland Is
(Islas Malvinas)
West Falkland
East Falkland

South Georgia

The boundaries and names on this map do not imply
official endorsement or acceptance by the United Nations

Tierra del Fuego
Santa Ines
Hoste Navarino

0   250   500   750 km
0   250   500   750 mi
Lambert Azimuthal Equal-Area Projection
Centre 15 S 60 W

SCOTIA SEA

South
Sandwich Is

MAP NO 3119 REV 1 UNITED NATIONS
AUGUST 1984

533

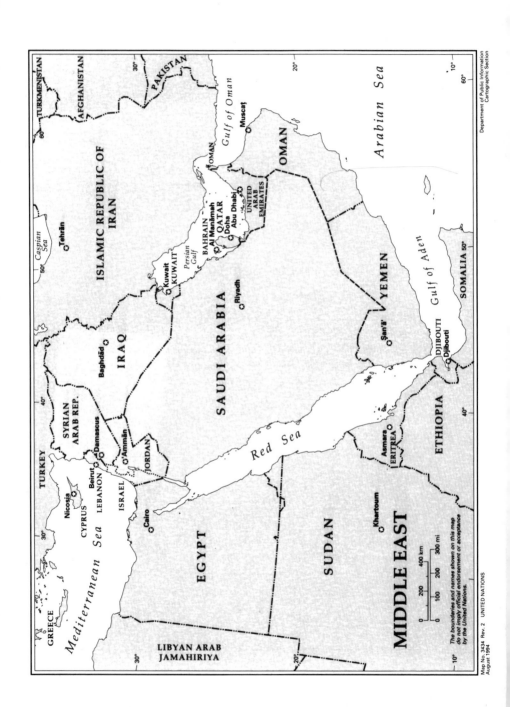

MIDDLE EAST

The boundaries and names shown on this map do not imply official endorsement or acceptance by the United Nations.

0   100   200   300 mi
0   200   400 km

Map No. 3434 Rev. 2   UNITED NATIONS
August 1994

Department of Public Information
Cartographic Section

Glossary

achieved status: A position people acquire through their own actions.

adaptation: Process by which organisms achieve a beneficial adjustment to an available environment together with the results of that process, i.e., characteristics that fit organisms to the particular environmental conditions where they are generally found.

agricultural society: A society that engages in large-scale cultivation of crops using plows drawn by animals.

anomie: A social condition in which norms are weak, conflicting, or absent.

applied research: Research designed and conducted to answer "practical" questions.

artifacts: Material elements of the society.

ascribed status: A position a person is placed in, usually at birth.

attitude: An individual's learned tendency to react positively or negatively to given stimuli.

basic research: Research designed and conducted to test hypotheses.

birth rate: The number of live births per year usually computed as a rate for every 1000 people.

bureaucracy: An organization that has a division of labor, hierarchical authority, formal rules, and impersonality among members.

case study: A detailed investigation of a single event, person, or social grouping.

caste: A social category to which one is assigned by birth and from which there is no escape.

cause and effect relationship: A statement of an association between 2 or more variables that state that one variable brings about, influences, or changes the other one.

class: A social category to which one is assigned because of economic, prestige and/or power factors.

control group: In an experiment, the subjects who are not exposed to the independent variable, giving the experimenter a basis for comparison with subjects who are.

correlation: A statement of an association between 2 or more variables that states that changes in one variable are related to changes in another but that one does not necessarily cause the other.

culture: All of a people's shared customs, beliefs, values, and artifacts.

cultural relativity: The principle that a culture must be understood and evaluated on its own terms, and not by the standards of another culture.

death rate: The number of deaths per year usually computed as a rate for every 1000 people.

deductive reasoning: The use of logic to infer a specific statement of conditions from a general statement of conditions.

demographic transition: A theory that birth rates and death rates are linked to a society's level of technological development.

demography: The statistical study of factors that alter the size and composition of populations.

dependent variable: A factor that changes in response to changes in the independent variable.

DNA: Dioxyribonucleic acid—the genetic material; a complex molecule carrying information to direct synthesis of proteins. DNA molecules have the unique ability to produce exact copies of themselves.

dyad: A group with two members.

ecology: The study of the way organisms respond to their environment.

empiricism: The belief that only sense impressions are a reliable source of knowledge.

experiment: A research design that exposes subjects to a specially designed situation. By systematically recording subjects' reactions, the researcher can assess the effects of several different variables.

experimental group: In an experiment, the subjects who are exposed to the independent variables and observed for changes in behavior.

ethnocentrism: The tendency to see one's own way of life as superior and others as inferior.

evolution: A theory that sees the development of humans, society, etc. from simple to complex.

fossils: Bones, impressions, or traces of animals or plants that lived in the past.

function: As used in the social sciences, the consequences or impact of something. It can be manifest (overt) or latent (hidden).

genus: A group of like species. Genus *Homo* includes *Homo erectus,, Homo habilis, Homo sapiens* (Neanderthal and modern), etc.

group: Two or more people who interact in patterned ways.

Hawthorne effect: The possibility of influencing subjects in an experiment simply by giving them the satisfaction of being noticed and studied.

hominid: Hominoid family to which humans belong; ground-dwellers with bipedal locomotion and significant reliance upon culture (learned as opposed to biologically determined or genetically programmed behavior).

hominoid: A primate superfamily that includes apes and humans.

Homo: A hominid genus characterized by expansion of brain and reduction of jaws.

horticultural society: A society that cultivates plants using hand tools.

hunting and gathering society: A society that uses simple tools to hunt animals and gather vegetation.

hypothesis: An empirically testable proposition about how two or more variables are related to each other.

independent variable: A factor that the researcher manipulates because he believes it will affect the dependent variable.

inductive reasoning: The use of logic to infer a general conclusion from specific facts.

industrial society: A society that uses machines to produce material goods.

instincts: Fixed, unalterable behaviors that are biologically inherited.

institutions: A stable cluster of values, norms, statuses, roles, and groups that develop around basic needs in a society.

interview: A conversational research technique in which questions are asked of respondents. It may be structured or unstructured.

megalopolis: An urban region that contains two or more metropolises and the land between them.

methodology: A systematic set of procedures by which knowledge is developed.

mesolithic era: Middle stone age, that is, that period of time around 35,000 B.C. when the human species assumed its present form.

metropolis: A central city with its surrounding suburbs.

natural sciences: disciplines that study physical and biological phenomena.

natural selection: The evolutionary process through which environmental factors (e.g., malaria, ultraviolet rays of the sun, lethal viruses) exert pressure that favors some individuals over others to reproduce.

neolithic era: New stone age, that is, that period of time around 10,000 B.C. when humans began to cultivate grains and domesticate animals.

norm: An expectation of how people are expected to act, think, or feel in specific situations.

objective: Capable of being observed empirically; elimination of the influence of personal values or emotions.

objectivity: Being free of bias, impartial.

paleoanthropologist: One who studies human evolution from fossil remains.

paleolithic era: Old stone age, that is, that period from 1,000,000 B.C. or earlier when humans used stone tools.

participant observation: A research design in which the researcher joins and participates in the groups he is studying in an effort to gain firsthand knowledge.

pastoral society: A society where subsistence is based on the domestication of animals.

personality: The organization of attitudes, emotions, and temperament of a person.

population: In a research study, all the people the investigator wants to learn about.

postindustrial society: A society in which the majority of people are not engaged in food production or manufacturing but in service and information related occupations.

primary groups: Small, close-knit groups characterized by intimate face-to-face associations.

race: A category of people defined by common physical characteristics.

random sample: A sample chosen in such a way that every member of the population has the same chance of being selected.

reinforcement: The strengthening of a response either through a reward or the removal of something unpleasant.

reliability: The degree to which a study yields the same results when repeated by the original researcher or by other scientists.

replication: Repetition of a research procedure to see if earlier results can be duplicated.

representative sample: A subgroup of a population that is believed to be typical of the larger population from which it is drawn.

research: Investigation guided by theory to collect and analyze data.

role: Behavioral expectations connected to a status.

sample: A limited number of people selected from the population being studied.

science: Both a method for obtaining information and a body of systematically arranged knowledge that attempts to discover and explain relationships among phenomena.

secondary group: Large or small impersonal groups where members do not know each other intimately.

social sciences: Disciplines that study various aspects of human behavior and the institutions which mold it.

socialization: The process by which people learn the ways of a society or group.

society: A group of people who live in a given territory and who share a common culture.

sociocultural evolution: The tendency for societies to grow more complex over time as their means of subsistence changes.

species: In biology, a population or group of populations capable of interbreeding but reproductively isolated from other such populations.

status: A position in a group or society.

stratification: A hierarchical system in which people are ranked into layers or strata. Basis for ranking includes such factors as skin color or parent's religion which would result in a caste system or such factors as wealth, prestige, or power which would result in a class system.

subjective: Not capable of being verified by others; dependent on values, judgments, or emotions.

survey: A research design in which a population or sample is questioned (through interviews and questionnaires) in order to learn specific facts about it.

theory: A comprehensive explanation of apparent relationships or underlying principles of certain observed phenomena.

validity: The degree to which a scientific study measures what it attempts to measure.

value: An ideal shared by members of a society about what is good and bad, right and wrong, desirable and undesirable.

value-free: The attempt to banish personal values and beliefs from the realm of scientific pursuits.

variable: Any concept or factor that has a value that may change or vary.

Made in the USA
Middletown, DE
26 May 2023

31535525R00210

**THE WAR AMERICA CAN'T AFFORD
TO LOSE**

GEORGE GALDORISI

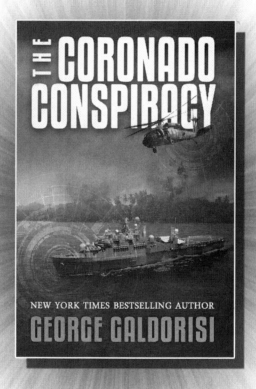

Everything was going according to plan...

WHITE-HOT SUBMARINE WARFARE
BY
JOHN R. MONTEITH

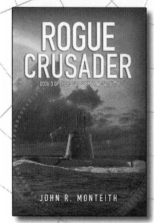

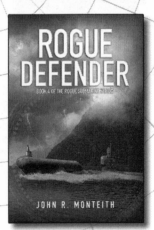

**CUTTING-EDGE NAVAL FICTION
BY**

JEFF EDWARDS

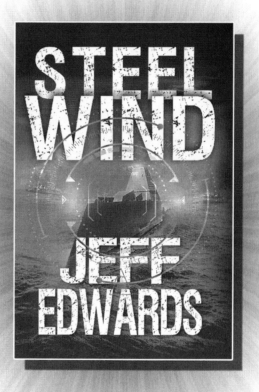

**A battle we never expected to fight, against an
enemy we can barely comprehend...**

CUTTING-EDGE NAVAL THRILLERS
BY
JEFF EDWARDS

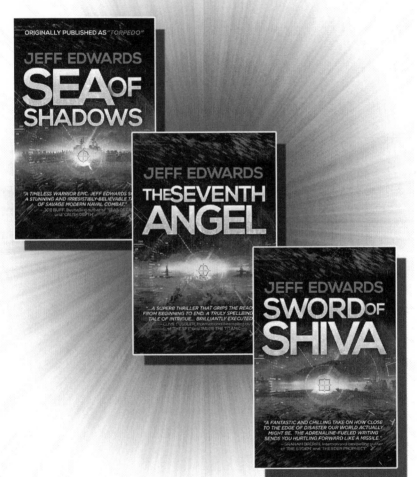

**FROM TODAY'S MASTER
OF CARRIER AVIATION FICTION**

KEVIN MILLER

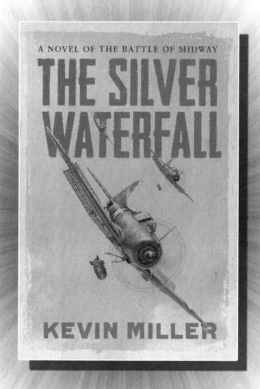

A NOVEL OF THE BATTLE OF MIDWAY

THE SILVER WATERFALL

KEVIN MILLER

Midway as never told before!

www.braveshipbooks.com

SUPERSONIC CARRIER AVIATION FICTION
FROM
KEVIN MILLER

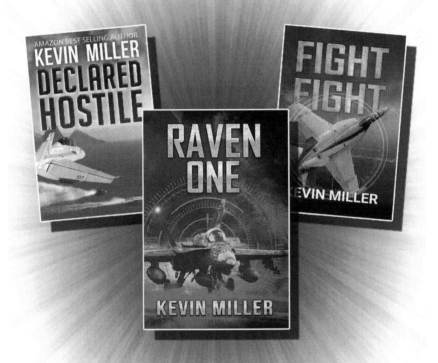

The Unforgettable Raven One Trilogy

www.braveshipbooks.com

Part I

Lord, guard and guide the men who fly
Through the great spaces in the sky,
Be with them always in the air,
In dark'ning storm and sunlight fair.
Oh hear us when we lift our prayer,
For those in peril in the air.

Navy Hymn Alternate Verse

CHAPTER 1

The formation wheeled right, steadied on a heading of 165, and accelerated into the cold darkness. With Mosul just off to the left, the pilot selected the target bullseye on his navigation display.

Penetrating Iraqi airspace, the four FA-18 *Hornets* led a package of aircraft *going downtown* on night one. The pilot shifted the position of his back and legs in a vain attempt to relieve the strain of being strapped into his seat for the last two hours. He had at least another two hours ahead.

Three miles below was "friendly" Kurd territory, but from this height it seemed dark and foreboding. He checked fuel, checked his position off the lead, and scanned the horizon for threats. His eyes, though, always came back to the mesmerizing confusion of moving lights on the far horizon: the lights of Baghdad.

"Ninety-nine *Buckshot, armstrong.*" The voice of the strike leader was calm.

The pilot raised the MASTER ARM switch to ARM. Pulling the trigger now would send off a radar-guided missile to find and kill its assigned target. The radar cursor bounced back and forth across the display like a metronome, but the display showed nothing ahead, nothing yet for the pilot or his wingmen to kill. *Where are you? Come on up! Come up, you dickheads, and fight!*

The lights of Baghdad loomed larger.

Breathing through his mouth, the pilot realized his throat was bone dry. His eyes tracked the occasional flashes of cruise missile impacts throughout the metro area, which he could see in its entirety through the windscreen. The flashes grew larger as they neared the city.

All around Baghdad, ordered rows of lights lifted slowly and silently from dozens of locations to fill the sky above the city. Some gracefully turned this way and that before they reached their apex and died out. These great tentacles of AAA, almost elegant in their beauty when viewed through the night vision goggles, formed gnarled fingers of light as they, too, looked for something to kill. They wanted to swat down some piece—any piece—of American aluminum so that it made a flaming, cartwheeling plunge toward a fiery impact on the desert floor.

3

The pilot imagined, if he had to eject, the gunners pointing at his parachute and the raging mob below waiting to beat him senseless—or worse. *This is the Cradle of Civilization.* The pilot couldn't help but think of the irony as he neared this web of death at nearly 10 miles a minute.

"*Brooms, Excalibur*, picture bullseye, single group cold, low."

"*Broom* Four One, declare."

He looked right with a start. His NVG field of view was filled with a *Hornet* centerline fuel tank and underside coming right at him. Seconds from midair collision, he instinctively pushed nose down. After he managed to recover, he looked up to his left and saw the aircraft stop its leftward slide and come back above him to take station. *Did I miss a call? Or did he?*

"*Brooms, Excalibur*, single group bullseye three-five-zero for ten, hot, climbing. Hostile, repeat, hostile."

Fighters! The Iraqis are coming up! Forgetting his near midair but keeping a wary eye on his wingman, the pilot ran his radar elevation down. A blip immediately appeared, and, with a flick of his thumb, he locked it.

The suppression element miles behind him fired their high-speed, anti-radiation missiles. As the missiles flew above the *Buckshot* formation, they resembled supersonic sparklers rocketing along unseen tracks, blazing forward to home in on enemy radar emitters and destroy them. That gave the pilots an opportunity to maneuver into a position to fire on the enemy "bandits." The bandits were coming right at him right now. *Yes! Yes, they're coming! We're gonna splash these guys!*

As he approached the target area, the radio came alive with calls of AAA and radar spikes, check turns and threat locations. For a few seconds, he noticed the contrast between the radio activity and the silent light show in front of them, especially as the impacts of the Tomahawks occurred with a greater frequency and the AAA arcs rose to their altitude. He could make out specks of radiance far to the south—formations of carrier strike aircraft coming up from the Persian Gulf. *Right on time,* the pilot thought. The slowly rotating tentacles of light grew closer.

He squeezed the trigger. With a lurch, a missile fell from the aircraft and ignited into a giant sun that sprinted ahead with a deep rumbling.

WHOOOMMmmm!

Even as the flash momentarily blinded him, he could see through his goggles that the missile seemed to run like a cheetah after its target. He saw another missile come off his wingman's aircraft and watched it rise into the star-filled sky toward its target.

Without warning, but accompanied by a muffled boom, he was jolted in his seat by something that slammed into his jet from behind. The airplane rolled right. Full left stick was useless to stop the roll. His headphones erupted into the cries of his airplane's death throes, recorded by an impassive female voice: *Flight Controls. Flight Controls. Engine Right. Engine Right.*

Warning and caution lights, too many to comprehend and too many of them red, popped up on the digital displays and lighted panels. As the rotations got tighter and tighter, he saw that the scattered lights on the ground below were also spinning in his windscreen.

"Get out!" he heard someone call over the radio.

Yes, get out! he thought, at the same time he sensed his airspeed increasing. He tore the goggles from his helmet, dropped them on the console and found the handle between his legs. He grasped the handle with his right hand and grabbed his right wrist with his left as he was trained to do. With his back against the seat and elbows in, he pulled.

The pressure and cold of the 500-knot airstream roared into his cockpit void and gripped him hard as the canopy exploded off the airplane. For a moment, he wondered if the seat was going to ignite, but then was compressed into it as the rocket he was sitting on blasted him into space with deafening and painful force as the slipstream violently wrenched helmet and mask from his head. Legs and arms flailing, he tumbled through the darkness...

When Lieutenant Commander Jim Wilson opened his eyes in the early morning shadows, the first thing he saw was the rack above him in stateroom 02-54-1-L aboard USS *Valley Forge*, a carrier en route to combat in the Persian Gulf. Breathing deeply, he realized the ejection had been a dream. *Just a dream.* But as he slowed his breathing, he actually considered it a flashback to what could have happened to him that March night in 2003. *Don't fool yourself. It can happen next month, or even next week over Iraq.* Then, just as suddenly, he berated himself. *Stop thinking like this.*

He looked at the clock: 5:52. Reveille in eight minutes, but he could go right back to sleep. Since he had a night hop scheduled, he could not break his 12-hour "crew day" by beginning his day too early, despite the fact that one could never escape "work" at sea.

He remembered yesterday's hop in the Gulf of Aden, a functional test hop on a clear, blue day, one of those days when he still couldn't believe they paid

him to fly. He was the last aircraft to trap, and after shutting his jet down on the bow, he had taken a favorite route toward the carrier's "island," the towering six-story superstructure that housed the bridge that allowed him to enjoy the sunshine. As he had trudged down the flight deck in 40 pounds of custom flight gear, he had taken in the scene and wondered if this would be one of the last times he would ever experience it. *It may be the last time this cruise...may be the last time ever*, he had thought. He was conscious of the fact that once the cruise ended—some five months from now according to the schedule—he may not come back here on a deployed aircraft carrier again. *Possibly by the Navy's choice—probably by my own.* He thought of the exhilaration of flying off the ship, being up on the "roof" and experiencing what only a handful of humans can even imagine. Experiencing life on a warship on the other side of the world—a reason to stay. And, at times, in his innermost thoughts, a guilty desire for combat, a reality which was now little more than 1,000 miles over the horizon, and getting closer with each passing minute.

A dread began to creep inside, bringing him back to the realization of what waited him later that morning and every morning, a reason he would resign his commission. *Five more months,* he thought, as he turned over and closed his eyes.

CHAPTER 2

At thirty-five years old, "Flip" Wilson was at the pinnacle of his flying prowess. As a *Hornet* pilot of some 3,000 hours, he had been in the cockpit each year of the twelve since flight school and was a decorated combat veteran. Approaching the end of his tour in the *Ravens* of Strike Fighter Squadron Sixty Four, Wilson was the Operations Officer responsible for both training the squadron pilots for any contingency and producing a daily flight schedule. Below him in rank were three more department heads and a gaggle of junior officer pilots. And, as mandated by the Navy's career managers, he had a desk job awaiting him after this cruise.

The *Ravens* consisted of 15 pilots, a small number of maintenance officers, a dozen chief petty officers, and some 160 sailors who maintained the 11 aircraft and performed various functions that allowed the operation to run without hiccup. The *Ravens* flew the multi-mission FA-18 *Hornet* strike-fighters, and were equally at home with anything from air-to-air fighter sweeps and combat air patrols to air-to-surface bombing and defense suppression missions with an array of weaponry each pilot mastered. VFA-64 was commanded by Commander Steve "Cajun" Lassiter, an easygoing former Tulane linebacker with a thick moustache and a shock of dark hair. He was known as the "CO" or Skipper to those inside the squadron. The second in command, the executive officer, or XO, was a sour-faced martinet. Commander William "Saint" Patrick was responsible for all squadron administrative functions and in line to succeed the CO. Patrick was a slender man of medium height with a thinning hairline he combed to perfection. Unlike any other air wing pilot, he wore his flight suit only from brief to debriefing a flight. Once the debrief ended, he changed into a khaki uniform within minutes.

Four hours later, Wilson rolled his six-foot frame out of his rack. *What is today? Day 25 of a six-month cruise?* He did the math as he stumbled to the sink... *No, day 21. Three weeks. With 21 more weeks to go.* And he knew almost every one of

those days would run together, a reason the crew called their time on-station "Groundhog Day."

Wilson thought of Saint immediately as he ran a razor under the water. *What bullshit crisis is it going to be today? Dental readiness report? Scratched tile on the deck?* He didn't technically work for Saint, but because the XO was a heartbeat from command and well-connected at the wing staff—and a senior officer—you didn't mess with him. *Yes, sir. Yes, sir. Three bags full.* Wilson shaved in silence and switched his thoughts to his upcoming day.

At nearly 1,100 feet long, *Valley Forge* was one of the largest warships afloat, a *Nimitz* class nuclear-powered aircraft carrier, one of twelve U.S. Navy aircraft carriers. Below deck, *Happy Valley*, as the crew referred to her, was a fluorescent world of overhead pipes, electrical cables, and steel bulkheads with strange number and letter combinations. Damage control equipment was spaced at intervals and oval openings, called "knee knockers," were cut into the steel frames. Yellow battle lanterns hung above the openings. The air smelled of fresh paint and machine oil, accented by sweat-soaked flight gear and the odor of jet fuel. The ship was a maze of right angles that provided a heart-pumping workout comprised of 18 decks of ladders—from bilge to tower. She now plowed through the Indian Ocean on her way to the location the Washington leadership had deemed she was needed: the northern Persian Gulf where she could launch close air support missions to support American forces on the ground in Iraq, hundreds of miles inland. For this purpose she was at her full combat load-out of over 100,000 tons.

The *Ravens* lived in Ready Room 7, located aft one deck beneath the flight deck's arresting wires. Ready 7 was situated between Ready 8, which housed the *Spartans*, who made up the two-seat FA-18F *Super Hornet* squadron, and the Marine squadron, and Ready 6, which housed the *Moonshadows* who flew older *Hornets* like the *Ravens*. Despite the common bond of service and having some individual friends in the *Spartans*, Wilson and most of VFA-64 liked and hung out with the marines, who shared the same airframe. The marines also joined in with the rest of the wing with their collective disdain for the arrogant and imperious *Spartans* of VFA-91 and their brand-new *Super Hornet* jets. With not a little scorn, most of them referred to the *Spartans* as "the girls next door."

Located amidships in Ready 3, the remaining *Hornet* squadron aboard *Valley Forge* was the *Buccaneers* of VFA-47. Like the *Ravens*, they also flew the FA-18C, and the two squadrons were known as "sister squadrons." These two squadrons were the only two of the eight aboard that were mirror images of each other, all reporting to the Commander of Carrier Air Wing Four, known as the CAG.

As "sisters," friendly, and sometimes not-so-friendly, competition was a part of their daily lives. The *Ravens*—from the Skipper down to the airman swabbing a passageway—wanted to outfly, outbomb, and generally outperform the *Bucs* in every area, and vice versa. In conversation, each squadron regarded the other as "Brand X."

Before going to lunch, Wilson opened the rear door of the ready room. His eyes immediately focused on the back of the XO's head in his front-row seat. The room was quiet now as most of the pilots were at lunch up forward. The squadron colors were blue and black, and each chair had a blue cover with black trim. The design depicted the squadron emblem—a black raven silhouette, wings outstretched as if swooping in for the kill. The image was simple, yet menacing, and a familiar tradition in carrier aviation over four major wars. Behind their backs, however, many in Carrier Air Wing Four and the fleet sarcastically referred to VFA-64 as the *Crows*.

Here it comes, Wilson thought. He grabbed a cup of water and made his way between the two groups of high-backed leather chairs to his own front-row seat.

"Hey, Olive," he said to the duty officer. Lieutenant Kristen "Olive" Teel wore khakis and sat at the duty officer console. Behind her was a status board with the day's flight schedule, each pilot's name written in grease pencil in bold capital letters.

Olive was nearly six feet tall, her slender body bordering on anorexia. The combination of her close-set eyes and long, dark hair pulled back into a tight bun made her a dead ringer for Popeye's girlfriend Olive Oyl, but without the squeaky voice. A no-nonsense woman of few words and fewer emotions, she participated on the periphery of any ready room hijinks only when avoiding it would call attention to herself. "Morning, sir," she replied to her department head, as she kept her eyes down and made a notation on the status board.

Wilson sat down in his chair in the front row, next to the Skipper's. He checked for something in the large drawer under his chair. He then sat back with his legs outstretched, took a breath, and waited. His wait lasted only a few seconds.

"Mister Wilson, I see you've not initialed the message board today," Saint said from across the aisle. He did not bother to look up.

"No, sir."

"An oversight?"

"No, sir. Haven't read them yet," Wilson said. He stood up and took a few steps, eyes locked on his XO.

Still looking down, Saint continued. "Do you know Strike-Fight Wing took all of our 2,000-pound practice bombs for noncombat expenditure and gave them to Air Wing Eight?"

"No, sir."

"It's right here," Saint replied, lifting the message board a few inches toward Wilson. Wilson noticed that a gaggle of JOs had arrived. *Oh, great!* Wilson thought. The XO continued with his quiz.

"Why did you not know? Actually, the more important question is, why did they take them?"

"The Wing did not contact me, sir. I'll e-mail them and find out." The JOs had stopped next to Wilson. Aware that he was in a serious exchange with his XO, they didn't dare interrupt. Saint noticed them, too…and liked having an audience.

"You're the OPSO of this squadron—for the next several months—and you're supposed to know these things before they happen. Had you reviewed this message board first thing this morning instead of rolling in here at 1030, you would have known about this before I did. You would have also had the chance to call the Wing and leave a message to find out *what the fuck. And* you could have had them e-mail you back to give the CO a full report. There could have been an answer in your mailbox *right now.*" For the first time, he raised his eyes to stare at Wilson. He couldn't have planned the moment for greater effect.

The JOs kept their eyes downcast, embarrassed to be part of the public dressing down of a senior officer and too discomfited to leave. From her perch on the SDO desk, Olive feigned inattention, but she was listening. Wilson's countenance remained rock steady.

"No excuse, sir. I'll find out."

"Thank you, Mr. Wilson. That will be all." Saint returned his attention to the message board, oblivious to the fact that the East Coast would not arrive at work to respond to Wilson's query for several hours.

"Yes, sir." Wilson responded. He managed to maintain control and repress his rage as he took his seat. *Company man,* he thought, scolding himself as he felt the JOs' eyes on him.

An hour later, Wilson's roommate, Lieutenant Commander Mike "Weed" Hopper, entered their stateroom. He found Wilson at the computer in PT gear. Weed took the measure of his roommate.

"Hey, man."

"Hmm," Wilson grunted without turning his head.

Weed clicked the light on above his desk. "Olive told me what happened."

"Hmm."

Hopper was the squadron Maintenance Officer, one place below Wilson in the *Raven* pecking order. Tall, with red hair, he possessed a big smile that matched his sense of humor. The *Ravens* were fortunate that these two department heads were friends, as they both had to work together to make the squadron flight schedule work.

"Five more months, my friend," Weed said with frown.

"Roger that," Wilson replied, and then added, "I can stand on my head for five months."

"He grabbed me earlier, too. Said there were *too many* boot marks on four-oh-two and the troops needed to be more careful. Imagine that— too many boot marks on a deployed fleet *Hornet*."

"Where is the skipper?" Wilson asked.

"He went to the wardroom with some JOs. C'mon man, let's do the same."

Wilson donned his flight suit and began to lace his boots. *Five more months.* He took stock of his situation. One thousand miles north kids were getting their legs blown off with IEDs on a daily basis. And that didn't even take into account the misery of living day-to-day in the 110-degree talcum-sand hell of Anbar Province...for a full year.

Compared to that, putting up with humiliation from known prick "Saint Patrick" is a small sacrifice. The bigger one is being away from Mary and the kids. Combat flying over Iraq would be a relief, and short of that, the routine flight schedule offered an almost daily respite from the XO. Wilson knew if he wanted to be a squadron CO, he would have to take it. All he had to do was *take it* for the remainder of this cruise. The question was whether or not his pride and vanity would let him.

Maybe I don't want it, he thought as he pulled tight on the laces.

CHAPTER 3

In her stateroom that evening, Olive wound down from a long day at the duty desk. She forced herself to e-mail her mother a birthday greeting full of the emoticon hearts and flowers her mother loved. The head cheerleader at Vanderbilt in the late 1970's, her mother was a Knoxville socialite, still stunning at age fifty. The hair, the teeth, the heels—Camille Bennett had it all. She also attended every important community event. Junior League. Democratic Party fundraisers. Garden Club tea parties. With one son in Vanderbilt medical school, and the other as Sigma Nu president at Ole Miss, no one could match her.

Olive's mother left her father, Ted Teel, when Olive was a small child—probably because she couldn't stand to hear "Camille Teel!" from her squealing sorority sisters one more day. She didn't mind Ted's six-figure salary at the prestigious downtown law firm of Smith, Teel and Martin, but that was adequate only until 50ish investment banker Mike Bennett came into her life with *seven* figures. Her mother was pregnant within a year, and Olive suddenly had a distant middle-aged stepfather to go along with her absent father.

From the time Olive was born, Camille wanted to use her as a dress-up doll, a role Olive fought for as long as she could remember. Olive could play the piano and had learned about white gloves and party manners at the cotillion. She could even navigate the make-up counter at Lord and Taylor, and her statuesque height and athletic prowess caught everyone's attention. But Olive knew how to draw boundaries; for example, she eschewed the cheerleader culture.

She liked the guys—but wanted to be around them on her terms, not as an arm piece—or piece of anything. Her mother cried when Olive was accepted into the Naval Academy and rarely visited. When she did visit on the yard, radiant in her navy-colored suit and stilettos, she would scoff under her breath and say, "Kristin, must you wear those mannish Oxfords?" Then she would spy a boy and whisper, "There's a cute one! Unbutton a few buttons and go up to him. Go on." Olive shook her head at the thought of it.

Camille cried again when Olive was accepted to flight school. "You *marry* a pilot, not become one!" Olive was a huge disappointment to her mother, and always had been. The calluses of emotional defense she had developed from

childhood were the foundation of the reserved personality she still maintained. Even now, whenever one of her Junior League friends asked about Olive, her mother politely said, "Kristin flies for the Air Force," and quickly changed the subject. Camille could not have identified an FA-18 *Hornet* to save her life.

Just as Olive hit "send" on the e-mail, her roommate, "Psycho," burst through the door.

"Hey, how was duty?" Psycho asked. Without bothering to listen to Olive's answer, she undid her hair and began peeling off her flight suit.

"Fine. How was midrats?"

"Awesome! Sat with a bunch of *Moonshadows*. You know Lester and Crunch? They crack me up every time! Smoke was there...Dutch...Sponge.... good time." Lifting her t-shirt over her head, she added, "You should go up there. They are probably still there."

"No thanks. Writing my mother on her birthday."

"Awww...Happy Birthday, Mrs. Teel!"

Olive waved off the reference to Mrs. Teel—Psycho didn't know and never listened—and then admired her roommate's shape for just a moment as she changed. Psycho had *curves*—curves Olive wished she had. She had had boyfriends in the past, but with her insecurities made it a point to catch them eyeing a full sweater or tight pair of jeans on other girls and then blew up at them. Because she had been hurt before, she now dismissed all men *(boys)* as incorrigible pigs—a belief she had thrown up to act as another layer of defense.

However, she was alone—and didn't like it.

With her pajama bottoms on, Psycho maneuvered into her top and began buttoning the buttons.

"Hey, what do you have tomorrow?"

"A night intercept hop with the skipper," Olive replied. "How about you?"

"A day dick-around with Smoke."

Olive glanced over and saw a flash of Psycho's perfect breast before the last button was buttoned. *I may need to get me some of those*, she thought.

Psycho flung on a robe, stepped into her flip flops, and opened the door to visit the female head down the passageway. "B-R-B!" she called out airily as she left.

Olive smiled to herself. *Psycho*, she thought, *if Mom could overlook the fact you "fly for the Air Force," she would love to have you as her daughter.*

CHAPTER 4

The ethos of fighter squadron life is competition. Against other squadrons and outside groups, between squadronmates, and even against oneself. The competition is daily and relentless, and, once at sea, there is no escape from it. Landing grades, boarding rate, interval timing, bombing accuracy, air-to-air training engagements won, aircraft system test scores, flight hours per month, career night vision goggle hours, career traps, night traps per month (high and low), squadron flight qualifications, ground jobs held (high and low), combat sorties, combat drops, strike/flight Air Medals, and squadron competitive ranking... In fact, practically every area of their lives—including beers consumed on liberty, facial hair quality, stock portfolio knowledge, video game victories, coolness of car, and hotness of girlfriend—become legitimate areas of competition for the aviators in a fleet carrier squadron.

For a pilot, and for some more than others, each flight is one big pass/fail test. However, each flight also includes dozens of little tests, some institutionalized but many self-administered. These tests allow the pilot to measure his performance against others but most importantly against himself in order to do one thing—get better. The pilots live with a constant undercurrent of anxiety; in no way do they want to embarrass the squadron or themselves. It is not surprising that the overwhelming majority are first-born perfectionists.

Even killing time in the ready room turns into evaluation and critique sessions as they watch their air wing buddies on the closed-circuit flight deck TV, called the Pilot Landing Aid Television or PLAT. The eyes of every pilot of every experience level are drawn to the PLAT whenever it is on. The pilots check the weather outside or how the aircraft are parked on the deck or "spotted," but more often than not, they just want to watch the minute-by-minute drama of carrier aviation. At night, the PLAT is genuine entertainment in its own right, depending on the weather conditions, with the ready room "cowboys" able to monitor the side numbers and recognize the voices—and voice inflections—of their fellow air wing pilots and naval flight officers as they struggle to make their approaches. Like everything else, the landings always create an environment for stiff competition between squadrons and individuals. A missed trap bolter for

"the girls next door" is almost always good; a bolter for a trusted squadronmate is the source of feelings of sympathy, or even of personal disappointment—however, for a rival squadronmate, not so much.

Despite the fact most of it is healthy, competition is ever present in a fighter squadron, and it is magnified by the hours spent going over every aspect of a flight in an effort to improve—to attain perfection. To this end, constructive criticism is a daily occurrence for a pilot of any rank, and every flaw—personal and professional—is identified. Most can handle the feedback, but those who can't are easy targets of ready room mockery until they succumb to a certain amount of humility. And if they refuse, squadron life is brutal for these loners. With so many healthy, if not huge, egos in close quarters, the near constant competition acts as a control mechanism to keep the egos of certain ones in check. Therefore, since no one can be number one in everything with so many overachievers looking over one's shoulder, the competitive atmosphere allows everyone to stake a claim someplace.

CHAPTER 5

As the sun set the following evening the ship began to pick up some appreciable movement from the long Indian Ocean swell. Wilson noted this as unusual in the IO. These waters off the Arabian Peninsula were often calm and sunny throughout the year. If seas were heavy at any time, it was during the winter months, when squall lines with heavy thunderstorms and occasional sand storms were not uncommon.

From his stateroom desk, Wilson checked the flight schedule: the XO and Sponge Bob were on the "pinky" recovery, followed by the Skipper leading a practice intercept hop with Olive. *Glad I'm not out there tonight,* he thought. Night carrier aviation was difficult enough without a pitching deck. He surmised the weather was deteriorating, and realized he had not been outside the whole day.

He clicked on the PLAT…the ceiling was down from earlier and the deck was slick from a passing rain cloud. The *Hornets* on the bow were preparing to launch and the camera showed one taxiing out of its Cat 2 parking spot. Wilson watched it taxi aft past the bow jet blast deflectors, take a 45-degree right turn to clear the aircraft parked amidships, and then turn left down the angle to the "waist" cats. The camera showed a close-up of the aircraft…side number *406*. Wilson clicked up two channels for the air ops status board: *406* was Sponge Bob's aircraft, and the XO was in *402*. He clicked again and checked the weather. Low broken-variable-overcast clouds, three miles visibility in rain, with occasional lowering to 500 feet overcast and one mile with lightning, freezing level at 14,000 feet and high gusty winds.

Not a good night at all.

Wilson wondered about the thought processes of the captain on the bridge, the admiral in flag plot, and the CAG in his office. *They've got all the information I've got, and more,* he thought, *and these guys are still taxiing to the cats.* He saw Sponge Bob on Cat 4, with the *Viking* tanker next to him on Cat 3. Ten minutes to launch.

The sound of an E-2 on Cat 2, two decks above, caused him to switch again to the PLAT. The screen was obscured by water droplets from another rain cloud as the *"Hummer"* extended its wings at a measured pace while its big turboprops

kicked up clouds of spray behind it. *Clackety, clackety, CLACKETY, CLACK-ETY, clackety, clackety* sounded overhead as the "shuttle," the above-deck catapult launching mechanism, was retracted aft for hook-up. Underneath the shuttle and below the metal catapult track, two large pistons, the size of a small car, moved into launch position. Once the aircraft was connected to the shuttle, and on signal, superheated high-pressure steam exploded into the piston cylinders to propel the aircraft forward to reach flying speed. The pilots likened it to being flung out of a slingshot.

Wilson exited his stateroom and headed for Ready 7. As he strode aft on the passageway, the noise of the *Hummer*, although at idle one deck above, surrounded him. He heard the familiar "thunk" as the catapult was placed in tension. That was followed by the increased engine reverberation as the aircraft props changed pitch at full power for launch. *Are they really going to shoot these guys?* he wondered. *They are going to have a tough time getting back aboard in these conditions.*

He made a right turn, then a left, as he continued aft to the ready room. He had to cover his ears as the familiar, yet annoying, din from the jet blast deflector pumps and the aircraft at full power pounded into his brain. A thud above and behind signaled the firing of the catapult, and the swift movement of the shuttle made a *zziiiiipp* sound as it moved forward pulling the E-2 with it. The sound of the E-2 engines also faded away at the instant a *THUNK* was felt forward on the bow: the sound of the catapult slamming into the water brake as it flung the *Hummer* into the air.

Just then a loud *CLACK, CLACK, CLACK* passed from inside the ship on his right side as the shuttle roared along the track. It stopped with a booming *THUNK* that rattled the ship's frames. This was followed by a faint whistle sound as the S-3 tanker was launched off the waist. *They're gonna do it.* Wilson smiled and shook his head as he stepped over a knee-knocker.

Halfway to the ready room he steadied himself as the ship took a starboard roll. Right after it stopped, the grim-faced Deputy CAG and his Operations Officer, whom he knew as "Bucket," passed him in a hurry.

"Sir," Wilson said. The DCAG passed with a barely audible acknowledgement and turned outboard toward the island ladder, shoulders hunched and head down.

As he trailed his boss, Bucket raised his eyebrows at Wilson to convey his thoughts: *I don't know what's going on.*

Wilson wondered where they were headed. *The bridge? The tower? Who knows where?* He walked past the S-3 and helo ready rooms, pushing off a bulkhead to steady himself as the ship took a roll. *It's getting worse.*

When he entered the ready room, Wilson's eyes were drawn to the Skipper, who was conducting his brief in the front of the ready room. Olive, two *Buccaneer* pilots and two aircrew from the *Sea Owls* listened intently. If Cajun Lassiter was concerned about the conditions his squadron pilots—and he—would face that night, he didn't show it. *Too professional for that.* But Wilson knew he would brief the aircrew on every contingency and would further brief Olive on pitching deck LSO calls and other heavy weather techniques he had picked up over 17 years of carrier flying.

LT Ramer Howard, known in the squadron as "Prince Charming," both for his dark good looks and as a sarcastic reference to his disagreeable personality, sat in his khakis at the duty desk. The blank look on his face belied the question they all had as the roar of a jet at full power filled the room. The Skipper raised his voice an octave to be heard above it. It was a *Super Hornet* in tension on Cat 3, and on the PLAT Wilson could see light rain falling from the low clouds that extended to the horizon. With a dull thud, the *Rhino* screamed down the deck and kicked up billowing clouds of water drops in its exhaust. The familiar sound of the water brake reverberated through the ship and the *Super Hornet*'s WHOOSH served as evidence it had cleared the deck—airborne over 500 feet forward. Wilson glanced at Prince Charming, but his face remained blank.

"Wanna get some food?" Weed asked.

"Yeah, let's do it," Wilson replied.

JOs Psycho, Smoke, and Guido had just left the ready room, also on their way to the forward wardroom. Before he reached the door, the sound of a strike-fighter in tension caused Wilson to return to the PLAT, with Weed right behind him. They could make out Sponge Bob's salute to the catapult observer, which was followed by the usual 10-second wait. When the cat fired, the *Hornet* thundered down the catapult track and into the air, another wake of wind-driven spray behind it.

The pilots proceeded out of the ready room and forward along the passageway. "Gonna be a varsity night," Weed began.

"Yes, it is," his roommate responded. "What's been happening down here?"

"Deputy CAG called about 45 minutes ago. The Skipper talked to him, and I discerned that DCAG wanted to know about Sponge Bob. Skipper said he was a solid pilot. If it were me, I would have asked about the XO instead!"

Wilson decided to keep the fact that he agreed with Weed to himself. "How are your guys doing up there?" he asked, as he glanced at Weed over his left shoulder.

"Drenched and loving it," Weed chuckled. "Guys are fighting to go topside so they can get some sea salt on their shoulders."

"Yeah…think that's what Sponge is thinking right now?" Wilson deadpanned.

"He looked confident as he walked, but the XO was real tense, more than usual."

After they walked a distance of two football fields over a series of frame knee-knockers, they came to the "dirty shirt" wardroom, which was located below and between the bow catapults. Cat 2 was still firing, and the sound of the shuttle roared through the wardroom overhead. The tremendous crash that came from the water brake, located on the extreme forward part of the flight deck some 200 feet away, shook everything in the room that was not bolted down. The pilots were used to the noises and the shaking and paid little attention—unless there was something unusual about them. Tonight, they noted the increased movement of the ship, well forward of its center of gravity.

Wilson and Weed picked up their trays, drinking glasses and silverware as they got into the already long buffet line. The junior officers were about ten ahead. Everyone in line wore a flight suit.

Wilson had experienced severe pitching deck conditions several times off the Virginia Capes and once near the Azores, but not out here in the IO. Regardless of where it was, the great 100,000-ton ship could bob like a cork in heavy seas. In fact, right now, the ship was creaking as the bow rose and fell in the deep swells. It pitched up and down, often accompanied by what the seamen called a Dutch Roll, a roll induced by the pitching oscillations. Pitching and rolling decks were difficult enough, but the seas could also heave the whole ship, lifting it up and down in the water.

All this was a recipe for a poor boarding rate, which meant lengthy recoveries, stressed aircraft components, and tension with everyone involved with flight operations exacerbated by the fact that each plane had limited airborne fuel. USS *Valley Forge* just signed up for it.

The two sat down next to the *Raven* junior officers. Each squadron had staked out their own "unofficial" table where they—as the trained creatures of habit that they were—almost always gathered for a meal. The *Raven* table was all the way forward on the port side.

"Anyone care to go flying tonight?" Wilson asked the group as they joined them.

"No, thank you," Psycho answered. Her voice carried throughout the room as she continued. "I flew last night and twice at night in the Red Sea. Think I'm covered for at least tonight."

"JOs complaining about flying at night," Weed said, shaking his head in feigned disgust. "Can we count on you for a full moon night? Waxing gibbous at least?"

"That would be nice—if you must fly me at night at all!" she giggled. Nugget pilot Lieutenant Melanie "Psycho" Hinton was an anomaly. The daughter of an admiral, she was blessed with California surfer-girl good looks. But she didn't act like she knew it, and she could keep up with any of the guys. Her loud and obnoxious commentary—on any subject—earned her the call sign Psycho, which stood for "Please Shut Your Cake Hole."

"It was clear and a million in the Red Sea, and last night was fairly pink, as I remember," Wilson interjected. "You'll just have to take it up with the schedules officer."

"He gives you the schedule to sign!" Psycho cried, her eyes wide in mock indignation, enjoying the attention.

"I just sign what Nttty gives me," Wilson said with a smirk as he reached for his salad plate, which slid to the left as the ship took a roll. "Nttty" was Lieutenant Junior Grade Josh Fagan, the Schedules Officer, who, after one memorable multiplane intercept hop, was christened with his call sign Nttty—"Not Time To Talk Yet."

"So does the CO. Take it up with him," Weed added.

Psycho also caught her plate in midslide and sighed. "Should have known the hinge-heads would band together in support of the front office. Next time I'll just take it up with my good friend, Nttty. Thank you, sir."

"Good answer," Weed mumbled, through a mouthful of food.

SLAP!

A swell slammed hard against the bow and rattled the dishes. The group heard the water gurgle down the hull.

"It's serious out there," Guido muttered into his food as he took a big gulp of fried rice.

Smoke agreed. "Yeah, they've gotta be thinking about canceling the night events."

Just then the loud *WHOOOMMMmmm* of a jet on a bolter filled the wardroom. The aviators exchanged knowing glances as the jet climbed back into the pattern. *The first of many bolters this recovery*, Wilson thought. He turned to Smoke, one of the squadron landing signal officers, and asked, "Were you guys working manual recoveries earlier?"

"NO!" Psycho howled and slammed her hand on the table. "I had a sweet OK going and then the deck pitched down—or came up—and I caught an ace

on the fly. They gave me a "fair." They said that was a gift because the ship did a little dance in close, but not so much that I couldn't have made a better correction. I mean, it's either a pitching deck OK or not! They should have rigged the MOVLAS, the *bastards*."

Sensing an opening, Smoke chided her. "Was the deck down, or did it come up?"

Psycho's eyes narrowed as she shook her head at him. "You A-holes stick together, don't you? I thought squadron blood might be thicker than LSO water. Guess not."

"Well," Smoke said, and grinned at her. "We have two senior aviators here who are charged with advising the commanding officer as to proper procedure, given the operating conditions we face. So what was it? Up or down?" Smoke folded his hands in front of him and held her gaze.

"It was UP!" Psycho shot back, fire in her eyes. "As in *'Shut up!'*"

"All right! I'm sorry." Smoke smiled and extended his hands in front of him. "Just wanted to get that straight!" His eyes remained on her as he mouthed *"LSO water?"* with a quizzical look.

"What did you get, Paddles?" Wilson asked Smoke, instantly wishing he hadn't. Pausing for effect, the LSO suppressed a grin. "OK three, sir."

"SEE!" Psycho exploded, her food barely staying in her mouth. "It's good-old-boy collusion out there!"

Wilson saw the Skipper and Olive duck into the room carrying plates of food. It was an hour and ten minutes before their launch, just enough time to eat a rushed meal before man-up. Lassiter found a few spots at the table and placed his tray across from Wilson.

"Hey, Skipper."

"Flip," Lassiter greeted him over a *WHOOOMMMmmm* from above—the sound of another *Hornet* on a bolter.

"What's the story on your event, sir?" Weed asked him.

Lassiter exhaled. "Nothing yet, we'll walk on time. My guess is they will make a decision in the next hour. CAG is recovering on this event."

Weed grinned. "Maybe that was him going around."

"Hope not," Lassiter said and smiled.

"I'm sure Paddles will no-count it for a pitching deck," Psycho chimed in, as she shot Smoke a look.

"As they should," Smoke retorted with a confident grin. "Paddles always does the right thing." Psycho responded to that with her most feminine sniff.

Wilson watched the exchange and figured there might be something going on between Smoke and Psycho. Lassiter shoveled another spoonful of rice into his mouth. He kept his eyes down, as if lost in concentration about his upcoming flight, and acted oblivious to the flirting between his junior officers. Wilson knew, however, the skipper was paying attention and was probably on to them.

"Smoke" was the call sign of Lieutenant Zach Offenhausen, a blond pretty boy of supreme confidence who, in fact, *was* a California surfer and had been a motocross champion in his teen years. Now a second-cruise JO, he aspired to TOPGUN training once the deployment ended. Both Smoke and Psycho—despite the fact that she never shut up in social situations—were good officers and solid pilots. Fraternization was one way to destroy that good standing. Here they were, attractive young single adults, working and eating together day after day for months—and, from what it looked like, maybe even sleeping together.

Wilson got up from the table and said, "Excuse me, sir," to the CO. Weed did the same, followed by Smoke and Psycho. Lassiter waved and nodded and swallowed a final mouthful. He and Olive picked up their trays, took them to deposit in the scullery, and hurried back to the ready room. They wanted to walk on time.

In the passageway, the JOs and Weed continued aft while Wilson ducked below to his stateroom to check for e-mail from home. The darkened room was illuminated only by the screen saver of his laptop. A note from Mary awaited him.

> *Dear James,*
> *Derrick rode the bike this morning without training wheels! He did great! I just ran behind him a little and then he took off on his own. He went to the end of the cul-de-sac and turned around. I was praying he could do it. When he got back to the house though he crashed—into the Hopper's car! Karen had just pulled up and we were standing by the car cheering him on as he rode toward us. He tried to turn away but hit the left front and fell off. He skinned his elbow and cried a little. No damage to the car, but Karen felt awful. Derrick was over it after a band-aid and a kiss. Just another day as a navy wife.*

Oh, great...

> *Brittany was so cute yesterday in her new winter boots. She drew a picture of herself wearing them just for you, which I'll send to you soon with some goodies. I miss you, my love.*

He looked at Mary's picture on his desk and daydreamed for a few moments. The photo, taken at the Strike-Fighter Ball, was sensational. It caught her beautiful face, her dazzling smile, which generated more wattage than all the sequins on her dress. He dreamed of her feminine shape. Thirty-three years old…and she had not changed since college.

Click, click…weeEEEEeeoowww!

The sound of a *Viking* recovery above brought him back to his O2 level stateroom and the realization that holding Mary was over five months away. With the *Viking* aboard, the recovery must be nearing completion. He checked the schedule again and verified his CATCC watch for the next recovery, fifty minutes from now.

Wilson composed a quick note to Mary and headed aft to the ready room.

CHAPTER 6

Thirty minutes later, Wilson walked into Air Ops, amidships on the O3 level. The cool, dark room was illuminated by a few small overhead lights over the work desks. The desks and two rows of Naugahyde-covered benches faced the event status boards.

Wilson was the first CATCC rep to arrive, and he took a spot on the back row. Commander Marty O'Shaunessy, the Air Ops Officer and a career naval flight officer, was hunched over his desk talking on the phone, his usual pose. Wilson knew O'Shaunessy was having a miserable night with this weather. He also knew that, as the sun sank below the horizon, the misery was going to get worse.

Wilson studied the acronyms and numbers on the status monitors for the information he needed. XO and Sponge Bob were checked into *marshal*, the aircraft holding pattern aft of the ship, at 12,000 and 13,000 feet, respectively. XO had 8,000 pounds of fuel, Sponge only 7,100. And that information was five minutes old. *If the launch goes on time, Sponge should get here with a little over 4.0.* That 4,000 pounds gave him two passes before he would need to be directed to the tanker overhead.

The ship was working "blue water ops" as normal, as if there were no divert fields in the area, but Wilson sought them out on the status monitors anyway. He needed to find a location in Oman where a divert aircraft, which required a climb and descent through icing conditions in order to make an instrument approach to an unfamiliar field at night, could land as safely as possible in the wind and rain. The ship was definitely where the pilots wanted to recover tonight... if the deck would cooperate. Wilson recalled a salty instructor pilot describe the cause of an aircraft mishap as a "box," where the sides are closed, one by one, by poor decisions and conditions. He thought tonight's operations had the construction of such a box well underway.

Wilson caught the eye of LT Mike Metz, the Assistant Air Ops Officer, and gave him a nod to join him. Metz glanced at O'Shaunessy, then got up and walked the few steps to the bench where Wilson was seated.

"Hey, Flip."

"Hey, how's it going?" Wilson asked in a low tone. "Are we going to continue?"

"Yes, sir. The weather should be improving with frontal passage. The Captain wants to fly, too."

"Great," Wilson muttered as he looked at the status board. "How was the last recovery?"

Metz glanced again at O'Shaunessy. "Took forever. The commander got reamed by the Captain for having too many tankers airborne. We had three sweet tankers and needed to tank four guys almost simultaneously, so we needed them. Hey, did you see that *Cutlass* bolter?"

Wilson shook his head. "Who was the pilot?"

"I think they call her Betty. It was *really* long. She went to the tanker but had to climb through some clag to find him, and she finally plugged with about 1,500 pounds. When she got back here, it looked like she trapped hard… She was determined not to go back up there again."

"I can relate." Wilson realized he was keeping Metz too long. "Hey, thanks, man. You have a great recovery."

"*You, too, sir,*" the lieutenant said with a smile and returned to his seat.

Wilson nodded. He was right. Air Ops was *the place* to be at night, especially a night like this. Dozens of decisions were being made that affected the human drama of operating high performance aircraft in the close vicinity of the ship. And, for the most part, that drama centered around fuel states. Airplanes could recover aboard a carrier only if they had a certain amount of fuel. The typical requirement was half of a full load; that amount would not overstress a 17-ton *Hornet* airframe as it smashed into the deck at the rate of 700 feet-per-minute. During the descent, the plane looked as if it were suspended a few feet above the flight deck and then dropped. At the moment of the "drop," the plane's tailhook grabbed one of the steel cables stretched across the deck and wrestled the jet to a halt, slowing it from over 140 miles per hour to zero within the distance of little more than a football field.

The hook sometimes skipped over the wires, or the pilot came across the ramp too high and landed long. Either circumstance resulted in a "bolter." Therefore, landing called for full power on each touchdown to ensure the aircraft could get airborne if necessary. Until it did, its hook clawed at the nonskid surface and kicked up a dazzling spray of sparks. The jet then zoomed off the end of the angled deck and struggled back into the air for a downwind turn and another approach.

Sometimes the pilot would get a "wave-off" signal from the LSO due to a poor approach or due to the deck status. Pilots liked recovering with "max-

trap" fuel in these conditions. More fuel meant more options, more chances to get aboard. All aircrew sweated fuel when operating around the ship, but "blue water ops" at night, especially with a pitching deck, put everyone on edge. Sometimes pilots cheated, bringing an extra 100-200 extra pounds of fuel aboard; that extra fuel equaled one or two more minutes airborne if they needed it for another pass, to rendezvous on the tanker, or to make the divert field, even if they had to fly on fumes. That was certainly better than flaming out and ejecting 10 miles short. The fuel gauge was, indeed, the most important instrument in the cockpit at times like these.

More pilots dropped in next to Wilson in the peanut gallery: squadron department heads and COs and XOs from the other squadrons were all there to act as subject matter experts, if the need arose. He exchanged greetings or nods with most of those who caught his eye, but they were all there, like Wilson, to assess the situation facing their pilots that evening. CDR Randy "Big Unit" Johnson, the *Buccaneer's* Executive Officer, sat down next to Wilson. Johnson shared the same name as the flame-throwing major league hurler, stood at six-foot-four, and had a bone-crushing handshake he had developed from regular workouts in the foc'sle weight room. He possessed the good looks of a movie star—with his thick, dark hair, brown eyes, square jaw and cleft chin—he was one of the nicest guys in the wing and a solid carrier pilot.

"Flip, ready for another fun-filled night of stupid human tricks?"

"Yes, sir!" Wilson responded, and then added, "How's Betty doing? Heard about her long bolter."

"She saw the elephant on that one. She said she had a ball, but she could sense the deck pitch down—it just slid out from under her. She knew she was going to bolter and just held what she had, but the deck seemed to fall further and further away. She saw nothing but water and lit the cans just as she touched down. My understanding is that she was pretty far up there."

"Yes, sir, my gunner saw it from the de-arming hole. His eyes were big."

"Yeah," Johnson chuckled. "I'll bet he could see *Betty's* eyes a mile away when she was abeam on downwind! After she trapped, she came into the ready room in her gear muttering 'Holy shit! Ho-ly *shit!*'"

Wilson laughed, having been there before.

Johnson continued. "You know, it always amazes me… Here we are in the middle of friggin' nowhere, flying in these varsity conditions, which is pretty dangerous when you think about it. Yet, we go to the ready room, watch the PLAT and *crack up* laughing as our friends risk their lives! No one else on earth has any idea this little drama is happening. And only about 50-60 people aboard

are intimately involved in it right now. That means *only* about one percent of the crew has a clue about how screwed up this is."

Wilson smiled and nodded. "Yes, sir."

"And we howl laughing and critique the finest pilots in the world doing their best under tremendous stress with very little margin for error." The Big Unit shook his head. "And before long, it will be our turn again."

"I promise I won't laugh at you, sir," Wilson said with a straight face.

"Bull*shit*!" Johnson whispered and smiled. "We heard the *Raven* ready room howl from a hund'erd frames away when Betty boltered!"

"I swear I wasn't there, sir!"

A loud roar filled the space and made further conversation difficult. A *Hornet* in tension was at full power on Catapult 3 above them. Two white cones of fire leapt from the tailpipes and licked at the jet blast deflector, the brilliant light washing out the camera. The sound inside Air Ops became a deep, vibrant, continuous boom. They watched the pilot select external lights—*ON*—and the pulsing aircraft glow illuminated the deck around him. That was the signal he was ready. Wilson watched the LED display on the clock: 17:59:49...50...51.... The *Hornet* remained stuck to the deck, burning fuel at a prodigious rate. A familiar pop and zipper sound started the *Hornet* down the track, its afterburner exhaust tearing at the deck. Wilson kept his eyes on the PLAT as the *Hornet* got to the end and went airborne. Another *THUNK* of the Cat 3 water brake shook the ship's frames down to the keel.

Ding ding, ding ding. The sound of four bells played over the 1MC loudspeaker, signifying 1800 hours. *Valley Forge* prided itself on "launching on the bells."

Another *Hornet* roared off Cat 2. Olive's husky voice sounded over the departure frequency. "Four-one-two airborne." Wilson watched her aircraft on the PLAT, and with a positive rate of climb, she deselected burner to save fuel to remain aloft for the planned 90 minutes. The skipper launched off the waist one minute later, and Wilson recorded their times in a log book. Seven more jets to go. Wilson had to steady himself as he wrote. The ship was still moving appreciably in the heavy seas.

The marshal frequency radio crackled over the loudspeaker as the first returning aircraft began its approach: *"Marshal, Spartan one-zero-three commencing out of angels six, state seven-point-eight."*

"Roger, one-zero-three, check-in approach on button fifteen."

"One-zero-three, switching fifteen."

CHAPTER 7

The recovery commenced. Each minute, as one aircraft, with the hook down for landing, pulled power and pushed the nose over, another pilot or aircrew entered a precision realm of absolute concentration. Airspeed, heading, and rate of descent were monitored to maintain position in an exact sequence as the aircraft lined up behind the ship. More than anything else, the fuel state of each aircraft dominated everyone's thinking.

The instrument scan, the voice calls, the procedures were rote, all trained into each pilot to become second nature, even to Sponge Bob at the beginning of this, his first deployment. Also common to all the aircrew was a level of tension that, at times, bordered on fear. Wilson knew tonight was going to be one of those bordering-on-fear nights; everyone faced low overcast with sporadic rain, a pitching deck, and unfamiliar divert fields that were over 200 miles away.

At sea, away from the cultural lighting of shore, an overcast sky at night blocks out even the moral support starlight can offer. With no discernible horizon, the sea and the sky become a whole. *Black.* Inside-of-a-basketball black. Nights like these bring out the inner demons harbored within each pilot. *Cold cat shots. Ramp strikes. Total electrical failures.*

Those who bolter or receive low state wave-offs are given vectors to a tanker located overhead in the gloom. Those pilots, sometimes near a state of desperation, must try to find it without becoming disoriented, without losing control of the aircraft, and without letting a moment's inattention cause them to collide with the tanker.

Pilots who experience brake failure on deck must make a frantic pull of the ejection handle before the aircraft goes over the side. The seat blasts them out of the cockpit and then blasts them again into a parachute. They have no more than a second after the disorientation of the opening shock (*OOMPH!*) to get their wits about them and to prepare for water entry.

Inflate! Pull at the toggles. *Raft!* Reach for the release.

Immersed in frigid seawater, they struggle to get free of the chute, conscious of the great ship parting the waves mere feet away. As the wake breaks over their heads, they get tossed about, get sucked under, gag constantly and spit out mouthful after mouthful of salt water. They must feel for their raft in the blackness, as icy cold numbs their fingers. Above all else, they hope the plane guard helo sees them and puts a swimmer in the water *now*. *Please, God, help me!*

It gets worse. If a pilot can't get aboard or tank, he may be directed to divert ashore. This requires that he transit alone over miles and miles of open ocean. If disaster strikes then, and the jet is no longer flyable, the pilot makes a desperate *Mayday!* call, giving his range and bearing before he ejects into black nothingness and a shivering cold descent. Added to that is the dreaded knowledge that *no human being is within 100 miles!* And even if a rescue helo is sent immediately, it won't get on scene for nearly an hour, and the pilot is in the cold water that whole time, fighting shock and hypothermia. They hope to muster the strength to signal for the helo if it, by miracle, finds the "needle in the haystack" of the black and limitless sea.

Wilson and the others were well aware of the sudden and violent ways aviators could meet their end. Episodes like this were quite rare. The Navy, as a whole, often went many years between such incidents. Their training was superb and they knew how to handle any situation placed before them. But the nightmares did happen on occasion, and deep in their minds—in the darker than night place where the demons lived—they knew that some gloomy night fate could choose them.

The external lights of a *Hornet* at full power came on, a signal to the deck crew the pilot was ready for launch. In the corner of the screen, however, Wilson noted the squadron troubleshooter with wands crossed over his head, the signal for suspend. He watched the Cat crew go through the suspend procedures and heard the Mini Boss make the radio call.

"Two-one-zero, you're suspended."

"Roger," the pilot replied. Another first-cruise aviator, he kept his left arm locked in order to hold the throttles forward until given the signal to throttle back.

A groan went up from O'Shaunessy as he reached for the phone once more.

"Two-one-zero, we didn't see a rudder wipe out. Let's try it again," the Mini-Boss radioed.

"Yes, sir," the young marine pilot answered.

O'Shaunessy turned to the peanut gallery, his eyes searching for any pilot with a high and tight representing the Marine *Hornet* squadron. *"Red River* rep, you catch that from the Boss?"

"Yes, sir, he'll be debriefed," the major responded.

"Good, and you can apologize to the *Spartan* rep sitting next to you if we don't catch one-oh-three," said O'Shaunessy as he glared at the major. Just then his phone buzzed, and he turned to answer it. "Roger," he spoke into the receiver, and raised his voice for all to hear. "Take one-oh-three over the top."

With a sheepish expression the major whispered, *"Sorry, man!"* to the *Spartan* pilot who sat next to him, who then took it as an opportunity to extract payment from the *Moonshadows.*

"I think, when we get to port, a beer for the one-zero-three aircrew will make amends, *and* a beer for me having to stay here in this pressure cooker longer than I should have, *and* a beer for the maintenance department for keeping one-oh-three airborne on this shitty night, *and* for the CO for general purposes. Hell, just buy the whole squadron a beer, and we'll call it even."

"We ain't *that* sorry!" the marine chuckled.

The PLAT screen shifted to the approach view and looked aft into space. Three aircraft showed on the screen as twinkling bundles of light set against the black. Two FA-18s followed 103, which was the largest bundle. They were all three to the left of the crosshairs, the lines in the middle of the screen that signified heading and glide slope. The ship was now on a 115 heading in the never-ending quest to put the winds down the angle.

As the pilots in Air Ops suspected, after what they had seen on the screen, the voice of the approach controller came over the radio loudspeaker with new coordinates: "One-zero-three, discontinue approach, maintain angels one-point-two, fly heading one-one-zero."

"One-oh-three, roger, one-one-zero."

As the *Hornet* on Cat 4 was placed in tension, Wilson heard the sardonic voice of "Saint Patrick" as he commenced his approach. "Four-zero-two commencing."

"Roger, *Raven* four-zero-two, take speed two-seven-five, say state."

"Two hundred pounds less than when you asked me *two minutes ago,*" Saint replied. Wilson cringed at the unprofessional sarcasm in his XO's voice.

When he heard this exchange, O'Shaunessy, whose attention had been on the situation regarding the deck status, turned his head and said to no one, "Who the fuck's in four-oh-two?" He answered his own question by looking at the

status board. He shook his head in disgust when he read "PATRICK" and turned to search for a *Raven* flight suit patch among the pilots seated behind him.

"If your XO would make proper voice calls, we wouldn't have to ask him for his state."

All Wilson could do was acknowledge him with a chastened "Yes, sir."

"*And* give him a speed change because he can't hit his marshal point on time," O'Shaunessy added. The room was silent except for the clipped radio exchanges from the final approach controllers and pilots.

The Big Unit leaned over to Wilson and whispered *"Bad hair day..."* Wilson nodded but wondered if he was talking about O'Shaunessy or his XO.

The marshal controller queried the *Raven* XO a second time. "Four-zero-two, say state."

Wearily, Saint responded, "Six-point-*one*."

Next, Wilson's ear was attuned to Sponge Bob's voice over marshal frequency as he began his approach. "Four-zero-six commencing out of angels thirteen, state five-two."

"Roger, four-zero-six, five-point-two."

Wilson did some fuel calculations in his head. Sponge had enough for a few looks at the deck before he hit tank state. The ship had two tankers overhead, a *Rhino* with 6,000 pounds to give and a *Viking* with 4,000. Outside the wind blew at 36 knots down the angled deck, most of it natural as the ship was making nothing more than bare steerageway. Glancing at the PLAT, Wilson saw a flash on the horizon. Thunder in all quadrants, varsity pitching deck, rain and dark, with the nearest *open* unfamiliar divert field 250 miles away. *Why do we do these things to ourselves?* He turned his attention to the *Hornet* above the crosshairs on the PLAT.

"Two-zero-one, three quarter mile, call the ball."

"Two-zero-one, *Hornet* ball, four-eight."

"Roger, ball, workin' thirty-five knots, MOVLAS." Wilson recognized the voice of Lieutenant Commander Russ "Shakey" McDevitt. He was the new Air Wing Four LSO who had reported aboard just before cruise.

Conversation stopped as everyone in Air Ops looked toward the PLAT. The first aircraft of the recovery, *Red River 201*, flown by a marine captain on his second cruise, was coming in. The light cluster grew larger and the external strobe lights on the *Hornet* blinked every half second as the aircraft approached the ship at over 140 knots.

"You're goin' *a lit-tle* high," Shakey said in his characteristic LSO bedroom voice. Wilson thought *201* looked *way* high, but Shakey was going to talk him

down. He added a pitching deck call. "Deck's movin' a little, you're high…coming down. You're a *lit-tle* fast."

Wilson felt the ship take a lurch and saw the crosshairs drop suddenly on the PLAT. As the *Hornet* reached the wave-off decision point, Shakey finally made the decision by squeezing the "pickle" switch. "Wave-off, pitching deck," he radioed. At once Wilson saw the *Hornet* add power and disappear out of the top of the screen as it passed over the deck, much of the sound penetrating the flight deck into Air Ops.

"Oh for two," The Big Unit said softly.

Wilson's guys were next. Saint was at one mile, and despite the deck motion, appeared low and lined up left, as he was for most of the approach. Wilson shook his head imperceptibly. *He just accepts being off*, he thought.

"Four-zero-two, slightly below glide path, slightly left of course, three quarter mile, call the ball."

"Four-oh-two *Hornet* ball, five-one."

"Roger, ball, thirty-five knots."

After the "ball" is called, radio communications are limited to the LSO only, and at that signal, the dozen pilots in Air Ops also ceased their whispered conversations. Instead, they watched the light cluster loom larger in the glide slope crosshairs. Saint was holding left, and Shakey, on the LSO platform, saw it, too, and coaxed him back to centerline. "You're lined up a *lit-tle* left...Lined up left...Deck's movin' a little. You're on glide path."

Wilson saw Saint correct for line up, and as he did, he carried too much power and drove himself high. Wilson thought, for sure, his XO would bolter, but suddenly the aircraft took a lunge to the deck.

"ATTITUDE! *PO-WER!" Raven 402* slammed into the deck hard, and the sound of the *Hornet* at full power, straining against the number one arresting wire, filled Air Ops.

"*Saint* wasn't going around," murmured The Big Unit. Wilson heard him, but kept his eyes on his XO in the landing area. As the arresting wire was pulled back, the arresting hook was retracted too early and fouled the wire between the hook and the fuselage underside. Wilson knew why it happened...Saint raised the hook before the yellow shirt signaled him.

The PLAT showed the *Hornet* stop and drop the hook to the deck. The hook runner, a sailor with a long steel crowbar, ran underneath the aircraft and pulled the cable clear of the hook, which was then raised again. Once untangled, the *Hornet* advanced the throttles to taxi forward and get clear of the landing area. The jet's exhaust blasted the water on the flight deck into another cloud that tumbled aft. The PLAT switched to Sponge Bob, the undercarriage of *402* visible as it taxied forward over the camera.

"Four-zero-six, on and on, three quarter mile, call the ball."

"Four-zero-six, *Hornet* ball, four-oh."

"Roger, ball *Hornet*, deck's movin' a little, you're on glide slope."

Wilson watched the deck status light indication flashing foul in the top of the screen as Sponge drew closer. *"It's gonna be close..."* he said to no one in particular. Shakey continued to guide the pilots with his calming voice, as if there were no worries. "You're on glide slope...*onnn* glide slope," he called to Sponge, keeping a careful eye on him but conscious that the deck was still foul since *402* had not yet cleared the landing area. Seconds from the decision point, the deck motion subsided for a moment. With the deck still foul, though, Shakey had to wave him off.

"Wave-off, foul deck," paddles called, just as the deck went clear.

Damn, Wilson thought. His XO caused the wave-off by retracting his hook too early and not waiting for the yellow shirt signal.

O'Shaunessy turned to him. *"Raven* rep, your flight lead shit-in-the-gear caused that."

Wilson nodded and said, "Yes, sir." O'Shaunessy kept his narrow eyes on him for a count and turned away. While Commander O'Shaunessy could be a dickhead, he was at least *fair*, taking on peers like The Big Unit to his face, or Saint behind his back, as well as lower ranking squadron department heads. The Irishman always looked pissed off, and who could blame him? He had to orchestrate the tension of carrier recoveries night after night after night, while the captain up there watched his every move and ripped into him when the airborne ballet was less than perfect. If air wing pilots were fouling up *his* pattern, they were going to know it, and *screw 'em* if they didn't like it.

Wilson looked at the status board with a grim face. This recovery was not going well, and no wonder! Varsity pitching deck, high gusty winds, rain and thunder in all quadrants, barely enough gas airborne on a dark night...and the divert fields practically out of reach, the best one of them closed.

Spartan 104 then trapped on a lucky four wire, and CATCC came on the radio to Sponge: "Four-zero-six, turn left to downwind. Fly heading three-five-zero. Report abeam."

"Four-zero-six," answered Sponge.

Wilson thought that Sponge Bob sounded cool. Despite his relative inexperience as an aviator, and despite a baby face that resembled the cartoon character, he could handle this. *Maybe this experience will be good for him*, thought Wilson. *He needs to add a few lines to that face.* CATCC was sending more aircraft to waiting tankers overhead. O'Shaunessy called to launch the alert 15 tanker, a *Super Hornet.* "Tell 'em I need it in ten minutes," he said.

Ding ding, ding ding...ding. The 1MC bells sounded again...1830. Wilson turned his attention to a *Hawkeye* lined up left on the PLAT and watched it settle on a one wire and roll out on centerline. The familiar *whooumm* of the turboprops at full power penetrated the space. That sound was followed by a deep *whhaaa* as the prop pitch reacted to the throttle setting on deck. Now, there were three *Hornets* and a *Viking* left to recover, and Sponge was first in line.

On departure frequency, Wilson heard "*Cutlass* three-zero-five, report plugged and receiving."

"Three-oh-five, *wilco*."

Wilson glanced at The Big Unit, whose eyes remained locked on the PLAT. Both watched the flickering strobes of Sponge on final at three miles, but Wilson knew he, too, had to be listening to the departure frequency transmissions and thinking about the young *Buccaneer* pilot struggling behind the basket overhead.

All the aviators in the room had been there. In their minds, they climbed off the bolter with the pilot, raised the gear, switched frequencies to receive instructions, activated the radar and commanded it to automatically acquire the assigned aircraft. Even as their eyes joined the pilot's eyes in search of the tanker, the idea of being in a low-state aircraft far from land lurked in the corners of their minds...

There it is! That cluster of lights at 2 o'clock high. The pilot levels off at 2,000 feet and holds 250 knots, on altitude, controls the closure, and gets on bearing line. The pressure is on to join up and plug on the first try. As the pilot draws near, the flashing strobe lights illuminate the outline of the tanker, and the basket suddenly extends out of the refueling store. With his left hand, the pilot reaches down from the throttle and extends his refueling probe. With his left foot, he feeds in some bottom rudder to align the fuselages. Stabilized on the tanker's left wing, he sees the tanker pilot make a circle with his flashlight—the signal to plug.

The pilot slides into position and, with no horizon to reference, attempts to line the probe up behind the basket. Rigid with concentration, and "*squeezing the black out of the stick*," the pilot attempts to anticipate the movements of the basket, which is constantly buffeted in the airstream. He adds a little power to ease forward, misses low, pulls a bit to back out, and lines up again for another stab. *Hurry back*, stabilize, now easy, *easy...* He takes a lunge with throttle and

stick to slam the probe into the basket. The hose buckles from the impact before the take-up reel returns tension. The pilot pulls some power, but not so much that he backs out. As he maintains that position on the tanker, he watches the status light on the store, willing it to go from amber to green.

Green. Good flow. Life blood enters the aircraft. *Time* enters the aircraft. A split-second glance at the fuel page on the multifunction display, followed quickly by another glance, confirms the increase in fuel. *Yes, yes.* Even as his eyes scan for the first hint of relative movement on the tanker, he relaxes a bit and exhales deeply, his mouth open against the mask's microphone. Another chance, more time to live.

Air Ops let out a collective sigh of relief when the *Cutlass* came up on the radio. "Three-oh-five, plugged and receiving."

"Roger, three-zero-five, take three-point-oh."

"Three-oh-five."

Wilson heard The Big Unit murmur. "Oh, thank you, thank you, thank you."

"Four-zero-six, two miles, going slightly below glide path."

"Four-zero-six."

O'Shaunessy assigned one of the tankers, *Spartan 102*, to keep their eyes on—or "hawk"— Sponge. As Wilson watched the PLAT, he could see the familiar strobes of the *Super Hornet* high in the screen. They crossed from right to left across the screen as the tanker passed behind the ship and into a position to catch Sponge if he needed their services. The final controller called to Sponge with "Four-zero-six, on glide path, slightly right of course, one mile," and followed that with "Four-zero-six, on and on three quarter mile, call the ball."

"Four-zero-six, *Hornet* ball, two-seven."

"Roger, ball, workin' thirty-six knots, slightly axial."

O'Shaunessy turned to Wilson with an amused look and, referring to Sponge's *below tank* fuel state, said, "At least he's honest."

"Yes, sir," Wilson said and smiled. He appreciated the small break in the tension and stood up to take full advantage of it. He heard Shakey assure Sponge of his position on glide slope just as the PLAT crosshairs moved up, then down. The screen displayed a sudden pitch of the ship's deck, one they also felt in their stomachs. The chance of catching Sponge on this pass was very low.

O'Shaunessy picked up the phone. "If he doesn't get aboard, send him to one-oh-two for two-point-five."

C'mon, Wilson thought, trying to control the motion of the ship. *Settle down.* Sponge was in close. *Maybe he can make it...*

"Wave off, pitching deck," Shakey said as he depressed the pickle switch. Sponge added full power and maintained his proper landing attitude as he flew away.

"Dammit!" O'Shaunessy sighed, and spoke to CATCC. "Tank him."

Seconds later, they heard approach call to Sponge. "Four-zero-six, your signal is tank, clean up, take angels one-point-two, *Texaco* is at two o'clock, angels two, report him in sight."

"Visual," Sponge responded.

"Four-zero-six, roger, take angels two and switch departure button two."

"Four-zero-six, angels two, button two."

After a short lull in the action, and while he was chatting with The Big Unit, Wilson heard Sponge's voice on the overhead speaker.

"One-zero-two, there's a heavy stream of fuel coming out of the basket."

Wilson's head snapped to the status board and looked at Sponge's fuel state...2.5 two minutes ago. He then looked at O'Shaunessy, but he appeared not to have heard the transmission.

"Roger, we'll recycle," the tanker pilot answered.

"Commander?" Wilson called to O'Shaunessy, who turned to him and cocked his head.

"I just heard four-oh-six say there's a heavy stream of fuel coming out of the basket."

O'Shaunessy whipped around and picked up the phone. "Get me a status on four-oh-six."

Sponge watched the basket retract into the refueling store and glanced at his fuel: 2,300 pounds. Roughly, he had 20 minutes. A wisp of cloud flew past; then they were in the clouds. He edged closer to the tanker to keep the position light on the red wingtip of *102* in view.

The *Spartan* tanker pilot pushed down to get out of the clouds, and Sponge saw a minor stream of fuel emitting from the back of the store as the small generator prop on the store turned. Minor, yet *disconcerting.* He hoped it was just

residual fuel from an earlier stream and, for an instant, when the basket started to move out of the store, he thought all was well. When it opened, however, a solid flow of fuel billowed into the airstream.

"Still streamin' heavy," Sponge radioed. His breathing was deep, and he squeezed tighter on the stick. Departure control called to him. "Four-zero-six, update state."

'Two-point-three," Sponge replied.

The tension in Air Ops ratcheted up as the focus shifted to *406*. O'Shaunessy rubbed his forehead. "What's the status on three-oh-five?" he asked Metz. The room was quiet except for the sound that came from the air conditioning vents overhead.

"Still on one-zero-seven, sir." At that moment the radio crackled. "Three-oh-five, tank complete."

"Get him aboard!" O'Shaunessy shouted and looked at the status board. "What's the story on one-oh-seven?"

"He's dry, sir, four-point-oh," Metz answered, his voice almost an apology.

"*Fuck!* Get him back here, *now!*"

CHAPTER 9

Wilson figured Sponge was good for 25 minutes airborne at low altitude—if he "hung on the blades" at a max conserve power setting. The two desired outcomes of flying an approach to the ship with gear and flaps down or joining up on a hoped-for tanker for a desperate "drink" would burn up more gas. He estimated Sponge really had 20 minutes before a third outcome was required: controlled ejection.

Wilson got O'Shaunessy's attention. "Sir, he's got about 20 minutes."

"I know… He's been doing good, hasn't he?" Wilson interpreted his question to be about Sponge's ability behind the ship.

"Yes, sir, if the deck cooperates, he'll get aboard."

Sponge remained on *102*, fuel still streaming from the basket. He edged closer to see if he could plug anyway and noted a heavier flow than he first thought. The flow was solid, as if the basket was engaged and fuel was being pumped into an invisible aircraft. If he attempted to plug now, he risked getting the windscreen covered with fuel that could then be ingested into the right engine. That could cause problems he didn't even want to imagine. When a bolt of lightning from a nearby squall exploded off their right wing, Sponge made up his mind.

"One-zero-two, recommend you stow the basket."

"Concur," *102* replied. He retracted the basket almost immediately.

When the prop was secured, Sponge radioed, "Good stow." After a moment, he added, "Departure, four-zero-six detaching," as he deflected the stick to the left.

"What's the story on one-twelve?" O'Shaunessy said to no one, then picked up the phone and asked the Air Boss the same question.

Wilson heard Sponge ask the question. "Departure, tanker posit?"

"Four-zero-six, we have no sweet tankers airborne. Launching alert *Texaco, Spartan* one-zero-five in five mikes. Your signal is max conserve. Say your angels?"

"Four-zero-six is at angels two."

"Roger, four-zero-six, take low holding."

"Four-zero-six...Ah, you want me to go to angels *eight?*"

"Affirm, four-zero-six."

With alarm, Wilson shouted from the back row. "Sir! *Commander O'Shaunessy!*"

Half expecting a vocal blast from the Commander, Wilson noticed that O'Shaunessy was shaken as he put down the receiver. He turned to Wilson as if to a friend who has a solution to his dilemma. "Yeah?"

"Sir, Departure told just told four-oh-six to take angels eight. Recommend you keep him down low so he doesn't chew up gas in the climb."

"Concur...because we're gonna barricade him."

Wilson stared at O'Shaunessy, not comprehending what he had heard. "*Sir?*"

"He's at barricade fuel. We're gonna catch the tankers and rig the barricade." O'Shaunessy saw the look of astonishment on Wilson's face and added, "Captain just made the call." His eyes remained locked on Wilson, as if to convey he understood but was powerless to overrule the Captain.

Wilson took a breath. "Sir, this is a night pitching deck barricade with a nugget pilot. My recommendation is to bring him aboard. He's got two more looks right now."

"What if we don't catch him?"

"Then a controlled ejection alongside."

"I thought you said he was good behind the boat."

"He is for a nugget, but why take the risk in these conditions?"

The Big Unit interjected, "Marty, I would recommend that for any pilot in these conditions."

O'Shaunessy studied both of their faces. "It's from the bridge. As soon as we get this *Bloodhound* aboard, we rig the barricade." He turned to Metz and gave more orders. "Get four-oh-six ten miles aft, max conserve."

"Yes, sir," Metz answered and picked up the phone.

Wilson got up and went to a J-dial phone circuit to call the CAG office. The Ops officer, known as Bucket, answered.

"Yes sir, Flip here in Air Ops. Four-zero-six is low state and the tankers are dry or sour. They're riggin' the barricade."

"Yeah, we just got the word. I'm tryin' to find CAG... We'll be right there."

"I'm tryin' to find my XO."

"Is your skipper airborne?"

"Yes, sir...my recommendation is to trap Sponge now or fly alongside and eject."

"OK, Flip, got it, thanks," Bucket said as he hung up. Wilson went back to his place next to XO Johnson, aware that the eyes of the other aviators were on him. Wilson dialed Ready 7 and Prince Charming answered. "Ready Seven, Lieutenant Howard."

"Prince, Flip, where's the XO?"

"He hasn't come in yet."

"Find him and get him to Air Ops *now*!" Wilson ordered.

"Yes, sir."

"Tell him they're gonna barricade Sponge."

"Holy shit!"

"Find Dutch and Smoke, maybe they can help the LSOs up there. Break out the premishap plan."

"Aye, aye, sir. Dutch is up there waving now," Prince said.

Wilson realized he was powerless to do anything. The Captain had decided to barricade Sponge, and that was that. He looked at Commander O'Shaunessy hunched over his desk with the phone receiver in one ear. He saw the PLAT crosshairs moving slowly relative to the S-3 on glide slope. Cajun is airborne. CAG isn't here. XO isn't here. Even if they were, he realized, they couldn't overturn the Captain's decision. The book says when a *Hornet* gets to 2.0 at night, you barricade him. The captain was nothing if by the book. *Rig the barricade! Yes, sir! Aye, aye, sir!*

The barricade was a nylon web net made of heavy-duty nylon bands that hung down vertically from a steel cable rigged across the landing area. It was held up by two great stanchions that lifted it some 20 feet above the deck. This allowed the aircraft to make a normal carrier approach with the barricade net stopping the aircraft. Typically, the arrestment ended with significant damage, and the pilot had no option to eject once the aircraft was caught. The pilot shut down the engines on LSO command as the aircraft crossed the ramp, which further reduced the scant 10-foot hook-to-ramp clearance. The aircraft had to roll into the net with little drift—drift would cause the aircraft and the net to veer over the side or into the jets parked alongside the foul line. Too high was disaster. If the top loading strap were to snag the hook or landing gear, the aircraft would be slammed to the deck with back-breaking force, and the fiery wreckage would slide down the angle and into the water. And once inside a certain point subjectively determined by the LSO, there was no way to wave-off.

It was rare for the Navy to barricade an airplane, maybe once a decade. And when it happened, it was an event felt throughout the fleet. *Hey, did ya hear Valley Forge barricaded a Hornet last night?*

I can't believe we are doing this, thought Wilson. *Night, dog-squeeze weather, pitching deck barricade! If all works well, if the barricade is rigged in time, if the deck steadies out, if we don't steam into a squall, if Shakey or Stretch give him the right sugar calls, if Sponge flies a solid pass, everything will be fine.* Just trap him! *He has one, maybe two looks. If he doesn't get aboard, then eject alongside.*

Wilson wondered if Sponge knew what was happening. He got up from the bench to review the NATOPS manual for barricade procedures when he saw his XO standing at the entrance to the room. Still in his flight gear, Saint scowled at him and cocked his head in a motion to come over. Saint then led them into the back office.

"Yes, sir," said Wilson.

"Mister Wilson, *what the hell* is going on?"

"Sponge couldn't plug because the tanker was sour, fuel streaming from the hose. The other tanker was dry from tanking all the bolters and wave-offs. They're gonna barricade Sponge."

"Did you recommend that?"

"No, sir…the Captain made the call. I recommended they trap him normally in these conditions. He's got two looks."

"And if not aboard he's out of gas. Then what?"

"Controlled ejection alongside," Wilson replied, keeping his face expressionless as he held the XO's gaze.

Saint looked down at the deck with tight lips steadying himself on a desk as the ship took a roll. The overhead creaked under the strain. He snapped his head up, eyes narrow with contempt.

"I expected more from my Operations Officer."

"Sir?"

"Why is that nugget out there in these conditions? I expect my Ops Officer to write a schedule that reflects the expected weather. But I don't expect him to then go and countermand an order of a Captain more than twice his seniority! *Unsat.*"

Wilson felt his upper body tighten.

"Sir, the Skipper signed the schedule almost 24 hours ago—before we knew what we would be facing tonight, before we knew we would be over 200 miles from *any* divert. Any senior officer in Air Wing Four could have broken the chain today with a recommendation to stop flying." He paused and lowered

his voice. "Any flight lead could have ensured his wingman came down with sufficient fuel for any contingency instead of showing up here at minimum fuel. Any flight lead could have sent his lower-state wingman down first. And any pilot could have gotten out of the gear clean so his wingman could trap."

The XO's eyes narrowed even more, and he forcibly exhaled through his nose. Wilson knew right away he had overstepped several boundaries. Back-talk to commanders, even when justified, was never career-enhancing. He waited for the blast. When Saint just glared at him, apparently unsure of how to counter, Wilson decided to change course.

"I didn't countermand anything, sir. I made a recommendation. Sponge has to fly a solid pass, and if he doesn't hit the barricade clean, he probably doesn't get a chance to punch if he needs to. My recommendation is made and noted. Our squadronmate is in trouble, and I made a call. Now I have to get back—unless you want to take over, sir."

At that moment the familiar sound of an S-3 catching an arresting wire filled the space, and through the armored steel of the flight deck, they heard the muffled voice of the Boss on the loudspeaker. "Rig the jet barricade. We've got a low-state *Raven!* Ready Cat 3 for the alert *Texaco!* Get movin'!"

The overhead fluorescent light shone down on the *Raven* pilots as they looked at each other, unyielding and firm. Either one apologizing for the exchange was unthinkable.

"Get up there," Saint finally said.

At least he kept his eyes on me, Wilson thought, before his thoughts turned back to Sponge. As soon as he returned to his place next to The Big Unit, but before he could sit down, O'Shaunessy motioned Wilson over to the console and handed him the radio handset. "Tell Jasper we're gonna barricade him in about five minutes. Do you guys have a procedure for that?"

CHAPTER 10

Sponge breathed deeply as he flew away from the ship eight miles aft. *Two thousand pounds... I've got a little over 20 minutes at this fuel flow.* He wondered why they were vectoring him out here and keeping him at angels two. When he looked over his left shoulder, he could make out a cluster of lights in the distance...*Valley Forge*...and home. He desperately wanted to be aboard her. A bolt of lightning flashed nearby and for an instant the ship was illuminated in a bluish light, before darkness surrounded it again. During Sponge's short aviation career, he had already become accustomed to being at low fuel states. Judging from their ready room conversations, the old guys like Flip and Weed loathed them as much as he did. *Sweating fuel* was part of life when a *Hornet* pilot was at sea.

So this is my night in the barrel, he thought, a sea story he could tell at the O-Club just like the heavies did when they held court there. Each story, it seemed, involved a black night, a tanker, and a low-state trap. However, if this was his rite of passage, he would gladly decline. *Damn XO!* Sponge had seen Saint's aircraft taxi over the foul line just before Sponge got the wave-off on the first pass. If Saint had gotten out of the gear sooner, Sponge would probably be aboard right now, drinking a cup of water in the ready room. He *was* thirsty, so he pulled out the plastic canteen from the left pocket of his g-suit and unscrewed the top. He then popped a fitting on his oxygen mask so he could drink.

Just as he took a gulp, the approach controller's voice filled his headset. "Four-zero-six, fly heading two-one-five. Take angels one-point-two. Stand by for your rep."

Sponge screwed down the canteen top and shoved it back against the left console. After fumbling for the mask, he brought it to his face and keyed the mike. "Four-zero-six."

"Four-zero-six, rep," Wilson called to him.

"Go ahead," Sponge replied, glad to hear Wilson's familiar voice. He then adjusted the mask against his face.

"Four-zero-six, the airborne tankers are dry or sour. We're starting one up on deck but still haven't been able to get him airborne. We're rigging the barricade."

Rigging the barricade. Sponge sat motionless as the message sank in.

"Four-zero-six, you copy?"

"Affirm" Sponge responded. "I'm still headin' away from mother."

"Roger, Sponge. Mark your father with state."

"I'm on the two-six-five for niner, one-point-niner."

"Roger, we're gonna hook you in soon, but first I'm goin' to go over the barricade checklist... Do you have any ordnance?"

"Negative."

"Roger, OK... We're gonna punch off the drop tanks. See anything underneath you?"

Sponge dipped his wing to the left, looked below, and saw nothing but black. "Negative," he said.

"Roger, then emergency jett your tanks. Big switch on the upper left...hold it in till they're gone. Let me know when you've done it."

Sponge placed his left thumb on the switch, looked at the tank under his left wing, and pushed. He heard a *ka-chunk* and felt a twitch as small explosive cartridges pushed away the empty 300-gallon drop tanks from stations on the wing and fuselage. He watched the left drop fall and disappear into the darkness.

"I'm clean."

"Roger, Sponge," Wilson answered.

The final controller followed immediately and said, "Four-zero-six, turn left fly heading zero-five-zero."

"Four-zero-six, left to zero-five-zero," responded Sponge.

Wilson proceeded with the checklist.

"Sponge, Paddles is going to come up in a bit and give you the barricade brief, but as you get lower in fuel, remember, no negative g. You have a fuel low light yet?"

"Not yet."

"OK, but when you do, the airplane still flies. Just don't horse it around."

The amber color of the master caution light suddenly illuminated the cockpit. The impassionate voice of the aural warning tone, which the pilots called *Trailer Trash Tammy*, sounded a warning in Sponge's headset. *"Fuel low. Fuel low."*

Sponge's eyes went to the FUEL LO caution on the left multi-function display. "Jus' got the fuel low."

"Roger that. Net's goin' up." Wilson regretted his last comment. The barricade was actually still in its locker, despite the high activity of the crew in the

landing area. They were busy making preparations so they could run it across the flight deck. "I should'a been straight with him," he said under his breath to The Big Unit.

The Commander replied, "He doesn't need to know. Just tell him everything's fine here."

CHAPTER 11

"WHAT?" Lieutenant Commander Russell "Shakey" McDevitt exclaimed to the LSO phone talker on the platform. *"Barricade?"*

"Yes, sir," the young sailor replied. Shakey saw the look of concern the sailor couldn't hide as he relayed the message. "After this *Rhino*, they gonna rig it for four-zero-six!"

Shakey looked aft at the blinking lights of the *Super Hornet* some five miles away. "Who's in four-oh-six again?"

"Jasper," a young LSO sang out, at the same time Dutch said, "It's Sponge."

Sponge, Shakey thought, and immediately his mind spat out a trend analysis: *Sponge tends to get overpowered and drive himself high in close and overcorrect to an early wire. He responds to calls, a solid nugget, trainable.*

Shakey then turned his attention to the aircraft at one mile. The rain started to pick up again.

As Shakey, with Dutch backing him up, worked to get the *Rhino* aboard, he fought to keep from thinking of the barricade approach he would wave less than 10 minutes from now. Mercifully, the deck cooperated with the *Spartan*, and it flew a solid pass. Shakey then walked over to call the tower, picked up the receiver, and dialed.

The call was answered after the first ring. "Air Boss."

"Boss, Shakey. Are we really going to barricade this guy?"

"Yeah, he couldn't plug. We've got an alert tanker, and we're shootin' him now. But we need to get four-oh-six aboard. How's Jasper been lately?"

"He's doin' good, sir. Tends to be overpowered."

"A few extra for the wife and kids. Nothin' wrong with that!" he said, in an attempt to lighten the mood. Then the Boss turned serious. "Can he handle this?"

"Yes, sir. We'll get him aboard." Shakey hoped he was right.

"You ready for this?"

"Yes, sir. We've got it."

"Good job, Paddles. We're workin' a 28,000 gross... Gotta go."

"Yes, sir" Shakey said as he hung up.

Seconds later the Boss came over the 5MC. "On the flight deck, we've got a low-state *Hornet* comin' in. *Rig the barricade.* Rig the jet barricade for *Raven* four-zero-six."

Shakey looked at Dutch, who was still stunned by the news. "You good to go?" he asked.

Dutch looked toward the horizon and back toward Shakey. "Yep, I'm right behind you—unless, of course, you want Stretch up here."

"No, his eyes aren't night adapted. You back me up."

"Roger that," Dutch replied, and grabbed a radio handset to listen to the CATCC controlling his sqadronmate.

Shakey still couldn't believe this was happening. He reached up to rub the tension out of his neck. The pain felt like an ice pick digging into the base of his skull. When the phone rang, which was barely audible over the wind and the roar of the *Rhino* engines up forward, one of the LSOs answered and turned to Shakey. "It's CAG."

Shakey walked over toward the console and took the receiver. "Lieutenant Commander McDevitt, sir."

"Paddles, CAG. Can we get this guy aboard?"

Shakey looked at the dozens of sailors swarming into the landing area to rig the barricade, their shouts audible above the din of the flight deck. "Yes, sir, but I would prefer, and even recommend, a normal arrest. When is that tanker gonna get launched?"

"They're workin' on it," CAG said, and then added, "Paddles, the Captain made the call. It's going to be a barricade, but if Jasper is not where you want him, pickle him and try again. If he's not there the next pass, don't take him out of parameters. If he flames out, he ejects, and we'll pick him up. Don't think you have to save the world here."

"Yes, sir, thanks CAG," Shakey said.

"You can do it, Paddles!" CAG said as he hung up.

Shakey took a few steps to the LSO console and picked up the radio transceiver. He felt the eyes of every LSO on the team focus on him as he moved toward the platform wind barricade. As he pressed his back against it to minimize his exposure to the elements, he opened his gouge book, his LSO platform "Cliff Notes," and quickly scanned the barricade brief.

I must convey confidence. Smile, he thought, and keyed the mike. "Four-zero-six, Paddles!"

"Go ahead," Sponge replied.

"Hey, Sponge, we're going to rig the barricade for this next pass. I know you've been workin' hard out there. You flew some solid approaches, but the

deck just didn' cooperate. I'm going to go over the brief with you... Ah, let's see... What's yer configuration, approach speed and gross weight?"

"I'm slick. Just punched off the tanks...estimating one-thirty knots and twenty-seven K."

"Roger that," Shakey said as he proceeded with the brief. "Deck's movin' a little, and I'll be givin' ya calls to back up what I'm showin' ya on the MOVLAS. Don't chase the deck. We're workin' thirty-five knots right now. Line-up is going to be *real* important, so keep that in your scan. We don't want any drift at touchdown."

He took a breath and continued with the checklist.

"Fly it on speed, and fly the ball I'm showing ya. Now, I'll be talking to you the whole way—advisory calls early, imperative calls in close." Shakey took another breath. "You can't execute your own wave-off in close. Jus' follow my calls, and, at the proper point, I'm going to give you a *cut*. When I do, shut down the engines and you'll roll into the barricade. Keep the throttle under control. Don't get overpowered and drive yourself high. If you do, I'll be talking to you. Big corrections early, *smaaall* corrections in close. Got it?"

"Roger, sir."

"One more thing, the ship's moving, and it's gonna generate a Dutch Roll...Fly your needles, and don't chase line-up at range. After the ball call, it's meatball, line-up angle of attack." Shakey paused to let it sink in.

"Roger," Sponge replied.

"Any questions?"

"Negative."

Shakey was encouraged by the confidence in Sponge's voice. He knew he held Sponge's life in his hands.

CATCC jumped in. "Four-zero-six, turn right zero-eight-zero to intercept the final bearing one-one-six."

"Four-zero-six," Sponge said. His mouth was parched with fear as he reached down to set the course line.

"Bingo! Bingo!" sounded *Tammy,* warning Sponge again of his emergency fuel situation.

Sponge had never been this low on fuel in a *Hornet*. Breathing through his mouth, Sponge thought he could hear his heartbeat. Even under his mask, he could smell a metallic odor emanating from his person. Adrenaline. *Fear.* The realization surprised him. *You can smell your own fear,* he thought, and fought to keep himself under control. *It's bad enough to be on fumes at night. But this is a night pitching deck barricade!*

Turning back to the ship, he double-checked the course-line, touched the hook handle to ensure it was down, and fiddled with the HUD intensity. He had any number of minor cockpit tasks to distract him. *Night, pitching deck barricade in the middle of fucking nowhere!* After his moment of self-pity, he realized he was the only pilot in the airplane. *You can do this,* he told himself.

As he removed his kneeboard and set it in the map case for a possible ejection, CATCC called again. "Four-zero-six, dirty up."

"Four-zero-six," Sponge acknowledged as he slapped the gear handle down and moved the flap switch to half. The aircraft ballooned with the increased lift, and the landing gear caused a dull roar behind him as it extended into the airstream. He countered the increased lift with a nose down bunt and retrimmed the aircraft. He tried to concentrate on flying the airplane so he would not think about the barricade.

A few moments later, though, he glanced at the ship to see if he could see it.

CHAPTER 12

"Tower, one-zero-five, we just lost nose wheel steering."

"*WHAT?! Dammit!! Mother-f...!*" Marty O'Shaunessy was not having a good recovery. He needed the alert tanker to launch immediately to get more gas in the air, and instead he gets this. He shook his head in disgust and grabbed for the phone.

"Roger, one-zero-five. Stand by," the Boss said.

Wilson heard O'Shaunessy plead with the Boss. "Can you put a tractor and tow bar on him? Push him to the Cat! We need that gas airborne!" Wilson knew there was no time even for that desperation measure, maybe not even time for 105 to taxi to the catapult normally.

Sponge was expected at the ramp in minutes.

"*Fuck!*" O'Shaunessy said, as he slammed down the receiver.

When Air Ops next heard the flight deck loudspeaker through the deck, it was the Air Boss. "C'mon! We've got a *Hornet* at five miles! *Chop! Chop!*" Things were obviously not going well on the roof.

The Boss was not happy with the barricade progress. The nylon netting was laid out on deck and was attached to the two barricade stanchions embedded into the deck. However, the heavy strands were tangled and bunched together, and some of the plates were not yet in position. The Flight Deck Officer and Bos'n were everywhere. They shouted orders, grabbed sailors, jumped over nylon straps, and checked the connections to the stanchions. While Shakey and the other LSOs watched, they were joined on the platform by a new LSO. It was Stretch.

"Are we havin' fun, guys?" he said with a grin. Stretch was a perpetual optimist.

"Hey, glad yer here," Shakey answered. "We're set. Just briefed him. He's about one-point-five now... See him out there?"

"Yeah...I'm not night adapted, so you and Dutch wave him. You've been doing great out here tonight. And remember, if he's not set up, pickle him early."

"Roger that," Shakey said.

The Air Boss exploded again on the 5MC microphone. "All right, get out of there! Raise the barricade on signal!"

From the platform they heard more shouting as dozens of sailors scurried away into the catwalks and behind the island. Moments later, the Flight Deck Bos'n gave the signal and watched as the barricade assembly rose into the air, carried aloft by the two large stanchions.

In the subdued Air Ops space, Wilson and the others watched the barricade ascend, its heavy vertical nylon straps fluttering in the wind, into the PLAT's field of view. In the distance, on the left side of the picture was Sponge, represented by the pulsing external lights of an FA-18. Saint was still there in Air Ops and still in his flight gear. He sat off to the side and concentrated on the PLAT.

A radio call from CATCC broke the silence. "Four-zero-six, lock-on six miles, say your needles."

"Fly up and left," Sponge replied.

"Concur, fly your needles," the controller commanded. Wilson recognized the approach controller's voice and thought, *They've got their best guy controlling him.*

"Four-zero-six, update state."

"One-point-two."

Damn, Sponge is cool tonight, Wilson thought as he returned to his place. *At least cooler than I feel right now with all these eyes on me. And Saint over there adding zero value.* Wilson wished Saint would just leave and watch from the ready room. Was he here because he cared about Sponge, or was he thinking about having to answer questions at the mishap board? That meeting would surely be convened tomorrow morning, no matter what happened right now.

"Four-zero-six, four and a half miles, right of course correcting. Mother's in a starboard turn. Expected final bearing one-two-six."

"Four-zero-six... Jus' got a *fuel hot.*"

"Roger, four-zero-six, right of course and correcting. Turn right to zero-niner-five to intercept final."

"Four-zero-six, zero-nine-five."

On the platform with Dutch standing behind him, Shakey held the headset to his left ear. He had his right arm tucked under his left elbow and looked aft into space. As he watched, the lights of Sponge's Hornet and those of the escort ship behind the carrier drift left. *We're in a fucking turn!* he realized. He listened to the exchange between Flip, CATCC and Sponge and was impressed by the calm in their voices. He felt anything but calm, but maintained a stoic exterior. The dull tension at the base of his skull spread to his shoulders and was intensified by the isolated raindrops that splattered on his back and head.

His mouth felt like cotton, but he had to sound confident on the radio. *Fight it!* he thought.

He took a deep breath, glanced at the wind speed indication, and willed his voice to be calm as he keyed the mic. "Workin' *thirty-four* knots…Barricade's up." He exhaled deeply and put the handset down to rub his shoulder. A bolt of lightning flashed from somewhere behind him.

"How ya doin', Shakey?" Stretch asked.

"I've got it…Just picked a bad day to quit sniffin' glue!"

The tension broken, Dutch chimed in, "Yeah, I've never waved a barricade either, but I did stay at a Holiday Inn Express last night." Although it was somewhat forced, the officers on the platform laughed. It was a welcome relief from the strain of the recovery.

A radio call from the final controller brought them all back to the task at hand. "Four-zero-six, approaching glidepath. Slightly right of course correcting. Expected final bearing, one-two-eight."

"Four-zero-six."

Stretch shouted over gusting winds to the controlling LSO. "Shakey, after the ball call, jump in early. Lip-lock him the whole way down if you have to."

"Roger that!"

To minimize the danger to the others on the platform, Stretch shouted, "Guys, let's clear the platform. Primary and backup LSOs, myself and the phone talker stay. Rest of you guys go below and hang out in Ready 8 until he's aboard. Sorry." Four of the LSOs nodded and walked to the catwalk ladders.

The J-Dial circuit buzzed, and Stretch answered it. "Lieutenant Commander Armstrong, sir."

"Stretch, Boss… Captain wants you to call him."

"Yes, sir," Stretch answered. He killed the connection and then dialed the Captain's chair on the bridge. After one ring, the Captain picked up the receiver and growled, "Cap'n."

"Lieutenant Commander Armstrong on the platform, sir."

"Paddles, time to stop screwing around and get this guy aboard. *Now!* Got it?"

"Yes, sir," Stretch said, then swallowed. "Will we have winds down the angle? Because…"

Before Stretch could finish the Captain boomed. "I'LL TAKE CARE OF THE WINDS! *Now you do your job!*" The Captain slammed the receiver down.

Stretch looked aft into the dark. He had received blasts from the Captain in the course of predeployment training. His temper was legendary, and over

time Stretch had built up a mental layer of protection. *Same shit, different day,* he thought, trying to reassure himself about tonight's display of temper.

"Stretch, who was that?" Shakey shouted to him.

Stretch smiled. "It was the Boss. Says barricade's set. Actual weight 27,000. The bridge is workin' on the winds. We're good to go!"

Sponge concentrated on his instruments but took a peek at the ship off to the right of his HUD. He was curious… *Will I be able to see the barricade from three and a half miles?* When he looked over his nose, he saw nothing but the outline of the landing area, the drop lights, and the tower sodium vapors…a cluster of yellow lights surrounded by black.

One thousand pounds of fuel remaining…this is it.

"Four-zero-six. You're on course, approaching glide path," the controller said.

"Four-zero-six."

He watched the glide slope indication steadily descend from the top of his HUD. He focused on obtaining the best possible start to the approach and let everything else—the fuel quantity, the aircraft cautions, the weather, the barricade stretched across the deck—become secondary to flying a night carrier approach. The tension left him as he entered a mental realm that took all his attention.

Most pilots made use of this type of compartmentalization. It allowed him to sit still in the ejection seat, with his hands making tiny corrections to the stick and throttles. His eyes rapidly scanned his HUD instrumentation, primarily centered on the needles. As he approached the glide path inside three miles, he pushed the nose over and pulled some power, and then reset it to hold the steep 800-foot per minute rate of descent.

"Four-zero-six, up and on glide path, begin descent," said the CATCC controller.

Sponge keyed the mike. "Four-zero-six."

"Four-zero-six, going below, below glide path, two-point-five miles."

Sponge corrected with deft movements of the throttle and stick. Once the plane was back on the four-degree glide slope, he reset power. This steep approach angle, where he was just able to see the ship over the nose, gave him the impression of peering down into a void from the opening of a well. He could see he was lined up right of course and nudged the stick to the left. Suddenly, the needles jumped left. *The ship must be in a turn,* he thought, a fact confirmed right away by CATCC.

"Mother's in a starboard turn, turn left five."

"Four-zero-*six*," Sponge replied, with some exasperation.

Here, on the pass of my life, the ship jinks on me—inside *three miles*. He quickly put the thought out of his mind and concentrated on the HUD display. He slid his velocity vector to the left then recorrected once on course.

The sound of raindrops increased and beat on the canopy in great sheets. The rain also reflected light from the ship as it streaked aft on the smeared windscreen. The white noise of the rain added to his tension and caused his breathing to deepen and his hands to tighten on the controls. He worked hard to stay on glide slope and on centerline. Through the sheets of rain attacking his windscreen at over 150 miles per hour, he looked out at the ship and sensed he was lined up left, but the needles showed him on-and-on. *Trust the needles!* he reminded himself. His fuel indicator showed 930 pounds.

"Four-zero-six, on and on, one-point-five miles."

"Four-zero-six," Sponge acknowledged, and then he saw it.

The barricade was raised perpendicular to the landing area and looked almost like a solid swath of amber as it reflected the floodlight from the tower. It felt like a dive-bombing run, a dive-bombing run into the side of a chalky yellow cliff spread across the deck. He fought the urge to stare at it. The rain subsided a bit as he concentrated on maintaining glide slope, but his breathing rate picked up speed.

On the platform, the LSOs watched in grim silence as *406* approached. The wind velocity increased to 38 knots, and the plane guard destroyer aft on the invisible horizon seemed to float in space, up and down with the changing pitch of *Valley Forge's* deck.

"Barricade set two-seven, *Hornet!* Clear deck!" The phone talker shouted for all to hear.

Dutch glanced back into the landing area out of habit to ensure it was clear and was mesmerized by the barricade, where the high winds buffeted the thick nylon strands. Through the strands he could see shadows on the island weather deck galleries. Dozens of sailors were gathered there to watch the approach from the aptly named, "Vulture's Row."

"Roger, clear deck," he said, and immediately returned his attention to the familiar FA-18 light pattern manifested by *406.*

Shakey picked up the handle of the visual landing aid system and showed Sponge a centered ball. The rain was coming down harder now, pelting them in their exposed position. They both straddled the coaming, with one leg each placed on the flight deck. *We're probably going right into a squall,* thought Shakey.

Subconsciously, he pulled the collar of his flight suit up to cover his neck. Dutch, right next to him, cared much less about the weather than the fact that his squadronmate Sponge was in that jet.

Dutch saw Sponge drift left, as did CATCC. "Four-zero-six, one mile, drifting left of course, on glide path."

"Four-zero-six."

"Four-zero-six, slightly left of course, on glide path, three quarter mile, call the ball."

"Four-zero-six, *Hornet* ball, point-niner." Sponge sounded calm.

Shakey did, too, when he responded. *"Roger ball, Hornet,* working thirty-seven knots down the angle. Deck's movin' a little, yer *ooon* glide slope."

Dutch sensed the escort ship on the horizon slide left. "Ship's turnin' right!" he shouted to Shakey, who immediately informed Sponge.

"Ship's in a turn, come left...on glide slope...*come left*...yer goin' high...on center line."

"Talk to him!" Stretch called out.

Shakey keyed the handset microphone and held it depressed while he raised the MOVLAS handle higher. "Yer high! *Easy* with it."

Sponge made an aggressive correction, just as the ramp pitched down. He was uneasy with his steep view of the deck and felt as if he were right on top of it—and already past the cut point. He lost the ball due to the barricade stanchion and his eyes became glued to the deck and the bewitching movement of the barricade strands. *I'm going to hit the top loading strap!* he thought. Reflexively, he pulled power and bunted the nose down, dangerously steepening his rate of descent.

On the platform, Shakey and the others immediately sensed disaster. The *Hornet* was high and fast, and at a quarter mile Shakey *heard* the strike fighter pull power to correct. The deck was coming up now, fast, and Sponge was in danger of overcorrecting and flying through glide slope. If he did, he could impale himself on the *ramp*, the opposite of hitting the top loading strap of the barricade.

"Pickle him!" Stretch screamed.

Shakey squeezed the wave-off switch and shoved the handle to the bottom. "Wave off! *Wave off!"* Within the next couple of seconds, the rate of collision between Sponge and the ramp or Sponge and the barricade picked up considerably. *He must have been way back on the power!* thought Shakey as he screamed, *"BURNER! BURNER! BURNER!"*

Dutch and Stretch shouted the same into their handsets. As a result, they saw the afterburners stage and the white burner plume leap from the tailpipes

as the engine pitch changed to a booming roar. The *Hornet* continued to settle and the ramp continued to rise, with the red glow from the wave-off lights now reflecting off the bottom of the aircraft. Sponge had stopped his rate of descent and was now safe from collision with the ramp. The LSOs, however, were horrified as they watched the plane head for the top loading strap.

If Sponge hit the strap, the aircraft would smash violently onto the deck. The potential results were ominous: Sponge might be knocked out; the ejection mechanism might be crunched; the aircraft might explode into a mass of twisted metal and fire; or the wreckage, whatever its condition, might slide off the angle into the dark sea.

Shakey froze as he focused on Sponge's hook point, time seeming to slow as the *Hornet* thundered over them. *Oh, God, please,* he prayed, and turned his body left.

Dutch shouted, "Holy *shiiit!*"

Traveling at over 130 knots, the hook point nicked the top loading strap. The hit started an undulating motion that quickly moved from the heavy steel cable to the stanchions. At that instant the burner plume passed over the barricade and shook it violently, the plume igniting a small grease fire at the top of two nylon bundles.

The LSOs, stunned by what they had just witnessed, watched the small fire struggle with the wind and rain. Sponge climbed out ahead of the ship at a steep angle, burner cans still white.

Dutch had the presence of mind to call *"Out of burner!"* That would help preserve what remained of Sponge's fuel.

"Clean up," added Stretch.

I can't believe it didn't break! Shakey thought, as the Boss yelled over the 5MC for sailors to put out the fire on top of the barricade.

Sponge was still climbing ahead of the ship, and CATCC directed him back for another pass. "Four-zero-six, take angels one-point-two. When level, turn to the downwind three-zero-five."

Shakey knew Sponge didn't have the gas to turn downwind for even a four-mile hook-in to final.

As the crash and salvage tractor drove out to the centerline to douse the small flames still flickering on the loading strap, he took matters into his own hands. "Four-zero-six, Paddles contact. *Turn downwind now.* Level off at cherubs six."

"What're you doing?" Stretch cried.

"He doesn't have the fuel. We've gotta get him back here now! Watch him, guys!"

CHAPTER 14

Sponge breathed heavily through his mouth and fought the urge to remove his mask. *Holy shit!* he thought. He had pulled the throttles out of burner when Dutch called to him, but what did Shakey want? *Level off and turn downwind?! Another first! A night pitching deck barricade out of a day visual pattern!* A look at his fuel, though, confirmed Shakey was right. *Five hundred pounds left!*

He pushed the nose over and banked left. To keep from becoming disoriented, he concentrated his attention on the instruments. In less than three minutes he was either going to be on that ship or in the water next to it. Sponge took a series of deep breaths to remain calm. *One step at a time.*

A sudden bolt of lightning in the downwind turn made Sponge flinch. His shoulders ached. They had been under strain for the last 40 minutes, ever since he had pushed out of marshal. And he could smell the adrenaline; the smell was stronger than ever, and it seemed to seep right out of his skin. *Concentrate!*

Shakey called to him again. "Cherubs six, no lower."

Sponge was concentrating so hard to maintain his tight turn, he didn't even answer. He was at 800 feet, and would descend to six once on downwind. As he leveled off, he took a glance at the ship, which looked about level with him to his left. He saw one helo close on the starboard quarter and another nearby. He almost wished the ship would just tell him to punch out. The rain was picking up too, another unwelcome sensory.

"Damn, this sucks!" he shouted into his mask.

Wilson and the others in Air Ops watched the raindrops bounce on the deck in front of the PLAT camera embedded in the centerline. Wilson was incensed. He couldn't believe that, after witnessing the near catastrophe, the ship was going to attempt another barricade recovery. *What else can go wrong tonight?* he thought.

O'Shaunessy, who had lost the bubble, was on the phone to somebody but overwhelmed by the crushing demands put on him by the Captain, the elements, the scheduled track, and the air wing tankers. And Shakey had now turned

Sponge downwind for a day pattern on a shitty night like this! Saint just stood off to the left and watched the PLAT. He offered no answers whatsoever.

"Sir?" Wilson called to O'Shaunessy.

"Yeah?" When O'Shaunessy looked over his shoulder, Wilson saw the deep circles under his eyes.

Wilson glanced at Saint, who still stared at the PLAT. Damn, he wished the Skipper were here now, but for the moment he was the only *Raven* representative thinking about Sponge's well being. He leaned forward on the bench.

"Recommend a controlled ejection alongside, sir." Wilson said in a measured tone, eyes locked on O'Shaunessy.

Saint "woke up" with a start. "Negative!" he exclaimed. "Barricade him! Mister Wilson, I've got it."

Despite the in extremis condition of *406*, O'Shaunessy and the others were astonished by this public display. After a moment, the Air Ops Officer looked to Wilson and said, almost apologetically, "He outranks you."

Wilson sat still and said nothing, but he felt his blood pressure rising. The silence was broken by Shakey as he talked to the lone *Hornet* abeam. "Sponge, nice job on that one, the ship jinked for winds, but you did a good job of getting that good start. You're real light, so keep that right hand under control and make easy glide slope corrections with power. We're gonna get 'cha this time... We've got a little raindrop here, so check windshield air... What's yer DME?"

"One-point-four," Sponge replied.

"Roger that, turn in level, dirty up. CATCC, say final bearing."

The approach controller, monitoring everything, was on top of it. "Final bearing one-three-seven."

"Roger that. Sponge, you have *bullseye* needles?"

"Affirm."

"OK, use them to help get set up. We'll show you a ball when you get in the window."

"Roger, *Paddles*."

As Sponge prepared his airplane for approach, however disjointed this one might be, his training took over and he became calm. He went through the checklist by memory: gear – DOWN; flaps – HALF; antiskid – OFF; hook – DOWN; harness – LOCKED. His hand touched each handle and knob to ensure they were all set as required. Keeping a good instrument scan and flying the ball was something Sponge could do. And, in his mind, he had resolved to wave off if one of the engines rolled back due to fuel starvation. He would then take a cut away from the ship—portside—and eject when abeam. He could do that, too.

Shakey also had a newfound confidence. Stretch, the senior partner, was letting him wave, not because Stretch wanted to avoid waving but because his vision was still not night adapted and because Shakey was handling this pitching deck MOVLAS recovery quite well. As *406* appeared and moved across the ship's longitudinal axis, Shakey picked up the handle and showed Sponge a slightly low indication. The steady rain pelted him and Dutch as all eyes looked aft toward Sponge. *Please help me, God,* Shakey whispered into the rain as the wind swirled around him.

"Two-seven *Hornet,* clear deck!" the phone talker called out.

"Roger, two-seven *Hornet, clear deck!*" Shakey bellowed back.

In Air Ops, The Big Unit leaned over and murmured to Wilson. "You made the right call. You're on record."

Wilson said nothing, but his eyes followed Sponge as his aircraft came into view on the right side of the screen. *Shakey is doing good,* he thought, *taking charge out there.* Wilson knew only prayers could help them now. *Our Father, who art in heaven...*

"Four-zero-six, got a ball?" Shakey called over the radio.

"Four-zero-six, *Hornet* ball, point-four," Sponge answered.

"*Ro-ger* ball, thirty-nine knots down the angle, workin' a little low... You're low and lined up left, come right...Come right...Approaching centerline, back to the left, you're on glide slope...Ooonn glide slope."

The ship heaved up and rolled right. Air Ops was silent, save for the radio transmissions from the platform. Throughout the ship all eyes were on the PLAT crosshairs, and hundreds of prayers were asked of God to help the young pilot.

"Deck's movin' a little. You're on glide slope, on course. *Oooonn* glide slope...a lit-tle power, a little right for lineup."

Sponge lost the ball behind the stanchion and cried, *"Clara!"*

"Roger, clara, you're on glide slope, going a *little* high, easy with it...power back on..."

"Ball!" Sponge sang out again.

"Right for line-up!" Dutch called. The deck steadied out a bit...they were committed.

Wilson saw the *Hornet* behind the barricade correct the drift. *C'mon!* he thought.

Shakey kept the calls coming as Sponge approached the ramp. "Roger ball, a little power...Now cut! *CUT! CUT! CUT!*"

"*Right for line up!*" Dutch added.

With that, the *Hornet* fell out of the sky, slamming on the right main-mount, followed by the left main and nose. A twisting motion sent the airframe into the barricade, which enveloped the aircraft in webbing, water and debris.

The LSOs saw the hook catch a wire somewhere in the maze of confusion, and the stress and strain of the arrestment was too much for the overstressed right main. As the main suddenly collapsed, the whole jumble slid down the deck into the centerline PLAT camera, where the wreckage and right wing dragging on deck kicked up a shower of sparks as it veered to the starboard side of the landing area.

On the PLAT image, Wilson saw Sponge's white helmet move in the cockpit. Sponge then opened the canopy as crash and salvage sailors swarmed the nose, some of them employing foam on a small fire underneath the aircraft. A booming cheer in Air Ops released a torrent of tension and anxiety. Wilson's air wing shipmates all patted him on the back.

"You got him!" The Big Unit said as he grabbed Wilson's shoulders. Wilson offered a weak smile in return, feeling he had done pitifully little. Wilson's eyes met Saint's scowl before the commander wheeled and left for the ready room.

Sponge had never wanted so much to get out of an airplane. Leaning to the right, his hands raced over the Koch fittings and seat manual release handle that secured him in order to get free of the cockpit. He opened the canopy normally and flipped off a bayonet fitting to let his mask dangle to one side. Instead of breathing fresh air, he gagged on a cloud of CO_2 from the crash crew's attack on the aircraft. He then got splashed by firefighting foam, supposedly pointed at the fire coming from somewhere by the right intake. The foam spotted his helmet visor and obscured his vision as the rain caused it to run down the front.

A hooded sailor wearing a silver fire retardant suit, a chief by the sound of his gravelly voice, climbed up on the leading edge extension. He yelled, over the chaos, to Sponge, "You okay, sir?"

"Yeah! I'm okay!"

"Nice goin', Lieutenant! Let's go!"

Sponge pulled himself up and over the canopy sill. The chief and three other sailors grabbed at him as he tumbled down to the deck. He got covered in foam, and some of it splashed into his mouth. Just as he got to his feet and tried to spit out the foam, they began to both pull and push him from the wreckage. Still spitting foam, he trudged 50 feet toward a throng of sailors.

"Sir, you have to get in the stretcher!" a sailor yelled. He pulled Sponge toward a wire mesh stretcher on the flight deck.

"I'm fine!"

"Sir, orders. Get in!"

"Lieutenant, it's procedure. *Get in.*" added another unfamiliar sailor.

Sponge tilted his head up and saw an older sailor under the cranial and goggles next to him— maybe an officer, a medical type. He decided not to fight. *I've had enough fighting for one night. I'll let someone else take care of me.*

"Lie down here, sir. You'll be OK," the first sailor said.

Sponge got in the stretcher and the medical department sailors strapped him in. Now on his back, Sponge faced the rain and had to squint his eyes to shield them from the raindrops. He heard the sound of helicopter rotor blades getting louder and louder. *Is that guy going to land on top of me?* The straps were cinched down to keep him in place, and he couldn't move his arms. White smoke was still pouring from underneath 406, the Air Boss was yelling orders over the 5MC he didn't understand, and rain was pelting his face. Sponge couldn't see well and that scared him. A sailor, or maybe the old medical guy, stood over him and talked into a portable phone. "Pull down my visor!" he yelled, but no one heard him over the din. Then someone bumped the stretcher, which sent a sharp pain into his left thigh.

Sponge snapped. The tension of the past five hours—beginning with the XO's bullshit brief, followed by launching in awful weather, dodging the embedded thunderstorms during the hop, marshaling in the clag, and finally ending with his night-in-the-barrel foul decks, sour tankers, jinking ships and a pitching deck barricade—turned to rage in an instant. *Everyone on this ship* really is *trying to kill me!* he thought.

Lieutenant Junior Grade Robert K. Jasper, United States Navy, drenched and immobile, had had enough. He took a deep breath, tensed his body and exploded with a roar he was certain could be heard by the plane guard destroyer across the waves.

"Get me outta here! *Now! RIGHT Fucking NOW!!*"

CHAPTER 15

From the desk chair in his stateroom, Wilson watched the E-2 grow larger in the PLAT crosshairs. When it touched down and rolled out on centerline, the nose gear tires, in a blur, rushed up and over the embedded flight deck camera.

With his legs stretched out in front of him and his hands folded on his lap, Wilson sat alone in the stateroom to escape, for a moment, the pressure-filled aftermath of the barricade. Cajun and Olive had diverted with most of the older *Hornets* to Thumrait to be out of the way while the crash crew removed *406* from the angle and swept the deck for debris. Making the deck ready for recovery took almost an hour, and Wilson was surprised that the ship then recovered the remainder of those airborne, the *Rhinos* and big-wing aircraft. At least the deck had settled down and the wind had subsided.

Valley Forge had lucked out. A busted *Hornet* and a bunch of jets on the beach was a small price to pay for the decision to fly tonight. And it was a foregone conclusion that the Captain was going to recover what he could after clearing off the deck. The conditions had improved and everyone got aboard with no fodded engines—as far as he knew.

As he watched the *Hummer* fold its wings and taxi to its parking spot abeam the island, Wilson realized the night's ordeal was basically over. But for Wilson, it was just beginning.

And everyone's okay. Nerves may be shot, but everyone has all their fingers and toes, and we're all breathing. Amazing. Wilson tilted his head back and yawned as he fought the urge to crawl into his rack and forget this night had even happened. *This is going to be a long deployment.*

The squadron, VFA-64, however, was not okay. Sponge's plane, *406* was likely down for the cruise, and might never fly again. Sponge Bob was in sick bay for who knew how long, and no one knew what kind of pilot would emerge when he was discharged. Would he bounce back, or would he lose the confidence the squadron had spent the past year building into him?

Word of Wilson's exchange with the XO was, no doubt, a major topic right now at midnight rations, or midrats. *Summarily relieved of CATCC watch.* Wilson replayed the image of Saint's face as he relieved him. His own face, as well as his

ears, flushed with blood as he fought to contain the flood of emotions that spread through his whole body—a mixture of rage, humiliation, and fear for Sponge's life.

Should I have gotten up and left? No, he thought. *I did the right thing.* Leaving CATCC—with the eyes of all those witnesses on him under the crushing silence of embarrassment—would have been an act of capitulation. It had been bad enough just sitting there. He knew that issue was also being dissected at midrats, and he could imagine the discourse. "Man, if it were me, I would have said, 'I stand relieved,' and shoved the book in his gut on the way out." Wilson slouched low in his chair staring at the gray locker in front of him, lost in his thoughts. *Can I get through the next five months?*

The door opened and Weed entered. He had just returned from the flight deck where he had accompanied the Maintenance Master Chief and airframe mechanics to assess the damage to *406.* The Air Department had placed it, slumped over as it was on one wing, out of the way on the starboard shelf. Still wearing his float-coat, Weed dropped his cranial on his chair and began to rummage through a drawer.

"Hey, man."

"Hey," Wilson replied. "What's the verdict?"

"Class Alpha mishap, no question. Right motor is toast, right wingtip launcher all but torn off, leading and trailing edge flaps worn down, right wingfold mechanism AFU. Of course, the right main is shot and the nose gear probably stressed, and foam covers the aircraft, including everything inside the cockpit. Nothing a year in the depot can't fix. And Station 8 is ground down with big divots in the deck. You seen Sponge?"

"Yeah, about 30 minutes ago in sick bay. A different Sponge—*pissed* like I've never seen him. They took him down there and made him remain on his back while they cut away his gear and flight suit. They then pronounced him fit to pee in the bottle and said they are going to keep him overnight."

"Does he get a shot of medicinal brandy?" Weed said, as he continued digging through the drawer.

"Not sure if Doc goes for that."

"You mean he's a gin guy?" Weed found the package of AA batteries. "Well, the boys in the Ranch will hook him up before long."

"Yeah," Wilson mumbled, his stare steady on the locker as his thoughts returned to his role as Operations Officer. "All of Sponge's gear is gone. Do the PRs have enough to outfit him?"

Weed placed the fresh batteries inside his utility flashlight. "I'm sure, between us and brand X, we can throw something together."

"I want to fly him within 48 hours. Thinking tomorrow we can get the MIR and human factors investigations well underway."

"Who's gonna do the human factors board for the XO?"

Wilson shot a glance at Weed, then looked back to the locker.

"You okay, OPSO?"

"Yeah, just need to sulk for another 20 minutes."

Weed looked at his exhausted and humiliated roommate. He knew what had happened in CATCC and knew Wilson *knew* that he knew. There were few secrets in the air wing, and a scene like what happened in CATCC tonight flew through the ship. He asked the question anyway to get Wilson to unload. "What happened?"

Wilson pursed his lips and said nothing.

"Just tell me, for crying out loud."

Wilson opened his mouth but couldn't vocalize anything. How does an experienced aviator like him, a *prideful* man like him talk about the *disgrace*, the *shame* of being relieved of CATCC watch? Finally, he was able to get it out.

"After Sponge nicked the top loading strap with fumes remaining, I'm thinking, 'Fuck it! Punch out now—and live! Break the chain.' I made a recommendation and Saint goes ballistic, adding no value." Wilson felt like he was whining.

"I'da done the same." Weed said.

"Well, better not, or you'll be relieved, too."

"Saint isn't qualified to carry your helmet bag."

Both pilots knew about Saint Patrick's carrier bona fides. As a junior officer, he had made one deployment, and, as a department head, was in a squadron that had a long turnaround between deployments. Saint had rotated out before they went across the pond.

Weed shook his head and resumed, "Three hundred and ten career traps. *Smoke* has more than that. And XO has never been CATCC watch on cruise in his life, not even this cruise. Hey, why don't you schedule him for one?"

Wilson allowed a faint smile. "Because I care about you guys."

Unfazed, Weed continued. "Saint knows paperwork though! *That's* the way to command. Admiral's aide, staff weenie, War College, Pentagon Joint Staff. Punch tickets and visit a cockpit once in a while, a long while. Having the right last name helps, too."

Wilson appreciated the comments of his indignant roommate. If he wouldn't—or couldn't—unburden himself, Weed would do it for him.

"And then a middle-management job as XO/CO... Let's send Saint to the *Ravens*. They are due to be brutalized. I mean, how much damage can one incompetent commander do in one tour?"

"*The horror, the horror.*"

"Yep. *Where do we get such men* indeed?" Weed got up and clapped his hands to end the bull session. "Been to the ready room?"

"Uhhmm...to help Prince with the initial mishap report. XO made the call to Norfolk."

"C'mon, man. Let's go to the ready room and help Dutch write up the follow-on message. Then we can go to midrats and get a slider."

Wilson lifted himself up in the chair and exhaled. "Those things can kill you, ya know."

"Yep, but since we are surrounded by machinery, tons of ordnance and jet fuel below us, teenagers everywhere, homicidal maniac XOs, the raging sea outside and hostile countries over the horizon, I'll take my chances. And I'll have mine with cheese."

"You forgot the nuclear water we drink."

"Which makes great bug juice and mixes well with scotch...or so I'm told."

CHAPTER 16

Riiinnnngggg.

Wilson jerked his head up from the pillow and stumbled toward the phone. He glanced at the LED digits of his clock: *7:12.* He had been asleep five hours. Light from the passageway filtered into the stateroom from under the door and through a grate on the bulkhead.

He cleared his throat and picked up the receiver. "Lieutenant Commander Wilson, sir."

"Flip, Nicky at the duty desk...XO just called an APM."

Wilson stood motionless as he let the message sink in. *An APM? Called by the XO?*

"Flip," Nicky continued, "it's for zero-seven-thirty."

Wilson exhaled. "Roger, we're on our way," he said and hung up the phone. "Get up...APM," he said to his roommate in a frustrated undertone.

Weed groaned into his pillow, but he began to stir. "What the fuck?"

"XO called an APM. Fifteen minutes."

The Maintenance Officer tossed his covers off and rolled his body over the bunk. He braced himself with one foot on the frame of the lower bunk and eased to the floor in one familiar motion. Wilson turned on the water and filled the sink to shave.

"Any idea what this is about?" Weed asked.

"No...and the CO's not here. Not good."

"When are they coming back?" Weed asked as he put on a fresh, black squadron t-shirt.

"Around 1500," Wilson said as he lathered. "Just one recovery today for the Thumrait birds. Then a RAS."

"So, with Cajun gone, the XO can play Skipper for a day." Weed pulled on his flight suit.

"Yep...not good."

At a hurried pace, the two pilots finished dressing, laced their boots and brushed their teeth. Wilson quickly checked his e-mail and saw a note from Mary. It would have to wait.

With only five minutes to go before the meeting, they headed toward the ready room. Most of that time was spent navigating 700 feet of ladders, passageways, hatches, and knee-knockers. They ascended a ladder in quick steps, pulling themselves up with their arms. At the top, they swung their legs into the passageway and darted left, crouching low under the Cat 2 track, and then onto the portside O-3 level "main drag" passageway.

Wilson acknowledged passing sailors with a nod and reflexively lifted his boots high over the knee-knockers. He was lost in his thoughts, and his thoughts were gloomy. *Why is the XO calling an APM? And why* now, *rousting everyone with only 20 minutes notice?*

Aviators, who were night owls by nature, ignored reveille and rarely went to breakfast. Their days were, therefore, skewed between a midmorning wake-up to a bedtime where they hit the rack long after midnight. These 16- to 17-hour days included one hop, maybe two (with hours of briefs and debriefs), all manner of meetings, assigned duties, and myriad admin functions relating to the pilot's "ground job." For Wilson, this meant a late night every night as he and Nttty, the Schedules Officer, wrote and refined the flight schedule for the following day. Although they could also find time for movies, exercise, video games, and e-mail home, everyone was always at and available for "work."

Wilson continued aft as the ship swayed back and forth on the swells. It was rare for an XO to call an All Pilots Meeting. The overall squadron leadership of pilots and flight policy was the unquestioned province of the Skipper, while the XO was charged with admin duties relating to personnel and work spaces. *Depending on his message, what Saint is doing—with the CO off the ship and after the night the squadron just experienced—could be insubordinate. And, with the hours we keep, such short notice certainly shows contempt toward us,* he thought.

Wilson recalled the first time he had met Saint, last year at the O-Club while Saint was still in refresher training. Cajun had introduced them. Without making eye contact with Wilson, Saint had given him a tight-lipped, perfunctory nod and a quick handshake. Saint then took a sip of beer and turned his attention back to Cajun. Wilson received the message loud and clear: *You are an underling, nothing more.* Since that meeting, Wilson had found that Saint's ignoring him had not been personal. Commander Patrick treated the whole squadron that way.

Weed and Wilson got to the ready room with three minutes to spare. Wilson was surprised to hear music blaring from the stereo. The bleary-eyed JOs were either seated or getting a cup of coffee, and all but Nicky were in flight suits. Bubbly Psycho bebopped between the chairs, mouthing the words to the song: *"Shake it like a po-la-roid pic-cha."*

Wilson poured a cup and strode up the aisle to his chair in the front row. "Anything from the beach?" he asked Nicky.

"No, sir, but both jets reported safe-on-deck last night."

Wilson glanced at the status board; LASSITER and TEEL were the only *Raven* sorties listed, their mission a fly-on at 1500.

As the 1MC sounded the first of seven bells signifying 0730, the XO walked in. He entered from the front door that connected to Maintenance Control. Dressed in his khaki uniform with full ribbons, he placed his notebook inside his footstool and turned to Nicky. "Turn that shit off. What if CAG comes in?"

"Yes, sir!" Nicky wheeled in his chair to comply. As the ready room became quiet, the remaining pilots started to move to their seats. Wilson spotted Sponge Bob as he entered from the back door and took the seat nearest to the door. It was obvious he did not want to call attention to himself. He was also dressed in khakis and stoically acknowledged the nods and smiles many of his squadronmates sent his way.

Saint looked at Wilson and bulged his eyes to convey his impatience to start. Wilson turned to the group and said, "Okay guys, attention to APM. Take your seats." Wilson took stock of the room as he returned to his own seat. Satisfied, he faced forward, but sensed the XO was looking at him.

Wilson met his eyes, and Saint asked, "Do you have anything to pass on the schedule?"

"No, sir."

Saint exhaled in apparent disgust and took the floor. He stood directly on top of the *Raven* emblem embedded in the deck tile, an act that violated an unwritten squadron rule.

"All right...I've called you here because we had a mishap last night, preventable like most mishaps are. I realize the CO is off the ship, but we have to talk about this now, while it's fresh in our minds. We may not get another opportunity before transiting Hormuz. People, we are America's first team right now. Next week we will be in combat over Iraq, and, in my view, it is likely we'll be involved in combat with Iran at some time during this deployment. Pakistan is also heating up, as is Afghanistan—which we will probably see at some point during the cruise. We have got to be prepared for any contingency, and we must know the procedures for any tasking in the CENTCOM Area of Responsibility."

Combat with Iran? Wilson thought and dismissed the XO's dramatics.

All eyes were on Saint as he continued. "Last night VFA-64 lost a significant portion of the combat power we took with us from Norfolk, provided and entrusted to us by the taxpayers. Four-oh-six is a class Alpha mishap that

may never fly again, but it was not shot down and it delivered nothing against the enemies of freedom. Right now, it just clutters up Hangar Bay 3, and it will become a daily reminder to CAG that the *Ravens* weren't ready when it counted."

Wilson could feel the tension building. He stole quick glance at Weed, who sat with his hands folded, his eyes focused on something on the tile floor.

"We had a full workup with which to train and to be on the step when we enter a combat situation. We cannot and *will not* regress now. *Basics*, people...from launch to recovery, they have got to become second nature, and they must be executed *without flaw*."

The front door of the ready room burst open, and Gunner Humphries emerged from Maintenance Control wearing a float-coat, his cranial perched atop his head. Gunner froze as he realized he was interrupting an APM. For a second, no one moved, and Saint glared at him from a few feet away. Embarrassed and caught off guard—but sensing the tension in the room, Gunner, the squadron joker, blurted out a salty verse learned from his younger days:

> *Get a woman, get a woman, get a woman if you can.*
> *If you can't get a woman, get a fat young man!*

As the room exploded into laughter, Gunner turned on his heels and exited the way he had entered. The deep, stress-releasing howling was welcome by everyone—except the XO.

"*SILENCE!*" he bellowed, now incensed.

The room went silent at once. The tension returned as fast as it had disappeared.

"That's what I'm talking about!" Saint began. He snapped his fingers at Nicky to place the Do-Not-Disturb sign on the door. "We can't even get the room secure for a meeting!" His face was flushed with fury.

"Here it is, people. The Skipper is *kicking my ass* because of the lackadaisical attitude of this ready room. Sleeping all morning. Playing video games all night. Complacency in the brief. Bolters, like we had last night. Poor interval and not maintaining proper airspeed on the approach. Your job is to land the airplane safely, not to slam it into the deck. And when you get a wave-off, you do it now!"

With that, Sponge got up and exited through the back door. Saint shouted, "Sit down, Lieutenant!" but Sponge ignored him. The XO, seething, turned to Wilson.

"Mister Wilson, Lieutenant Jasper is in hack until further notice."

"Aye, aye, sir," Wilson replied, eyes downcast.

"In his khakis and out of his rack."

"Aye, aye, sir."

Saint surveyed the room to assess the mood. The pilots were tight lipped and sullen. Few looked at him.

"This is *nothing,* people. We are in a dangerous business, and the slightest inattention to detail can be fatal. Our job is to execute the plan given to us by the admiral's staff and by CAG. We *do not* question their actions."

Wilson realized it was now his turn.

"When a decision is made by a senior officer responsible for any evolution, you do not question it. When we are airborne, the ship owns us. And when they need the advice of a squadron rep, they will ask."

The pilots sat still, taking it, but they could not wait to leave. Wilson felt the eyes of the JOs, *his* JOs, watching him. He did not bolt out like Sponge, but he mentally condemned himself. *Company man, that's me.*

"The CO is disappointed with our performance so far. My job is to ensure that the CO looks good and that VFA-64 is ready in every respect. So, let's turn it around, *now.* Any questions?"

The room was silent. Nobody believed Cajun had chartered the XO to *fix* the ready room, much less confide in him. Nevertheless, Saint looked at every pilot to ensure his message was received.

"Good. Dismissed."

The JOs got up and headed for the back door. Wilson wanted to follow them, but he knew he would not get the chance.

"Mister Wilson," Saint motioned him over.

"Yes, sir."

"I understand the pressure you must have been under in CATCC last night—with a low-state nugget pilot in the pattern. Commander Johnson spoke to me and said you did a good job working the situation. Receiving praise from an officer of his caliber is commendable, and mitigates the momentary lapse in judgment regarding your call to have him eject alongside. We'll just call this a learning point in your department head training. As far as I'm concerned, the matter is closed." To Wilson, Saint looked more compassionate and understanding than he had ever seen him.

"Yes, sir."

"What happened last night is between us. No need for the CO to know."

Between us and the entire air wing, Wilson thought. "Yes, sir," he replied as he fought to keep emotion from his face. Wilson kept his eyes on the XO, but he sensed Nicky listening over Saint's shoulder.

"That is all," Saint said as he turned to his chair.

CHAPTER 17

A few minutes later, Wilson was forward on the O-2 level. He knocked on the door of the JO's bunkroom.

"Enter," answered a voice. Wilson recognized it as Guido's.

Wilson entered the six-man bunkroom. The furnishings consisted of three top and bottom metal racks behind blue curtains, six metal built-in desks, and sets of drawers along each bulkhead. Everything was painted gray. Two sinks and mirrors occupied the other bulkhead, and towels and robes hung on hooks nearby. Fluorescent desk lamps from two open desks provided some subdued lighting. A small TV was rigged in a corner of the overhead for viewing in what passed as the common area, a space little more than 8 by 8 feet. Guido and Sponge were seated, Sponge at his desk with his jaw set.

"Hey, Flip," Guido said. Sponge remained motionless.

"*Guido,*" Wilson replied, and then added in a low tone, "How about taking a walk topside?"

"Yes, sir," Guido replied, grabbed a pair of sunglasses from his desk, and exited the stateroom.

Sponge did not move as Wilson pulled up a chair. Sponge kept his eyes forward.

"I've never met anyone that flew a barricade pass," Wilson began.

"Paddles graded it an OK, little right wing down to land—*crash,*" Sponge hissed. Wilson did not recognize the junior officer before him. The old Sponge Bob was gone. He needed to get him back.

"That was a night pitching deck barricade," Wilson continued, "…on fumes, after essentially a day pattern in varsity conditions. Damn impressive flying."

"The jet's trashed."

"Screw the jet," Wilson responded, with a casual wave. "They'll send us another one."

Sponge didn't answer. Wilson kept his eyes on him and began.

"You've now been in this squadron one year. You've made the entire workup: Fallon, the Key West det, probably 250 hours of hard-core tactical flying—everything the Navy says a *Hornet* pilot needs to go on cruise a full-up round.

Now we're on cruise, and in two days, we're going through Hormuz and will enter the Gulf. Two days after that, you will probably be in an aircraft with green bombs under the wings on your way up to Baghdad."

Sponge's eyes remained down.

Wilson continued, "There are Marines and soldiers down there who are going to need us—that are going to need *you*. You know any Marines in the box these days?"

"My college suitemate… He's an infantry Marine in Anbar," Sponge replied.

"Well, you never know, he may need you one day. And it doesn't matter, really, if it's him, does it? Whoever calls us in wants fused ordnance on target, and you and I have to deliver it—on target, on time. That's our job. That's what we've been trained to do. You ready to go up there?"

Wilson saw Sponge's jaw tighten.

"Sponge, you are a hell of a pilot, and you did good last night. I doubt anyone else on this ship has flown a barricade, much less night pitching deck. When the pressure was on, you came through."

Sponge looked at Wilson. "I just crashed a jet, my flight gear is *literally* in tatters, the squadron XO blames me in public and puts me in *hack* when I refuse to 'sit down' for more humiliation. I've got to write my statements for the mishap board, the JAG investigation, the human factors board, and who knows what else. Oh, yeah, my girlfriend knows—already, knows it's me! I just got an e-mail from her. Which one of my air wing buds sent *that* news home? She's freakin' that *I* didn't let her know—not that I've had a spare *minute* the past thirteen and a half hours."

"Should'a married her," Wilson deadpanned, "and, as a wife, she'd get an official call. And at least a *chance* at $400 grand in life insurance."

Sponge shot him a look at first and then sensed the humor. A wan smile crossed his face in response to Wilson's barb.

"Sponge, you'll be ready to go soon. We'll scrounge up some flight gear, hack will end, and you'll be on the flight schedule before you know it. Take today to do your statements, write to your girlfriend and your family, and blow off some steam with the guys. Guido and them will bring you food. In 48 hours, though, we're in the Gulf. We're gonna need your game face."

Sponge held Wilson's gaze. "You've got it, Flip."

"Good man."

"One thing though," Sponge added.

"Go."

"I don't want to fly with the XO again this cruise."

Wilson listened to his words and thought for a few seconds.

"I mean it. I flew with him a lot on workups; he's my fighter section lead. He gives a shitty brief, and then he shits on you in the debrief when things go bad—which they often do. Know what we did last night? We were supposed to do 2v2 intercepts with the *Bucs*. XO calls their Skipper before the brief and bags out with some BS excuse about the weather and my training requirements. So we brief breakup and rendezvous training for me, like I'm back in flight school. We did *six* of 'em—him in the lead the whole time and me chewing up my gas. There was *no* discussion of the weather, the diverts, pitching deck procedures, how many incoming and off-going tankers airborne. Flip, *I* should be the lead for *him*. No more. I'm done."

Leaning forward in his chair with his elbows on his knees, Wilson stroked his chin. "That's a tall order. I can minimize your time together, but it's a long cruise. Once we draft it, the CO can still tweak the sked, and you could be paired with Saint."

"Flip, I need a break from the XO." Sponge looked almost desperate.

"I'll keep you apart in the short term—no promises about the entire cruise."

"Thank you, sir."

"What are you going to do first?"

"Honestly, sleep. Too keyed up last night."

"Good. We'll find you some flight gear and bring it down for fit later. Don't expect to fly tomorrow or the next day, so do the admin stuff you need."

"Yes, sir. Thanks, Flip."

"No worries," Wilson replied as he got up to leave.

CHAPTER 18

"He did *what?*" Cajun exploded, both angry and dumbfounded. His eyes narrowed on Wilson.

"Yes, sir, he called it early this morning." Giving up the XO gave Wilson the perverse pleasure he had wanted all day.

"What did he say?" Cajun asked with disgust, as he got ready to study the flight schedule. With the JOs at dinner up forward and Nicky out of earshot at the duty desk, the ready room was more or less deserted.

"He said we're entering a combat zone, and we've got to be at the top of our game. Need to look good around the ship, brief everything, and fly the brief." Cajun knew Wilson was telling the truth, but sensed there was more. The fact that Saint had called the APM was transgression enough, but Cajun wanted to know if he had done anything else over the line.

"Flip...everything."

Wilson drew a breath. "Sir, he said you've been kicking his ass about the 'lackadaisical attitude' of the ready room. Sleeping till lunch, the video games. He also implied that Sponge gooned the approach, and that's what led to the foul-deck wave-off and the low-fuel barricade. Sponge got up and bolted out the back with the XO shouting for him to stop. When he didn't, XO put Sponge in hack. I visited Sponge a few hours ago and he's pissed—no longer the happy-go-lucky Sponge. Skipper, Sponge flew a night barricade in *varsity* conditions. The jet's broke, but he did well."

Cajun looked away with his jaw clenched. "What happened in CATCC last night?" he asked. Wilson told him. As the CO stared at the bulkhead, his jaw tightened even more.

In his mind, Cajun summed up the results of the past 24 hours. *Raven 406* in a heap below with such catastrophic damage she would probably never fly again. One of his nugget pilots banished to his stateroom with who-knows-what damage to his confidence. His Operations Officer and, by extension, VFA-64 publicly humiliated in front of the senior pilots in the Wing. His own authority usurped by the XO. He could hardly comprehend it all. Less than one month into the deployment, and just days before commencing the combat operations

they trained all year for, the *Ravens* were in the shitter as the scuttlebutt topic of *Valley Forge,* and soon the Atlantic Fleet—once the e-mails started flying, which they surely had. He would visit Sponge, free him, and put him back on the flight schedule. Beginning the process of rehabilitating him as an aviator was all important. *Get back on the horse.* He would also need to have a "come-to-Jesus" with Saint and visit CAG. But first, he needed to repair the damage to Wilson.

"Flip, I believe you handled the situation in CATCC well," he said softly. "It takes two years to build a jet, but 25 to place a 'Sponge' in a squadron. You made a call, a *recommendation*, and your logic was sound. I want you to know I'm always confident when you're in CATCC." Wilson knew the CO was much too professional to bad-mouth his XO in front of a subordinate, but the message was clear.

"Thank you, sir," Wilson replied.

Cajun turned to depart and over his shoulder said, "All Officers Meeting, followed by APM tomorrow."

"Yes, sir."

When he reached the ready room door, he turned again and added, "Put me with Sponge on the next event, preferably a 1v1 with him leading." Cajun winked with the trace of a smile.

"Aye, aye, Skipper," Wilson said, relieved that Cajun was back aboard.

Wilson stepped out onto the well of the catwalk ladder and looked down through the grating. Some 50 feet below, the ship made huge waves as it pushed through the Gulf of Oman. He climbed up a few steps to the starboard catwalk to assess the weather: clear, sunny, warm, gentle wind. Considering the speed the ship was making, Wilson was surprised by the wind and figured it around 20 knots…and out of the south since the ship was headed north by west. He walked aft and found the small ladder that led to the flight deck. He kept his head down, climbed the steps and crouched low in order to step over the deck edge coaming and onto the deck. Still ducking, he moved under a *Hornet* horizontal stabilator and moved along the aircraft, avoiding obstacles such as tie-downs, trailing edge flaps, and the external fuel tanks hanging on the wings. The engine turbine blades turned freely in the breeze. Their steady chatter created the ever-present wind chime of the flight deck.

He had eaten lunch only a short time ago, but this was the first time he had been outside that day. Across the deck he saw a squadron maintenance crew working on an aircraft; to his left a plane captain stood in a *Hornet* cockpit as he polished the windscreen. Dozens of joggers ran up and down the 1,000-foot flight deck as they followed a deformed racetrack pattern that avoided parked aircraft and yellow flight deck tractors. He spied Smoke and Lieutenant "Blade" Cutter, the squadron strike fighter tactics instructor, moving in long strides—down the deck and with the wind. A leisurely no-fly day on the flight deck.

He walked aft behind a *Raven* jet; his trained eye scanned its skin for signs of corrosion. When he found an area between two aircraft where he could stand with an unobstructed view of the horizon, he looked across the Strait of Hormuz. Miles to starboard—Wilson estimated over 20 miles—he saw the shadow of a ridgeline. Just visible in the distance. *Iran.*

Each time he had been to the Gulf, Wilson was struck by the desolate and forbidding landscape. To him, the entire Arabian Peninsula was simply inhospitable. Centuries of crushing heat and simoon winds had baked and eroded the land into one of the most continuous bodies of sand in the world. When he

looked at the charts in the ready room, Wilson noted one could go *hundreds and hundreds* of miles and see nothing but sand dunes. Called The Empty Quarter, this inland sea of sand was so barren that the borders of Saudi Arabia, United Arab Emirates, and Oman were not distinguishable. From Aden all the way up to Baghdad, the terrain, and everything on it, was a light shade of sand marked with occasional patches of tan. Even the towns were tan; the only things not tan or sand were the black asphalt roads and the blue gulf along the coast. Flying over Arabia was like flying over a giant horizon-to-horizon *sandbox*, which is what three generations of American military personnel called the U.S. Central Command Area of Responsibility.

As he surveyed Iran in the distance, Wilson reflected on the times he was high over the Persian Gulf at night. To the south and west, the countries of the Gulf Cooperation Council were illuminated with bright clusters of lights in the cities and settlements. Natural gas flare stacks flickered and burned off at the well heads at oil fields ashore and on platforms dotting the Gulf. Desert roads in the middle of nowhere were lighted as if the roads were in a large city. Far to the south the modern metropolises of Dubai and Abu Dhabi shone brightly, and further up the Gulf, the cities of Doha, Manama, Dhahran and Kuwait City glowed—evidence not only of life but of prosperity. In this part of the world, light meant money, and under the sandy desert of the Arabian Peninsula, the former nomadic peoples of the region sat on a pile of it.

To the east and north it was another matter. Aided by the fact that the Iranian coastline was mountainous, and to a great extent devoid of humans for some 400 miles—from Bandar Abbas to the Bushier/Kharg Island complex—Iran gave the impression of being dark and foreboding. Even well inland, there were few lights to signify settlements. Basra in Iraq seemed to have a greater degree of lighting than a comparable Iranian town. Wilson found the Iraq/Iran comparison a perplexing metaphor—free enterprise on one side and essentially a command economy on the other, with both dominated by a religion that oversaw every aspect of its believers' lives. Despite their similarities, the two peoples regarded each other with deep suspicion, and in the case of the sheikdoms, fear of their powerful and populous Shiite neighbor to the north. They disagreed about much, even the name of the body of water that separated them. *Persian* Gulf. *Arabian* Gulf. To be fair, it could not be said that the GCC sheikdoms were *free*, but when he could actually view the paradox in the light patterns he saw whenever he flew high over the Gulf at night, he found it fascinating.

All around *Valley Forge* merchant ships plied the strait, visual proof that 30% of the world's crude oil passed through this vital strategic waterway. Behind

the ship, and all the way to the horizon, a line of black-hulled oil tankers rode high in the water as the Indian Ocean funneled them into the Gulf to pick up loads of crude from Dhahran or Kharg Island--or maybe from Iraq. Far to the south, he could make out the white superstructure of a very large crude carrier, its hull obscured by the horizon.

One mile to port, a full tanker rode low in the water and pushed the sea before it as it lumbered into the open ocean with another 100,000-ton load of crude. Wilson scanned the deck and peered into the bridge—no sign of human life. In all his years of observing merchant ships on the high seas, even when he flew right over them, he never saw sailors on deck. For a moment Wilson wondered where the tanker was headed, and thought of Norfolk. He then noted the flag flying from the mast; it appeared to be Japanese.

Further to port, the mountainous and seemingly deserted coastline of Oman was visible, a landscape dominated by dull sandy browns and grays, with a touch of olive drab vegetation, but mostly a light beige color, or coffee with cream, which was the primary shade of the whole Arabian Peninsula. Wilson walked further up the angled deck to get a better view. Merchant ships dotted the horizon; *Valley Forge* was passing a blue-hulled containership that had shipping containers stacked high over all available deck space to bridge level. The officers on the carrier's bridge had much to contend with while avoiding traffic in these restricted waters. Their efforts were compounded by dozens of speedboats crisscrossing the narrowest part of the strait between Iran and Oman. *Smugglers.*

Wilson got to the end of the angled deck and stood there to watch the speedboats bound north and south over the waves. They left thin, white wakes as they weaved between the large merchants heading either east or west in this portion of the strait. Carpets, gold, knock-off clothing, watches, CD's, and who knows what else stashed in those fiberglass hulls... He surmised some of the boats were *boghammars*, the ubiquitous Iranian Revolutionary Guard speedboats with small arms and RPGs used to harass shipping. *Modern day pirates following centuries of tradition in this God-forsaken place. The vessels change shape, but the business stays the same*, he thought.

From his perch at the end of the angled deck, Wilson saw *Valley Forge's* bow cut into the Strait of Hormuz, the sea flaring out into a large wave that emanated from the hull and crashed over itself, leaving a frothy white blanket on the water as the ship sped past. He thought of how American Navy ships, and the waters they visited, had changed over the ages. The Navy's mission, however, remained the same: prompt and sustained combat operations at sea.

CHAPTER 20

Wilson went below to his stateroom. The first thing he looked at was his laptop. As he had hoped, a new e-mail, a long one from Mary, waited for him.

> *Dear James,*
>
> *I miss you very, very much and so do Derrick and Brittany. When I heard about the crash the other day, I was just sick about it. Stephanie told me Bob was the pilot and is okay. I'm so glad he's okay, but what happened? She said it was at night with rain and lightning. Why don't you just stop when it's bad outside? Can you advise the Skipper to stop flying? Bob's girlfriend Meagan just flipped out – she comes across as this sweet-as-she-can-be sorority girl, but when Billie Lassiter called to tell her about the crash, she just blew up and snapped at Billie because Billie didn't know the answers to all her questions. She wanted Bob to come home and when Billie said that was not going to happen, she went off about how dumb the Navy was and why is an aircraft carrier involved with a land war – a war she hates, etc. She called back to apologize to Billie the next day, saying she's new to this and loves Bob so much. Billie is a saint, having to put up with this chick – who is not even a wife yet! I used to wish they had gotten married before the cruise, but now I'm not so sure. She said the pressure of him being gone <u>one month</u> is getting to her. I say she doesn't know the half of it.*

Wilson saw where this was going, and, with the AOM in twenty minutes, he knew better than to continue reading. Yet, he couldn't help himself.

> *Sometimes I just don't know why you go on these cruises. Isn't it enough that you've already been on four cruises? And each one was a combat cruise, even before 9-11. I counted last week – in our nine years of marriage, you've been gone almost four years, counting the cruises, workups, and detachments. When you return in May, you'll have been gone 20 of the last 36 months. Haven't you – we – given enough to our country? I'm proud of you, James, and I know you are a good pilot and do a great job of teaching the new guys*

and keeping them out of trouble. You are now, and always will be, my hero! But does it always have to be you? Can't someone else step up? Unless they do, all I can see is more of the same for years to come.

After you leave VFA-64, you'll get that admiral's aide job you want, and after we move to Washington, you'll be working all day. And once again, you'll be gone on travel with the admiral, and I'll be stuck in a new and expensive town, not knowing anyone, with two little kids. Then you'll get command, and we'll move again back here, or to Lemoore, or Japan, and like everything else, it will probably be "get here right now." When the war started, you flew back here to join the squadron. Then I drove from Fallon across the country by myself with a two-year-old, found a house, and moved us in while you did shock-and-awe over Baghdad on CNN. I am not going to do that again.

James, I look at Billie Lassiter and think, do I want that? Not only does she take care of her own houseful alone, but she has to put up with bitchy wives – and now girlfriends – as she leads our support group. She does it with a smile, and I do admire her because she is doing it with no help because your XO doesn't have a wife. But I'm not sure that I can do it or want to do it.

And after command, there will more moves into key 12 hour-a-day jobs and then CAG, with more deployments, and then admiral... The point is, we'll never see you. Your kids will grow up and graduate from college, and you won't be there. Do all of us have to pay the price?

Wilson inhaled deep and exhaled long. Mary must have had this building up inside her for months or years. She was not prone to emotional outbursts in e-mails or letters. Sponge's mishap must have been the catalyst. The next part hit him hard.

It kills me that you have missed so much of Derrick and Brit growing up. You are a wonderful father and have so much fun with them – when you are home. They miss you, Derrick especially. He's enjoying first grade and he's really doing well. Many of the dads in his class (and one mom – ugh) are Navy and deployed, but when they have parent events like the Thanksgiving pageant, it's so nice to see the dads there. Derrick said he wished you could have seen him. (He was the Pilgrim leader.) By the time this cruise is over, you will have missed Thanksgiving, Christmas, and then Easter...all the big family holidays, not to mention my family reunion in August while you

were on workups. In fact, you have missed half of Brittany's life. It is not fair to the kids that their father is gone so much of the time – by choice.

James, I need you too. Not only to help with them but as a woman. I knew you were a Navy pilot when I met you, and I went into this marriage with my eyes open, but after nine years the reality is I have a part-time husband. I want a full-time husband at home and in my bed. I'm lonely, and a future Navy career means more loneliness. Haven't I supported you through your service to our country? I love you for that and America owes you and everyone out there everything. You, and I, have given so much. Can't someone else step up and save the world? You have lived your dream, and every time you go out, you come back with more medals. At what point is enough, enough? Is it worth sacrificing your family?

This is not an ultimatum. I know we've got five more months ahead of us. But you need to know what it's like for me, and I want you to give this serious thought. With your talents I know you can get a good job that will allow us to live as a family. Lots of our friends are airline pilots, and your brother has a good job in Chesapeake. You can fly for the naval reserves, can't you? That seems like a good balance. You've done much more than your share, and have nothing to be ashamed of. Come back to me, James.

I love you so much, and pray for you every day.
Love always,
Mary

Wilson sat back and propped up his chin with his fingers, reeling from her words. He stared at Mary's Strike Fighter Ball picture, a photo taken about four years earlier. He thought of their years together as he studied her face and her gorgeous smile. *She has not changed from the day I first laid eyes on her,* he thought.

Or had she? She *was* older, and in his mind's eye, he studied the face of the woman who dropped him off at Oceana four weeks ago. It was a long morning, the culmination of what to Wilson always felt like the countdown to a death sentence. It began two weeks before each deployment. Two weeks to go. Ten days to go. Four days. Tomorrow. Two hours. Fifteen minutes. Wilson remembered standing next to the hangar gate in his flight suit as he watched Mary pull the minivan out of the parking lot that morning. His heart begged her to look at him and wave one last time. Instead, she drove off without a glance. *That* face, discounting the puffiness around her eyes as she had hugged and kissed him goodbye moments earlier, had lines in it. Lines he and his profession had put there over the years.

Then he remembered the glimpse through the tinted back window of little Derrick from his car seat. As Mary made the turn onto 1st Street, Derrick lifted his hand to wave. Wilson fought to keep his composure as they faded from view. Then he turned to salute the gate sentry and walked toward the hangar to get ready for the flight that would begin his fifth deployment. And Mary was right. It was a deployment he *wanted* to be part of.

"Damn," he whispered, as he pushed himself out of the chair to go to the ready room.

Chapter 21

Zydeco, the kind of music Cajun loved, blared from the stereo speakers as Wilson entered Ready Room 7. Most of the officers were in their seats, but several gathered around the water cooler. Gunner held court with the JOs in the back and sipped on a glass of red bug juice that complemented his red flight deck jersey. The pilots were in flight suits except for khaki-clad Psycho at the duty desk. The XO drank his coffee hunched over the message board with his green pen, oblivious to the laughing and banter around him.

Four bells over the 1MC signified 1400, and Wilson stood to face the group. "Okay, guys, seats. Attention to AOM." Psycho killed the music and the room came to order.

In a familiar routine, each officer with a message to pass addressed the group, followed by the XO. Then, it was time for the CO to have the last word. Typically, the ground pounders were excused at this point, while the pilots remained to repeat the ritual in order to cover pilot-specific issues, but as he stood before his squadron officers, Cajun's message was one the CO wanted all of them to hear.

"Okay, guys, welcome, or welcome back, to the Persian Gulf," said Cajun. "In forty-eight hours we'll be up in *carrier box four* and fly our first OIF hops into Iraq. We are going to spend the next four or five months flying combat missions—long ones—day and night in support of our troops. First we go to Iraq, then to Afghanistan later in the cruise. Here's the bottom line... For the foreseeable future we are here to answer *their* tasking and the tasking of National Command Authority. That's one main reason we are here. The guys on the ground are going to need us sooner or later, and we have to be on station with fused ordnance available, and we must deliver it when and where they want it. After a while, the kill box geography, and most everything else, will become routine. You'll know the procedures by heart, and even the controller's voices will become familiar to you. However, it is *not* routine for the guys on the ground. They are in a firefight, or they got hit by an IED or they see the bad guys planting one. For them it's very, very personal, and when they need 'fast mover' support, they need it *right now*. They are in combat—and so are you.

"If you, *all* of you, do not have your game face on right now, you are late. If you have not made a Gulf divert chart that includes the divert fields inside Iraq, make it. And if you do not know the JDAM max release airspeed, are confused about how to preflight your expendables and set a program, do not know the Mk 80 series frag patterns in diameter and altitude, are not intimately familiar with your survival radio, have not preflighted the items in your survival vest in months, learn it or do it. Any one of dozens of small details can bite you if they drop out of your scan. So, you've got 24 hours to get your act together. Ask yourself where your deficiencies are and use this time wisely.

"Last cruise we drilled around a lot in the box and didn't drop much. I admit it was hard to stay focused week after week as we lugged bombs north only to bring them home. This time, though—if what *Ike* and *Enterprise* have done recently is a guide—we are dropping plenty. If we find an IED, we aren't screwing around. If there are some bad guys holed up in a hut, *level it* once you are given the 'cleared hot.' Remember, though, if there is a doubt *there is no doubt*—don't drop. Work with the controllers, but unless you are 100 percent sure of the target, don't drop on a hunch. Bring them back. The last thing we need is to give CNN and Al Jazeera incidents to fill their air.

"The other main reason we are here, and have been at least since 1979, is to deter Iran. We are not at war with Iran, but Iran certainly is not friendly to us or to the GCC countries in the Gulf. Those countries are scared to death of Iran, not only because of Iran's military capability but also because of the exportation of Shia Islam and revolution to their populations. Anything more is above my pay grade. The bottom line is maintain a 12-mile standoff and don't thump Iranian oil platforms, dhows, *boghammars*, or Iranian P-3s. They have rights in these waters, too. If you see an Iranian unit, tell the ship and stand by for tasking. This is a rough neighborhood, but believe me, they are more afraid of you and your intentions, so it's smart to give everyone a wide berth out here. The overwhelming majority of Iranian people hate their government and the ayatollahs are afraid of the people and repress them. The Iranians are looking for a reason to fight us and unify their population in order to take the heat off themselves. Let's not give them a reason by doing something dumb.

"One more thing. We must guard against complacency *every single day*. We can hurt ourselves on this ship dozens of ways in *peacetime*, not just during combat ops. This affects everyone in this squadron, and we are all susceptible to it. When each day becomes like Groundhog Day and you lose respect for this environment, and if you pilots get into the mindset that another kill box

hop is just a routine cross-country with bombs, you have got to step back and *compartmentalize* why you are out here."

Wilson immediately thought of Mary's e-mail, but willed himself to concentrate.

"We saw the other night that this can be an unforgiving business. Weather, the deck, tankers…the situation can go south real fast. Sponge found himself in a box, not because he placed himself there, but because of the way one event built upon another. Sponge, your recovery on a night pitching deck barricade was a fine piece of flying under extreme pressure. None of us here have done what you did, and I'm not willing to say I would have done any better. The airplane *is* broken—but we'll fix it. As soon as we can, we'll get you back in the air, and I hope that is tomorrow."

What a great leader, Wilson thought. He stole a glance at Saint who listened with eyes down. Regardless of the Aircraft Mishap Board outcome, Cajun knew enough to absolve Sponge of responsibility for *406* in public and, by extension, disagreeing with Saint in public. Wilson wondered if Cajun had already had a one-way conversation with his XO behind closed doors.

"Okay, anybody have anything for me?" asked Cajun, ready to wrap it up.

No one did.

He clapped his hands and said, "Okay, ready, *break.*"

"QUOTH THE RAVEN!" the room responded in unison.

Wilson got up and projected his voice over the sudden disorder. "Okay, pounders, excused. Pilots, back in yer seats in five minutes." Psycho turned and pushed the play button, and the high-spirited sound of accordions and washboards once again filled Ready Room 7.

CHAPTER 22

A few minutes later, Wilson called the room to order. The pilots went around the room again, this time with their pilot-specific discussion items. When it was his turn, Wilson stood up to go through a PowerPoint presentation on flying in the Gulf. "Okay, guys, this is the gouge, so listen up. The Skipper just got our minds right about flying here. Now, I want to give you a brief on how CAG Ops is going to build the Air Plan and what a typical fly day is going to be like over here.

"First, stand off. NAVCENT gets their ass kicked if we even get close to territorial airspace, so know where you are and don't press the limit. Even if you know you are safe according to your system, realize that if you fly right at a limit, you are going to set off alarms inside the host nation's airspace. Especially if you get close to Iran.

"Also, we need to follow the standard routes into Iraq, and those are basically along the al-Faw Peninsula with altitude deconfliction. They are *not* over Iran. If you are going to be off, be off to the west." Wilson stomped his foot to emphasize the importance of the point, and several pilots nodded. He changed to the next slide.

"The action right now is in Diyala, north and east of Baghdad, southeast of Baghdad around Salman Pak, and in Mosul. The Marines out of al-Asad have Anbar. Chances are you won't go there this cruise—but you may—so be ready. Get ready to be strapped into the seat for eight hours at a time, and the hours are going to accumulate. The guys on *Enterprise* were getting 70-80 hours a month. If you want to bag flight time and traps, you've come to the right place. For those of you who haven't experienced it, 80 hours a month kicks your ass.

"You heard the CO. Get ready.

"We are loaded for bear each hop," said Wilson, as he shifted gears, "but we have to adopt the mindset that we do *not* want to drop. Our job is to support the guys on the ground who are in a battle for the hearts and minds. When we drop, even if we're on target and are killing bad guys, it doesn't help us with the populace if we break windows and make babies cry. We have got to determine through our own assessment of the tactical situation—through the voice inflection of the JTAC and through the passdown of the flights ahead of you—whether

it's right to drop. Remember, the bad guys *want* you to drop, that's why they are holed up next to mosques and in the middle of neighborhoods. Ask the JTACs to declare *troops in contact*, and if they report TIC, support 'em with fire. If the JTAC can get the bad guys to hole up or to cease fire by calling you in to make some noise, that's mission success. So, we have to assess the situation and assess when it's smart to release, and it's going to be *you knuckleheads* who are gonna make this call on the spot. Remember, you do *not* want to be on CNN by making the wrong call.

"So, triple-check the coordinates, use a run-in that minimizes collateral damage and your exposure to the threat, listen to the JTAC. If he wants you to hit something in the middle of a city, question him. Have him declare TIC, see if he's taking fire. Like the CO said, if you need to drop or strafe to support these guys, *do it*. But there should be no doubt. We cannot make a mistake."

Wilson reminded them to make area divert charts and to study the terrain around Diyala and along the Tigris to Mosul. When he finished, Cajun looked over his shoulder at the group, pointed toward Wilson and cracked, "What *he* said!"

"QUOTH THE RAVEN!" boomed the pilots inside Ready 7.

After dinner, Wilson went down to the "clean-shirt" wardroom and was grateful there was no one using the satellite phone to call home. It was early afternoon in Virginia Beach, and Wilson hoped Mary was home and in the mood to talk. She had been distraught when she wrote the e-mail, and he knew the stress of facing another holiday season alone was what was really bothering her. He dialed the number and took a deep breath. After two rings she answered.

"Hey, baby," Wilson said softly.

"James?"

"Yeah…anybody else callin' you baby?" he chuckled.

She giggled. "No! No one else! How are you? I'm glad you called!"

"Doin' good. Just finished dinner." Wilson sensed by her voice she was having a good day.

"Did you get my e-mail from last night?" she asked. Wilson didn't expect it to come up so soon in the conversation. He paused and answered flatly.

"Yeah."

Wilson could also sense, from thousands of miles away, the wave of emotion that swept over Mary as she broke down.

"Oh, James, I'm *so* very sorry! Please forgive me!" In an instant she was sobbing.

"Baby, don't cry, it's okay."

"As soon as I sent, it I wanted it back!" He heard her sniff. "It's just that with you gone *another* Christmas and the disposal broken…"

"The disposal's broken?"

"Yes, but I handled it. It's okay, but, James, I *don't* want you to worry about that or the kids or me."

"Well, I always *worry*," he replied.

"I know you love us and worry about us, but you are over there flying that airplane, and I want you to concentrate on that." She gasped a little for breath. "I don't want to distract you from your job."

"I can…" The short delay in the satellite transmission made the conversation stilted.

"I don't want you to *crash*…" Mary blurted. Wilson imagined her shoulders heaving as she spoke.

"I'm not gonna crash. Have I crashed yet?" he joked weakly. Mary ignored it and passed her message to him in a stream of consciousness.

"I need you to come home to me after this cruise is over, not before. You are in my prayers every day, and I know you are a good pilot. Billie tells me Steve thinks the world of you. The new guys need you to get them home safely. But right now, I know why you are there, because those Army and Marine kids on the ground need you. You are my knight in shining armor!"

"We'll be okay. We're ready." He sensed she had regained some of her composure, but he needed to find out more. "What's wrong, Mary?"

"James, nothing is wrong. We're okay. Please concentrate on your flying. I'm okay, really, and I don't want you to be distracted. We'll talk when you return home."

"I won't be distracted. We're prepared, and we have the best equipment and best training. Bob did a great job flying his airplane; everyone involved did a good job to get him aboard. We'll fix the airplane."

"Is the airplane broken?"

"It's fine. Just needs some minor repairs," Wilson lied.

Mary exhaled. "I miss you already. Five more months?"

"No, only four months and three weeks."

"Oh, great."

Now that he knew the emotional storm had passed, Wilson desperately wanted to hear her laugh. "Did you say we'll talk when I get back?"

"Yes."

"*First* thing?"

"Well," Mary coyly replied, "maybe not the *first* thing!"

They continued to talk about the kids and her holiday plans until Wilson noticed one of the marine pilots waiting to use the phone.

"I gotta go, baby. I know you support me out here, and it's okay to blow off steam. I can take it."

"I promise I won't do that again, James. We're fine here, surrounded by friends and family. Get another medal, will ya."

"Medal of Honor this time?"

"If it will keep you home, yes."

"Okay, I'll work on it," Wilson said, smiling.

"I love you very much."

"I love you, too."

"Bye, baby."

"Bye."

Part II

OH, East is East, and West is West, and never the twain shall meet,
Till Earth and Sky stand presently at God's great Judgment Seat;
But there is neither East nor West, Border, nor Breed, nor Birth,
When two strong men stand face to face, tho' they come from the ends of the earth!

The Ballad of East and West by Rudyard Kipling

CHAPTER 23

Wilson looked over at his wingman, Smoke, inside his *Hornet* in tension on Cat 1. Seconds prior to launch, Smoke's head was back against the headrest, left arm locked against the throttles at full power. All around Smoke's aircraft, *Raven 410*, the troubleshooters and catapult crewmen held thumbs up aloft to signify ready. The catapult officer, topside on this clear blue day, had returned Smoke's salute seconds earlier and was in a crouch pointing toward the bow. The green-shirted crewman in the catwalk looked left and right, arms raised, and then dropped his arms and depressed the FIRE button on the console in front of him.

As the catapult fired, Wilson saw Smoke's body compress, due to the sudden forward motion. It then seemed to bounce in the cockpit as the 44,000 pound aircraft was slung down the track by the shuttle attached to the nose gear. The aircraft accelerated from zero to 180 knots with an instantaneous 3 g-force that drove him further into his seat and caused the stabilators to deflect down to lift the aircraft up on the climb out. Wilson saw the burner cans stage open with yellow fire halfway down the track as Smoke selected afterburner. In a fraction of a second, the aircraft departed the ship, accompanied by a sharp *Boom* as the catapult shuttle crashed into the water brake at the end of the stroke. Two seconds from the first motion, Smoke's bomb-laden *Hornet* was airborne 60 feet above the peaceful waters of the Gulf, accelerating as the pilot gently picked up the nose and turned right, away from the ship, while raising the gear and flaps, then reversing his turn to the left to parallel the ship's course.

A *Prowler* roared past on Wilson's left off Cat 3. The pilot banked left, cleaning up and climbing into a mirror image of Smoke's flight path. As both aircraft receded from view off the bow, Wilson grew impatient to launch. He wanted to minimize the distance building each second between him and his wingman.

The catapult crew now focused their attention on him, and at the instant the yellow shirt gave him the "take tension" signal, Wilson brought the throttles to military as the engines thundered to life behind him. On signal he lifted the launch bar switch to "UP." In rote sequence, he extended the flight control stick to full travel in a deliberate motion forward... back... left... right.... Simultaneously,

he pushed the rudder pedals to their limits with each leg and kept his eyes on the engine instruments.

Satisfied, Wilson turned to the catapult officer, made eye contact, and popped a jaunty salute before he, too, placed his head back in the head rest and braced for launch. Off to his right he saw the catapult officer return his salute and make his final checks of the aircraft and the cat track. Leaning into the 25-knot wind, he then looked forward, touched the deck with his hand, and pointed to the bow on one knee. Remaining motionless but taut, with his left arm locked and pushing the throttles forward to ensure they didn't come back to idle during the stroke, Wilson's eyes shifted left. He saw the green-shirted crewman with arms raised look up and down the track, then lower his arms.

Unseen and instantaneous force pinned Wilson's shoulders back into the seat. His oxygen mask pushed tight against his face and caused his eyes to squint behind the helmet visor. The FA-18 seemed to bounce down the deck as it accelerated to flying speed, and like Smoke moments earlier, Wilson shoved the throttles past the military stop into burner. He heard the shuttle increase speed and saw the bow rush up to meet him. The 3 g's against his body felt good as he hurtled down the track, and the airspeed box in the HUD rapidly scrolled above three figures. With an abrupt lurch forward, the g-force disappeared and a deafening boom sounded below as the shuttle slammed into the water brake beneath him.

At that, Wilson was also thrown into the sky above the glassy blue-green Persian Gulf. His right hand dropped to take the stick and command his own gentle climb and turn to the right. His left slapped up the gear and the flaps in a practiced motion. Still in burner, he rolled back left to parallel the course and bunted the nose to level at 500 feet. With the radar on, he pushed the weapon select switch forward to sweep for contacts, as an instructor had taught him years ago: *Get the radar searching ASAP, like you are going to kill something.*

Wilson's radar detected something about five miles ahead, and he bumped the castle switch to lock it. An aircraft heading northwest at angels five closing at 150 knots. *Must be Smoke*, he thought. Minutes later, as he closed on the left bearing line, the bright afternoon sun illuminated the black *Raven* insignia on the vertical stab and confirmed his assumption.

Earlier, they had briefed to join northwest of the ship, but Smoke knew Wilson was next off the bow and had slowed his acceleration to allow his flight lead to catch up. Smoke had, thereby, expedited the join-up and had minimized the time needed to get to the tanker south of Baghdad. None of this was discussed on the radio. After two years of turnaround training and combat flying together

in VFA-64, Wilson and his favorite JO wingman were at the point they could anticipate each other's thoughts.

Wilson crept up to Smoke in a shallow climb. He inspected *410*'s left side and, in a graceful maneuver, slid under to repeat the procedure on the right. He then pushed up next to Smoke, who had been looking over his shoulder, waiting for him. Using hand signals Wilson took the lead, led them through a frequency change, and checked the drop tank fuel transfer. Then, with an open-palm hand signal, he pushed Smoke out into a more comfortable formation for the long flight north.

Wilson prepared them to test their decoy expendables. "Stand by for confetti checks…from lead."

Wilson's left thumb rocked forward and back on the chaff/flare switch, expending one bundle of chaff and one flare. His headset clicked as they were released, and even in the bright sunlight, he could see the flash from the flare reflected off his left drop tank. He looked over at Smoke 400 feet away, and soon saw the metallic fibers of the chaff bundle blooming, followed by the dazzling yellow flare as it ejected from below his aircraft, and rapidly fell behind.

"Good checks," Wilson said. Satisfied the go/no-go criteria from their brief were met, he added, "Lead's fenced, eleven-eight."

"Two's fenced, eleven-four," Smoke replied.

With both aircraft now combat ready, there was no need for Dutch. He had launched a few minutes after Wilson and was there to serve as the airborne spare if one of the two primary *Ravens* was not fully mission capable for the assigned combat mission. Dutch was now free to go on an alternate mission for the ship, such as sea surface search around the strike group ships. He would look for contacts of interest like dhows or unusual watercraft and would recover on the next recovery.

Wilson called to him on squadron tactical. "Dutch, we're fenced and outbound."

"Roger that. Have fun," he replied.

Wilson clicked his mike twice in acknowledgement as they continued north and into combat.

CHAPTER 24

The "Surge," which had begun in earnest earlier in the year, was paying big dividends for the Commander, Multi-National Force Iraq. The strategy of trying to limit the Iraqi footprint of the Multi-National Force—by garrisoning the troops in fire base enclaves, making only high-speed patrols through towns, and by treating IEDs as a law enforcement problem—had failed in 2005 and 2006. The Iraqi people, fed up with the violence but unsure of the American commitment, withheld their allegiance until they could be confident of U.S. resolve. They did not want to back the loser in the struggle with the Al-Qaeda insurgents.

The surge strategy—enter a town, clear it of insurgents, stay to ensure the personal security of the inhabitants, and support the fledgling government and Iraqi security forces—involved heavy firepower up front. If people were observed digging alongside a highway in the wee hours, they were taken out immediately. If mortar fire was observed from an urban dwelling, it was obliterated with a 500-pound bomb.

Nowhere were the results more striking then in al-Anbar province, known for years as "the Wild, Wild West" to the Marines responsible for that area. Through the coalition's aggressive destruction of insurgents and the engagement of the tribal sheiks by mid-grade officers, the formerly restive region came to trust and to communicate intelligence to the Americans. The officers were schooled in classic counter-insurgency tactics which suggested that by working with the coalition Anbar could have a better future than that which al-Qaeda offered.

The "Anbar Awakening" was a success story many Americans were aware of by late 2007, but Iraq was not a place where one political solution or one counter-insurgency model fit all provinces. Several pockets of resistance remained north and south along the Tigris River, and it was likely Wilson and his wingman would find evidence of one of those pockets on this flight.

They continued northwest and climbed above 30,000 feet in their transit of Kuwait. As they talked to air traffic controllers at various stations in Kuwait, in

Iraq, or in AWACS aircraft, they noticed the occasional detached accent of a Brit ex-pat controller. Wilson selected his mission computer destination for *Padres*, the aerial refueling track. It was located southeast of Baghdad, 345 miles away from their present position, or about 50 minutes away. They were scheduled, or "fragged" to be on station 30 minutes later. Wilson set his fuel flow to burn 2,800 pounds per hour per engine and engaged the autopilot.

Below to his right, about 10 miles away, were the twin oil pipeline terminals Al Basrah and Khawr Al Amaya, thin angular man-made "islands" set on the blue Gulf and connected to Iraqi oilfields by underwater pipelines. Wilson observed one tanker at each terminal: a large, traditional, black-hulled crude carrier with white superstructure at one and another of similar design, but smaller and painted bright orange at the other. He locked up the larger vessel on the radar and slewed his infrared aiming diamond on it. The crude carrier showed up as a ghostly white image on his digital display, the wisps of its mooring lines visible on the infrared display because of the midday heat.

The two terminals dispensed the economic lifeblood of Iraq to eager customers from around the world. Wilson knew that SEAL teams lived on the platforms in austere conditions, and in triple-digit temperatures, to provide security. Off his left nose, he saw one of the strike group frigates, stationary in the water, but within close visual range of the platforms ready to serve as another layer of defense for the vital terminals. Further off his left side, and to the south, numerous oil platforms, some Saudi and others Kuwaiti, dotted the Gulf. He craned his neck to the right and behind in order to study Iran's Kharg Island oil complex. Some 40 miles distant, the island had several bright flare stacks scattered about the sandy terrain. Nearby more tankers stood off from the island.

The nose of Wilson's *Hornet* passed over Bubiyan Island, a large plug of barren land dividing the al-Faw Peninsula from the mainland of Kuwait. A small vessel was transiting up the Shatt-al-Arab waterway, the confluence of the Tigris and Euphrates rivers. This narrow ribbon of brown water, less than a half mile across, separated Iraq from Iran.

Wilson shot a glance at Smoke, flying in loose tac-wing formation, and in the distance saw the large metropolis of Kuwait City, with the distinctive Kuwait Towers dominating the northern shore. The city blocks were tightly packed into irregular geometric shapes that all converged on the north of the city and the Grand Mosque. Outside of the great city were only small scattered settlements.

Wilson's daydreaming was interrupted by the radio hand-offs from controller to controller.

"*Nail* four-one, contact Basra Control on Red one-five," the controller said, using the call sign assigned by the Combined Air Operations Center, or CAOC, for this mission.

Wilson responded, "Roger, *Nails* switching Red one-five," and in a command intended for Smoke, added, "Go button six."

He punched in preset button six, waited several seconds, and then keyed the mike. "*Nail* check."

"Two," Smoke replied.

Wilson then called the new controller. "Basra, *Nail* four-one flight with you enroute *Padres* at flight level three-five-zero."

"*Nail* four-one, Basra center. Radar contact, cleared direct *Padres*," answered the voice, which had a definitive Iraqi accent.

"*Nail* four-one."

Crossing into Iraq, Wilson noted the range to *Exxon 55*, the aerial fueling tanker orbiting at *Padres* for their fragged mission give of 8,000 pounds. With over 300 miles to go at 435 knots ground speed, they had almost 45 minutes of cruising ahead of them.

Although he had flown through this narrow band of airspace between Kuwait and Iran dozens of times in his career, Wilson was once again struck by the landscape below. He scanned the desert floor of northern Kuwait both with his eyes and aircraft sensors for scars left over from Desert Storm some 17 years earlier. Scattered over the entire region, which was pockmarked with craters from coalition bombs, were long berms with irregular breeches that marked former Iraqi fighting positions and bunkers.

Wilson could only imagine the terror of the Iraqi boys who had lived for months on the cold, winter "moonscape," as they faced the daily onslaught from above. Death came suddenly and with little warning through many means: iron bombs, LGBs, *Rockeye*, artillery, rockets, *Mavericks*, *Hellfires*, 20 or 30 millimeter, 105 millimeter. Mere *movement* in the open likely meant death, the stuff of their regular nightmares…

Outside on a cold, clear February night, three scared, hungry and chilled conscripts from Saddam City share a cigarette after relieving themselves. Enjoying the moon and stars and thinking of home, they are grateful to be out of that wretched bunker, ignoring their sergeant's warning about lingering outside. The three soldiers watch the gunners to the east shoot their 57mm into the air and cheer them on to find a mark among the formations of invisible jets high above, the sound of which

bathes the air in a low-frequency rumble. An American bomb flashes on the horizon, and they time the seconds until they hear the muffled *Wump...8 kilometers? 10?*

Without warning, the guttural roar of a fighter pulling out of a dive rips through the air just above. Wordlessly and in unison, they bolt for the bunker like scared rabbits, wide-eyed with fear, not by conscious thought but by instinctive terror, knowing what it could mean. *They saw us!*

Exhorting each other to run for their lives, they hear an almost imperceptible "crack" over the noise of their boots and the rattle of their canteens under their winter coats. Gasping lungfuls of heavy desert air and searching for the bunker, they sprint wildly with gripping fear through the sand and the darkness toward the soft glow of light from the bunker entrance, hoping that they or their bunker are not targeted.

Only 30 meters to go! Keep pumping! Then a sound, a high-pitched whistle close above them, registers louder and louder in their brains, *dozens* then *hundreds* of whistles slowly melding into one terrifying *shriek* as the boys whimper for their mothers. A sparkling flash to the left, accompanied by a sharp *POP*, causes them to hunch over by reflex and as a second and third *FLASH! POP!* hit near them, they throw themselves headlong (*Mama!*) into the dirt as reality registers in their consciousness. *Cluster bombs!* They claw at the land in a vain attempt to pull themselves into the sun-baked dirt as the whistling becomes a piercing din, and lethal bomblets pepper the ground all around them causing the earth to erupt in a deafening cacophony of horror and death.

And after the last fragment comes to rest, calm...as the low rumble of jet aircraft permeates the stillness of the now lifeless desert floor.

Wilson imagined what it must have been like for those kids almost 20 years ago.

Time and wind-driven sand had eroded the earthen fortifications and covered the vehicle hulks—and the bodies. Desert Storm—the "Mother of all Battles." Wilson glanced at Smoke, where he should be in stepped up tac-wing, the same formation American fighters had been using to enter Iraqi airspace almost daily since the long ago winter of 1991. The battle was still not over, morphing, over time, into this routine Iraqi Freedom patrol.

CHAPTER 25

An asphalt road, running from east to west, formed a distinctive black-on-sand visual cue of the Kuwait-Iraq border. Berms and lines of other man-made objects ran parallel to either side of the road. A great oilfield straddled the border, dominated by features of Iraq's Ar Rumaylah complex: storage tanks, pipelines, various earthworks and the ever-present flare stacks. The stacks blazed through the midday haze and sent dark gray smoke aloft, where the prevailing winds carried it to the northeast. Underneath the smoke were large swaths of black, oil-stained sand. From Wilson's vantage point five miles above, the swaths looked like giant ink spills on the desert floor. Though far from human settlements, environmental considerations were not high priorities on this bleak landscape.

Wilson shifted in his seat. Yesterday, Shakey and Dutch had dropped two GPS-guided Joint Direct Attack Munitions apiece on an insurgent stronghold in western Diyala north of Baghdad. They were the first weapons CVW-4 had released in a week, and the Air Force had done some "good work," too. Before he had walked, he learned the *Spartans* and *Moonshadows* had released on targets in Diyala that morning. Wilson's two-plane "section" carried a mixed load of two 500-pound JDAM and two LGBs split between them. Each also carried several hundred rounds of 20mm. Wilson wished he had a *Maverick* missile to shoot at a vehicle or something moving. He had never had the opportunity to shoot one before. Positioning himself more comfortably, he settled in for the next 200 miles to *Padres*.

After 15 minutes of looking at the brown countryside of southern Iraq, the airspace controller broke the silence. "*Nail* four-one, switch up *Exxon* five-five on Violet three."

Wilson keyed the mike and replied, "*Nail* four-one, roger. Switching *Exxon* five-five on Violet three. *Nails* go."

"Two," Smoke acknowledged.

His radar swept back and forth in the 80-mile scale. Wilson picked up a contact in the top half of his display and bumped the castle switch to the right. The cursor went to the contact and locked it, showing an airborne contact 10 degrees left of the nose at 24,000 feet heading east. On the left display his FLIR

showed the bogey as a white image, which to Wilson's trained eye was a KC-135 *Stratotanker*, call sign *Exxon 55*. In his HUD was displayed a course to intercept, but Wilson ignored it, knowing that the tanker would begin the racetrack turn to the west before long.

Minutes later, when the tanker turned, Wilson set an intercept course to the northwest, listening to two *Buccaneers* line up behind *Exxon 55* for a long drink. Through his FLIR, he discerned two white dots behind the tanker. Raising his head, he could see with his naked eye a small dash set against a lone cumulonimbus cloud 30 miles away on the northern horizon, with two tiny dots behind it.

The boom operator called to one of the *Hornets*. "Three-zero-seven, that was 7,200."

"Three-zero-seven, roger." Wilson recognized the voice of one of the VFA-47 JOs.

Sliding closer, Wilson positioned them on the tanker's left wing, using geometry to close the distance. Inside 10 miles he could discern the tanker aspect, and hoped they would hold this heading to affect an expeditious join up. He wasn't in too much of a hurry. The second jet had just plugged, and 8,000 pounds took eight minutes.

Soon Wilson joined up on the left wing of the gray *707* airframe using visual cues, while *Cutlass 310* was still plugged in on the boom. Smoke drew in closer in a loose cruise, and using hand signals, informed Wilson of his fuel state—5.7. Wilson gave a thumbs up and passed his own state—5.9— with an open hand (five) followed by four horizontal fingers (nine).

As *310* backed out with a small puff of fuel vapor over his fuselage, the basket swung like a mace in the relative wind before it steadied. The boomer radioed *310* that he had taken 9,000 pounds, and *310* crossed under to the outside of his own wingman.

Wilson called, "*Exxon* five-five, *Nail* four-one flight joined on your left wing as fragged, nose cold, switches safe." He took a glance over his left shoulder at Smoke, who nodded an acknowledgement.

"Roger, *Nails*, cleared precontact," the boom operator replied.

"Roger, precontact," Wilson answered. He then reached down with his left hand to extend the air refueling probe, which extended into the airstream from his right nose.

In a practiced motion, he dropped his right wing and pulled a bit of power, gliding back to a position behind the boom. For a few moments, the five aircraft flew as one at 300 knots. However, as Wilson drew closer to the basket, the

Buccaneer section banked right and opened away from the formation at a measured clip. Wilson noticed their weapons were still secured under their wings, weapons they would take home with them on the one-hour return flight to the ship.

When he lined up the probe five feet behind the basket and stabilized, he could make out the face of the boom operator. The "boomer" wore sunglasses and headphones as he watched Wilson from a window on the bottom of the fuselage.

"Precontact," Wilson transmitted.

"Cleared contact," the boomer replied.

The tanker then began a right turn to remain on the track, and Wilson compensated by matching the roll and adding a bit of power. As his probe inched closer to the basket, Wilson maneuvered his aircraft with tight deflections of the stick. Satisfied with the angle, Wilson added a little power and flew his probe into the basket, then took a bit off to cause the six-foot hose to bend a little, but not too much.

"Contact."

Fuel flowed into the aircraft while they completed the turn to the right and rolled wings level. Wilson concentrated to keep the probe engaged with the basket. For the next eight minutes he maintained this position by holding the aircraft within an area no more than three feet square, down and to the left of the tanker. Fuel transferred through this connection filling his internal tanks and centerline drop. Wilson made his corrections to stay engaged almost by reflex. This allowed his mind to speculate on where, and for what purpose, *Falcon*, or the CAOC airborne coordination controllers, would send them once refueling was complete.

Once transfer was complete, he was careful to get aligned with the end of the rigid steel boom as he slid aft to unplug. The basket came off the probe with a little whip motion and then steadied out into the relative airstream. Wilson waved thanks to the boomer and retracted the probe, sliding over to the tanker's right wing.

"Four-zero-seven. That's 8,400."

"Roger, eight-point-four," Wilson replied and scribbled *8.4* on his kneeboard card.

While Smoke went through the same procedure, Wilson was able to relax a bit on the right wing and study the tanker. Painted a dark shade of gray with a black nose, it had four fat turbofan engines on the wings. At the top of the tail the word "MISSISSIPPI" was spelled with large interlocking "Ss," the style

common to the state's promotional literature. Wilson knew this Air National
Guard refueling squadron was based at Key Field in Meridian, just across town
from where Wilson had gone to flight school 12 years earlier. He pulled acute to
the cockpit, some 60 feet away, and saw that the copilot was looking at him. The
pilot next to him then popped his head into view. When another face appeared
in the window behind the copilot, Wilson gave them a thumbs-up, which the
three Air Guard aircrew returned. The copilot pointed at the ordnance under the
Hornet's wing and slammed his right fist into his left palm, then bared his teeth
and flexed two clenched fists in front of his face. The message was unmistakable,
and Wilson nodded an acknowledgment.

CHAPTER 26

Despite the ever-present haze, it was a nice day over central Iraq. Wilson slid back and looked below at a town hard along the Tigris River. The town consisted of packed brown rectangular structures set within a crosshatched street pattern amid larger streets that funneled out from a central square near the river. The whole scene resembled a huge spider web. Wilson checked his digital moving map—Az Zubaydiyah. From this altitude everything appeared as an earth tone: the buildings, the streets, the surrounding fields, even the river. Though he was rather familiar with the topography and the landmarks of Iraq, this town was one he had never worked.

Five minutes later Smoke was complete and joined Wilson on his right wing. Once Smoke was stabilized, Wilson waved to the still fascinated copilot, whom Wilson surmised had not seen many Navy fighters. As they took a gentle cut away and opened distance from the tanker, Wilson activated his radar and was careful to keep his head on a swivel to watch for nearby tanker traffic.

After they exchanged their new fuel states by hand signal, Wilson tapped his helmet and showed Smoke one then two fingers with his right hand. Smoke nodded.

Wilson switched up Button 12 on his radio, waited a few seconds, and then transmitted. "*Falcon*, *Nail* four-one and flight off *Exxon* five-five at *Padres* with you as fragged."

After a long pause, *Falcon* replied, "*Nail* four-one, roger. Proceed to eighty-nine ALPHA, ten to thirteen K. Keypads eight and nine hot all altitudes. Switch *Bowstring* on Indigo five."

"*Nail* four-one, roger. Proceed to eighty-nine ALPHA, ten to thirteen K. Eight and nine hot. Switching *Bowstring* on Indigo five. *Nails* go!"

"Two," Smoke said into his mask.

The airspace over Iraq was crowded with aircraft of all types. While the controlling agencies provided traffic calls as best they could, pilots were wise to look outside the cockpit. Wilson descended them down under 20,000 feet, sweeping in front of his flight path, as well as across the horizon, for other aircraft. The previous week, north of Baghdad, he and a *Predator* UAV had had

a close call, close enough for Wilson to see the *Hellfire* missile it was carrying under its left wing.

He was pleased they were currently heading to a position in Diyala, where Shakey and Dutch had dropped their JDAM the day before. Leaving the Tigris behind, they glided north in a lazy descent, Smoke following on his wing. Both pilots moved their heads from side to side, pausing for a second on one "piece" of sky at a time and focusing their eyes for movement at range, scanning more for traffic than ground threats.

Wilson examined the surface below, a mixture of desert wasteland and anemic-looking irrigated fields in small slapdash rectangle shapes, canals feeding what meager water was available to them and the occasional village. Under 15,000 feet and able to see better through the desert haze, Wilson began to pick up color in the fields, an olive drab green. He spotted a lone vehicle, a sedan, moving on a road at a normal speed toward a village, resumed his scan, and keyed the mike to contact *Bowstring*, the terminal area controller.

"*Bowstring, Nail* four-one flight checking in mission one-three-one, one Mk 38 JDAM and one GBU-12 each plus twenty mike-mike, ATFLIR. Playtime zero plus four-five. Sitrep."

"Roger, *Nail*, proceed to eighty-nine ALPHA, cleared to roam north and south. Quiet now."

"*Nail* four-one, roger."

The two *Ravens* cruised at a max endurance fuel setting in an area 75 miles northeast of Baghdad, which was obscured from their view by the haze. Wilson edged to the western border of their assigned area, which paralleled the north/south road from Baghdad to Mosul, a notorious insurgent corridor that included the town of Tikrit. As *Bowstring* had said, it was quiet, or so it seemed from altitude. The minutes ticked off one at a time, and he shifted uncomfortably in the seat he had strapped himself into three hours ago.

They flew in a 30-mile racetrack up and down, as Wilson scanned for puffs of dust on the surface or palls of smoke. He was reminded of a pilot's axiom: *Flying is hours and hours of boredom interrupted by moments of sheer terror.* Nothing was going on down there, and Wilson, hoping to hit something today, was ashamed to realize that the satisfaction he derived from releasing a weapon was to a great extent dependent on American kids first getting ambushed by the enemy.

Wilson called to Smoke on his aux radio. "Lead's seven-point-oh."

"Two's six-point-seven."

Heading south and initiating an easy climb, Wilson informed *Bowstring* that they were departing for *Padres* and more fuel. *Bowstring* answered, "*Nail* four-one, standby. We've got a mission for you. Contact *Bowser* on Yellow Fourteen."

Wilson bunted the nose, pulled a handful of power, and turned away from Smoke as he rogered a response. With the *Exxon* refueling track some 80 miles away, Wilson figured they could squeeze 15 minutes before departing for a drink. He looked up the UHF radio frequency for Yellow 14 on his kneeboard package and entered it into the radio keypad.

"*Nail* check."

"Two," Smoke replied.

"*Bowser, Nail* four-one flight checking in mission one-three-one as fragged with two Mk 38 JDAM, two GBU-12 and twenty mike-mike. Standing by for nine-line."

Bowser was the call sign of a Joint Terminal Attack Controller, a young soldier on the ground who needed help. By the sound of his voice, Wilson guessed he was a southern kid in his early 20s, and anxious.

"Rog' that *Nail*, copy all. We're in Balad Ruz on Highway 82. Got a sit'ation here, where y'all at?"

Wilson checked his sector chart and made a calculation. *Bowser* was 25 miles to the east. Smoke was to his right in combat spread. To get them moving east, Wilson keyed the mike and said, "Tac right—go," as he rolled the aircraft on its right side and pulled across the horizon toward Smoke.

"Two," his wingman replied. Wilson went back to *Bowser* on his primary radio.

"Be there in about four minutes *Bowser*, and we'll have about ten minutes on-station for you. Need us sooner?"

"Ahh…yeah…need you *NOW, Nails,* for a show o' force. Lemme know when you have the town."

Wilson keyed aux and said, "Gate," as he shoved the throttles to burner and unloaded for knots. Out of the turn Smoke matched him as their indicated airspeed increased rapidly, still in spread but now to Wilson's left.

"Roger, *Bowser*, be there in 2.5 minutes for a show of force, wilco."

Wilson wondered what lay in store for them in Balad Ruz. Was *Bowser* and his squad facing some angry townspeople, or did they get hit by a roadside bomb? Through the haze, he followed Highway 82 toward the town, located about 50 miles from the Iranian border. The town was in the middle of an agricultural area characterized by small, rectangular fields and ditches, some partially flooded by recent winter storms.

In the air-to-ground mode, Wilson selected "GUN" to ready his 20 mm cannon. He called "Tapes on... *armstrong*" to Smoke on aux, then lifted his own Master Arm switch to ARM and energized the video tape recorder.

"*Nails*, need you to thump this town, low and loud."

Sensing the rising tension in *Bowser's* voice, Wilson nevertheless asked for more details. "*Bowser*, what heading do you want us on?"

"*Nails*, don' matter, any head'n will do. Do you see the town?"

Through the milky haze the town, another packed jumble of small, boxy structures surrounded by disorganized fields, came into view south of the highway. Wilson called to *Bowser* that he had it in sight.

"Roger, *Nail*, we're near a small minaret on the southwest part o' town. Jus' took a mortar. How far you out?"

"One minute, *Bowser*. Looking for you," Wilson assured him. He told Smoke to take high cover and continued down in a shallow dive to the deck. In his mind he recited the low-altitude training dive rules: *15 for 750*. The airplane intakes were moaning at high speed, and he looked at his fuel: *5.4*. With the ground rushing up at a steady pace, and a large bird whizzing past his left side, he realized he was no longer bored.

CHAPTER 27

Taking a cut to the right to set up a southwest-northeast run over the city in order to put the low afternoon sun at his back, he leveled off at 200 feet and scanned the fields in rapid motion for signs of small arms or MANPADS. There were single trees here and there, and he saw a stand of trees to the south.

Bowser's excited call filled his ears. "Gotcha in sight, *Nail!* Bring it!"

At treetop height over the fields, Wilson approached the low wall that surrounded the town at over 500 knots, a high transonic airspeed that would rattle the windows but not break them. When he saw *Bowser's* minaret, he made a quick jink away from it, then rolled out to fly over the center of town at 200 feet. Smoke, 5,000 feet above, watched for threat fire.

The town appeared quiet as he approached. A few people walked along the dusty streets and alleyways and cars were parked here and there, but very little moved. Color in the form of green date palms and various Arabic signs dotted the cityscape, a light brown hodgepodge of row houses and courtyard walls, everything cut at right angles by east-west streets and north-south alleys. An Iraqi flag flew from a modest building to his right.

At this speed the people could not hear Wilson approach until his was right on top of them. He noticed a man flinch on the sidewalk as the jet thundered past, and a second later he caught a glimpse of an *abaya*-clad woman trudging down an alley with a small child dressed in a nightgown. Wilson threw up a wing and jinked right a few degrees to look for telltale flashes of small arms fire and MANPADS launches. A brown blur of rooftops covered with water tanks, antennae and satellite dishes whizzed underneath him. Another minaret, this one larger, passed down his left wing. More people were outside in this part of town, and as they saw him approach, they darted inside buildings and alleys. He rolled up on his left wing and looked down, just in time to see the face of a boy, mouth agape, looking up in wonder from a courtyard below.

He traversed the town in less than 10 seconds, and at the eastern wall pulled up and to the left. He traded airspeed for altitude and punched out some flares as he looked over his left shoulder for threats.

"I'm high at your left eight, six clear," Smoke called.

Wilson replied, "Visual, six clear," and continued up.

"*Fuckin' sweet!* I mean nice job, *Nail*. That's jus' what we need. We were startin' ta' get some trouble down here. I've got 'nuther mission for you, right now!"

Wilson had about five minutes of fuel before he had to bingo to *Exxon*. "Make it quick, *Bowser*. We've got five minutes of playtime."

"Yes, sir, this will be a talk-on. See the road 'long the town's southern border? See where it kinks?"

Wilson saw it and replied, "Affirm." He leveled off at 8,000 feet in a shallow bank north of Balad Ruz.

"OK, that corner is bisected by a dirt road that leads southeast, connectin' with the corner of a parallel road, 'bout a mile."

"*Nail*, four-one contact."

"OK, using that measure of distance, 'bout two thirds of the way down from the city and to the north of the dirt road is a maroon sedan parked in the field. Need ya t' hit that with a GBU on a zero-niner-zero run in. You've got friendlies to the north in town."

"*Nail*, four-one, roger. What's in the car?"

"We filled it with a bad-guy arms cache and IED explosives. The car belonged to an insurgent we captured, and his friends are pissed, 'specially his ol' lady!"

"Roger that…looking."

Wilson extended to the west, and slewed his FLIR on the road south of town, running the aiming diamond to the kink in the road. He was now at bingo fuel, but could stay a few minutes more for *Bowser*. He widened his field of view, took a guess at the distance, and narrowed his FLIR picture. A white smudge stood out in the display, likely the "hot" infrared image of a car left out in the midday sun. Wilson kept his turn in and was now flying east and closing the "smudge." Several seconds later the smudge began to take on the shape of a sedan. He overbanked and pulled his nose down to put the aiming diamond image in his HUD. It showed a vehicle in the distance, the maroon color discernible—but barely—against the dark green field.

"*Nail*, four-one, *captured*," Wilson said and took a fleeting look at Smoke, who joined to the inside in tac-wing. "Switches set, *armstrong*," he relayed on aux while pulling up to level off.

"Two has contact, visual, roger, *armstrong*."

The mission computer calculated a heading and a time to release the 500-pound, laser-guided bomb: …14 seconds, 13 seconds, 12 seconds…. Wilson triple-checked his switches: weapon – SELECTED; laser – ARMED; tape – ON. He monitored the greenish FLIR imagery and slewed the aiming diamond with

small corrections to keep the diamond centered on the target. It was now easily identifiable on the FLIR as a compact sedan with the hood open.

"*Bowser, Nails* are five seconds, wings level," Wilson called.

"*Nails,* gotcha in sight. Yer cleared hot," *Bowser* responded.

"Roger, cleared."

In the last few seconds before release, Wilson "sweetened" the computed solution and saw no life around the vehicle. With three seconds left, he placed his right thumb on the pickle switch and pushed.

The 500-pound weapon left the aircraft with a familiar twitch from the sudden release. He looked over his shoulder at Smoke, flying a little above on his right side in time to see Smoke's LGB release and fall away, wings extended. He turned his attention to the FLIR and looked at the time of fall countdown …10 seconds, 9 seconds… then returned his focus to the diamond to prevent drifting off the car.

At one second to impact, a white dash shot from the top of the display and into the sedan, causing the display to burst into images of explosive flash and smoke. Wilson selected "WIDE" field of view and rolled up to his left in time to see Smoke's weapon enter the maelstrom of smoke and fire. It detonated with a white concentric shock wave that expanded in rapid fashion away from the explosion. One huge secondary explosion, then another, caused additional shock waves to ripple away like high-speed rings. Wilson saw tumbling fragments thrown into the air, leaving thin smoke trails above the dark roiling cloud. Debris pelted the field hard enough to kick up small dust clouds all around the sedan's former location.

"*Nails—SHACK!* A hun'rd over a hun'rd!" In the background, Wilson overheard one of *Bowsers'* mates exclaim, "*Fuckin' –A!*" to his buddy as they watched the scene.

"Roger that, *Bowser.* We are bingo for the tanker. You guys take care."

"*Nail,* are you guys done for the day? Can you all come back?"

Wilson answered, "We've gotta get a drink, but we've each got a JDAM and bullets left." After a pause, he added, "We'll let *Falcon* Control work it out." He reached down and marked his position over Balad-Ruz.

"*Nail,* four-one, roger. Think we are the only game in town today. Hope t' talk t' y'all later."

"Roger that, *Bowser,* we'll expedite. *Nails,* switch *Bowstring* on Indigo five, go."

"Two," Smoke replied.

"Switches safe, camera off," Wilson added on aux.

"Two."

CHAPTER 28

The *Raven* pilots worked their way back through the controlling agencies to the *Exxon* tanker, now 60 miles away. As they climbed to the tanker track over eastern Iraq, the landscape below was again transformed through the haze into an overall beige patina. Wilson surveyed the scene and unclipped his oxygen mask bayonet fitting and took a drink from the plastic flask he kept in his g-suit pocket. The haze reminded him of the smog that so often covered the Los Angeles basin. He set the power to rendezvous on the tanker with 3,000 pounds of fuel, and checked the bingo to Al Asad as he clipped his mask back into place.

Nail 42 broke the silence. "There's hope for those Army guys—they swear like Marines." Smoke was close enough to see Wilson's white helmet move up and down in the affirmative as he searched the sky for *Exxon*. Minutes later they joined on the same Mississippi tanker they had tanked from earlier. The boom was all theirs, and both pilots plugged and took on fuel in turn. Although they could have topped off with more, Wilson directed Smoke to take 10,000 pounds to shave some time tanking and to get back to *Bowser* in a hurry. In a little over 20 minutes they completed their tanking. While Smoke was still in the basket, Wilson was coordinating their next mission...back to Diyala and *Bowstring* control. Ten minutes later they were enroute to *Bowser*.

"*Bowser*, *Nail* four-one, flight of two, checking in with one JDAM and twenty mike-mike each, play time 0+40." Wilson saw the outline of Balad Ruz, just visible through the haze, in his HUD field of view.

"Rog' that, *Nail* four-one, welcome back! Y'all ready t' copy nine-line?"

"Go ahead."

"OK, head t' Wizards...and stand by for brief."

Bowser read off a standardized close air support targeting checklist. It consisted of nine lines in sequence, each line corresponding to a piece of information required to build the tactical picture with a minimum of transmissions. These nine lines would give the aviators all the information they needed to release their weapon on target at the precise second required. This precision also served to avoid fratricide and the targeting of noncombatants.

After half a minute, *Bowser* keyed his mike.

"Nail four-one, nine-line as follows...

"...Wizards...

"...Zero-sev'n-five...

"...Six-point-four...

"...One-three-two...

"...building, insurgent stronghold..."

Bowser read the detailed latitude/longitude info for the JDAM, and continued.

"...not applicable...

"...southwest three thousand...

"...egress north back t' Wizards...

"...advise when ready to copy amplifying remarks, over."

Wilson finished scribbling the nine-line into his kneeboard CAS card and answered, "Ready to copy remarks."

"Rog-o, *Nails,* need jus' one JDAM fer now. Restriction for collateral damage is a mosque west one thousand...troops in contact. Time on target when able." The JTAC sounded nervous.

Wilson hit his countdown timer. *Bowser's* assignment to the *Nails:* leave the initial point *Wizards* on a heading of 075, and 6.4 miles later, hit an insurgent building at an elevation of 132 feet with a single JDAM. *Bowser* and his squad were southwest at 3000 meters, and a mosque was west at 1000 meters. Once the weapon was delivered, the *Nails* were to come off north and return to Wizards for more tasking. From what Wilson could see, and from the inflection of *Bowser's* voice, they needed fire support *now.*

Wilson answered, "Roger...about five minutes." *Bowser* asked him to read back line six, and Wilson complied. The contract was set.

Wilson directed Smoke to take high cover. He then set his own destination for the target and readied himself for a busy five minutes filled with mental time-distance-heading calculations, triple checking the lat/long entered into the computer, and verifying the numbers with his wingman. He selected his JDAM on Station 2, and set a course line of 075 from Wizards. He maneuvered west of town at 7,000 feet, over open fields, and saw no movement below him. As he approached the run-in, he pushed the throttles to burner and pulled to the northeast.

"Nail four-one, IP inbound."

"Rog-o *Nail,* continue."

Upon reaching a tactical air speed, Wilson pulled it out of burner and lined up on his steering. The town floated under his nose ahead of him. On his FLIR

he saw a clutter of square shapes—buildings—and as he drew closer, he was able to break them out on the north/south streets. He selected his tape ON and noted 25 seconds to release.

"*Nail* four-one, wings level."

"Cleared hot, *Nail*"

"*Nail* four-one"

Wilson lifted the master arm switch to ARM and continued at high speed toward the town.

Smoke called to him. "Got a puff to the southwest. Maybe near *Bowser's* posit...Yep, there's an impact flash."

Wilson looked over his right leading edge extension and saw two small smoke clouds wafting up from a nondescript neighborhood. He was well above small arms fire, but was concerned about hand-held SAM launches, even though no firings had been reported in this area for some time. With seconds to release, he concentrated on the release cue and accelerated. *Bowser* seemed like a guy who wouldn't mind a JDAM a bit early. The airplane jumped as another 500 pounds of ordnance, guided by satellite signals all the way to the target, fell earthward to the precise point *Bowser* wanted it to hit.

Wilson went to military power and rolled up on his left wing to egress north and watch the impact. The FLIR showed a car approach the targeted building; in anticipation he looked over his left shoulder to watch the weapon impact. He saw a massive explosion in the middle of the city, the shock wave raising a concentric cloud of dust above the structures around the building covered in smoke. Secondary explosions shot out of the burning building, and projectiles rammed into the houses across the street. One missile-like projectile flew crazily over the houses and landed in a dirt field north of the highway. The driver of the car he saw before impact reversed down the street in a panic. Wilson was surprised it was still running. A raging column of flame and black smoke towered over the targeted building.

Wilson was transfixed by the scene until the radio crackled. "*Nails*, we gettin' mortared! Gotta move, out!"

Wilson overheard a soldier in the background shout, "*Andy, let's go!*"

"Roger, *Bowser*, we're standing by."

With his wingman in trail, Wilson orbited northwest of the city, the pall of black smoke showing no signs of abating. To the southwest he also saw a tight group of small puffs caused by mortars. *Bowser* must be in that area.

Wilson called to Smoke. "Let's make some noise south to north. Follow me after I come off."

"Roger!"

To keep the insurgents' heads down, Wilson commanded Smoke to take trail as he led them from the south over the narrow part of the city in another show of force. With airspeed increasing, he descended in a left-hand turn to begin his run. Approaching the city, he popped out chaff and flares and initiated jinking in three dimensions. From the secondary explosions he saw, Wilson figured they had just hit an even larger weapons cache than the one they had destroyed in the sedan. The throttles were at full power, showing 550 knots indicated, as Wilson flew over the city and pulled up to the left to watch Smoke begin his run.

Wilson made a call to *Bowser*. No answer.

After Smoke's run, Wilson overflew the town again, higher and slower. He and Smoke were in a perfect wagon-wheel orbit, which would allow one of them to pounce on a pop-up contact while the other maintained a position to provide support.

"*Nail* four-one, y'all up?" It was *Bowser*.

"Go ahead, *Bowser!*"

"We got a vee-hicle, a white SUV, movin' outta town on Highway 82. Movin' west now. Bad guys in there."

Smoke called a tally. "*Nail* four-two has a white SUV passing the northwest corner of the city on the highway." Without warning, a bright flare separated from the SUV and climbed into the sky leaving a gray corkscrew trail of smoke.

"SAM at your left seven! Break left! Flares!" Smoke cried.

Wilson saw the launch and turned hard into it. He sensed, though, he was not the target because the missile veered low and behind him well before the rocket motor burned out. He expended some flares and kept an eye on the SUV, which continued to barrel west away from town.

Smoke called to *Bowser*. "*Bowser*, *Nail* four-two, that guy just launched a MANPAD at *Nail* four-one. Request clearance to engage with twenty mike-mike."

"You're cleared, *Nail* four-two. Take that mo-fo out!"

"*Nail* four-two's in hot."

Wilson watched Smoke roll in on the white truck. Although it sped away from the town, it was now completely in the open and stood out in contrast to the black asphalt road that stretched across the desert. Smoke extended a little to the south to get a better run in, and when he turned back, the SUV was still moving west at high speed. It was going to be a 90-degree crossing shot for Smoke, and Wilson took up a position in trail. Wilson selected GUN, and armed up.

Smoke bore in on the SUV and kept his eyes padlocked on it from two miles away. Wilson saw a car on the highway heading east and called it to Smoke.

"I've got it... *Nail* four-two's in hot on the SUV," replied Smoke.

"*Nail* flight, *Bowser*. I've lost y'all. Engage at pilot discretion."

"Roger, *Bowser*, engaging."

Wilson watched Smoke in his strafing run. Once the eastbound vehicle passed the SUV, a faint white trail of vapor emerged from Smoke's aircraft. Wilson saw the tracers as they flew toward the insurgent truck.

Dust kicked up along the highway 50 yards in front of the SUV, and one ricochet spun into the far field with a wild trajectory. Smoke had calculated too much lead and missed.

The bullet impacts stitched across the highway, however, and startled the driver. In what must have been a panicked state, the driver slammed on the brakes and turned south onto a side road. Wilson saw right away that the insurgents were trapped.

The dirt road ran between two partially flooded fields in flat farmland—about three miles west of Balad Ruz. Despite the fact he was driving an SUV, the driver couldn't change course to turn left or right through the muddy fields. The only chance the insurgents had was for the driver to drive straight ahead and limit Wilson's firing window by closing the range and making him aim steep.

Wilson watched the SUV come right at him, trailing a cloud of dust. Although the target was moving, all he had to do was aim short and walk the rounds up to the vehicle, or let it drive into the bullets. He felt as if he were rolling in on a strafe target run-in line, with Smoke, on a local training mission back home over the Dare County target range in eastern North Carolina. He keyed the mike.

"Lead's in hot," he said with a calm voice. *Oh, yeah!* he thought and rolled left.

His g-suit squeezed him and the horizon tilted as he overbanked and looked out of the top of his canopy at the SUV. He pulled his nose to a point on the road ahead of the vehicle. For Wilson, the situation was ideal: Against the landscape, the vehicle appeared to be a white dot moving toward him. The brown cloud of dust it kicked up behind was proof of the driver's desperate attempt to avoid another strafing attack. Wilson stabilized in a shallow dive; pulled some power; placed his gunsight "pipper," in front of the SUV; and watched the range ring unwind on the reticle.

As the truck and the fighter drew closer, Wilson wondered if the insurgents could see him. A faint muzzle flash from the passenger side of the vehicle an-

swered that question. Wilson squeezed the red trigger on the stick with his right index finger and held it for *three...long...seconds.*

A cloud of white gun gas formed above the nose of the aircraft as 20-millimeter rounds flew out of the six-barrel cannon. The deep *BURRRRRRRRP* sounded similar to the noise of a large chain saw. Wilson noted the tracers explode away from his aircraft at supersonic speeds, but he kept his concentration on the green pipper, the "death dot," in front of the white truck. His hand clenched the stick hard as he pushed forward a hair to keep a tight bullet grouping; he released some pressure to "walk" the rounds up and then back down the road. The first rounds of the bullet stream kicked up the dirt in front of the truck. They were followed by bright impact flashes that ripped open the vehicle and churned the dirt around it into a brown cloud. Approaching 500 feet, Wilson yanked the stick up and rolled left, looking down to check his work.

Below he saw the burning truck. Peppered with huge holes and missing jagged chunks of its body, the vehicle had emerged from the confusion of dirt and metal and careened into a field, splashing water as it came to a halt. The road behind it was pockmarked with bullet impacts. As Wilson whizzed past the smoking vehicle, and as it receded into the distance, he saw no further motion on the dirt road.

"Good grief! You Winchester now?" Smoke asked on aux. He then added, "I can see your nose glowing from here! Sierra Hotel!"

Wilson ignored him and called to their JTAC. "*Bowser*, the white SUV is neutralized and burning approximately three miles west of your position. We've got one JDAM and a few bullets left for you."

"Way t' go, *Nail*! Those a-holes been screwin' with us for days! Nice shootin', sir!"

"Roger that, *Bowser*. Happy to help. We'll orbit high for now. Have 'bout twenty mikes left. Where you from, *Bowser*?"

"Hardeeville, South Carolina, sir! Goin' home in two weeks, too. In time for the Super Bowl!"

"I know Hardeeville... You guys okay down there?"

"Yes, sir, we're good. Happens ever' now and again. An' next time you're in Hardeeville, we got some good home cookin' restaurants, too. Not just that fast food on the highway."

"Roger that, and safe trip home, soldier. You're a damn good JTAC," Wilson replied.

"Thanks, sir. Great hits today."

CHAPTER 29

One hour later, Wilson and Smoke were headed back to the ship, having tanked a third time. Wilson made mission reports to the CAOC in Qatar and to the ship via E-2 radio relay. *Nail 41* flight had completed an eventful Iraqi Freedom patrol, and the ship would want to hear all about it ASAP.

As he and Smoke transited to the southeast in silence, Wilson thought about the white SUV. The insurgents had never had a chance once they made the turn onto the dirt road, not that they had had a much better one on the main road. *Who was in that vehicle? Iranians?* They had taken a shot at him with a MANPAD. *Where could they have gotten that but from Iran?* Wilson could not get the image of the SUV—coming right at him—out of his head. With a cool demeanor, he had placed his 20-mm aiming reticle on it and shot the truck to pieces in one massive burst. They had been trapped; it was as if he had been holding them in his hand and had shot them point blank. *They didn't have a chance. Was it* murder? They had shot at him twice, including the potshot the passenger took at him seconds before he died. *Was the weapon an AK? Another gift from Iran?*

Over the course of his career, Wilson had dropped bombs and shot anti-radiation missiles against fixed targets. Enemy buildings. A bridge. A radar in a field. Maybe enemy personnel had been inside…maybe not. Regardless, Wilson had always slept well afterwards. But an hour ago, he had seen human beings in that truck, human beings that Wilson had reduced to lifeless, and probably unrecognizable, bodies. *That guy took a shot at me. This is war,* he thought. They were *clearly* enemies, but they were humans, nonetheless, with human reflexes and emotions. He tried to imagine what it must have been like to be inside the SUV and to see his aircraft looming larger, unable to turn left or right to avoid the bullets that were only seconds away. Wilson could only guess about how close the AK bullets had gotten to his jet…the guy who took the shots must have been a bad mother or scared to death.

Weren't they all scared kids in a foreign land, like *Bowser* and his squad, thinking about home? Like those Iraqi soldiers freezing in their bunkers? *Maybe so, but these guys were fighting in the shadows, behind civilians, and not in uniform.*

Getting in the SUV and making a run for it was as stupid as it was suicidal, Wilson rationalized to himself. *The world now has two, three, or four fewer terrorist insurgents to cause mayhem and murder—here or anywhere.*

The sun was just above the horizon, and Wilson watched it over his right shoulder, his dark visor sitting on top of his helmet. Smoke's aircraft formed a sharp silhouette against the bright western sky as he flew a loose cruise formation next to Wilson.

From altitude the desert sunsets were often spectacular. Airborne particles turned the horizon a deep red, and sunlight from the now orange ball illuminated the bottom of stratus clouds over 100 miles away, the sky transitioning to a yellow band, then deep blue. Above them, several miles away in the blue, he saw an airliner heading southeast with twinkling anti-collision lights. The setting sun turned its four long contrails into platinum. Wilson wondered, *Where is it going? Dubai? India?* He thought of the wealthy passengers sipping cocktails in first-class comfort, oblivious to the combat below them. He studied the aircraft a little longer and identified it as an *Airbus.*

As Wilson contemplated the western sky, his thoughts turned to Mary. *Can she see this same sun right now?* He realized today was a Sunday. Eight time zones away—maybe she was packing the kids in the van for church. *They have no idea what just happened here,* he thought, and he was glad that was so. He would keep it that way. *And tomorrow is New Year's Eve back home. Out here, it's just another fly day.*

On the surface, the desert floor was a dim grayish blue in the twilight. Scattered lights shone here and there and the wispy outline of a river—*Tigris or Euphrates?*—meandered to the Gulf. A large cluster of lights from Basra loomed ahead off the nose, and oilfield flare stacks were visible to the west. Another 30 minutes to the ship… Wilson adjusted the cockpit lighting and checked his fuel.

Soon Wilson's mind drifted back to Balad Ruz. He reached up and turned the rear view mirror down toward him. His eyes reflected back over his oxygen mask; the eyes of a hunter… the eyes of a trained killer.

That day, combat became personal for James "Flip" Wilson.

Mary awoke the next morning to the sound of the *Virginian-Pilot* hitting the driveway while it was still dark. With so much on her mind, she hadn't slept well. Her parents were coming down from Baltimore to spend New Year's with her, and her plan was to put them up in her room. She still had to clean the

bathroom, pull sheets off the bed, do the wash, move her things into Derrick's room (for three days), vacuum the house, and go to the grocery store. She then had to make something for when they arrived and get ready to go out with some of the squadron girls to a New Year's Eve party in Lago Mar. When she thought about that…the outfit, the shoes, the small nub of her favorite lipstick left on her dressing table…she wondered, *Is that enough for tonight?* She looked at the clock: 5:55 a.m. *Ugh!*

After she fixed breakfast and dressed the kids, she threw on a sweatshirt and looked in the mirror, groaning at what she saw. *I hope no one sees me at Safeway.* She made a mental note to get nacho chips. *Dad is going to watch a lot of football tomorrow.*

Damp winter cold greeted her as she opened the door and loaded the kids into the minivan. Fumbling with Brittany's car seat, she saw the paper at the end of the driveway.

"Derrick, please get the newspaper."

At once he spun around and sprinted to retrieve it. *He sprints everywhere,* she thought. *How does he get the energy, and how can I bottle it?*

"Here it is, Mommy!" Derrick said as he proudly handed her the newspaper. Still struggling with Brittany, she kissed him, asked him to get into his car seat, and tossed the paper onto the floor of the vehicle under Brittany's feet. Inside, in the "News in Brief" section on Page Six, was a wire service story:

U.S planes bomb al-Qaeda safe haven east of Baghdad

BAGHDAD, Dec 30 (Reuters) – U.S. warplanes bombed a suspected al Qaeda safe haven east of Baghdad, a U.S. Air Force spokesperson announced, the latest in a series of strikes aimed at disrupting the Sunni Islamist group's operations.

The operation, which began Saturday night and continued through Sunday, involved B-1 bombers and F/A-18 jets. It targeted Balad Ruz, an area 50 miles east of Baghdad.

"This particular mission targeted an area where al-Qaeda laid obstacles in the way of improvised explosive devices and took up safe haven at the same time. They also used the land to send fighters into Baghdad," the Air Force spokesperson said in the statement. Several houses booby-trapped with explosives were destroyed in the air strikes. Six U.S. soldiers were killed in Diyala province north of Baghdad at the start of the offensive when the house they were searching blew up and collapsed on top of them.

A U.S. military spokesperson said 117 militants, including 82 characterized as "high-value targets" were killed in the operation, including three fleeing in a vehicle that was destroyed by machine gun rounds from an F/A-18 jet fighter.

Upon returning from the store, Mary received a cell phone call from her mother as her parents traveled along Interstate 95. With the phone in the crook of her neck, she removed Brittany from the car seat and scooped up the newspaper, still in its wrapper, and deposited it in the garage recycling bin, never to be read. It dawned on Mary that she had forgotten the nacho chips, and she asked her mother to pick up a bag on the way.

CHAPTER 30

The January sun shone brightly on *Valley Forge* moored at Jebel Ali. In the company of containerships and other merchants, the carrier dominated the main UAE seaport south of Dubai. The piers were covered with loading cranes, warehouses, thousands of containers, and all manner of modern port equipment. The whole area hummed with constant activity. The carrier was there on a port visit to provide liberty to the crew in Dubai, the region's mega-trade center to the north. Sailors dressed in civilian slacks and collared shirts departed the ship via two brows, officer and enlisted, and stepped into busses for the 30-minute drive to the city.

Taking care to avoid their male squadronmates, Olive and Psycho got off the ship as soon as they could. Olive was fascinated by Dubai. She watched its spectacular skyline, a sharp gray outline against the white sky, loom up through the morning haze. In a dozen directions huge skyscrapers alternated with construction cranes.

When she had visited the city on the last cruise, she had marveled at its variety: the soaring buildings and opulent hotels with lush gardens; cars everywhere on the roads but the traffic did not choke them; locals in both traditional Arab garb and western clothing. So far, this visit was no different. The signs were in English and Arabic. A woman on the sidewalk, dressed in a black *abaya*, dragged a small child in shorts and a Mickey Mouse t-shirt behind her. Two Arab men held hands while they walked by an electronics store. A western man in a stylish business suit talked on his cell phone. To Olive it was a land of contrasts—ancient tribal customs blended with 21st century modernity.

And then there were the sights, sounds, and smells of money—everywhere. On every visit she found a new world-class building or complex to gawk at from inside the plush, air-conditioned motor coach.

Psycho was on her first trip to Dubai, the first time she had set foot in Asia. She either dozed during the bus ride or became otherwise lost on her cell phone. About halfway to Dubai, Olive noticed Psycho crack her eyes open, survey the scene, and close them again as she murmured, "I can't wait to get some sun."

Olive looked away. *Yeah, it will be nice to relax by the pool*, she thought. *I wonder when I should bring Psycho in on my little plan for this evening.*

An hour after they departed the ship, they were checked into the luxurious Regency Plaza Hotel in the Deira district of Dubai. Now fully awake, Psycho's eyed darted everywhere as they stepped into the lavish lobby. Indian bellhops carried their luggage past middle-aged Arab men in flowing dark robes—a sign of money—and past both Asian and western women in chic business suits and heels. The American officers, easily identified by their "liberty uniforms" of cotton slacks and polo shirts, couldn't take their eyes off the other women in the lobby. As they admired the hairstyles and makeup, they determined that's what they wanted to wear and *feel like* again—if only for their few days on liberty.

After checking into their $400-a-night room, they skipped lunch and went straight to the rooftop pool. *"Yes!"* Psycho said when she learned it was "Women Only." Less than 20 minutes after they checked in, they were lounging under the hot Arab sun in their swimsuits.

Olive smoothed sun block on her long legs. *Ahhh. I'm off the ship. I have a cool drink. I'm sitting by the pool.* Only 18 hours ago she had recovered aboard *Happy Valley* on a glorious full-moon night in the southern part of the Persian Gulf, the glittering lights of the coastline and diamonds-on-velvet lights of oil rigs and shipping scattered about the dark waters adding to the beauty. *Yep, I'm getting paid for this*, she thought.

She looked around her. Who among the dozen European women sunning themselves would suspect Olive and Psycho were combat-experienced fighter pilots? Through her oversized Dolce sunglasses Olive spied on the others, somewhat unnerved by an older woman with close-cropped blonde hair lying topless across the way, adding more rays to her leathery brown skin. Olive dismissed her. *Fine*, she thought. *Tomorrow she can deal with melanoma, and tomorrow I can deal with the ship. Up here she's a woman without a care in the world—like me.*

Psycho rolled over and unhooked her bikini top before dozing again. Olive just lay there sunning, her mind wandering.

"Hey, I need your help tonight."

"Wha…" Psycho answered. She was half asleep with her head turned away. After shifting slightly, she said, "What's the plan?"

"Karaoke. There's this place the air wing goes to every time. I'm going to sing."

Psycho spun her head toward Olive. "You sing? *Cool!* Are you good?"

"Okay. My mother pushed me—in all kinds of ways—but I can sing."

"Yes! What are you going to sing?"

"You'll see. I need you to help me get ready. I have a dress and some shoes. Tonight I want to be 'Kristin' for a change."

"You've been holding out on me!" Psycho boomed as she rolled over onto her back.

Horrified, Olive whispered, *"What are you doing?"* She was surprised the pool boy did not appear to notice Psycho's bare chest.

"Just giving the girls some sun. It will be good for them. When else can I this cruise?"

"But that guy over there!"

"The Filipino kid? He's gay. How else do you think he got this job? Look." Psycho lifted her arm, and the boy jumped up immediately and began to walk toward them. Stunned, Olive watched him approach. None of the other women seated around the pool seemed to take notice.

"Yes, miss!" The pool boy gave Psycho a huge smile.

"Hi." Psycho smiled back and said, "Could you please bring me a towel?"

"Yes, miss!" he responded as he smiled again and bowed.

Staring at his nametag, Psycho asked him, "What is your name?"

"Homobono, miss."

"Homo-bono… What a lovely name!"

"Yes, miss. Thank you, miss!"

The boy spun to retrieve a towel, and Psycho turned to Olive with a smug smile. "Ha," she giggled, "he has the perfect name, too. And he didn't look at my boobs once." Psycho then shimmied her back into the lounge chair for full effect.

Olive realized that, despite the fact she was older and a more experienced pilot than Psycho, up here in the glorified air of Dubai, her junior roommate was, in fact, the flight lead. She settled back into her own chair and thought, *Yes, Psycho will be the perfect "wingman" for tonight.*

CHAPTER 31

With a surgeon's steady hand Psycho placed the false eyelash on Olive's left eyelid. *"Ohhh,* girlfriend, they are gonna be creamin' their jeans when they see you up there."

Next to the bathroom counter covered in make-up and hair products, Psycho worked on her roommate while she sat on the toilet seat.

"And I *love* your dress. Where have you been hiding it?"

"In my locker...been there the whole time." Olive said, eyes closed while Psycho applied the finishing touches.

"You've been planning this..."

"Yes."

"Are the hajis going to freak when they see you in it?"

"No, I've seen local women wear minidresses here. So long as the shoulders are covered and there's not too much cleavage—not that I have to worry about that. Hey, why don't you go get yourself a minidress at the boutique downstairs."

"Nope, I'm the wingman tonight. This is *your* run through the target-rich environment of Carrier Air Wing Four. I have skinny jeans and a cami top, a jacket, and some heels to dress it up. The best outfit to kick in the balls of any dickhead who hits on me. But tonight I won't have to worry about that because they will be rolling in on *you.*"

"Hardly."

Psycho pulled a handful of Olive's hair into the curling iron. "Who are you going for tonight?"

Olive thought for a moment. "I don't know. Maybe Crusher, if he's there."

"Ohh, I'd love those big Marine Corps arms around me! Look, I'm going to find him and keep him occupied before you come out so that hobitch from the *Knights* doesn't get close to him. Don't even need a reason to kick *her* in her balls."

"He can have her."

"No! Listen, *fighter-goddess,* you told me to never give up in a guns situation. You haven't even turned at the merge, and you offer your throat to that skank. Here's what we do... I sweep the bandits ahead of you and then you

schwoopenhousen in for the kill. That dress, those shoes, *those legs*…you have a full weapons load out, and I want to see them expended!"

"Thanks, wingee."

"And this voice of yours…it's the siren song. You want me to spend the night in the lobby?"

"No!" Olive turned her head in protest. "*Oww!*" she then cried as Psycho's grasp pulled on her hair clamped to the iron.

"*Relax!* I know you are a nice southern girl. How are you going to snag him?"

"I don't know. We'll see what happens."

"Just unbutton an extra button and laugh at their stupid jokes. Works every time."

"That's not me, and I need every button I can."

"For *once*, Olive, can you not be an officer and a gentlewoman? Look, right now, there is no wash-khaki material within miles of us. You've got silk and lace tonight, and if you don't know how to use them with these guys 5,000 miles away from the Oceana groupie-sluts, you are *never* gonna get laid."

Olive stared ahead and said nothing in an awkward silence.

"I'm sorry," Psycho muttered. Unspoken between them was what they both knew. Olive was *plain*, and while the makeup and clothes helped at the margins, they had their limits. And her businesslike personality didn't help matters.

"It's okay. I'm going out of my comfort zone for tonight. I'm glad you are here to help me."

"Me, too!"

The officers turned some heads as they clicked through the hotel lobby. Psycho stuffed wads of dirhams into the hand of every bellman who held a door open for them. The bellmen figured the tall woman in the short dark dress was a famous movie star accompanied by her personal assistant. After the women stepped into a waiting cab, the bellmen argued among themselves in Hindi as to who she was.

It was a cool but pleasant evening in Dubai as the cab departed the hotel and entered the wide boulevard. "The Highlander my good man! How many doo-dahs?" Psycho asked the driver.

"Thirty-five dirham," the Pakistani driver replied.

"Thirty-five!" Psycho exploded. "No, no, twenty."

"No, no! Thirty-five, but for pretty ladies, thirty."

"Thank you, but do you know who this is? Ms. Jolie is going to be upset and may not make her next movie here. Twenty-five," Psycho said as she playfully flinched from Olive's jab to her side.

The driver inspected Olive through the rearview mirror as he navigated the traffic through the canyon of tall buildings. His dark eyes burned a hole in hers before she turned away.

"Twenty-five and Ms. Jolie gives a big tip if you get us there in 10 minutes." Psycho could not be stopped, and was picking up the bargaining thing quite well. Olive rolled her eyes.

"Okay, okay. Twenty-five and big tip, I get you there safe and fast."

"Thank you, sir," Psycho replied. She then turned to Olive and added, "Ms. Jolie, everything will be fine ma'am, and you won't have to worry your pretty little citizen-of-the-world head." Psycho was having too much fun to stop.

"Would you shut up?" Olive muttered as she suppressed a smile.

"I have been to the United States," the driver said suddenly. The women froze.

"Where?" Olive asked, sensing the jig was up and attempting to salvage what little dignity she could.

"Orlando. Disney World. I took my wife and son. Very nice place."

The women did not know what to say. Olive wondered how a third-world cabbie could afford that, and even converse with them in English. Maybe he was pulling *their* legs.

"Disney World *is* very nice," Olive volunteered.

"I've never been," Psycho added wistfully.

Minutes later they pulled up to the Highlander nightclub and Psycho put two 20 dirham bills in the driver's hand, the promised big tip for their Ugly American conduct. When she turned toward the entrance, Olive spotted some air wing guys walking up to the door.

"*Hide me!*" she ordered Psycho under her breath.

"Here," Psycho said as she pulled her coat up and wrapped it around herself and Olive. "Guys see two women huddling under a coat in front of a Middle Eastern nightspot, and they don't give it a second thought."

Once the men disappeared inside, they entered and Olive took the lead, moving fast to another hiding spot near the stage, not making eye contact with

any of the Americans there. A favorite watering hole for Brit expats and American sailors on liberty, the Highlander boasted wood paneling, velvet seating, Fosters beer and flashing lights. A disco ball hung over the stage. A Filipino ensemble, three young men with guitars and a keyboard accompanied by two women singing and swaying in tube tops, performed a remarkably accurate "Dancing Queen" on the cramped stage.

Dozens of *Happy Valley* aviators, identified by their clean-cut appearance and American denim, dominated the tables and dance floor. Most of them nursed a Fosters bottle. None, however, were dressed as glamorously as Olive was. If she did not stay out of sight, she would be noticed before she wanted to be, but not as Olive. *No one* would think that the *Amazon* with wild, dark locks in the black minidress was Lieutenant "Olive" Teel from VFA-64.

Still hiding near the stage, Olive and Psycho surveyed the crowd. "Tally-ho on Crusher, left eleven," Psycho said. "Good, there's *slut-bitch* working a gaggle of *Rickshaws* over there."

Olive then spotted a group of *Ravens*: Sponge Bob, Little Nicky, Blade *and* Crusher were talking with some marines. Suddenly, a group of three tall young women entered, flowing blonde hair, sleek outfits...they were clearly not from the ship. The air wing guys locked on immediately. This was big game.

"Oh, oh. Brit flight attendants. Or Aussies," Olive surmised. Turning to Psycho she briefed her wingman." Okay, *wing-girl*. Get over to Crusher and keep his attention away from those flying baristas while I get on stage. After I'm done, meet me back here. We will then bolt to a pub I know downtown, one with leather, scotch, and Brit guys."

"Why? This is..."

"Never leave your wingman, girlie. Besides, I want to leave *him* wanting more, and I'm not going to be pawed and ogled by the rest of these assholes all night. Trust me on this one."

"Okay, fine, I've got your 6 o'clock," Psycho said. She inspected Olive. "Hey, you look *incredible* and your legs go on *forever!*"

"Let's hope he's a leg guy," Olive deadpanned as she nervously assessed the performers on stage.

"They *all* will be after they see you." Touching Olive's arm, Psycho added, "Have fun with this, Okay?"

"Okay, now go." As Olive shooed Psycho away, she took a moment to get into full combat mode. She had planned this "coming out" for months: the outfit, the song, the Highlander, the right moment on the stage. Now, even though she tottered a bit on her fresh-out-of-the-box stilettos, she was ready.

And despite the pounding adrenalin, she felt a calm confidence spread through her.

She *did* look good. If only Camille could see this... The thought of her mother reminded Olive of Camille's recital stage coaching tips: *One foot in front of the other, suck in your tummy, shoulders back, chin up.* Never forgetting she was an officer 24/7/365, Olive checked her outfit again and was satisfied it did not cross the line of *too* much.

After speaking to a stagehand, Olive went back to observing the crowd. Three JOs from the *Spartans* took the stage to perform a Black Eyed Peas favorite. By playing with her hair and laughing at whatever he said, Psycho had successfully cornered Crusher. The flight attendants were completely surrounded by air wing JOs and were not a factor. *Perfect.*

After a momentary lull, the DJ's Filipino accent boomed over the speakers. "An' now, ladies and gem'men, please welcome, *Miss Kristin!*"

Smile! Olive thought again of her mother as she took the first step.

Olive walked up and tried to gauge the hushed crowd but could not with the blinding and hot spotlight on her, hearing the whispers as the air wing tried to figure out who this creature *was.* Unfazed, she grabbed the microphone.

CHAPTER 32

The following day Wilson and the others who had remained behind for duty departed the ship and headed to the rented squadron hotel room, the *admin*, which the first wave of *Raven* officers had set up the day before. Wilson enjoyed Dubai, but even with this first Gulf port call of the deployment, he'd been there and done that. Dubai would be here for several more nights before they got underway again, and, no doubt, for several more visits this cruise.

Once off the bus, he and Dutch took a cab to the hotel, admired two Asian women employees in fashionable business suits in the lobby, took an elevator to the 15th floor and found their way to the *admin*. This room, which they had each chipped in for during the port visit, served as a base from which the officers could relax, explore Dubai and, in many cases, spend the night after an evening on the town. When they entered the room, a familiar sight, no matter where the *Ravens* set up shop, met their eyes.

Sleeping bodies were sprawled across couches and chairs. Some still wore clothes from the night before; one, with his head back and mouth agape, slept on a chair wearing nothing but boxers; and yet another had rolled up in a ball under the desk and covered himself with a sheet stripped from the bed. At first, Wilson couldn't place the sheet-covered body but soon identified him as Blade.

Empty Fosters beer cans littered the room. Pieces of open luggage and other detritus from the previous night's activity were strewn about or heaped up on the floor. Room service items cluttered every furniture surface. The curtain to the sliding glass door was open, and sunlight streamed into all corners of the room except into the brains of the "dead bodies" sleeping it off. The squadron drinking flag with the *Raven* emblem was still flying in proud defiance above them, despite being held aloft by only two of three rings.

Wilson and Dutch walked into the adjoining bedroom. Wilson identified five bodies in the darkened room, two each on the double beds and one on the floor under a blanket. Everything smelled of beer. One of Wilson's sleeping squadronmates stirred to see who was there. It was Sponge Bob. "Hi, OPSO," he croaked.

Dutch was quick to roll in on his hungover LSO trainee. "Sponge, did we get a little *large* last night?"

"Yeeesssss..." he groaned.

"And your impression of Dubai?"

"Needs more water," Sponge said, rolling over and hoping Dutch would go away.

"No, *you* need more water. Did you take your aspirin?"

"Noooo."

"Man, I told you to take a preemptive aspirin and hydrate. You never listen."

"Yes, Dad," came the muffled reply from Sponge, face down in his pillow.

One of the "dead bodies" spoke up from the other bed. "Dutch, shut the fuck up or leave, or both." It was Stretch.

"Paddles, is that *you?*" Dutch replied, feigning hurt. "I'm a brother, know the secret handshake, two mike clicks on the ball and all that." Dutch relished any attention, and, despite his low tone, his voice boomed throughout the suite.

"But today you're a dick," Stretch answered.

Sponge added, "*Today* he's a dick?"

"LSO, dick, Dutch, all the same thing." Clam spoke from under a bedspread.

"Hi, Admin O!" Dutch replied with an exaggerated cheer. "XO was just asking for you before we left the ship. I'm sure there's a dental readiness report that AIRLANT needs right away, or tomorrow's plan of the day to be chopped by you. 'Where's Lieutenant Commander Morningstar? Where's Lieutenant Commander Morningstar?'"

"Eat me, Dutch," Clam mumbled, motionless under the bedspread.

"Glad to see you doing so well, sir! And it's a beautiful day in this neighborhood—this exotic desert country! Say, any of you guys wanna get up and *drink?*"

In unison, and with their heads pounding, the *Raven* officers pummeled him with obscenities and ordered him to leave. Wilson took it all in with a knowing smile. Same morning-after scene, different port.

As Wilson went back to the living room, the door of the *admin* opened. Weed entered, saw Wilson, and said, "My brother, how're things *bak sheep?*"

"Fine, where's the skipper?" Wilson asked.

"CAG rounded up all the COs and XOs to play golf at Dubai Creek. They left at eight...Cajun was *huge* last night, booming till 0400. I don't know how he does it."

"XO was still aboard when we left. Where were you guys last night?"

"The Highlander, and it was amazing. The whole air wing was there." Now, from across the room, voices of the veterans from the previous evening's activities, joined in.

"They had this Filipino karaoke band with this *smokin'* hot lead singer chick. They were real good, and the place was rockin'," Blade said as he got up from the floor. "Then they opened it up for volunteers, and Killer, Hondo, and Wanda from the *Spartans* took the stage and did *Pump It*. They were damn good. Killer had the rhyme down, and Wanda did this dead-on Fergie impersonation. Even the Filipino chick was impressed."

Little Nicky took over. "Then from out of nowhere comes Olive. She's in this black minidress with stiletto heels, hair flowing, makeup. I mean, she looks *good*—for *Olive*. We'd been there for hours, but hadn't seen her all night. Then she takes the stage and does *Zombie*. Flip, I'm tellin' ya, nobody moved. We were captivated. She can sing, and she knew how to move on stage. *Incredible*."

Prince Charming rolled over and added, "She belted it, especially that last part. You would have sworn it was off the CD."

Nicky continued. "She finishes, and the place goes *nuts*. I mean *our Olive* owned that place, and now the Filipino girl thinks she's out of a job."

"Where has she been keeping this?" Wilson chuckled.

"That's what the CO said," Nicky replied. "So we're yelling at the *Spartans*, 'You got served!' And we're trying to find Olive, and she disappeared. Gone."

"Where'd she go?"

"Dunno. I guess back to her *admin*...She and Psycho went in on a cathouse someplace."

"I knew under that zoombag and hair bun was a hammer," Dutch chimed in.

"Still a head case though," someone shouted from the other room.

CHAPTER 33

Wilson slid into the hotel pool with Dutch and Nttty. They had all gone shopping that morning for polo shirts and CDs and now had a plan to relax in the company of friends. They headed toward the swim-up bar, ordered a Fosters and surveyed the scene. Several groups of air wing officers were lounging about, some playing full contact water basketball. The first wave of *Ravens* was back in the fight.

Wilson sipped on his beer at the shaded bar, truly enjoying the warm water that covered him from the waist down. He was seated next to two *Buccaneer* department heads, Gramps, their maintenance officer, and Rip, the administrative officer. The Filipino bartender eyed Wilson warily, but he ignored it.

"Wonder what the poor people are doing today," Gramps thought out loud as the three lieutenant commanders surveyed the pool scene. Nttty had made his way to the other side of the pool to make friends with two bikini-clad flight attendants, while Dutch hung on the edge in an effort to be noticed by them.

"They have the duty *bak sheep*," Rip answered as he pulled on his beer.

Wilson had gotten used to the fact that when he was surrounded by pilots, the conversation always came back to flying. He hardly noticed that, even in this resort setting where they wanted to decompress from shipboard life, they couldn't help talking about it.

"Been anyplace interesting lately?" Rip asked Wilson.

"Lots of stuff in Diyala and Salman Pak. Haven't been to Mosul yet. How about you?"

"Had an interesting hop in Al-Amarrah the other night. We were working with a Shadow UAV along the river and found some guys planting an IED on the road north of town. The JTAC talked us on the target and we each dropped a LGB. We were watching them dig on our FLIRs...oblivious... diggin' all the way till impact." Rip shook his head in wonder. "Can't believe they didn't hear us."

"I had a hilarious hop up around Mosul last week." Gramps added, while looking at Wilson. "It involved your XO."

"Oh, great!" Wilson exhaled in mock embarrassment. He looked forward to hearing the story, but he still cringed at the thought.

Keeping his voice low, the *Buccaneer* pilot began. "Me and Dog checked in with *War Eagle*, a JTAC we worked with a few weeks ago who was really good, so I was looking forward to workin' with him again. We switched up the freq' and I hear *War Eagle* talkin' with Saint.

"'Shotgun flight, acknowledge nine-line.'

"'Can you clarify the target?' Saint asks.

"*War Eagle* gives him the lat/long and says, 'Target is open field west of the hamlet.'

"Saint says, 'Still not clear on the target. All I see is a field.'

"*War Eagle* wants a bomb to go off on the field because his colonel is telling the hajis that, as colonel, he can make one go boom on command. *War Eagle* imagines the Army colonel looking over his shoulder as he talks with the locals. 'Now, I will summon *fire* from the *heavens*...uh, Sergeant, bomb...now!'

"Saint repeats, 'There is nothing in the field.'

"*War Eagle* says, 'I need a bomb in the field NOW.'

"'Where in the field? What quadrant?'

"*War Eagle* is cool, and says, 'Anywhere in the field you want. Go ahead. Just need a bomb in the field ASAP. You're cleared hot. Come on in.'

"Saint, still pressing, asks, 'What's in the field? Troops in the open?'

"*War Eagle* grabs the lifeline Saint has offered and says, 'Yes, sir, troops in the open. Yeah, we're in contact with a whole *division* of al-Qaeda. Cleared hot.'

"'I don't see any troops on my FLIR,' Saint counters.

"*War Eagle*, his ass now gettin' ripped by his colonel, says, 'Shotgun, do you have the field west of the village, south of the tree line bordered by a north/south road to the west?'

"'Affirm,' Saint says.

"'Roger, *Shotgun*, bomb that field with any weapon in any delivery. You are cleared hot.'

"I mean, I take a look at Dog on my wing and he's got his mask off he's cracking up so bad. I've never seen him laugh that hard." Gramps was on a roll.

"'Roger, *War Eagle*... What *crop* is in the field?'

"And *War Eagle* loses it! 'SIR - just bomb the fuckin' field! NOW!'"

Gramps realized his voice was carrying too far and too loud. He looked around him with a half-apology on his face as he reduced his howls to a snicker. Rip tried to suppress his laughter, but failed miserably, Wilson noticed the bartender looked at them with a disapproving frown. *What's his problem?* he thought. *Or is it just me?*

"Saint is upset and says, 'Hey, soldier, watch the language on the radio. Do you *know* who this is?'

"*War Eagle* swallows it and says, 'Sorry, sir, it's a soybean field.'

"There's a pause, and then this gruff voice comes on and says, '*Shotgun* flight, this is Colonel Johnson of the 2nd battalion, 16th Infantry, 1st Division' … I dunno … *Royal Armored Fusiliers*, whatever. 'If you fast movers can put a weapon on the field we've requested, do it!'

" 'Roger, sir,' says Saint.

" '*Much obliged*,' the colonel responds, his voice dripping with sarcasm."

Rip was wracked by convulsive laughter, and his eyes were glassy slits. Wilson had to grab him to keep him from falling off his stool. Wilson had gamely smiled through the embarrassment his XO had caused the squadron, but, for the most part, he just looked down and shook his head.

Rip was still laughing. "Was he a radio colonel or full bird?"

"He sounded like the real deal to me—he sounded like fuckin' Patton!" Gramps' answer elicited another roar from Rip.

"There's one thing I want to know. Did he ever hit the field?" Wilson asked.

"Oh, yeah," Gramps said, as he finished the story. "He drops a LGB right in the *middle* of the field."

"*War Eagle* says, 'Good hit, sir.'

" 'Roger, bomb impact assessment please?' Saint asks, and *War Eagle* tells him 100 over 100, anything to get him out of there!"

"How do you paint a soybean field on the side of a jet?" Rip asked, with a chuckle. He was rewarded with a guffaw from Gramps.

Wilson groaned and looked across the pool. The flight attendants were now surrounded by a gaggle of *Raven* pilots who had tired of "basketball." He was grateful Gramps hadn't told the story with the JOs around, but by now, no doubt, the details of this flight had made it to the bunkroom. He made a mental note to find out who the wingman was for the flight when he got back to the ship.

"Your boys bagged a few over there," Gramps said as he looked at the girls across the pool.

Wilson nodded. "In the process. Looks like it will be another big night at the Highlander."

CHAPTER 34

One week later, Wilson returned from a night hop, deposited his flight gear in the paraloft, and plopped down in his ready room seat to watch the PLAT recovery of the last event. The CO was flying with Blade on an intercept hop against the *Spartans*, and Weed was out doing a night sea surface search around the strike group. Guido was at the duty desk watching "The Office" on the ship's closed-circuit TV.

A copy of *Navy Times* was on the skipper's footstool. Wilson picked it up and thumbed through the pages: articles about pay raises, new uniform standards, the usual stuff. He then came across a familiar section highlighted with photos of American personnel who had lost their lives in recent weeks in Iraq and Afghanistan. Most of the time the photos were formal poses, but he often found a boot camp photo of a 19-year-old Marine in dress uniform or a candid shot of a soldier. On occasion he came across a photo of a young woman, a girl really, or a senior officer. They were almost always young—too young.

When he scanned the photos in this issue, he found the photo of an Army major. Age 35. His own age. He wondered if the major had a family at home. Chances are he did.

The photo next to the major was of a young man in his early 20s. Clean shaven and wearing cammies, he had big, dark eyes, a full mouth and a square jawline. Just under the cap Wilson could make out bushy eyebrows. Something caused Wilson to dwell on this soldier. He looked at the name: Spec. Donnie Anderson.

He studied the photo again. Anderson. *Anderson. Andy, let's go! Was Andy short for Anderson? Was this "Bowser" from Balad Ruz?* He stared at the photo of the fallen soldier. No unit, no hometown. *Specialist? What the hell is that? Are JTACs Specialists? Balad Ruz was three weeks ago—would the* Times *publish a photo so soon, even if he lost his life the day after we worked with him?*

Driven by the need to know, Wilson got up and logged on to the classified computer at the back of the ready room. He would contact the Air Wing rep on the CAOC staff in Doha, a naval flight officer on temporary duty from the *Spartans*.

Subject: JTAC track down
  Hey, Biscuit, Flip.
  I was working with a JTAC around Balad Ruz on New Year's Eve; his call sign is "Bowser." We were Nail 41 flight that day. Don't know what unit he's with but he did a good job and other guys in the wing have talked about him. Said he's from Hardeeville, South Carolina. He may have rotated home but I want to send him an attaboy through his CO. Can you ask the JTAC guys there to track him down; name, unit and contact info? Thanks man.
  It's dark out here, you aren't missing anything. They have cold beer where you're at?
  Thanks again,
  Flip

He hit send and went back to his seat to watch the recovery. An hour later, after the uneventful recoveries of his squadronmates, he returned to the computer to check for an answer from Biscuit. One was waiting for him.

Subject: RE: JTAC track down
  Flip, we tracked him down but bad news. "Bowser" was hit and killed two days after your hop with him. He entered a booby-trapped house in Balad Ruz after some of his buddies were hit inside. The hajis waited for rescuers to enter before they set off the bigger charge.
  Apparently "Bowser" was the first to go to their aid. The house collapsed and he was killed. The only one though...another guy lost a foot.
  His name was Spec. Donnie Anderson and he was from Hardeeville, SC. He was 20. He was a good JTAC; had a great mission effectiveness record.
  Sorry, Flip,
  Biscuit

Wilson felt his body going numb as he stared at the screen. *Bowser*—Specialist Anderson—was 20 years old, just days from going home to watch the playoffs. He was so excited to be going home to watch football "live," as well as to leave that hellhole town. Wilson thought of Bowser's photo in *Navy Times*: the square jaw, the distinctive features. *Such a good-looking guy. Did he have a wife or girl-friend? Did he ever get to experience the love of a woman?* he wondered. *Whatever he experienced, his life was too short.* Wilson's throat tightened, and he swallowed hard.

That night in his rack Wilson's mind drifted back to *Bowser* in Balad Ruz. *Just a kid. Twenty!* Though they had never met, fate had brought them together at a moment in time to fight a common enemy. Wilson wondered, *Why am I alive and why is Bowser dead? Why is any of that fair? So young, so much to live for...*

In the darkness, he was surprised by a tear that escaped his left eye and dampened the pillow.

CHAPTER 35

"Flip, XO wants to see you in his stateroom."

Wilson looked up at Olive. She waited behind the duty desk, her face as expressionless as usual, for his acknowledgement. "Thanks. Did he say what it's about?" Wilson asked.

"No, sir."

Wilson placed the message board on his chair and walked to the sink with his coffee cup. He gave it a quick rinse it and hung it on the wooden peg above the sink that said "OPSO." In place, the cup blended in with all the others emblazoned with *Raven* logos and individual call signs.

Stepping out of the ready room and into the starboard passageway, he strode toward the XO's stateroom up forward. He made his way, as if on autopilot, past the knee-knockers and through the sailors inspecting damage control gear, his mind trying to figure out what the XO wanted. Halfway there he realized it was pointless.

Commander Patrick's stateroom was aft of the Cat 1 jet blast deflector on the starboard side. Next to him was the stateroom of the Spartan's XO. Commanders bunked alone in individual staterooms on the O-3 level, but Wilson disliked this part of the ship. The XOs lived on a very public passageway and right under the deafening catapult. During launch operations, conversation in the staterooms was impossible. Quiet is a relative term on a carrier, of course, but he liked his O-2 level quarters. He would certainly miss them if he stayed in and was promoted to squadron command.

Unlike other squadron stateroom doors, the XO's door was bare—except for a placard that read KNOCK TWICE THEN ENTER. Wilson rapped twice, paused, and opened the door. He stepped inside and said, "Yes, sir."

Saint sat sideways at his desk, scribbling in an open notebook on his lap. He wore his usual khaki uniform with full ribbons, the only officer aboard to do so. Without looking up, he motioned to the couch and said, "Mister Wilson, good morning. Please have a seat." Wilson did as he was told and took a place in the middle of the couch with both feet on the floor, hands folded.

Saint pored over the notebook and said nothing, his familiar and unnerving tactic. Wilson looked around the room for anything new, any window into the

soul of his executive officer. The room was not only immaculate, but devoid of personal effects, as if he had just moved in yesterday. The television displayed the Ship's Inertial Navigation System (SINS) screen, a series of numbers showing the ship's position, course and speed. His desk held nothing but a plain coffee cup that stored pens and pencils. On a hook near the sink hung the XO's blue bathrobe, emblazoned with a gold naval academy crest. The robe was the only item of sentiment Wilson could find.

"Mister Wilson, I'm looking at the Navy Relief Society contributions by department. The Administrative and Safety Departments are at 100 percent, Maintenance is 77 percent, and the Operations Department is 50 percent. The squadron goal I set last fall was 100 percent for all departments. Do you recall my discussion on this at an AOM?" The XO's voice was calm and measured.

"Yes, sir."

"Then why is the Operations Department so deficient in meeting this squadron goal?" For the first time Saint lifted his eyes to look directly at Wilson. He waited for an answer.

Wilson kept his eyes on his executive officer. "Sir, may I ask who has not contributed yet?" He regretted adding the word *yet*.

"Certainly, and I like your modifier 'yet.' Let's see… Airman Ayala and Petty Officer First Class Johnson. Your other two sailors made modest contributions."

He once again waited for Wilson to answer.

"I have no excuses, sir. I will ask Ayala and YN1 Johnson about it."

"Very well…I look forward to your answer after lunch." Saint made a mark on the notebook spreadsheet.

"Sir, Ayala is on night check and doesn't report 'til 1830. I'll…"

Saint jerked his head up, eyes wide under his thin eyebrows. With his mouth slightly open, he held Wilson's gaze for several seconds. "I look *forward*… to your answer after lunch," he responded with a cold stare, struggling to keep his fury in check.

"Yes, sir," Wilson said meekly, his eyes locked on Saint.

"Very well," Saint replied, the fire gone from his face as fast as it had appeared. Drawing a deep breath, he then launched into a new subject.

"You are leaving the squadron soon. Why don't you have orders?"

"I'm still working with the detailer, sir."

"What does he tell you?" Saint asked, with a hint of a smile.

"Washington, War College, Joint staff duty—the usual career path." Wilson lowered his defenses a bit.

"The CO tells me you are dragging your heels. What do you want?"

Wilson realized his answer had to be the truth.

"I'd like to stay in the Norfolk area. My family needs a break."

"Yes, the family. Isn't it always so... You have four kids?"

"Two, sir."

"Two. Are they young?"

"They are," Wilson responded, his defenses going back up. To know the answers to these questions, Saint only needed to take a basic interest in his people.

Saint looked off at the bulkhead in thought. He turned back to Wilson. "Are you going to resign?"

Wilson fought to remain calm. "No, sir." The answer was technically true, but he had been giving the idea a lot of thought lately.

"Mr. Wilson, despite your many years of service and family sacrifice, the Navy needs fine young black officers like you to stay for a career."

So there it is, thought Wilson, Saint's motivation for this talk. Officer retention figures, especially minority officer retention figures, drew great scrutiny in Washington. Wilson saw right through it...*Saint doesn't care about me as a person. I am just one of his statistics. Can't have a minority officer resign under his watch.*

"XO, does the Navy want me, an officer who happens to be black, to command a squadron, or an air wing...or a ship?"

Saint hesitated for a second and looked down, then recovered. "Yes, of course, but you won't get there if you continue to underperform or if you fail to meet established squadron goals. You can't do that to get to the next level. In addition, you must obtain every possible qualification. There are lots of officers with records like yours who didn't screen for command last year. You can't just coast along, depending on..."

"On what, sir?" Wilson asked, feigning ignorance.

Saint knew he was losing control. "To screen these days you have to go the extra yard."

"XO, I have every qualification available to me in this squadron—from functional check flight pilot to Strike Fighter Tactics Instructor. In fact, I have more qualifications than you and the CO, sir. There's no syllabus training hop I can't instruct, much less fly. What further qualifications do I lack?"

"We've established that your ground job performance needs significant improvement, that you are not meeting squadron goals." Saint was beginning to lose his temper.

"Yes, sir, I've not met the personal goal you set for the squadron, and I'll address that by encouraging my sailors to contribute something. I will do every-

thing short of *compelling* them to contribute to the Navy Relief Society. Will do, sir. But I would still like to know…. Is there a Navy-wide performance standard I'm not meeting? One that directly affects the combat readiness of this deployed strike fighter squadron?"

"Mr. Wilson, I will remind you to watch your tone."

"A little too uppity, sir?"

"Dammit, Wilson!" Saint thundered, as he rose to his feet. "Get the hell out!"

Wilson, also enraged, sprang to his feet and took a step toward the senior pilot, who flinched ever so slightly. "XO, I'm a naval officer and *Hornet* pilot who happens to be black. Nobody *gave* my wings to me. I earned them myself. The airplane does not care who's flying it, male, female, black or white. The Navy does not need quotas. It needs warriors to stay for command, and I am a warrior. If I do resign, this meeting will feature prominently in my letter."

"DISMISSED!" Saint roared back, inches from Wilson's nose. Wilson stepped to the door, and as he passed through, Saint added, "And take that chip on your shoulder with you!"

Wilson closed the door with a firm grip. When he turned to head forward, he met the eyes of the Spartan's XO who had opened his door half expecting to break up a fight. Trembling with anger, Wilson passed Dutch without acknowledging he was there. "Hey, Flip," said Dutch and stopped to watch his department head bound forward. Finally, Wilson realized someone had addressed him. He stopped and turned to see a bewildered Dutch about five frames back. He then saw Saint appear from his athwartship passageway. Their eyes met, and Wilson spun for his stateroom. Dutch looked at Wilson and then at his XO. *What just happened?* he wondered.

Wilson burst into his stateroom to find Weed typing on a laptop. "Kimo sabe," Weed greeted him, without taking his eyes off the screen. When Wilson answered only by yanking open a drawer, Weed knew something was wrong. "What happened?"

Wilson unzipped his flight suit and worked open the laces of his boots. "Oh, just a come-around with the XO. Seems my department's Navy Relief numbers are short of the squadron goal."

"Bummer. Should we call a stand-down to address the problem?"

"Yes, we should," Wilson answered. "Your department is only at 77 percent, but the OPS department is making you look good. We're last at 50. Admin is

at 100 and the one-person Safety Department is also at 100. We're both on his shit list, but at least you aren't last." Wilson slipped out of his flight suit and put on his black gym shorts.

"Thanks for the heads up and for making me look good. What else?"

Wilson bent over to tie one of his sneakers. "Well, we then had a counseling session. Seems the Navy needs black officers to stay, which it does. What I got from Saint, though, was that he doesn't particularly care for black *commanding* officers, but he wants me to 'please stay' for the retention numbers." Wilson pulled the laces tight.

Weed looked at Wilson as he worked the other shoe. "I may have over-stepped," Wilson added.

"Whad'ya mean? He throw you out of the room?"

"Yes."

"Oh..."

"I will not be placed in a box!" Wilson continued, still furious. "I'm a Navy fighter pilot. I am not a *black* Navy fighter pilot. I've only had to deal with two guys in my whole career who judged me for my color. You know, one guy in flight school, and now the XO."

"Master Chief Morgan?" Weed added.

"Oh, yeah, okay. Three guys in 13 years."

"Not a bad track record."

"Concur! The Navy's been great to me every step of the way, and I've had it a lot easier than my dad did in his day, with the race riots and everything else. At least here you get promoted on merit. You work hard, play by the rules, and compete. I love that."

"Why don't more African Americans come through the front door?"

"*Hell if I know!* I'm tellin' 'em all the time! I go to friggin' Norfolk State, family gatherings. I'm spreadin' the word, tellin' the homeboys they got nothin' on my posse. Brothers are joining and they have bright futures, but not many go air."

"Why're you so fuckin' pissed off?"

Wilson stopped and looked at Weed, who was giving him a wry smile. *Weed is right. I am furious—but why?* Wilson already knew, everyone knew, the XO was an arrogant bastard...and he had still let him get under his skin, especially with the "chip on your shoulder" crack. Was he angry that Saint treated him like a number, a quota, instead of a key member of the squadron, even a person? Did that surprise him? Was he angry that it did? Was he angry with the Navy and the sacrifices it demanded of Mary? He looked forward to his run so he could think.

Weed then added a typical Weed comment. "It could be worse, you know. If you were a woman, the XO could be after you!"

Shaking his head in disgust, Wilson turned for the door. "Man, you are one sick puppy!"

"I'm thinking Tyra Banks with a big—ah—Adam's apple."

"I'm outta here," Wilson said, still smiling in spite of himself.

"Where ya goin'?" Weed asked.

"Topside for a run."

"It's 30 knots up there."

"Perfect," Wilson replied.

Chapter 36

"Lead's air speed, angels on the left." Prince transmitted from a mile abeam.

"Two's speed 'n' angels on the right," Wilson replied.

"Take a cut away," Prince ordered.

"Two," Wilson acknowledged.

With that, both pilots pushed the throttles to military and banked away from each other for the last of three engagements they had briefed for this good deal flight, a 1v1 air combat maneuvering training sortie. This was Wilson's favorite part of the hop: the neutral setup where both aircraft extend away from each other to build separation and then, on signal, turn back toward one another. The track the airplanes flew on this maneuver resembled a butterfly wing, hence the name, "butterfly set."

Wilson steadied out on a heading of 210 and scribbled some notes on his kneeboard card, with a drawing of a God's-eye picture of the two aircraft heading 180, and taking cuts away from each other. He drew a circle to depict the sun ahead of them and wrote the number "60" to indicate 60 degrees up.

Prince was leading because he needed the hop for his flight-lead-under-training syllabus. After 15 months in the squadron, it was time for Prince to become a *section leader*, the flight lead of two aircraft. Wilson was disappointed with Prince's performance on this qualification flight. It began with the brief, when Prince did not know the ship had moved south during the night. His perfunctory preflight briefing was nothing more than satisfactory, and his performance on this flight, so far, was *unsatisfactory*.

In both his offensive and defensive setups Prince had mismanaged his air speed and lift vector. In the first, Prince allowed Wilson to escape when he began the engagement behind him in a firing position. In the next setup, when beginning from a defensive position, Prince was unable to shake Wilson from shooting him with a tracking guns shot. Although Wilson possessed 2,000 more FA-18 hours than Prince, and was a *TOPGUN* graduate, he was upset. *"C'mon, Prince, pull!"* he had muttered as Prince arced above him and let up on the pressure. Wilson liked to win an engagement as much as anyone, but it was as if Prince had been just going through the motions, not challenging Wilson or

himself. The two pilots were not friends and there was a clear superior/subordinate relationship, but as Operations Officer Wilson wanted and *needed* Prince to qualify as section lead to allow more flight scheduling options. After the last fight, as they climbed to altitude, Wilson had radioed a simple comment to him on how to improve his lift-vector placement. Prince had answered with a glum *"Roger."*

An overnight cold front had left behind a gorgeous winter sky, clear and crisp, and the visibility was unlimited from horizon to horizon, rare anytime in the Gulf. From 18,000 feet, Wilson had a clear view of the Saudi coast, with Dhahran off his nose and Bahrain just to the left. Offshore were numerous oil rigs, and the two dominant colors were the blue of the Gulf and the beige of the Arabian land mass. He could see the frontal clouds far to the east over Iran. Wilson loved moments like this: high over the water in a single-seat jet with a sparring partner to bump heads with and log some great training. He remembered how a friend once described air combat training: *the sport of kings.*

Even if Prince would not give him a good fight, Wilson was ready...no, *eager...* to kick his ass if he again ignored his advice. *No holds barred, full up air combat maneuvering*, he thought. *This day is too perfect and the fuel too short to waste.* Brimming with anticipation, he looked at Prince over his left shoulder some three miles away.

Thirty seconds later Prince broke the silence. "Turnin' in, tapes on, fight's on."

At the *"f"* in "fight's on," Wilson slammed the throttles to afterburner and snapped the *Hornet* over on the left wing in one motion, pulling hard across the horizon in a slightly nose-low energy sustaining pull. "Tapes on, fight's on," he responded.

Keeping sight of Prince through the top of his canopy, Wilson pulled hard across the horizon and put the "dot" of Prince's airplane in the middle of the HUD. The radar locked on and formed a box around the jet 2.5 miles away. Wilson pulled tighter and was on the inside position as they accelerated to the merge. The aircraft were now pointed at each other with air speed building to over 900 knots of closure. By the geometry, Wilson could see a right-to-right pass forming as they approached like knights in a jousting match.

"Right-to-right," Prince radioed.

"Right-to-right," Wilson responded, as he pulled the throttles out of burner.

A 1v1 fight with a modern forward-quarter missile threat aircraft like the *Hornet* calls for a one-circle or *pressure* fight to stay close and deny the opponent the forward quarter missile, often a heat-seeker like the *Sidewinder*. In

like-performing aircraft the initial move inside was vital to gain angles that allowed one to position the opponent out in front of the canopy, or even to take a gun shot if one presented itself. Such fights often degenerated into slow-speed scissors, or "knife fights," as the aircraft kept close. They also often ended up with both aircraft groveling at slow speed just above the 5,000-foot "hard deck," which simulated the ground. Wilson knew he had to pressure Prince, and noted the sun up and to the right. If he pulled hard across Prince's tail and into the oblique, after 180 degrees of turn he could be inside his turning circle and lost in the sun above him, able to pounce once Prince lost sight. Wilson decided on this strategy in an instant. In essence, he would be toying with Prince instead of pulling hard into him and going for the jugular.

As they drew closer, Prince drifted right on Wilson's windscreen. The norm was to pass close aboard, 500 feet, but Prince did not correct this drift. The added distance meant *turning room* for the pilot who was willing to "bite" and take advantage of an early turn to get angles, and Wilson wasn't going to pass up free angles. *You give me room, I'm gonna take it,* he thought. With Prince's *Hornet* growing and lateral separation building greater than 500 feet, Wilson took a sharp breath—*Hookkk!*—while tightening his muscles, relit the burner cans and pulled hard into Prince.

Wilson snatched the jet up and to the right at the instant a force of 6.5 times his body weight pushed and squeezed every square inch of him. At the same time, a cloud of white condensation formed on top of the aircraft as he flew into and above Prince's flight path. Straining to keep sight of Prince over his right shoulder, he sensed the horizon elevate and go perpendicular on the canopy.

To Wilson's surprise, Prince held his lift vector on as he went up with Wilson. *Well, well,* Wilson thought, as he watched the outline of the *Hornet* going up a mile away. *Prince is showing some aggressiveness.*

Wilson sensed his sun strategy was now superseded by Prince's nose-high move. He kept his left arm locked against throttles, pushing them against the burner stop as he pulled the nose through the vertical and to the horizon. He rolled into Prince with a boot full of rudder to knuckle his own aircraft down and inside the younger pilot. The horizon rolled underneath Wilson as he reached the apex of his modified loop and put the top of his canopy, his lift vector, on Prince. The dark silhouette of Prince's *Hornet* zoomed past less than 500 feet away. Wilson dug his nose down to regain needed air speed, ruddered the jet to the left and kept the top of his airplane facing Prince in a nose-low pirouette.

The extensive training the two pilots had been through allowed them to maneuver by instinct, each managing air speed and angles to get behind the

other and into a firing position. If one of them allowed too much separation, the other would fire a missile shot. If the other got too close, the "knife fight inside a phone booth" could lead to a position change at best—or a raking guns shot at worst. They rolled and pulled in three dimensions, the background changing from water to sky to water, as they craned their necks to full extension in an effort to keep sight.

With his experience, Wilson got every angle he could with his available air speed, and moved Prince forward on his canopy. After less than a minute, they were passing 10,000 feet in a rolling scissors, with Prince going up and Wilson coming down, building knots. Prince fell off right, and Wilson had the energy to loop—if he remained patient and resisted the desire to keep pushing Prince around the sky. Wilson got off the g and let the aircraft ride the burner cans into a loop, a graceful pull into the vertical that stopped his downrange travel. His purpose was to flush Prince out in front and underneath.

For an instant, the two pilots saw each other in the cockpit as they passed on the horizon, their visor-covered eyes padlocked on their opponent, mouths gasping for air in short, deep breaths against the pressure. *Hold it! Hold it!* Wilson said to himself as he watched Prince descend and gain air speed. He fought the urge to overbank and allowed the optimum separation to build. Wilson slowed below 100 knots and let his nose track down to the horizon. About a mile below, sharply set against the blue Gulf, he saw condensation stream off the wingtips of Prince's gray fighter as Prince pulled to meet Wilson once again. As Wilson's nose fell through the horizon, he mashed down on the weapons select switch. The familiar *Sidewinder* growl sent a greeting through his headset. One second later, the growl changed to a high-pitched *Scrrreeeeeee!* as the seeker-head locked on to Prince's engine heat. Wilson squeezed the trigger.

"Fox-2," he radioed to Prince.

"Out of burner, chaff, flares," Prince replied.

"Continue," Wilson answered.

Sensing Prince had little air speed to counter, Wilson closed the space between them. He pulled up at the bottom of the loop and turned to align his fuselage with Prince, who was only 2,000 feet above the hard deck. Selecting GUN on the control stick with his right thumb, Wilson rendezvoused on the inside of Prince's turn. Prince appeared to be motionless in the sky, doing little to throw off Wilson's impending shot.

"*C'mon, Prince!*" Wilson shouted into his mask as he pulled the green pipper to the back of the nugget's aircraft. Prince was arcing again, not pulling down and into him, not making his aircraft skinny. In essence, he had rolled over and

exposed his neck for the kill. He had given up. From 1,000 feet away, Wilson pulled the throttles to idle and squeezed the trigger.

"Guns, *knock it off!*" Wilson transmitted his disgust along with his words.

"Lead, knock it off, *joker*," Prince replied.

Wilson saw that he, too, was a few hundred pounds below joker fuel as he maneuvered to join on his flight lead. Both aircraft accelerated to 300 knots and began a long climb to high altitude. The pilots routinely climbed to *bladeland*, as they called it, in an effort to "hang on the blades," or to conserve every drop of fuel they could as their jet turbine blades turned in the cold, thin air. They would need it for the recovery 35 minutes hence.

Wilson slid into position on Prince's right side and inspected Prince's aircraft for popped panels, fluid leaks, or anything out of the ordinary. He glided below the *Hornet* to check the bottom of the aircraft and then moved to the left side, bottom and top. Satisfied, he drew forward to where Prince was waiting for him to take the lead so Prince could inspect Wilson's fighter using the same procedure. When the checks were completed, Prince resumed the lead. Via hand signals they learned that each aircraft had roughly 6,000 pounds left.

Wilson eased away from Prince as they leveled off at 28,000 feet, turning left and to the east as they drew too close to the Saudi coast. *Dammit, Prince!* he thought. *Not getting it is one thing, but not trying is something else.* Wilson scribbled notes, mixed with arrows and symbols, on his kneeboard card. First, he recorded his recollection of how the fight ended and followed that with notes about the initial nose-high move they took at the first merge and how that became a rolling scissors. He wrote ARC at a point in the engagement where Prince arced to lose angles, and recorded his estimation of his *Sidewinder* shot range. Once on deck, they would review their video tapes before the debrief. Wilson knew it would not be a smooth one. He hoped Prince could end the hop on a positive note by managing their fuel before leading them into the break. The post-flight debrief was not going to be easy.

CHAPTER 37

The formation steadied up on a heading of 060, with Wilson 400 feet away in loose cruise. Wilson looked down as a heavily laden southbound tanker plied the textured blue surface below. It left a wide wake behind, as the load of hundreds of thousands of tons of crude began its long voyage to Japan, or Europe…or Houston. Forty miles to the north he could make out *Valley Forge*, escorted by the guided-missile destroyer, *Stout*. Though they were at a max endurance fuel setting, the two *Hornets* cruised along at 250 knots indicated air speed. Wilson checked the winds at altitude: 125 knots on the tail, cooking right along after the frontal passage. He looked about the sky for other traffic and scanned his radar in range-while-search mode. *Clear.*

Wilson's thoughts returned to Prince. He was *different* from the others, different from any other pilot he knew. First, Prince was a loner. Despite his good looks, he had no wife or girlfriend. Wilson realized the same could be said of the XO, but with Prince it was different. Saint could be engaging when he wanted to be, particularly with his superiors, but Prince always looked angry and impatient. He thought he knew all the answers and bristled at constructive criticism about his flying or division paperwork to the point he almost *talked back*, even to seniors. Prince was careful not to cross the line, but he went right up to that line way too often. Among the department heads and senior JOs, Prince was a "project." They needed him to pull more of his own weight, but after a year in the squadron, it seemed they had made little headway with him. Wilson tried to put the upcoming debrief out of his mind and enjoy the day, even though it had turned out to be a day in *bladeland* on Prince's wing.

They were nearing the Iranian coast, but Prince had given no indication he was about to turn away from it. After giving Prince every opportunity to monitor his own navigation, Wilson began to fear an embarrassing call from *Alpha Whiskey* and keyed the mike.

"Let's bring it west."

Prince remained silent and continued ahead.

"Now!" Wilson growled over the radio. The lead *Hornet* still did not respond. *He can't even stay out of Iran!* Wilson thought, considering this the last straw in an unsat check ride.

When Prince didn't respond, Wilson guessed Prince had switched up to another frequency on the secondary radio.

"Prince...*Prince!* You up?"

Growing concerned, Wilson added some power and nudged the stick to get closer to his flight lead. Prince wasn't moving, and as Wilson slid closer, he saw Prince's head slumped down.

The two aircraft were headed right for Iran. Over his nose Wilson saw a long, barren island. It formed a natural harbor, but Wilson saw no settlement anywhere on the deserted coastline.

"*Prince!* Bring it *west!*"

The radio crackled with a reminder that the ship, too, was watching their progress. "*Raven* four-one-two, *Strike.* Vector west for airspace."

Wilson answered, "Roger, *Strike*, standby." Wilson got into parade formation right next to Prince, who remained motionless in the cockpit. Was it hypoxia? "Prince, PRINCE!" Wilson shouted into his mask in an effort to wake him up. Prince stirred, but he remained slumped forward in his straps. "PRINCE! WAKE UP!" Wilson roared.

Wilson got as close as he could to see if Prince's mask was hooked up, but he could not be sure. He chopped power and pushed the stick down and left, then reversed the motions to come up on Prince's left. He was then able to see that the mask dangled to one side. Prince twitched again.

"Prince, NOSE DOWN, PUSH YOUR NOSE DOWN! GET YER MASK ON!"

Not knowing that one *Raven* pilot was incapacitated, the strike group air warfare commander saw the *Ravens* heading into Iran and scolded them for their poor navigation on the GUARD emergency frequency that was broadcast for all aircraft to hear. "*Raven* four-one-two, this is *Alpha Whiskey* on GUARD. You are approaching *Waterloo* red. Turn left heading two-four-zero immediately."

"NOW, PRINCE, DO IT NOW!" Wilson shouted. Prince had "altitude hold" set in his automatic pilot which was carrying him, unconscious, into Iranian airspace.

Another strike group ship called to them on GUARD. "*Raven* four-one-two, this is Mike One Kilo. You are standing into danger. Turn left *immediately* and contact *Alpha Whiskey* on two-eighty-nine-point-five."

Wilson keyed the mike and said, "*Strike*, four-zero-two... Four-*one*-two appears to be incapacitated. He may be hypoxic. We are steady, heading zero-six-five at angels twenty-eight."

"Four-zero-two, *Strike*. Say again?"

Exasperated, Wilson repeated the transmission and ignored another call on GUARD for them to turn. After several seconds, *Strike* responded, "Roger four-zero-two, standby and turn left to two-four-zero."

"*Strike*, four-*zero*-two is declaring an emergency. I *can't* turn left because my flight lead is incapacitated! I'm next to him on his wing. Get a *Raven* rep ASAP."

"Roger, four-zero-two. Emergency declared. Say your state and stand by."

As they passed over the Iranian coastline, Wilson inserted "7700," the international distress code, into his transponder. He continued to watch for signs of consciousness from Prince. Wilson maneuvered high on Prince's left side and pulled forward, flying as close as he dared, his right wing tip over Prince's fuselage. This time he saw that Prince was holding his green canteen in his right hand, a viable explanation for his mask hanging down: He had been taking a drink. Suddenly, Prince twitched.

"*Prince!*" Wilson transmitted. "WAKE UP!"

Strike came up on the radio, "*Raven* four-zero-two, we copy your emergency squawk. Squawk zero-one-four-two."

While *Strike* was talking, Wilson heard Cajun on the squadron tactical frequency. Manning up his jet for the next launch, the CO said, "Flip, Cajun, what's goin' on?"

Wilson responded, "Sir, Prince is unconscious—think he's hypoxic from taking his mask off. We're at angels twenty-eight with altitude hold on and heading into Iran. Actually we're in Iran."

As soon as he finished with the skipper, Wilson called to *Strike*. "Negative, *Strike*, I'm keeping 7700 set."

A new and strange voice with a foreign sound came up on GUARD, a detached voice with perfect English diction. "*Raven* four-one-two, this is Bushier Approach Control on GUARD. You have violated Islamic Republic airspace. Please return to international airspace at this time. Thank you."

Taken aback, Wilson selected GUARD and answered. "Bushier, *Raven* four-zero-two on GUARD is declaring an emergency. The pilot of *Raven* four-one-two is incapacitated. He appears to be unconscious."

Then Cajun broke in on tac. "Flip, shout at him. Thump him if you have to... Are you feet dry now?"

"Yes, sir, I've been shouting at him, and we've been feet dry for several minutes."

"What are you carrying?" Cajun asked.

"Nothing but a CATM, sir." And then it dawned on him. He and Prince were alone over Iran with no weapons, no expendables, no sidearm—and none of the

accoutrements one would carry on a combat sortie. They weren't at *war* with Iran, but the country was by no means friendly.

"Is he moving at all?"

"He twitched a minute ago. Stand by."

Wilson slid back and crossed under to Prince's right wing. He had an idea... If he could place his left wingtip under Prince's right wingtip, the airflow over his wing could force Prince to roll slightly left. If Wilson could do that in a way that did not cause Prince's altitude hold to kick off, maybe Prince's aircraft could at least return to the Gulf. It would be a long shallow turn, but Wilson needed to try something. They were flying into Iran at a rate of over seven miles per minute.

Suddenly, GUARD frequency sprang to life and another strike group ship called out: "*Raven* four-zero-two! *Waterloo* Red! *Waterloo* Red!"

"*Shut up!*" Wilson snarled into his mask and punched off GUARD, conscious of both his anxiety and his loss of patience over the situation.

Wilson eased up next to Prince's right side and looked over this left shoulder as he placed his wingtip a few feet under his stricken squadronmate's wing. *Strike* asked him again about Prince's condition, and, as he concentrated on keeping his wings steady, Wilson responded with a terse "No change."

Holding his wingtip position under and forward of Prince, he clicked nose up trim once, then again. This did nothing but make the stick forces greater. What he was doing—looking over his shoulder as he placed his wingtip dangerously close to another aircraft travelling at 250 knots of indicated air speed—was unnatural. Every impulse ordered him to back off, and he fought these instincts to remain in position.

Wilson's slipstream caused Prince's aircraft to develop a slight left-wing-down attitude. Prince's wingtip suddenly dropped into Wilson, who had to push the stick down and away to avoid collision. He realized he was squeezing it hard, and, as he repositioned himself, he took a deep breath.

Strike inquired about his fuel state, and Wilson answered, "Five-point-one."

Prince's shoulder twitched. Wilson immediately reported this to *Strike* as he prepared for another attempt to nudge Prince to the west. At least Prince still appeared to be alive. "PRINCE! NOSE DOWN!" Wilson commanded him, in vain, on the tac frequency.

Cajun, helpless to do anything but desperate for information on his two pilots, called from his position on the flight deck. "What luck, Flip?"

"He just twitched his shoulder. I got under his wingtip and tried to lift it, but his autopilot fought me and leveled him back. It appears we gained a few

degrees. I'm tryin' to get us back feet wet by nudgin' him with my slipstream. You monit'rin' *Strike?*"

"*Firm...how far in are you?*"

"About 25 miles."

Wilson looked underneath him at the desert floor, an uninhabited coastal plain that rose into a karst ridgeline to the northeast. A series of ridges and valleys were arrayed in front of him.

"What's your pressurization showing? How long has he been out?" Cajun asked.

"Twelve K, and it's been about ten minutes now. We had just finished a fight and climbed to altitude."

"Rog, must have a pressurization leak," Cajun surmised.

Wilson checked the outside temperature...-42 degrees centigrade. If Prince's cockpit was at ambient outside pressure, he was in trouble.

BOOOP.

Wilson glanced at his radar warning display. The Iranians were looking at him with an air-search radar.

CHAPTER 38

Are they scrambling fighters on us? Wilson wondered. Iran possessed two fighter bases in the region: Bushier, some 90 miles northwest, and Shiraz, on his nose for 100. He asked *Strike* for help from the E-2 *Hawkeye* on station. "*Strike*, are you working with a *Knight?*"

Knight 601 answered immediately. "*Raven, Knight,* radar contact, picture clean."

"Roger, *Knight*," Wilson replied, recognizing the voice of their XO.

"*Raven* four-zero-two, Bushier approach is trying to call you on GUARD."

"Roger," said Wilson and reselected GUARD on his up front control, wondering what they wanted, but then realized they wanted to know why and how long he would be in their airspace. Wilson keyed the mike, still in parade formation on Prince.

"Bushier Approach Control, *Raven* four-zero-two on GUARD."

"*Raven* four-zero-two, Bushier, do you require assistance?" the faceless Iranian replied.

Now what? Wilson thought. If Prince also had 5,000 pounds remaining, at this fuel flow and with the tailwind, they would remain airborne little more than an hour. That would put them well into central Iran. He also realized that, at some point, he would have to go back to the ship, almost 100 miles behind him and opening. He had to get Prince turned around and down to a lower altitude.

"Bushier, *Raven* four-one-two appears to have a cockpit pressurization leak, and the pilot is unconscious. I'm trying to use my slipstream to maneuver him out of your airspace. Request you move away traffic ahead of us and to the north."

"Thank you, *Raven* four-zero-two, Bushier has your request… Interceptors are inbound to assist escorting you out of Islamic Republic airspace."

Wilson felt a shot of adrenalin shoot through him. Iranian fighters were inbound…but what would they send? *Phantoms? Tomcats?* Those he could handle in an engagement, but with Prince incapacitated, he was worse than alone. *Fulcrums? Flankers?*

He drew closer to Prince and positioned his wingtip for another attempt, his neck muscles straining as he craned his neck left and fought through the tension of the moment. Once stabilized, he tweaked the throttles forward and added a tad of back stick pressure. The wake turbulence from his wing created a high pressure area under Prince's wingtip that pushed it up, and they started to turn left. Although he sensed the aircraft ease left, Wilson, breathing deeply and rapidly, did not dare to glance inside at the heading. *Hold it. Hoooollld it.*

Cajun's voice came over the radio again. "Flip, how's it goin'?"

Wilson was concentrating too much to answer.

All of a sudden Prince's right wingtip slammed down onto Wilson's left. *Crack!* Frantically pushing away from Prince, Wilson stabilized low and to the right. He was stunned to see Prince steady after the collision.

"Oh, that was close," he said over the radio.

"What happened?" Cajun asked.

"Just swapped a little paint, but we turned a few degrees. Surprised his altitude hold is still working," Wilson replied.

"Don't worry about touching, go ahead and hold him with your wingtip if you have to," Cajun said.

As he got back into position next to Prince, he noticed a film had developed inside Prince's canopy. Wilson studied it. It appeared to be condensation, and drawing closer, he noted small glimmers of light from the reflected sun. *Frost!* Prince was unconscious inside an icebox of a cockpit, an almost definite indication of cockpit pressurization failure.

Wilson's radar warning receiver lit up with a tone in his headset. Off his nose the fire control radar of an aircraft was tracking him. He eased away from Prince to better scan the horizon and called to the *Knight* E-2.

"*Knight*, four-zero-two is spiked at twelve o'clock. Picture!"

"Four-zero-two, single group, 330 at 60, hot… Looks like they are the bogeys out of Bushier."

"Four-zero-two, roger," Wilson replied.

Those guys are off to the northwest, he thought. *What caused the radar spike from the northeast?* The spike had disappeared, but he lifted his dark visor for a moment and scanned the eastern horizon for aircraft. Far down to the east the cold front had formed an irregular mass of white and gray clouds that could highlight an aircraft. He noticed a white nub of cloud on the horizon a bit higher than the others. He willed his 20/15 eyes to search the horizon, focusing them on one spot, then moving to another. At the same time his radar searched in AUTOACQ as he moved the elevation at intervals to search a band of air-

space. Wilson stole glances to the northwest, suppressing the urge to turn in that direction to meet the bogey group…and to abandon Prince.

DEEDLE, DEEDLE, *DEEDLEDEEDLEDEEDLEDEEDLE…*

Wilson's RWR again lit up. It appeared to be a lock on from a fighter radar. With a sense of urgency, he called to *Knight* to reconcile it. *"Knight,* I'm spiked at zero-five-zero and clean. Picture!" Wilson eased away from Prince—about 200 feet. His senses were on heightened alert.

"Four-zero-two, *Knight.* Picture clean to the northeast, the E-2 answered. "Single group three-two-zero at forty-five, hot, medium."

Wilson was dumbfounded. *Knight sees* nothing *ahead of me? What's going on here?* he wondered, eyes wide with apprehension.

Flying formation on Prince, he sensed something above in his field of view. A blurred object streaked toward his wingman. Before his mind could identify it, a tremendous flash centered on the top of the Prince's *Hornet* behind the cockpit, covering the airplane with fragmentation impacts and igniting a huge, orange fireball at the fuselage and on top of the wings. The impact was accompanied by a muffled *Boom!*

Transfixed with horror, Wilson watched the *Hornet* yaw left, trailing monstrous flames and black smoke. Smoldering pieces of debris fell away to the earth, some four miles below. *Raven 412* then snapped down hard as its right wing was ripped off at the fuselage. Tearing itself apart, the aircraft became a tumbling, hurtling mass of yellow flames and charred debris. He saw a large, pointed piece fall end-over-end, trailing white smoke from the break in the fuselage.

That piece was the nose of the FA-18—and Prince was inside.

"Prince!" cried Wilson, recovering from his momentary shock. He crammed the throttles forward and pulled the jet down and away to the right. During the maneuver, his eyes picked up a single-target track lock on the radar display. Something heading at him and above him, with a high air speed, slid off the display to the left as the radar reached the gimbal limit. Rolling out, Wilson pushed the nose down in order to go weightless and increase air speed. Still floating off the seat, he strained to reach the MARK button on his display to record his current latitude and longitude—to reference the spot Prince was hit.

Returning to one g, he reached up and hit the EMERGENCY JETT, button, which blew off his empty wing tanks and caused the *Hornet* to leap forward from the sudden release of weight and drag. His mind raced to understand what he had just witnessed. Through the sounds of the RWR's *deedle* and the 450-knot rush of the airstream past the canopy, Wilson realized what had happened.

Prince was hit by a radar missile, coming from that contact on my nose!

CHAPTER 39

Wilson's training took over. Instinctively, his left thumb activated the chaff button in a vain attempt to expend chaff he didn't have. His right thumb selected *Sidewinder*, and his headset filled with the familiar growl of the seeker head—on a dummy missile. As a brown ridgeline grew larger in his windscreen, Wilson realized the contact off his nose was the fighter that had put a missile into Prince and was now targeting Wilson with an air speed and altitude advantage.

Retreating to the Gulf, some 50 miles away, was not an option. The bogey—no, the *bandit*—would just run Wilson down from behind. He looked high to the left for a sign of either the bandit or a missile in the bright blue sky—*anything*, a glint off the wing, a wingtip vortice, a missile rocket-motor plume, a dark speck... He saw nothing.

At least Wilson was no longer spiked, and the bandit, looking down toward the desert, would have greater difficulty picking him out of the backdrop. When he passed mach one, Wilson pulled the throttles out of afterburner and slid forward in the seat. Within seconds, as he passed 20,000 feet in a shallow dive, Wilson's training again formed his game plan. He would turn to engage.

Realizing he needed to get a quick report to the ship, Wilson keyed the mike. "*Knight*, they shot down four-one-two! I'm engaging a bandit to the northeast!"

"*Say again!*"

"Four-one-two is shot down. Didn't see a chute, and I'm targeted! *Turning to engage!*"

Wilson grunted through clenched teeth as he pulled his *Hornet* hard into the unknown threat. Despite his senses and mind working overtime, and despite his confusion and anxiety, he had never felt so alive.

A feeling of déjà vu came over Wilson... Everything reminded him of his *TOPGUN* graduation hop high over the Nevada desert: going into a merge with an unknown bandit, the intense pressure to succeed, even the topography below. Even his thoughts were the same. *What will I meet? Who will be flying it? The* difference? This was not a training sortie but deadly single combat—and he was unarmed.

Wilson rolled out and up into the expected threat position, pulled the throttles to idle, bumped the radar mode into WIDEACQ and searched the sky around him for the bandit. Close to hyperventilating, his mouth was bone dry and his eyes were frantic to find Prince's assailant. To the left, several miles away, he saw a dark gray cloud suspended against the blue sky. An irregular trail of smoke led to the desert floor, smaller trails of debris fanning out along the path of the main plume. Pieces of Prince's *Hornet* continued to flutter down. Still, Wilson saw no chute.

A radar spike at 10 o'clock jerked his head left. Wilson saw a large fighter pointed at the *Hornet* less than two miles away, slightly low. He yanked the stick left and put his nose on, selecting VERTACQ to place the bandit inside the two dashed lines formed on the HUD. He was rewarded with a lock at once, and the *Sidewinder* seeker tone screamed loud in his headset. With over 700 miles per hour of closure rate between them, Wilson was inside a mile in seconds and pushed the throttles into burner to regain the air speed lost in his uphill glide. By instinct he looked for a wingman …the empty sky reminded him he was alone. His eyes returned to the big fighter. Wilson feared being peppered by a high-angle snapshot from the fighter's gun, but the bandit was not pulling a great deal of lead.

"*Knight*, four-zero-two's engaged, visual!"

At first Wilson identified the bandit as a Russian-built MiG-29 *Fulcrum*, but as they drew closer, he sensed a larger, *longer* aircraft with a square intake under a huge nose and a big missile on a wing pylon. The bandit took his nose off, and the geometry on both sides dictated a left-to-left pass. Wilson pressed it inside 500 feet.

He was awestruck at what flashed past him.

The aircraft was something he had never seen before. The small nose section was stuck far forward of an enormous single intake, behind it a long fuselage with delta wings. It was painted in shades of sky-blue camouflage with a beige nose cone and the circular red, white, and green Iranian Air Force roundels on the wingtips, but it possessed characteristics of a Russian design. He saw only the one huge missile under the right wing and an unusual feature—two wing canards over the intake which signaled to him an ability to fight slow. The twin vertical stabs sat on large booms adjacent to the massive engines. He realized he was fighting something big and powerful: a fifth-generation Russian with great turning capability, top-end speed, and probably a lot more gas than he had. The fighter bowed in a graceful curve from the needle-nose cockpit down to the empennage.

What is this? he thought.

As it flashed past, Wilson inhaled and held his breath, making an audible *Hookkkkk* as he closed his windpipe. When he pulled the stick hard into his lap, the top of his aircraft turned white with condensation as the force of seven *g*'s gripped the *Hornet* and inflated his G-suit. The familiar anaconda-like pressure squeezed his legs and abdomen as his horizontal stabs dug into the clear winter air and pitched his nose up. The combination of g force and his muscles resisting its pressure affected every part of Wilson's body. Wedging his head between the seat box and canopy he continued to fight against the pressure and keep sight, inhaling and exhaling—*Hookkkkk*—ah, ha, *Hookkkk*—ah, ha—keeping his lift vector on and bleeding air speed fast. *I have to get inside this guy.*

Wilson managed the presence of mind to keep a running commentary on strike frequency. "*Knight,* I'm, *Hookkkkk,* ah-ha, one-circle with a single-seat twin engine fighter," he gasped into his mask between breaths. "Never seen b'fore. *Delta wings.*"

If the E-2 responded, though, Wilson did not hear it. He was completely absorbed with the unknown aircraft he was fighting. He pulled everything he had and got inside the Iranian's circle. Despite the fact Wilson was unarmed, he reasoned he could push around the mystery jet and hold him off long enough that the Iranian would have to disengage because of low fuel. Wilson then looked at *his* fuel—3,700 pounds. His F404 engines were devouring it at well over 10,000 pounds per hour. Wilson had no choice but to stay and fight.

At the second merge, Wilson guessed that both aircraft bled airspeed to around 250 knots, and he unloaded while reversing his turn to take a 30-degree bite. With looping air speed he planned to take it up at the merge. By taking advantage of his superior slow-speed controllability, he could park his nose high and flush the Iranian out in front of him. *Maybe I can spook this guy,* he thought.

As they passed, he fed top rudder, eased his angle of bank and took it up, *skates on ice,* milking the most of every knot of air speed to get above and behind the bandit. He looked inside for just a moment, a second, to check his fuel. When he returned to the bandit, he was stunned by the image of the enemy plane. Just a few hundred feet away, it went up with him and even out-zoomed him as it stood on two long pipes that belched a cone of fire visible even in the midday sun. Soon Wilson would be below and out front.

For a moment Wilson froze and looked at the white-helmeted pilot who sat high on the nose of the colossal fighter. Across the small void, he saw the pilot's eyes peer over his mask. Dark, chilling eyes…looking right at Wilson.

Holy shiiiit!

Wilson kicked right rudder to slide closer and jam any chance for a bandit gunshot. When the bandit pulled all the way over, almost on its back but in control, he cursed in frustration at what he knew was coming next. The hostile fighter reversed over the top in a negative *g* maneuver, his nose tracking down on Wilson like a falling sledgehammer in slow motion. Horrified, Wilson realized he faced an imminent snapshot. With the little air speed he had, he inverted his *Hornet* to avoid it. His aircraft still rolling, Wilson saw that the monster had another weapon at its disposal. *Thrust vectoring!*

Wilson managed to float, barely in control, in front of the bandit. Shocked at the gaping maw of the intake only 200 feet away, Wilson, upside down, looked out his left side. At that moment, the right side of the Iranian's fuselage unleashed a bright tongue of flame. Inside the flame was a nearly solid stream of what looked like flaming supersonic baseballs. Under Wilson, an earsplitting *POP-POP-POP-POP-POP* penetrated the canopy. A low guttural BORRRRP sounded in the background as the cannon rounds missed low, mere feet from his head.

Mo-*ther-FUUUCK!*" he cried into his mask.

Petrified, Wilson pulled hard and down, rolling and kicking the controls to the left. Straining to keep sight of the bandit hovering above him, Wilson saw the nose of the fighter drop to pounce once again. He let out an involuntary whimper of fear as he slammed the stick forward to unload. In the back of his mind he acknowledged his cry and recognized it as a signal of the panic that he must fight in addition to his adversary. Over the years, Wilson had known apprehension and fear. Taxiing to the bow on a pitch-black night. Caught inside a thunderstorm. Far from land trying to find a tanker at night in bad weather with low fuel. He had been afraid before and knew how to handle it through compartmentalization and preflight preparation. But this was different.

Twenty minutes earlier Prince's poor navigation had been Wilson's biggest problem. Then Prince had been blown out of the sky right next to him, and now Wilson was unarmed over a hostile country fighting an unknown aircraft with a pilot who was trying to kill him. Those flaming balls represented a stream of death that had just passed underneath him by mere feet. That stream, delivered by a thinking human, was about to reach out to him again in seconds. This realization was more than fear; it was terror.

Get down, Wilson thought.

He had two immediate and conflicting needs. First, he had to stay out of the Iranian's gunsight by maneuvering hard once he felt threatened, although that bled air speed. His second need was to get into the weeds. To do that he had to re-

gain maneuvering air speed at the cost of providing the bandit with a predictable flight path, one that would almost surely invite a missile or a gunshot.

Wilson's senses were on fire. With his neck stretched back as far as possible to keep sight, he flew the aircraft by feel. The big fighter opened to 500 feet of separation and began to pull lead. Just seconds before the Iranian let go with a burst that missed to the right, Wilson instinctively pulled up and rolled away to avoid the shot. The rapid popping noise filled his cockpit for a second time.

Gaining confidence, Wilson thought he could hold off his pursuer. And, right now, the Iranian was about to overshoot his flight path because he had his nose buried. This gave Wilson some valuable time. Wilson chopped the throttles and popped the speed brake, stepping on right rudder to spiral into his opponent while keeping the air speed on the edge of stall. The Iranian fell underneath Wilson and pulled his nose up in an attempt to stop his downrange travel and to slide behind Wilson for another shot. Wilson's maneuver had the effect of locking horns with the strange aircraft. As heavy, white vapor poured off the tops of both fuselages, and as their wings shook violently under the deep airframe buffet, the aircraft fell, more than flew, down to the deck.

For a moment, their relative positions were unchanged. Locked in this spiral for a few turns, Wilson saw the pilot's menacing eyes stare at him again across a space less than half a football field away. Wilson warily studied the fighter's lone missile to identify it either as radar or infrared guided. *It's a radar missile,* he concluded.

Now furious at, more than fearful of, the man who had shot his helpless wingman out of the sky, Wilson's left arm swiped up *his* helmet visor to show the Iranian *his* eyes. The enemy pilot reacted with a combination upright roll aided by vectored thrust. The maneuver stopped the Iranian's downward vector, but it also immobilized him in midair for a few moments. Wilson seized the opportunity to increase their separation. He shoved the stick and throttles forward as far as he could and fed in some rudder to maintain sight as the *Hornet* rapidly picked up precious air speed. He passed through 7,000 feet in a steep dive as the enemy floated above him. As Wilson whipped his head from the HUD to the bandit, he saw the bandit's nose was now tracking down and falling off left to line up for another shot.

Wilson was still twisting his neck to keep sight when he heard *FUEL LO, FUEL LO* in his headphones. *Dammit!* he cursed through clenched teeth. Fuel was now a real factor. With only 1,800 pounds, his *Hornet* would flameout in minutes if he kept both engines in afterburner. The Iranian was at the edge of gun range as Wilson unloaded for knots.

Both aircraft were now close to the ground. They entered a narrow desert valley ridged on the east by a steeply rising mountain range of chocolate-colored karst. To the southeast Wilson noted a complex of green fields—an indication that people were nearby.

"Four-zero-two, *Knight*. Status?"

Before he answered, Wilson picked the nose up to shallow his dive. "Four-zero-two's defensive. Heading for the deck. State one-eight."

Wilson jinked into the Iranian and then pushed away in an effort to throw off any gun shot. When he sensed the ground looming below them, he flipped the radar altimeter switch into priority. He employed a maneuver that got *Hornet* pilots to the deck quickly and safely. *25 for 15...*

The desert floor rushed up to him, scarred with deep fissures that again reminded him of the badlands in Nebraska. *No people out here.* The Iranian remained above and to Wilson's 5 o'clock, inside a mile. *Why doesn't he shoot his missile?* Wilson wondered. He jinked into him again and pulled up sharply, passing 1,500 feet in gently rising terrain. Through a mixture of bunting the nose and pulling up hard, Wilson leveled at 200 feet. He continued alternately to snap his head forward to clear his flight path and aft to keep sight of the Iranian. He now had two enemies to fight: the ground and the bandit.

Wilson eased down to 100 feet above the ground, as low as he dared having to divide his scan between the ground and the threat. He sensed his pursuer holding off above him but gaining advantage. When he saw two small hills or mounds ahead, he reversed his turn in order to aim for the pass between them. He reasoned that, even for a second, the hills might shield him from a shot or cause the Iranian to lose sight. Wilson knew that, even if he avoided the enemy's gunfire, he wouldn't be able, at this fuel flow, to get back to the *coast*, much less the ship. He had little choice but to defend himself until the engines flamed out.

As he approached the pass, Wilson regained sight over his left shoulder and saw the fighter high and behind a mile, nose off but accelerating. Wilson, too, was accelerating past 400 knots, and the turbulent air caused him to bounce in his seat. Although still breathing hard from fear and adrenaline, he saw the Iranian was lagging too much which gave Wilson some lateral separation with which to maneuver. He had an idea.

With the bandit no-factor for the moment, he concentrated on putting his wingtip into the narrowest part of the pass, a few dozen feet above the rocks. He chopped power to decelerate and approached the backside of the left mound. Suddenly, he came upon a dirt trail and saw a man in a brown pajama-like outfit with a vest and turban trudging up the hill, leading a pack animal. As the *Hornet*

roared past, the startled man dropped the animal's reins and jerked his head up, face frozen, wide-eyed, from a combination of awe and fear. For an instant, Wilson's eyes again met those of an Iranian. As the startled animal skittered away and the man quickly receded from view, Wilson put his plan into action. He was momentarily concealed from the bandit and pulled into the mound as close as he dared. *One-potato, two... Now!*

Tightening his muscles and throwing the throttles full forward, Wilson, almost in one motion, pushed, rolled, and pulled right and into the bandit. Again he grunted, *"Hoookkkk,"* as the g enveloped him like a vise. At this dangerous altitude he gave his full attention to staying out of the rocks, betting the Iranian would not see him reverse. A bird appeared out of nowhere, just above his flight path, and instinctively tucked its wings to avoid collision with this strange, speeding object—even before Wilson could think to evade it. *"Fuck!"* he yelled as the bird passed over his jet above his right wing.

Wilson picked up the Iranian at 5 o'clock, moving counterclockwise with his nose off. Wilson's trick had worked. The big aircraft was arcing with too much air speed to remain offensive, and Wilson's bleeding high g turn and lower air speed had put him inside the enemy circle. Wilson saw a high-deflection snapshot opportunity develop and pulled his nose up. He held the GUN trigger down as his green gunsight aiming reticle flew along the bandit's fuselage from left to right. Despite the fact he had no bullets to use in this vain attempt to shoot down the bandit, Wilson felt a sense of satisfaction.

The Iranian seemed to stop fighting—he was holding too much air speed and appeared to be as low as he was willing to go. Wilson left it in burner and with only 1,000 pounds left resisted the urge to reverse his turn behind the enemy. They passed 500 feet apart with the Iranian holding a shallow left angle of bank. Wilson watched the bandit fade away down his left wing line, without turning to engage. He kept his turn in and pulled the throttles out of burner to military. As he floated up a little to make it easier to keep sight, Wilson picked up the strange aircraft over his right shoulder, heading in the opposite direction and climbing, receding from view.

He's had enough!

CHAPTER 40

Now Wilson's biggest problem was fuel. He glanced at his moving map for the nearest heading to the blue safety of the Gulf, over 50 miles to the southwest. The *Hornet*, now light and *slick,* accelerated rapidly to 490 knots and began an emergency-fuel "bingo" climb. Getting to the ship was no longer an option. Wilson just wanted to get feet wet, and as far from the Iranian coast as possible, before he ejected.

On the way up, he searched the sky for the Bushier group *Knight* had been calling, and he took cautious glances over his shoulder to ensure his opponent had not changed his mind. He peered northwest down the valley and saw the black pall of smoke rising up from the desert floor some 10 miles away...*Prince.*

His eyes alternately scanned the cockpit instruments and outside in the familiar pattern he'd practiced since flight school. His eyes dwelled, however, on the fuel indicator, mentally noting every 10-pound drop. His engines would suck fuel until the tank was completely dry, and, the way he figured it, that was a real possibility in less than 15 minutes. The profile called for a climb to 20,000 feet at .83 mach, then an idle descent holding 250 knots at 32 miles. *Eight hundred pounds, seven hundred and ninety pounds, seven eighty, seven seventy...*

He had to get a voice report to *Knight,* and to the ship. "*Knight, Raven* four-zero-two."

"Go ahead, four-zero-two!"

"*Knight,* four-zero-two is passing angels twelve on a bingo profile, state seven hundred. The bandit disengaged, and I don't see any other bogeys. Didn't see a chute or get a beeper on four-twelve...There's a column of smoke on the desert floor about 10 miles north of me. Believe that's him. Get a tanker out here, now."

"Roger all, four-zero-two... Will pass to Mother," *Knight* replied.

Still concerned about the Iranian fighter threat, Wilson called, "Picture."

"Stand by, four-zero-two... Picture. Single group, BRA zero-two zero at sixty, medium, nose cold."

"Roger, declare." Wilson continued with the cadence.

"Hostile...70 miles now, no factor."

"Roger."

Wilson rolled the aircraft left and right and scanned the ground below for threats, but the landscape was barren: no twinkling AAA muzzle flashes or MANPADS missile plumes. He took a last look at Prince's crash site over his right wing. The smoke appeared less dense, as if the fire were burning itself out.

The Gulf beckoned him. Although it filled his forward view with clear blue water, he was still over 30 miles from feet wet and over 40 from international airspace. He was also fighting a headwind. Leveling at 20,000 feet, Wilson pulled the throttles to idle, which allowed the airplane to decelerate to 265 knots.

Wilson's fuel reading was just over 500 pounds, which translated into roughly five minutes of flight time. He could squeeze a few more minutes at idle power, but the ship was almost 100 miles away—over 20 minutes of flight time.

Knowing he had a chance if he acted fast, Wilson switched up to departure control frequency to back up his request for a tanker. "*Departure, Raven* four-zero-two checkin' in on Mother's one-zero-zero for ninety, angels twenty-five, low state five hundred pounds. *Texaco*, you up?"

"*Redeye* seven-zero-four's up. About 50 miles away, Flip. Comin' to ya." Wilson did not recognize the S-3 aircrew's voice, but he now knew *they* knew *he* was in *402*. The use of his personal call sign reassured him that they were apprised of his grim situation. The fact that he did not know the aircrew didn't matter. He took charge.

"Roger, seven-zero-four. *Buster*," he said, pulling the throttles all the way to idle and bunting the nose down to maintain 250 knots. He bumped them back up a bit to pucker the nozzles, which would squeeze more thrust, and precious range, from his engines.

Then he called *Knight* to shape his backup plan. He wanted them to send the SAR helo in case tanking was unsuccessful. "*Knight*, better get *Switchblade* out here."

The E-2 controller replied, "Roger, already enroute."

Wilson continued his mental calculations. His ground speed was about four miles a minute and he was descending at 1,500 feet per minute. In seven minutes, he would be at the coast passing 10,000 feet, with 300, maybe 400 pounds left. He increased his rate of descent to 2,000 feet per minute, accepting a faster air speed for a lower altitude at the coast. The FUEL LO caution remained illuminated on his left display as a constant reminder.

His radar picked up a contact 30 degrees right at 40 miles. Bumping the castle switch, he locked it, revealing a bogey with hot aspect approaching him at .7 indicated mach, 16,000 feet.

"*Knight*, four-zero-two, contact two-nine-zero, thirty-five miles, sixteen thousand, Declare."

"*Raven,* that's *Redeye* seven-zero-four to the rescue."

"Roger that – break, break – *Redeye,* four-oh-two. Descend to angels five. Turn right ten degrees to intercept. Keep your knots up."

"Roger that, *Raven*... What's your state?"

"Fumes," Wilson replied, not far off the truth.

"Roger, we're at red-line air speed."

Wilson knew the only way to affect the rendezvous with the tanker before he flamed out was for the S-3 to meet him over the coast. That would mean a third American violation of Iranian airspace during the past 30 minutes. *Screw it,* he thought. The damage is done.

But would *Redeye 704* comply? Wilson needed to know. "Seven-oh-four," he said with meaning. "I need you to help me in here."

"No worries, *Raven,*" came the reply.

Wilson could not wait to find out who was in *704.* He planned to buy them a drink in the next liberty port. However, right now, he had to face the reality of a possible ejection in the next five minutes. He removed his kneeboard and placed it on the right console. He had worn that kneeboard on his right knee since flight school, and he would hate to lose it forever if he needed to blast himself out of the cockpit. However, there was just no need for it during an ejection.

"Flip, Cajun." The skipper was calling on tac frequency, which meant he was still on deck monitoring what he could from the line-of-sight radio transmissions.

"Yes, sir, on the bingo descent. Still feet dry. Less than four hun'erd pounds. *Redeye* joining."

"Roger, glad you're okay. Will let you fly the jet... Get out when you have to."

"I think Prince is gone, sir. Didn't see a chute," Wilson added.

"Roger, take care of yourself now. We'll talk about it when you're back."

Wilson thought about the CO absorbing the probable loss of one of his pilots, one of his kids. Prince was a favorite of no one, but even now, in extremis, Wilson was already mourning him. He was almost certain Prince had not survived the aircraft break-up to eject. In fact, he feared Prince had already frozen to death from the well-below-zero outside air temperature that had worked its way into the unpressurized cockpit. Wilson recalled the image of Prince slumped over in his ejection seat just before the missile impact.

He had to put Prince out of his mind when he saw the S-3 transition into the 20-mile radar scale as the *Viking* raced to meet him with its life-saving fuel.

Things were going to happen fast now, and this was his only chance. He bumped the stick to sweeten the intercept heading.

Suddenly GUARD erupted. *"Redeye seven-zero-four, this is Mike One Kilo. You are standing into danger! Turn right to two-seven-zero!"*

Damn, Wilson thought. *That small-boy* still *doesn't have the picture.* Wilson ignored the transmission and hoped *704* would do the same. He noticed, for the first time, the muscle tension that had built up in his body over the past 30 minutes. It had seemed to localize in his right shoulder and neck region, and he rubbed his shoulder through the torso harness strap.

Wilson visually picked up the *Viking* inside 15 miles, a speck against the white haze on the western horizon. Thankfully, it was descending as Wilson had instructed. He rolled the jet up to check below him and saw a dirt road meandering along the coastal plain. His inspection found nothing on it—no motion whatsoever.

Now five miles from the coast, he called to the *Redeye* tanker. "Seven-oh-four, I'm gonna call your turn. Maintain air speed. On my signal, I'll need you to break right and bleed to extend the basket. I plan to be on your left wing when you roll out."

"Roger that, *Raven.* Standing by," *Redeye* replied.

The aircraft were approaching each other fast, but once Wilson gave the order to break right, he would have no other options; he would be committed to the join up. Without extra fuel, Wilson had to plan it perfectly. He would have to direct the S-3 to roll out and to slow to the basket extension speed of 225 just as Wilson got there. The radar scale decremented to 10 miles, and the small rectangular "brick"–that signified the S-3–was now moving fast toward him. He looked outside and saw the S-3 on a collision course. The *Viking* was at five miles with lots of closure, and Wilson fought the urge to have him break well in front of him. *C'mon, c'mon...now!*

"*Redeye,* break right heading two-three-zero. *Go!*" Wilson commanded.

"Roger."

Immediately the S-3 threw his left wing up and pulled hard away from him and toward the water. Wilson watched the S-3 roll up and pull, streaming thin vapor trails from the wingtips. He checked into him a few degrees but held his rate of descent and air speed as he drew closer. Wilson's eyes were outside now assessing the closure, and he saw the *Viking* roll out a quarter-mile ahead and below him, speed brakes open and slowing to extend the basket.

"*Redeye,* check left ten," Wilson called to sweeten the rendezvous.

"Roger, Flip, checkin' left."

Wilson approached the S-3 one thousand feet above at his 7 o'clock, his fuel indicating only 250 pounds. He pushed the nose over to gain a few more knots of closure, almost directly above the tanker and practically came down on top of it. Sensing the development of an overshoot, he extended the refueling probe to slow himself, and the increased drag of the probe bled a few knots. Because he was in danger of passing the tanker, he popped the speed brake for a few seconds and then retracted it to remain co-air speed.

Wilson fed in top rudder to bleed air speed and descend, and the *Viking* extended the basket from the wing-mounted refueling store, which payed out the basket via a 40-foot hose into the airstream.

"Hold that air speed," Wilson said.

"Roger."

Wilson noticed, while holding top rudder and assessing closure, that they had passed over the coastline. *At least we are feet wet,* Wilson thought, He took another glance at the fuel—180 pounds. *This is it.*

Wilson pushed the nose down for the final 50 feet and pulled it back up to level himself as he slid behind the tanker and stabilized. Bringing the throttles up for the first time in ten minutes, he placed the probe three feet behind the basket, which was mercifully steady in the clear air. He goosed the power and gripped the stick as he maneuvered his probe inches from the basket. He was surprised one or both of the engines hadn't failed yet due to fuel starvation. He then gave it a shot of power and rammed the probe home. The impact caused the hose to make an undulating sine-wave motion back to the store. When he didn't see the green transfer light on the store, he thought, for an instant, of backing out for one more shot to seat the probe. Then it illuminated, and a sense of relief flooded over him. The fuel gauge increased to 240, 280, 350...

"*Departure,* four-oh-two's plugged and receiving," *Redeye 704* called to the ship.

"Roger *Redeye,* you are cleared to give 5,000."

The S-3 began a shallow right turn toward the ship. Wilson, still plugged in, concentrated on staying in position behind the store to receive fuel. Although he took glances at the fuel gauge—*passing 1,000 pounds!*—he did not have to think for a moment. *Let someone else navigate,* he thought. *Let someone else talk on the radio.*

At that moment the same distinctive Iranian voice came up on GUARD and jolted Wilson back to reality: "U.S. Navy warplanes, you are leaving the Tehran Flight Information Region and Islamic Republic airspace. Contact Bahrain FIR on frequency three-one-seven-point-five. We hope you enjoyed your stay. Please come again."

CHAPTER 41

CAG Tony Swoboda and Cajun greeted Wilson at the ladder as he shut down *402* along the foul line. Wilson was exhausted, and despite the piercing whine of jet engines all around him, he just wanted to sit there in the ejection seat with his head back and his eyes closed, feeling the warmth of the sun on his face. Mindful, though, of hundreds of eyes focused on him, he turned off the displays, the radios, the computer and all the other avionics components—and made sure he used the same method he always used postflight. He then gathered his nav-bag and, double-checked his seat safe, and pulled himself out and onto the left LEX and down the ladder.

Once on deck, Wilson turned first to Riley, the plane captain, and three flight deck troubleshooters. "Jet's down for overstress, guys, and the top of the left outer wing panel was impacted by four-twelve." They nodded, tight-lipped, but understood the significance of the statement. "Thanks guys, nice job." He turned to slap the young plane captain on the back and said, "Riley, thanks."

"Thank you, sir. Glad you're okay," Airman Riley replied with searching eyes, still trying to make sense of the apparent loss of Lieutenant "Prince" Howard.

Wilson then turned to CAG, who extended his hand and grabbed his arm. "*Welcome home*, Jim. You did an *outstanding* job today," he shouted over the din of the flight deck, squeezing Wilson's hand like a vise grip. "Let's talk about it below," CAG said. "The admiral wants to see you."

With a grim smile visible under the dark visor of his helmet, Cajun patted Wilson on the back. CAG led them below to the Captain's passageway and flag country. CAG Swoboda was an F-14 radar intercept officer by trade, and commanded one of the last F-14 squadrons. Short and stocky, with a weathered face and squinty eyes, he could pass for a mob boss, an impression exacerbated by his Philly street accent. In the wing, he was popular, respected as a fair leader who knew his business. As they navigated the labyrinth of passageways, Swoboda peppered Wilson with questions: *How many missiles did you see? Was there any ground fire? How many Iranian aircraft did you see? Are you sure Howard didn't get out?* Rounding the corner to the main starboard passageway Wilson looked

aft and saw Psycho. She gave him a smile and a look that conveyed her thoughts: *Good to see you back, Flip.*

When they got to the admiral's in-port cabin, Wilson was led to the large, well-appointed living area, which was full of flag and air wing staff officers, including DCAG and intel officers from CVIC. Wilson, face etched with lines from his oxygen mask and his flight suit stained with perspiration, felt conspicuous in flag country. When the flag lieutenant brought him a glass of water, Wilson downed it in one gulp.

Captain Swartzmann emerged from flag plot in his navy blue sweater, glasses perched on the tip of his beak-like nose. *If he's not the oldest officer in the Navy,* Wilson thought, *he looks like it.* He resembled a dour, pasty-faced Puritan out of the Massachusetts Bay Colony—someone like Ichabod Crane. He walked up to Wilson as if to inspect him. Without even looking Wilson in the eye, he opened his notebook and asked, "So, what were you guys doing over Iran?"

Taken aback by the implication, Wilson's mouth opened and his eyes widened in shock. Before he could answer, CAG did it for him.

"Gene, his wingman was incapacitated over the Gulf and flew into Iran on autopilot. Jim stayed with him in an effort to revive him—and even tried to nudge him back to the west with his own airplane. Very dangerous. The Iranians shot Lieutenant Howard down, and Jim—with some damn good flying—fought his way out in an unarmed airplane. Barely made it back."

Swartzmann, unmoved, peered down at CAG. "I asked *him.*"

A chill filled the room, and 30 people looked at CAG to see how he would react. Swoboda, used to the cutting sarcasm of the Chief of Staff toward his aviators, was having none of it.

"This pilot is *mine,*" he exploded, "and I haven't had the chance to properly question him yet. I haven't even had the chance to review his tapes! I was ordered to bring him here directly from the jet and here he is. But I *resent* your insinuation that he or Howard were doing anything less than a by-the-book routine training mission."

Just then Admiral Smith, wearing khakis and a green flight jacket, entered from flag plot. Everyone in the room came to attention. "Flip," he said in his rich baritone as he walked up to Wilson with his hand extended. The admiral was short and wiry, with salt and pepper hair and a long, weathered face. His eyes were big and brown under bushy brows, and his booming voice did not match his slim body. "Well done today, and I'm sorry about the loss of your wingman." Turning to Cajun, he added, "Skipper, I'm afraid national assets indicate he's dead. Not *official* yet, but there doesn't appear to be much of a chance. I'm very

sorry. When we're done here, I want you to call the commodore back home to prepare him for the official word when it comes. Gene, make that happen, please."

"Yes, sir," the Chief of Staff replied.

Turning to Wilson, Smith said, "Flip, let's hear it. What happened?"

"Sir, we'd just finished a 1v1 south of the ship and were on the ladder. We went up to hang on the blades at 28,000. We motored a while, and as we neared the Iranian coast, I came up on the radio for him to turn around. He didn't respond, and I got short with him to turn, but nothing. When I joined up, I saw him motionless, but I also saw his mask dangling down and his canteen in his hand. I started yelling at him to wake him up, figuring it was hypoxia. So I'm yelling at him, and then all the strike group ships and everyone else starts giving us *Waterloo* calls, so I have to deal with trying to explain to them what we've got here."

Smith nodded as Wilson continued.

"We entered Iran about 80 miles south of Bushier, a pretty deserted area, but we were tracking northeast at 450 knots ground. I figured we had to get out of Iran, so I tried to get underneath his wing to see if my jet wash could roll him up a bit. It worked a little, but his autopilot fought it. At one point we swapped paint when his wingtip slammed down on me. By then Prince was not moving, and his canopy started to freeze up. My cockpit was at 12K, and I'm thinking he's got a pressurization problem, and he's hypoxic with his mask off. I was talking to *Knight* the whole time, and he called some bogeys out of Bushier at my 9 o'clock long. At the same time, I started getting some RWR hits off the nose. My scope was clean, but something didn't feel right. I opened up a bit off Prince, and a minute later a missile came down on him. It looked like a streak—white—and I'd say it hit just behind the cockpit. No warning. No plume. Just a huge fireball, and his jet started breaking up. Never saw a chute."

Everyone in the room was focused on Wilson, and behind the crowd of officers Wilson noticed a sailor setting the admiral's dinner table. He, too, was listening.

"Go on," Smith said.

"I turned to engage—training took over—and we went to the merge. At first I thought it was a MiG, but this jet was something I've not seen before. Never seen anything like it. It had a long fuselage with a small nose, a huge intake, canards up forward, delta wings..."

"Was it *this*?" the Air Wing Intelligence Officer asked, showing him a photo of a jet. Wilson studied it...the long bowed fuselage, the huge intake, the slight "V" to the vertical stabs, the canards.

"Yes, sir, it is," he replied. "What is it?"

The "spy" answered. "It's the Mikoyan Project 1.44, also known as the MiG-35. It's a fifth-generation technology demonstrator designed and built by the Russians in the late 90s. The NATO designation is *Flatpack*. Stealth design, two big engines, 1-to-1 thrust to weight, supercruise, thrust vectoring. Russia built five of them, but rejected the design because of the poor radar in the nose and low airframe g loading. Little power out and low range—they rely too much on GCI control. And, despite the large fuselage, it's fuel limited. Hariri launched with half a fuel load anyway, like all the Iranians do."

Wilson looked puzzled. "Hariri? Who's Hariri, sir?" he asked.

"Their wing commander, a colonel," Admiral Smith said. "You fought him." Wilson absorbed the information, and recalled the pilot's eyes. The eyes had a name...*Colonel Hariri*.

The Intel Officer continued. "He's the wing commander at Shiraz. Our dossier says he flew *Tomcats* in the Iran-Iraq War and got three kills."

Smith waved his hand and cut him off. "What happened postmerge?" he asked Wilson.

"Sir, we went one-circle," Wilson said, "and I pulled inside him. I had angles at the second merge and pulled hard across his six, but he just *stopped*. Just stood on the cans and stopped in midair. He then did a cobra-like maneuver and flushed me out in front. Incredible. He took a snapshot that *just* missed low. Then we spiraled down to the deck. I had an opportunity to extend and got down into the weeds. He never took that second missile shot, and I figured it was hung. He chased me a bit down low, but I reversed. He then pitched out of the fight and headed to the northeast, probably back to Shiraz, if that's where he's from."

Wilson looked directly at the admiral to ask about Prince. "Sir, the vis was great, and I never saw a chute. But do we have *definitive* proof he's dead?"

Smith looked at Cajun and CAG, then back at Wilson. "That's what Washington says. And your eyewitness account seems to confirm it. We tend to think he didn't survive, but—for now—he's officially *missing*. We're workin' it, with Washington's help." He then changed the subject.

"Jim, again, *superb* job staying with Howard and trying to save him. And your survival against this *Flatpack* was eye-watering, not to mention your driving the join-up with *Texaco* to save your jet. The phones and e-mail are turned off now due to this ruckus, but I want you to call home to your wife. Gene, set that up, please."

"Yes, sir," Swartzmann replied, scribbling something in his notebook.

Smith drew closer to Wilson. "Lieutenant Howard is missing and we are searching for him. Tell your wife that. Tell her you are safe, and we're not going to fly tonight. She'll sleep soundly after hearing your voice."

"Thank you, sir."

"Then go to CVIC for a debrief and write your statement. Then get some food and rest. Got it?" the admiral asked with a wink.

"Aye, aye, sir." Wilson said.

"CAG? Skipper?" Smith asked each of Wilson's superiors.

"As ordered, sir," CAG Swoboda answered, and Cajun nodded in the affirmative.

"Good," Smith said with a smile, as he grabbed Wilson's arm. *"Good job, good job,"* he whispered to him before leaving.

Wilson then looked at Swartzmann who nodded for him to follow. Wilson was led into the flag staff office, and Swartzmann ordered one of the staff officers to set up a SATCOM line. Wilson wrote his number on a piece of paper for the officer, who was curious about why this pilot was receiving a special privilege. The officer dialed and handed Wilson the phone once it rang. Wilson looked at his watch – almost 0500 there. After two rings, Mary answered, still half asleep.

"Hellooo?"

"Mary."

"James? *James,* is that you?"

"Yeah, baby," Wilson answered self-consciously, as he looked up at Swartzmann's unsmiling face.

She exhaled. "You're calling *so early*...I need my..."

"Mary...Mary?"

"What...?"

"Mary...something's happened."

Chapter 42

Colonel Reza Hariri, a colonel in the Islamic Republic of Iran Air Force, lay on his back, awake in the darkness. He listened to the low tones of the muezzin from the minaret three blocks away as he summoned the people for *fard salah*, the first of five calls to prayer. Off in a different part of the city he could hear the faint sounds of another muezzin call the Shiite faithful to prayer. The mournful lines of the *Adhan* from that other minaret were broadcast across a scratchy loudspeaker.

For almost every morning of his 48 years, Hariri's brain had absorbed the message of the Holy Men chanting in Arabic…a language he little understood. He did know most of the meaning of the morning call to prayer: *I bear witness that there is no deity except God. Make haste towards prayer. There is no deity except God.*

He looked out the window at the mountain ridge to the east, outlined by a dim glow provided by a sun that would not spill over and upon the Iranian city of Shiraz for about two hours. He glanced at the alarm clock LCD display: 4:40. *He's late today*, he thought.

Hariri would have enjoyed the extra 10 minutes of sleep, but he had been awake all night, reliving yesterday morning's fight. He couldn't get the image out of his head: the American was *right there*, out of airspeed and inverted, almost hovering in the sky in front of him—less than a soccer pitch away. The F-18 had filled his windscreen as Hariri's nose tracked down to cut him in half with a cannon burst. His pipper was well above the *Hornet* when he squeezed the trigger—and nothing! Nothing for a split second until Hariri's nose fell, and he missed low. No! *He* didn't miss—it was the damned Russian aircraft and the inferior weapons system! How he wished for his beloved F-14 at that point, with a reliable gun and accurate sight.

As the Wing Commander of the IRIAF base at Shiraz, *Sarhang* Hariri happened to be inspecting the strip alert facility when the call had come in that American fighters were crossing the coast. A young *sargord* scrambled for the MiG-35, but Hariri stopped him, grabbed his helmet and ordered him to remove his g-suit, which fit Hariri to an acceptable level. Within minutes, Hariri had

the MiG taxiing for the runway and his rendezvous with destiny. *I was meant to be here,* he thought.

His mind wandered to his last guns kill, an execution really. Winter of 1988, northwest of Kharg Island. A lone Iraqi *Mirage* returning to Iraq flew in front of Hariri and his wingman moments after Hariri had shot down another F-1 with a *Sidewinder,* causing the Arab to spin out of control into the white cloud layer below.

He saw the *Mirage* a few miles ahead, crossing left to right off his nose and low. The fighter was just cruising along straight and level after its own attack on a tanker, oblivious to both the destruction of his countryman seconds earlier and the presence of his assailant now coming out of the sun. With calm resolve, Hariri rolled in behind him, pulled power and popped the speedbrakes while Hariri's useless radar intercept officer cried *"God is great!"* over the intercom.

"Shut up and look for the enemy," Hariri scolded him. He lined his *Tomcat* up on the Iraqi's 6 o'clock—he still hadn't budged—and squeezed the trigger from 200 meters behind. He saw the first 20mm tracers hit the fuselage; massive yellow flames and black smoke erupted from the fuselage and wings. Hariri overtook the fighter as it slowed in its death throes—now covered in flames. He saw inside the cockpit and watched as the pilot's arms frantically reached for the ejection seat face curtain through the fire. He was being burned alive. The canopy then blew off and flames poured out of the cockpit into the slip-stream, followed in an instant by the ejection seat and pilot exploding from the inferno—completely engulfed. Hariri watched the fireball, now a flaming arc, pick up speed and rate of descent as it disappeared into the same undercast as his mate moments earlier. Despite two aerial victories inside three min-utes, Hariri could not erase the sickening image of the burning pilot from his mind. Once he crossed into a safe area south of Kharg, he wretched into his glove.

In 1979, when the Shah of Iran fell from power, Hariri was weeks away from starting flight school with the American Navy at Pensacola. Twenty years old at the time, he was identified as pilot material, and he was blessed with 20/10 vision and exceptional athletic ability. His physical stamina and hand-eye coordination as a soccer midfielder, coupled with his quick mind, caught the attention of the military representative at the University of Tehran. His father's position as the head of Tehran's electrical generating facility also was helpful in obtaining a flight school slot for young Hariri. When the revolutionaries took over, the Hariri family was spared from the purges of those bureaucrats close to the Shah...the lights still needed to work, no matter who was in charge.

Hariri was not devout growing up, but to deflect unwanted attention, he grew a beard and made the daily prayers in the mosque. His newfound religious "zeal," together with his physical and mental gifts, led to a marriage of convenience between Hariri and the revolutionaries. In order to fight Saddam's attacking air force, they needed young pilots to replenish those they had purged after the revolution. Hariri turned out to be the natural his superiors had suspected, and he soon was flying the frontline F-14 *Tomcat*, compiling an enviable combat record and moving up fast. Though he had missed his chance in Pensacola to learn from the best, Hariri was determined to prove he could succeed as a fighter pilot without U.S. training.

After his double-kill flight, Hariri was a hero of the Islamic Republic. Then, when he scored again over Kharg later that year, he thought his childhood dream of becoming a fighter ace would come true. But the Iranians had flown little during the last months of the war, and the times they did encounter Iraqi fighters, Hariri was elsewhere. The horrific ground war had ended with half a million slaughtered, and the air force had not engaged in aerial combat since.

However, Hariri's single-minded focus was to prepare himself, and then his squadron, to fight and to defeat the Gulf Sheikdoms, the Americans, the Pakistanis.... It did not matter who threw down the gauntlet, Hariri would pick it up. He eschewed women and lived like a warrior-monk until the higher-ups thought it would look better if he married. Therefore, a few years ago he had married Atosa, a beauty sixteen years his junior. She had dark almond eyes and long, flowing hair she covered with stylish Italian scarves, showing as much of it as she could at the bazaar and still keep the religious police away.

In the dawn twilight, he thought about the pilots he had defeated. *Arabs!* Arabs, who for years had proved themselves inept against the superior equipment and training of the Israelis and the Americans. Arab pilots who seemed incapable of thinking for themselves, tied as they were to strict instructions from the ground. Hariri's last Iraqi foe had at least held him off for a full-circle before Hariri's missile found its mark, but the fights were almost not fair.

Like his fourth kill yesterday—a forward quarter missile against a half-dead American in a non-maneuvering aircraft. *Nothing more than simulator training, a chalkboard exercise! A video game! What pride can one take in that?*

But his wingman.....*that* was the challenge he'd waited a lifetime for, the fight he'd dreamed of. An American F-18 *Hornet*, avenging his mate's death, coming to the merge with a knife in his teeth and turning hard... *This* was a worthy opponent. Hariri was ready, knowing how he would maneuver his aircraft at the merge and bait the American to give everything away. He would then stand

his MiG on its tail and let the American fly out in front. It worked to perfection, the way Hariri had dreamed it would, the way he had *planned* it. Unlike so many religious pilots who called on God to vanquish the enemy, whether they were prepared or not, Hariri had planned such a moment for years. He had studied his own aircraft, smuggled journals from Western intelligence sources, and searched out every bit of information he could on the Internet—all for that moment...

His nose tracked down.... His finger squeezed the trigger...

Damn! Blast! His weapons system let him down, and the enemy escaped, avoiding more gun shots and never having to face his remaining missile—which was *hung on the rail! Dammit!* The final insult had been running low on fuel and having to break off the engagement... all because the Iranian air force didn't trust its pilots to take off with full loads, afraid they would defect. *After I've given 29 years of faithful service, the monkeys think I, the bloody Wing Commander, will fly across the Gulf to Bahrain,* he thundered in his mind, exhaling deeply with disgust.

After landing, Hariri had exploded into a profanity-laced tirade at everyone: his crew chief, the armorers, and the avionics technicians, saving his best salvo for the Russian technical representative. During the flight debriefing, he was asked endless questions about the *Hornet*: What was it carrying? How did the American fly it? And, the question that caused his blood to boil—*Why didn't he shoot that one down, too?* While the mouthpieces in Tehran rejoiced on the BBC and CNN about downing the imperialist American fighter over Islamic Republic soil—proving to the world that the Americans are girding for a fight and that Iran would destroy anyone violating her sovereign airspace— Hariri had to hear over and over from the generals and the bastard religious officer about how *he* let down the Islamic Republic. *Swine! Imbeciles!* Despite their ignorance, it was almost too much to bear.

Then, a shock—they told him the pilot was an African! *How can an African fight for the Great Satan?* Hariri wondered. *If this pilot—named Wilson—is Muslim, is he devout? Do the Americans conscript Africans to fly their planes?*

When told Wilson was also a graduate of the legendary U.S. Navy Fighter Weapons School, or TOPGUN, Hariri had heard everything. He had fought, and all but defeated, an American TOPGUN, who was also an African—and possibly a brother Muslim. Hariri's initial confusion soon turned to anger and determination. *Muslim or not,* he thought, *Wilson had aligned himself with the Great Satan. If the Americans gave him a jet to fly, nothing can hold Wilson back from defecting and pledging his allegiance to the Islamic Republic.*

No matter…Hariri had proved to himself that, even without Western train-ing, he could engage and defeat an American in a frontline F-18…a TOPGUN no less! He craved a win, he *must always* win, and prayed that the international situation would escalate so he could have another shot at the Americans. *If I am lucky, it will be this TOPGUN-trained African,* he thought. He would then become an ace and join the elite list of *Persian* aces formed during the Iran-Iraq War.

Atosa, still naked, stirred next to him. She had offered herself to him last night, but he had rebuffed her, unable to forgive the Russians, the generals, and even himself for not downing the second American. The thought of this Wilson consumed him. Exasperated, she whispered, "Why can you not sleep, azizam?"

Hariri grunted. "Too much adrenaline."

She turned to him and pressed her body close, her French perfume filling his nostrils. "You defended us from the Americans. You are a hero, *my* hero! Why can you not sleep?"

Hariri said nothing. He then took a breath, as if to talk, but only exhaled deeply. *She wouldn't understand,* he thought, but he knew she was going to rebuke him for his refusal to make love last night and to talk now.

"Let it *go*, Reza, and next time shoot them *all* down, or *don't come back.*" She rolled away and pulled the covers up over her shoulders. They remained motionless in the dark, lying in the same bed, but emotionally separated by a sea of anger, his anger.

Damn Iranian women, Hariri thought. Even though Atosa usually proved herself to be easygoing and supportive, she was an Iranian woman first, and they were *tough* on their men. Hariri let out a breath. Since the excitement of yesterday, he *had* been an ass to his young wife. Nevertheless, she was not afraid to stand up to him.

Hariri placed his hand on the warm skin of her smooth hip. She flinched, and then allowed it to remain. Hariri wondered, *Does Wilson have a wife next to him on that cursed ship three hundred kilometers away?*

CHAPTER 43

Day is done, gone the sun,
From the lake, from the hills, from the sky.
All is well, rest in peace, God is nigh.

In his service dress blue uniform, eyes locked straight ahead, Wilson saluted from his position in front of the officers and chiefs. The rest of VFA-64 stood at attention behind him in Hangar Bay Two while the bugler played taps. As he listened to the haunting notes, he thought about other times he had stood at attention in ranks and saluted other fallen comrades over the years. How many? Nine? Ten? He figured it was too many, whatever it was. Most of those comrades had been lost to pilot error...and it appeared Prince was another. Even at this moment, Wilson's mind continued to analyze the situation. Removing his mask at altitude wasn't smart, and a probable pressurization leak made the poor decision deadly. Hariri's missile destroyed Prince's *Hornet* and may have killed him outright, but if he was not dead in the cockpit before impact he was minutes from it. Hypoxia or an air-to-air missile—both can kill.

For Wilson, the past 48 hours had been a blur: debriefings, investigative queries, written statements, SATCOM calls from TOPGUN staff officers, classified email messages, well wishes from air wing friends in the wardroom and passageways, department head meetings, memorial service planning meetings, and retelling the events of the shootdown and MiG-35 engagement. Added to that mix now was the necessity to avoid the media, which had sent a dozen reporters out to the ship the day after the shootdown. He was shocked at the speed they arrived onboard, with Navy support at every level.

The swarm diligently set about finding the pilot who was with Prince and who had fought the Iranian after Prince was shot down. In a display of unity, the air wing pilots removed their identifying squadron patches from their flight suits to throw off the snoopers, but try as he might to avoid the intruders, and despite the efforts of the ship's public affairs officer to protect him, Wilson sensed they were closing in on him. Yesterday, a reporter with large glasses and a graying ponytail had stopped him on the way to the wardroom. "It's you, isn't it?"

he asked with a smirk. Wilson gave him a blank look and continued on his way, but asked Weed to bring a plate of food to the stateroom that evening to avoid another confrontation. The word was out though. Just this morning he had passed two sailors in the hangar bay and overheard one whisper to the other, *"He's the guy."*

Most of the air wing aviators were at the memorial service and were seated in rows of folding chairs, with the admiral, CAG, and captain sitting in the front row. A *Raven* helmet and brown boots—signifying Prince's body—had been placed on a pedestal near the speaker's lectern. A sailor with a video camera recorded the proceedings for the family, catching, through the cavernous elevator opening, the characteristic hazy sky above the mirror-flat Gulf water, the bright morning sun glinting off its surface.

As the commanding officer, it was Cajun's responsibility to preside over the ceremony. He had asked for a JO volunteer to give a eulogy of LT Ramer Howard, the person, and that task had fallen to Nttty, Prince's bunkmate in the six-man *Ranch*. Nttty did a good job of relating the "PG" version of some fun times the two had shared: their days in flight school, how Nttty had marveled at the ease with which Prince made female friends in Virginia Beach, and a story or two of their madcap adventures with cab drivers while on liberty in Dubai. Nttty also told the audience that, in college, Prince was a lead vocalist in a cover band and once auditioned for *American Idol*, getting a trip to Hollywood but no more. Standing in ranks, Wilson reflected about how he had not known that about his dead squadronmate; he regretted he had learned it too late.

Cajun returned to the lectern head down, tight-lipped and somber under the visor of his combination cover. At this point in his career, a memorial service was a familiar ritual, yet one that was always difficult, and he had hoped to never speak at another one. Wilson knew Cajun would speak without notes, from his heart, and that the message would be powerful and consoling not only to those assembled in the hangar bay but to Prince's family who would receive a videotape of the proceedings. After perfunctory acknowledgements of the senior officers present, he began:

"Ladies and gentlemen, take a moment, if you will, to look at the sea and sky though the elevator opening. This sea...flat, with its brownish tinge, sometimes with strange sea creatures on its surface...different from the familiar seas back home off our own coasts: the choppy waters of the Atlantic, the serene blue waters of the Gulf of Mexico, and the long swells of the Pacific that crash so spectacularly into the shores

of our west coast. This sky…typically a milky brown haze like today that does not change for days or weeks… different from the brilliant blue skies of our homes which are often dotted with puffy cumulus clouds and accompanied by dramatic lighting displays that bring life-giving rain to our land. This sea. This sky. They look different. They *are* different.

Lieutenant Ramer Howard volunteered to leave the safety of his home and country and come *here*, to these strange and oftentimes hostile surroundings, to *defend freedom*, not only for ourselves but millions of others he never met. He was a talented and gifted young man, a man of accomplishment and promise even before he decided to volunteer. That he volunteered was enough, but he chose to pursue a career as a carrier pilot, a profession that is fraught with danger even in peacetime, and he accepted the challenge, and excelled at it. Alone over the open ocean far from shore, or high above an enemy country, carrier flying is always demanding, and often unforgiving. He met and passed the test of combat, striking blows against those who would kill and maim civilians. His loss, known to enemies of freedom around the world, gives them pause. An American volunteered to come here and risk his life to oppose tyranny. Those who use terror may now think twice about any cracks in American resolve. In his short life, he made a difference."

Wilson listened to the words of his skipper. While he knew Cajun was right, he could not grieve for Prince—and was ashamed by it. Wilson was the last person Prince had spoken to on earth, and Wilson had not felt a personal sense of loss. Had the specter of violent death so hardened him that he could no longer feel?

While Cajun finished his tribute to their fallen comrade, Wilson scanned the horizon through the open elevator door. He noticed the ship was turning, a routine occurrence in the confined waters of the Gulf. As the Chaplain closed the proceedings with the benediction, Wilson felt the ship vibrate underneath him and recognized the ship's increasing speed through the water. Once the ceremony ended and the squadron was dismissed, the sailors dispersed to their work centers and berthing spaces. Wilson ambled to the deck edge, squinting his eyes toward the western horizon. The ship was moving fast now, and he watched one large bow wave after another radiate away from the hull. Weed joined him at the edge.

"We're goin' somewhere in a hurry," he said.

"Yeah, southeast," Wilson responded, also wondering what it meant. Stepping away, he saw Lieutenant Metz approach them on his way up forward. Wilson walked over to intercept his path.

"Hey, Mike," he said, "where we goin' so fast?"

Metz stopped and looked at the two pilots. "Just got a message from NAV-CENT. We're heading out to the GOO."

CHAPTER 44

The shoot-down death of an American fighter pilot over Iranian soil was front page news all over the world. The story generated predictable glee in most African, Middle Eastern, and Asian communities, and indifferent resignation in other parts of the globe. The incident had now resulted in a diplomatic fight between Washington and Tehran, and the Iranians, masters at exploiting American misfortune, had the upper hand.

"God willing, American imperialist aggression will meet its end in the waters of the Persian Gulf!" thundered the Iranian foreign office. "The Great Satan is no match for the forces of God and has delivered to us an American angel of death who violated Islamic Republic sovereignty. Further American acts of war will be met with the full fury of Islamic Republic forces. They will guide more arrows of destruction to American planes that defile the Islamic Republic, and send their vessels of war to the bottom of the Persian Gulf to rid our waters of this wicked pestilence for all time, praise be to God."

While Washington issued a public apology for the violation of Iranian airspace, its expressions of dismay at the unprovoked downing of an incapacitated airman without warning after repeated calls to this fact on international radio distress channels was met worldwide by skepticism, if not disbelief. Many nations viewed the incident as an American probe, or as a precursor to a wider war with Iran, which in some Washington circles was viewed as inevitable. The GCC nations, always wary of their northern neighbor, quietly asked Washington to tone down their profile in the Gulf and to give assurances that this was not a sign of an American attack.

Intercepted Iranian communications, however, did show command and control confusion on part of the Islamic Republic Air Force. The Iranians were just as surprised as the Americans were at the sudden turn of events that led the two FA-18s into their airspace, and there was uncertainty in Tehran from conflicting field reports received from the south. The civil air traffic controllers correctly identified the incursion as pilot incapacity, with one aircraft in extremis accompanied by a wingman. However, airspace controllers from the military sector painted a picture of an imminent American attack. Regular

saber-rattling discourse by Iranian leaders likely conditioned those on watch to default to the military analysis, and with only minutes to decide on a course of action, they scrambled strip alert fighters from Bushier and Shiraz.

Control broke down further when different military sector controllers sent out conflicting orders to the fighters. The Bushier group was ordered to intercept and escort. The Shiraz group—which consisted of Hariri alone—was ordered to engage. American analysis was that the difference in orders could be explained by the vector of the *Raven* flight path, which was almost straight at Shiraz. The intelligence community analysts in Washington surmised it was more than the proximity to Shiraz that led the local air defense sector to engage without warning and without explicit orders from Tehran. On some satellite photos Washington had found an apparent cement production facility near Shiraz, but they were unsure of its true purpose. The analysts assumed that when the Iranians saw the Americans heading right for the facility, they took preemptive action. An unanswered question about this facility in Washington may have found an answer.

Even when the story moved off the front page, it remained the number one topic of conversation in the Virginia Beach fighter community. When the Strike Fighter Wing held a memorial at the chapel, most of the Oceana community, and all the *Raven* spouses, attended the service. Prince's parents, as the guests of honor, were awash in grief, especially because they were still in the midst of a diplomatic battle to receive the remains of their son from the Iranians.

Every spouse there knew that abrupt loss could be "part of the package" in naval aviation, but it was never discussed. Even veteran wives like Mary Wilson, who were friends with more than one young woman suddenly widowed, lived in a state of denial most of the time. Mary had been the first to know her husband was involved in Ramer Howard's last flight, and though her husband downplayed it at the time of his call to her, she had learned through the Oceana grapevine that her husband had literally dodged bullets over Iran. Hearing about the danger he had been in from people other than James scared her more than anything else she had experienced in her nine years of marriage to a Navy fighter pilot.

Several days later, she e-mailed a message to him.

Dear James,

Hearing your voice when you called the other day, despite the dreadful news you told me, was a big relief. I slept soundly that night knowing you were safe aboard the ship. You've been in the news quite a bit—well, not

you, but you as the "lost pilot's wingman, name withheld." So, you've been relegated to anonymous wingman. I guess that's better than nothing, huh?

The newspaper stories say you tried to save Ramer by placing your airplane close to him to get him to turn away from Iranian airspace. Then, after the missile hit and killed him, you were able to avoid the Iranians and return to the ship. I've heard rumors about what you did after Ramer was hit, that you were in a dogfight against a new type of fighter and that you almost got shot yourself. No one told me this directly, but the girls here have heard it from their husbands—the word gets out—and a friend told me. Not telling you who, it doesn't matter. And I'm glad she did. I don't blame you for not telling me yourself. You don't want me to worry, and I understand that.

You know I've seen you at parties, when you guys all gather in the corner with your beers and start talking with your hands and "shooting your watches," like you do every time. The other girls and I just roll our eyes and ignore you. But, as I watch you from across the room, you are at your most animated, doing more talking at that session than you will the rest of the evening. I used to think I knew what you do when you fly, but at times like this, I realize I don't have a clue. I can visualize you landing on the carrier and even dogfighting—but I really have no idea about the weapons you carry or the weapons you face. The complexity of what's going on around you with the thousands of little things you must monitor and consider is way beyond me. Sometimes, when you've tried to explain your flying to me, my eyes have glazed over. I want to know more, but at the same time, I really don't. In fact, I try not to even think about it until things like this make me think about it.

James, you are a good pilot, and while I understand it's dangerous out there, I'm confident in your ability, and I know you will come back to me. But I want you to know something else. The Iranian government has been causing problems and killing Americans for years. They are trying to get the bomb and they'll use it. They killed Ramer without warning and they tried to kill you. You probably wouldn't even be over there now except for them. I'm not sure what's going on, but I imagine you guys will be in the middle of it. Focus on them. If they start something with us, I want you to beat them. The kids and I are fine but America and the world must be able to live in peace. We need you and the Ravens to keep them at bay and defend freedom. Is that asking too much?

So, if the President sends you, don't worry about us, just concentrate on what you have to do, defeat them, and come back with that big shiny medal!

James, I love you so much and I am so proud of you. It's times like this—actually for the first time, during this cruise—that I realize just how important your job is, and that it's really just you guys out there on the frontline. You'll do great, too. Won't even be a fair fight!

So you've got the green light, Flip Wilson! Roger ball... Kick the fires... Hit the burner... Pull g's... Do all that pilot stuff and do it well. We're fine. We miss you tons, but lead those JOs to victory and bring everyone back soon!

Love,
Mary

Wilson smiled, and then read Mary's note a couple more times. What a woman. Alone with two little kids and bucking *him* up. He recognized her fear, but she was reassuring him, building *his* confidence and allowing *him* to compartmentalize for any eventuality in the coming weeks. He hit "Reply" and began typing:

Hey, Baby... Did you mean "light the tires?" ☺

CHAPTER 45

Where is he?

Wilson, in growing panic, searched the sky to his left. The Iranian was just there, going up in a left-to-left pass as Wilson unloaded for knots. He had been at the top of his arc and passing through the sun when Wilson had glanced inside and saw 450 knots in the HUD and the valley floor rushing up to meet him. Wilson yanked the throttles to idle and pulled on the stick as he returned his head to the top of the canopy, straining his neck and eyes back to see his foe. The g swallowed him at once, the anaconda-like squeezing of his torso and legs and the vise-grip pressure on his chest forced him to exhale. He gasped for breath as his mask slid down his nose. He heard a cockpit deedle, followed by *Tammy's* laconic warning: *Flight controls. Flight controls.* He figured he had just overstressed the airplane, but his first concern was sight, sight that had narrowed to a cone, a fuzzy gray cone—with nothing inside it! *Lose sight, lose fight.* He had just committed an error, and time—time now measured in mere seconds—would determine if the error was fatal.

As he leveled, Wilson kept the left turn in, re-engaged burner, and remained outside, looking for any moving object against the eastern horizon. He was in a large valley, karst ridges on either side about five miles away from him. *Where is he?* Wilson held his left angle of bank and searched for Hariri. He realized he was arcing and didn't know why. Wilson thought, *He's here, but where? And why am I arcing? I can't stop arcing!* His adrenaline had elevated to the point his mouth felt like it was stuffed with cotton.

Wilson's blood ran cold as he overbanked and picked up his foe. The MiG was below him at his 7 o'clock, a mile and closing—nose on. Breaking out of his funk, Wilson overbanked further and put the top of his aircraft on Hariri. With a good maneuvering air speed, Wilson continued to pull into him to throw off his shot. Hariri appeared motionless against the valley floor, and Wilson saw the speed brake open on the top of his airplane—a huge panel that made the *Flatpack* appear even bigger. Wilson was fascinated by the scene. He looked down into the gaping intake of the big Russian fighter, those powerful engines delivering 80,000 pounds of thrust. He saw white missiles on the pylons—pointing right at him.

Wilson had a sense of being "frozen," flying but unable to move through the sky. The Iranian seemed to be holding him in place—holding him by the throat before striking. Even in full afterburner, Wilson couldn't escape. It was as if he were running on sand in heavy boots, his antagonist drawing closer, showing more of the bottom of his aircraft. *He's pulling lead to shoot me,* Wilson thought, transfixed.

A bright, flickering light flashed over the right intake. Time compressed. Smaller lights floated off the fighter, then accelerated toward him. Wilson saw several whiz past, sounding a loud *pop* under his left wing. He wondered what they were…23 mm? 30 mm? He knew he needed to roll down and into the threat, make his jet skinny, gain more time, throw him off…but he couldn't. He was cornered, held in place as if the wily Iranian had pasted him against the sky like a cloud, a soft puffy cloud. Wilson was giving up, and he knew it.

Wilson watched the first round strike dead center on the left outer wing with a loud *crack*. The airplane shuddered as the black composite material splintered. He kept the pull in, into the threat over his left shoulder. For an instant the flashing stopped, but when it resumed, a great tongue of fire leapt from the Iranian's gun muzzle, and Wilson thought he could see the shell casings ejected into the air stream. The hits were almost instantaneous on his left wing, and he heard and felt another *crack* on the leading edge flap, followed by two impacts that sounded like a pencil punching through aluminum foil stretched across a tin can. These impacts caused small explosions on the top of the wing and fuselage. The alarms followed. A cacophony of warnings burst into his earphones in rapid succession: *Flight controls. Engine fire left. Engine left. Engine fire right.* More aluminum punches were accompanied by a chorus of pops as the rounds whizzed past at supersonic speed. The *Hornet* shook with each hit. More cockpit warning lights illuminated in unison, led by *both* engine fire lights.

The airplane *felt* different.

When Wilson snapped his head back over his left shoulder to find Hariri, fuel-fed flames filled his entire field of view. The bright orange fire, fanned by his 200-knot indicated air speed, covered the top of the aircraft and licked at the canopy. A sudden, loud *clank* threw Wilson hard against the left side of the cockpit, and his helmet slammed into the canopy with such force he thought he cracked the Plexiglas shell. The negative g caused his arms to fly up, and the force pinned him against the canopy. He couldn't reach the controls! His mask was pushed up against his eyes, and when he managed to open one of them, he saw nothing but orange fire and black smoke…then blue sky…brown earth…orange…black…blue… brown…. He was tumbling, and through the sounds of

aluminum and composite tearing into pieces, he noted that the aural warning tones had stopped.

Then a sickening sight flashed in front of him. The flaming fuselage of a *Hornet,* missing one wing and throwing off burning debris, corkscrewed through the air. When the *Raven* emblem on the tail emerged from the thick smoke, he realized in horror he was trapped in the tumbling and disintegrating cockpit now separated from the fuselage. His mind called out, *Eject! Eject!* but his arms would not, could not reach for the handle, pinned as they were against the canopy.

At that moment, the MiG flashed into view. It was Hariri! Then, a crushing explosion of pressure from rapid decompression pushed down on Wilson from all sides as the canopy was wrenched off the cockpit. A simultaneous roar of wind ripped at his helmet and pulled it off his head with the mask still attached. Wilson couldn't feel his left arm, and his feet and legs took blows from debris as the cockpit disintegrated around him. His mind again said, *Eject!* but he couldn't reach the handle. He wasn't sure if he was strapped in the seat anymore, and sensed a passing burst of heat in front of him. He heard a succession of loud pops with no idea of the source. *Reach for the handle! The handle!*

But he couldn't…his arms would not respond. With eyes closed against the cold wind lashing his body and whistling in his ears, he hurtled through space. Falling…. Waiting….

Wilson opened his eyes wide and realized he was inhaling and exhaling long and deep through his nose, his neck bathed in sweat. He rolled over and looked at the time on the digital clock: 4:37. Light streamed through small openings in the passageway bulkhead, and he heard footsteps walking past his stateroom door. Weed snored in his rack. The air conditioning blower thrummed as normal.

A nightmare. He had fought Hariri and lost—again. *Gunned! A tracking guns kill!* But worse than that, worse than the image of tumbling to his death, was the fact that he had *given up.* Jim Wilson did not give up, had never quit anything in his life. It was part of the fighter pilot creed: *Never give up.* You never give up on the count, never give up on a putt, *never* give up in a guns defense situation. That he gave up in his dreams scared Wilson, and as he lay in bed slowing his breathing, he thought about the implications. Was he afraid? The OPSO of VFA-64? The Strike Fighter Tactics Instructor who taught half the guys in the air wing about basic fighter maneuvers, about the importance of keeping sight, about last-ditch maneuvers to defeat a guns attack? Who was better than Flip Wilson in a 1v1? Hariri? The combat-proven Iranian flying

a monster jet that had power and an ability to point the nose unlike anything Wilson had ever seen before?

Was he afraid?

Wilson lay on his back in the darkness and looked up at the bottom of Weed's rack for the next hour.

CHAPTER 46

Approaching midnight, the guided missile frigate USS *Richard Best* cut through the murky waters of Hormuz on an outbound transit, her gas turbine engine emitting a steady high-pitched whine as she proceeded at 15 knots. In her darkened bridge, soft red lights used to preserve night vision and the green symbols displayed on the radar repeater, illuminated a group of shadowy figures. The watch team peered into the gloom—the haze reducing visibility to three miles—and plotted the course through the strait using radar and GPS navigation. Oman was 10 miles to the south, and the barren coastline offered few sharp objects or known lights from which to shoot bearings for fixes, even if the night had offered one of those rare moments of clear visibility.

The fracas between the *Valley Forge* FA-18s and the Iranian jet was several weeks past, and things appeared to be settling down between the two countries, now that the carrier was operating in the Gulf of Oman. However, what the *Airedales* did mattered little to the crew of *Richard Best*. After four long months in the North Arabian Gulf guarding the damned Iraqi oil platforms and dodging the lumbering tankers that seemed to have no one on the bridge, they were one month away from San Diego and home. The crew was more than ready to say good-bye to this hellhole.

Ready, but only after they passed one more challenge—a night transit of Hormuz. Following the shoot-down incident, NAVCENT had directed night transits of Hormuz in an effort both to minimize and to conceal the American presence among the north/south traffic on the waterway, much of it potentially hostile. *Best's* captain, Commander Mark Albright, blond and athletic at 39 years old, sat up straight in his chair, trying to discern the faint lights off his port bow. His left hand nervously stroked his chin. His helicopter was down with a transmission-line leak, and he wanted it airborne, scouting for contacts ahead of him in the outbound lane. He wanted, and needed, it *now*. He picked up the sound-powered phone to the flight deck.

"Yes, sir," answered one of his aviation lieutenants.

"What's the story, Eric?"

"Sir, we found the leak, and the chief is patching it up. We're going to run it to make sure it holds pressure...10 minutes, sir."

"*Expedite!* I need it airborne right away."

"Yes, sir."

Albright cradled the receiver, and queried the watch team. "Range to the *skunk?*"

"Eight thousand yards, sir," the officer of the deck replied.

"CPA?" Albright could just make out a white light on a masthead, stationary on the black horizon, as he waited for a reply.

"One thousand yards. He's tracking south at 3 knots," the OOD responded.

Dammit, Albright thought. From the other side of the bridge the young conning officer under training gave a command to the helm to maintain their track in the outbound lane. "Come right, steer course zero-seven-seven."

"Come right, steer course zero-seven-seven, aye," the 20-year-old helmsman answered. Moments later, he added, "Ma'am, my rudder is right five degrees...coming to new course zero-seven-seven."

"Very well."

Albright assessed the situation. The unidentified surface contact was tracking left to right and closing his ship. Not knowing what it was and with no airborne aircraft to tell him, he wanted to give it a wider berth. The only problem was that shoal water ahead on his right allowed him only so much sea room.

He spoke in a low voice to his officer of the deck who was standing next to him. "John, let's give this guy some more room. What's the CPA if you put us on the southern border of the lane?"

After consulting the radar repeater, Lieutenant John Reynolds answered, "Three thousand yards, sir."

Albright grunted. "All right, give me that and some change—as much as you can. Call him bridge-to-bridge."

"Aye, aye, sir," the officer of the deck replied, as he charted a course to comply. Within 10 seconds, he turned to the conning officer. "Conning officer, come right to new course one-one-zero."

"Aye, aye, sir. *Helm*, right standard rudder, steady course one-one-zero."

The helmsman turned the wheel while watching the rudder position indicator and repeated verbatim, "Right standard rudder, steady course one-one-zero, aye."

Just then the phone talker piped up. "Sir, signal bridge lookout reports surface contact bearing three-three-five relative, range 7,000 yards as a dhow, sir."

"Very well," Albright said. *A dhow*, he thought as he studied the solitary light in the distance. *But who's in it? And what are they doing?*

"Are they inside the lane, John?" he asked.

"Just outside, sir, but should cross into it in a few minutes."

"Rog," Albright replied.

He was tired, tired of four months in these restricted waters with obstacles everywhere, unidentified threats all around: above...and below the surface...sometimes even on his bridge in the form of junior officers who were for the most part competent, but who could suffer, without warning, a momentary lapse of judgment. Albright was on edge, and had to control himself so as not to alarm the crew.

Six hours to sunup, where we'll be pointing south and steaming fair into the Indian Ocean, Albright thought. He looked forward to opening her up to flank speed and leaving a wake behind him pointing aft at this god-forsaken patch of water he'd spent years of his life operating in. Never got a summer Med cruise, never got a Caribbean swing. Every single deployment of his 18-year career had taken him *here.*

"*I hate this fucking place,*" Albright muttered under his breath, staring ahead into the black night. Again, he rubbed the stubble on his chin.

"Sir?" the OOD inquired.

"What?" Albright answered, surprised he had spoken out loud. "Oh, nothing."

In the pilothouse of the dhow, the master walked to the port bridge wing and stepped outside. He looked down at a cluster of eight speedboats, each crewed by three or four Revolutionary Guard irregulars. The motley fleet of *boghammars*, as they were known to the Americans, consisted of everything from small, open-cockpit cigarette boats to a glorified skiff with an outboard motor. The boats were armed with RPGs, recoilless rifles, and sometimes frame-mounted mortars, with other light infantry weapons aboard. He motioned them to cast off their lines from the dhow and from one another, but warned them to keep close and out of sight of the American frigate. He then went inside and bumped the diesel throttles forward with his open palm. The engines growled deeper as the dhow increased speed on a course to intercept.

"Cap'n, the dhow's pick'n' up speed and appears to be heading southeast."

Albright snapped his head to the port bow. Because the dhow showed only a single light, it was nearly impossible to discern aspect in the darkness. Other lights on the horizon signified strait traffic, but this vessel, instead of falling off to port as per the rules of the road, had increased speed and had set a course to intercept or to cross in front. *Why is this guy screwing with me?* Albright wondered.

"Range to the contact?" Albright barked.

"Five thousand yards, sir. CPA one thousand."

"Increase speed to full," he responded.

"*Increase speed to full,* aye sir. Helm, engine ahead full. Indicate one four two revolutions for 20 knots," the conning officer commanded.

Once the lee helmsman repeated the order, Albright calmly said in the hushed darkness, "Sound general quarters."

"Sound general quarters, aye, sir!" the bosun acknowledged and reached up and hit the Klaxon.

BONG, BONG, BONG, BONG... "General quarters! General quarters! All hands, man your battle stations! Now set Material Condition Zebra throughout the ship!" *BONG, BONG, BONG, BONG...*

The bridge watch could hear the scramble of sailors running to their stations and closing watertight doors and hatches. Like the others, Albright broke out the gas mask stowed under his chair and pulled his socks up over his blue coveralls. All the while, he kept an eye on the dhow. Others in the bridge already had their flash gear and helmets on. Albright smiled at how much faster his people could do it for the real thing vice scheduled exercise. The whine of the LM 2500 gas turbine increased in intensity and permeated the bridge as the ship increased speed.

Albright shouted across the bridge, "Mister Reynolds, keep us outside 10 fathoms, but give me as much room as you can between me and this idiot."

"Aye, aye, Captain!" the OOD responded.

Richard Best was now hugging the southern border of the outbound shipping lane in order to run past this unidentified dhow that was getting dangerously close. Some three miles to starboard was shoal water and Omani territorial waters. Ahead was clear, with radar showing a very large crude carrier making the southbound turn in the lane at eight miles.

"*Range?*" Albright barked the question.

"Twenty-five hundred yards and closing, sir!"

"Five short blasts."

"Five short blasts, aye, sir!"

The ship delivered five blasts from the ship's horn, a deep resonating *hmmm* that carried across the water. The blasts, a message common to mariners, signified danger or disagreement. "Battle stations manned and ready, sir!" the bosun bellowed from his station amidships.

"Very well," the OOD answered.

Just then the phone talker sang out.

"Officer of the Deck, signal bridge lookout reports multiple contacts bearing three-three-zero relative at 2,000 yards. Identified as possible *boghammars*, sir!"

Albright snapped his head to the left and shouted, "Put a light on him! *Now!*"

A few seconds later a searchlight illuminated the water off the port bow, and the watch team saw several small bow waves cutting through the serene water a mile away—and pointed at *Richard Best*.

Boghammars!

"This is the Captain. I have the conn!" Albright shouted for all to hear. "Right standard rudder!"

"Right standard rudder, aye.... Sir, my rudder is right standard. No new course given!"

"Increase your rudder to right full," Albright said in a sharp tone, and grabbed the sound-powered phone. He snarled into the receiver. "We are under attack! Get that helo airborne *right now!*" Turning to his OOD, he added, "Mister Reynolds, give me a course between the sandbar and the coast. I want to scrape these guys off before we reverse to the east." The ship heeled to the left.

"Aye, aye, sir. We're going into Omani waters though," Reynolds replied.

"They'll get over it...*Rudder amidships*, mark your head!"

"Rudder amidships, aye, sir. Sir, my head is one-four-eight!"

"That should work for now, sir," Reynolds chimed in.

"Very well, steady as she goes. *Engine ahead flank*," Albright added.

As the helmsmen shouted over each other responding to the Captain's orders, the ship's *Seahawk* helicopter, *Talon 42* took off and flew past the port bridge wing. *Finally*, Albright thought.

The bridge was a flurry of activity, with Albright issuing orders to the helm and to his XO in combat concerning weapons status. He also sent a report to the task force commander with a call for assistance. His officers shouted navigation bearings and depth soundings to the team, and lookouts reported range and bearing to the lead *boghammar*. The Iranians were engaged in a tail chase with Albright, who planned to use the sand bar to port to prevent the Iranians from cutting the corner once he turned east. Maybe he could even cause them to run aground in the darkness, despite the fact the shoal was well marked with a

light. The lead boats were inside 1,500 yards and gaining as *Richard Best* sped through the water at 27 knots. Albright did the math in his head. They would be in effective RPG range in less than five minutes. The aft lookout had already reported sporadic small-arms fire from two of the boats.

"XO, any guidance from Fifth Fleet?" Albright shouted into the sound-powered phone.

"None yet."

That was all the captain of *Richard Best* needed. He was not going to subject his ship and crew to any more risk from these clear acts of war. "XO, this is the captain. Weapons free on the *boghammars* in trail approximately 1,000 yards."

"Aye, aye, sir," he replied.

Okay, Albright thought. *The wheels are in motion.*

"Sir, we're approaching shoal water in two minutes on this heading. Recommend come left to zero-nine-five."

Just then the CIWS 20mm cannon mounted above the helo hangar sprang to life with a loud guttural *BORRRRRRRPPP* as it targeted the first *boghammar*. Albright shouted over the din. "Mister Reynolds, you have the conn. Take us close aboard the sandbar, but stay outside 10 fathoms!"

"Aye, aye, sir. On the bridge, this is Lieutenant Reynolds and I have the conn. *Belay your reports!*"

Before Albright headed to combat one deck below, he stepped out on the port bridge wing and looked aft, covering his ears at the din. Another angry burst from the CIWS sent a streak of yellow tracers aft. They lit up the back of the ship and appeared to float toward the *boghammars*, almost hovering in space before hitting its target. He observed numerous ricochets and, for a moment, was awestruck at the display. At least one boat was now out of action, but Albright counted muzzle flashes from five or six other boats nearby. The ship heeled to starboard as Reynolds initiated his turn, unmasking the 76mm mount. The gun immediately unleashed a series of deafening metallic *BOOM*s, accompanied by a bright muzzle flash every second as it worked over a target. *Talon 42* got involved as it rained down a sudden band of machine-gun fire on the easternmost boat. Albright had pulled himself away to go below when a splash close aboard surprised him: then another splash slid past him as high as the bridge wing. *This isn't small arms*, he thought, and as he stepped back inside the pilothouse, he heard the lookout report. "*Boghammars* at three-one-zero relative going to three-two-zero. Five hundred yards!"

Recoilless rifle fire tore into *Richard Best's* superstructure and against her bridge windows, causing the watch team to duck down and scramble for cover

in order to avoid the shattered glass and flying debris. The .50 cal mount opened up on their swarming attackers, contributing to the confusing racket. The scene became a kaleidoscope of flashing light, screaming and shouting, heat, concussion...and blood. Just as Albright grabbed the sound-powered phone, a tremendous explosion blew through the bridge overhead, knocking everyone down. Once Albright regained his senses, the first thing he saw was an arc of sparks from a severed electrical cable. Then light from a battle lantern allowed him to see that several men were down on the starboard side of the bridge. His OOD Reynolds looked at him from under his helmet in wide-eyed shock. "Are you okay?" Albright shouted.

"Yes, sir!" Reynolds answered, touching his ears to indicate he could not hear Albright well.

"Let's get out of here!" Albright shouted as he picked himself up.

The OOD worked the helm on a course to get them back into open water. The port side of the frigate delivered a broadside of withering fire into the nimble Iranians, even as additional RPGs arced over the ship. Some hit the rigging and sprayed shrapnel on exposed personnel. Three members of the bridge watch team were down, and one wasn't moving. Cries of "Corpsman!" and "Get the Doc!" pierced the air.

The running gun battle lasted 10 minutes before *Richard Best* could speed away from her attackers, re-enter the outbound lane, and turn south. A line of impact marks marred her port side, and some rounds penetrated into the ship, killing one man in a damage control station. One "lucky" RPG found its way into the open helo hangar. Topside personnel took severe casualties, with one lookout and one gunner dead.

The Iranians took heavy losses: Eleven of nineteen *boghammars* were put out of action; few survived the well-aimed 20mm and 76mm fire. The .50 caliber gunners claimed two, and *Talon 42* was a key force multiplier with their 7.62mm gun. Once the Iranian boats had turned around in retreat, *Talon* had also seen mortar positions on the sandbar and silenced them.

Albright walked across the bridge and knelt over the conning officer where she had fallen. He held her cool hand, fighting the urge to recoil at the ghastly scene. She struggled to breathe, her breaths coming in gurgling fits that wracked her small body. Her lower jaw was gone, and her neck and khaki shirt were covered in blood. *What is she? Twenty-two years old?* he thought. A sailor with a battle lantern shined it near her face. Her eyes reacted, following the light, and then settled on her CO. Skin the color of porcelain surrounded her pretty blue eyes, all that was left of her face. Albright held back sobs.

"Molly," he said, just loud enough to be heard over the whine of the engine and the wind whipping through the bridge. She studied him for a moment as her body heaved and struggled. Then she looked ahead...and stopped struggling.

The corpsman began CPR immediately; "One, two, three... C'mon, Ensign O'Hara! *C'mon!* ...six, seven... C'mon ma'am! Please don't! *Please!*" With each compression, blood oozed out of an opening in her neck, and Albright placed his hand on the sailor's arm, a signal for him to stop. Tears streaked down the young man's face and his shoulders heaved. He opened his mouth and cried out to anyone who was listening. "She was e-mailing my little sister with tips on baton twirling. *She did that for me.*" Albright put his arm around the young sailor and knew that he, too, would miss the energy Ensign Molly O'Hara had brought to his wardroom.

Looking up to the dark sky, the corpsman wiped away a tear and streaked his face with the blood of an officer, now dead, who had cared about him as a person.

Part III

That he which hath no stomach to this fight,
Let him depart; his passport shall be made,
And crowns for convoy put into his purse;
We would not die in that man's company
That fears his fellowship to die with us.

from Shakespeare's *Henry V*

CHAPTER 47

Wilson stepped into his stateroom and flicked on the overhead light. "Wake up, sunshine, we've got tasking," he said.

His roommate was still under the covers in the top bunk. Groaning, Weed rolled over and said, "What now?"

"The Iranians hit a frigate in Hormuz last night, swarmed 'em with *bogham-mars*. USS *Richard Best* was transiting alone. Five dead, a bunch wounded."

Pulling himself up on his elbows, Weed looked at his roommate in shock. "*Holy shit!*" and sensing the increased vibration of the ship, asked, "Where are we going?"

"Southwest at 30 knots. Heard something about Masirah. Should be in the vicinity by sundown."

Weed climbed down from his bunk, went to the sink, and drew some water. "Are we meeting in CVIC?" he asked as he opened the medicine cabinet to retrieve his razor.

"Yep, zero-seven-thirty for all strike leads. CAG's kicking it off and Intel's going to give us the run down." Wilson answered as he ripped the Velcro patches off his flight suit and tossed them on his desk.

"And to think I was just getting used to seven-hour hops over Afghanistan with an oh-ridiculous-thirty recovery," Weed deadpanned, applying shaving cream to his cheek. "Oh, well. Care to grab a bowl of fruit loops with me before we join CAG?"

"No thanks, my brother. What time did you get in last night?"

"Zero-three."

For a few moments they were silent, Weed at the sink shaving and Wilson at his desk busy with some routine paperwork. They both thought about the Iranian targets they could be hitting, very soon. Wilson's mind wandered. It was incredible. The Iranians had taken on an American warship with no provocation. Did they want to start World War Three? Surely this was the big news in every capital across the globe. Wilson imagined world leaders calling Washington and imploring the Americans not to send waves of nuclear bombers to obliterate Iran...which Washington could do. *Why do world leaders defend Iran every time*

Iran kills or acts out some way? He further imagined there were some politicians in Washington calling for that. *Tehran, a city of millions—wiped out.* Or would they nuke Bandar Abbas? *Five sailors dead and we are spinning up. Rightfully so! But the frickin' Iranians kill that many soldiers each week in Diyala with IEDs and booby traps, and we look the other way.* Wilson wanted revenge, wanted to pop off a nuke and end the nearly 30 years of Iranian-sponsored terror and instability they exported around the world. *We'd be doing the whole world a favor.* He then remembered the Bible verse: *"For the sake of even ten good people, I will not destroy the city."*

Wilson broke the silence. "Gonna be a long day in CVIC."

"Yea, verily."

Thirty minutes later in the Carrier Intel Center, Wilson and Weed sat together in the third row. They waited, with other department heads from the *Buccaneers* and *Spartans*, for CAG Swoboda to address them with the tasking from above. Sitting in front of them were the air wing COs and XOs, and behind were assorted JOs, as well as officers from the flag and air wing staffs. Cajun sat in the front row next to the E-2 skipper, while Saint was at the opposite end of the row chatting up the Big Unit. Before them on the bulkhead were charts depicting Iran, with smaller charts and satellite imagery of the areas around Bandar Abbas, Jask, and Chah Bahar. Across the room the aircrew studied the charts, murmured about threat concentrations, and imprinted the surface-to-air threat rings on their brains. In the corner, Wilson noticed the SINS readout that confirmed the steady vibration of the deck below his feet. *Valley Forge* was on a southwest heading at 30 knots.

"'tenshun on deck!"

Chairs shifted and conversation stopped as the room sprung to attention, eyes locked forward. CAG's purposeful footsteps broke the silence, and halfway into the room, he grunted, "Seats." Everyone relaxed and sat back in their chairs. DCAG followed, and to Wilson it looked as if neither had slept during the night. The bare Velcro of CAG's flight suit, devoid of any patches but ready for imminent combat, was somewhat disconcerting. It indicated a *mindset.* Swoboda's face was set in a taciturn frown as he prepared to address his aircrew. Weed noted it, too, and whispered to his roommate, *"That's a game face."*

Swoboda wasted no time getting started:

"All right. You guys know the Iranians hit *Richard Best* last night as she was transiting Hormuz. Ambushed by a double-pince of *boghammars.* Five dead, sev-

enteen wounded. The ship took heavy damage to the bridge and topside spaces from RPG's and recoilless rifles on the boats and from *mortars* they staged on a sand bar in the narrowest part of the strait. You gotta hand it to them. Although I'm told the ship was alert for trouble and the captain did a great job, the Iranians waited till the last moment to show their hand. Their timing could not have been better. *Richard Best* did good work though…eleven *boghammars* sunk, several damaged and some 30 Iranians dead.

"The Revolutionary Guard conducted this attack. Iran has two navies, the Islamic Republic of Iran Navy and the Revolutionary Guard, or *Pasdaran*. They can work in concert or independently. This appears to be the Revolutionary Guard working solo. Since last night, commercial shipping through the strait has stopped. As a result, oil futures have shot up over thirty dollars per barrel, and the Asian markets are down five percent from their opening yesterday. You've seen CNN. Hormuz is the focus of the world right now as the Iranian action is a clear act of war. In Washington last night, the first question was *"Where's the nearest carrier?"*

Wilson's eyes wandered to the chart of Iran, figuring the distance from Shiraz to Bandar Abbas. *Three hundred miles? Two fifty?*

CAG continued:

"National command authority has tasked NAVCENT with the following objectives: severely degrade Iran's ability to harass shipping in the strait, hit the *Pasdaran* bases of operations, and eliminate the Iranians' *Kilo* subs wherever they are found. Imagery shows one of those subs in dry dock at Bandar Abbas. That's the first one to go away. The others will be found and *sunk*, at their moorings or on the high seas. If the Iranian surface navy stays in port, we'll leave them alone. But, if they come out, they are fair game and we'll put them on the bottom. The friggin' *boghammars* are what we're after, and we're going to hit them in their nests and degrade their ability to operate by destroying their fuel supply or maintenance facilities. Any *boghammar* we find underway? Gone."

The room was silent, every aircrew focused on the air wing commander. He was clearly incensed at the Revolutionary Guard. Behind him, Wilson overheard a shipmate whisper, "CAG's *pissed.*" Swoboda pointed to the chart.

"Our tasking is to hit targets in Bandar Abbas, Jask, and Chah Bahar. We will also conduct SUCAPs in the GOO and Hormuz to find any *Pasdaran* or Iranian navy assets underway. The coastal targets will take a couple of nights, and we'll be flying a dozen or so strike packages to accomplish it. The international waters stuff will take as long as it takes, and the priority is to locate and to neutralize the *Kilos.*

"We're going to have help, too. In the Gulf, SEALS are going to raid *Pasdaran* facilities on the Tunb Islands and Kisk. The *Tinian* ARG is coming up from the Horn of Africa with *Harriers* and *Cobras* to augment our SUCAP posture; they should get here by tomorrow. Air Force *Buffs* and B-1's from Diego Garcia will fly with you on several strikes. P-3's out of Masirah, with another four inbound, will help with the ASW picture. AWACS and more are coming. We are also going to have *Tomahawk* shooters from our own strike group and some more TLAM from one of the ARG small boys coming up. We've got lots of assets, and they are at *our disposal*. Right now *we* are the focus of national command authority."

Wilson glanced at Cajun, who remained focused on CAG. As Cajun's assistant strike leader, Wilson wondered what target they would receive, and surmised CAG would assign the skipper a tough one—probably in and around Bandar Abbas.

"Iran isn't a pushover like Iraq was five years ago. *Two hundred and fifty* combat aircraft, many of them fourth-generation, and as we found out last month, *fifth*-generation jets. Double-digit SAMs. Effective triple-A ranging from light to 100 millimeter. Modern, sea-skimming antiship missiles. And hundreds of *boghammars* using swarm tactics. These guys don't have what we have, but they present us with a formidable military problem. They are *smart* and they have *will*. They know we are heading back to the GOO, and they are dispersing their forces and getting their defenses ready. Again, our goal is not to invade Iran or even destroy the Iranian Navy, but to degrade their ability to conduct these raids in and around Hormuz and the GOO. This response option is limited and proportional, and it needs to be timely. That's why we are doing this now, because we don't have time to wait for help, and these guys need to know that we can smack them down with just a portion of the forces we have in theater. We need to make them think twice before they engage in another act of war, against us or anybody.

"Our first strike is tomorrow night in Bandar Abbas, followed by packages going to Jask and Chah Bahar. So as not to tip them off using any land-based activity, these strikes will be Navy and Marine only, from us and *Tinian*, and lots of TLAM in a coordinated manner. This could run just one night, probably two, with the Air Force bombers joining us then."

Wilson studied the known SAM rings along the Iranian coastline, as well as the fighter bases at Bandar Abbas and Chah Bahar, defenses which offered little in the way of sanctuary and reached well into the Gulf of Oman. Coordination, timing, and contingency planning, from launch to recovery, were going to be

extensive. His mind raced through what they needed to plan within the next 36 hours: the weapons plan, the launch sequence plan, the tanking plan, the defense suppression plan, the strike plan, and the search and rescue plan. Each had myriad requirements and considerations, and each carried its own set of variables that required detailed answers.

For the air wing strike leaders—senior squadron aircrew such as himself—striking anywhere along this heavily defended coastline would become a monumental challenge of coordination and execution. They had to accomplish the mission and keep losses to an absolute minimum. He knew the air wing would be up all night planning it, and up the following night flying it. *And* the next night, according to CAG. Air Wing Four and *Valley Forge* were up to the task, but CAG was right: by no means would this be *easy*. And by the looks of the huge black circles on the chart that signified the SAM threat rings, it was damn dangerous. CAG finished his message to his aviators.

"Ladies and gentlemen, we have frontline aircraft with *stand-off* weapons, accurate cruise missiles, superior sensors, and state-of-the-art electronic warfare capability—both active and passive. And we have you, the most highly trained and combat-experienced aircrew in the world, all purchased at great expense by our country. We will prevail, but we've gotta be smart and keep mistakes to a minimum. Keep it simple, and maximize the effectiveness of your blows. USS *Richard Best,* our sovereign U.S. territory in the Gulf, was there to defend the economic lifeline of an allied country. While conducting innocent passage through a vital international waterway, she was attacked by the forces of Iran, an attack which killed Americans and has thrown the world into economic turmoil. The Iranians miscalculated, and whether it was on a national or local level doesn't matter. Washington is tasking us with significantly degrading Iran's short-term ability to attack again, and to keep Hormuz open for commerce. Maybe the diplomats will de-escalate this, but you and I are going to be ready to go tomorrow night with fused ordnance on our aircraft and a detailed plan to use it. After the *spy* briefs you on the order of battle, each strike planning team will be assigned a target...and a secondary target for night two, if we get to that. Strike leaders, today at 1500 I want you and your assistant strike leads to brief me or DCAG on your thoughts and plans regarding your primary target. Later tonight, once we approve your choices, you'll visit the admiral's staff and brief him. Just give an overview, and we'll provide any rudder you need at that time. Obviously, this is all classified, and the crew can see we are transiting west at high speed, but we are to discuss this only in cleared spaces—not the wardroom, not in the passageways."

Once CAG finished, the air wing Intel officer provided an order-of-battle briefing, and the aviators listened in tight-lipped silence. Iran possessed the latest in high-tech military equipment, purchased from Russia, China, North Korea and even Europe. And the United States had sold Imperial Iran the F-14 *Tomcat*, which the Islamist regime had used to great success in skirmishes with the Iraqi Air Force during the 1980s. Even the venerable F-4 *Phantom II*, also provided to the Shah by the United States, was a serious airborne threat.

The SAMs were numerous and also modern, led by the Russian-built S-300, and had a range of over 100 miles. The Iranians had lots of tactical SAMs and modern MANPADS, some developed indigenously. While all of *Valley Forge's* fighter aircrew were combat experienced, very few had experience dodging a radar-guided SAM, or even seen one fired in their careers. It was common knowledge that CAG Swoboda and Admiral Smith had seen several of them during Desert Storm, and Wilson knew of Cajun's close encounter with a SA-6 over Kosovo, but that was it. With his talk, the CAG had done his job. Although they already knew the facts, everyone in a flight suit had been reminded that Iran possessed a major league defense. CAG had also reassured them, just by his demeanor, their leadership was not asking them to face anything they had not.

When the meeting broke up, groups of aircrew gathered around the chart and discussed the defenses and targets. Rows of long tables allowed planning teams to pore over the charts and weapons manuals in order to devise the best plan for success. Banks of computer terminals along the bulkheads were manned by JOs inserting target coordinates for closer review. Cajun's eyes met Wilson's, and Wilson walked over to join him.

"Yes, sir."

"Let's you and I look over this folder. It's the first strike—Bandar Abbas. Have the ready room pass the word for our strike planning team to join us here at 0900. Also, *Raven* AOM in the ready room at 1300. No, make it 1230."

"Aye, aye, sir."

"This is a big one," Cajun added as he leafed through the contents of the folder. He then gave Wilson an intense, direct look to ensure his meaning.

"Yes, sir," Wilson responded, expecting nothing less from the man CAG tasked to lead the first strike.

CHAPTER 48

Wilson and his CO reviewed the tasking for Strike 1A: fourteen designated mean points of impact, or DMPIs. The two pilots studied the target imagery, all in and around the harbor area of Bandar Abbas. A nest of *boghammars* along the wharf. A SAM site. A storage and repair facility. The fuel farm. Located at the top of the Strait of Hormuz, Bandar Abbas was essentially surrounded on three sides by land, with the restricted waters of the strait to the south. To the east, on the other side of the city, was an Iranian tactical air base with MiG-29s and F-4s. Assigned time on target was the next night at 2315 local. Coincident with this strike were two smaller strikes down the coast at Jask and Chah Bahar.

Once the strike planning team, consisting of an aircrew from each air wing squadron, got together, Cajun briefed them on the overall plan and assigned various tasks: the launch sequence plan, the electronic warfare plan, the combat search and rescue plan, and the weapons delivery plan. He assigned the last to Wilson. All around them in CVIC were dozens of other aircrew in flight suits, working on their assigned targets, the room an orderly hum of activity.

After about 45 minutes, while the team worked quietly, several of them studying charts, others building the aircraft load out on the computer, Smoke leaned over to Wilson. "Sir, can we talk for a minute outside, please?" Smoke spun to leave before his department head could answer, and Wilson, puzzled, watched him for a few seconds before he got up to follow him, grateful for a break. Cajun and the others continued, lost in their concentration.

Smoke entered the passageway and went forward, and Wilson followed, thinking, *What's this about?* Over his shoulder, Smoke gave him a clue. "We have to go see Psycho," he said, continuing forward toward the stateroom Psycho shared with Olive on the O-2 level.

"What about her?" Wilson asked. "Why doesn't she contact me herself?" Smoke stopped and turned. "She asked me to bring you to her room. You can hear it directly from her, sir."

"Hear what?" Wilson asked, and wondered why Smoke was *sir*-ing him so much. As Smoke left Wilson's question hanging in the air and continued

forward, a feeling of dread came over the VFA-64 Operations Officer. *Oh shit,* Wilson thought.

When they arrived at her stateroom, Smoke knocked twice. "Come in," Psycho responded.

Lieutenant Melanie Hinton sat on her bunk in her flight suit, dabbing at her puffy eyes. She came to her feet as Wilson stepped inside. Smoke closed the door behind them.

"Please, be seated," Wilson said to Psycho. "What's goin' on?"

Psycho drew in a breath. "I'm pregnant."

Wilson looked at her and let it sink in. Turning his head to Smoke, he lifted an eyebrow.

"Yes...sir," Smoke nodded.

Wilson took a deep breath and exhaled through his nose.

"I didn't know until today! This morning. I had my flight physical yesterday, and Doc Laskopf called me back in this morning to tell me."

"Who else knows?" Wilson asked.

"Just us," Psycho answered, taking a seat on her bunk.

Wilson needed more. "Who *exactly?*"

"Us and Doc Laskopf," Psycho answered. "I *just* found out an hour ago!" she added, exasperated and looking away.

Wilson continued to pull the string. "Doc, or the corpsman who did the test? They haven't told anyone?"

"Sir, I *pleaded* with Doc not to tell, to let me handle it inside the squadron first. He said he would. I know we are planning to hit Iran tomorrow night, and I want to be a part of it. And you'll need me as a pilot for the flight schedule."

"Why didn't you keep quiet then?"

"Because Zach...Smoke... said I needed to tell you to schedule me in the best manner. But I feel fine! I'm ready to go tomorrow night."

"Morning sickness?"

"No, not counting when I threw up after Doc told me."

Wilson smiled, and then thought for a moment. Pregnancy was a grounding condition. Psycho could not fly anything while pregnant, and the news was a serious blow to his ability to schedule pilots for the upcoming operation. "Smoke is right. You did need to tell me, and you need to tell the Skipper."

"*No!*" Psycho exploded. Looking at Smoke with fire in her eyes, she added, "See, I *told* you this would happen! I could have flown these hops...!"

Wilson cut her off. "Psycho, it's *his* squadron. He makes the call. That's why he's paid the big bucks."

"He's gonna *shit* when he finds out, and he's going to shit on me...and Zach." Psycho was shaking her head. She began to tremble.

"Psycho..."

Seething with rage, Psycho lashed out. *"You don't know what it's like!"* she cried. "I'm a *Hornet* pilot with combat experience, but to the rest of this ship I'm just a piece of ass! Half the guys in the air wing have tried to get in my pants: JOs, *chiefs*, even officers senior to *you*. I'm doing my job and doing it well, but I have to deal with this crap *all the time*. Zach protects me from you guys, and if we've fallen in love and gone too far, then *guilty*. We can *handle* it!"

Smoke, horrified, watched as his department head absorbed the outburst from the petulant junior officer. Wilson glared at Psycho, his blood boiling. The look on her face indicated that she knew she had crossed the line.

Rubbing his hands together in an effort to control himself, Wilson began. "I would tend to accept what you've just told me better if you put a 'sir' on the end of that, *Lieutenant,* and I resent being lumped in as 'you guys.'"

"Yes, sir," she replied, her eyes downcast.

He's going to rip her spine out, Smoke thought to himself, his heart pounding.

"And I would add that, yes, I *do* know what it is like to be judged by appearance, and I do know the resentment that can bring. And I know that I must outperform white officers in every aspect of my job."

"Yes, sir, I'm sorry."

"What separates us, Lieutenant Hinton, is that instead of feeling sorry for myself, because I cannot control the color of my skin or what people *may* think any more than you can control your sex, I channel any resentment I may have into building qualifications and learning more about the airplane and displaying the best officer-like behavior I can for my people. And I've found, over the years, that that behavior leads to success for any officer—no matter the skin color, whether male *or* female. Yes, I must work a bit harder. But I can hack it, and I take great satisfaction in that. And I've been richly rewarded by the great meritocracy of naval aviation."

Psycho, eyes still downcast, answered, "I have to outperform 90 percent of the pilots in the air wing to be taken seriously."

"At this point I'd say a 100 percent! You aren't going to *win this*, Psycho," Wilson replied. Again on the verge of losing his temper, he let his words hang for effect. "In the air and with your ground job, you can outperform all the aviators in the Navy, but if you don't stop the valley girl act in the wardroom—and if you don't stop treating this whole cruise as a high school musical—you *won't* be taken seriously, ever. You are a beautiful woman, a talented aviator, and you,

as you say, have half the players in the air wing after you. From what I see, any other woman on this ship, any of them, would love to be you for a day. But the difference is most all of them would eliminate 90 percent of the unwanted attention up front by carrying themselves as *adults*. But here you are expecting me to deal with this for you when you are closer to 30 than 20, face combat tomorrow, and are pregnant with child. Time to grow up!" Wilson saw Psycho's lip quiver.

"Where's your roommate?" Wilson asked, referring to Olive.

"Down in CVIC, strike planning," Psycho replied, eyes still down. She was barely able to keep her composure.

"That's right, where the three of *us* should be right now, instead of dealing with *this*. What I need, and what the skipper needs, is for you, both of you, to be on your game because, for the next 72 hours, we need every ounce of ability from everyone in the squadron." Motioning to Psycho he added, "You represent a significant portion of the combat power of this squadron. Are *you* ready to go? Can *you* compartmentalize?"

Springing to her feet she responded, "Yes, sir!"

"Don't *bullshit* me, Psycho! A few minutes ago you were whining to me about your lot in life!"

"Yes, sir, whatever you need me to do. I can do it. I *can*, sir." Their eyes locked, and Wilson knew she meant it. He turned to Smoke.

"And you?"

"*Yessir*," Smoke answered, jaw set.

Holding Smoke's gaze, Wilson nodded his understanding, and turned back to Psycho. "Okay. *After* the 1230 AOM, you and I will have a private meeting with the CO. You will tell him the situation, *including* who the father is. I don't know what the Skipper's gonna do, but I'll recommend we fly you because we'll need everyone tomorrow night. If you can convince him that you can compartmentalize this and not cause harm to yourself or others in formation, that would be good. After that, it's *his* call. Copy?"

"Yes, sir," she replied. "I'm ready."

"All right. Let's get back down there and help."

CHAPTER 49

The *Raven* officers took their seats while Cajun stood resolute at the front of the ready room, leaning against the white board tracks with arms folded. The mood of the room was pensive, with all eyes on their commanding officer in anticipation of his message. The 1MC sounded a single *Ding* signifying 1230. Wilson turned in his seat and surveyed the silent room behind him, sensing the eyes shift on him.

"Everyone's here, sir," Sponge Bob said from his duty desk perch.

Wilson turned back to the front, nodded to his CO, and said in a hushed voice, "Skipper," the signal for Cajun to begin. All hands knew that Cajun would be the only one to speak at this AOM.

"If you've watched CNN and Sky News, checked the SINS screen, or been topside and seen the huge wake behind us, you know we're heading west in a hurry. And you don't have to be a pilot who spent the morning in CVIC to know why. Iran attacked one of our small boys last night, killing our sailors. This is an act of war. National Command Authority tasked NAVCENT with a response, and we are now planning to carry out that tasking sometime tomorrow, probably after sundown. We should arrive at our station late this afternoon, and we're gonna fly maintenance test hops and get some air wing guys in night qual. Our SUCAP alert posture begins later this afternoon, and the ordies are loading the jets now.

"We'll be facing the Iranians, who have a modern air force and navy, with sophisticated weapons and a formidable integrated air defense system. They have a history of innovation, and they want to surprise us and *hurt* us, as they did last night, *and* with Prince last month. Remember, he was unarmed and incapacitated when they shot him down with no warning. They should *not* be underestimated, and we have a tough job to suppress their defenses and hit the assigned targets. However, they aren't 10 feet tall, and if anyone should be afraid about any upcoming action, it should be *them*, afraid of what this strike group, and you guys in particular, can do to them. We will prevail, but we have to be smart. *Pilots,* until further notice, your schedule consists of flying, eating, sleeping, and planning. No mindless video games or movies, no division paperwork,

no spending hours in the gym. Part of flying consists of briefing and debriefing, and standing watches in CATCC or Pri-Fly."

Cajun pointed to the duty officer, Sponge, and said, "Or this duty here… Want to make sure you frickin' *sea lawyers* don't use my words to get out of it." The comment elicited smirks from the JOs and served to ease some tension.

He continued:

"Ground pounders, we need you guys to run the squadron. If routine paperwork can wait for the department heads or me and the XO to review once this is finished, then let it. Or, if you can handle it at the Assistant Admin or Maintenance Material Control Officer level, then do it. Now, if you deem that there's something I or the XO or the department heads must deal with immediately, bring it to our attention. Whatever call you make will be the right one; I'll support you. Don't worry about how much sleep I get.

"Now Weed here, he's a different story. *I* worry about how much sleep *he* gets." The room snickered, and Wilson heard his roommate chuckle at the needling from the CO. Cajun returned to business.

"We are four months into this deployment. We're experienced operating in this part of the world, we've been in combat in two theaters, we're looking good around the ship, and the jets are flying great. We are on the step…. We are *ready* for this. If we just follow the *basics* of solid preflight planning, comm discipline, section integrity, combat checklists and flying smart tactics with our superior weapons and sensors, we'll do fine. Plan for contingencies. Take a good look at your wingmen's aimpoints, and be ready to flex if you have to. Know the geography. If you are hit and can still fly, get feet wet. If you can't do that, get away from populated areas. If your wingman punches out, mark the position, sing out immediately, identify an on-scene commander and call away the CSAR. Your priorities for ejection are over water followed by any country but Iran, and if you can find a deserted area you may be able to evade before we pick you up. That's what I mean by knowing the geography. Have a plan up front, such as 'Safety is 10 miles east, or west, or whatever.'"

Raven One paced a few steps and exhaled, gathering his thoughts. Wilson and the others remained riveted.

"Once again, our friends and enemies around the world are calling for *us* to restrain ourselves. Europe reminds me of the cowardly lion, and Canada, who we protect like our own country, is AWOL. The GCC sheikdoms are petrified that we'll do something to ruin their holiday plans in Switzerland. Russia warns against American military adventurism, and China denounces our movement as reckless saber-rattling that only increases tensions in the strait. Japan, who

gets almost all its oil from the Gulf, and much of that from Iran, is silent. Only Australia has spoken out against the Iranians and is expressing regret at the loss of American lives.

"That's always the case, isn't it? When the victims are American service personnel, at a Khobar Towers or aboard a USS *Cole* or even at the Pentagon, nobody in the international community, including many in our own country, much cares about it except for the fact they can get a few days coverage for their news media. But the world community, with the exception of the North Koreas and Venezuelas, secretly wishes that we *do* respond to the Iranians. They *want* us to swat them down, so they'll stop causing problems. They also know that we will continue to guard against flare ups, and that will allow the world to go back to living what passes for normal.

"Therefore, it has become the responsibility of this strike group, and you and me in particular, to handle this for them, and to do the dirty work. Myself, if I can strike a blow that allows my family and your families and millions of families around the world to live in *real* peace and harmony, I welcome the opportunity. These Revolutionary Guard assholes are causing my wife to worry and my kids to cry—and have been for years. In my small way I want to prevent them from doing so any more. They are smart. We must be smarter. They fight dirty. Within the limits of the rules of engagement, we'll fight dirtier and hit where and when they don't expect. *They shot down our shipmate* experiencing an airborne emergency. For me, this is personal, this is payback, *they* overreached, and any action we take will be proportional and justified and professionally carried out. If Washington decides to throttle this back, then aye, aye, it's their call. But for now, I plan to go up there tomorrow night, and you're coming with me."

Wilson and the others sat in their seats with backs straight, soaking in Cajun's intensity and purpose, ready to burst out of the room and man the jets. The pilots shared his grim determination to prevent the *Pasdaran* from causing any further loss of life or any further disruption of international commerce. With the opportunity the *Richard Best* attack had afforded them, they would literally follow Cajun through fire to do it *now*, despite the fearsome Iranian defenses.

"Anything for me?" Cajun asked, as he met the eyes of each officer in the room. When no one spoke, he said, "Then let's do it. Ready, break," Cajun finished, as he clapped his hands together.

"*QUOTH THE RAVEN!*" boomed from Ready Seven, rattling the photos on the *Spartan* and *Moonshadow* ready room bulkheads.

Sponge hit play on the stereo and cranked up the volume to George Thorogood's "*Bad to the Bone*" as the pilots broke up into smaller groups. Some headed

back to CVIC and others moved to the front to study the Iranian coastline on the pullout chart.

In the midst of the activity Wilson approached Cajun, who was now head down searching for something in his seat storage drawer. "Skipper, can we talk for a moment, in private?"

Cajun looked up and into Wilson's grim face. He noticed that Psycho hovered behind him in an apparent state of distress. Knowing Wilson's request indicated some kind of problem, he stared for a moment at both of them. "Yeah, let's go," he said.

Chapter 50

"Dismissed," Cajun whispered. As she got up to leave, a shaken Psycho glanced at Wilson and stepped outside.

After she closed the door, Cajun gave Wilson a disappointed look. "When did you know this?"

"Four hours ago, sir. I wanted to wait until after the AOM."

"Right before my brief to CAG?"

"It was a trade-off, sir. I made a call."

"What's your recommendation?" Cajun asked, still not convinced.

"Sir, she's five weeks, and says she feels okay. This is combat, and we need her. We don't have enough pilots as it is to cover all the strike packages, SUCAP, and alerts. Recommend a waiver."

"And Doc Laskopf? You think he's going to agree to remain quiet when he sees Psycho on the flight schedule? He works for CAG, too."

"Recommend we ask him for two days, sir. Both of you can tell CAG that you kept it from him because he has more pressing issues now. Just like you asked the ground pounders to handle the routine stuff and leave you out of it during this operation."

"This isn't small stuff."

"No, sir—but in the context of the next 48 hours, it actually is."

They were interrupted by two raps at the door. "Come in," Cajun answered.

XO Patrick entered, and appeared surprised to see Wilson.

"Yeah, what'cha got, Saint?" Cajun was irritable, leaning back in his chair with his hands folded behind his head.

"While in the passageway, I saw Lieutenant Hinton leaving here, so I thought I'd catch you and ask for a quick ruling on AD2 Moran's request for MEDEVAC due to his rotator cuff. He says it hurts, but Doc Laskopf thinks he can handle light duty."

Cajun looked at him for a few moments, and then looked away. He tried and failed to hide his disgust. "Light duty... Is there anyone in the squadron Doc Laskopf hasn't seen today?"

"What do you mean?" Saint replied.

Wilson's heart beat faster. *Don't do it, Skipper!*

"Psycho was just in here. She's med down. Pregnant."

Damn! Wilson thought.

"Are you going to tell CAG? He'll need to know," Saint responded, incredulous.

"No, I'm not. We need her for the flight schedule. We've got 15 pilots, and after they are scheduled for strikes, spares, CAPs and everything else, we're tapped out. She's not bleeding, is in possession of her faculties, and wants to fly. So she's flying. Flip, keep her off the overland stuff—just SUCAP, alerts, Iron Hand escort...relatively easy stuff and away from the threat to the max extent. It's two days; then we can proceed."

Saint protested. "You *can't* do that. It's cut and dried. We have to tell CAG, and..."

"No, we, *don't!*" Cajun shot back, glowering at Saint through clenched teeth. The two commanders locked eyes on each other, refusing to blink, both conscious of the fact their subordinate department head was observing them. Cajun was enraged at having his authority questioned in public. When Saint's countenance remained defiant, Cajun detected what he was thinking and lowered his voice to an icy growl.

"XO, I swear, if you go to CAG, you will *never* command this or any squadron. *Is that clear?*"

"*Yes,* Skipper." Saint's eyes narrowed as he stared at Cajun, and both men breathed deep while Wilson held his breath. This display among seniors was shocking, and, for a moment, Wilson thought Cajun was going to choke the XO.

His hands balled into fists, Cajun continued to fume with rage. "I'll go right to CAG and the Commodore and tell them how you've usurped my authority and suppressed morale in my ready room. *I* am the CO of VFA-64, *not you. I* make policy. *I* decide on waivers. And *I* ground my pilots or *unground* them. *Do you...?*"

Cajun caught himself before he went too far. For a moment he looked for something nearby to throw, but then he slumped in his chair and looked away, face red and muscles taut. During their years together, Wilson had had several opportunities to observe Cajun's volcanic temper, and he now watched as Cajun struggled to keep it in check.

After a few moments Saint spoke. "Will that be all, sir?"

Cajun lifted his head and folded his hands in his lap, eyes again burning into Saint. "*Yes,*" he answered. Saint left without making eye contact, closing the door behind him.

The two pilots listened to Saint's footsteps recede down the passageway. "Sorry you had to see that," Cajun said, closing his eyes and rubbing his temple.

"It's okay, sir."

Cajun looked up at Wilson. "Tell Psycho—and Smoke—I need them to get their minds right and I need them to fly. We are in combat. I'll contact Doc Laskopf and ask him to give us 48 hours. He'll work with us. And if those two *can't* get their minds right, then I need to know ASAP. No more secrets."

"Yes, sir," Wilson replied. He noticed a single gray hair in Cajun's moustache.

"Tell her I'll talk to her tonight, after the flag brief."

"Yes, sir. How about *you*, Skipper?"

"I'm fine. Just give me 10 minutes, Flip. I'll meet you in CVIC," Cajun added.

"Take 20, sir. We've got well over an hour before we give CAG our game plan, and it's pretty much set already."

"Roger that. Thanks," Cajun answered, his weary fingers again rubbing his temple.

CHAPTER 51

While the world nervously watched the Strait of Hormuz and wondered if the United States was going to send a nuclear missile into Tehran, Cajun looked at his watch. "Okay, time to go."

He then stood to leave and gathered up all the pages and put them in his strike planning folder while Wilson rolled up the chart of Bandar Abbas. Wilson followed him out of CVIC, where the bright fluorescent lights illuminated the activity of dozens of aviators in various stages of strike planning for *their* assigned targets. Admiral Smith and his staff expected Cajun and CAG Swoboda to brief them in 10 minutes. The so-called "lap-brief" would consist of big-picture items—such as strike composition, other assets assigned, and enemy order of battle—interspersed with myriad details concerning timing, tanking, target area tactics, and of critical importance, the aimpoints for the strike aircraft. CAG had approved Cajun's thumbnail sketch of the plan earlier, which had allowed Cajun and his team to refine the plan and add detail for this brief with the strike group commander.

Cajun and his team had been assigned several aimpoints and a time on target from NAVCENT, with recommended weapons load outs and available intelligence and support assets at his disposal. However, the strike leader had the responsibility to orchestrate the plan and to obtain flag-level validation prior to execution. Cajun left CVIC confident of the plan his team worked on all day. Soon after turning right on the starboard passageway, he and Wilson entered the blue tile area and arrived at CAG's stateroom door. Cajun knocked twice.

"Come in," CAG said from inside.

Cajun opened the door and saw CAG and DCAG sitting at the table. "Ready to go sir?" Cajun asked.

"Yep, let's do it," CAG replied. Both of the seated officers rose to lead the way to the flag briefing spaces, eight frames aft. As the junior in the group, Wilson brought up the rear. In this meeting he would remain silent, but he would watch the proceedings carefully and take detailed notes of any of the admiral's concerns.

CAG led them to the conference table in the empty briefing room. The admiral's chair was at the head of the table, and Cajun staked out a position to its right, with Wilson next to him. CAG and DCAG sat down as their mirror images on the other side of the table.

Soon Captain Swartzmann entered wearing his blue, pullover sweater and carrying his ubiquitous notebook and coffee cup. He was followed by the Air Ops officer in a green flight jacket and another sweatered surface warrior. CAG Swoboda greeted Swartzmann with a cordial *"Gene."* The chief of staff made a face but otherwise ignored him, and Wilson saw that CAG's informal greeting got under Swartzmann's skin. He, no doubt, preferred the formal *Captain Swartzmann* to his given name. Wilson suppressed a grin. Even the heavies found ways to bug each other.

Moments later the admiral arrived wearing his flight jacket and also carrying a cup of coffee. The room came to attention and Smith responded, "Seats. Seats, please." Placing his coffee on the table, he surveyed the room and nodded at each of his air wing guests, greeting them by name and with a smile. "All right, Skipper, you are the first out of the block. What'cha got here?"

"Package 1A, sir, Bandar Abbas," Cajun answered.

"Yeah, yeah…okay, go ahead," Smith said, focused on the imagery slide Cajun placed in front of him.

Cajun began:

"Sir, this package is going after several aimpoints in and around the naval base at Bandar Abbas to interdict *Pasdaran* and Iranian Navy ability to harass shipping in Hormuz. As a premier naval base, you can see it's heavily defended—with long range SAMs here, here, and here and with tactical weapons in and around the harbor areas. These islands in the strait are inhabited with triple-A of all calibers, and we can expect MANPADS everywhere. Bandar Abbas is also a fighter base, and we've imaged *Phantoms*, *Tomcats*, and MiG's at the airfield. If they come up tomorrow night, we have a dedicated sweep to deal with them. And the strikers will be loaded out to deal with any leakers."

"*Phantoms* and *Tomcats*," Smith grumbled, shaking his head at the irony his pilots would have to face American-built aircraft.

Cajun described the aimpoints, the weapons load out and the delivery profile for the strike aircraft. Each of the senior officers leaned in to capture his every word and ensure their understanding—and Cajun's complete mastery—of the reason for this strike. Because errant bombs were unacceptable, the strikers needed to be 100 per cent certain of their aimpoints and release parameters.

Smith looked at the satellite imagery, puzzled. "What are these?" he asked.

Cajun looked at the aimpoint. *"Boghammars* in a nest, sir."

"Then what are *these?*" Smith added.

"Dhows, sir, also in a nest." Cajun saw where the admiral was going.

"Well, they look a lot like *boghammars* to me."

"Yes, sir, but the dhows are larger and pretty much uniform. *Boghammars* are smaller and have irregular shapes, as you can see."

"Yeah, I can. But tomorrow night, will one of your tired and stressed JOs, or even you, be able to positively ID it on a targeting FLIR before you release? We can't have the media bastards beat us over the head because we blew some fishing boats out of the water."

Wilson noticed that Swartzmann gave Cajun a sanctimonious look, and CAG did not appear to want to help in this situation. Wilson's CO was on his own.

Cajun frowned at the imagery photo and looked up at Smith. "Sir, I can't *guarantee* you the strikers, or even myself, can discern a dhow or a *boghammar* in every instance, but we can put a bomb in the middle of any nest along that wharf. The target is *boghammars,* but if a dhow is in among them, then they picked the wrong night to go alongside. They used dhows in the *Richard Best* operation."

"That's another question," Smith added. "What if there's nothing there? How old is this imagery? Hell, it doesn't matter. It could have been taken today, and it wouldn't matter. The Revolutionary Guard can move these boats in hours…less."

Wilson watched as Swartzmann's eyes burned holes into Cajun, then shifted to Wilson, who held his gaze for a moment. *Screw you, sir*, he thought, and returned his attention to the admiral.

Cajun didn't flinch. "Yes, sir, and the answer is a radar-to-FLIR-to-visual delivery. We can see on the radar if anything is along the wharf, sweeten it on the FLIR, and then roll in visually on goggles to refine the aimpoints. Wherever they moor these guys, we can hit them. And if nobody is home, we have alternate targets. There's a boat crane here and a gasoline pipeline pump here connected to the fuel tank that services everything on the wharf."

Smith studied the targets again. Bandar Abbas was a tough nut, and his A-team had to get in there. With an element of surprise, and led by Cajun Lassiter, they could suppress the defenses *and* take a toll on the *Pasdaran* before they could even react. Follow-on strikes along the coast would attrite *Pasdaran* assets to prevent further raids in Hormuz, of that he was certain, but could they destroy *boghammars* in numbers? *Damn things could hide in every cove and along every breakwater, or in some shack along the beach.*

Smith motioned for Cajun to continue and followed him through discussions of the expected weather, DMPIs, contingencies, show stoppers, command and control nets, rules of engagement…. The list was exhaustive, and Smith let him move along, knowing they could anchor down on any of these subjects—and be here all night discussing the nuances and contingencies. *Damned media!* Smith surmised the Iranians could blow up a dozen of their dhows anywhere and blame America. He knew CNN and the BBC would run with it without questioning the source. Smith looked at the threat rings: big and lethal. *How many of my aircraft and aviators will I lose?*

"Any questions, sir?" Cajun was finished. Jolted from his daydream, Smith rapped his pen on the table and spoke in his low baritone.

"Skipper, I'm confident in your plan and in your ability to lead this strike. But go back and take a look at the suppression plan. If you need more assets, ask. Much can still be done in the next 24 hours. This is the first strike, and it needs to be effective. We all want to provide you with what you need."

"Yes, sir, Admiral. We'll give it another look with that in mind. Thank you," Cajun replied.

"How about you, Flip?" Smith changed the subject with his wry smile. "Ready to meet up with that MiG-35 again?"

Sensing the approving nods from all but Swartzmann, Wilson answered with a confident smile of his own. "I'll be armed this time, sir. Let's do it."

The admiral's word touched a nerve; tomorrow night he would be shot off the bow with a full load of ordnance. Headed for Iran.

Smith smiled, his eyes lingering on Wilson for a second. Turning his head to CAG, he then signaled the meeting was over. "Okay, guys, thanks for coming. Press on."

Cajun and Wilson took their cue and left, but CAG stayed behind. Smith caught his eye. "Whada'ya think, Tony?"

Swoboda answered with assurance. "Sir, Cajun has a sixth sense tactically, and Flip Wilson is the finest pilot in the wing. They are my go-to warfighters. They'll get everyone in and out and bring back video of their hits. Color these aimpoints gone."

Smith nodded, and looked up to see that the next strike leader had arrived for his lap brief. *CAG's right,* he thought. *Package 1A will deliver the initial hammer blow we need to set these guys back on their heels.*

Chapter 52

Back in CVIC, surrounded by his strike planning team poring over charts and entering info into the computer for kneeboard cards, Wilson looked at his watch. Almost 2200... 14 hours since CAG had gathered them there. Psycho's announcement, Cajun's pep talk, the scene with the XO, briefing Admiral Smith. It all seemed like days ago. Wilson rubbed the stubble on his face, then reached over his shoulder to massage the kink out of his neck. Two more hours...then sleep. He thought of tomorrow night—24 hours until launch.

Thinking out loud and hoping for guidance, Dutch worked on the tanking plan. "If we join up overhead in high holding, it's easier, but we may tip off the Iranians if we break the radar horizon. If we join up on a radial toward Bandar Abbas, we can save transit time and gas."

One of the *Moonshadow* captains countered. "What if that radial is clobbered by the marshal stack?"

Wilson turned to join the conversation. "I'm not sure we'll have an event up when we launch. If we can get away with joining low the guys on the beach won't see us until we climb up, giving us time to close the target. Anyway, let's check with Strike Ops on the schedule.

"JD, how about it?" Wilson asked one of the marines at the table.

Just then the 1MC sounded a whistling *taa-weet,* followed by the bosun's message: "Now stand by for the evening prayer."

Dutch, oblivious to the 1MC announcement, continued. "We have two packages of aircraft, the strikers and..."

With his head down and straining to listen, Wilson raised a hand to stop the conversation. Dutch and the others looked at him, and then bowed their heads when they realized what he meant. While much of the room continued to work, Wilson and his team listened to Chaplain Dolan's prayer. His familiar voice was rich and soothing.

"Heavenly Father, as this day comes to an end, we, Your servants, thank You for our many blessings: a letter or e-mail from home, the friendship of shipmates, a kind word from a superior, a moment of solitude, good food to eat, and a warm bed. Lord, many of us are busy with the serious tasks our nation has assigned us. We ask You to

give us strength as we prepare for the challenges of tomorrow and each day, so that each of us may better serve You and one another. In Your name we pray. Amen."

Wilson reflected on Father Dolan's words. With day-to-day duties and distractions, Wilson often forgot that, in this life, we are here to serve one another. Caught up as they were with whatever duty was assigned and their own self-important roles in it, the need to fulfill that obligation was regularly lost on Wilson and many of the 5,000 sailors aboard *Valley Forge.*

The evening prayer complete, the conversation about the tanking plan resumed where it left off. A few minutes later, the 1MC sounded four bells, followed by an announcement: "Taps, taps. Lights out. Maintain silence about the decks. Now taps."

For the most part, activity throughout the ship continued unabated, especially in CVIC. Wilson continued his study of the chart, the bells serving as another reminder that time was passing quickly.

Cajun leaned back in his chair and stifled a big yawn. As he stretched one arm behind his head, he looked at the bulkhead clock: 0115. His strike planning team was exhausted. After considering and answering hundreds of variables, they had produced a PowerPoint briefing and kneeboard cards for strike 1A. Although it seemed they had reached the point of diminishing returns over an hour ago, five of his team were still at work. The remnants of several other planning teams were scattered about, but they also looked as if they were going to soon call it a night.

Cajun then spoke up, stifling another yawn.

"Guys, let's knock this off for now and hit the rack. How about we meet tomorrow—today—at 1400 and wrap up the kneeboard packages and briefing slides? We're looking to brief at 1900 in Ready 7."

The team responded with enthusiastic *yes sir's* all around, gathered their planning materials, and put them in folders to be placed in the safe by the intelligence officers. Wilson was more than ready to shut down for the night. He gave his CO a casual "See you tomorrow, Skipper," and departed CVIC.

The darkened passageways were illuminated by red lights. Exhausted, Wilson made his way forward toward his stateroom, pushing off a bulkhead at one point to steady himself. Many frames forward he saw the shadow of a sailor walking aft toward him, then disappearing as he turned into a starboard passageway. He heard the engine of an FA-18 howling one level above on the flight

deck; apparently, night-check maintenance was doing a high-power turn to check some component. *Valley Forge* never slept completely, but most of the crew was asleep now, and Wilson's body craved it.

He trundled down the ladder and aft, shielding his eyes from an area of bright fluorescent lights. Entering officer's country, he navigated the dim maze to his stateroom on autopilot. Opening the door, he switched on his desk light to minimize the disturbance to Weed, asleep in his rack. Or so he thought.

"Hey, you guys done?" Weed mumbled. Facing the bulkhead, he was a motionless lump in the top bunk.

"Nah, still have some element brief stuff…kneeboard cards. How about you?" Wilson replied, unfastening the laces on his boots.

"Pretty much the same."

Wilson was wiped out, and neither pilot was in the mood to talk. He removed his boots, hung his flight suit on a hook, and crawled into bed, pulling the covers up around him. *Rest, finally. What a day!* The news about *Richard Best.* Psycho. Strike planning all day and night. *Hitting Iran tomorrow. No, tonight!*

Wilson put all of it out of his mind. He had to sleep, knowing it would be the only uninterrupted rest he got in the next 36-48 hours.

"G'night, man," he mumbled to his roommate.

"G'night."

Wilson woke and looked at the numerals of the LCD clock: 4:30. *Oh-ridiculous thirty.* He had been asleep only three hours and had popped awake now because of adrenaline and stress. *Calm down,* he thought. *Go back to sleep.*

Over the next hour, Wilson tried to sleep, but he couldn't shake the image of a *Hornet* in formation next to him, ghostly green under the illumination of night vision goggles. The cultural lighting of Bandar Abbas slid closer and soon the AAA appeared as a reverse waterfall of small lights rising into the air in a graceful arc. The heavier stuff followed, which to Wilson looked like flashbulbs popping in a cluster. It seemed much closer when viewed through the NVG light intensifiers.

Wilson marveled at the serene background of aerial combat. It was for the most part silent. He recalled how, in 2003, the armada of American and Brit aircraft had approached Baghdad in waves. The floating waves of aluminum pummeled the Iraqi capital with precise violence while the defenders fired barrage AAA into the air in a desperate attempt to hit something, anything… but

still unsuccessful after 12 years of trying since the truce in 1991. He remembered the muffled flashes as *Tomahawks* hit their targets around the brightly lit city from many miles away. He also watched the tentacles of AAA rising into the air like fingers of a rotating hand looking for something to grasp. The sight was fascinating to watch, and both the *beauty* of the light show and the *silence* of the scene held him spellbound as he approached the target at transonic speeds. His only interruption might be a terse *"Ramrods check right twenty"* from an element leader on the strike common frequency. Dozens of aircrew experienced this incongruity from inside their warm cocoons, the rumble of the engines behind them and the hum of the cockpit their only company, as they are drawn by their mission plan into this hornet's nest of defenses. In contrast, it must have been hellish on the ground as numerous AAA pieces fired their ear-splitting staccato bursts into the air, frantic crews reloaded, and soldiers shouted angry orders or cried out in fear. It was not silence that permeated the background of these scenes but the haunting sounds of air raid sirens and the thumps and booms of ordnance hitting its targets.

Would it be like that over Bandar Abbas? *Probably so, and worse,* Wilson surmised. Would he be able to pick up a SAM amid all the cultural lighting? Would the Iranian gunners be better than their Arab counterparts? Was there a lucky BB up there with his name on it? He thought of Hariri. Would he, or other pilots in MiG-35s, rise up to meet him? As the fear built up inside, Wilson focused on the rise and fall of his chest in an effort to control his breathing. *Please God, let us all come back.*

He looked at the clock: 5:40. *Damn.* He needed to sleep but was wide awake. He thought about checking the computer to see if Mary had sent anything during the night but decided against it. He needed to stay here and get rest.

Weed stirred above him, and Wilson heard him mutter under his breath. "Fuck."

"Can't sleep either?" Wilson asked.

Weed rolled over and exhaled. "No."

"Where are you going tonight?"

"Jask—Skipper Sanderson is leading it," Weed answered, referring to the *Spartan* CO. "You guys going to Bandar Abbas?"

"Yep."

Lost in their thoughts and fears, they didn't speak for a while. They knew they were the finest tactical aviators flying the finest aircraft with the finest weapons in the world—their "blade" honed sharp during months of combat in *Iraqi Freedom* and *Enduring Freedom*— but they also knew the Iranians were

serious opponents. Wilson recalled the Skipper's words: While the Iranians were not their equal in the air, they definitely had a way of hurting Americans in the past.

"You afraid?" Weed asked in the darkness.

Wilson contemplated the question as he continued to stare ahead into the shadows of the frame of his roommate's rack. He admitted to himself he was afraid of dying and of getting himself captured, but he was even more afraid of hitting the wrong target or making a mistake in the planning that could render strike 1A unsuccessful. While confident of his ability and training, he was not infallible. What was he missing? Why the anxiety? Did he and the others have to be *perfect*? Was it Hariri?

"Yeah. But I'm ready to go up there and strike those dickheads. If not now, when? If not me, who?"

Silence returned to the stateroom, both men still thinking about what the next 24 hours would bring. Wilson returned the question. "How 'bout you? Ready to go, big guy?"

"Yeah, I'm ready. Just apprehensive, like the night before the high school district championship game. And I'm not sure how this story ends, either. Do we knock this off after a few nights? Do the Iranians escalate? What happens to traffic in Hormuz, oil prices, all that?"

"So, you're worried about your portfolio?" joked Wilson.

"You know, we've been in combat every cruise since we were nuggets in the 90s. Yet it gets harder, not easier. Like night traps. Guess a little apprehension comes with age."

"Yeah. Sometimes I think about the World War II guys. They flew out hundreds of miles from their ship using heading, airspeed, and time on a damn *plotting board* to fight their way through the Zeros and roll in on a carrier in a near vertical dive. Imagine diving into that ring of fire, every gun on the ship pointing at you. Then they had to use dead reckoning to get themselves back to their ship. Or the Vietnam guys—*two or three times a day*—dodging SAMs and going to the merge with MiGs that could out-turn them. We won't have to face what they faced."

Weed grunted. "Um, hmm. Yeah, we *are* fortunate. You know, I hate it when you're right and make me feel like shit."

Wilson chuckled, but knew they needed sleep. "Let's sleep 'til 10, get cleaned up, get some food, and press on."

"Sounds like a plan," Weed replied, and they both rolled over and closed their eyes in an effort to will themselves to sleep.

After several minutes four bells sounded over the 1MC: "Reveille, reveille, all hands heave to and trice up. The smoking lamp is lighted in all designated spaces. *Now reveille.*" Wilson pulled the covers up to shield his eyes from the white light that, when switched on in the passageway, leaked under the door. Aboard *Valley Forge* a new day was beginning. He thought about the time: 0600. Sixteen hours to go.

CHAPTER 53

While her department heads conversed in their racks, Olive, 40 frames aft, had no one to talk to.

Unable to sleep, she had pulled herself into a fetal position and wrapped her arms around her long legs. She figured other Air Wing Four aviators were struggling for sleep, but the reality of this night had hit her in the deep recesses of her mind.

Tonight, as a senior JO, she would be flying on Cajun's wing in the first strike going against an alerted and capable enemy. *Combat.* This was not an Iraqi close-air-support bomb toss. Tonight they would face SAMs and AAA, and maybe even Iranian fighters. *Downtown* Bandar Abbas with multicolored and interlocking threat rings. She knew their defenses would be effective. Determined. And only hours away.

Like everyone else, she had long ago come to grips with the knowledge that death could come any day with no warning. A routine cat shot suddenly transformed into a crash. A shipboard fire. An unexpected and lethal jet of scalding water in the shower. Electrocution. The list was almost endless both aboard ship and in the air, and the fact that it hardly ever occurred was little solace. Sometimes it *did* occur, and putting oneself over Bandar Abbas tonight raised the odds significantly.

As a warrior she would go. There was no doubt of that.

Her worst nightmare was capture, which would soon be followed by rape. Repeated and vicious. And, if there were a captured American male in the next cell to hear her screams, the enemy would continue the brutality to get *him* to talk. She would be alone, and she would be singled out night after night. While she had long realized and accepted that fearful reality, it was now a much greater possibility...a possibility she may have to experience within the next 24 hours.

Compared to rape, death—fast and painless in an exploding *Hornet*—would be welcome. But what if she were conscious in a spinning, burning jet? Would she pull the handle, be it consciously or reflexively, at the chance to live? Even if that meant consigning herself to the living hell that would await her in captivity? She shuddered when she realized that, yes, she would.

Olive knew all about loneliness, but she had never felt more alone than she did at that moment. Twenty-eight years old. Had any man, even her father, ever loved her? Olive's only sexual experience had come two weeks before she entered the academy, and the boy's drunken premature finish had left her ashamed and confused. That was it? Where were the supposed fireworks? There were certainly no bells or singing birds. She didn't even remember his name anymore, and she knew he had forgotten hers within days.

The only real remnant of the experience was anger...which revealed itself in her cold and always professional demeanor. Both her anger and her loneliness had become a burden. When was the last time she had laughed as a carefree girl?

During the past 10 years, as she had entered adulthood and become a capable woman, Olive had been *surrounded* by men in this testosterone-drenched, male-dominated culture. Many were still *boys*, for sure, but they were technically men. Legal, adult men who could pursue Olive if they wanted—but chose not to. Who was she kidding? Even the "boyfriends" of her youth had taken her on a few unexciting dates before they moved on. Her athletic body and mysterious way had gained their initial interest, but they dropped her with no explanation.

In the darkness, she felt her face, felt the skin around her jawline. The only fat on her body was *right there*. With her fingers, she measured the close distance between her dark eyes, touched the high forehead, glided over the acne scars, felt the coarse hair. She had followed this routine every time she had moments like this—ever since she was in seventh grade. That was when the image of Camille's disappointed and disapproving expression was seared into her memory. Her mother had touched Olive's face in the same way, and then with hands on hips, said to her the words that had set the course of her life: *"How did I end up with a plain Jane like you?"*

Not now! Olive thought as she rolled over and hugged her pillow. She fought mentally to keep her finely constructed emotional barriers from sagging under the stress of impending combat. Her thoughts, though, soon turned dark again.

As a student of history, she knew that on the eve of combat men of every culture traditionally found women—*any* women they could find—and deposited their seed in an instinctive human desire to spread their genes and leave as many offspring as they could before they died. Doughboys on their way to the trenches of France. Bomber crews out in London before a mission. Japanese soldiers with "comfort women" sex slaves before their banzai charges. The examples were many over the millennia. Men could find a woman for release, could spread their genes, and it was all accepted.

But a female warrior on the frontline was relatively new to human history. And, as a woman, Olive had to be selective. Sure, she could remove her clothes and get any number of sailors within a thousand feet to screw her in a fan room or dark alcove, right now or practically anytime she wanted. The problem was she had to carry *his* genes with hers, and she had to deliver and care for a child—forever. Her instinctive need for love included a need for a strong father to support a baby, and that could not be met unless a man was committed to her and *loved* her. For Kristin Teel, that was not going to happen tonight. No one had ever offered.

Resentment began to build when she realized that Psycho, sleeping so peacefully above her, *did* have all this. The thick, silky hair, the high cheekbones, the blue eyes, the creamy skin, the fun personality—and a killer body. And inside that killer body was a growing baby, *Smoke's* baby, spreading *his* genes, a fact that would keep Psycho from the heavy overland stuff tonight. While Olive was risking everything over the Bandar Abbas meat grinder, "poor Psycho" would be flying quick-reaction surface combat air patrol high over the North Arabian Sea with a near-zero threat. She would then go back home for maternity leave with her Air Medal while baby-daddy Smoke passed out cigars. Later they would get to move into the house with the picket fence.

Olive suddenly hated Psycho, her admiral father, Smoke, and the whole Navy. Psycho was just like the rest of the party girls in high school and at Bancroft Hall in Annapolis. They were loyal to Olive—until their guys came by and picked them up. She thought of the dozen bridesmaid dresses she had worn to their weddings.

Bitches.

Stop this! Olive hissed into her pillow. When Psycho stirred above her, she froze. After a moment, though, Psycho settled back down into silence, sleeping as peacefully and as carefree as a *Hornet* pilot could be on the eve of combat—and loved by a man.

Olive rarely allowed herself to wallow in this much self-pity. She resolved that the timing of this episode would not deter her from walking to the jet tonight. She would launch, fly into the maw of Bandar Abbas, and deliver her JDAM with cold precision. Lieutenant Teel didn't need either a baby or a man. Or want one. Maybe she never would.

Maybe she would.

CHAPTER 54

Wilson and Weed awoke midmorning and were among the first in line for lunch. They joined most of the Carrier Air Wing Four aircrew, many of whom they recognized from the previous long day's planning in CVIC. The mood was quiet, if not a little tense. Most of the aviators were still tired after a fitful night's sleep, and each one was preoccupied with thoughts of the Iranian coast. Wilson remembered a similar feeling just before launch time on the first night of *Iraqi Freedom,* and all the aircrew knew that tonight would be much hotter than "routine" patrols over Iraq. After lunch, the aircrew spent time checking gear and studying their procedures. Many of them also tried to catch a few moments to write a note home, some writing "the letter" to their families in case they did not return. Wilson already had such a letter for Mary stashed in his desk drawer in a sealed envelope.

Wilson was always amused, if not a little put off, by the disposition of the sailors before major combat. To the majority of them, many of them teenagers, it was just another day at sea. Their major goal, from the time they rolled out of the rack, was to survive the day, mentally if not physically. They thought of the pilots as the guys who flew the planes over the horizon and returned hours later. Who knew what they did, and if knowing was not going to make the job any easier, then who cared? Over four months into the deployment, fatigue and tension wore on everyone, and sailors bore the brunt of it.

While the aviators were well aware of the historic significance and geopolitical consequences of the missions they flew, the sailors, for the most part, were oblivious. Wilson smiled at the idea that, despite what they may think, the aviators were not the center of the universe to thousands of kids just trying to make it through the regimentation of another day at sea. The young sailors were proud of their roles and welcomed opportunities to learn more about the aviators' missions, but not all of their leaders took the time to visit them in their shops and explain. Time, after all, was a precious commodity at sea for everybody.

For Wilson and his team the afternoon went fast as they folded updates on the tactical situation, the weather, and expected ship's position into the strike

plan. When Wilson joined Olive and Dutch afterwards for dinner, he sensed the disposition of the air wing had picked up and ranged from quiet confidence to eager anticipation. Wilson was familiar with those feelings, too. *Let's get this show on the road.*

After he finished dinner, Wilson went below, for no particular reason other than he wanted to be alone for a few moments. He stepped inside his stateroom and flicked on his desk lamp.

He looked at Mary's framed picture on his desk, his favorite of her at the strike fighter ball. She had looked stunning that night. He leaned in toward her image and stared at her beauty, drinking her in, trying to seek comfort.

Wilson fought against the empty feeling in his stomach, the foreboding tension always felt prior to combat in a high-threat environment. *What will Iran throw at us? What are they preparing up there?* He answered his own question. *Bandar Abbas is going to be hot. Compartmentalize, dammit!*

Wilson stood to head aft to the ready room for the Skipper's strike brief, but paused to pray instead. Holding his folded hands against his chin, he closed his eyes and whispered, *"Please, God, bring us all back. Let us do well. Give us strength. And your will be done, not ours."*

Before he flicked off the light, Wilson took another long look at Mary's photo, and said, "I'll come back to you, baby." He glanced at his watch: four-and-a-half hours until launch.

On a whim, Wilson decided to take the long way to the ready room—via the hangar bay. Sunset was in 15 minutes, and sunsets on the open ocean were often breathtaking in their beauty. Going this way he could look out to the horizon through the open elevator doors.

He walked aft, through a hatch, and down two ladders to the hangar bay. Winding his way through the parked yellow tractors, drop tanks on dollies, hydraulic jacks and various other pieces of hangar bay equipment, Wilson walked past a *Raven* aircraft, *401*. Wearing a respirator, a young, female petty officer maneuvered an orbital sander on a piece of wing in preparation for some routine touch-up paint. He looked at the name on the cockpit:

CDR STEVE LASSITER
CAJUN

Wilson realized the skipper wasn't going to be flying "his" aircraft that night. While *401* had a reputation as a solid flyer, maintenance would put Cajun, and the rest of the pilots, in full mission-ready aircraft, right now being loaded and fueled topside.

Wilson walked under a *Prowler* tail and over to the Elevator 1 opening. The sea was a deep blue, and where it met the sky, he saw the white superstructure of a tanker, brilliant from the reflected sunlight, peeking over the horizon. Realizing the carrier was pointing north, he scanned for other ships and noted another tanker, this one less than 10 miles away, and heading east. Several miles away to the southeast, he recognized the familiar outline of a guided missile destroyer in escort, paralleling the carrier's course. Further east, dramatic cumulus buildups, illuminated by sunlight, formed a sharp line in the sky, all the way to the horizon. Great visibility.

Wilson savored moments like this, alone with his thoughts in the vastness of the Indian Ocean. But he couldn't help thinking of what was in store after the sun set: the tension of the man-up, taxiing among dozens of loaded strike aircraft, joining up in the darkness and pushing toward Bandar Abbas, the radar cursor sweeping like a metronome as it searched for contacts, with terse, clipped radio transmissions interrupting the electronic hum of the cockpit. *SAMs.* They would see SAMs tonight, probably in numbers. Wilson imagined his RWR lighting up, accompanied by loud *deedles* in the headset, if his aircraft were caught in the electronic snare of a missile-tracking radar. His head would snap in the direction of arrival in a frantic search to pick it up visually and maneuver to defeat it. Known AAA sites surrounded the target area. It was also likely the American formations would be ragged and confused once they reached the release points. He visualized more arcs of AAA rising up to meet them, giant rapiers swinging through a swarm of bees in a desperate effort to hit one, just one. Would it be him?

And MiGs. Would the Iranians launch their fighters tonight? All of the fighter aircrew actually welcomed a fight, and prayed for the chance to down a MiG or *Tomcat* or *Phantom.* So did Wilson, but in the back of his mind, he knew more than the others how formidable the MiG-35 could be: invisible to radar, possessing an incredible thrust-to-weight ratio, slow-speed maneuverability. He wondered if the IRIAF would deploy them down here? *What is Hariri thinking right now?*

Enough! Wilson scolded himself, still trying to scan the horizon out to 1,000 miles. He was the operations officer in a deployed *Hornet* squadron and a TOP-GUN instructor with as much green ink as anyone in the air wing. *You can do*

this, he thought. *If anything, it should be the* Iranians *who are worried right now, knowing we are just over the horizon.* And if there was a golden BB out there for him, then so be it. He could not be more prepared for this moment.

Wilson said another prayer. *God, please take this anxiety from my shoulders. Please allow me to do Your will now and always. And please bring us all back. Your will be done. Amen.*

The apprehension left him at once, replaced by quiet confidence and assurance. There was no need to dread this mission; he would prosecute the assigned targets with aggressive energy. He was ready.

Wilson ambled along the length of the hangar bay and took in the scene: sailors and marines working on airplanes, yellow shirt directors talking in a group by Elevator 2, two young sailors in dungarees walking forward and nodding to him with respect as they would on any other day. Yep, to most everyone aboard, this was just another late afternoon at sea.

Hoping to view the sunset through the Elevator 4 opening, Wilson continued aft through the jumble of parked aircraft, each separated by mere inches from its neighbor. The tight spacing sometimes required him to lower his head or contort his body to squeeze past. Coming around the tail of an S-3, Wilson froze. Ahead of him, about 20 yards away, he saw a lone aviator in a flight suit. Standing motionless at the edge of El 4 and looking out to sea, with arms folded, was his CO...Cajun Lassiter.

He did not want to disturb Cajun, but decided to observe him for a few moments. Redness from the sunset reflected off Cajun's pensive face as he looked to the west, eyes squinting from the light. Wilson walked to the starboard side of the bay well behind Cajun, who was now silhouetted against the radiant setting of a red sun over a gray mountain range of clouds. Beautiful streaks of light broke through the clouds and illuminated distant patches of ocean. Though Wilson rejected an impulse to join Cajun—because he especially wanted to stay and take in the beautiful scene—Wilson realized that he himself could be discovered. Knowing Cajun would be embarrassed if caught in a quiet moment, even by Wilson, he headed aft to a starboard-side hatch by the jet shop. Wilson had to stop, though, to take one more look at the *Raven* skipper—who remained a statue—before he proceeded to the ready room where Cajun himself would arrive shortly.

CHAPTER 55

Ready Seven was standing room only as the aircrew assigned to strike package 1A met to brief. The aviators, most from other air wing squadrons, studied a stapled "kneeboard package" of briefing cards that contained the aircraft lineup, frequency plan, navigation plan, drawings of target area tactics and aimpoint photos. Some talked among themselves as they sat in the high-backed chairs. Others clicked open their ballpoint pens to write notes in the margins.

Cajun stood at the front of the room with a projector screen behind him. He looked at the clock: one minute to go.

"A'tenshun on *deck!*" one of the lieutenants sang out, and all rose as CAG Swoboda entered from the back.

"Seats," said CAG as he strode to the front of the ready room, nodded a greeting to Cajun, and took his seat in the front row next to Wilson. Cajun handed Swoboda a kneeboard package and asked the room if anyone else needed one. With 20 seconds to go, he reminded all to synchronize watches with the SINS clock.

At 1900, six bells sounded over the 1MC, and Cajun began:

"CAG, welcome to strike 1A, a strike designed to degrade and attrite the IRGC maritime forces in support of national tasking. We've got two groups of strikers—accompanied by dedicated sweep, defense suppression and jamming packages—going into Bandar Abbas. Launch time is 2200. We'll tank overhead from two dedicated *Redeyes.* We will push out along this route, with my flight, *Hammer* one-one, in the lead." As Cajun spoke, Dutch advanced slides on the projector. The "snapshots" of key events during the strike gave the aircrew a sense of the plan.

After the overview, Cajun turned the brief over to the Aerographer's Mate from the ship's meteorology office for the weather forecast. The clear weather Wilson had seen from the hangar bay was to hold, with probable low-scattered clouds in the vicinity of Hormuz, and a partial moon rising just before recovery time. Next, the Intel officer, the *spy*, gave the rundown on the Iranian order of battle. It appeared the MiG-35s could not be found in Shiraz and may have been dispersed nearby. Wilson again thought of Hariri. *Those eyes.*

Once the spy finished, Cajun resumed his brief and, for the next hour, led the aviators through the step-by-step details of the roll call, the launch sequence plan, the tanking plan, navigation, target area formations, off target egress and return-to-force procedures. And contingencies: dozens of them from unexpected weather conditions to communication backups, from search and rescue procedures for a down plane to go/no-go criteria. Cajun reinforced the "snapshots" from earlier so each aircrew would have a good idea of where their formation was supposed to be at a given time and in relation to the others. The cadence of the brief was familiar to the aviators and offered no surprises. They had practiced power-projection strikes many times during stateside work-up training off the Virginia Capes, and after months of flying from the ship, things like in-flight refueling, formations, and weapons carriage were easy. Even night operations around the ship, which were particularly dangerous, were also routine. However, a large power-projection strike package into a well-defended target area was *not* routine, and the aviators paid close attention as Cajun led them through the actions to take if they confronted their worst nightmares. After answering a few questions, Cajun offered CAG a chance to address the group.

CAG Swoboda stood and turned to the group.

"Skipper, good brief, thanks. Ladies and gentlemen, Bandar Abbas is the first of several heavily defended targets we're going to hit tonight along the Iranian coast, and because it's the *Pasdaran* HQ, we want to ensure we hit hard and with precision. Any element of surprise will be expended on this strike. We've got a smart suppression plan with exposed DMPIs and standoff precision weapons. In your element brief, talk contingencies: your backup delivery, comm degrades, the jamming plan if you get a pop-up emitter you didn't expect. We have to do some serious damage on this strike because the others build on it. So, continue to brief it in detail, fly the brief, and use those blocking and tackling skills we've practiced all cruise. Fly solid formations, know and use the code words, do combat checklists early and double check 'em. And study the targets and how you'll use funneling features to find them. If they send up fighters, shoot them down. *But* if you accept a commit, know what you are flying over. Be aggressive and be smart. That's all I've got. See you out there."

The room jumped to attention as CAG walked down the aisle to the door. "Seats," he said as he left, his Ops Officer "Bucket" following him out. The room then broke up into groups. Some talked in a corner and others left for other ready rooms where they would go over their formation tasking in detail in their element briefs. A few flight leads sought Cajun to clarify a point. Within five

minutes only the *Hammer* and *Iron* formations remained. Cajun took the floor again to brief the target areas and how they would attack them.

The *Hammer* division, also led by Cajun, consisted of Olive, Wilson, and Dutch, and would hit several aimpoints around the harbor. A wharf, where imagery showed the *Pasdaran* berthing and servicing their *boghammars*, was the primary target. Each pilot was assigned a particular aimpoint in order to deliver their GPS precision-guided weapons. To get to the release points, they had to fly past two inhabited islands, one of which they figured to have a SAM site. They knew for sure both islands housed AAA in all calibers. The *Sweeps* would clear the skies ahead of them of any airborne threat. Then the suppression aircraft, call signs *Tron* and *Zap*, would take out the surface-to-air missile sites allowing the four *Hammers* and the *Irons* unencumbered access to the target area. After release, both formations would flow south and away from the threat.

At that point, the *Iron* pilots, made up of marines from the *Moonshadows*, departed and Cajun spent another 10 minutes going over standard launch and recovery procedures, formation lighting, and aircraft emergency procedures. One hour and 15 minutes to go.

Wilson spent a few minutes alone in his chair with his eyes closed. He imagined himself as he taxied to the cat, climbed away from the ship, joined on the tanker, pushed out in formation, adjusted his goggles, set up his switches, and funneled his eyes to the target on his radar and FLIR displays. He saw the silent streams of AAA, graceful white lights climbing single file into the black sky, and he saw a SAM blast off its launcher with city lights in the background. He reviewed the procedures to deal with each. He saw his weapon, signified by a white infrared dash, fly into the FLIR display and explode. The blast covered his aimpoint in fire and smoke as it hit. All the while, Wilson kept sight of the others in formation and followed Cajun out of the target area. He imagined a push out of marshal on time and flying a centered-ball pass all the way to touchdown.

Wilson routinely used this personal preflight ritual to *visualize* his success in every phase of the flight; it had become part of his habit pattern. The *Raven* pilots knew not to disturb Flip prior to launch whenever he got into his "zone."

Wilson looked at his watch. Ten minutes to walk time. He went up to the duty desk and was the first to pick up a personal sidearm, a clip, and a "blood-chit" guarantee from the United States Government. Written in dozens of languages, it offered a reward if this pilot—Wilson—was returned safely to friendly forces. He also signed for a pair of night vision goggles.

Ensign Anita Jackson, one of the maintenance "ground pounders" was at the duty desk and offered him a log and a pen to sign for the items. A former

airframe chief who came up from the deckplates, Jackson was soft-spoken and sweet in demeanor, but could be a ball of fire if pushed.

She smiled at Wilson as he finished signing his name. "Kick their ass, sir," she whispered so only he could hear.

Wilson smiled and said, "Will do, Anita."

He then stepped outside into a passageway that ran along maintenance control and picked up the book for *Raven 403*, the aircraft with his name stenciled on the side. He reviewed the aircraft discrepancies, or gripes, and the actions taken over the last several flights, but *403* was a familiar bird and a good flyer. While reviewing the book, he sensed the maintenance master chief and Ted Randall, both in their green flight deck jerseys, were watching him with interest. He glanced up at Ted and back to the book.

"Any problem, OPSO?" Ted asked.

"Nope, looks great, Ted. As usual!" Wilson replied with a smile.

He returned the book to a young female airman who took it with a look of concern in her eyes. Wilson smiled at her, understanding and appreciating her unease. He realized she did not know what the pilots would do tonight or the threats they would face. She just knew it was serious and hoped that Lieutenant Commander Wilson and all the pilots would return in three hours.

As Wilson grabbed his helmet bag, a burly chief slapped him on the back and said, "Blow 'em away, sir."

"We will, Chief," responded Wilson.

He grasped, in that instant, that it was here, and in squadron spaces throughout the ship, where personnel showed their appreciation for the human risks their pilots were taking. Such moments also allowed them, through their comments to pilots like Wilson, to strike a vicarious blow against the enemy. He knew he was representing them, and could not let them down.

CHAPTER 56

Wilson entered the ready room and noted that the skipper, Olive, and Dutch were at the duty desk signing for their gear. He walked through the room and stepped into the passageway where he saw Gunner Humphries coming into the ready room from the flight deck.

"Hey, Gunner, all loaded up there?"

"Yep, which one are you?"

"Four-oh-three."

"Four-oh-three… Yeah, you're on the bow, one row."

"Great, thanks." Wilson turned toward the paraloft to suit up. Before he could walk away, the gunner stopped him. "Wait, I've got a joke for you."

Wilson stopped and chuckled. "Go ahead."

Humphries was in his element. "What's the fastest thing known to man?"

"What?"

"The water that shoots up your ass after you take a shit. What's the second fastest thing known to man?"

Still chuckling, Wilson took the bait. "What?"

"Your asshole when it slams shut to catch it," he replied with an expectant look, suppressing a grin.

Wilson smiled and laughed, shaking his head at the absurdity of Gunner's joke. With his years of experience, Gunner knew how to keep pilots calm.

"Have a good one, OPSO. Hit 'em hard," he added with a knowing smile and a squeeze to Wilson's arm.

"Thanks, Gunner, will do." Wilson replied as he turned for the paraloft, still smiling and shaking his head.

Wilson entered the paraloft, or "PR shop," and greeted Petty Officer Zembower, the shop supervisor. Pulling the first item of flight gear from his hook, Wilson donned it in his same superstitious manner: g-suit around the waist, zip it up, followed by right leg, then left. The butterflies returned as he anticipated what lay ahead, not the least of which was a night cat shot. Cajun, Olive and Dutch entered together and went to their own hooks from which their flight gear hung.

Cajun, apparently, was also thinking about the dark night. "Flip, when did he say the moon was coming up?"

"About 2330 or thereabouts, sir. Just in time for the recovery."

"It's actually 2334, Skipper," Dutch chimed in.

Cajun looked at Dutch. "Next thing you're gonna tell me is the percent illumination, aren't you?"

"Actually, sir..."

"Yeah, *I know* you know, Dutch!" Cajun replied, feigning mock disgust. "JOs know these things, like days between duty, so you guys can wheedle your way out of it with some BS excuse. Seniority among JOs is like virtue among whores."

Wilson and the others smiled at the CO's rambling. After a few moments Cajun looked at Olive. "Do *you* know the illumination?"

"Yes, sir, 72 percent," she answered with a smug smile, working her straps.

Vindicated, Dutch puffed out his chest. "See sir, the JOs have you covered!"

The aviators were all aware of Petty Officer Zembower on the bench, polishing a helmet visor and enjoying the pilot's banter without appearing too interested.

Cajun shook his head. "All right then, *Dutch*, tell me this: Is the moon *waxing* or *waning*?"

"Ah, sir, so long as I have a night light for the trap and know the percent illumination, even at only 72 percent, I'm good."

"And you call yourself a naval officer," Cajun replied in retort as he worked his g-suit zippers, shaking his head. While the skipper was pulling Dutch's chain, Wilson knew he was halfway serious.

The four aviators finished dressing in silence as their thoughts returned to the bow catapults, or Bandar Abbas, or the recovery. On the PLAT Wilson noticed an E-2 hooking up to Cat 3, the deep hum of the *Hawkeye* engines reverberating as background noise in the shop.

Wilson was the first one done, and as he stepped to the door, Cajun raised his voice. "Good hunting up there, OPSO."

"You too, Skipper. See you guys out there," Wilson replied.

He noticed that Zembower looked up at him as he walked past to the door. "Have a good flight, sir," he said with a smile.

"Will do, PR1. Thanks," Wilson answered and exited the space with a confident grin.

Wilson stepped into the starboard passageway and began his familiar trek to the bow, trudging over knee-knockers and through open hatches to the "point" area of the flight deck some 700 feet away. *I wonder if they're going to turn this off,*

Wilson thought, imagining the mixture of disappointment *and* relief he would feel should Washington decide not to launch the operation.

While lost in his thoughts, a sailor traveling aft passed him and muttered, "Good flight, sir."

Startled for a moment, Wilson turned and responded, "Thanks!" The nameless sailor was one of hundreds of teenagers aboard.

When he had almost reached the wardroom, he turned outboard, passed underneath the Catapult 1 trough, and stopped in front of a hatch leading to the catwalk. He lowered his visor and pulled his gooseneck flashlight from his survival vest. Opening the door, he stepped into a black vestibule and flicked on the flashlight. His watch read 2110. Fifty minutes to go. Wilson reached down and grasped the bar to undog the hatch, and yanked it up.

A torrent of salt air, wind, and turboprop noise bombarded his senses as he stepped outside onto a small steel platform and dogged the hatch behind him. Lightening holes in the deckplate allowed him a view of the froth generated by the bow wave on the dark water 50 feet below.

Wilson grabbed the railing and stepped up the ladder and into the catwalk. He kept his head down and swept his flashlight ahead to locate any fuel hoses or electrical cables that might snake along his path. As he crouched low and steadied himself against the wind, he stepped up another small ladder onto the flight deck. The illumination provided by sodium vapor lights high on the island gave everything an eerie yellow tint. He directed his light on the tail of the *Hornet* next to him and read the side number: *403*.

Airman Muriel Rodriguez greeted him at the ladder with a salute, her big eyes visible through the cranial goggles even in the low light. A slight girl of only 19, she had entered the country from Mexico at age 10. Without any knowledge of English, she worked hard to learn the language and graduated from high school with honors. She had joined the Navy last year, and this was her first deployment.

Wilson returned her salute and ascended the ladder to stow his gear inside the cockpit while maintaining a precarious balance on the LEX with one hand, holding the flashlight as he did so. He returned to the deck and did his usual preflight inspection. Working his way around the nose and aft, he inspected the aircraft panels and circuit breakers and then ducked into a wheel well and checked the tires and struts. He paid particular attention to the JDAM on the parent stations.

Two of the red-shirted aviation ordnancemen lingered near the JDAM hanging on the right wing. "Sir, do you have a message for those fucks that killed our guys?" one of them asked, handing Wilson a black magic marker.

Wilson smiled, took the pen, and thought for a moment. *Hmmm.* The Navy's politically correct leadership frowned on such messages, but they looked the other way as long as one of the media's cameras didn't pick it up. Not wanting to disappoint the young sailors, Wilson asked one of them to point his flashlight on the weapon as he wrote:

LIGHTS OUT, ASSHOLES – YOU PICKED THE WRONG NAVY

"There you go, guys," Wilson said as he finished.

"All right, sir!" The *ordies* nodded in approval.

"Thanks for loading these up for us. Don't expect you'll have to download," Wilson replied.

"Thanks, sir, have a good flight," the sailors answered and moved to the next bird in line. Wilson continued with his preflight, the familiar nerves returning. He wondered if they were due to Bandar Abbas or the cat shot. He could see some stars overhead through the broken clouds. Although he'd seen blacker nights than this, it was still very dark. On the horizon he noted the running lights of a ship, one of the escorts. He forced his mind to concentrate as he folded himself under a wheel-well door to check the APU accumulator pressure, strut pressures, and landing gear links.

Wilson ascended the ladder with nimble steps and, after checking the ejection seat, slid in and began to hook up his fittings. Airman Rodriguez was right behind him, hooking up the oxygen and comm cords and helping Wilson with his Koch fittings. "Sir, are you going to attack Iran?"

Wilson nodded as he slammed a fitting home. "Yep, looks like. They attacked our ship in international waters and killed sailors. We're going to prevent them from doing that again."

"Sir, look!" Rodriguez called out, pointing to port.

On the distant horizon a slow-moving light lifted off the water like a faraway sparkler. It then picked up speed and moved in a northerly direction. Another missile burst from its vertical launch tube amid the fiery smoke generated by its rocket booster and lit up the superstructure of the guided missile cruiser on the horizon. It followed the path of the first missile north to an unknown target.

"Are we under attack, sir?"

"No, those are *Tomahawk* cruise missiles. We're attacking *them*." As he watched the two small lights climb away and pick up speed, Wilson realized that the United States had just crossed the Rubicon. There was no turning back.

Valley Forge aircraft would soon deliver the main strike power against Iran. *Holy shit. We're really doing it,* Wilson thought. He looked directly at the young plane captain. "Rodriguez, you are part of history tonight."

She returned his look, slightly uneasy. "Have a good flight, sir," she said as she descended the ladder.

"Thanks, Rodriguez! See you soon!" Wilson said. With a reassuring smile over his left shoulder, he added, "We'll be okay."

The plane captain lifted her head, and Wilson could detect a faint smile through the darkness before she disappeared under the LEX.

CHAPTER 57

Wilson's thoughts returned to Bandar Abbas, and as he set up the cockpit for launch, he noted a third *Tomahawk* arc away from its launch vessel. He noticed his deep breathing as he checked that the circuit breakers were stowed and the rudder pedals were set to his liking, only two among the dozens of little cockpit checks he had to perform. Then, with a start, he froze as he looked at his left knee. His kneeboard was attached to it. With his mind on autopilot, he had attached his kneeboard around his *left* leg, something he had never done before in nearly 13 years of flying. It shocked Wilson to see it there, and after a moment, he unhooked it and placed it on his right knee where it belonged. The nerves were returning, and Wilson fought them as he continued the rest of his checks. *Calm down, buddy. Step by step.*

The E-2 was now in tension on Cat 3, its big turboprops digging into the air with a deep hum heard throughout the ship. The pilot illuminated the aircraft's external lights, signifying readiness for launch. Moments after the catapult officer touched the deck, the aircraft shot forward as the shuttle hurtled it down the angle to obtain precious flying speed. *Knight 600* whizzed past the bow with a *WHOOOOMM* as the pilot set the climb attitude.

With the E-2 gone, the flight deck became quiet again, save for the wind that whipped through the aircraft stacked on the bow. Finished with his checks, Wilson savored the quiet, but his eyes scanned through the cockpit again and again. *Nerves*, he thought. He sat in the cockpit and glanced at Cajun finishing his checks in the *Hornet* next to him. Olive, in her cockpit on the other side, sat motionless with her head back, as if asleep. Rodriguez stood at parade rest and watched him from her position on deck. *He* watched dozens of ordies and maintenance technicians behind her as they milled about in preparation for engine starts. He looked up at the stars and sensed the ship in a turn. Thirty minutes to go.

Just then the Boss came over the 5MC. "On the flight deck, aircrews have manned for the 2200 launch. Time for all personnel to get in the proper flight deck uniform." As the boss continued with the standard prestartup litany, the tempo on deck picked up as plane captains and troubleshooters moved into position in anticipation of his finish: "Let's start the 'go' aircraft. *Start 'em up!*"

Over a dozen *Hornets* scattered over the flight deck reacted to the command as the mournful sound of auxiliary power units cranked to life in order to provide starting air to the jet engines. With his APU online, Wilson gave the two-finger start signal to Rodriguez. She then approved and authorized him to start the right engine. As soon the generator kicked on and the *Hornet* sprang to life, Wilson's hands flew through the cockpit and turned on displays and radios in another ingrained routine. Within minutes, the flight deck had become an ear-splitting cacophony of jet engines, and once Wilson got the other engine started, he lowered the canopy to drown out the din. He wanted to concentrate on the navigation and weapons displays he would soon need.

In a businesslike manner, after 36 hours of thorough preparation, *Valley Forge* was in the final stages of thrusting the "tip of the spear" into an enemy of the United States. At command and control operations centers in Manama, Tampa, and Washington, staff officers and their commanders monitored the status of Air Wing Four's Strike 1A and counted the *Tomahawk* launches and tracked their progress. They also relayed the latest intelligence regarding the surface picture and enemy readiness to Admiral Smith and his staff who would pass it on to the pilots once they were airborne. National intelligence, surveillance and reconnaissance assets all had their sensors focused on this part of the world in support of both the *Valley Forge* strike group and the *Tinian* amphibious ready group. Inside the great carrier, the next wave of pilots were already signing out their maintenance books and getting dressed in squadron paralofts for Strike 1B—even while others gathered in a ready room to brief Strike 1C, a strike package that would launch and recover in the wee hours.

Ten minutes after engine starts, observers on the bridge and in pri-fly watched as the first *Hornets* pulled out of their bow parking spots. The directors used yellow light wands to funnel them aft and guide them, with only inches to spare, down the narrow opening between two rows of fueled and loaded strike-fighters. Hundreds of officers and sailors, each with a vital job, were scattered about the flight deck. Each sailor, depending on his or her job, wore a cranial helmet and float-coat of a certain color, marked with reflective tape that showed as bright gold when illuminated by the island spotlights.

One by one the aircraft moved either aft, or forward from the fantail, to feed the catapults. By design, two *Viking* tankers moved into position on the waist cats. They would be shot early to take station and top off the *Hornets* after they

launched. In the blackness, the stars rotated overhead and the running lights of the escort ship moved steadily along the invisible horizon, clues that the carrier was turning to a launch heading. The flight deck was a screaming whine of jet engines as waves of kerosene exhaust and sea air cascaded down the length of it. The aircraft began to form patterns familiar to the crew as the yellow shirts arranged the deck to launch one jet every minute off the four catapults.

Wilson's eyes were locked on his yellow shirt director as he moved past the island and aft to a spot behind a *Super Hornet*. Once stopped, he checked his FLIR operational and finished his comm checks.

Cajun came up on strike common for the roll call: "Ninety-Nine *Tomahawk*, stand by for check-in. *Hammer* one-one."

"*Hammer* one-two," Olive replied next.

Wilson keyed the mike. "*Hammer* one-three."

"*Hammer* one-four," Dutch responded, followed by the other air wing strikers answering in order until all were accounted for.

With everyone up, Cajun switched back to departure frequency and waited with the rest of them. Wilson sensed the ship steady out and looked over his shoulder as the *Viking* on Cat 3 hooked up to the shuttle. Seven minutes until launch. He looked over his left shoulder toward "Vultures Row" and saw that the galleries were full of off-duty sailors wanting to witness history. If Wilson could have been, he would have been pacing to settle his nerves. Buckled as he was into his little cocoon, he had to be satisfied with drumming his fingers on the canopy bow and waiting his turn. He did the combat checklist again.

The *Vikings* whizzed down the cat tracks in order and launched, position lights slowly receding into the black as they climbed away. Led by two *Prowlers* on the waist cats, this allowed the conga line of aircraft to move up. He looked over his right shoulder and saw 400, Cajun's jet, behind him, painted in a colorful scheme with the *Raven* emblem taking up the entire vertical tail. Even under these conditions, Wilson admired the sharp manifestation of squadron pride. *One more minute*, Wilson thought. He saw the sailors on the waist look at the island for the signal to begin.

"Green deck."

On signal, and with a metallic shriek, the first *Prowler* roared to life. The pilot cycled the controls and, once ready to launch, flicked on the external lights. Seconds later, the big jet thundered down the track and into the Indian Ocean air. Almost immediately, Wilson heard another aircraft go into tension up on the bow so that, one minute after the *Prowler* was airborne, a *Rhino* followed it into the night sky. Strike 1A was on its way. The yellow shirts continued

to feed airplanes to the hungry catapult crewmen who hooked them up and shot them in a practiced sequence, as if it were any other night on deployment. The airborne aircraft climbed out and began to form a jagged string of blinking lights ahead of the ship.

With eyes locked on his yellow shirt, Wilson maneuvered behind the waist catapult aircraft in a familiar succession. He saw he was being led to Cat 4, and as he taxied behind Cat 3, *Raven 403* was buffeted by the jet blast from a *Rhino* in tension. Once the *Rhino* was airborne, the *Hornet* on Cat 4 went into tension, and this time Wilson's jet bounced and rocked in place. Shielded only by the steel jet blast deflector mere feet from his nose, Wilson was bombarded by waves of exhaust from the white hot burner plume of the jet. At maximum power, it produced a deafening sound of deep, continuous thunder. Finally, the jet roared down the track, the fire and thunder tearing at the deck as it accelerated to flying speed in less than three seconds. When it reached the deck edge, a loud *THUNK* was felt throughout the ship. As the jet rose into the darkness, the pulsing heartbeat of its anticollision lights receded in the distance.

A yellow shirt straddling the catapult motioned Wilson to inch forward with yellow light wands and signaled slight turns that Wilson responded to with a gentle push of a rudder pedal, causing his aircraft to lurch this way and that. Wilson's eyes remained fixed on the yellow shirt, dutifully following his orders. Billowing steam clouds swirled about the director and nearly obscured him from view even while the lighted wands called Wilson forward. On signal, Wilson stopped and turned the handle to spread his wings.

Cajun was next to him on Cat 3 and would be shot first. Once Cajun went into tension, Wilson watched him wipe out the controls and then, on signal, select afterburner. Wilson shielded his eyes from the dazzling twin 20-foot cones of white hot fire to his right and watched as two *Raven* troubleshooters crouched low. They lifted their arms high, with a thumbs up, to signal ready. Suddenly, the strike leader shot down the angle and into the sky, afterburners blazing. The observers in the tower saw the glow reflect off the water below and move away from the ship.

With 400 clear of Cat 3, attention turned to *Raven 403*. With his heart beating faster, Wilson lifted his arms above the canopy rail as the ordies armed the gun and the *Sidewinder* missiles on the wingtips. Once complete, he inched forward on signal until he felt the holdback catch him, and pulled the throttles to idle. A *Hornet* roared off the bow, and Wilson knew he would be next to launch. His eyes darted across the cockpit for a last-minute check. His breathing deep and body tight, the adrenaline began to flow.

The cat officer turned and signaled to the sailor tending the launch bar underneath Wilson. The yellow shirt director then looked up and down the cat track and spread his arms in the take-tension signal. Wilson slammed both throttles to military power, and the engines roared to life. He felt the catapult assembly "grab" his aircraft, and looked at each engine instrument as he cycled the control stick and rudder pedals with his right arm and feet. Engine and flight controls good. One last check of the cockpit displays.

Wilson's machine strained hard against the catapult, begging to be released. He glanced at the catapult officer who signaled him for afterburner. Wilson shoved the throttles all the way forward, locking his arm in place. He felt the power behind him and saw it reflected in his rearview mirrors. Satisfied, he grabbed the towel rack and placed his head on the headrest. His little finger flicked on the external lights, and the flight deck around him seemed to pulse as the red strobes flashed on and off.

It will come any second now. Wilson's eyes scanned the instruments. Arm muscles locked in place. Heels on the deck. Braced. Waiting. In tension.

Walking to his airplane, Weed popped his head over the catwalk aft of El 3, and saw a *Hornet* in burner on Cat 4. He noted the side number: *403*. With a little jump, the jet shot forward and accelerated down the track, on its way to join the rest of Strike 1A forming up overhead.

"*Vaya con Dios, roomie.*"

CHAPTER 58

The tanker pilot extinguished the green light on the refueling store, which was Wilson's signal to back out of the basket. It also signified that he had received all he was going to get from this *Viking. Two thousand pounds.* An extra thousand would top him off, but Olive was next in line and needed her share for the long drive to Bandar Abbas.

Wilson tweaked the throttles and slid back as the basket popped off the probe and stabilized in the relative wind. He retracted the probe and slid to the right to join Cajun and Dutch information on the *Viking's* right wing as Olive took her turn in the basket. Once stabilized next to Dutch, he glanced up and saw the light clusters of the *Iron* division aircraft on their *Viking* 1,000 feet above. The three of them waited for Olive to plug, and once fueled, she backed out of the basket and slid over to Wilson's right. The *Viking* retracted the basket and illuminated its anticollision light, banking away from the *Hornets*. Cajun led his three wingmen in an easy right-hand turn—away from the tanker and toward the initial point some 30 minutes away.

The strike aircraft were assigned exact target times, which allowed the sweep, suppression and jamming aircraft, all coordinated by the E-2, to know where each formation was at a given time. As they pressed out, Wilson took a position abeam Cajun, and the two wingmen got into formation on their respective section leads without a voice call. All four pilots clicked their night vision goggles into place on their helmets and, while maintaining their place in formation, made the necessary adjustments. To the west Wilson saw the desolate coastal plain of Oman rising to rugged mountains, with the glow from the metropolis of Dubai dominating the horizon beyond them. On this side, the town of Fujairah was the major settlement and shone brightly off their left nose.

The radio crackled. "*Sweeps* pushing, no alibis."

Looking north, Wilson found the *Sweeps*, four dots of light moving among the stars, each one representing a *Super Hornet*. At his 4 o'clock was the *Iron* division, moving fast to catch up. At his left seven, well aft, he picked up the suppression aircraft, the *Zaps* and *Trons*. He noted Dutch in position and then

looked north again at the long coastline of Iran, punctuated by the cultural lighting of the scattered settlements along its length.

A moment later Cajun keyed the mike. His *"Hammers* pushing" was quickly followed by *"Irons* pushing" from the *Iron* lead.

Though flying at hundreds of miles per hour, the formation glided as one unit high over the Gulf of Oman. The radio stayed silent except for an occasional "picture clean" call from *Knight*. The route they took funneled them into Hormuz, closer and closer to the Iranian coast. Their green radar cursors bounced back and forth across the displays while the pilots scanned the horizon through their goggles to pick up any movement. Below him, Wilson saw the scattered lights of the Gulf's merchant shipping, and noted one very large crude carrier stopped dead in the water. *Maybe they're waiting for this operation to complete before entering the Gulf,* he thought. *Maybe they know something.*

Looking toward Hormuz, Wilson saw a muffled flash in the vicinity of the target. A *Tomahawk* impact, he guessed. *They know we're coming now.* A minute later, he noted a second flash, then two more in rapid succession. His radar warning receiver was clean. No enemy radars were painting his aircraft. Wilson looked over at Cajun and Olive, then over his right shoulder at Dutch. They were all flying perfect form, and the *Irons* were where they should be. They glided on in silence, scanning their radar and FLIR displays and trying to keep busy without spending too much time looking at the Iranian coastline as they edged closer. Fifteen minutes to go. Wilson took another look at the target imagery on his kneeboard card and, following ingrained habit, checked his fuel.

Suddenly, Wilson got a *boop* in his headset and his eyes flashed to the RWR display. Now someone out there *was* painting them, and before long, they would enter several threat envelopes. Up ahead, the *Sweeps* committed on an airborne contact north of the target. Though the contact was not "hot," any unknown airborne aircraft ratcheted up the level of excitement for everyone. The *Sweeps* were there to shield the strikers, and this unknown aircraft could turn and become a threat to the Americans at any moment. The *Super Hornets* tracked the contact while searching for others, ready to blow the bogey out of the sky should it be identified as hostile. The *Hammer* and *Iron* divisions had almost reached the initial point—where they would split to go after their respective targets.

"Ninety-nine, *armstrong.*" Cajun's firm tone was evident as he called on strike common.

His second message came over *Hammer* tac: "Let's bump it up. Check right twenty. *Go.*"

In unison, the *Raven* pilots rolled right to the new heading and accelerated to their run-in speed, each one lifting the MASTER ARM knob to ARM.

An *Iron* pilot called out. "*Iron* two-three, SAM launch zero-two-zero!"

Wilson and the others looked right and saw a plume rising fast from the coast but falling aft as they continued north. "Doesn't appear to be tracking—*ballistic*," the *Iron* lead responded, with each *Iron* pilot reporting "clean."

Nevertheless, all the pilots tracked the missile's bright, elongated tail. It looked much closer when intensified by NVGs, but it soon fell aft. Wilson figured it to be a tactical SAM.

One of the *Zaps* called, "*Magnum* from *Zap* two-five."

Looking high out his right side, Wilson saw a supersonic HARM missile fired by one of the *Zaps* climb high into its profile, searching for a threat emitter to home in on.

As they neared the target area, they began to pick up some AAA off to the left from one of the islands south of the harbor. Unguided barrage fire, this heavy stuff resembled popping fireworks. It was no factor as the *Hammers* pressed on without reacting.

Cajun came up on aux. "Anyone having trouble with their weapon?"

Wilson punched up his weapons display and selected both JDAMs that were to be dropped on separate DMPIs near the harbor. At first all looked normal, then NO GPS flashed up on the screen. A chill of foreboding came over him as he deselected and reselected the weapons.

Dutch came up and said, "Mine are degraded."

"*Hammer* one-two concur," Olive added.

Dammit, Wilson thought. *We're less than two minutes from release!*

Cajun came up again. "*Irons* from *Hammer*. How are your weapons?"

"Good so far," the *Iron* lead replied.

"Roger, *Iron*, continue as fragged. Break, break, any luck, *Hammers*? Check BIT status." Cajun asked his pilots, who each answered *negative*.

Why are our *weapons bad?* Wilson wondered. *When the* Irons *only a few miles away are receiving good guidance?* Localized GPS jamming? Were they tracking his division and spoofing the JDAM somehow?

Wilson looked at his display in disbelief. The target area was passing under their nose! And the RWR was suddenly cluttered up with threats, sending distracting *deedles* into his headset.

Cajun Lassiter had a decision to make and, at their transonic run-in speed, less than a minute to make it. Without GPS guidance the JDAM accuracy decreased, and near misses on the assigned aimpoints were unacceptable. JDAMs

could be delivered with a tolerable degree of accuracy from a visual dive, but that would bring the *Hammers* down into greater concentrations of AAA and would significantly increase each pilot's risk. Lugging the bombs out of the target area meant degraded maneuvering off target and not accomplishing the mission. Simply dumping the JDAMs in the ocean before recovery was a non-starter for Cajun.

With 40 seconds to the roll-in point, Cajun keyed the mike. "Okay, *Hammers*, we're gonna put 'em all on the wharf. One run. Standard visual division roll-in to the left. I'll take the southernmost boats...Olive and Flip the middle...and Dutch the northern *boghammars*. Egress left and south. Check right twenty. *Go!* Olive, cross under."

Now alarmed, Cajun's anxious wingmen responded in order. They set up their switches, found the wharf on their FLIRs in the remaining seconds before rolling in on their targets, and designated where Cajun wanted them to aim.

Wilson eased closer to Cajun and took a look over his LEX at the harbor. He noted several blinking AAA guns, some sending near solid streams of fire into the sky. It was into that image he and his squadronmates would soon dive. Through the goggles he could make out the clusters of *boghammars* moored along the wharf.

"Don't ferget yer chaff program," Cajun reminded them. "Four miles to go," he added. *"Tapes on! FLIR!"*

Wilson's mouth felt like the desert below. He fought to control the quick breaths through his mouth that seemed to suck in his oxygen mask. Between the *Sweeps* and *Knight* clobbering strike common about the will-o-the-wisp contact to the north and the *Irons* calling in and off on their aimpoints, his mind neared sensory overload. Even more insistent, though, was his own RWR screaming threat indications in all quadrants with near incessant threat tones in his headset. It was all Wilson could do to ensure his switches ready and to maintain position in formation. Adrenaline coursed through his body.

What Wilson could not hear was the AAA below his aircraft, but he sensed the muffled flashes of shells going off underneath him. He moved his head constantly to keep situational awareness inside and outside the cockpit. With too much closure, Olive slid into her new position between Wilson and Cajun and had to throw a wing up in a desperate move to stop her overshoot. Dutch was high and even with Wilson's wingline. *Ready to go.*

Was that another SAM to the east? Wilson ignored it and focused on the next 15 seconds...the reason they were there.

"*Hammer* one's in hot," Cajun called in a calm voice. He pulled his jet across the horizon then overbanked and pulled down into the target area—a move he had performed hundreds of times during his long career.

Once Cajun's nose was down, Olive followed in the same manner. Through his goggles, Wilson observed the hot exhaust gas that shot from her tailpipes as she selected military and pulled the airplane around. Bright explosions of chaff expelled behind her from buckets on the bottom of her jet. Once her nose committed, Wilson said, *One potato,* and pushed the throttles to military, rolling left and pulling his nose across the horizon.

For an instant, Wilson looked out his left canopy at the wharf below him. He observed muzzle flashes from several guns, including one big one with a slow rate of fire north of the wharf. He then rolled further left, pulled the stick in his lap so his g-suit inflated, and then sucked the throttles to idle. When he banged out a chaff program and craned his neck to full extension to keep the target in sight, his goggles picked up multiple rows of tracers crisscrossing his view. Some moved fast and some slow against the stationary lights of the harbor and the dark water in the background.

Holy shit! he said to himself. They were diving into a confused buzz saw of AAA, heavier than he had ever seen.

CHAPTER 59

Pulling his nose down to the target, Wilson unloaded and rolled out wings level in a steep dive. As his *Hornet* accelerated and raced downhill carrying a heavy load of ordnance, his years of training took over. Wilson noted Olive still in her dive, but he didn't see Cajun. He shot a glance at Dutch, who was behind him with adequate separation, and brought his attention back to the HUD to track his target. Wilson struggled to line his aircraft up on the green HUD aiming cues, which required a lightning quick scan to ensure proper weapons delivery. He made crisp corrections with the stick while slewing the aiming diamond on his exact aimpoint —the middle group of *boghammars*.

With release altitude fast approaching, he heard Cajun call, "Lead's off." Wilson made a last-second azimuth correction, pressed the red "pickle" button on the stick with his thumb, and held it down hard. His HUD release cue "flew" through the velocity vector and signaled the computer to eject the bombs. The airplane shuddered as hundreds of pounds of ordnance was suddenly released from each wing.

Wilson heard *Boom! Boom! Boom!* in rapid succession off his right side. He pushed the throttles to military and hauled back on the stick to stop his dive. He sensed a bright flash to his left, banged out another chaff program, and jinked hard right into Dutch for a count. He then rolled back to wing's level in order to catch his bombs' impact on the FLIR.

He then heard an alarmed Olive call out. *"Skipper!"*

Wilson looked left and saw a wild, gyrating fireball. The dazzling, white-hot light almost washed out his goggles, but he saw the unmistakable planform of a *Hornet* wing poking through the flames before it, too, became engulfed. Horrified, he looked under the goggles and saw the yellow and orange flames of the fireball spinning in a steepening dive. Flaming pieces of debris ejected from it and trailing black smoke could be seen against the radiance of the city lighting.

Two huge flashes underneath him caught Wilson's attention, and he overbanked to see concentric circles emanating from tall geysers of water and smoke. Flaming pieces of debris cartwheeled through the air from where the skipper had laid his bombs, bullseye hits. Two more flashes erupted next to them, one

on the wharf pier and another one on an adjacent warehouse. They produced circular supersonic shock waves as more debris floated into the air in slow motion.

Wilson pulled hard up to the left and watched the flaming wreckage continue to gyrate out of control. "Get out!" he cried on strike common, and then repeated, "*Hammer* one-one, get out!"

Receiving no response, Wilson called to Olive, "Olive, keep your knots up, egress southeast! Dutch, you with us?"

"Affirm, visual two, coming out your left seven high. No chute yet!"

"Roger, bug southeast!"

Wilson noted AAA fire above with more streams in front of him as he kept his turn in to egress. His fist banged out more chaff, as he violently maneuvered the jet in order to keep sight of Olive above him. He then overbanked to see *Raven 400* in its final plunge. The aircraft had now disintegrated into several flaming pieces, with the largest one falling toward the mouth of the harbor. He checked his airspeed—a slow 300 knots—*Dammit!*—and crammed the throttles to burner as he punched off his drop tanks. Looking down, he saw only splash circles on the water south of the wharf—all that remained of his skipper's aircraft.

Wilson keyed the mike on aux frequency and shouted in vain. "*Cajun! You up?*"

As he jinked left, a bright flash burst to his right. *Fuck!* The flash was followed by a rapid *bap, plink, plink* off to his right. *Did they hit me?*

Wilson bunted the nose to regain precious airspeed while his threat receiver was going off—the aural warnings in his headset were constant. He could barely think. Instinctively, he continued to jink in three dimensions to throw off the gunners aim and ran away from the threat on brain stem power and a very human will to survive. He spotted Olive and Dutch several thousand feet above as all three aircraft clawed their way toward safety.

A transmission from the *Iron* lead broke through Wilson's fog. "*Hammers*, you guys okay?"

Still jinking and searching the ground for threats, Wilson recognized the voice of the *Moonshadow* XO and answered between breaths. "*Hammer* one-one could be down. Any *Hammers* see a chute?"

"*Hammer* one-two negative."

"One-four negative."

"*Hammers* from *Iron*, we have the impact marked."

"Roger," replied Wilson.

Now running to the briefed get-well point, with the threat from the AAA appearing to subside, Wilson almost allowed himself to relax. But he couldn't. No chute. No emergency beeper. Instead, the horrific image of Cajun's jet being torn to pieces by both an antiaircraft shell and the forces of nature. His skipper, Cajun, *gone*. Yet, if anyone could survive, it would be Cajun.

The familiar voice of CAG Swoboda broke the short silence. "*Hammer* lead, this is *Sweep* zero-three. I've got the on-scene command with *Sweep* flight. *Hammers* and *Iron*, RTB. *Tron* three-one and *Zaps*, remain at your orbit, max conserve. *Knight*, pass to mother…*Hammer* one-one is missing and appears to be down. Launch the Alert CSAR and send bucket brigade *Texaco* to the briefed get-well point."

Still jinking south of the target and looking for any AAA batteries on the islands, Wilson remained beneath Olive and Dutch who were in formation above him. He fought the urge to disagree with CAG, but impulsively keyed the mike. "*Sweep*, from *Hammer* one-three, request remain behind to help, have the posit marked." He got the answer he expected.

"*Negative*, one-three. I *understand*, but get your people home and send your post-strike report."

Embarrassed, Wilson replied, "*Hammer* one-three wilco." He banged the top of his instrument panel in frustration at his inability to help. At this distance from the ship, CAG knew that the *Hornet* strikers were marginal on fuel even after they topped off from the *Viking* tankers and pushed out.

Once out of the AAA envelopes, the *Hammers* transited over the strait and into the GOO. They hugged the Omani airspace to put as much distance between them and the Iranian coastline as possible. This allowed Wilson to flick off a bayonet fitting and take in lungfuls of air. His *Hornet* was flying fine—no flight control anomalies or engine problems—so, if he *had* been hit, it was superficial. Still thousands of feet underneath his wingmen, Wilson pulled the canteen from his g-suit pocket for a long drink, taking wary glances north and east for SAM launches. He then stowed the canteen, reset his mask, and climbed up to their altitude on the left.

"Flip has the lead on the left. Check in with state," Wilson transmitted.

"You've got the lead on the left. Two's five-point-eight," Olive replied.

"Three's six-point-one," Dutch added.

Wilson responded, "Lead's five-point-three. Everyone get their hits?"

"Affirm," Olive said.

"Got everybody's," Dutch answered. His FLIR tape had picked up the impacts from all four *Hammers*, invaluable intel once the analysts in CVIC could review it.

With this information, Wilson made his report through the *Knight* to relay to the ship. He also added the aircraft status and a request for a tanker once they got to *Valley Forge.*

Transiting to the southeast, Wilson looked at the port of Jask to their left and saw faint streams of AAA, then two bright flashes on the waterfront, followed by two more. On the goggles he strained his eyes to see the 1B strikers overhead, but could not discern them, lights out, among the stars. Nevertheless, something was hitting Jask, and Wilson figured Weed was involved. It was fascinating to watch, live, from over 40 miles away.

"Check out the action to the east," Dutch transmitted on aux. Wilson acknowledged him with two mike clicks.

As they continued in glum silence, Wilson's thoughts soon returned to Cajun. *No way was Cajun going to bring those bombs back.* But why were *their* GPS receivers bad when the *Irons* had no problem? Was the AAA too hot? Should they have aborted? Was that level of intensity the go/no-go standard now?

Wilson thought again of the World War II aviators diving into the ring of fire, and the Korean War and Vietnam aircrews facing sophisticated integrated air defenses. They had set the standard his generation had to uphold. Cajun, too, was on government time—and he had delivered. *Did he get out?*

Wilson thought of Billie Lassiter in Virginia Beach. *What is she doing now? Welcoming the kids home from school, figuring out what to feed them?* Maybe turning on the TV to learn right now that American aircraft are attacking Iran in response to the *Richard Best* attack. Billie has been around this business long enough to know that the *Ravens* would be involved, with her husband leading from the front. In less than two hours, the Commodore and the chaplain could be knocking on her door with bad news, or uncertain news… Either way, it would be devastating.

To the east, the moon peeked above the jagged cloud-lined horizon. On its slow journey across the black sky, its glow created a welcome line that helped the pilots distinguish up from down at a glance. Though the pilots could see the moon from four miles up, far below on the surface it was still well below the horizon, and, to the left, the dark Omani coastal plain was almost indistinguishable from the sea. This region was one of the most desolate and inhospitable places on earth. Its desolation, however, possessed a beauty of its own, and Wilson had observed it many times during his deployments here. The ugliness, in contrast, was pronounced: the cruel heat of midday; the wind-blasted and sun-scorched wasteland; and a strange, unfriendly people whose ways were so foreign and views so absolute—yet accommodating, if it suited them.

Wilson had been forged a warrior here, and the region held a special place in his heart. At the same time, he hated it, hated coming back…but could he *walk away* after this cruise? Wilson looked over at Olive and Dutch, dutifully following their flight leader. At the moment, they were mere position lights in the darkness.

The radio crackled, and Wilson returned to the task at hand: Get everyone home.

Then it hit him, pent up and long suppressed emotion welling up from inside, the tectonic plates of service before self and the desire to live a normal life with Mary and the kids that ground away at each other for months and years suddenly shifting at this time and place, alone in the cockpit of a low-fuel-state warplane high over a dark and hostile sea on the other side of the world, surrounded by strange combinations of numbers and letters on his night-dimmed cockpit displays, hearing and comprehending short and clipped radio transmissions that are all but indecipherable to only a few thousand people on earth.

A question, a cry rose up from a place he did not know he possessed. *What am I doing here?*

As he looked up at the Milky Way, as if asking someone, anyone, for an answer, he let the question hang and then repeated it in his mind. What made him come *here*, again and again, fighting the Iraqi's, Al Qaeda, the Taliban, and now the Iranians? Going back home to recharge, retrain, and reload? And repeating the cycle for *another* deployment? And another? And if successful in his career path, he'd have *many* more deployments, all of them here in this literal hellhole of a region. And was that it? Promotion? Advancement? The all-consuming obsession with *command?* Was he thinking only of himself on the way up, willing to miss vast swaths of his children's lives in the process and even to risk making Mary a widow at worst? He thought of what she was doing now—at home watching the kids during the midafternoon doldrums. Soon the phone would ring and someone would tell her to turn on the news, and she would start wondering and worrying and praying. Then, she would receive another call with the shocking news that Steve Lassiter is missing, and she would rush over to Billie's house with the other girls to support her. They would each begin living their own personal hells while they watched one of their own experience it for real. His career choice was going to do that to her in mere hours.

"Damn you!" he shouted at himself in guilt and frustration.

"*Raven* four-zero-three, Strike?"

Wilson snapped out of it and keyed the mike to answer the ship over 100 miles away. "Go ahead."

"Check in with flight number and state."

He took a deep breath and responded. *"Ravens* checking in with three, low state four point one, requesting *Texaco."*

"Raven four-zero-three roger, vectors for *Redeye* seven-zero-two is one-five-zero at sixty, angels fourteen, switch up departure on button two."

"Strike, four-oh-three copies. *Ravens* go, button two," Wilson said as he punched in the tanker frequency and prepared for another night tanker rendezvous in a thirsty jet over a dark ocean.

Almost an hour later he climbed down from *403* on the foul line, emotionally and physically spent. Airman Rodriguez met him at the bottom of the ladder with a salute, but Ted Randall and the troubleshooters were there with some news. "You took some dings on your right wing, two in the aileron and one in the trailing edge flap. One of the aileron hits went clean through, a hole about the size of a quarter. Did it give you problems?"

"No, no problems," Wilson said, walking past the group to see for himself, while Ted and two of the troubleshooters following. He looked up at the folded right wing and saw the top of the aileron with its composite fibers exposed. Then he inspected the trailing edge flap with his flashlight, running his fingers over a one-inch exposed shard of metal embedded in the skin.

They hit me, he thought. If he had been a little closer, or if the frag had hit him in a vital area, he, too, would be in the dark waters of Hormuz—or worse.

"Can you patch them?" he shouted over the whine of nearby jets. Before Ted could answer, a *Prowler* trapped and rolled out some 60 feet away, and they waited for the deafening roar to subside to continue the conversation.

"Yeah, won't make the last go, but tomorrow for sure. What happened to the drops?"

"Had to punch 'em off, needed the airspeed," Wilson answered, still fascinated by the damage, albeit light, to his aircraft.

They hit me.

"Is the Skipper okay? Is he going to be late?" Ted shouted. The troubleshooters leaned in to hear the answer.

Wilson sensed they already knew what it would be. He looked at Ted with a pained expression. "I don't know. Doesn't look good, Ted. What have you heard here?"

Ted shook his head and said, "Nothing. Just that he didn't check in."

The troubleshooters drifted away in grim silence, but Wilson stopped one of them and shouted close to his ear. "Petty Officer Mansfield. I want that frag, please."

"You got it, sir," the metalsmith replied with a solemn nod. "I'll deliver it myself."

"Thanks."

Wilson turned to complete his post flight and saw that Airman Rodriguez stood in his path. She looked up at him in confusion and disbelief. "Mister Wilson, is Commander Lassiter coming back tonight?" She had to shout in her accented English to be heard over the din.

"Don't know, Rodriguez. We're looking for him." Wilson didn't know what else to say.

The girl refused to believe it.

"Sir, you said everyone would be okay." She looked at him as if he had deceived her.

Chapter 60

Wilson sat bone tired in his ready room chair, head back, legs stretched out in front. He tried—and failed—to nap while waiting for Saint to show up from his early morning strike. Shortly after his own return, Wilson had answered endless questions from the CVIC *spies* about the enemy defenses, the hits, Cajun's last known position, the JDAM indications, and routine coordination procedures. He was then led to flag plot to relay the story, again from the top, while Admiral Smith, with his staff looking over his shoulders, studied target photos and charts of Bandar Abbas. He learned from the admiral that CAG and the *Sweeps* could not raise Cajun on his survival radio. Neither could they remain in the area where he went in due to the heavy concentration of AAA and a tactical SAM launched at them. Their assessment was that *400* went in several hundred yards off a jetty near the harbor entrance with no indication that Cajun made it out; but there was no proof he was dead, either, so the search and rescue effort was ongoing. Nobody wanted to turn it off and declare him missing—or killed—too soon.

Smith had dark circles under his eyes. Every person in the room did.

Wilson then went on to the strike debrief, which he held in place of his CO. With Cajun's hits on a nest of *boghammars* included, Strike 1A had done significant damage to the *Pasdaran*, and the *Irons* were four for four with no JDAM problems. The suppression plan was also a bright spot. But to the aviators gathered in the somber ready room the strike was a failure: One of them, the strike lead himself, had not returned.

Air Wing Four had hit the other coastal targets with good results and no additional losses. The last of the early morning strikers were returning. This included the XO, who was now the de facto commanding officer of VFA-64.

Wilson raised his head and looked around at everyone in the silent ready room, which continued to function as a fighting force, even wrapped as they were in the pall of loss. Anita remained at the duty desk, and behind Wilson were several JOs. Among them were Olive, trying to nap; Nttty, in his alert flight gear; and Smoke, taking a sip of water.

Wilson got up and spoke to the group as a whole. "Guys, if you aren't briefing or debriefing, standing an alert or eating, go and get some rest. We have another big day and night coming up."

Smoke put down his cup and left without saying anything, and others filed out in glum silence. They didn't know what to do and were too keyed up to sleep. Wilson felt the same way. Nttty, however, settled in to doze, and exhausted from the flight and her restless sleep from the previous night, Olive remained in her chair with her eyes closed. Wilson sat down next to her and waited for her to respond. Sensing a presence, Olive opened her eyes and turned to Wilson.

"What did you see?" he asked.

Olive looked at the back of the chair in front of her as she formulated her answer. "Just as he pulled off, his right side exploded, as if a round went down the intake. The wing was blown off, and the jet became a tumbling fireball, flaming pieces thrown out. No chute...just...*fire*... just a shower of fluttering, flaming debris."

"Yeah...I was releasing when you made your call."

"What call?"

"You called '*Skipper!*' "

Olive looked away. "I don't remember," she said. Wilson studied her and noted lines on her face he had never noticed before.

"You okay?"

"Just whipped. I'll be fine."

"I need you to go back up there tomorrow night. Can you do it?" Wilson asked.

"Yeah, I'm good," Olive replied as she again closed her eyes.

Thirty minutes later, Saint came into the ready room still in his flight gear. Wilson rose to his feet as the XO asked, "What happened to the skipper?"

"Just as we passed the IP, the four of us had NO GPS indications, and the skipper flexed to a visual roll-in, standard high-dive, one run and off. Skipper took a triple-A hit on the pull off. Olive watched him explode right next to her. No chute, no indication of ejection. We marked the wreckage in the water south of the harbor, and CAG relieved me as on-scene commander. However, he couldn't stay in the vicinity because it was too hot."

"Yes, I heard you took a few rounds yourself."

"Yes, sir, superficial damage."

Saint handed his weapon and blood chit to Anita, and then continued with Wilson. "What do you think?"

Wilson looked away, then back to Saint. "I *hope* he's captured, sir."

"Concur, but is that what you think?"

"No, sir...don't think he got out." Nttty and Anita didn't dare move.

Saint wriggled out of his torso harness and nodded. "I tend to agree with you from everything I've heard. I'm going to visit CAG and report as the acting commanding officer of this squadron. You are now acting XO. CAG Ops says he has new strike tasking from above—that's coming to Skipper Lassiter's strike planning team—that I will now lead. Meanwhile, we've got another day and night of CAPs and strikes coming up. You need to schedule your people smart."

"Yes, sir."

Saint grabbed up his flight gear in one arm and headed toward the door. Halfway down the aisle, he turned and said over his shoulder, "Oh, yes, about Hinton. She is now grounded, effective immediately." He then craned his neck fully to lock eyes with Wilson and ensure his message was received.

"Yes, sir," Wilson answered and stood still as the new commanding officer of the *Ravens* exited the ready room.

Nttty and Anita exchanged looks and wondered what they had just witnessed.

CHAPTER 61

Valley Forge had completed her interdiction strikes for the night, except for the helicopters and S-3's monitoring the surface picture. Two hours earlier, a formation of *Tinian* AV-8's had come across two *boghammars* well south of Chah Bahar that were transiting at a high speed into the Indian Ocean—on an apparent suicide mission to find and attack anything they came across. Each *Harrier* shot a *Maverick* guided missile into the boats, blowing one apart and setting the other on fire. After reporting the action on GUARD, the Americans had given the Iranian search and rescue helicopter plenty of sea room to affect the rescue of survivors, which appeared to be small in number.

Just after *reveille*, Wilson followed Saint along the passageway of blue tiles that led to CAG's stateroom. Arriving at a blue door emblazoned with a large CVW-4 emblem, Saint knocked twice.

"Come in," CAG answered, and Saint opened the door.

CAG and DCAG were seated at a table in the middle of a living area. The room was spacious and plush by modern warship standards, yet spartan for a man responsible for more assets and people than the CEOs of many Fortune 500 companies. It featured a desk in one corner, with a squawk box and built-in shelves in another corner, where CAG displayed several personal and professional mementos. Two couches were arrayed against the wall, and another door opened to a bedroom that was little more than a closet.

CAG motioned them to take a seat at the table. "How you guys doing?" he asked.

"We're making it, sir, but still in shock," Saint answered. "Any more news?"

"We've got some assets in the vicinity of Bandar Abbas watching. The Iranians know where he went in and were observed trolling the area with something like a johnboat to pick up anything they can. Still no contact from Cajun. We have to figure that if he's not dead, he's captured. You saw him go in, Flip?"

"Yes, sir, but it was lots of flaming pieces and debris heading for the water, last I saw of him."

"How many would you say?"

"A handful, sir. Three? Five? Lots of smaller pieces."

CAG looked up and rubbed the stubble on his chin. Wilson figured he, like all the others, had not slept well, if at all, during the past 48 hours. "Okay—Saint, you are obviously leading the *Ravens* now until we get Cajun back, and we need you guys. We are going to continue with strikes against the *Pasdaran* tonight as planned, but we've got pop-up tasking for one more.

"The GCC countries are wringing their hands that Iran is going to strike them with a ballistic missile, and they're leaning on Washington hard to prevent it. We've got several Aegis ships in the Gulf, but they can't be everywhere. And Iran is threatening anyone and everyone who provides sanctuary to the Great Satan. These missiles aren't Saddam's SCUDs either, these guys can target and hit what they aim for. They rattle their sabers and test these things, and the GCC Arabs are deathly afraid they'll strike them. GCC mouthpieces are already condemning our strikes to placate the street, but their front offices all know they need us here in the region or Iran takes over everything."

CAG pulled some imagery from a folder and placed the photos on the table. Saint picked them up and studied them for several moments.

"Saint, your target is a missile final assembly facility in south central Iran called Yaz Kernoum. You can see it's a hike from here, and it looks like some kind of cement plant or mine out in the middle of nowhere. According to DIA, though, it's the one place in Iran that can fuel the rockets and install the guidance section and warheads. The GCC thinks their counties are targeted next because who knows who is controlling the IRGC these days. Frankly, they have a point. We know Iran has been working on nukes for a long time, and although the experts say they are years away, the *experts* have been wrong before."

Wilson noticed a sudden look of disdain on DCAG's face as he stared at Saint's khaki uniform shirt. Wilson glanced at it himself and saw why. Saint had affixed a command-at-sea pin, which signified an officer in active command of a sea-going unit, over his right pocket.

Bastard couldn't wait to put it there, Wilson thought.

CAG pointed out the targets on imagery. "You have eight aimpoints, and I'm going to give you two divisions of strikers—plus a dedicated *Iron Hand* package. We'll be in this vicinity for the next 24 hours. Time on target is 0530 local, just after sunup. And this strike has to be covert from the get-go, with perfect comm discipline. We must show our hand only at the last moment. We'll have made an announcement that the current operation is over, then hit 'em with this a few hours later...part of the "fighting dirty" I mentioned a few days ago. You'll have AWACS for target area control and the dedicated mission tankers you need from Air Wing Four. This is an add-on—after we finish the scheduled strikes

tonight. I want a brief at 1600 with your plan. Then we go to the boss for his blessing."

CAG paused for effect, then added, "This strike *has* to go. Losses are acceptable."

Saint looked up at CAG, then back at the imagery. Wilson noticed Saint's discomfort and the minute shift of his body. "What weapons do you want us to use, sir?"

"You tell me, but give me as much heads up as you can so the ship can break 'em out and build 'em up. Given our GPS hiccup or spoofing from last night, I want a solid backup plan."

Wilson looked at the chart. One hundred miles northwest of the target was Shiraz. "CAG," he asked, "any indications the MiG-35s flew last night?"

"Thought you would recognize this place. And the answer is no, not as far as we know. But Yaz Kernoum is just down the street from Shiraz. Plan for it."

CAG signaled it was time to leave. "Lots of work to do, and my staff is here to support. See you back here in 10 hours."

DCAG spoke up as Saint rose to leave. "I see you wasted no time pinning that 'sheriff's badge' on your uniform." He was not smiling.

Saint, eyes downcast, said nothing as he gathered up the folder. CAG noticed the pin and then looked away, embarrassed. The two *Hornet* pilots turned to leave.

"I spoke to Billie," CAG said, just as they reached the door. They both turned back to face him, waiting for more.

"She's holding up well, knows Steve is a fighter, and, even now, is a rock of strength to the other wives. She said the outpouring of support is overwhelming. I imagine all the squadron wives are with her right now."

Wilson knew he was right, and noted the time…approaching midnight in Virginia Beach. It was going to be another very long day and night for all the *Ravens*.

CHAPTER 62

After breakfast Wilson and Saint met in CVIC, in a small room set off from the main planning spaces to review the target folder CAG had given them. Wilson looked at the overland navigation chart first and plotted the distance: over 500 miles on a direct line and right over Hormuz, a place Wilson did not want to see again with its layered defenses. However, as with any layered defense, there were seams to exploit, and areas that would provide concealment from radar detection, allowing the strike package to expose itself at the last possible moment...if they stayed low on the ingress. At some point, though, they would have to climb to stay out of any local defenses and give themselves the best chance of acquiring their targets. The time on target was troubling, too, just after dawn, which degraded night vision goggle and infrared sensors. It also required a daylight egress, which increased the threat of scrambled interceptors from any number of fighter bases in the region, which to Wilson meant Shiraz—and Hariri.

While Saint stepped out for a moment, Blade joined Wilson in planning. Within 10 minutes, they both knew what they needed, and they had determined the "A" team to fly it. Wilson called down to his stateroom and summoned Weed to join them. The *Raven* division would be Saint, Blade, Flip and Weed, with Saint as the strike lead and Wilson backing him up.

Saint returned and spent a few moments looking at the chart while Wilson and Blade worked in silence. After a few moments, Saint took a straight edge and drew a line from the ship's position to the target. "Hmm..." he said, "if the ship can launch us in order, we might be able to do this without tanking up front. Mister Cutter, give me a max-range profile to the target area, high all the way, and the fuel when we return feet wet. Maybe we won't need to ask CAG for so many tankers."

Blade, incredulous, looked at Wilson and back at Saint. *"Sir?"*

Commander Patrick looked up and coldly assessed the senior lieutenant. Pointing with his finger on the chart, he repeated himself. "Here to *here*, max range, with this bomb load, two tanks, standard self-escort load out. We brief our plan in eight hours. I need the answer in five minutes. *Am I clear?"*

Blade swallowed hard and said, "Sir, that takes us right over Bandar Abbas, with double-digit…"

"I see exactly where it *takes* us, Mister Cutter," Saint shot back. "We'll surprise them off the cat with our audacity and high speed. Thinking we are already done for the night, they won't be able to react until we've passed over them."

Blade chuckled and shook his head in disbelief. "Those guys are going to see us coming for miles, and their gunners will still be at their posts from our previous strikes!"

"I am leading this strike, not you!" Saint fired at Blade, now visibly upset.

Wilson spoke in a low tone. "Blade, *leave us.*"

"This is *bullshit!* You can't…" Blade said through clenched teeth before Wilson interrupted him.

"*Lieutenant Cutter!* I said, *leave us!*" Wilson's words thundered at Blade and shocked him into silence. Regaining his composure, Wilson added in a low voice, "Now. *Go!*"

Blade abruptly pushed away from the table and stepped out. Wilson and Saint looked at each other. Saint spoke first.

"He's off the strike. Why did you even select him?"

"Because he's the TOPGUN trained squadron tactical expert—and a damn good pilot. He stays."

Saint's eyes narrowed as he stared at Wilson. *"What did you just say?"*

"He *stays*, sir, because *I* need him." Gesturing at the chart, he added, "And we aren't going to fly this profile, either."

Incensed at Wilson's insubordination, Saint fired back. "Let me warn you now that *you* can be replaced, Mister Wilson. I will forget I heard this mutinous talk coming from a senior department head and *subordinate*, obviously affected by the stress of combat, once we complete this strike as fragged."

Wilson was prepared for this confrontation and decided, at this point, he was unwilling to needlessly risk his life and the lives of the others.

"Commander Patrick, when we launch tonight, we are two individuals trying to do the job, and we're also trying to give ourselves the best chance of survival. We aren't going to highlight ourselves and motor straight up there like flying pincushions for their missiles. We are going to stay low and tank enroute, under the radar until we get into the Persian Gulf. We will then ramp up over a less heavily defended area, hit the target, and egress to safety the way we came. I am going to plan this, and you are going to brief it and lead it and *take the fucking credit*. But if you deviate from my black line by so much as a mile, I'm gonna take it back. You'll know when you hear me transmit on strike common,

'Flips, go alternate tac.' We will then wheel away from you *en masse,* and you will be *alone,* sir."

Saint leaned in and whispered, "You're fired."

"As you wish, sir, but who are you going to get to help you? Weed? Blade? They aren't stupid. Clam? He's not a qualified strike leader. And CAG thinks the lineup is already set. Tell him that the *Raven* department heads are off the strike, and then brief him and the admiral on your flawed plan. He's right down there in his stateroom just 10 frames away, probably trying to nap." Wilson pointed to the starboard side of the ship for effect. "Go ahead, sir. Wake him up, and get this news to him early so he has time to flex." Pausing for a moment, he then said, "You *need* us, sir, and we'll come through with a plan that's tactically smart and meets CAGs objectives and gives us *all* a chance at survival. Now, *commander,* shall we proceed? Or am I still fired?"

Wilson watched a crimson flush of color race across Saint's face, still locked in its piercing stare. Wilson knew Saint didn't have the guts to follow through on his threat.

After several seconds, Saint pushed back from the table and looked at his watch. "When I come back at noon, I want the plan and the weapons load out, in detail. CAG needs the load out ASAP."

"Aye, aye, sir. You'll have it." Wilson nodded slowly with determined eyes.

CHAPTER 63

Fifteen minutes before launch time, Wilson released the parking brake and taxied, under the skillful control of the yellow shirt, from his spot on El 3. In the 20 hours since their confrontation in CVIC, he and Saint had managed to plan the add-on strike to Yaz Kernoum with a minimum of friction. When disagreements did occur in front of the others, a raised eyebrow from Wilson was all it had taken to get Saint to defer.

The plan was to launch the package after a routine "dawn patrol" launch of two S-3s and two *Hornets* to monitor the surface picture around the strike group and deal with any threats. *Valley Forge's* two nights of retaliatory strikes against IRGC and Iranian Navy units was complete. There had been no additional American losses, and the last of the strikers had recovered the previous hour. Just before walk time, Wilson had stolen a glance at CNN and heard a Pentagon reporter say the strikes were over. The report was accompanied by an Iranian-manufactured propaganda videotape of burning residential areas and frenzied crowds chanting "Death to America."

Wilson had shrugged it off, too tired to care anymore. Messaging was not his job.

He *was* tired. During the past 48 hours, he may have slept three hours, maybe four, grabbing fitful catnaps whenever he could. He had forced himself to remain alert during the strike brief, which Saint delivered to the equally exhausted aircrew in his flat monotone.

Now, in the early morning darkness, the typical nadir of human performance, he and the others had to perform at their peak to make this strike a success.

An E-2 and two *Vikings* were soon launched into a clear night, half-moon almost overhead. They were followed by two *Buccaneers* off the waist. On routine patrol, these aircraft would make themselves known to the Iranians, and keep their attention, while the strikers worked their way, unseen, into position low on the water. The deception plan was beginning to come together.

In line behind the waist catapults, Wilson fidgeted in the cockpit of *405*, his familiar nighttime butterflies returning. Weed was behind him in the queue

in *407*, hands resting on the canopy bow, and Blade was going through final checks on El 4 in *411*. Dutch was the airborne spare, turning on the fantail in *413* with his canopy down, ready to go. Saint was starting up in *404* someplace on the bow. The *Raven* division call sign on this raid was *Anvil*, and the *Spartan* division was designated *Sledge*. The two divisions would be joined by the *Tron* self-escort suppression element of one EA-6B and two *Moonshadows*. Tonight there would be no check-in on strike common, no post launch voice calls from the strikers. To a great degree, the strike's success hinged on their ability to maintain communications discipline, waiting to expose themselves at the last possible moment.

The *Rhino* tankers were next off, as a *Prowler* taxied down from the bow to feed the cats with airplanes. Wilson looked at his kneeboard card: just a few minutes behind schedule, time Saint could make up.

Off to his right, Wilson sensed motion, and looked down to see Chief Grant waving to get his attention. Pointing to the bow, Grant raised four fingers, then a fist, then four again, followed by a thumbs down. Wilson immediately grasped the meaning: Saint's jet was down and, as alternate strike leader, this would now be his mission to lead.

Yes! Wilson thought, as he returned a thumbs up in vigorous acknowledgment. He caught Weed's attention and, through hand signals, passed on the news. His roommate shook a thumbs up in return, followed by two raised fists of encouragement. In the last moments before the launch, Wilson shook his head with contempt. He *knew* Saint would find some reason not to go, but at the same time he was relieved he would not have to deal with Saint's airborne leadership.

In short order, the *Sledge* and *Tron* elements launched. Then, Wilson, a mix of adrenalin and rage coursing through his bloodstream, impatiently waited for his turn at the catapult to do what he trained a career for: lead a long-range power projection strike deep into enemy territory, which would *make everyone happy*. Make Washington happy, make the GCC happy, and make the admiral's staff happy. *Just hook me up, dammit!* and put Yaz Kernoum out of action *now* and bring everyone back and everything will be okay. Saint, Cajun, Psycho, CAG, the admiral…even Mary and the kids… *all* was blocked out when he was finally hooked up to the catapult, checking the cockpit, cycling the controls, watching for the burner signal, and then shoving the throttles to max, locking his left arm hard against the stops, like a caged animal, impatient to be set free, furious to get off the friggin' ship, breathing deeply as he scanned the blackness off the cat track ahead of him, full of resolve to do his duty and *make everyone happy*.

With a familiar jolt, Wilson was shoved back in his seat. The deck edge rushed up and under as he accelerated into the void, fiery thrust lifting him into the night, a free man.

Saint exploded, in a barely suppressed rage, into the ready room, followed by Ted asking for more detail on *404*. Saint threw his helmet into his chair, but it bounced onto the deck with a crack. At the duty desk, Psycho rose to her feet in shock, and Nicky froze in his back-row chair.

Saint turned and let loose a salvo at Ted. "Is it too much to ask to have a fully mission capable jet for the biggest strike of the year? I'm the damn strike lead and you put me in *that?*"

"Sir, four-zero-four flew last night, no problem. It's a good flyer. We had no indication the TACAN was bad until now. We're swapping it out."

"Too late, Mister Randall. Launch complete! My strike is going up there without me, and I have to explain to CAG why I'm not leading it." Beads of sweat dotted Saint's forehead as he placed his sidearm on the counter. He then removed his blood chit and flung it at Psycho.

"XO, we could have made it, but you downed the jet just as they began to taxi you, and the deck wouldn't let us work on it until you were respotted." After the hectic maintenance pace of the previous two days, Ted's own patience was wearing thin.

Saint's jaw remained set as he continued to remove his gear. "The TACAN is a vital piece of equipment—*every* component of the jet is vital—and when it's down, especially in combat, the jet is *down!*"

"Yes, sir, no argument. We had a small window to make and we couldn't. At least you and the jet are safe on deck."

"*Fuck! Fuck! Fuck!*" Saint muttered audibly to himself. Nicky was sure he was witnessing a breakdown, and everyone in the ready room was embarrassed by the display.

Psycho broke the silence. "Excuse me, sir, but you should have another pistol clip…"

Saint reached into his survival vest pocket and answered, "Yes, another clip for the combat mission I'm *not* going on because of the unsat jet I was assigned." He tugged on the clip once, and when it didn't come free, he yanked on it hard.

With a loud *hiss,* an orange smoke, tinged in pink, shot from his vest and formed a billowing cloud in the front of the ready room. While others scrambled away, Saint dropped the vest to the floor in disbelief.

"Cut it!" somebody cried.

That call propelled Nicky forward. He took his XO's shroud cutter from the pile at his feet and cut the lanyard to the still-firing flare. Gunner Humphries appeared beside him and reached over Nicky to grab the flare and get it out of the ready room. *"Make a hole!"* Gunner shouted as he opened the door and walked briskly past astonished onlookers in maintenance control. He turned aft and then outboard to toss the flare over the side from a hatch under the LSO platform. The high-visibility smoke, however, lingered in the passageway and compartments as sailors fanned it away from their faces.

The ready room was still in shock, when Psycho yelled, *"Attention on deck!"* The room popped to attention, and Saint's face fell, and then turned white, as he looked through the wafting smoke.

Swoboda stood, stunned and incredulous, at the back of the *Raven* ready room.

"CAG…yes…sir."

CHAPTER 64

This would be no "ordinary" power projection strike.

The strike package stayed low on the water under strict radar emissions control and veered northwest in a running rendezvous with *Super Hornet* and *Viking* tankers. Each pilot judged range, bearing, and closure by means of the sight picture provided by a cluster of lights from the tanker and the aircraft that may have already joined on it. The pilots had rarely used this method since flight school. Flying without the aid of their radars, especially when they could not even use the radio for a dark night *"comin' left"* sugar call or to check everyone in on the proper frequency, was disconcerting. The key, though, was to remain as covert as possible.

Wilson eased up next to Weed's darkened jet while Blade was in the basket. The airborne *Anvil* spare, Dutch, appeared on his bearing line. To the north several miles and 1,000 feet above were the *Sledges* on their tanker, and he hoped the *Tron* division was somewhere nearby. The aircrew in these aircraft was the best A-team Air Wing Four could put together on such short notice after the previous night's schedule.

Once Blade and Weed completed their refueling, Wilson extended his probe and slid behind the basket as the formation motored northwest in silence, still over an hour from the target. While in the basket, he noted a small light on the water, maybe a merchant—or a dhow—just off their nose with no chance to avoid. They would hear the jet engines and maybe even see a position light.

Damn. Who was on that vessel and what would they make of it? Would they radio someone about what they observed? After the recent action, he surmised it was unlikely to be an Iranian vessel way out here, but not knowing gnawed at him as it always did.

Wilson finished refueling and crossed under Blade and Weed as they waited for Dutch. Donning his goggles, he scanned the surface of the water and saw some lights well north—not a factor. He found the *Tron* division behind them and to the south, but at least they were there. *Good, we're all aboard and on timeline,* he thought.

Wilson checked his fuel: two hundred pounds low. Despite needing every drop to hit the target and escape with a reserve, two hundred low was not bad. Now the strike package would accelerate ahead, staying low, while the tankers joined on another tanker to top off and meet the strikers at the get-well point in the Arabian Gulf for post-strike tanking.

Dutch finished refueling and crossed under. A minute later, the *Super Hornet* retracted the refueling store basket and veered away left in a shallow angle of bank. The *Anvils* were alone on their track.

In silence, they shuffled the formation, Blade and Dutch flying cruise on Wilson's left wing, Weed on his right. Wilson completed his combat checklist for the second time since launch and popped out a bundle of chaff. To the others it looked like a flashbulb under Wilson's jet and served as the signal for them to complete their checklist and check their systems. Wilson noted each pilot expend a bundle in order. *Even at 0445, we are on our game tonight*, he thought.

In the distance, Wilson saw the mountains of Oman rise out of the northwest horizon, and aided by his NVGs, he could see the glow of cultural lighting from the Iranian coastline. Scanning the sky, he saw no aircraft lights over Iran, but he did see a few over the GOO. He surmised they were American, and those he saw over the Persian Gulf could be American or civilian. On his moving-map, the distance to the coastline was 45 miles, but it looked much closer on goggles as the moon backlit the rising terrain. To his right, he sensed a muted flash and noted Weed's *Hornet* was now without its drop tanks. When he looked left, he saw Blade punch off his tanks and watched them tumble away. Wilson noted he had only a few hundred pounds remaining in each of his tanks and prepared to jettison them once they were dry. This would reduce both his weight and drag and would increase maneuverability.

As the little formation continued through the darkness in silence, each pilot busied himself in the cockpit monitoring the navigation and thinking about their individual weapon deliveries and the enemy threats they might face.

As they approached the coast, Wilson hit SELECT JETT, and, as he felt his tanks leave the aircraft, he cracked the throttle back to compensate for the increased airspeed. He veered the formation left to lead them into a fissure in the rising Omani wilderness, which offered a place of concealment from visual or electronic detection. He looked back to see Dutch clean off his tanks, just in time, as the coastline loomed ahead.

Low-altitude on NVGs in mountainous terrain—in the wee hours—was varsity flying, and each of the *Ravens* worked hard to accomplish three things: to keep position on Wilson, keep themselves out of the rocks, and look for threats.

The half-moon bathed the terrain in all the light they needed as they turned their heads right and left to scan through the green-tinted spotlight their goggles provided. Wilson led them up the illuminated side of the ridge face, and the wingmen held tight positions above their leader, which allowed them to maintain formation and monitor ground clearance as well. The nearby *Sledge* and *Tron* formations did likewise over a moonscape of rugged, uninhabited land. As they transited over the ridgelines, they maintained radio silence, avoided the shadows and stayed as far away as possible from scattered settlements that would be alarmed at the sudden thunderous rumble from the jet formations breaking the stillness of the desert night.

The *Anvils* made an easy left turn on a westerly course. Wilson led them down the backside of the Omani range to the sea as he increased his groundspeed for the next leg, which led into the Persian Gulf. He noted that the cultural lighting from Dubai dominated the southwest horizon and bounced off a high overcast that bathed everything in a greenish NVG glow. Numerous lights from shipping and oil platforms dotted the Gulf ahead of them.

He checked the clock… Inside 30 minutes to go.

Losses are acceptable. He remembered CAG's words and the punch they sent to his stomach. Air Wing Four was going to take no chances. The strikers were loaded with laser-guided bombs each pilot would manually guide into their assigned aimpoint with a laser beam…all while flying formation and monitoring the threat. Because they still didn't know why the *Raven* division had NO GPS indications over Bandar Abbas, the strikers needed a weapon that didn't depend on GPS guidance. Laser deliveries, however, required clear line-of-sight, so if a cloud deck got in the way over the target, the *Anvils* and *Sledges* would be forced to get underneath it. That would mean exposing themselves to the threat to a much greater degree deep inside a hostile country. Looking in the direction of Yaz Kernoum, Wilson couldn't see any weather. They were on time and Wilson's fuel was as planned. Things were looking good.

Now on the water, Wilson took them down as low as he dared, his obedient wingmen still in loose cruise as the eastern sky began to lighten behind them. He looked under his goggles to assess the ambient light and decided to keep them on as long as he could before the rising sun compelled him to remove them.

Wilson reached down to find the fuel dump switch and held it for a second before he secured it. He then switched on his radar. The others saw a shot of fuel burst from Wilson's fuel dump masts: a welcome sight, their briefed signal to energize their own emitters. Now led by the radar, it was as if they had been

blind and could suddenly see. Each of the pilots immediately devoured the tactical information the electronic eye provided them about the surface and the air contacts ahead. They avoided the islands in the Gulf, some Iranian and some Arab, as they continued west just above the tranquil waters. Wilson was struck by the lack of tanker traffic—there wasn't any.

A new voice filled his radio headset. *"Thor,* picture clean."

Wilson transmitted, *"Anvil"* to answer the AWACS controller orbiting high over the Gulf in an E-3 *Sentry,* the Air Force aircraft providing early warning and tactical control for the strike package with an aircrew he had communicated the strike plan to the day prior. In succession, he heard the others.

"Sledge."

"Tron."

All were up strike common and another potential disconnect appeared to be solved. *Thor* responded with "Houseboat," the code-word to continue. No last-minute reprieve from Washington; the strike was going to go.

Wilson got to the end of the navigation leg and turned northwest on the established route. When he could see Weed's helmet next to him with his un-aided eye, he decided it was time for his goggles to come off. The first warm rays of sunlight creeped up from the eastern horizon and silhouetted the sharp shadows of *Hornets* next to him. The formation sped closer to a remote area of the Iranian coastline where they would enter the Islamic Republic to begin their final run-in for Yaz Kernoum.

CHAPTER 65

In his alert facility bed, Reza Hariri had finally gone to sleep after another restless night of waiting in vain for the Americans to come to him. It had been a long and frustrating two nights at the Shiraz alert strip, his armed and fueled MiG-35 parked in a shelter off the end of the runway, just beyond the wall of his small sleeping area. The setup allowed him and the other alert pilots to be in their aircraft and taxiing for takeoff within minutes.

The action around Hormuz had been disappointing, with IRIAF fighters recording no kills and maintaining CAPs far from the American strike groups in an effort to distract them and lure them away from the targeted areas—and into the teeth of the defenses. To Hariri it was all foolishness. *No, idiocy*. Iran possessed *dozens* of modern fighters with beyond visual range weapons, including the MiG-35!

Let me get down there, at night, and every one of my missiles will have a target, he thought, railing against the Iranian leadership that kept the MiGs *here* on strip alert, hundreds of miles from the action—while his F-14s and *Phantoms* were given worthless CAPs well inland. It was like a bullfighter waving a red cape at a charging bull from the safety of the grandstands. *No, we need to get down there, take some losses, but bloody their nose—much more than we did two nights ago.*

One (*one!*) *Hornet* had been shot down by antiaircraft guns over Bandar Abbas. He was surprised the Americans even *continued* their strikes after that loss, so risk averse and pampered a people. The intelligence collectors said the dead pilot was the commander of Wilson's squadron, and Hariri reflected that Wilson may have been inspired by the example of this man, a commander who *led from the front*. Pity that more in the IRIAF did not lead that way. They were worried, instead, about currying favor in Tehran!

Wilson. Surely he was involved with the actions to the south, and Hariri chafed to get another shot at him. He realized, though, it would be most coincidental if fate put them together again. He was certain he would have at least gotten a chance last night, the reason he spent the night here, hoping for a scramble in his *fully fueled* monster that would have covered the distance to

Hormuz in minutes at Mach 2. But the Klaxon had never sounded, and his excited junior pilots had returned hours ago with their weapons still attached to their aircraft and bogus stories of "standing up to the Americans." Knowing the pilots had been safe on CAP stations miles away from the *Hornets* while the enemy attacked his homeland with impunity, the stories had filled Hariri with contempt. At least the *Pasdaran,* and even the Islamic Republic Navy, was willing to shed blood against the Great Satan. Hariri would have sacrificed himself, and a squadron of his pilots, to down just *one* American fighter last night.

Indications were that the Americans had accomplished whatever goal they had after two nights of limited retaliatory strikes along the coast: an example of their clumsy and predictable military-stick-followed-by-diplomatic-carrot approach. Exhausted and unable to believe he and the IRIAF had missed the opportunity of a lifetime, he fell into his alert bed with his boots on, thinking of fat generals in Tehran, and fighting a TOPGUN, and squeezing the trigger one last time.

Vehicle headlights moved east on a desolate stretch of the two-lane coastal road—just as the *Anvils* approached from the south at low level. *"Damn!"* Wilson muttered to himself. Too late to avoid them, he led the *Hornets* feet dry into Iran as the vehicles passed underneath. Wilson imagined their startled drivers reaching for their cell phones to warn authorities of a sudden roar of jets crossing the beach in the twilight. He rolled up on a wing for a second to ascertain the vehicle types, which looked like sedans in the early morning murk. Wilson whispered more than transmitted, *"Fly ball,"* on strike common. The code word commanded the strikers to arm up and signified to *Thor* they were feet dry, a fact that was soon transmitted to eager staff officers monitoring their progress at command centers in the region, in Tampa, and in Washington.

If they had not been spotted until now, Wilson liked their chances. That meant they had avoided detection from sailors on "innocent" vessels in the GOO and Gulf and Iran's own early warning net...a combination of luck and solid planning. He noted 10 miles to the "pop" point. Within minutes, the Iranians would be alerted to their presence, and if Wilson's plan worked, they would be powerless to counter the Americans with anything like defense in depth.

Because of the rugged terrain, he elevated the division a bit but remained under the radar horizon and out of the shadowy darkness of the desert floor. The desert was now a dim, gray-blue surface, but the growing radiance from

the east was beginning to highlight the ridgeline off to his right. This low-light situation *at low altitude* was dangerous, and once they crossed the coastline, the strikers moved out into combat spread formation. In 15 seconds, they could climb.

Wilson brought the throttles up, eased back on the stick, and commanded his *Hornet* to enter a shallow energy-sustaining climb; his wingmen followed in mirror image. Off to the east a few miles, he saw the *Sledges*, four dark *Super Hornets*, outlined against the pink sky as they, too, started up. The radar cursors in every cockpit swept back and forth in search of any airborne threat on their nose. With their senses sharpened by fear and adrenaline, the pilots scanned the horizon for threats, monitored their navigation, checked their fuel state, and fiddled with their weapons programs. Throughout, they kept their knots up in a steady climb as they pressed further into Iran.

About halfway up, Wilson looked over his right shoulder and saw the orange sun burst above the eastern horizon and spread its warm rays of light from north to south. While observing this tranquil scene, he noted his first RWR hit—an early warning radar at 4 o'clock. *Not bad*, he thought. They had avoided Iranian radar detection until now, exposing themselves only when they had gotten behind the lines, minutes from the target. The strikers continued their transonic climb, knowing they were now drawing the attention of a hostile and surprised integrated air defense system.

In his semicomatose state, Hariri's mind attempted to grasp the meaning of the first sounding of the alert Klaxon. With open eyes, he heard it again accompanied by rapid footsteps and excited shouting outside. He bolted out of bed as a junior pilot, running to his own alert fighter, flung the door open and shouted, "*Sarhang* Hariri, the Americans are coming!"

Knowing every second counted, Hariri whipped his g-suit on with swift tugs on the zippers, grabbed his helmet and dashed to his jet. His mind raced. *Where? What are they doing? How many?* He bounded up the ladder and dropped himself into the cockpit in the same manner he had 20 years ago defending his homeland from the Iraqis. Sergeants shouted commands and linemen pushed open the shelter doors as Hariri, with help from his crew chief, hooked himself into his parachute harness. With a loud *whoosh,* a giant hose connected to the MiG became rigid and forced air through the turbines as Hariri initiated the fuel and spark required to begin the continuous cycle of jet propulsion.

Hariri taxied out from under the fluorescent lights and into the dawn twilight, cleared for immediate takeoff. He was given an initial vector of southeast, following a section of F-4 *Phantoms* that were already thundering down the runway ahead of him. He looked over his shoulder into the adjacent shelter and saw that the other alert MiG-35 had its canopy up and was surrounded by maintenance technicians. *Russian morons!* he shouted to himself before ignoring his wingman's plight.

The alert shelters were located adjacent to the runway, and Hariri didn't even stop as he taxied onto it. He brought the throttles up to afterburner, and his jet roared over the concrete behind two giant pillars of white-hot fire: a horizontal rocket ship accelerating to flying speed within 2,000 feet. Hariri picked the nose up and rolled right on course, in his single-minded focus to find and kill the enemy.

Chapter 66

The strike package leveled off high over a stark desert landscape of erosion-scarred ridges. The predawn light showed deep crags and fissures on every surface. During the planning, Wilson had picked this area for the ingress because it was devoid of surface threats but, as he looked at the dim surface from high above, he thought it the most uninviting terrain he'd ever seen. Harsh. Foreboding. The land below was *ugly*, and Wilson wanted to minimize his time over it, if for no other reason than to get to the target before the Iranians could mount a threat.

With fewer than 10 minutes to go, the pilots took last-minute glances at their assigned aimpoint imagery and double-checked their weapons switches set. Yaz Kernoum was located in a small valley separated from a village to the west by several miles. Nearby, and typical of this region of the world, were long green agricultural fields that reminded Wilson of Balad Ruz. The topography was also reminiscent of the Fallon training complex in the high desert of Nevada. Wilson's aimpoint was a rectangular building that looked like an abandoned industrial facility. It was located between two identical buildings on a road that bisected the complex. Weed's target, a missile final assembly tower, was nearby. Blade and Dutch were to hit fuel storage magazines set apart from the complex to the northwest, and the *Sledge's* target was the missile component storage warehouses on the eastern perimeter.

The idea was for all eight strikers to release on their aimpoints, guide the laser weapons from their cockpits while flying formation and scanning for threats, and then egress with mutual support while the *Tron* division behind them provided defense suppression. All the aircraft, except the EA-6B, were loaded with air-to-air missiles to defend themselves from enemy fighters. Wilson and the others knew the Iranians were now watching them on radar as they raced to the target with their heads on a swivel.

At the initial point, no one was reporting any radar contacts. Wilson selected AIR-TO-GROUND and transmitted, "Tapes on!"

Just then the radio crackled as *Thor* provided the strikers with their first contact report, a God's-eye radar view of the situation around Yaz Kernoum. "*Thor* picture–single group, bullseye, three-four-zero at sixty, medium, hot."

"*Anvils*, roger, *declare*," Wilson responded, asking the AWACS controller if the airborne contact was hostile, already knowing the answer.

"Hostile," *Thor* replied.

"*Anvil* one-one."

Though separated from the enemy by 80 miles, the Americans now faced a problem that called for a decision from Wilson. The two groups of aircraft were approaching one another at well over 1,000 knots of closure and would merge in minutes. Knowing the strike package would be at their release points in about half that time, and the target must be hit—*Losses are acceptable*—pressing to the target was required. But if they were shot down by fighter-launched, forward-quarter missiles before the bombs impacted, all was for nothing. It was going to be close.

Wilson keyed the mike. "*Sledges*, send a section and take the bandit group. Everyone else continue as fragged."

"*Sledge* two-one, wilco... Break: *Sledge* two-three flight, target bandit group, bullseye three-four-zero at sixty, medium, hot."

"*Sledge* two-three. *Thor*, *Sledge*, two-three committing group three-four-zero, sixty, declare."

"*Thor*, group three-four-zero, sixty, hostile."

"*Sledge* two-three, hostile."

Wilson's decision effectively cut the American firepower against Yaz Kernoum by 25 percent, but it was a contingency they had planned for as the *Sledges* were all going against the missile storage warehouses and could spare some overlap. The *Rhino* weapons system operators worked the intercept with the two AMRAAM missiles the larger aircraft carried. Wilson's *Anvil* division each carried only one AMRAAM for self-protection. All the fighters were loaded with two *Sidewinder* heatseekers.

On time line, Wilson commanded his radar and FLIR to find his assigned aimpoint. His targeted building came into view on his FLIR, as if viewed through a soda straw. In a deft motion, he slewed his aiming diamond over it. He checked that his wingmen were in position and noted the trajectory of a HARM missile fired by one of the *Trons*.

"*Thor*, new picture. Bandit group bullseye, three-three-five at fifty, medium, hot. *Second* group bullseye, two-niner-zero at sixty, low, hot!"

Damn, Wilson thought. Another bogey group to complicate the picture. He queried *Thor*. "Declare!"

"*Hostile!*"

The fact the Iranians had sent two groups of interceptors, separated laterally by some 40 miles, posed an even more difficult problem for the Americans, who

were already limited by available fighters to counter this new threat. Wilson could picture the geometry in his mind—these guys could pose a problem for their egress to the get-well point in the Gulf.

Weed came up on the radio. *"Anvil* one-two is spiked, zero-two-zero, chaff, defending."

Wilson saw Weed pull away and down in order to free himself from the electronic grasp of a SAM missile radar. He also noted the two green bombs on Weed's wings and realized he needed them, and all the remaining bombs, to hit their assigned aimpoints. Wilson searched the ground ahead for a launch plume and found it: a bright flare trailing a white plume that rose in the distance. The missile picked up speed as it ascended but was not tracking Weed, who, still in his defensive maneuver, was now 90 degrees off and descending. Wilson called out to his friend.

"Anvil one-two, tally on the *light post,* out your left nine o'clock long. No factor! Resume!"

"One-two, ah, *visual,* roger."

Wilson saw Weed reverse his turn to come back to his place in formation. Ahead and to his left, Wilson noted some black AAA puffs suspended in air, then some flashes from fresh air bursts underneath them. On his HUD, the seconds counted down to release. Switches set. The aimpoint grew larger in the FLIR display. A glance at Blade and Dutch confirmed they were in perfect position abeam.

A call from *Tron* filled his headset: *"Magnum* from *Tron* five-two."

Things *were* happening fast. Another picture call from *Thor* reminded him of the new threat to the west and the need to counter it.

"Trons, can you take the group to the west?" he asked.

"Affirm!" one of the marines answered.

"Roger, inside 30 seconds to release," Wilson acknowledged, just as his RWR lit off.

DEEDLE, DEEDLE, *DEEDLEDEEDLEDEEDLEDEEDLE!*

Wilson snapped his head to the spot from which Weed's SAM had launched and saw another missile lifting from the shadows of the ridge to the east. Weed saw it, too.

"Light post lifting at the *Anvil's* one-thirty!"

"Anvil one-one is spiked with a tally," Wilson replied, knowing he couldn't defend himself without throwing off his delivery. With five seconds until release, he kept his thumb pressed down on the pickle switch and held steady on the steering cue. At the same time, he kept one eye on the SAM that was now passing above the horizon and tracking toward him. Three...two...one...

The bombs left his jet with a lurch, and Wilson whipped the aircraft left and pulled hard, spitting out chaff to evade the missile. Looking straight down, he saw his bombs begin their earthward journey, a trip that would take over 30 seconds to complete—time he would need.

The confused predawn sky over Yaz Kernoum was dotted with black clouds of AAA fire, SAM plumes arcing here and there, and laser-guided bombs en-route to their aimpoints. Waves of RF energy filled the air performing diverse tasks in the service of each adversary. The cockpits were populated by highly trained professionals in their 20's and 30's, their minds trying to grasp what they saw and heard, identifying who made terse, nervous radio transmissions to build a mental picture for themselves and their wingmen. The men struggled to maintain as much situational awareness as they could while maneuvering hard in three dimensions to survive and guide their weapons to impact. It was the culmination of years of training from habitual drill to replicating this type of power projection strike in a permissive environment, and in the low morning light over the central desert of Iran, the intensity of this mission was the most they had ever experienced.

Wilson picked up "his" missile, but it was drifting aft on his canopy and going ballistic as he pulled back to the target. He rolled out to unmask his FLIR and reacquire the aimpoint. His mind absorbed a transmission from *Thor*—the northern group was 20 miles away—as he found the middle building and held the aiming diamond on it, while taking peeks at his wingmen who were also heads-down in their cockpits. He heard a "Fox-3" call and looked right to see *Sledge 23* and *24* launch AMRAAMs at the lead bandit group. Slender fingers of white smoke produced by the bright "lights" of the missile rocket motors moved away from the fighters at high speed and began a graceful climb to intercept the enemy aircraft the Americans could only see with their radars.

Ten seconds till impact. Wilson corrected some aiming diamond drift with a deft slew to the middle of the building. His ears picked up the voice calls of his wingmen and the *deedles* from his RWR, but they did not register now, lost as he was in the concentration needed to hold his aiming diamond on target. The seconds counted down and the FLIR view shifted as the *Hornets* flew over

the target, the countdown always too slow for the impatient aviators who just wanted to get out of *Indian Country* as soon as they could.

On the FLIR he saw his bombs, two white dashes, enter the screen and hit the building, the infrared image turning white from heat and smoke generated from the impact. Selecting WIDE, he saw Weeds' bombs explode on his aiming point with two concentric shock waves flying out from the middle of his target. Returning to NARROW, Wilson noticed a strong surface wind had blown away most of the smoke, and he could now see that a majority of his building was destroyed. A steady flame, resembling a blowtorch, shot from the target.

"*Anvil's* Miller Time!" Wilson broadcast on the radio. He overbanked left to begin their direct route to the Gulf.

"*Sledge* two-one and two-two clear, visual on *Anvil*."

"*Sledge* two-three, timeout on the lead bandit. Tally smoke! Splash one!"

"*Sledge* two-four, timeout on the trailer. Tally ho! Splash two! Visual, six clear!"

In the northern twilight the pilots saw two black puffs with fiery trails falling to the desert floor. Two down.

"*Sledge* two-three, flight visual, six clear, egressing."

Having dispatched the lead group of bandits, their type still unknown to the Americans, *Sledge* 23 and 24 jinked through the target area to join the lead section who were now trailing the *Anvils*—with all aircraft heading southwest, the shortest direction to the coast. On the surface, the muzzle flashes of over a dozen guns sent familiar arcs of deadly tracers skyward. Though the AAA was heavy, it was ineffective, and the SAMs were still lifting off their rails. With the extent of the defenses, they now had no doubt this area was more than just a cement plant next to a rural village.

Wilson's RWR lit off again. A SAM was tracking him from his 8 o'clock, and he picked it up visually. Breaking into it, he bunted the nose—and saw the missile mimic his move. *Oh shit!*

"*Anvil* one-one spiked, defending!"

Straining to keep sight of the missile against the dawn sky, Wilson bunted the nose again to pick up knots, and realized that he was surrounded by AAA puffs. He lit the burner and jinked into the missile, this one tracking his movements, watching it draw near from above the horizon, waiting for the right time...*Damn, it's fast! Now!*

Wilson rolled and pulled into it, crushed by instantaneous g that made it difficult to keep sight. Trailing a residual plume, the missile flew underneath him. He flinched when it exploded close to his jet with a sharp *BOOM* heard

through the Plexiglas canopy, the warhead making a blooming circle of flame and frag.

"*You okay?*" Weed called with concern.

Wilson rolled through the horizon and was relieved that he saw no cautions in the cockpit.

"Yeah, can you bug southwest?"

"Affirm, I'm at your right five, comin' to four."

"Visual, six clear. *Let's bug two-three-zero,*" Wilson directed.

The strike package was now sprinting southwest to the coast and safety, leaving the heavily defended caldron of Yaz Kernoum behind, columns of smoke from burning aimpoints rising into the sky. The *Tron* escort was off a few miles to the northwest, prosecuting the western group of bandits, acting as a blocking force for the rest of the package. After defending from the SAM, the two *Raven* department heads were now supersonic, several miles behind the others, as they all ran to the safety of the Gulf.

Wilson noticed a contact on his radar inside 10 miles, crossing left to right. Alarmed, he locked it, and soon identified it as the *Tron* EA-6B, alone, and going in the wrong direction.

"*Tron* five-one, *Anvil* one-one is at your right two o'clock long. Bring it southwest!"

"*Tron* five-one, roger," the *Prowler* answered, immediately turning southwest. The AWACS controller then called to inform them of a new threat.

"*Thor*, new group, bullseye, three-four-zero, fifteen, medium, heading one-eight-zero."

From this call, Wilson knew the bandits were nearby and probably gaining. "*Thor, Anvils* on the egress. BRA from *Anvil* one-one. Declare!"

"Standby, *Anvil*...*Anvil, Thor,* hostile BRA zero-one-zero at twenty-three, medium, hot."

"*Heading?*"

"Two-zero-zero."

With his arm locked against the throttle stops and the airframe moaning from the supersonic airspeed, Wilson did some mental calculations. The Iranians were 20 miles aft and on an intercept course, with the Gulf sanctuary over 50 miles away. However, the *Tron* EA-6B was up ahead with Wilson and his roommate set to pass them soon. A heading change would buy a bit of time.

"*Tron* five-one, check left twenty! Gate—*everything you've got! Unload for knots!*"

"Five-one, roger!" Wilson saw the *Prowler* bank left a few miles ahead.

"*Thor*, picture. *Tron* five-two, hostile BRA, three-one-zero at twenty-five, medium, hot."

"*Tron* five-two, sorted left."

"Five-three sorted right!"

By listening to the comms Wilson formed a picture in his mind. The *Tron* escort fighters were running on the bandit group to the northwest, their right flank. The other bandit group was running them down from behind, and, with its limited top-end speed, the *Prowler* would be easy prey. Well ahead, the other strikers were egressing hard with the coast in sight.

"*Tron* five-two, Fox-three on the western bandit!"

"*Tron* five-three, Fox-three on the eastern bandit." Wilson saw two more AMRAAM plumes appear in the distant sky, about 10 miles away. They headed toward the still unseen bandits to the northwest.

"*Anvil, Thor*, threat BRA three-six-zero at seventeen, medium, hot."

DEEDLE, DEEDLE, *DEEDLEDEEDLEDEEDLEDEEDLE!*

Wilson was locked up by a fighter radar behind him.

"*Anvil* one-one is spiked at six. Spike range?"

"*Thor*, fifteen miles."

"One-two's spiked, six o'clock!" Weed added.

CHAPTER 67

Although Wilson and Weed were gaining on the *Prowler* less than two miles ahead of them, the bandits at their six were gaining on all three American aircraft due to the airspeed limitations of the EA-6B. At their current speed, Wilson and Weed would pass the *Prowler* in a minute and leave it exposed to the gaining threat—an unacceptable condition for their impromptu high-value escort mission. Wilson guessed the Iranians had radar missiles that could catch them from behind, and due to the speed differential, the Iranians could easily run down the Americans and employ short-range weapons in minutes.

Looking over his shoulder to the north, Wilson tried to find the bandits but could not discern them in the dawn light. Then, his heart skipped a beat when he saw an object, a thin shadow, cutting through the eastern horizon. It passed 100 feet behind Weed from high to low as a white mist trailed in its wake. The missile had been fired from the bandit group just outside the range that would have turned Weed into a fireball. Wilson knew what they had to do, fast, to avoid the next enemy missile from finding its quarry.

"Weed, we've gotta engage now. Short-range set, I'm high, out of burner. *Go.*"

"Two," his wingman responded as both aircraft reduced power. The pilots were held in place by their straps as the aircraft slowed through the invisible barrier that separated supersonic and transonic flight.

"*Tron, Anvil,* lean right, descend for knots," Wilson directed the *Prowler,* still running for its life. "We're going to engage with these guys."

"Roger, *Tron* five-one leaning right. You can only push a barn door so fast!"

Wilson got another quick transmission in before they turned. "*Thor,* you copy? *Anvils* one and two engaging to the north."

"*Thor,* roger. Bandits now twelve miles, hot."

"Roger! One-two, you ready?"

"Affirm!"

In measured cadence, Wilson keyed the mike. "Roger, in-place-left, go!"

"*Two!*"

In unison, the two *Raven* pilots slammed their throttles to afterburner and yanked the jets left. Still not sure what type of aircraft they would encounter, they

pulled hard in a nose-low, energy-sustaining turn back to their pursuers to the north. With his head all the way back and straining against the pressure, Wilson struggled to look out the top of the canopy and pick up the bandits at the same time his fingers selected the radar mode and a *Sidewinder* missile. What they were doing was a dangerous last-ditch defense of the *Prowler*, running as fast as it could to the coast in a desperate attempt to escape the closing Iranian fighters.

Rolling out of his turn, Wilson got a lock at his 11 o'clock, 10 miles slightly high. He noted the distinctive planform of an F-4 *Phantom* closing the distance. Despite the screaming *Sidewinder* launch acceptability tone in his headset, but not wanting to take a chance, he selected the more powerful AMRAAM and pulled the trigger hard, holding it down. After what seemed like a long pause, the missile fell from its fuselage station. The rocket motor then ignited and shot the missile forward with a loud WHOOOM, trailing a big white plume as it sped away from under Wilson's jet.

Before his radar-guided AMRAAM impacted, Wilson saw it was tracking the "eastern" of *two* fighters, now crossing over the companion *Phantom* to engage Wilson. Just then Weed got a call out before he pulled his own trigger. "*Anvil* one-two, Fox-2 on the eastern bandit!" Wilson saw Weed's *Sidewinder* zoom away and twitch twice before tracking one of the two enemy aircraft. Wilson's AMRAAM impacted the "eastern" *Phantom* first and instantly turned the aircraft into a bright torch, tumbling through the sky and shedding flaming pieces as it tore itself apart. "Hey!" Weed cried out after Wilson's missile hit what Weed thought was *his* bandit. Weed's *Sidewinder* obediently tracked and exploded inside the plummeting inferno with no added effect.

The surviving *Phantom* was now coming straight for Weed, who quickly recovered. "*Anvil* one-two engaged with a *Phantom*. Chaff! Flares!"

Wilson was three miles away and headed to his roommate's rescue. He made a hard right turn, watching the two aircraft come to the merge on his nose, the *Phantom* turning his tail toward Wilson and inviting another shot. As Weed turned hard to go one-circle, Wilson's sixth sense caused him to do a belly check to the left. A few miles in the distance, Wilson instantly saw the dark planform of a big fighter, nose on, with a huge intake crowned by a high nose fuselage section. Seconds after he spotted it, a bright light erupted from underneath the fighter—and headed straight for him, trailing heavy white smoke.

Sonofabitch!

Wilson snap rolled left and pulled nose-down to sustain energy. He also went to idle and spit out expendables as he watched the missile arc up and then down toward him.

Time slowed. Placing the missile on the top of his canopy generated the maximum angles off for a potential overshoot if Wilson could anticipate the right opportunity to give away everything and break into it. The fiery dot seemed to lunge toward him, and he snatched the stick back in a break turn into it, banking for the second time that morning on a last-ditch maneuver to make a missile go stupid. Though straining hard, he was mesmerized as he watched the missile go horizontal as it tried to turn the corner—*right next to him.* Instead, it fell off with a twitch and shot past him, the rocket motor still burning brightly, on its way to land on the desert floor. Wilson looked up and saw his assailant high and to the west, ready to pounce. At that angle, he at once recognized the strange planform of a MiG-35. *Is that Hariri?*

"*Anvil* one-one engaged defensive!"

"Roger, I'm engaged offensive," answered Weed, "Should have a shot in 20 seconds!"

Wilson saw the MiG overbank and pull down toward him. He pushed the nose down to regain valuable knots and, reselecting burner, floated in his seat while he kept sight high behind him and slightly left. With the bandit's nose buried, Wilson pulled his lift vector up and into the MiG in an effort to force it into an overshoot. Awestruck, he watched the aircraft, cloaked in a white cloud of condensation, rotate from nose-down to nose-on as if it were stationary in the sky. He was certain another missile—or tracking guns shot—was imminent.

Wilson stood his *Hornet* on its tail to close the distance and, maybe, generate an overshoot. *Just hold him off until Weed comes to the rescue.* He felt the *Hornet* shudder and saw the flight control surfaces behind him move in computer-generated spasms in response to his efforts to keep the aircraft on the edge of controlled flight while his airspeed bled to 100 knots. Feeding in rudder, he veered left and watched the MiG slide behind him as both aircraft held their noses high.

The *Flatpack,* painted in a light blue air-superiority camouflage, with the IRIAF roundels visible on the fuselage and wings, was still behind him. The bandit now pulled his nose even higher to flush Wilson out in front, the canards working hard to keep the big Russian in controlled flight. Wilson craned his neck to the right to keep sight and watched the Iranian slide his nose back left and pull lead for a gun shot. Just before the enemy nose came to bear, Wilson pushed forward on the stick to foil the shot, which missed high. The all too familiar sound of large-caliber bullets snapped the air outside and penetrated his canopy. Once the MiG fell off to reposition, Wilson pulled up again, stood on the cans in full blower and fed in right rudder to force another overshoot. As he threw out chaff and flares, he also squeezed every bit of energy he could from

his aircraft to throw off his attacker. The MiG then countered as the *Hornet* redefined the fight once more.

Wilson heard an exuberant Weed call on the radio. "Splash the *Phantom!*"

"Roger, man, get over here! I'm engaged defensive!" Wilson cried.

"Looking!" Weed answered.

"In a flat scissors...I'm high, angels eleven!"

In heavy buffet, Wilson held his nose up as high as he could, ruddering his jet into a weave to hold off the MiG. He was using every pound of thrust his twin engines could deliver in an effort to fly *slower* than his opponent. The *Flatpack* recovered and pulled up next to him. Wilson froze as he looked into the cockpit.

Those eyes. Hariri! He was fighting Hariri for a second time!

For a moment, both aircraft were suspended 100 feet from each other, each pilot looking at his opponent from across the void, oxygen masks covering all but their eyes. Hariri with enough excess power to cut his opponent in half with a multi-barrel buzz saw and Wilson on the edge of stall knowing he could be blasted out of the sky in seconds. The dawn sun glinted off Hariri's canopy; it was definitely him. Cunning, dark eyes, determined to kill.

"Flip, tally, visual. Break left!"

"I can't, man!"

Hariri lifted the MiG up and over on its back, the hooded cobra ready to strike again and deliver the coup de grâce. Wilson knew he could not stay with Hariri and watched in helpless horror as the *Flatpack* drifted back on his canopy. Unable to run, unable to maneuver away—and with Weed unable to help—Wilson squeezed every knot he could from his jet to hold off the Iranian. He was trapped. With his heart pounding almost in time to the shake of the airframe in the heavy buffet, Wilson knew he was unable to avoid another shot. Breathing heavy with fear, he sensed he was about to die.

"C'mon, man! *C'mon!*" he shouted into his mask, coaxing his jet to give him more power.

Then, Hariri's jet began to shake.

With the MiG's nose parked high, it fell off right from its own heavy weight and began to backslide. Finally, out of power to bring his nose to bear on the American or to outzoom him, the huge fighter fell straight down under Wilson.

"Yes!" shouted Wilson and, with rudder, slid his aircraft right as he watched the light blue aircraft fall away. *Turning room!* Wilson took just enough separation to gun him and rocked back on the weapon select switch. Hariri sensed he was becoming defensive and pushed his nose down to gain knots and reposition. Wilson had to make his move—*now*.

Selecting GUN, Wilson slammed the stick forward hard to the stops and pulled the throttles back. The airplane pivoted nose-down in one g flight. When he pulled the stick to neutral, his HUD was filled with MiG-35, the green gun reticle positioned just in front of it.

Hariri saw the shot coming and tried to roll left underneath Wilson, but, at his speed, the *Flatpack's* roll rate was too slow. Wilson squeezed the trigger from less than 500 feet above and riddled the right wing of the MiG. The impact explosions were followed by an eruption of fire from the right side of the aircraft, a huge fuel-air explosion that buffeted Wilson's *Hornet* and reached right out to him. The wall of bright yellow-orange flame, mixed with black smoke, enveloped him for an instant before he flew through the edge of it. Wilson snapped his head left to watch the MiG roll right, belching huge quantities of flame and smoke. Finished.

"Shit hot!" Weed crowed from a mile away. "I'm at your right four high!"

"Roger, bug southwest! Check six. Lead's three point one."

"Three point five…comin' out your left seven."

"Visual, six clear."

"Visual, six clear."

The MiG rolled out of control toward the desert floor, flame consuming the right wing root. Wilson continued to watch its descent and soon noted a white parachute bloom next to the smoke trail that marked its path. *Hariri got out to fight another day.* In the distance, Wilson saw two other chutes, which he figured were the aircrew from Weed's *Phantom* kill.

The *Raven* pilots climbed up in combat spread, searching the sky and surface for additional threats as they brought up the rear on the strike package egress out of Iran. Going feet wet over the Gulf, they descended for their tanker rendezvous, with low fuel states as usual. Above them a CAP of Air Force F-15 *Eagles* was present to discourage any Iranian fighters from pursuing them into international airspace. Weed, mask dangling down to show his wide smile of joy and exhilaration, joined up in cruise position on Wilson's left. Wilson flicked off his bayonet fitting and smiled back. Pumping both fists, gulping big lungfuls of air, the two veteran pilots were as excited as little kids at Christmas. Relieved—and alive. Wilson then made a gun-cocking motion with his left hand, followed by a slashing motion across his throat to safe the switches. They had done it.

Hariri grimaced in pain as he looked up at the canopy of white nylon above him. The seat-slap from the ejection had caused something to snap in his lower back, and the shock of the parachute opening seemed to have pulled a muscle in his groin. Floating above the desert wasteland, he saw his burning aircraft pointed straight down in a tight corkscrew just before it slammed into a fissure and exploded into a fireball. The flames soon became a black mushroom cloud rising into the morning sky, the sharp *boom* of the impact reaching his ears after several seconds. To the southeast, he could see two other palls of smoke rise from the surface. He was then conscious of the low rumble of jet engines to the southwest but unable to see them. *Probably the bloody Americans.* And then it was quiet, save for the gentle wind whistling through the nylon shrouds above him.

As Hariri descended from 3,000 feet above the desert floor, his mind tried to comprehend what had just happened. The *Hornet* he had tried to shoot down had a black bird on the tail, like Wilson's aircraft from last month. He wondered if it was Wilson. Regardless, the American was lucky, defeating his missile by doing a belly check at the last minute—and then engaging him in a slow-speed scissors. Once again, Hariri's equipment had failed him: the stupid missile didn't guide, his gun pipper was *right on him* yet the aircraft missed high.

Damn you! Hariri shouted into the still desert air—at everyone but himself.

When he had flushed the American out in front, his MiG couldn't stay with it. The tons of fuel in the wings and fuselage had caused it to fall under its own heavy weight. He knew what was happening and cursed his jet as he fell below the *Hornet*, pushing the throttles forward with all his strength, almost bending them, in a vain effort to get more power out of the burner cans. When the American had pivoted down in midair, Hariri knew he was trapped.

The bullet impacts on the wing sounded like a string of holiday firecrackers, but they were followed by the roar of fuel-fed flames mere feet away. Time slowed as he pulled the handles by instinct, watched the canopy fly off, and winced in pain as the initial impulse of the seat motor slammed into his butt and rocketed him out of the aircraft. Hariri saw the canopy rail fall below him followed by the flames and smoke of his doomed jet.

He immediately regretted ejecting. *It would have been better to ride it in.* Now he would have to face the scrutiny he would receive from Tehran and his pilots, even from Atosa.

The sun that rested on the eastern ridgeline fell below it as he continued his descent. He knew there was a settlement on the other side of the ridge, but he saw nothing here but a dry stream bed among the shadowy limestone fissures.

Maybe he would die out here: of dehydration, of a broken back when he landed, or by wild animals. *A just fate*, he thought.

He heard shouting and scanned the surface for its source. He determined the language he heard was Farsi, and soon saw a village man with two boys and a pack mule on a dusty trail. *"We are coming to you,"* the man bellowed, and the excited boys ran ahead to the spot where he was about to land.

I can't believe there are people out here! Right under me! Hariri then realized he would probably live, a fact that filled him with a deep sadness.

CHAPTER 68

After Yaz Kernoum, *Valley Forge* and the other strike group ships stood down from further combat. Remaining vigilant, they flew only routine sea surface search hops in the GOO and made single-ship transits of Hormuz to ensure freedom of navigation, but otherwise kept a low profile. The Iranian maritime forces did as well, not only due to attrition from the American attack but from a practical sense, so as not to invite a further and possibly more damaging response from U.S. forces.

Reaction from world capitols was characterized by predictable expressions of regret at the American action, with little condemnation of the Iranian recklessness that had precipitated the use of force. The statements of American condemnation were accompanied by demonstrations in several European population centers, as well as damaging comments from some American left-wing politicians. However, the Arab world was silent for the most part, save for government expressions of shock at the American action and a few chanting mobs for local media consumption. Privately, the GCC governments thanked Washington for the prompt action at Yaz Kernoum that placed Iranian missile forces in check, if only in the short term. The United States also received quiet congratulations from many of the same governments that publicly expressed regret or worse. Even the Chinese remained officially silent but conveyed their approval behind the scenes.

Tehran loudly claimed victory over the Great Satan, feeling triumphant in the fact they had absorbed the best blow the United States could deliver and still had their blue-water maritime capability intact. They also sent out ominous warnings of devastating retaliation against American and GCC installations at a time and place of their choosing. Surviving *Pasdaran* assets were back at sea for the benefit of cameras, but they stayed inside the 12-mile territorial limit and went nowhere near the international safe passage lanes of Hormuz. Crude prices began their slow decline from the previous week's spike, and the Iranians communicated through the Swiss embassy the identity of the pilot the Americans had lost on the first strike over Bandar Abbas: Commander Stephen J. Lassiter.

The great majority of Iranian people, however, were unnerved at the military action their government had initiated with the world's only superpower. They saw through the pompous indignation of the Revolutionary Guard leaders who were acting independently of the central government that itself raised regional and world tensions on a routine basis. In essence, the Iranian people were in the back of a vehicle careening down a mountain road with a wild man driving, or in this case, two wild men—Guard and Government—fighting for control of the wheel. They were tired of Iran's international pariah status, and the daily hardships it placed on them, and wished only for what the West had, what the *United States* had…a representative government and a free-market economy that could unleash the vast untapped potential of the Persian people.

The current situation began, as it so often does, with young people, students unwilling to accept the lifetime of misery their parents had endured. They rejoiced at the fall of the brutal Pahlavi government, but their joy was short-lived when they found a brutal kleptocracy, cloaked in Islamic fundamentalism, had taken its place. They protested with nonviolent sit-ins, marched with placards, staged strikes in factories and questioned the legitimacy of the regime. The smuggled video of the vicious government crackdown was difficult to watch, but Iran's youth stood firm as the protests spread to Shiraz and Bushier, and even to Bandar Abbas. The people there envied the bright free-market light that gleamed from the Emirates cites on the southern horizon each night. Claims by the government that the Americans and Israelis wanted to conquer Iran fell flat—the people knew who caused trouble for the region and for themselves in their daily lives. The Islamic Republic government found itself with a more pressing problem than the regional proximity of the American military or the existence of Israel. The loud demands of their own people were at the moment a serious threat to the regime.

Life changed little for the sailors aboard *Happy Valley* as they watched the news from Iran. Their job was to orbit a piece of water in the North Arabian Sea in order to provide an American presence that sent a message to the Iranians and reassured others in the region. Days drifted by, and when the news that *Harry S. Truman* had gotten underway from Norfolk to relieve them was announced over the 1MC, a cheer went up throughout the ship. With tensions in the region lowered to a simmer, *Valley Forge* could soon point her bow southwest and transit the coastline of the Arabian Peninsula on the first leg of her 8,000-mile journey home.

In CAG's stateroom, however, a sensitive conversation was taking place, a conversation that had a great bearing on the future of the *Ravens* of VFA-64.

CHAPTER 69

"So, I come out of the admiral's office, and Bucket tells me Saint's jet is down and he's out of the airplane. What the hell for? His *TACAN*, for crying out loud! His people are launching on the biggest strike of the year, and he's not leading it for what I would consider an "up" gripe. An irritant, yes, but for a strike of this magnitude, and considering he's the lead with jets taxiing to the cat, you take it."

DCAG Allen listened, nodding his head in understanding and approval. Swoboda continued.

"I'm like, *what the fuck*, and walk direct to Ready 7. I open the starboard-side door and see Saint up there ripping his people, just having a cow about the airplane with his MMCO. I thought he was having a nervous breakdown. The duty officer asks him for his extra ammo clip, and Saint's still out of control, screaming. He reaches into his vest, rooting around in there and friggin' *heaves* on the clip to free it, and sets off the day end of his flare! Smoke goes everywhere, but his people swing into action. And Saint…he's just standing there…deer-in-the-headlights. They yell 'Attention on deck.' Then, he's looking at me—with real fear. I mean, his lip was quivering. Darth, I think he's lost it."

"The Human Factors Board said it was the stress of combat."

Swoboda grimaced and shook his head. "Not buying it. He had a strike against Chah Bahar, lots of standoff, low threat. No, he was in over his head going to Yaz Kernoum."

"Maybe he knew it."

"Maybe he did."

"You think he effectively turned back under fire?"

Swoboda paused and looked ahead in thought. After a long silence he lifted his head. "Yeah, I do."

Allen watched him, but said nothing. Swoboda exhaled deeply.

"You know, as a nugget I had this CO who flew *Phantoms* in Vietnam. He was a fire-breathing dragon and kicked our ass. He said turning back under fire was unforgivable. I think you have to temper that—especially as a CO. You don't want to lead guys into a meat grinder and lose half the strike group. But

on the other hand, you go. You take the jet and make a call on scene because *you* have the experience, or at least the seniority, to know what's acceptable. Saint abdicated that to his subordinate because of fear—of either screwing up the lead or getting shot down. It doesn't matter. He couldn't handle it. I mean, he's an administrative wizard, but he's hard on his people. When the pressure was on, he went to pieces. I'm sorry, but he's just not ready for command of that strike-fighter squadron. Maybe he slipped through the cracks to get here, but I've gotta make a call here and now."

"*Devil's advocate,*" DCAG said, raising a hand, "but I've got to touch on this. Cajun took his division into that meat grinder and paid for it with his life. Not excusing Saint, but couldn't Cajun have pumped once to troubleshoot the friggin bombs or dropped them in a level delivery using his radar and FLIR? He and the jet would still be here."

"Sure, on Monday morning that's a reasonable call, but Cajun made the call then on the first strike of the operation, with one minute to go. And he got the job done—he was *committed* to it. He stepped into the arena." Swoboda took a breath and his voice trailed off. "We need more Cajuns."

"You flew into that shit as the on-scene commander—after they were stirred up down there."

The CAG nodded. "Cajun would have done the same for any of us."

The two men sat in silence and stared into space, each pondering the next move that they knew would lead to the "firing" of a senior officer. It was the same agonizing decision they had watched others make during their 20 plus years in the military. CAG broke the silence.

"I'm going to relieve him."

The Deputy Wing Commander looked up and held his gaze for a moment. "You really sure you want to do that? The board says otherwise. It's his first day as CO after Cajun's shootdown. You can make a case that a TACAN is a downing gripe. He developed a plan, and the strike package executed it successfully. They are going to second-guess you in Norfolk. Besides, we're leaving here and heading home soon."

"*He* didn't develop that plan. Flip Wilson did, and Flip took the lead for him and did an *outstanding* job. After witnessing Saint's display, *I* should be relieved for assigning him the strike lead."

"You were out of strike leads; he was next in the rotation."

"Yeah, but for the same reasons you stated, I should have thought it through better—should have assigned it to you."

DCAG smiled.

Leaning forward with his elbows on the table, CAG made a pyramid with his fingers and brought them to his lips in contemplation. "Can we agree that Saint is a project?"

"No doubt."

"You'll be CAG next year. Do you want one of your squadron COs to be a project?"

DCAG looked at his shoes and exhaled, then lifted his eyes. "No," he said quietly.

Swoboda nodded in agreement.

"Who will you get to take over?" Darth asked. "The Big Unit?"

"Jim Wilson."

"*Flip?* He's too junior."

"He's the right choice. Who knows the squadron better? Who has proven himself under fire, time after time? Who has more credibility in the air wing? If anyone, it's Flip. I'm adamant about that. He'll take the *Ravens* home as acting CO, and the Commodore can get a short-term relief in another month or so. Flip will then go on shore duty, and he'll screen for his own squadron in a few years."

"I hear rumblings about him resigning."

"Doesn't matter. He's still the guy I want."

"Are you going to talk to the admiral?"

"After the fact...not gonna ask. When in command, *command*, right?"

They again sat in silence, thinking about the next difficult step.

"How are you going to do it?"

"Not going to humiliate or shame him. I'll bring him in tonight at 2100. Want you here, too. Let him pack his trash and manifest him on the COD tomorrow. If he wants to address the squadron, fine. In the meantime, we will keep it quiet that he's leaving so he can do so with as much dignity as he can. *Forgive* him...but he's done."

"Roger," Allen said. As he rose to leave, he added, "Tough business."

"Yeah...but there are tougher things. Oh, by the way, call Flip yourself, and have him report here at 2130."

"Yes, sir."

CHAPTER 70

At reveille, Wilson rolled out of the rack after a night of fitful sleep. Saint Patrick had been relieved for cause—and CAG had informed him that he would be the acting CO. He was sworn to secrecy until tonight after the humiliated officer was off the ship.

For months he had hated Saint: hated the dressing downs, the incivility to the troops, the bullshit busywork, the incompetence masquerading as effective leadership. Saint was an anomaly. *Nobody* liked him, and he had no friends among his peers. Not long after returning from the Yaz Kernoum strike, Wilson had learned about the flare going off in the ready room. How that scene had played out in front of CAG was amazing, even for Saint. Since then, the JOs had treated Saint with thinly veiled contempt—*Coward*—and Wilson had known it would be just a matter of time before CAG acted.

How had Saint gotten this far? The Navy that had promoted warriors like Cajun, CAG, and the Big Unit had also promoted Saint. How could the system have gotten this one so wrong? Somebody along the way had liked his abilities, but was Cajun—and now CAG—the first to see through him?

Restless, and knowing he would be alone at this early hour, Wilson donned his flight suit and went up to the wardroom for breakfast. He grabbed a tray, poured himself some coffee, and went through the speed line for bacon and eggs, oatmeal and juice. Sitting down at the deserted *Raven* table, Wilson picked up the ship's "newspaper" and began reading a wire story about the NCAA Final Four. Someone placed a tray down opposite him. When he looked up from his reading, he jolted back in surprise. Saint, impeccable in his khaki uniform, stood in front of him.

"May I join you, *Skipper?*"

Wilson didn't move.

Saint waited for an answer and, when none came, proceeded to take a seat. Wilson kept his eyes on Saint as he arranged his silverware, poured cream in his coffee, and stirred it in silence, eyes down. After a long pause, Saint poked at his eggs, looked up, and spoke.

"You know, *Skipper*—or are you the CO yet? I'm told there's a big change of command ceremony in the ready room tonight."

Wilson held his gaze. A sailor was wiping down an adjacent table, but they were essentially alone.

"I won't be attending, of course, since I'm on the COD this afternoon. But congratulations just the same," Saint said between mouthfuls of eggs. He stopped and looked at Wilson as a question formed on his mouth. "Jim...may I call you Jim? Did you ever see reruns of the show *Branded*? If you haven't, it was a show in the 60s about an Old West cavalry officer unjustly accused of cowardice. His reputation precedes him wherever he goes, and he has to prove himself at every stop. You may be familiar with the opening...the accused humiliated in public, epaulets ripped off, buttons pulled off, sword broken in two, then drummed out of the fort, never to return. Are you familiar with that show?"

Wilson nodded. "Yes, sir."

"Thought you might be," Saint replied, and started humming the theme song. *"Branded... scorned as the one who ran. What do you do when you're branded, and you know you're a man?"*

Wilson pushed back from the table.

"Won't you *stay*, Lieutenant Commander Wilson? Or are you, yourself, a coward?"

Baited by Saint's insinuation, Wilson remained seated. He watched Saint closely, certain he was witnessing a breakdown.

Patrick took another bite of his food.

"That will be me this afternoon...walking down the passageway in my civilian slacks and collared shirt, carrying my sea-bag, 5,000 pairs of eyes judging me, condemning me, banished from this ship forever, but, unlike the guy in the TV show, without a word. *What do you do when you're branded?"*

"Sir, when you get home, I hope you get..."

"Oh, *spare me*, please! You don't give a *fuck* about me, Jim. I hear they are putting you in for a medal for leading *my* strike. Bravo Zulu, Commander! Here, take my command, while you're at it."

"You would have failed. You know it. I know it."

"Perhaps so. Flying was never my strongest suit, you know. But one thing I *am* good at is *working the system*. Yes, and I cannot wait to *work it*, Mister Wilson. I mean, *Skipper*, sir, to put doubt in a promotion board's mind about *you*, your crybaby whining and insubordination, how *you* left Howard to the wolves, how *you* undercut me, ignoring regulations and essentially lying to CAG because *you* had a sexual relationship with Hinton, Mister '*Family Man.*'"

With that, Wilson stood up, eyes narrowed. Saint began to laugh.

"My, the dramatics, and look at that balled fist! A fistfight in the wardroom, Mister Wilson, on your first day in command? The other side of the story *will* be told when I get home, professionally, of course, not to besmirch the sterling reputation of a *war hero* such as yourself. Despite what I say, you'll probably do fine. After all, you do have your skin color to hide behind."

"You pathetic racist sonofabitch."

"Do I get under your *skin*, Jim? Hey, no pun intended. Play that race card, Jim. Press charges! You see I have nothing to lose. I'll deny it of course; it's basically us here, alone at this early hour, *hours* before your precious lieutenants wake up. Did anyone ever tell you that when you wrestle with a pig, both get dirty—and the pig likes it! I will *like* getting dirt on you, Mister TOPGUN Golden Boy."

"You are going *down*, Commander, and I will lead the witnesses at your mast hearing."

"Are you going to take me to *mast*, Skipper? Can I go *down* anymore than I already am? Heh. You know I always wanted to tell a CO to go to hell. Fuck you, Wilson. Fuck you. *Fuck you*." Saint spit the words out under his breath, seething as he also rose to his feet. From across the room, two shocked sailors watched, wondering what was going on between the pilots.

Wilson kept his eyes on Saint as he walked around the table toward him, wondering what he would do when he got there. Saint stood his ground, smiling at him and whispering, "C'mon and hit me, Jim. Hit me. You've been waiting for this moment. *Do it*." Wilson stopped, nose to nose with Saint, fury barely in check, hating him. Saint smirked back at him with satisfaction.

"*You pussy*," Saint spewed, his face suddenly contorted in contempt.

Wilson inhaled deeply through his nose. He could go to CAG immediately and make several charges: threats, racist comments, conduct unbecoming. How he wanted to shove Saint through the bulkhead, to *show him*, to exact *revenge* for the months of public humiliation and derision. Flashbacks of the knotholes Saint had dragged everyone through, the pain and embarrassment he had caused the squadron, exploded in his memory as he stared him down.

A smile slowly spread across Saint's face, a wide beaming grin that showed his perfect white teeth. Wilson couldn't let Saint *win*. Leaning in toward him with narrow eyes, Wilson simply whispered, "*Go*." He let the word hang there between them, and turned to leave.

Saint chuckled. "Turning your back on a senior officer? More ammo."

Wilson stopped and faced him. "There's only one officer in this room, and it's not you."

CHAPTER 71

Ready 7 was standing room only except for the two empty chairs in the front row that had belonged to Cajun and Saint. The officers were in their seats, the chiefs standing in the back or filling a few empty seats. The *Ravens'* Command Master Chief opened the door to the ready room and barked, "Attention on *deck!*"

All hands jumped to their feet as CAG Swoboda strode to the front in his khaki uniform, DCAG behind him. "Seats, please, relax," CAG commanded, and the assembled personnel complied. DCAG took Saint's chair, but, out of respect, no one sat in Cajun's seat.

Swoboda clasped his arms across his chest and began. "Ladies and gentlemen, I've called you here this evening to convey to you my admiration of and appreciation for your performance on this deployment, and particularly these past few weeks. During our recent combat operation, VFA-64 led the wing in sorties flown, ordnance expended and enemy aircraft shot down. That's no surprise to me as the *Ravens* have always been my go-to warfighting squadron, a winning team I can depend on to deliver fused ordnance on target, on time. You in this room have lived up to the high standards set by your ancestors in Korea and Vietnam.

"You've had some tough breaks on this deployment, not the least of which is the loss of your fine CO, Cajun Lassiter, to enemy fire. Even after that devastating blow, you compartmentalized and never missed a beat during your subsequent combat hops over the beach. I thank you, your Navy thanks you, and our nation owes you a debt of gratitude.

"By your performance, from you guys in flight suits, the maintainers and admin personnel, all led by a superb chiefs' mess, you've earned the best leadership the Navy can provide. As your immediate senior in command, I did not feel you had the leadership you deserve. No doubt you've heard that I relieved Commander Patrick of his duties, and he left the ship this afternoon for Oceana and reassignment. I offered him the opportunity to address you, and my understanding is he did not take it. This is a decision I did not come to hastily, and it was not one incident that caused me to act. I didn't ask for 'approval' either. It is my decision who remains in command of my squadrons. Commander Patrick

is to be afforded every courtesy befitting an officer of his rank, and I encourage you to reach out to him should you desire to do so."

Wilson thought of the morning's wardroom exchange, and found it ironic that CAG had just bestowed honor upon a wretched man who deserved none. Swoboda then motioned with his hand. "Lieutenant Commander Wilson, come on up here."

Wilson rose, and standing next to CAG, faced his squadronmates. Swoboda put his hand on Wilson's shoulder and said, "This is your new skipper."

The room was now energized, but the muffled cheers and scattered applause showed that the *Ravens* were not sure if it was appropriate to unleash their joy in front of CAG. Wilson noted, though, big toothy grins from Dutch and Sponge, and Pyscho nodded with an approving smile. CAG continued.

"Flip Wilson is a proven warrior, and he has my complete trust and confidence. During our remaining time in this AOR, he's the guy I want leading you, and he'll bring you home in the coming weeks. The Commodore will get you a new CO, but, until then, Lieutenant Commander Wilson is your acting CO. *Congratulations, Flip!*"

As the room erupted into applause and cheering, Wilson accepted the small gold pin that signified command at sea. "Thanks, CAG," he replied, shaking hands with a humble smile, still not knowing what to make of it.

"You're the right man for the job, Skipper," CAG said. "Well done."

A call for *"Attention on deck"* rang out, and the Air Wing commander departed the way he had come. DCAG offered Wilson a handshake of congratulations, with a wink, before he followed CAG out of the ready room.

Wilson was mobbed as his squadronmates shook his hand and slapped his back. He was touched by the sincere well wishes from the chiefs. After the commotion died down, Dutch asked, "Skipper, what's your first command?"

Wilson looked around. "Let's get some music going in here."

"QUOTH THE RAVEN!" boomed from inside Ready Room 7.

Before he left the ship, Saint Patrick took a last look at his empty stateroom. Not the sentimental type, he nevertheless knew he would never see the inside of another one, much less set foot on a warship again. His meticulously planned career had come to an end—here.

Wearing his grey slacks and blue polo shirt, Saint hoisted his bag and walked aft on the starboard passageway toward the Air Transport Office. He felt the

stares at once...dozens of nameless sailors noticed he was out of uniform, in civilian clothes. Silently, they braced up against the bulkhead so he could pass, blank faces watching him leave while they stayed. Bitter bile formed in his mouth—in essence, they were tearing off his epaulets, seizing his sword and breaking it over a knee. *These idiot sailors who know nothing, judging me,* he thought. He then saw The Big Unit coming in the opposite direction, both uncomfortable to see each other. Averting his eyes until the last minute, Saint looked up in time to see the *Buccaneer* XO slow down to say something with an anguished face.

"Bill, I'm sor-"

Saint silenced him with a look as he trudged past. *He's one of them,* he thought.

In the ATO shack, alone in his bitterness, he was surrounded by sailors and junior officers waiting, like him, to board the COD and return to staffs in Manama or Doha or travel home to the states. During the hour-long wait, his silent anger and sullenness was noted by everyone, and some sailors stood rather than sit next to him. After the scheduled event launch was complete, he heard the COD trap and listened to the hum of its engines as it taxied to its spot abeam the island.

Suddenly, the Air Transport Officer entered and said, "Okay, everyone, put on your cranials and float-coats." Like a condemned man being led to the gallows, Saint stood and donned his cranial and life vest, and, befitting one so senior in rank, was the last person to board the aircraft. The ATO Chief cheerfully offered him one of two window seats, which he took without a word, ignoring the crewman's brief as he cinched down the straps to his four-point release.

With the engines started, the cargo ramp slowly closed, swallowing up the flight deck scene in front of him. Saint then looked out the small window, only to see a *Raven* jet outside, prolonging the agony. He looked at the pilot, face covered by the visor and mask, elbows on the canopy sill and hands on the towel racks. He noticed the pilot looking in the small C-2 window, staring at him, as the *Hornet* waited for the next yellow-shirt command. Saint wondered who was in that cockpit, motionless, eerily judging him from across the flight deck. *They never gave me a chance,* he thought. His resolve stiffened. He would have his revenge.

Once in Bahrain, he bought some groceries at the commissary and went to his transient quarters for what became a five-day wait for his flight to the states, during which time he did not bathe or shave or step outside, but instead stared silently at the walls. He thought of his father, Vice Admiral William S.

Patrick: Vietnam MiG-killer; carrier CO, fleet commander; life-of-the-party with a broad smile and deep laugh; a work-hard, play-hard flag officer. His father had been distant to William Jr. as a boy; being on deployment, putting in the extra hours to advance his career and cheating on his wife left little time for games of catch or helping his only child with homework.

In spite of all that, like most sons, Saint wanted to please his father and gain his approval. An appointment to Annapolis was the first step, the first of *hundreds* of steps to get this far. Then *command at sea...*a middle management rung on the career ladder to four stars. He had worn the pin on his uniform! But CAG had taken it away because of the moron Randall and the stupid TACAN. And the sonofabitch had given it to the insubordinate Wilson.

Saint cleaned up in time to board the charter flight for Philadelphia in the wee hours, with stops in Sigonella and Lajes, sitting silently and staring out the window between bouts of fitful sleep. Over 30,000 feet below were clouds and water and, in the distance, North Africa and more miserable brown sand. Over the long day of flight, he ignored the Air Force sergeant sitting next to him, not saying a word to anyone, just staring at the endless water below.

Landing in Philadelphia, Saint had an overnight layover for the flight to Norfolk. However, being wide awake, he rented a car and drove down the Del-Mar-Va Peninsula to his home near Virginia Beach, arriving at his Sandbridge beach house as the eastern horizon was lightening. The long drive had given him plenty of time to think. For years, Saint had considered wives "distracters," so there was no family to greet him, no food in the refrigerator. He was not expected by his neighbors. *He was not supposed to be here.*

He entered his bedroom and opened the top drawer of his dresser to retrieve the large command-at-sea pin given to him 20 years ago by his father. His full-dress white uniform was ready in the closet where he had left it in November, and to it he affixed the pin above the ribbons on the right breast pocket, its rightful place. He thought of his father's words: "Get your reports in on time and stay out of trouble in the air, and you'll do fine."

Thanks for the great fucking advice, Dad.

The red sky to the east brightened as he buttoned the last gold button and placed the hook from his sword belt through the opening in his uniform. Annapolis. Noon formation at Bancroft Hall. *Pre-seeennnnt!...Hoh!* Hundreds of mids in his regiment, standing in orderly ranks of navy blue uniforms on a crisp autumn day, entering Bancroft for the noon meal in sharp formations under *his* command. At 21 he knew he was on his way, and no matter how many stars Dad had received, he would have one more.

Medals clanking, he walked out to the beach and into a stiff Atlantic wind that kicked up angry surf. Looking left toward Dam Neck, he saw a couple in the distance. To the south, he saw nothing but white mist along the shore. He thought again of his father, who, a few hours from now would join his retired flag cronies for their early tee time at the North Island course. The golf course was in sight of the Third Fleet Commander's home where, as a boy, he had spent so many lonely and troubled hours looking at the blue Pacific.

Saint pulled the .45 from his belt and looked at the eastern horizon: red, menacing, *angry.*

Red sky at morning, sailors take warning, he thought as he placed the muzzle inside his mouth.

CHAPTER 72

Nine *Raven* FA-18s, flying as one, descended in a shallow left-hand turn just east of Cape Henry. Now less than 10 miles from home, they would make up that distance in little over a minute. As Wilson lined the formation up on Runway 23, he glanced left at Little Nicky who maintained parade position, with Clam on his wing in the background. Both concentrated on flying sharp formation as Wilson rolled out in a measured rate. On his right side, Guido and Weed followed his moves as they remained welded to his wing line. Even though their faces were covered by helmet visors and oxygen masks, Wilson could recognize them, after months of flying together, by their body types and how they sat in the cockpit.

The pilots had been airborne just over an hour, launched 470 miles east into a gorgeous spring morning scattered with columns of cumulus clouds that hovered over a blue ocean. Wilson and the fly-off pilots had found it hard to sleep the night before, so excited were they at the prospect of seeing, in mere hours, the families they had said good-bye to six months earlier. For the first half of their flight, the pilots saw only water and clouds. From their vantage point at 28,000 feet, though, it wasn't too long before they could see the thin beige strand of the Outer Banks leading north from Cape Hatteras to Virginia Beach and Cape Henry. When they checked in with controlling agencies that had familiar names like GIANT KILLER and Oceana Approach, their excitement grew. Wilson looked over his shoulder at his wingmen and chuckled to himself when he noted they had all eased into parade formation, even though they were well out to sea and no one four miles below could admire their skill.

While the others concentrated on him, Wilson stole quick looks at the scenery. Dozens of sport fishing boats and motorized yachts poured out of Rudee Inlet leaving sharp white wakes behind them. The sun-washed, high-rise hotels along the strip boasted beaches covered with sunbathers, and the cars jammed Atlantic Boulevard as usual. To the north, beyond the green space of Fort Story, he saw the merchant ships lined up on their way past the north and south entrances of the Chesapeake Bay Bridge-Tunnel. Various containerships, bulk carriers, and crude oil tankers headed for the ports of Norfolk, Baltimore,

or Philadelphia, on the final leg of their long journeys from Rotterdam or San Juan...or Hormuz.

Wilson keyed the mike. "Oceana Tower, Navy Alpha Hotel four-zero-zero, flight of nine, seven miles northeast for a flyby."

"Navy Alpha Hotel four-zero-zero, Oceana Tower, winds one-niner-zero at five. You are cleared for a flyby. Welcome home, *Ravens.*"

"Four-zero-zero, roger. Thanks, great to be back."

Raven One eased them down to 350 knots over Virginia Beach Boulevard and lined them up on the squadron hangar. From three miles away, he could make out a faint cluster of colors in front of the hangar bay doors and allowed himself a small smile. Mary, Derrick and Brittany were in that cluster with the rest of the *Raven* families, and he put them in the middle of his HUD as he signaled the others to level off.

In a tight wedge, they thundered over the crowd and disappeared behind the hangar, leaving behind a group of giddy women, hugging each other in their tight dresses and sunglasses. The children jumped up and down, and a few startled babies cried from the sudden noise.

South of the air station Wilson detached Weed and Clam to lead their own formations back to the field. He took his three-plane echelon into the break, whipped his jet over to the left and pulled power to idle, waving at the crowd below. Wilson then dropped the gear and flaps and called the tower for permission to land, the first time in six months he would land on a runway.

Once they were all on the ground, Ensign Jackson, who had left the ship early with members of the advance party, drove out to meet them in the flight line truck. As they taxied up to their hangar in order, Anita delivered a bouquet of roses to each of the pilots. Wilson's heart soared when he spied Mary in a black and white dress, new to him, with one kid clinging to each of her hands. As the pilots had briefed it in the ready room, they shut down 18 engines on signal and popped their canopies in unison. Wilson grabbed the roses and a few other items, bounded down the ladder, and removed his helmet.

"Welcome home, Skipper!" Senior Chief Nowlin said as he took Wilson's helmet.

"Thanks, Senior Chief. You doing good?"

"Doin' good, sir," Nowlin answered, smiling. "Now go to your family."

"Roger that, Senior!"

Wilson donned his squadron ball cap and had taken only a few steps before Derrick broke loose from his mother and ran at him full speed. In one motion, he gathered his son up and squeezed him tight. "Oh, I missed you!" he said.

"Me, too, Daddy!" said Derrick, his voice muffled by the flotation collar of Wilson's survival vest.

As other families squealed with joy around them, a beaming Mary walked up with little Brittany in her arms. Wilson deposited Derrick on the concrete and looked at Mary. "Hi, baby!" he said before he wrapped his arms around his wife. As he kissed her lips and held her tight, the bottled-up tension of the past six months ran right out of him. He then took his daughter from Mary and smiled at the three year old, who was still not quite sure what was happening.

Thank you, God.

The *Buccaneers* had returned for their homecoming before the *Ravens* and were gathered in the hangar space next door. A small party followed. With smiles all around, the *Raven* and *Buc* families put aside their competitive spirit in their adjacent hangar spaces to enjoy an abundance of food and drink with excited kids showing their fathers missing teeth or new toys and with the relieved women clinging to their men. Wilson shook hands with his pilots and hugged their wives or girlfriends. He spied Olive smiling with an attractive middle-aged woman dressed as if she were at Churchill Downs for the Kentucky Derby, a woman he learned later was Olive's mother. The rest of the squadron personnel would come home the following day when *Happy Valley* shifted colors at Pier 12 in Norfolk.

But Jim Wilson had one more task to perform before this cruise was over.

CHAPTER 73

That evening, Mary got a sitter for the kids and the Wilsons paid a visit to a suburban residence several miles south of the naval air station. Mary drove them into the familiar driveway of a brick colonial, grass neatly trimmed, porch light on.

"You ready for this?" she asked him.

"Yeah. Let's do it."

They walked to the porch in nervous silence, and Mary pressed the doorbell. After a few seconds, Billie Lassiter opened the door.

"Jim," she said with a warm smile and threw her arms around him. "Welcome home."

Wilson didn't know what to say as he hugged her back, but knew he needed to be there. Billie invited them inside and poured everyone a cup of coffee. Her oldest son, Drew, a strapping, dark-featured high school junior, came downstairs to join them. He sat close to his mother, both surrounded by the memorabilia from Cajun's career on every wall of the family room. A middle-school daughter was out with friends, and their 10-year-old boy played video games in a nearby room.

After a few moments of awkward small talk, Wilson asked, "How are you?"

Billie sighed and looked at her son. "We're doing okay. My parents just left, and Mary and the girls have been wonderful. The support from the whole Oceana community has been great. The President called…and we had a nice conversation. The governor of Louisiana called, too, as well as the Chief of Naval Operations. Everyone is supportive and has said to call if I need anything."

"They mean it."

"I know, but we have what we need now. My family has some money, and we're okay. Jim, how was the ceremony on the ship?"

"Very nice. We did it topside on a beautiful day in the Indian Ocean in our white uniforms. The admiral said Skipper Lassiter was a gentle soul with an iron will. We then did a missing man flyby. As the missing man pulled up into the sky, the aircraft went into a cloud and 'disappeared.' That symbolism was moving to all of us who saw it. It was a solemn, very beautiful ceremony. The squadron took his loss hard. He was a popular CO."

"Who flew the missing man plane?"

"Olive... Kristin Teel."

"Ha! Missing woman! Steve would have found that funny!"

Mary giggled to release her nervous tension, and Wilson smiled. For the first time, though, Wilson noted Drew was not listening. He looked sullen and detached. *Angry.*

"I was shocked about Bill, so sad. The poor man. Why did he do it? Did he think Steve's death was his fault?"

Wilson's pained expression revealed he didn't know how to answer. "I don't know. We were shocked, too. He was... *different.*"

Billie then asked the question Wilson had known was coming. "Jim, what happened?"

Drew now looked at him, eyes cold, waiting for his answer. Wilson looked down and swallowed.

"After the Iranians made the initial attack on our frigate, we were tasked with a series of strikes along the Iranian coast to degrade their ability to close the Strait of Hormuz. The skipper was assigned to lead the first strike into their main naval base at Bandar Abbas. We launched and formed up, but, close to the target, we noted our weapon guidance system was degraded. Skipper immediately made the call to roll in, to deliver the weapons in a dive, which exposed us to greater threat. All of us got our bombs off, including the skipper, but, as he pulled up, his jet was hit by antiaircraft fire and exploded. He had no chance of survival."

"Did you see it?" Billie asked him.

"I saw the wreckage as it fell to the surface."

"You didn't see it blow up?" Drew asked, with definite hostility in his voice. Billie looked at him.

"No, Olive—that is, Lieutenant Teel—did. She was right next to him."

"He didn't eject? Are you sure? The Iranians didn't capture and murder him after you guys abandoned him?"

"*Drew!* You will treat Commander Wilson with respect!" Billie scolded.

Wilson raised his hand. "It's okay, Billie." He looked at the teenager's fierce, accusing eyes and knew he had to try and reach out to him with compassion and understanding. "I saw your father's jet tumble out of the sky, burning and breaking up until it impacted the water. None of us saw a parachute, and a parachute would have been obvious on our night-vision goggles. There was no emergency beeper, no radio call, no flares, no raft in the water, no reflection from your father's helmet. We would have seen that, too.

"We stayed until Captain Swoboda directed us to leave because we were low on fuel. After we left, he directed the pilot of his *Super Hornet* to make runs over the crash site. They took heavy fire the whole time and saw no sign of your father, no evidence he was alive. Over the next two days, we continued with the operation, but we also searched for your dad, until the Iranians identified him. We have some national assets that verify he was never alive on the surface. He probably died instantly and never knew what hit him."

"That's what you think," Drew replied, looking at Wilson with contempt.

"That's my professional opinion, as an eyewitness to your father's final moments."

"So Tony Swoboda's dad sent my dad to his death."

"DREW!" Billie was mortified.

Wilson remained calm and answered, "Your father was the finest strike leader on that ship, and CAG Swoboda knew it. The target your father was given was a tough one, and he devised a plan to get the job done at a minimum of danger to us. Captain Swoboda was devastated by the loss of his trusted friend and shipmate. He'll be here to visit with you tomorrow because I asked him to let me come over tonight."

"But the stupid weapons didn't work!"

"The Iranians did something to upset their guidance. We still don't know what they did or why the other aircraft weren't affected like we were. But your dad knew we had to succeed right then to take advantage of the element of surprise we had, before the Iranians could disperse their assets or hide 'em. He was a man of conviction and accountability—and courage. If he didn't do his job at that moment, then someone else would need to do it the next night—and it would have been a lot tougher for them. He reacted immediately, exposing himself to danger so others wouldn't have to."

At that moment, Drew Lassiter broke down in heaving sobs. Tears had already lined his cheeks before he could cover his face in embarrassment. He choked on the words he forced out of his mouth. *"But I don't have a dad!"*

Mary's hand flew to her lips to hold back sobs, and Drew slumped into his mother's arms. His six-foot body was wracked by waves of pent-up emotion as Billie patted his back with stoic resolve. Wilson struggled to remain in control, and remembered one last image of his fallen commanding officer.

"Just before your father briefed us that night, I spied him on the hangar deck. It was sundown, and he stood by himself, looking west, the pink glow reflected on his face. It was a beautiful scene and, as he stood there taking it in, I have no doubt he was thinking of his handsome family far over that horizon. He had

much to live for, and I'm sure that one of them was the pride he felt in having a young man like you as his son."

Her stoicism gone, Billie's lip quivered as she looked at Wilson. She mouthed the words, *"Thank you,"* and continued to comfort her son. She tried to fight back her own tears but failed. With a start, Drew bolted into the next room.

The Wilsons took that as a cue to leave. Billie wiped her tears and fanned her face before Mary surrounded her with a hug.

"Thanks for coming. I'm so sorry you had to experience this on your home-coming night," Billie said with a nervous laugh. "Drew didn't mean it."

Wilson hugged her. "We know, Billie, and we are here for you now and always. Whatever you need, you call us."

She pulled away and held him at arm's length. "He loved you, you know."

"And I him. He was the greatest CO I'll ever have."

CHAPTER 74

A brisk November wind churned the fallen leaves into a small cyclone outside the Pentagon Metro Entrance. Mary Wilson led her two children toward the metal detectors, her parents and Wilson's parents behind her. Mindful of the growing line of businessmen waiting to get through the security checkpoint, she tore the jackets off the children, and then realized she needed to go through first. As she removed her overcoat, it caught on her brooch. Her mother helped her free it while she became increasingly frazzled. Finally free of her coat, she walked through the detector and set it off—the brooch! She removed it before trying again and avoided eye contact with the impatient businessmen who looked at their watches and with the disapproving security personnel who monitored the checkpoint.

Once inside the building, they were met by Wilson in his service dress blue uniform, a loop of gold braid high on his left arm, and Weed in his khakis. Both men were there to escort them to the E-ring for the ceremony. Once up the escalator and into the open hallways, the children broke free and dashed ahead, dodging the endless stream of adults in business suits and harried action officers of every rank and service carrying folders of paper. An amused general watched Mary scurry after the children in her heels as they weaved through the crowd, first in one direction and then another. Mary looked over her shoulder at her husband, and Wilson got the message. "Excuse me, Mom, Dad. I think I need to lend a hand here."

After navigating corridors and escalators for several minutes, they found themselves in *Navy Country*, a command-suite corridor on the fourth deck with a décor characterized by wood paneling, paintings of former Navy Secretaries, and glass-encased ship models that showed the evolution of U.S. naval vessels through the years. The reduction in foot traffic allowed them to see people nearly a football field away as they walked down the corridor. The group peeked in at the furniture and paintings of some well-appointed offices and passed by others that had certain signs above the doors: "Secretary of the Navy" and "Chief of Naval Operations."

Wilson led them into a wood-paneled conference room. Empty of furniture, a ceiling-to-floor navy blue curtain at one end of the room served as a backdrop

to the "Stars and Stripes" and the Navy flag. Through the windows they could see people working in the offices of D-ring.

Many guests were already assembled, including several *Ravens:* Dutch, Blade, Psycho and Smoke had driven up from Oceana, and Olive had taken the afternoon off from Test Pilot School at NAS Patuxent River. The former squadronmates caught up with each other in the back of the room, and Wilson found a moment alone with Olive.

"How you doing?" he asked.

"Good. Okay. Studying hard."

"Great. Flying a lot?"

"Yeah," she said and smiled. "Flew a *Seahawk* the other day. Pretty cool. I mean, you are right in the weeds, and you have to *fly* that thing."

"I'll bet. Thanks for coming."

"Wouldn't miss it."

"It was an honor to be in the same squadron with you. You are a hell of a naval officer."

Touched, Olive nodded her thanks. "Thank you. If I stay, it will be to serve with you again."

As Wilson smiled, another lieutenant commander wearing a gold braid loop walked up to him and whispered, "The boss is on the way."

Wilson excused himself from his squadronmates to greet his boss. The Chief of Naval Operations was a surface warfare officer in his late fifties, tall, with thinning dark hair accented by a touch of gray around his temples. His engaging smile, a smile especially suited for ceremonies like this, lit up the room as he walked in. Wilson introduced him to his family, and the CNO shook each person's hand warmly and gave special attention to the children, both of whom were taken by this gregarious stranger. The sleeves on his blue uniform were weighted down by bands of braid that signified his four-star rank. The junior officers, who had never met a four-star, much less a CNO, were dazzled. After he worked the room, the CNO stepped with Wilson to the front and welcomed the crowd, recognizing everyone he had just met by name.

"Those of us in the Navy know it is a *family*, and we especially see that today. Retired Chief Warrant Officer Raymond Wilson, with whom I served over 20 years ago, stands here as the proud father of Jim. You may not remember, Warrant Officer Wilson, but I was the XO of *Sampson,* and your SURFLANT inspection team found a few discrepancies with our damage control equipment, discrepancies that you laid out to me in no uncertain terms—with a few 'sirs' thrown in there to keep everything professional."

The audience chuckled, and Wilson's father beamed. "*Sampson* was a good ship, CNO."

"Well, *yes, she was*, and she was made better by the great job you did inspecting us and pulling no punches, and I mean *no punches*, in your debrief to me. So thanks, Warrant—I think—and welcome!"

After laughter and polite applause, the CNO turned serious.

"Again, everyone, thanks for coming today. It's an honor for me to preside over this ceremony, the first presentation of this prestigious combat award to a naval aviator since the Vietnam War. When I met Jim Wilson, and interviewed him to be my aide, I was immediately impressed by his professional demeanor, his attention to detail, and, of course, his quick, friendly smile.

"While I was aware of his combat record during his recent deployment aboard *Valley Forge*, it wasn't until I read the justification statement for this award that I realized just how *eye-watering*, to use an aviation term, his aerial performance was over the skies of Iran. A close-in dogfight, twice, the first time completely unarmed, with one of Iran's most experienced pilots, who flew a secret fifth-generation fighter.

"Jim also planned and led a key strike on a vital facility that we needed to neutralize. With minimum time to plan and a small number of aircraft to accomplish the mission, this was an awe-inspiring performance. Jim Wilson's feats are already legend throughout the aviation community.

"Jim, I think you will agree that, to a great extent, the awards we receive are a reflection of the outstanding job done by our subordinates. This award, however, is truly a reflection of your superb flying ability and preflight preparation. *You* took the aircraft and training our country provided you, and with your own aggressive spirit and a resolute commitment to excellence, you contributed to a big win for our nation. This award Jim, is *yours*, and your Navy and your country thank you."

The CNO picked up the Navy Cross and motioned to his flag writer. "Linda, go ahead…"

As the military members in the room came to attention and the award citation was read, the CNO placed the Navy Cross, second to the Medal of Honor in precedence, on Wilson's chest, speaking in a low tone only Wilson could hear.

"Jim, I can't tell you how honored I am to present this distinguished award to you and to have you on my staff. Well done, sailor. My very best wishes to you and your family." With a smile, the admiral then added, "We'll go downtown to celebrate a bit. After that, take the rest of the night off, and I'll see you tomorrow at zero-six-hundred!"

Remaining at attention, Wilson smiled slightly and said, "Thanks, sir."

The ceremony concluded, and Weed walked Wilson's family back to their cars in south parking. The CNO offered Wilson and Mary a ride in his staff car to the reception, and they walked down to the River Entrance to wait for it. While standing next to the heavy columns, they looked north toward Rosslyn, and watched as a 757 airliner weaved along the river on final approach to Reagan National Airport.

"You wish I was flying that?" Wilson asked Mary.

"You want to?"

"Well, I'm flying a desk here. That looks kind'a fun right now."

Mary studied the airliner. "No."

"No?"

"No, that kind of life isn't for people like us. Gone half the time. Chaotic schedule. Low pay. Inexperienced pilots who barely shave. No, not for us. Who needs that kind of stress?"

Wilson smiled, put his arm around her, and looked at the next jet in line.

Navy Cross Citation

The President of the United States of America takes pleasure in presenting the Navy Cross to Lieutenant Commander James Daniel Wilson, United States Navy, for extraordinary heroism in action against the enemy on 17 February 2008 and 20 March 2008 as a Pilot in Strike Fighter Squadron SIXTY-FOUR (VFA-64) embarked in U.S.S. VALLEY FORGE. During a routine training mission over the Northern Arabian Gulf, his incapacitated wingman drifted into Iranian territory. Demonstrating exceptional aeronautical skill, Lieutenant Commander Wilson used his own aircraft in an attempt to return his wingman to international airspace. After Iranian alert fighters destroyed his wingman without warning, he engaged, completely unarmed, a heretofore unknown fifth-generation fighter, successfully evading fire and safely returning to force. On 20 March Lieutenant Commander Wilson displayed exceptional professional skill and sound judgment in planning and leading an extremely dangerous, low-level night, power projection strike on the strategic and heavily defended Yaz Kernoum missile assembly facility in Iran. Seconds before bomb release, an enemy surface-to-air missile was observed to be tracking his plane. Undaunted by this threat to his personal safety, Lieutenant Commander Wilson avoided the missile and then proceeded to complete his attack, releasing all weapons with extreme accuracy and dealing a significant blow to Iranian ballistic missile delivery capability. After release, he guided his plane through intense antiaircraft artillery fire and on the egress defended a valuable strike asset by turning back to the threat and pressing his attack, engaging and downing two enemy interceptors including one confirmed fifth-generation aircraft. His superb airmanship and courage reflected great credit upon himself and were in keeping with the highest traditions of the United States Naval Service.

ABOUT THE AUTHOR

Captain Kevin Miller, a 24-year veteran of the U.S. Navy, is a former tactical naval aviator and has flown the A-7E *Corsair II* and FA-18C *Hornet* operationally. He commanded a carrier-based strike-fighter squadron, and, during his career, logged over 1,000 carrier-arrested landings, made possible as he served alongside outstanding men and women as part of a winning team. Captain Miller lives and writes in Pensacola, Florida.

RAVEN ONE is his first novel.

I hope you enjoyed reading *Raven One* as much as I enjoyed writing it. Whether you found it good or "other," I'd sincerely appreciate your feedback. Please take a moment to leave a review on Amazon or Goodreads.

Thanks and V/R,
Kevin

IT HAD ALL GONE TO HELL SO QUICKLY...

KEVIN MILLER

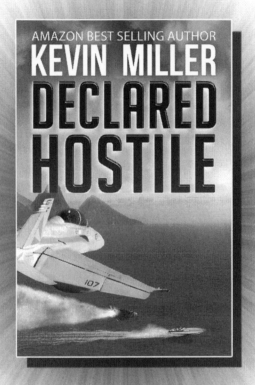

When does a covert mission become
an undeclared war?

www.braveshipbooks.com

DECLARED HOSTILE

Prologue

(Over the Yucatan Channel)

Doctor Leighton Wheeler suppressed a yawn as he arched his back and stretched his arms. With nearly two hours to go in the cockpit of the Beech *King Air*, he fought the urge to sleep. A half-moon high above kept him company and provided a horizon out in the middle of the Gulf of Mexico, but he slapped his face to stay awake. He knew he was now, at this 1:00 am hour, in the trough of human performance, and he had to concentrate on his gyro horizon and altimeter. Five hundred feet—even with altitude hold engaged, it was unnerving to be so low over the black water underneath. He figured it didn't make much of a difference. One hundred feet or one thousand feet; it looked the same over a dark ocean. He was tired, and the energy drink he had downed before take-off was now wearing off. He considered another one, but the physician in him rejected the idea. He twisted off the top of a plastic water bottle instead and took a long swig. He replaced the top, and as he put the bottle back in the cup holder, glanced at his fuel…a little over 2,200 pounds with 453 miles to go and fifteen knots of wind in his face. He would make it, but barely.

Wheeler twisted the heading select switch to 324, and the aircraft rolled gently right as it steadied up on course. *Nothing out here,* he thought, unlike the Yucatan Channel some forty minutes earlier. He had not been able to avoid flying right over a half-dozen lights below him. Not knowing what they were had bothered him, but they were most likely fishing boats, Cuban and Mexican. He knew it was too early for the motor and sailing yachts, most of which spent the winters in and around the Virgin Islands, and the Belize yacht traffic was another month away at least.

The moon illuminated the low scattered clouds, so typical above Caribbean waters. They cast splotchy shadows on the surface below. Wheeler knew the next hour would be boring, so to pass the time, he thought of his favorite subject…himself.

A youthful forty-seven years old, Wheeler owned, with three partners, the Women's Cosmetic Center, the top plastic surgery clinic in Birmingham, Alabama. They offered everything from rhinoplasty to Botox…the whole gamut

of services, many on an outpatient basis. The overwhelming majority of the procedures were boob jobs, with augmentation surgeries leading the way. For nearly two decades the Women's Cosmetic Center had offered hope and delivered results, with the ladies (and their men) gladly paying top dollar for their services. It was a gold mine.

Just last month two of Wheeler's clients had brought in their teenage daughters for consults. Cullen, his own teenage daughter, wanted him to perform an augmentation for her 16th birthday—to a tasteful C-cup that would "allow her clothes to fit better," an argument that was part of the tried and true cover story. He certainly wasn't about to let his lecherous partners touch her. Cullen would go to Atlanta with her mother, Tammy, for the procedure, allowing time to recuperate before her birthday party next month.

Tammy. A former homecoming queen at Alabama, Tammy had never allowed anyone to augment *her*—not even her husband, despite how much he had wanted to add some strategic curves to her tall and leggy figure. She was all for her husband performing plastic surgery for *other* women, and Wheeler had done work on several of her girlfriends. He had even had an affair with one of them that Tammy probably knew about but didn't press him on. No, all was perfect with Tammy: hair, makeup, body, clothes, house, kid, husband…in that order. Between the Garden Club, the Tri-Delt national vice-presidency and innumerable shopping trips to Atlanta and Nashville, Tammy had little time for her husband. That was all the excuse he needed.

Ten years ago he had taken up flying and now was the instrument-rated owner of a *King Air* twin. He used the plane for trips to South America to perform *pro bono* reconstructive surgery on cleft palates for Doctors Without Borders, giving deformed kids a chance for a normal life. Yes, the guys at the Club admired him for it, *giving back* to underprivileged third-world kids and all that.

He accepted their kind words with aw-shucks modesty, never letting on for a minute about his *other* motive: holding heavenly bodies in Bogotá and Cartagena and watching what the owners of those bodies *could do* with them. The coke, the money, the nightlife, and the girls—always the girls. *I'm an American surgeon, here to help children.* He would say it with a shy smile, looking down at his drink. And the girls crumbled before his eyes; leaning in, grateful, fawning, *buying it,* cooing in English or Spanish. It didn't matter. Within the hour, they would lead him out of the hotel lounge and to their rooms or apartments—rich European girls on holiday, local gold-diggers, sophisticated American businesswomen, Asian flight attendants on layover, ages ranging from 22 to 50. A citizen of the world like Doctor Leighton Wheeler believed in diversity.

The first year he flew to South America twice, and now he was on his fourth trip in the past 12 months. Surely Tammy suspected something, but his altruistic alibi provided cover for both of them. She took advantage of his absences with shopping outings with her girlfriends to Atlanta or New York. Both felt entitled.

Yes, the coke! How it felt when it entered his nostrils, the euphoric explosion of his senses. The girls fed it to him! They carried it in their purses and formed neat lines for him on their creamy thighs. And the guys at the airport loved to look at the plane, crawl around inside, talk flying. *Señor Doctor, want a blow before you take off?* And he would take a hit and fly hundreds of miles to the Caymans in what seemed like minutes, alert like he had never been before, feeling like he could fly on to Alaska if he had the fuel. Cocaine just didn't seem to be a big deal south of the U.S. border.

One day a guy he had befriended during a previous trip was at the airport and asked if he could take a package of "product" with him back to Birmingham. "C'mon, man. No one is going to suspect you, Mister Save-the-Children Surgeon!"

The guy tossed a worn duffel bag in back with his other luggage and handed him a black zipped-up folder. Wheeler glanced inside and quickly closed it, but once he got airborne with the autopilot engaged, he laid the contents out on the seat next to him and counted: *five hundred* Ben Franklins and one typed note.

"Mike" met him at the FBO in Birmingham to park him and to service the aircraft, just like the note said. He smiled as he pulled the bags from the compartment, placed the duffel in his tractor, and helped Wheeler button up the airplane. Chatting away, he was a really friendly guy, one of the nicest guys Wheeler had ever met. When they were finished, Mike offered his hand, just as a golf partner would coming off the 18th green. "Enjoyed it!" he said.

Wheeler had found yet *another* double life to lead, one that paid very, very well, more than enough to cover any of Tammy's activities. *Sure, Honey, go to Lenox Square Mall in Buckhead. Take Cullen. Anything you want. Have fun!*

Tonight Wheeler was on his fourth "mission," and it was a big one. He had told Tammy he was going to spend a couple of nights in the Caymans and rest—and get something nice for Cullen—before he took off for home. Once he arrived at George Town and parked his plane, "Luis" met him and led him to a different *King Air*, one loaded with product worth over $100 million on the street. With a box lunch and a five-hour energy drink, he set off in the aircraft for a dirt strip along the Mississippi coast called Goombay Smash Field. He would abandon the airplane there—the cost of doing business—and "Rich" would pick him up, drive him to Diamond Head, and put him in a G5 for a sprint back to

the Caymans. The morning sun would still be low in the sky by the time they landed back at George Town.

After a day of rest at the hotel, maybe a little *senorita* overnight, he would fly his own plane to Birmingham the next day for another hero's welcome—and a $5 million payday. A yacht. Yes, a yacht would look good parked next to their condo in Orange Beach. He would go to Miami next week and make a down payment on a 53-footer. Once the purchase was sealed, he would make a house call on a former augmentation client—to perform an important post-op examination, of course. That client, and many, many others, inspired the name with which he would christen his new yacht: *Two For the Show.*

A sudden *whoomm* on his right startled him. He studied the eastern horizon but saw nothing but ghostly clouds overhead—no lighting flash. He held his gaze and strained his eyes for several seconds. Nothing. He wished this airplane, expendable or not, had weather radar in it and cursed the cheap-screw *narcotraf-ficales* for not getting him a suitable plane for a long, overwater flight. Instead they had put him in this rattle-trap to save overhead dollars. He checked the INS and noted he was making 265 knots ground. The wind must have shifted to the east. And, for the umpteenth time tonight, he checked the fuel, doing a mental time-distance calculation.

What was that? he thought. *A bird? Did I hit a bird?* The airplane hadn't twitched, so he reasoned it may have been an engine surge...but all seemed normal. There were no indicator lights. He shifted in his seat uncomfortably, wishing he had a blow right now, and turned his thoughts back to Miami.

As if jolted by electricity he flinched by the loud *pops* coming from the right engine. Wheeler let out an involuntary *Fuck me!* as the airplane rolled hard right and the engine, mere feet away, exploded into flame. *Oh, God, please!* he cried, instinctively pulling the airplane left and up, away from the water below. Red and yellow lights flared on the instrument panel, and the annunciator bleated shrill warnings of danger. He pushed the throttles forward and felt heavy vibration from the right side, so he retarded the right throttle to idle and fed left rudder to stay balanced. He was already passing 1,000 feet, hyperventilating, and was nearly paralyzed with fear at the persistent flames coming from the right engine nacelle. Whimpering in confusion, he noted airspeed decelerate through 120 knots. *Don't stall the damn thing!* He let out another involuntary sound as he pushed the yoke down.

His heart pounded as his hand lifted the right throttle around the detent to shut down the engine. *Mayday!* he cried without thinking, then realized he was truly alone over the invisible sea, the nearest land over 100 miles away. Should

he turn right to Cuba? Left to Mexico? He hit the right engine fire light which doused the flames, and turned the yoke easy left. *What the fuck?* Still breathing hard through his mouth, his eyes went to the RPM gauge in an attempt to identify why the right engine had burst into flame. He was in a positive climb—even a shallow 100 foot per minute rate of climb was welcome—and he calmed down enough to think about a divert into Cancun. As he rifled through the maps to find the low altitude chart and dial up Cancun's VOR/DME, he made a decision. This was it, no more trips to South America, *ever.*

With a deafening series of staccato hammer blows, the right side of the cockpit erupted into fragments. As the instrument panel exploded in front of him, Wheeler drew his hands and arms in by reflex to defend himself from the flying debris. The windscreen shattered, then caved in from the airspeed. Wheeler was conscious of only three things: the rubbish and forced air swirling about him, the loud roar of the left engine permeating the cockpit, and the fact he was crying out in terrified shock.

Bullets? Is someone shooting at me? Why? Who? Mexicans? Cubans? Out here, at this hour? Then, without warning Wheeler was slammed against the left side of the cockpit with more force than he had ever experienced. A metallic wrenching sound accompanied a violent roll right, and he realized he was upside down and still rolling. *An aileron roll in a* King Air! His control inputs were powerless to stop it, and sensing flames again, he began to scream, *Please, God, no! This can't be happening!* Watching the altimeter unwind, not knowing what caused it, not knowing what to do, Wheeler feared the unspeakable. *Not now! Not here!*

Pinned as he was amid the churning chaos, Wheeler's charmed life flashed before his eyes. Brian, his childhood best friend, smiling at him, hair flowing behind as they rode their sting-ray bikes down a steep hill. Tammy's loving brown eyes looking up as they walked hand-in-hand to her dorm. A group of med school classmates laughing as he told a joke at the pub near the hospital. A beaming five-year-old Cullen running up to him as he got out of his car after a day at the clinic. Sitting in the church pew during Easter Sunday services, looking up at his mother—his beautiful young mother in a smart suit, her smooth skin and dark hair in its sixties flip highlighted under a pillbox hat. Her red lips forming a tender smile as she took his hand. *"God loves you, Leighton."*

The *King Air,* one wing gone, corkscrewed through the darkness in a near vertical dive. Trapped by the force of it, Doctor Leighton Wheeler, tears pushed *back* toward his temples, was filled with regret.

"*I'm sorry, God,*" he shouted with eyes closed. "*I'm sorry.*" He cracked open his eyes in time to see the yellow light from his burning plane reflected on the surface of the Caribbean as it rushed up to meet him.

Follow Flip Wilson on his next deployment and order *Declared Hostile* today!
https://www.amazon.com/dp/B01KNGFCAS

"Most of us, most of the time, live in blissful ignorance of what a small elite, heroic group of Americans are doing for us night and day. As we speak, all over the globe, American Sailors and Submariners and Aviators are doing something very dangerous. People say, 'Well, it can't be too dangerous because there are no wrecks.' But the reason we don't have more accidents is that these are superb professionals; the fact that they master the dangers does not mean the dangers aren't real.

Right now, somewhere around the world, young men are landing aircraft on the pitching decks of aircraft carriers – at night! You can't pay people to do that; they do it out of love of country, of adventure, of the challenge. We all benefit from it, and the very fact that we don't have to think about it tells you how superbly they're doing their job — living on the edge of danger so the rest of us need not think about, let alone experience, danger."

George Will commenting after the loss of the
Space Shuttle Challenger, January, 1986

CVW-4 "TOMAHAWK" CALL LETTERS AH "ALPHA HOTEL"

Squadron	Nickname	side number	Callsign	type aircraft	ready room #
VFA-91	Spartans	(100)	"Spartan"	FA-18F	RR 8
VMFA-262	Moonshadows	(200)	"Red River"	FA-18C	RR 6
VFA-47	Buccaneers	(300)	"Cutlass"	FA-18C	RR 3
VFA-64	Ravens	(400)	"Raven"	FA-18C	RR 7
VAQ-146	Sea Owls	(500)	"Rickshaw"	EA-6B	RR 1
VAW-111	Knight Riders	(600)	"Knight"	E-2C	RR 2
VS-36	Bloodhounds	(700)	"Redeye"	S-3B	RR 5
HS-12	Golden Angels	(610)	"Switchblade"	SH-60F	RR 4

STRIKE-FIGHTER SQUADRON SIX FOUR (VFA-64) OFFICERS

CDR Steve Lassiter Commanding Officer *Cajun*

CDR Bill Patrick Executive Officer *Saint*

LCDR Jim Wilson Operations Officer *Flip*

LCDR Mike Hopper Maintenance Officer *Weed*

LCDR Walt Morningstar Administrative Officer *Clam*

LCDR Ted Randall Maint. Material Control Officer *Ted*

LT Sam Cutter Strike Fighter Tactics Instructor *Blade*

LT Mike Van Booven Safety Officer/LSO *Dutch*

LT Kristin Teel Training Officer *Olive*

LT Zach Offenhausen Quality Assurance Officer/LSO *Smoke*

LT Nicholas Nguyen AV/ARM Division Officer *Little Nicky*

LT Ramer Howard Airframe Division Officer *Prince*

LT Tony Larocca Line Division Officer *Guido*

LT Melanie Hinton Personnel Officer *Psycho*

LTJG Josh Fagan Schedules Officer *Nttty*

LTJG Bob Jasper NATOPS Officer/LSO *Sponge Bob*

ENS Anita Jackson Material Control Officer *Anita*

CWO4 Gene Humphries Ordnance Officer *Gunner*

Rocket One — another term for Skipper in a tailhook squadron. *Rocket Two* is the XO, and so forth down to *Rocket Last*, the most junior pilot. A variation is the using the squadron callsign, such as *Raven One*.

ROE — Rules of Engagement

RPG — Rocket Propelled Grenade

SAM — Surface-to-air missile

SAR — Search and Rescue (CSAR is *Combat* Search and Rescue)

Seahawk — popular name for MH-60 series multi-mission helicopter

Sidewinder — popular name for AIM-9 infrared heat seeking air-to-air missile

SINS — Shipboard Inertial Navigation System

Strike — tactical airspace controller/coordinator in vicinity of ship

SUCAP — Surface Combat Air Patrol

Super Hornet — popular name for upgraded FA-18E/F single seat or two-place Strike Fighter with increased range and payload; also known as *"Rhino"*

Texaco — nickname for a tanker aircraft, typically S-3B

TLAM — Tomahawk Land Attack Missile; long range cruise missile launched from surface ships and submarines

TOPGUN — Navy Fighter Weapons School, Fallon, NV

Trap — arrested landing

VAQ — Fixed Wing Electronic Attack squadron

VAW — Fixed Wing Early Warning squadron

VFA — Fixed Wing Fighter Attack squadron

Viking — popular name for S-3B Sea Surveillance aircraft, also known as the *Hoover*

VMFA — Fixed Wing Marine Corps Fighter Attack squadron

VS — Fixed Wing Sea Control squadron (formerly Air-Antisubmarine squadron)

Winchester — out of ordnance

Wire — A 1.25" diameter steel cable stretched across carrier landing area to arrest tailhook aircraft, also known as "the cable" or "cross deck pendant."

XO — Executive Officer

HUD — Head-Up Display. Glass display in front of FA-18 pilot that depicts aircraft and weapons delivery information.

IED — Improvised Explosive Device

IP — Initial Point

IRGC — Islamic Revolutionary Guard Corps

IRIAF — Islamic Republic of Iran Air Force

JDAM — Joint Direct Attack Munition – GPS guidance kit placed on a general purpose bomb body. Also known as GBU (Guided Bomb Unit).

JO — Junior Officer - lieutenant (O-3) and below

JTAC — Joint Tactical Air Controller (formerly FAC – Forward Air Controller)

Knot — nautical mile per hour. One nautical mile is 2,000 yards or 6,000 feet.

LEX — Leading Edge Extension. Narrow part of FA-18 wing leading to the nose of the aircraft.

LGB — Laser Guided Bomb – laser guidance kit placed on a general purpose bomb body. Also known as GBU (Guided Bomb Unit).

LSO — Landing Signal Officer, also known as "Paddles."

Marshal — designated holding airspace prior to landing; also name of landing sequence controller.

Maverick — popular name for AGM-65 infra-red or laser guided air-to-ground missile

Military — Military Rated Thrust, the maximum engine power without selecting afterburner.

Mother — radio reference for the aircraft carrier

MOVLAS — Manually Operated Visual Landing Aid System – LSO depiction of pilot position on glideslope – typically used for pitching deck operations

NAVCENT — Central Command (CENTCOM) Naval component commander…three-star flag officer

NFO — Naval Flight Officer

Ninety-Nine — radio broadcast call used to gain attention; i.e. "listen up"

Nugget — first cruise pilot

NVGs — Night Vision Goggles

OPSO — Operations Officer

Plug — take fuel from tanker

Prowler — popular name for EA-6B Electronic Warfare Attack aircraft

RAS — Refueling at Sea, also known as Underway Replenishment, or UNREP

RWR — Radar Warning Receiver. Cockpit display of threat radars.

CENTCOM — U.S. Central Command

Charlie — come down and land now. "Signal Charlie"

Cherubs — altitude in hundreds of feet. "Cherubs three" = 300 feet

CIWS — Close-in Weapons System; surface ship 20mm gun primarily for terminal airborne threats

CO — Commanding Officer; in aviation squadrons known as "skipper;" on ships, "Captain."

COD — Carrier On-Board Delivery. The C-2 *Greyhound* logistics aircraft is known as "the COD."

Commodore — functional wing commander, shore based; supplies aircraft, pilots and maintenance personnel to air wings as required.

CPA — Closest Point of Approach

CVIC — Aircraft Carrier Intelligence Center

CVW — Carrier Air Wing

DCAG — Deputy Carrier Air Wing Commander

Delta — hold, delay. "Delta six" means delay 6 minutes

Dhow — small boat typical of southwest Asia region

Flag officer — admirals *or* generals…but typically a navy term for admiral

FLIR — Forward Looking Infra-Red. Targeting pod that detects heat contrasts. Aka ATFLIR.

Fox — radio call associated with firing of air-to-air missile with type. "Fox-2" = *Sidewinder*.

Fragged — as planned or previously assigned. "Proceed as fragged."

g — the force of gravity. "4 g's" is four times the force of gravity.

GCC — Gulf Cooperation Council (Saudi Arabia, Kuwait, Bahrain, Qatar, Oman, United Arab Emirates)

GOO — Gulf of Oman

GPS — Global Positioning System

Gunner — squadron ordnance officer; typically a Chief Warrant Officer specially trained in weapons handling and loading.

HARM — High Speed Anti-Radiation Missile (AGM-88) used to home in on radar energy

Hawkeye — popular name for E-2C Early Warning aircraft, also known as the *Hummer*

Helo — helicopter

Hornet — popular name for FA-18C Strike Fighter

HS — Helicopter Anti-Submarine Squadron

Glossary of Jargon and Acronyms

1MC — ships public address system

5MC — flight deck loudspeaker system

20mm — Twenty millimeter cannon round, the size of an FA-18 and CIWS bullet, also known as "twenty mike-mike"

AAA — Anti-Aircraft-Artillery; Pronounced "Triple-A"

Afterburner — FA-18 engine setting that provides extra power by igniting raw fuel creating a controlled overpressure. Also known as "burner," "blower," "max," or "light the cans."

Air Boss — Officer in Primary Flight Control (ship's control tower) responsible for aircraft operations on deck out to five miles from ship.

AMRAAM — Advanced Medium Range Air-to-Air Missile (AIM-120)

Angels — altitude in thousands of feet. "Angels six" = 6,000 feet

AOM — All Officers Meeting

AOR — Area of Responsibility

APM — All Pilots Meeting

ARG — Amphibious Ready Group

ATFLIR — Advanced Targeting Forward Looking Infra-Red. IR targeting sensor placed on fuselage mounted missile station.

Bandit — confirmed enemy airborne contact; also known as "'hostile."

Bingo — emergency fuel state divert from ship to shore base

Bogey unknown airborne contact

Bolter — tailhook flies past or skips over arresting wires, requiring a go-around for another attempt.

BRA — Bearing, Range, Altitude

CAG — Carrier Air Wing Commander; formerly Commander, Air Group

CAOC — Combined Air Operations Center

CAP — Combat Air Patrol

CAS — Close Air Support

Cat — catapult

CATM — Captive Air Training Missile

CATCC — Carrier Air Traffic Control Center

(Ret.), both prolific and accomplished writers in this genre, freely offered solid suggestions and were encouraging to me when the publishing process got me down, as was CAPT Tom Schneider, MC, USN (Ret.) who added sage advice about his experience with modern publishing. Thank you shipmates, one and all. My brother-in-law retired NYPD Lieutenant John Dove, also an accomplished professional writer, provided much appreciated suggestions, observations and encouragement. Throughout the years of writing and refining, my wife Terry — herself a veteran of those deployments but from the perspective of the spouse back home — and my late mother Margaret, also a career Navy wife, provided timely observations and edits in company with the love and support both of them have shown me all my life. I love you!

When *Raven One* was in need of an editor, I found a superb one in Linda Wasserman of Pelican Press Pensacola. Linda, another Navy wife and mother, had very little background in naval aviation and had not edited a military action-adventure novel such as this one. Once we set out on this journey I did not know what to expect, but soon realized Linda's exceptional literary knowledge and remarkable attention to detail was vital to make a good manuscript great. We discussed every sentence and did not move on until we found the right combination of words to convey the intended message with precision and flair. Readers of *Raven One* owe Linda a debt of gratitude, and, had she chosen another avenue for her life, would have made a fine fighter pilot.

Many thanks to Jeff Edwards and the superb authors at Stealth Books for their belief and support. Great to be aboard.

I never flew a perfect flight, and suspect most (honest) pilots haven't either. While we all strived for perfection, flaws were identified and corrected. If readers find flaws with *Raven One*, I take full responsibility.

Okay, reader. Are you ready to strap in and head up north?

Acknowledgments

Not long after I retired from the Navy, my friend Captain Dave Wooten suggested I write a book. Though flattered I demurred, claiming that my career experience and "war stories" were not particularly noteworthy in comparison to several of my friends. He said, "No, you have stories." He was right—I do have some stories, and memories.

My goal in writing Raven One is to answer the question I have often been asked: *What is it like?* This novel, I hope, serves to answer that question, and while it is compelling and entertaining for those who are familiar with the world of carrier aviation, it is written primarily for those who are not. Readers of *Raven One* are going to experience a deployment as part of a strike-fighter squadron. Not all deployments, however, are the same. Each of the several I made in my career was different, and the scenes in *Raven One* are not necessarily autobiographical nor are the characters based on actual people with whom I served. That said, I spent years of my life on carriers and each extended deployment took me to the Middle East. The memories of the flight decks, the ready rooms, the bunkrooms, the wardrooms, the training hops, and daily interaction with the finest men and women I'll ever work with remain vivid.

Before they lead a strike, fighter pilots get a "sanity check" from their seniors and fellow pilots to ensure success. I wish to thank CAPT Chuck "CAP" Nash USN (Ret.) for his invaluable observations on squadron culture, CAPT Rich Thayer USN (Ret.) for his keen thoughts on leadership decision making, and CAPT Kevin "KC" Albright USN (Ret.) for his thorough editing and content suggestions, as well as his observations on leadership. RDML Greg (and Mrs. Liz) Nosal USN (Ret.) were instrumental and enthusiastic in the editing process and storyline improvement, as were CAPT Will Dossel USN (Ret.) and LCDR George Walsh, USNR (Ret.). CAPT Don Gabrielson USN provided vital feedback and suggestions on surface combat and descriptive prose, and CDR Gordon "Dart" Fogg USN (Ret.) was instrumental in explaining modern close air support procedures with which I was not familiar. LCDR Gillian V. Jaeger, MSC USN (Ret.) was also helpful with her excellent observations and suggestions. CAPT George Galdorisi USN (Ret.) and CDR Ward Carroll USN

To Terry, who once had
the toughest job in the Navy

RAVEN ONE

Braveship Books

www.braveshipbooks.com

Aura Libertatis Spirat

This book was edited by Linda Wasserman, owner of Pelican Press Pensacola:

Pelican Press Pensacola

PO Box 7084
Pensacola, FL 32534
850-206-4608
http://www.pelicanpresspensacola.com

Cover Design by ZamajK, 99Designs

Back cover photo courtesy of *Rusty Buggy*

Map courtesy of University of Texas Libraries (Public Domain Resources)

Book layout by Alexandru Diaconescu
www.steadfast-typesetting.eu

ISBN-13: 978-1-939398-22-2
Printed in the United States of America